Inhe

The house was quiet next morning; quieter perhaps than she would have wished, for her own reflections were poor company. A dreadful sense of helplessness pervaded her mind. For all her experience, maturity, determination to protect Liza, she was helpless in the face of this unquiet spirit, straying so far from its home. How to fight a woman dead these two centuries? She stared through the window open to the colours and scents of early summer . . .

She brushed her hair and applied lipstick with care, never heavy-handed now. Old . . . sixty-three could not even pass for late middle age, could it? Strange, how she can see this reflected face and know with her brain that it is hers, yet feel inside her ageing skin no different than she had felt for years. She pulls a face, smiles at this ageless woman imprisoned in the body of a sixty-three-year-old, and is aware that every older human being must share the same sense of unbelief.

Margaret Evans is the author of five previous novels, including *Song of the Hills,* the novel which began the story of Hannah Hywel. She has spent much of her life in Wales or on the Welsh borders, but now lives in Wiltshire.

Also by Margaret Evans

The Hall in the Field
And the Little Hills Rejoice
The Wild Sky
A Place of Eagles
Song of the Hills

MARGARET EVANS

Inheritors

Published in the United Kingdom in 1997
by Mandarin Paperbacks

3 5 7 9 10 8 6 4 2

Arrow Books
The Random House Group Limited
20 Vauxhall Bridge Road, London, SW1V 2SA

Random House Australia (Pty) Limited
20 Alfred Street, Milsons Point, Sydney,
New South Wales 2061, Australia

Random House New Zealand Limited
18 Poland Road, Glenfield
Auckland 10, New Zealand

Random House (Pty) Limited
Endulini, 5a Jubilee Road, Parktown 2193, South Africa

The Random House Group Limited Reg. No. 954009

www.randomhouse.co.uk

A CIP catalogue record for this book is available from the British Library

Papers used by Random House are natural, recyclable products made from
wood grown in sustainable forests. The manufacturing processes conform to
the environmental regulations of the country of origin

Printed and bound in Great Britain by
Bookmarque Ltd, Croydon, Surrey

ISBN 0 7493 1918 6

For Ted, with grateful thanks

With thanks for help from Mr John Vivian Hughes,
Local History Archivist, Swansea Library,
and Mr Tim Bowyer, Magistrate.

Prologue

South Wales 1768

Rachel Hywel heard the first shouts over the roar of the flooding river Avan. It boiled through its valley below the hillside where her cottage sheltered by a stand of sombre pines. As the ragged crowd approached, some holding aloft flaming brands to light their way, Rachel drew her toddler twins close.

'Stay by me, sweetlings . . . do not fear.'

They waited silently as the shouting crescendoed, and after a moment the first stone smashed against the low door of weathered oak. The little boys gripped their mother's skirts and their big slate-grey eyes sought her dark ones for assurance. More stones followed from the soaked, miserable rabble outside, their faces contorted with rage and grief. They had all lost kinsmen that day in the landslip at Llety Harry colliery; they held Rachel Hywel responsible and they wanted revenge, an eye for an eye. Rachel's man, too, had perished in the disaster. But that was her own doing. She had put a curse on her man for his alleged misuse of her – had they not heard the witch? And the curse had brought down the rocks and earth upon not only Ben Hywel, but their own folk. A dozen men and boys now lay drowned in the flooded mineshaft and their sons, daughters, wives and parents had toiled up the track in the stormy night to confront the perpetrator of their present misery.

Rachel glimpsed the blazing brands outside, hissing

in the downpour. She knew why they were there, her husband's brother had come earlier to warn her. She also knew that she had no power to bring floodwater into the mines, even had she a mind to do so. Her man had broken her finger just this market day, attempting to wrest money from her for drink when she was buying food, and she had rounded on him publicly for his sins. This oath was the reason for the mob about her now . . . this, and the fact that Rachel was a healer, a talent by its nature suspect. Some of the crowd outside tonight had doubtless benefited from her gift, with a cricked back freed, an arthritic joint eased, a boil swayed away. Now, they bayed like wolves for her blood.

A brand was tossed through the broken window and she tried to douse the flames with a jug of water. But sparks had fallen on her basket of logs and when it quickly fired, igniting the straw matting, Rachel feared for her children. She saw too that the thatch must have caught, for thick smoke was drifting down the ladder to the sleeping-loft. Her twins huddled together, mute with terror: Rachel gathered them up, opened the door and deposited them on the muddied pathway. Then she stepped back to the threshold of her home and faced the crowd with her head high, the night wind blowing her dark hair about her face and the room behind her now bright with flames.

'Are ye now content? This is more wickedness than I ever committed in my life!' Her voice rose strong on the wind. 'Go mourn your dead like Christian souls, and not lay their deaths at my door. I've grief aplenty of my own.'

A man whose only son lay dead in Llety Harry mine flung a stone and it struck Rachel on the temple; without a sound she fell back into the blazing cottage, leaving her babies crying on the path.

No one moved for a moment, no one spoke. Then a woman pushed forward and snatched up the children.

Within minutes the crowd had melted away. Increasingly torrential rain doused the thatch; the fire dimmed and died about the body of Rachel Hywel.

The twins survived. A Hywel cousin, indebted to their father for a favour once done, took little Joss with him to the Americas when he went to seek his fortune there. Thomas was taken in by another cousin, Marged, who had a smallholding in Taibach. Marged knew the benefit of another pair of strong young hands to hoe her vegetable rows, to scrub out dairy pans, to feed chickens and pigs and cut wood. So Marged was charitable, and took over the infant Thomas.

Folks talked for many years of the great floods of 'sixty-eight' and how water had entered St Mary's church. Those who knew the truth of Rachel's fate on that dreadful night would feel unease then, and would keep silent. What could they have done more? Two babes had been orphaned . . . but life was hard and brief, and children were expendable.

Chapter One

August 1949 Port Talbot, South Wales

'That OK for you then, Han? It won't cause problems, bringing Carl along this trip?'

Joe's voice, so often spliced with static, was today clear enough for him to have been alongside Hannah in the little hall of Morfa Cottage, rather than in his New York apartment. She looked up at Liza, sitting on the stairs in her blue cotton sunsuit undressing her doll.

'No problems, Joe. It'll be fine.' Her daughter hung out the doll by one foot between the banisters. 'He'll be company for Liza, and Matthew likes children.' The doll crashed to the hall floor and Liza's head jerked up to assess her mother's reaction.

'He's twelve,' Joe reminded Hannah. 'A cut above entertaining a four-year-old for too long, I'd say. But he'll fit in with the company, I'll see to that. He's at a real loose end this vacation, having opted out on the Montana trip with his parents and the twins. And he's been keen to do the Atlantic crossing even though we can't make it on one of the Queens this time. He angled for an invite last year, but I said better wait a while.'

Hannah directed a stern shake of the head at Liza and a smile into the phone for her brother. 'Any godson of yours is a friend of mine, Joe. I'll be at Southampton next week, then. Same dock as last year, is it?'

'Far as I know. Thanks.' The line was so clear

Hannah could almost hear Joe hesitate, then take a breath. 'Strange to think that I killed a guy when I was his age, eh? Love to you all for now, then. Bye.'

Hannah sat abruptly on the bottom stair, still cradling the receiver. She felt winded, as though she had been dealt a blow to the stomach. Joe had never spoken so of his past, his tone almost flippant . . . never written so in the twenty-eight years of his exile from Wales. He had in fact never referred in any way to what had happened in any of the many letters he had written, first from London, then Pittsburgh, then New York.

She frowned, staring at the phone. Was he intending to shock? Why should he want to do that? Was he rethinking his attitude to the events of that hot July day of 1921 and trying it out on her? A painfully pointless flippancy, even so – and he might well be regretting it at this moment. To hear a secret she had carried so many years let out so casually was shocking in the extreme. Not even Matthew, her new husband, knew Joe's story.

Joe. Oh, Joey. Hannah's hand still lingered on the phone. 'I killed a guy.' But it had not been that way. Not *that* brutal, *that* simplistic. A tragic accident . . . and paid for long since in fear, guilt, permanent isolation from his family, his own place. Her dress stuck damply to her ribcage, as she remembered twenty-eight summers back to that clammy, breathless evening. Mam had been dead two years and Dada, four. She had looked up from making tea in the crammed little kitchen in Incline Row to see Joe's face sickly white beneath his freckles.

'I got to go out again, Han. Can't stay now, honest.'

He had backed away, twisting his cap with frantic hands. Hannah, at first unbelieving – for what strong, healthy twelve-year-old refuses his tea? – became suddenly rigid with premonition of tragedy. She had leaned towards her brother, willing him to disclose what she needed to know. 'Why, Joe? Tell me what's happened. You *must*!'

'He's dead.' Joe's voice was a dry jerked-out whisper. 'No doubt about it. Neck's broke, Han. I c'n tell. He was sayin' these awful things –'

'Who's dead?' Hannah gripped his arms. 'Say right out. *Who*?'

Joe seemed not to breathe, staring at her, brown eyes glassy with terror. 'Norman Madoc. I hit him and he fell in the quarry.' He began to shake then and Hannah had held him close, whispering comfort. He was a child; her brother. She would help him. Whatever had happened she would find a way out.

She remained where she was on the bottom stair now, her face stiff, remembering. They had gone back to the quarry after dark. They had pulled the body to the top, and dragged it over to the river. The farmer, Norman Madoc, was a heavier man than she had judged, and it had taken hours, and almost more strength than they could summon. The water had been low, but just sufficient. A month later the body had been washed up on a beach seven miles away, and eventually a verdict of accidental death by drowning recorded.

Liza, irritated that her doll's spectacular fall had not attracted her mother's full attention, pushed at her shoulder. 'I can't pick up Ginny if you don't move, you know,' she complained. Hannah collected herself up from the past and regarded her third daughter, love-child of her middle years.

'Did she fall or was she pushed?' She watched as Liza, wildly curling auburn hair escaping as usual from its restraining ribbon, picked up the doll from the slabbed slate of the hall floor. A piece of triangular-shaped forehead parted company from the rest of the pink china face. Liza looked at it, then at her mother; her brilliant aquamarine eyes became limpid and she smiled, and the hint of wistfulness coupled with deep dimples was so reminiscent of her father that Hannah winced.

'She jumped.' Holding the section of china forehead between two fingers, Liza attempted to reunite it with the bulging infant brow of the doll. 'Will you mend it? She was trying to jump on to the rug but missed. It wasn't her fault.'

'Indeed not,' said Hannah grimly. Liza might be a touch young at four to differentiate between fantasy and lies, but this aspect of her education would shortly merit attention. 'Now look, Liza . . . Uncle Joe's just said he'll be bringing a boy when he comes to stay next week. His name is Carl, and he's twelve. I would really like you to help Carl have a nice time. Can you do that, do you think?'

She took the doll from Liza, and the triangle of forehead, and seemed to weigh one against the other in her hands. Liza studied the doll; her best doll, given her by Uncle Tom last May for her birthday. She liked Uncle Tom, who was a baker and smelled excitingly of currant buns. She liked Ginny too, she was nice to cuddle at night. Her wide curved skirt of royal blue satin with rows of yellow braid had a clever little compartment to hold Liza's pyjamas during the day, and to the skirt were sewn blue satin slippers with yellow rosettes on the toes.

Liza nodded slowly. Twelve was older than she could easily imagine. But she saw no harm in agreeing for the moment to tolerate him at least.

'Well, I'll try to mend Ginny – if you're sure she won't jump over the banisters again.' Grey eyes met aquamarine and the arrangement, fragile and elusive, was made.

When Liza was in bed Hannah walked in the garden, full now of secret rustlings and scented dusk. Daisies scattering the little lawn were closed for the night, as were tall marguerites in the border behind sweet-smelling pink and violet phlox. By the wall, giant foxgloves hung the last of their heavy, speckled bells over fragrant mats of late-flowering dianthus, and mists of gypsophila. A frog the size of Hannah's fingernail dived from a yellowing iris leaf into the stone-edged pond, panicking a young hedgehog come to drink. The pond had been dug last autumn by Hannah's younger brother Tom, and was maturing effortlessly into the informal charm of the rest of the garden. All was enclosed by a drystone wall built up painstakingly by Tom the year before the war, to give protection from salt wind off the sea, and from the tough encroaching grasses and gorse of the hillside.

Hannah pushed bare arms into the sleeves of her cardigan and leaned on the wall, chin in her cupped hands, to stare over the roofs of houses below to the coastline. Her face was a pale oval in the fading light, with a square set to the jawline. In repose, the curved lips drooped a little, as though tragedy had been faced and overcome, but at a cost. The night wind lifted a swirl of nut-brown hair from her temple to reveal streaks of grey; she smelled the wind, and smiled. She loved this familiar blend of salt and seaweed, of mosses and wild herbs, of engine sheds and coal, of smoke from the vast spread of the steelworks where once had been dunes and heathland between sea and town. This was the remembered wind of childhood, reliving for Hannah the loving security of her father's hand as they would walk together.

Eyes closed, her hands reached across time to the slight, beloved figure of Thomas Hywel. So vivid, so close in the mind's eye . . .

'Dada.' Her hands became warm as a golden vein of love connected her to her father, bringing peace and refreshment; stress lines smoothed out and her eyes when they opened were clear and tranquil.

Since childhood, Hannah had known that she had inherited powers of second sight. Thomas had listened attentively when, twelve years old, she had finally confided in him; he had already guessed that his daughter saw things, and people, that others did not. His own grandmother – Hannah's great-grandmother Hywel, who had married her cousin and so was a Hywel twice over – had possessed the gift, as had other Hywels over past generations. He had urged Hannah not to fear the powers invested in her, but to accept what she was; to accept the gift. She had struggled throughout her life to live up to Thomas's wishes, not always with success. She had known ridicule, prejudice, censure. At times, she had faced a desolate sense of isolation, for how could she be part of a family, a community, who could not comprehend her strange inheritance? Time was, women were burned at the stake for less . . .

For her own part, Hannah felt she might have accepted her powers as naturally integral to her personality, as she had when a small child. But others' perceptions coloured her own view, forcing her to see her gifts rather as a curse, to be hidden from ignorant eyes. Perhaps subconsciously, she had blocked off their source of energy, channelling it into her fierce will to succeed materially, acceptably. At thirteen she had healed the sprained leg of their terrier, Fly, but only five-year-old Joe had shared this first small miracle with her. At fifteen, she had contacted briefly the spirit of a young man killed on the Western Front. This ability had terrified and repelled her, as had also certain premonitions that at times assailed her. While with later years had come a degree of the acceptance urged by her father, Hannah still knew herself to be far off full understanding of her powers.

She turned from the sea to examine Morfa Cottage. Her ambition for so many lean and desperately insecure years had been to own a home, a place of safety for herself and for her brothers Joe and Tom. She had eventually made it happen by force of will, and by the strength and stamina to work all hours, every day of every year. Before she reached her goal she had made a disastrous first marriage, to be widowed after seven years with young daughters Jonet and Serena to support and Tom still needing help. Joe by then had been long gone . . . to London, then America, a terrified adolescent flying from the spectre of Norman Madoc's lifeless body. And Hannah herself had, in the last months of the recent war, left Morfa Cottage – and her bakery, shop and restaurant in Swansea, all built up over twenty years' endless hard graft – to give birth to David Vaughan's illegitimate child Liza, alone in London.

Hannah frowned into the dusk. Alone . . . as Joe had been alone in his self-imposed exile. Hannah's exile too had been self-imposed. She had been isolated by the shame of her situation from family, home, business, in the alien greyness of the exhausted, war-torn capital. Yet now she knew she had been right to leave, and right to stay away. Jonet at seventeen had been horrified by her mother's pregnancy, and Hannah had judged that the least she could do to help her daughter would be to make herself scarce until the scandal waned. But Jonet had not been placated; Hannah was condemned for failing to be the perfect, socially acceptable mother Jonet demanded; blamed for bringing her into disrepute by association. For Jonet, appearances were all-important. Serena, Hannah felt certain, would not have judged her so harshly. But Serena had been killed by a US Army truck on her fourteenth birthday, two years before Liza's birth. Serena was dead.

The wind suddenly cold on her skin, Hannah pulled the cardigan up about her throat and moved back towards the cottage as bats began to fly in the dying light. Sweet, beloved Serry . . . She put out a hand in a clumsy gesture. It found the cottage wall and she spread her fingers, feeling the stored warmth of the day in the beautiful old stones. The pain of Serena's death lay always in waiting to claw at her in a vulnerable moment.

Joe had never known Serry, never seen her bright face and corn-gold hair. He had met Jonet on his first visit home three years ago, when passenger liners had shed their wartime camouflage to resume the Atlantic crossing. His niece had been polite but cool, keeping her distance; dark-haired Jonet had never possessed her sister's warmth. Joe's reunion with Tom though had lacked nothing; the boys who had been twelve and four when they parted had, twenty-five years on, come together with tears of joy. Tom, always a little slow from birth and lovingly protected by his sister, had continued to live at Morfa Cottage during Hannah's absence, working contentedly in her bakery. She had come from London this weekend to check on the provisioning for Joe's visit, but knew of course that dear, painstaking Tom would have everything in hand for his brother's comfort. The fatted calf itself would have been served up, did Tom but have the meat coupons.

Hannah turned at the door for the last view of the dimming land. Across the bay, beyond the massive panorama of the steelworks the hills beyond the bay had become flat monochrome, and a tug lay on the silver sea like a discarded toy. A tongue of flame from a newly fired furnace split low clouds above the steelworks; a weak segment of moon emerged from behind a giant chimney stack. Blackbird silhouettes dropped noiselessly to the lawn in a late quest for grubs, and a plover cried on the slopes behind.

This was Hannah's place, rooted deeply by generations of Hywels, by centuries of common memory. She did not doubt but that at some future time she would live here again; for now, she at least retained contact, and would not sell up.

She shut the door, crossed to the hall phone and dialled the number of her home in London, where Matthew would be waiting for her call. She smiled, tapping her sandalled foot lightly in rhythm to the ringing tone, looking much younger than her forty-seven years when her smile broadened in anticipation. Thinking of Matthew Stourton, Hannah was joyously aware that she had found gold.

Joe, pressed against the liner's rails with Carl, saw the crowd on the seaward corner of the big recreation ground, and strained for a sight of Hannah. So many pin-sized people, come to watch the berthing of the ocean liner, or to welcome loved ones. His brown eyes narrowed to focus down, and the brisk wind forced back his hair, thick and dark as his mother's had been.

Han; I know you're there. No way, would you not be there.

Then he saw her; Joe recognised the minute figure by her very immobility, eye-catching in the shifting groups. He imagined the smile with the mind's eye, as the liner edged through the channel of deep water towards the New Docks estate. He was quite certain about the smile. It would be unrestrained, whole-hearted, as Joe had remembered from infancy, when that smile had held the reassuring warmth to banish childhood nightmares.

Now he could swear she raised a hand, palm out as if to touch his. Could she actually see *him*? She bent to lift a tiny figure, who waved energetically. Joe blew back a kiss in case they had by a miracle pinpointed him, far above them as the liner inched past the recreation ground.

'See, Carl? There – standing by herself, holding a little girl? That's Liza.' Joe dropped a hand on the shoulder of a boy with thick fair hair and a narrow-cheeked, handsome face. Keen eyes, light blue and deep-lidded, homed in and Carl Cline nodded without comment.

'Can't tell you how good it'll be to see Han.' Joe paused, not taking his gaze off the woman and child as they receded. 'Mother and father to me, after the war . . . the one before last,' he added with a dry smile. Carl nodded again, uninterested in some far-off conflict so long before his time. Joe lit a cigarette, shielding the weak flame from the wind.

'Same with Tom, my kid brother.' He seemed to be talking to himself now. 'Han raised young Tom from a tot. I imagine neither of us would have made it beyond the nearest orphanage without that lady down there.'

'That right, Uncle Joe?' The tone was polite but Joe's words were meaningless to his godson. Han, Tom, Liza . . . not part of his scene. Carl was counting on this trip being more fun than the Montana drag with his folks. He was still put out on account of not making the Atlantic crossing on one of the Queens, and hoped that the visit to the UK would improve on the time already spent on this tub. He squinted down on the waving crowd, then across to where they would berth, and over the tops of the passenger and cargo sheds, the rail terminals, to the great flour mills served from the docks by huge gantries. It all looked shabby, rusty, tired. Not like New York . . .

'Southampton took a pasting from the bombers.' Joe might have divined the boy's thoughts. 'They're building a new Ocean Terminal now – should be open next year. That'll be quite an improvement. If you want to make a trip with me then, we'll book a Queen well in advance, eh?'

Carl nodded again. On tiptoe, head craning for a view, he gave himself up to the complexities of the berthing process. Hawsers were hauled ashore, gangs of dockside hands straining on their ropes. They gathered in, steadied and dropped the great rings of rope over the bollards. As each hawser was secured, the men stood back, waiting for the final winching to bring the liner to its berth. The hawsers tightened and creaked as the vessel was drawn the last few feet of its journey. The narrowing water seemed to bulge, then break, to foam away fore and aft as the wall of steel reached for the protection of dockside fenders. The hawsers, their strain easing, appeared to relax as the liner settled into position. Gangway hands stared up with heads tipped back and legs splayed, or smoked and chatted, ignoring the familiar scene until the time came for their own effort. Men in suits stood about waiting to board, looking important with their various burdens of paperwork.

'They make it look easy, don't they,' said Joe. 'Come on then, boyo. Down to our cabin to get things moving, eh?'

Hannah, grasping Liza's hand, made her way through the dock gate. Not long now . . . soon she would see him. Thank God he was prepared to come to her. She imagined the distant, terrifying stretch of ocean . . . she could never have conquered her fear of water sufficiently to sail over the limitless leagues between here and America. She smiled as Joe was smiling, both content in these final stages of the year-long parting. Once a twelvemonth may not seem often to have sight of a beloved sibling; but having once endured a separation of twenty-five years, Hannah and Joe were grateful for it. Then back to Waterloo, where Matthew would meet them, and home to Clapham. At the weekend they would go to Wales for a few days; fill the little rooms of Morfa Cottage with talk and laughter. One day surely, Joe would bring home a wife; he would be forty next month. Hannah was uncertain of the wisdom of probing in this personal area . . . for now, it must suffice that he had finally faced up to Wales last year, had walked to the quarry, confronted the tragedy of that July day twenty-eight years ago. Now, it *must* become easier each year.

'Mummy?' Liza pulled on her hand. 'Can I have an ice-cream?'

'If we can find any. Uncle Joe and Carl might like one too, we'll look for some when we get to the train platform.' Hannah's smile returned. Any minute now.

Joe came out from customs with Carl in tow, looked

right and there she was, walking towards them holding Liza by the hand; a calm, poised woman. No showy beauty . . . rather, a subtle blend of fragility and strength, of animation and deep stillness. Only at their first reunion had Joe become aware of his sister's physical attributes; all he had known – or cared – in childhood was that Hannah was the beloved rock to which he might cling when first Father, then Mother had gone from him. Joe figured out later that, in the end, she had probably saved his life. Maybe they did not hang twelve-year-olds for murder, simply incarcerate them for ever. Joe had not waited to discover which, but had fled.

Standing by his American godson he watched Hannah approaching with her free swinging walk. She wore a simply cut linen coat that fitted close before flaring from a neat waist, of a muted green that reminded Joe of the sage bush in their allotment, so long ago. A toning straw hat turned off her brow to reveal a wave of hair that curved above almond-shaped, calm grey eyes. Strange, how he had recalled the eyes so clearly in the long years apart. Her eyes, her smile, her strength under fire . . . enough to sustain the scared, lonely lad in the early years of struggle. So far from his own place; from where his heart cried to be. He had remembered enough of Hannah to drive himself slowly, precariously up the ladder of survival; Joe was certain that he must amount to something for Hannah's sake, if not for his own.

'Joe! Joey!' She took the last steps fast and they clung together, laughing. 'Oh, Joe – another year gone! Seems no time since last August.'

'What the hell –' He held her at arm's length, searching her face. 'Let's hope we've a few more

Augusts in hand yet, eh?' Joe hugged her again, for all the years when he'd have traded his soul to do just that. 'Now – here's Carl, looking forward to meeting everyone.'

Hannah put out her hand quickly. Carl took it, looking straight at her and she had no idea why a trickle of, not fear surely? slid down her backbone. *Fear*? Of this twelve-year-old New Yorker, the son of Joe's long-standing friend Alex Cline? Ridiculous. But yet . . .

'Carl, we're so pleased you wanted to come.' Hannah felt the grasp of strong fingers, the hard, direct appraisal of blue eyes that flicked to her daughter then back to her. Carl smiled, and his assured, handsome bearing, sophisticated beyond his years, had the strange effect of an affront. When he released her hand it felt heavy, and dropped to her side. How different Joe had been at twelve . . . She looked up at her brother, now a well-built man with brown hair, brown eyes, an open-featured, pleasant face. Then unaccountably, she was drawn to confront again the bold gaze of his godson, and this time the small shock was that of recognition.

Liza pulled at Joe's trouser leg.

'I'm here,' she said pointedly, and stood on his foot with her blue Clark's sandals. Joe grinned, delighted, and swung her up.

'I'm not likely to forget that, young Liza. My, but you've grown. Four now, is it?'

'You know it is. You sent me a card with four pigs on.' Liza poked a finger into the buttonhole of his beige hopsack jacket. 'And you sent roller skates. I fell down on them.' She regarded Joe severely, as though doubting his sense in offering a gift in advance of her ability to master it. Joe suspected that the brilliant eyes and auburn curls, legacies of David Vaughan (according to Hannah, for he'd never seen the man), gave his sister no chance to forget who had fathered this stubborn, emotional small person. He nodded cheerfully.

'I'll get you going on 'em, that's for sure. You'll be roller skating round the Common full speed before I board ship again.' Joe settled her comfortably on one arm. 'Carl – meet my niece, Liza. She'll lead you a dance but you'll cope, I guess.'

Carl and Liza scrutinised one another in silence. Watching, Hannah had the impression of an electric current sparking and she looked away, unaccountably discomfited. Better, perhaps, if Joe had left this slightly disturbing boy in New York this trip . . .

'Shall we make a move?' She smiled at Joe and tucked a hand round his free arm. 'Get your luggage organised, then we'll hunt for ice-creams before the train.'

'What d'you make of young Carl, sweetheart?'

Matthew, who had been sitting in bed reading the newspaper, lowered it to watch Hannah's reflection in her dressing-table looking-glass. She was massaging Ponds cold cream into her face with rhythmic strokes, eyes closed and head tilted back. When Matthew spoke she opened her eyes and met his gaze, hands stilled.

'Matthew; how did you know that I was at this very moment about to ask you the same question?'

'Because I am such a perceptive and aware chap, my love.' He cast down his eyes with an air of modesty so comical that Hannah snorted with laughter. She had realised, since their first meeting over two years ago, that one of the things she most loved about this tall, skinny man was his capacity to make her laugh without apparent effort, and sometimes even, without apparent intention. There had been very little laughter in her life, until Matthew. Fighting to keep her family and her business afloat through the increasing poverty of the depression, she had clung always to the dream of one day having enough ... enough food, enough warmth; enough love. And of course, enough money, earned by hard work and careful planning, to buy a home. Meanwhile, loving letters had sailed regularly across the Atlantic between Hannah and Joe, each giving heart and strength to the other as they walked their hard and separate paths.

She blotted her cheeks with cotton wool and patted on a few drops of freshener, smiling at Matthew through the looking-glass.

'So. What did *you* think of Carl?'

'I'm not certain yet.' Matthew's reply was serious, as was Hannah's question. 'He's a more sophisticated lad than either of my pair, certainly. More ... knowing, perhaps? Hard to put a finger on it at a single meeting. I think he may have been a bit on his guard, faced with his first family of Limeys.'

'Mm-m.' Hannah peered at her reflection then came to sit on the bed by Matthew's knees. She looked round the pleasant room they had shared since May, liking what she saw. Greystones was full now, with Joe and Carl in the bedrooms occupied when they were home by Matthew's sons Jake and Nick, and Liza in her own room. But whoever was in residence, this room overlooking the garden offered her peace and privacy. It had a small balcony, with doors left open on summer nights for them to hear a nightingale singing from a nearby willow.

'We'll look for something else if you're the least bit unhappy about it,' Matthew had said last spring, uncertain if she would want to live in a house he had once shared with the wife killed with ferocious unexpectedness by a flying bomb. 'Though heaven knows where we'd find anywhere for a few years yet.'

'It's a perfectly lovely house, darling.' Hannah had squeezed his arm. Indeed, she was most content. Greystones, in a quiet tree-lined road, had a tranquil, friendly ambience; she sensed well-lived years permeating its graceful Georgian contours. She was aware of her good fortune in having such a home, when thousands of families were crammed into old, inadequate dwellings in bomb-damaged cities, or in prefabs, dropped in rows on any site that could accommodate them. Now she said:

'Joe thinks a lot of him; of Carl. And he seems very attached to Carl's father, Alex. I haven't sorted out that relationship yet. But after meeting Carl my interest deepens.' She frowned. 'The only thing Joe ever said apropos the Clines, was something about them and the Hywels being related. When I asked "how on earth" he said he'd tell me when we had both time and privacy.'

'They're always at a premium,' Matthew agreed. 'It sounds quite intriguing though.'

'I'm determined to make progress with the story this visit, if I have to tie him to a chair while he tells me.'

Hannah went to the window and pulled back the rose velvet curtains to uncover the night sky. Such a luxury to expose a lighted room, even four years after war's end. She recalled time spent under the kitchen table at Morfa Cottage, an eiderdown draped over to muffle the noise and protect from flying glass. The wireless would be turned up, *ITMA* or *Forces' Choice* or a good loud concert, and Wedgewood the cat would lie shaking in Serena's arms, sometimes opening his pink mouth in voiceless misery. After the All Clear they would crawl out and drink cocoa made with half-water, and eat broken oatcakes from Hannah's shop. When Jonet and Serena had gone yawning to bed, Wedgewood had relaxed sufficiently to wash his genitals before the kitchen stove and Towser the hamster had emerged to play on his wheel and ladder, Hannah would switch off the light and pull aside the blackout curtain to peer at the sky, so lately filled with alien aircraft. As always – as now – it was huge, mysterious, unaffected by trauma. And thus, oddly comforting.

'I wish each year, each visit, that Joe could have known Serry,' she said softly, staring into the tangle of willow. She turned back to the comfort of the gently lit room and her husband. 'I hope Jonet will see him this year, anyway. She's found a perfectly good excuse not to be around since that quite brief meeting, his first visit. I can't think – well . . . however she feels about me, Joe's her uncle, and had nothing to do with *anything* –'

Hannah's hand swept the air in a vague, hopeless gesture. Matthew said reasonably, 'They mayn't have been excuses, love. You mustn't look for Jonet to be prickly before you're sure she is being. I know how her hurt, hurts you . . . Come here and I'll give you a cuddle.' He patted the bed. She said with sudden force:

'What I can't work out is why you don't agree with her! How could *you* – a solicitor, a respected professional – actually come to marry a woman with a child born out of wedlock? No better than she should be, isn't that the phrase?'

Hannah stared at him with eyes suddenly bright with unshed tears. Then relaxed her shoulders, gave him a rueful smile and a shake of the head. He patted the bed again and now she came to him.

'Listen to me.' Matthew laid his big, strong-fingered hand over hers. 'I know all about you, Hannah Stourton. Well no; correction, no one ever knows *all* about anyone. But I know what you've told me and it wouldn't occur to me that you'd lie. I also know what I observe, have observed ever since I've known you. You told me about loving only David Vaughan since you were sixteen. No other man; not even your first husband from what I deduce. Twenty-seven years later you had Vaughan's child. An accident – of course you didn't set out to become pregnant in your forties. But no promiscuity – absolutely not. And being you, a strong but compassionate soul, in my book a *good* person in every sense of the word, you do the best you can with this situation. You care desperately that Jonet is both personally offended, and feels deeply embarrassed socially. You say you understand why she is. Yet still it wounds you deeply that she can't distinguish between you, who became pregnant after a deep, long and constant relationship, and the poor kids who were swept along by a glamorous uniform, some sweet talk and a pair of nylons. It wounds you that she can't seem to recall those years of loving care for her, all your hard work and effort to give her every possible advantage.'

Hannah dipped her head. So strange, that this man could pinpoint with such gentle accuracy her complicated, half-formed thoughts. It caused a relaxed warmth to soften her tense face, the beginnings of a smile to light her eyes.

'I hope so much for her to understand one day.' She spoke almost to herself. Matthew stroked her neck, and she leaned on his hand as would a cat, loving the contact.

'She can't be *made* to understand, however obvious it seems to us.' Matthew's voice was soft in her ear. 'We can only hope she'll come to understand. Be patient . . . just go on being patient.'

'Yes. I have to be, I know. I say . . . Carl and Liza didn't hit it off that well, did they?'

'Why should they?' He cocked an eyebrow. 'Your daughter, my darling wife, has in the brief time I have had the privilege to be bossed about by her, never relished a situation she could not entirely control. She has quite possibly already divined that young Carl is putty in no one's hands, not even hers. The odd jousting bout between them might make compulsive viewing.'

In his room at the corner of the house nearest to the gravelled driveway, Carl Cline pulled aside a curtain and stared at the unfamiliar shapes of trees, gateposts, the interrupted outlines of roofs in the lamplight. His first night in England . . . in any country but his own. He yawned, released the curtain and climbed into the single bed that belonged to Jake Stourton. Carl had already made a thorough examination of the framed school photograph on the wall, of three tiers of boys with tidy hair and stern faces interspersed with masters in caps and gowns; of the leather football and studded boots tucked into a corner, the row of *Eagle* annuals stretched along a shelf beside a handmade model of a Spitfire in balsa wood, and more plane models attached to the ceiling with cotton and drawing pins. They moved gently in the air from the open window. He lay back now with his arms behind his head and gazed at the planes, English, American, German. They swung on their cotton and the effect was hypnotic.

Carl's blue eyes followed their drifting rhythm. Blurred, half-discerned images formed behind them of smoky pale mountains with clouds hanging low, and somewhere a glint of water. Wales . . . he would see Wales in a couple of days; another country, talked about by Uncle Joe way back as far as Carl could recall. Wales . . . strange word for a place, that. He gave a tiny shiver as if a door might be about to open a crack, to reveal a long-kept secret that he was not certain he wanted to know.

Carl's eyes took in the planes' swing one more time, and closed.

Chapter Two

August 1949

'Mummy! Uncle Joe! Watch me – I can nearly fly!'

Liza appeared over the brow of the hill behind Morfa Cottage, running towards Hannah and Joe. Her legs, in her fifth year beginning to lose the soft curves of infancy, pumped furiously over the rough ground but failed to obey her urgent will to defy the laws of gravity.

'She thinks anything is possible if she wants it enough.' Relaxed in the shade of a little scrub oak, Hannah watched with resigned good humour. Arms at full stretch, Liza held aloft her mother's gauzy headscarf for it to catch the breeze. It billowed and rippled above her bouncing copper hair and hot face; a knicker leg slid below the hem of her cotton frock and a tendril of bramble had anchored itself to her sock.

'See me?' Oblivious to where her feet were taking her Liza tripped on a stone and sat down hard, the scarf descending like a collapsed parachute about her head.

'You resemble a cross little angel more than an aeroplane right now,' Joe called. 'But you'll fly one day right enough, sweetheart. You'll fly across the ocean to visit me in New York, for one thing.' He rolled on to his stomach to regard Hannah. 'She'll maybe want to visit her dad in Canada one day too, Han. Have you told her about him yet?'

'No. But it's fast becoming an issue. She asked me outright where her dad was last week. I managed to divert her – but it gave me a jolt, I need to have an explanation ready for next time. She'll hear Nick and Jake calling Matthew 'Dad' again when they get back from school camp, and she's sure to refocus on why "Dad" to them is "Uncle Matthew" to her.'

'Have they all moved over to make room for you and Liza?' Joe hesitated. 'You know; in their lives? Can't be too easy the second time around . . .'

'Everyone collects emotional baggage, of course. Matthew's boys . . . well, I wouldn't presume even to make an attempt to replace their mother. They're away at school a lot of the time of course, so I don't see that much of them, but they're likeable boys, we get on fine. What Matthew and I hope will emerge are new relationships between all of us; different, rather than "better" or "worse". Patently they could never be the same, because I am not Myra. I can only be me, and hope that will be acceptable.'

Hannah looked over the hill, chequered in bleached light and violet shade under clouds drifting up from the bay. Seven miles as the crow flies Dada had told her, clean across Swansea Bay from their house to the blur on the horizon that was Mumbles. She'd not questioned how he would know about the crow; Dada's words could be taken for gospel.

'I do worry about Liza, Joe.' She turned to her brother. 'She misses so much, doesn't she? If you think back to when we were small; what Dada meant in our lives?'

Joe had no difficulty recalling that Thomas Hywel had meant everything of value to him . . . love, warmth, a rock-firm security. And laughter. He had of course loved Mam too; but it had not been in Betsy's gift to communicate, and a sharp word came more readily than a hug or a smile. Betsy Hywel had seen life not as a laughing matter but as a daily battle to survive. When his father was killed in France, it had been to Hannah that eight-year-old Joe had turned; Hannah who had held him in the night while he sobbed out his misery, Hannah who promised never to leave him.

Nor had she. It had been he who had left her, running like a frightened rabbit from another nightmare. He'd loused it up for Han, left her to manage on her own with Tom to care for and support.

'I feel responsible, Joe, for what Liza misses out on.'

'How the devil can you be? That was her father's doing, surely?' Joe was quick to target his own guilt on David Vaughan, who had also deserted Hannah.

'He came back, actually.' Hannah stared at a ladybird clambering over the hairs on the back of Joe's hand. 'In April – just five weeks before Matthew and I were married. I'd come here for the weekend with Liza; he saw me in a shop and came round to Morfa Cottage that evening.'

She pulled a blade of grass, invited the ladybird to board it. The creature walked the length of the blade, shook out its wings and flew to a clump of heather.

'David said he'd flown over from Canada to wind up the family business after his mother's death. He began to question me; he'd apparently heard that I'd moved to London and started a business there. Then Liza called down from bed for a drink of water.'

Hannah pulled the blade of grass into fragments. 'When I came back downstairs he asked who she was.'

'You mean he didn't *know*?' Joe sat up. 'Good grief Han – why not? I'd no idea you'd never told him!'

Hannah looked up with a hint of appeal. So often

she'd longed to confide in Joe, when he'd been so hopelessly far off. So often, she had needed him to understand both her doubts and her certainties; understand decisions she'd been forced to make over all the years of their separation. Now, she needed him to agree the wisdom of not having told David of their child, in a situation of such delicate complexity.

'I had truly intended writing, Joe. Every week I thought, I must tell him. But somehow –'

'He was her father, Han.' Joe still looked doubtful.

'True. But with absolutely no rights.' Her voice was firm now. 'You know perfectly well that he'd chosen to remain married to someone else, and live halfway across the world. Well, *I* chose to be responsible for my own child, after a great deal of heart searching. Only . . .'

'Only now you're not always so certain? Well, sure, that makes sense. But you're doin' a good job on Liza, Han. And Matthew seems to take her in his stride; that's one decent guy you finally came across. Anyway, what did Vaughan say? About Liza?'

'Oh . . . he was a bit annoyed I suppose. He got quite upset, actually.' Hannah examined her left hand where her new gold wedding ring still looked unfamiliar. 'Anyway, his wife had recently died, so we could be together – the three of us. But it was all too late, Joe. I love Matthew now; I really do. And I think that after all those years of waiting, hoping, dreaming of David, his ghost had been laid at last. Only – well, he begged me at least to *tell* Liza about him, and allow him to see her sometimes. I said I would tell her when the time was right, then maybe they could meet if she wanted that. Now I have to tell her, for good or ill; but I admit I'd prefer to have left things as they were.'

'That's natural enough.' Joe covered her hand with

his. Hannah felt the pressure of Matthew's ring and was grateful anew for these two men in her life, where five years ago she had wanted only David Vaughan.

Her attention turned again to the child she had conceived then; a love-child in the fullest sense, born of what had been passionate and long-term devotion. Liza, still kneeling in the grass, had with a child's sure instinct abandoned the unattainable for the available. One day she would of course fly; for now she observed, rapt, the community of ants under the stone. A boy's breathless whistle impinged on her concentration and her head came up as Carl Cline rounded the bend of track, slashing at the air with a bracken frond. He looked foreign in a way Hannah found difficult to define, in narrow khaki sailcloth pants and a loose shirt of striped knitted cotton. Of course: British boys would wear old school clothes on holiday, no one had coupons to spare for purpose-made leisure clothes, even were they available. She recalled the made-over frocks and skirts of Jonet and Serena, the blouses made from coat lining, Liza's infant nighties cut from an old flannelette sheet. Wars were not just men fighting in distant places ... knickers sewn from used parachute silk also figured.

'Been having a look around, old man?' Joe's voice was a touch too hearty; his godson was behaving differently down here in Wales, though the change was barely detectable. Carl never had been the easiest child to handle, but as his best friend Alex's son, Joe had made an effort. He had dealt in a reasonably relaxed manner with earlier childhood tantrums and more recent touches of surliness, but these last days a hint of – danger was not the word, an overstatement, but perhaps a barely discernible note of alarm? Joe hoped that this was no more than his imagination;

why the devil should Wales affect the boy adversely?

Carl struck about with the bracken again. 'I went along there –' he nodded back towards the shoulder of the hill. 'Nothin' much going on though, just a load of sheep.' He stopped by Liza and peered down.

'Ants,' Liza told him. 'Some are carrying things, like that dead beetle – see? And see those, aren't they running fast? P'raps they're very late for something.'

'They won't run anywhere now.' Carl stamped his foot hard and ground the ants into the earth. Liza stared down at the mutilated colony, then up at Carl's now smiling face, her eyes intensely blue-green and expressionless. Then she lunged at him in one fast springing movement, fingers tearing at him.

'Wicked! Wicked!' She shrieked with fury and kicked him hard on the shin. '*Why* did you do that! I hate you!' She pummelled him with bitter ferocity, fingers stretching for eyes and hair. Carl staggered under the attack before regaining his balance and making use of his far superior size and strength to fend off her blows.

'Liza!' Hannah pulled off the struggling child. Carl moved out of harm's way, straightened his shirt and pushed back a wing of light hair, his face reddened with anger.

'Jesus! Some temper.'

'No need to do that though, was there?' Joe frowned. 'I mean – why?'

'Why not?' Carl was turning sullen, facing away from Liza who was still making efforts to tear free from her mother's grasp.

'We don't usually kill creatures who're doing us no harm, Carl,' Hannah said reasonably. Carl shrugged.

'A few old ants. No big deal . . .' He began to walk. 'See you back at the cottage, I guess.' His whistle was one of defiant bravado and he picked a fresh bracken frond to beat off flies. He'd felt all along that Wales was bad news, and his hunches were always on target. London would be better, with a trip on the river and a look around the tower; more his scene.

'Horrible boy!' yelled Liza after him and burst into a flood of tears, burying her head in Hannah's skirt. Joe squatted by her, touching her tentatively as though he feared she might set on him too.

'Come on, sweetheart. Let's mop you up, then you can feel in my pocket for one of those jelly-beans, eh?'

Liza subsided gradually, hiccuping and drying her eyes on the skirt of her frock, beyond which the knicker leg had descended further in the mêlée. Joe wiped her nose on his handkerchief. Children were not absolutely familiar territory though he had excellent recall of his own boyhood, and had observed Carl's moods and stratagems over twelve years. He felt no compulsion to contribute himself to the post-war population boom. Joe had his own long-term secret reason for walking alone – but he did recognise a certain affinity with children, and this small niece would have the affection he had been unavailable to give Hannah's other daughters. Serena could never now be more than an image, a laughing face in a treasured photograph, and Jonet was already a stiffly reserved young university student when they had first come face to face three years ago. He would like to know her better, but realised that the chances of that were slim.

'Will I get to see Jonet at all this trip?' He spoke over his shoulder, starting down the hill with Liza on his back.

'I do hope so.' Hannah paused, the knot of distress always apparent at the mention of Jonet's name tight in her stomach. Jonet. Come and see us soon, *cariad* . . . forgive us our trespasses. Her birthday coming up, her twenty-second. She had worked so hard, done so well, an excellent English degree from Durham and now a first step on the ladder in Bristol library. Why Durham, Hannah had wondered; had that been the furthest she could go from the mother who had disgraced her? Had the secret of the illegitimate young half-sister been safe there?

'I still cannot bear that she took it so hard, Joe.' She spoke with sudden force. 'You know . . . I wonder if she will *ever* not mind. Probably not.' She touched Liza's hand as it rested on Joe's shoulder and her daughter smiled down sleepily, worn out by her tantrum.

'Not mind what, Mummy? Who?'

'Oh – no one you know, Miss Sharp-Ears.' That was almost true; the half-sisters barely knew one another and had no relationship, or prospect of one. From her first view of the infant Liza at eight weeks Jonet had been at best studiously noncommittal, at worst awkwardly cool. Don't blame the baby, Hannah had wanted to beg; it cannot be Liza's fault, it is mine. But she had held her peace. Joe smiled at her over his shoulder.

'Don't fret about it, Han. Time changes things – you know that.'

'Sure. It may sort out.' She looked at the huge spread of the steelworks unfolding below as they descended the hill. Almost impossible to believe the mills' growth since at about Liza's age Jonet had walked down there with her, hanging on to baby Serena's old pram. She had flinched at the gouts of steam hissing from tall chimneys, at the screaming of giant chains in the scrapyard, at intimidating dockside gantries silhouetted against the sky like giant birds of prey. Jonet abhorred noise and disorder of any nature. Serena had from babyhood been excited by the size and power of this industrial heartbeat that gave life to the town, but Jonet had turned from it, frowning at its grubby chaos. Perhaps she also saw in her mother's affair with a married man, and in Liza's birth, only shocking disorder of the worst kind. Well . . . Hannah's gaze rested for a moment on the 'old' steel mills; the first part of the industrial conurbation around the docks. They had been her father's working world. They were part of her own good memories of childhood, and a closeness to Thomas Hywel that remained undiminished. If she could pass a part at least of this to Liza – a sense of family, of place – perhaps her lack of a father would be less acute. If only Jonet would help. If only family bonds would re-establish . . .

Early next evening she waved the three of them off to the fair, along the coast road at Porthcawl, Joe undertaking to have Liza back no later than 7.30. Carl remained a touch defiant, Liza continued to glare at him with disapproving eyes, and Joe sat between them on the long back seat of the bus to avoid any danger of open conflict. When Hannah reached the wicket gate of Morfa Cottage again Tom was in the garden watering the runner beans. Of middle height and build, Tom had light brown hair that was already thinning at rising thirty-two, and his calm grey eyes reminded Hannah of their father's. There was, too, a look of Thomas Hywel in the squared jaw. Born six weeks after Thomas's death in Flanders, young Tom had learned, through Hannah, to know and love his lost father. They had only one small likeness of Betsy and Thomas Hywel, a sepia miniature taken on their wedding day and given to Hannah by their mother just before her death. The miniature, on a thin gold chain, was kept in a small velvet-covered box on Hannah's dressing table at Morfa Cottage. She had told Tom to look at it any time, and to keep it in his own room if he wished. Tom had, with Hannah's constant support and encouragement, drawn confidence first from becoming a master baker in her business and then by completing his wartime army service in the Catering Corps without noticeable mishap. A slow learner he might be; but he could bake fine bread, could grow rows of first-rate vegetables, and he now lived in quiet content at Morfa Cottage with the familiar Mrs Lloyd on a Friday morning to polish, wash and iron. Tom did indeed look sometimes at his parents' photograph; not for emotional support, but because he felt – thanks to Hannah – a strong continuity between his life and theirs.

He had, though, missed Hannah badly since she had gone to London to live. He missed his two nieces, and still grieved for the loss of Serena. But Tom had listened carefully to Hannah's reasons for leaving her home, had accepted that she must do what she felt was right. Now they wandered together round the garden, a source of joy and renewal to both, admiring the profusion of beans, the orderly patch of onions ready to harvest, the happy tangle of pea plants in their hazel twigs. Tom pulled them a pod each, and munching, they moved to where a yellow rose was coming gloriously into its second blooming of the summer. Serry's rose . . . She had saved her pocket money for months, and her twelfth birthday money for it, and in November of that year had helped Tom dig the hole, and trowel in well-rotted horse manure from the mare of Williams the Coal. Then the three of them had stood back to admire the scrawny, bare little plant, and Jonet had been summoned from her homework to join the fan club. It stood in the sunshine now, as vigorously beautiful as Serena had been.

'She'd be proud of it now right enough.' Tom's voice was soft. Hannah nodded, touching one of the fat buds springing from glossy foliage.

'Shall we take her a few of these, Tom? I haven't been down yet this visit.' Tom nodded, pleased, and went for the secateurs while Hannah picked half a dozen of the unfolding buds with some maidenhair fern and put them in the basket of her bicycle. They cycled down from the cottage on to the coast road running west towards the Afan bridge that divided the districts of Taibach and Aberavan. On their left was the gigantic new Abbey Works, under construction these two years. Hannah had loathed the idea; the last of the ancient *morfa* to go. Sixteen hundred acres in all, she'd read. Seeing the slabbing mill taking shape, Hannah wondered what her father would have made of it all. Now they were passing Margam Works, begun during the Great War. Inland, rows of streets ran up from the coast road to peter out as the gradient of the mountain halted them. They drew level with Incline Row and both slowed a little . . . there was the terraced house in which Tom had been born, opposite the school. Hannah's lifelong friend Florence lived there now, married to Hannah's favourite cousin Harry. Florence managed and had recently bought a half share in Hannah's Swansea restaurant, but they had worked as a team from the time of Hannah's first bakery stall in the market. Years later when Hannah, pregnant with Liza, had left for London, it was to Florence she had turned for help; Florence who had run the Swansea business successfully, coped with the intimidating Ministry of Food paperwork. And Harry, though still handicapped by the effects of a severe head wound suffered on the Somme, had thrown in every ounce of energy he had to support them both.

They swung over the Afan bridge and up to St Mary's church. Here were buried Serena, Hannah's mother and grandparents, and her two brothers who had died in infancy before Joe's birth. She had always longed for her father to lie here too, but he had no known grave; Thomas Hywel had been blown to eternity by a British bomb in a German field hospital.

Serena lay close to the gate, in a spot dappled pleasantly by light and shade. Hannah always caught her breath on seeing the small neat plot, as if in disbelief at what had befallen her loving, vital Serry. But she walked steadily forward with Tom and when he went to fill the flower bowl with fresh water, sat back on her heels and waited, hands folded quietly and face composed. When he returned she seemed for a moment not to be aware of him. Then he leaned to touch her shoulder; the lightest pressure of fingers, but Hannah looked up. I am here, he was telling her wordlessly. I won't leave you. She smiled at him.

'Dear Tom. Thank you.'

They arranged the roses, talking quietly in the still August evening while sweethearts strolled through the churchyard and children playing hopscotch in a nearby street called and laughed, and gulls cried from the roofs. Then they moved across to water the low-growing white rose spreading fragrant on their mother's grave. Thirty years back, Hannah had followed Betsy's coffin here with toddler Tom astride her hip and Joe, scrubbed and impossibly tidy, clutching her hand. The oak coffin upon which she had insisted had emptied the funeral fund but for the price of a small posy of summer flowers. When Uncle Griffith, the senior of Hannah's uncles, let drop the first clod of earth, Tom had suddenly whimpered, Joe had begun to shake with silent sobs and Hannah had stared hard into the depths of the yew tree, eyes wide open to hold back her own tears.

She had seen the shadow of her father then, just discernible beneath the yew. He had smiled at her, lifted his hand . . . and Hannah had felt so deep an answering swell of peace and certainty that she had bent to tell Joe, pointing. Though Thomas Hywel was gone when she looked again, the peace remained. She had sworn then that however difficult, she would provide for them, keep them together as Betsy and Thomas would have wished. And when Joe clung to her with desperate tears that night she had been able to comfort him, telling him that Dada and Mam were happy together again, and would not want more tears.

Remembering all this, Hannah looked again at the ancient yew. But she imagined another shadow now, to make her shiver in the sun . . . It was here at St Mary's that she had after painstaking research discovered the identity of Rachel Hywel, her ancestor. Two centuries ago, Rachel had married Benjamin Hywel at St Mary's, and the baptism of her twin sons Thomas and Joss was also recorded. But all Hannah's efforts to unearth further details of her fate had failed. She would have given much to learn Rachel's story . . . to learn why her spirit still lingered by the ruins of the cottage on the hill; why it had on three occasions materialised there before Hannah. Fear of Rachel Hywel had melted over the years, but unease remained . . . She had, the last time, begged the spirit to go in peace on its journey, seeing no way to help, whatever tragedy had left it here in limbo. Hannah had, though, no certainty that her plea would succeed in freeing her from Rachel's attentions. She experienced an unexpected *frisson* of apprehension now, half believing she did indeed see that other, unforgettable shadow . . . the dark blowing hair, the pale narrow face above the grey shawl and heavy folds of skirt.

'Shall we go?' She smiled at Tom and he smiled back, reassuringly warm and real. 'Did I tell you we are having toad-in-the-hole? Carl didn't believe there could possibly be such a dish so I told him he should sample it tonight. And plum crumble. Tom – isn't it wonderful to have *custard* again whenever we want?' Arms linked, they walked down the mossy path to their bicycles, leaving the old churchyard to the gold and green silence of early evening.

When they returned to London there was a note from Jonet saying that she could stay over Saturday night to meet Joe, but would not make it until around five o'clock, and must leave Sunday morning for a train back to Bristol.

'Better than nothing,' said Hannah to Matthew with an edge in her voice. She was tired after the journey into Paddington on a train crowded with holidaymakers, Liza and Carl were still sparring, and she'd just had a phone call to say that a promising young girl she had been bringing on carefully in her Clapham restaurant had left without warning in her absence. She dropped Jonet's note on the kitchen table, put her arms round Matthew's waist and rested her cheek against his ribby chest. He stroked back the hair from her forehead and planted a kiss on it; they stood quietly together, taking pleasure in their reunion.

'It *is*, isn't it, sweetheart? Better than nothing?' He rubbed the nape of her neck gently, lifting the hair that clung damply in a humidity threatening to turn thundery. 'I mean, you were afraid she might not see Joe for a second year on the trot.'

'Yes . . . of course,' she acknowledged. They picked up their cups of tea and moved into the garden by mutual consent as the strains of 'My Old Man's a Dustman' played loud on Liza's gramophone wafted from her bedroom whence she had taken Joe. High summer excess was everywhere outside; plants and shrubs grew into each other with ill-mannered exuberance and twigs from overgrown branches caught in their hair. Lawn daisies had closed for the evening; a blackbird sang with piercing sweetness from an apple tree whose fruit was colouring up in the dark foliage. Hannah and Matthew idled down to the vegetable patch and examined the onions, the tops lying over now ready for harvesting.

'We'll get them out tomorrow,' decided Hannah. 'It may rain before old Jonas comes on Tuesday. Tell me – did you really intend proposing to me here by the onion bed, darling?'

Matthew screwed up his eyes to consider. 'Probably not. But it seemed comfortable, as I recall . . . you counting out the sets from that brown paper bag and then handing 'em to me for planting. It just struck me as an excellent idea that we do it together every spring. *Ad infinitum*.'

'As long as it's not *ad nauseam*.' She grinned then added seriously, 'You know, I feel quite nervous about seeing Jonet. My own daughter . . . and then I'm angry with myself for feeling that! I keep thinking, if I refuse to recognise any awkwardness there won't be any. I tried hard to make that work when she came to our wedding, but when we were face to face I knew it was simply not true.'

'If you'd blinked you'd have missed her there anyway. An hour, was it, before she sloped off?'

'Long enough to lower the bride's radiance factor, I recall.' They started back to the house, seeing Joe at the open french windows. 'She may have been thinking of my last wedding . . . to her father. She was old enough to remember him, after all, though she's never keen to talk about him.'

'Don't tie yourself into knots about it now, darling.' Matthew dropped a friendly arm over her shoulder. 'We'll make her welcome on Saturday, lean over backwards.'

'We must hope Carl behaves while she's here. Further dollops of temperament being flung around will be distinctly unappreciated.'

'You poor old thing.' Matthew laughed outright, the open gutsy laugh that Hannah found impossible not to enjoy. 'All these neuroses to handle! Isn't it lucky that I at least am such a model of equanimity!' He dodged the bit of dead branch she flung at him and made for the terrace, but as usual failed to look where he was going and tripped, long legs flying awkwardly. Joe, watching Hannah laugh again as she helped Matthew to his feet, saw the brightness of her happiness and hoped devoutly that this time it would last.

'It hasn't been easy for me to get today off,' Jonet said in her light clear voice, from which the Welsh accent was fast disappearing. Hannah glanced at her profile, which still bore an endearingly strong resemblance to the small girl of six, crayoning in a colouring book at the kitchen table in Incline Row. Jonet dipped her head to study the beige hand-crocheted bag on her lap and her hair, straight, dark and glossy as her father's, fell forward in a shining protective curtain. Hannah was swamped by a forceful emotion that she recognised with shocked surprise as pity . . . she was remembering Jonet at thirteen, sent home from school with that hair tied back with a bootlace because it had been allowed to grow long enough to touch her blazer collar. For her, the disgrace had been huge, and her distress out of all proportion, so that Hannah had wanted to slap the mistress who had inflicted this cruelty on her vulnerable daughter. Serena would have laughed it off, made a joke to amuse her many friends; Jonet had shut herself in her room and brooded over the public humiliation.

'Well – thanks for making the effort to come, dear. Uncle Joe would have been disappointed to have missed you a second year.' The profile with the small straight nose and pretty chin appeared to harden and Hannah realised that a criticism had been detected. 'We remember how busy you were last August,' she added hurriedly.

Blast; was it going wrong so early? She sat back in the taxi, depression overtaking pity. Why on earth could Jonet not *relax* . . . She looked at her daughter again, and saw the large, round eyes, dark as her father Darrow Bates's had been, appear sad now as heavy lids drooped over them. She covered the hand curled over the beige bag with hers; it was thin but soft as a child's, soft as Liza's.

'Jonet. I really am very happy to have you here. I wish so much that we could have time together more often. I haven't seen your new digs yet, have I?'

'They're nothing special.' Jonet's voice was flat. She did not remove her hand from beneath Hannah's but it lay stiff, full of tension. 'There are no decent places to be had after all the bombing. They're putting up prefabs, but families take priority of course.'

'All cities are the same now, it will be years before there are enough houses again. Greystones is beautiful; I'm very lucky.' When Jonet said nothing Hannah added: 'You know there's loads of room for you at Morfa Cottage if you could get a transfer from Bristol to Swansea. Tom would be delighted –'

'I wouldn't want to do that,' Jonet said decisively. 'But thank you.' Hannah removed her hand and Jonet stuffed hers into the pocket of her grey flannel Utility suit, which though plainly tailored looked very good on her neat little figure.

'Why would you not?' Hannah hoped to not sound argumentative. 'Do you have a special friend in Bristol?' Lord; could that be construed as prying? Thank heaven they'd be home soon. Now she could swear that Jonet was just a shade set back – was that the faintest blush on her creamy skin? A boyfriend? Hannah closed her lips firmly over any further probing but she could hope at least; falling in love might be the making of this constrained young woman.

'It's not to do with friends, it's to do with work. I'm studying for my first librarian's exams, and Bristol is where I plan to do that.' The voice was cool as night rain. Of course; Jonet had had Plans since she had known the meaning of the word; Hannah had been privy to the earlier ones such as getting such and such marks in exams and so many credits in School Certificate. But after Hannah had broken the news of her pregnancy, a steel shutter had slammed down between mother and daughter. Plans, now, were what Hannah might only be told after they had come to fruition.

'I'd no idea what you might like for your birthday,' she said abruptly. 'I thought of a whole lot of unlikely things and then gave up. Is there anything? If not, I'll send a cheque.' You can't buy love, she reminded herself, grim-faced.

'A cheque would be lovely, thanks. There's things I still need for my rooms.'

Which I would know about had I been allowed to see them. Hannah squared her shoulders as the taxi turned into the road. It did rather seem as if the evening might be a long one. For a second she felt the warmth of tears threaten to blur her vision, but coughed fiercely and rustled in her bag for fare money. Self-pity would get her nowhere.

In fact the evening passed quite pleasantly. Hannah had been lucky to find a chicken, for which meat coupons were not needed, and fresh vegetables were in abundance including delectable kidney beans, fresh picked. There were still raspberries from the garden, and 'ice-cream' made in the top of the refrigerator with cornflour, passing for the real thing. They sat until dusk at the big oval table in the dining room, its french windows open to the fragrant evening. They nibbled at cheese and the first of the English apple crop, crisp and fizzing with juice; drank the coffee Joe had brought over from New York, a rare treat after years of wartime substitutes.

Observing Jonet, Hannah saw her relax gradually over the course of the meal and was devoutly grateful. It had become easier once Liza had been noisily persuaded into bed, for Jonet had failed – as she did whenever she and her small half-sister met – to handle the relationship with the casual ease required. Liza of course had no idea there was a problem so made no concessions to one, and was her usual charming, exasperating, high-profile self. She had put out her tongue at Carl, who, intending to make a good impression on the guest, had not retaliated. Hannah had to concede that Carl Cline could be both agreeable and attractive when he decided to be, but found the manner in which he could present different aspects of his nature to serve different purposes quite unsettling. Tonight he appeared older than his years as he discussed the American college system with Jonet, then listened attentively as Matthew tried to explain the intricacies of British petrol rationing.

'That's a great car you have, sir,' he told Matthew, who beamed with pleasure, being deeply attached to his ten-year-old Wolesley.

'You think so? She's a good old bus, quite a goer on an open road too. I'll take you out for a spin; though it can't be far, I've all but used up my coupons for this month. Can't think when we shall be allowed to fill up at will again. What does your father run?'

'A Packard. I've driven it on a field track at our place in Long Island – it's a beaut. I've been telling Uncle Joe he should get himself one.'

Jonet had been listening to this; Hannah had been watching her. Although the gulf between them had widened, she still knew her daughter well enough to guess what was going on. A Packard . . . a place in the country . . . Carl Cline was from a family of substance.

'What is your car then, Uncle Joe?' Her lovely dark eyes turned to Joe, who suddenly became aware that his coolly intelligent niece was also quite a stunner in her own way.

'I run a Buick right now. Why? interested in American automobiles, are you?'

'Well – I don't know that much about them. But with the poor old pre-war tin lizzies we still have on the roads here they always seem marvellous. On the screen, that is.' She smiled, displaying a delicious dimple. 'I've only seen an American car in the cinema.'

'Any time you can take a break from that job of yours you're welcome to visit me in New York,' Joe offered, pleased to have made something of a breakthrough. 'You'd see enough autos there to satisfy anyone.'

'I'd really love that, Uncle Joe. I shall have to see what might be done.'

'You could meet my folks, if you came,' Carl told her grandly, and Jonet bestowed her dimple on him too. Hannah, leaving the room quietly to answer a persistent call from Liza for a drink, reflected on how it could be possible for Jonet to take a holiday in America, when she had not a day to spare for a visit from her mother. Might just a touch of her father's cruelty have been inherited along with the lustrous dark eyes, or did she believe Hannah would not note the remark? Consider others before yourself, she had regularly encouraged her daughters; but Jonet appeared to pursue her own aims with disquieting single-mindedness. Always had done, if Hannah cared to remember back. Quietly implacable, her eldest daughter had from early childhood attempted to organise affairs to her own best ends. Hannah would smile over the careful plans, the steps by which the young Jonet would attain success and status in the eyes of the world . . . she had, perhaps, closed her eyes to the degree of ruthlessness also attained. Poor Jonet . . . the siren call of social standing was clearly as strong as ever for her. Perhaps she never would come to terms with her small beginnings in Incline Row; with a mother who had cooked for other people to earn money for them to live. And that she had been further disgraced by that mother producing a child out of wedlock. Strange, how pity and anger can rise together to produce sadness ... she swallowed it down hard before it ran over.

Breakfast was staggered and leisurely. Endless tea, from a dark blue teapot painted with white ox-eye daisies, brown eggs from a source not to be divulged by Hannah, toast from a crusty loaf she had saved from Saturday's restaurant order. They took big blue breakfast cups outside and sat chatting on the terrace in pleasant sunshine and shade, with Sunday papers folded on the slatted wood table by a dish of apples and early plums. Before it seemed possible, the morning had moved right on ... Jonet was consulting her watch and collecting up her things, and Matthew, knowing Hannah would like to make the most of Jonet's brief time allowance, suggested she take the Wolseley to Paddington and they would economise elsewhere on petrol. Goodbyes were hurried; Liza, who had attempted to kiss her half-sister, was left standing, pushing a finger through her hair in perplexity. Hannah gave her a hug, and a promise of a game of ball after taking Jonet to Paddington, and her face was suddenly hot with resentment against the elder daughter on behalf of the younger one. As they moved down the gravel driveway Jonet turned to wave then settled back with a little sigh. After a moment she said:

'Uncle Joe really has done well for himself, hasn't he?'

'He has, yes. Though not without a tremendous struggle early on. He's worked very hard always and taught himself everything he knows about the antique business.' Hannah's voice was unfamiliarly cool as she struggled with mounting anger.

'And now he has his own shop . . . in a pretty good district too he said – Manhattan?'

'That's right.' As they crossed Battersea Bridge Hannah added briskly: 'When he was eight he had a little cart that he pushed around Taibach, picking up any oddments he thought might sell, then offering them to Mr Jacobi for his stall on the market. He helped support himself that way after our parents died. So he started early, getting his eye in for a saleable object. When he worked in the Pittsburgh steel mills he built another cart to take round evenings and weekends. When the crash came in '29 women would sell off things to buy their children food, so Joe benefited from that as the mills shut down and he had no other means of support.'

Jonet was quiet. Hannah wanted to go on – to say that both she and Joe were *proud* to have survived by their own efforts; proud that they had fought so hard for security rather than have it handed to them on a plate. She felt a nauseous tide rising, of remembered terrors and hardships, and also of anger. Jonet cut into it with her cool clear voice.

'What made Uncle Joe go to America?'

'His search for a future,' said Hannah shortly.

'When did he meet Carl's father? Is he an antique dealer too?'

'I believe he owns an interior design firm. His father used to own the steelworks Joe worked for in Pittsburgh.'

'Oh, well. It certainly would be nice to visit New York . . .'

'You and I and Liza could go together. I'd have to find someone to manage the restaurant here for a couple of weeks but that's possible. I'll help out with the fare; how about that?' Hannah felt a sudden wild freedom from having to watch her words with Jonet. She noted that her change of tack had certainly left her daughter at a loss for words.

'Oh; perhaps it might not be . . .'

'A good idea?' Hannah finished with suicidal abandon. 'Probably not, as you like to spend an absolute minimum of time in my company, and make your distaste for your half-sister patently clear.'

Jonet's face drained of colour. She hung to the ceiling straps as Hannah swung the car around Marble Arch into Edgware Road before saying thinly: 'Do we need to have this conversation, Mother?'

'I think it may be time to call a spade a spade. I've always tried to show you by example what values to foster –'

'Such as having a baby by a married man?'

'There are so many worse crimes than that. Lack of compassion. Lack of straight basic *kindness*. I would find your values almost laughable sometimes Jonet – if they didn't make me want to cry.'

'Yours have certainly not made me laugh these past five years,' Jonet retaliated. 'Really Mother, I cannot imagine what has just got into you –'

'To rock the boat this way?' Hannah took the corner into Sussex Gardens too quickly and stepped on the brakes so that the Wolseley juddered and the tyres gave a scream of complaint. 'OK; I'll tell you. When Liza held out her arms to be picked up for a goodbye kiss just now, and you pretended there was a bad smell under your nose and looked away, I thought it unforgivable of you. Whatever sins you lay at *my* door, Jonet, there is absolutely no excuse for laying a single one at Liza's. She did not choose to be born; she is innocent of any misdemeanour. It shocks me that your nature is so utterly alien to – well, to mine.'

'Perhaps I take after my father.' Jonet's rejoinder was bitter. 'That I will never know; I had no chance to know *him*, did I?'

'My God – you can't possibly be trying to blame me for that as well?' Hannah could hear her heart knocking hard, seeming to make her whole body shake as the situation spun out of control. 'Jonet; your father was killed in an accident in the Light Bar mill. I was given the news after he was dead.'

She drove along Praed Street in a daze; Sunday traffic was light or she might not have negotiated successfully a turn into the station. She slammed to a halt and looked at Jonet, who was now struggling against tears but said in a choked voice: 'Maybe you put a spell on him. I heard someone call you a witch once.'

'Jonet!'

Hannah felt a tide of insane, uncomprehending laughter flood her throat. She reached across to find her daughter's hand, to limit the damage, but Jonet had opened the door and was out. She pulled her overnight bag from the rear seat, slammed the door and put her white face down by the open window.

'Goodbye. Thank you for the visit. I hope you're pleased with what you've done.'

She turned and ran, disappearing fast into the concourse. Hannah, stunned by the bitterness of the altercation, drove slowly into a side street, shut off the engine and stayed there quietly for half an hour.

Chapter Three

August 1949

Hannah always enjoyed the walk to work; down pleasant roads of well-maintained villas showing only slight signs of bomb damage to the Common, across the corner through a stand of chestnut trees, past the big clock and over to The Pavement, a row of shops on a curve lying back from the road. Earlier, Hannah had taken Liza to Ursula Mallow's flat in the spacious Edwardian house where she herself had lived until her marriage in May. Ursula had become a loved and trusted friend over the years. In her sixties, when Hannah had first taken on the management of the Pavement Restaurant she had offered to have Liza during working hours. 'A challenge' would be nice, she had said; life was quiet after the excitement of being an ARP warden in wartime London. She met the undoubted challenge of Liza with flying colours; the two had now a finely tuned understanding of one another's strengths and weaknesses, the territories to be respected on either side.

Small and wiry, Ursula Mallow had white hair and a heart-shaped face with finely lined, baby-soft skin, and round alert eyes. She was a widow, telling Hannah briefly at one point that her husband had been killed in the first weeks of the Great War, and showing no inclination to confide further. Though clearly a gentlewoman, Ursula had a restricted income; she and her small charge had been together for two years and both gave profit and delight to the other in equal parts. Knowing this gave Hannah the ease of mind to build up into a success the restaurant she had bought from the elderly, war-weary couple anxious to leave London. She had met her own challenge of building a new life for herself and her daughter, and like Ursula had triumphed.

Today though, Hannah felt not triumphant but wrung out. The scene with Jonet had had a dire effect. Matthew was a perceptive man and when finally they had achieved the privacy of their own room, had made efforts to discover the problem. At that point Hannah was still too confused to feel able to talk . . . confused, guilty and ashamed, in alarmingly varying proportions.

'It's Jonet. It's something Jonet has said,' he insisted. 'Wouldn't you feel better to spill the beans, so we could maybe sort it out?'

'I'll tell you when I know what there is to tell you,' Hannah promised, grateful anew for him. So he had given her an all-the-way-down cuddle, big and warm and morale-boosting, and she had slept the sleep of exhaustion. But today she was torn between writing a letter of apology to Jonet and vowing never to make any further effort to mend fences between them. Joe and Carl had gone 'up West', Matthew had left early to handle a brief in court and Hannah intended shelving the problem for a few hours at least.

'Hannah's', of The Pavement, Clapham, had never given her quite the lift that the little Taibach bakery and adjoining café had done in the early days. That had been a supreme achievement; a triumph both of her will to choose her own path, and of her strength to master adversity in following it. In the early days, a few pennies had been the margin deciding if she and her young brothers would enjoy one of her meat or fruit pies, or eat bread and scrape after she had sold her entire baking on her market stall. The margins were as narrow when she first took the momentous decision to rent the small shop in High Street; rent must be paid, ingredients bought, and coal for the ovens in the little kitchen. For Hannah, that shop had been a door out of the dire poverty in South Wales in the 1920s, a way to rise above the lowly status of a working-class orphan with a brother – and soon two daughters – to support.

As it had taken root and gradually flourished, Hannah's business also gave her both the confidence and the deep fulfilment that her marriage denied her. A work ethic developed, which was to become permanently ingrained long after the need for work had passed. It had already – Matthew would have been delighted to see her at home, as were the wives of his professional friends. But since Liza's birth, Hannah had worked to provide them with a secure base away from Taibach and the censure of the community whose rules she had flouted. This restaurant served a different purpose from the Taibach shop. It brought not life-or-death sustenance, but the satisfaction of a continually improving business that she actually enjoyed, and full independence. It had, until her marriage to Matthew, taken the place of a relationship missing from her life.

The premises now had recognisable style. Nearby bomb damage had all been made good, and the small parade of shop fronts refurbished. Hannah had made an attractive job of hers, with double-fronted bow windows and an upmarket entrance door with thick pebbled glass and door furniture of solid brass. All had been recovered from bomb-damaged premises and carefully restored. The interior too was inviting, with round polished oak tables on which stood hand-written menus with a yellow check border. There were delicate bowls of flowers, and above the panelled dado half a dozen watercolours, crisp and full of light. Two long gilt-framed mirrors lit the room's darkest corners, soft lamps lit shining brasses; the ambience was one of restful, cheerful comfort.

Hannah longed for the day when food would again be varied and plentiful, when she could offer menus unrestricted by what was 'available'. Rations and shortages had, though, undeniably worked in her favour over the last decade. Customers had not in the least minded restricted choices then; they were simply grateful to buy a well-cooked meal of basic ingredients to augment their own household's rations. Whatever Hannah served them was a bonus. But the situation was changing imperceptibly, even though four years after the war's end, austerity still ruled. Bread rationing had been in place until a year ago; meat, tea and other staples were still on coupons. But now a tide of longing for the return of normality was rising, slowly but inexorably – normality being, in this reasonably affluent district, freedom to eat as much as one desired of whatever one chose.

People were utterly weary of going short. They'd won the war, hadn't they? Where then were the spoils of war? Only the far-thinking few had appreciated that there were to be no spoils . . . that the island had all but bankrupted itself by the gargantuan effort of waging six years of total war; that the promised 'sun-lit uplands' were still a long march distant and that the boots for the trek were not yet available in the shops.

At midday today, a trio of housewives with full

shopping baskets still lingered over coffee and scones, and two tables were beginning early lunches, though the professional people rarely came in before one o'clock. Hannah slipped through to the kitchen, which was warm and full of good smells. Miss Chalker was in command of operations here, though never at her best on Mondays owing to something mysterious that happened each Sunday to give her smudged eyes and an air of chronic fatigue the following day. With a martyred expression on her large features she basted two outsize chickens. The birds would be cooked to perfection, as were the roast potatoes and parsnips sizzling fragrantly in their pan, and the apple charlotte which would have precisely the ideal amount of cloves, cinnamon and lemon peel grated over it. Rose Chalker was an intuitive cook. Whatever went on in her life on Sundays, Hannah prayed it would never cause her sufficient grief to stop her working during the week.

They were busy for a Monday. Shirley was waiting at table, a stick-thin seventeen-year-old with a pale, pointed face which could light with a dimpled smile that transformed it utterly. Shirley lived with her mother, a widow of about Hannah's age who was housebound with arthritis, and Ben, an exuberant mongrel whom Shirley walked in the park early each morning and again after work. She also fitted in the shopping and changing her mother's library books, leaving housework and laundry for the evenings. Hannah, full of admiration for the care Shirley lavished on her two dependants, made certain she was never kept late, and told her always to take home any leftovers for Ben's supper.

'The rolls were late again,' Rose Chalker said tersely as Hannah hung up her cardigan on the back of the door leading to a small courtyard. 'And two of Rossiter's eggs were cracked. You can see –' She nodded to a basin. Hannah stifled a sigh; she was always pleased to see Tuesday, and a return to Rose's equitable self. No need to stay long today anyway; August was a quiet month, enabling her to spend time with Joe. Quickly she gathered up salad ingredients and mixed a simple dressing, hands moving deftly and leaving her mind free to consider Jonet. By the time lunches were over she had decided to let things sweat for a week. Jonet might herself make a move, although that was unlikely; it was more likely that Hannah's own feelings might have crystallised. Maybe that was unimportant, and all that mattered was to repair fences quickly and regardless. But this time Hannah felt unusually sore about it all . . . not so easily inclined to eat humble pie, make a wholesale blanket apology. Let it wait a few days.

Joe was feeling tired. He had failed to foresee the difference that having Carl with him for the entire trip would make in depriving himself of time alone. This was new to Joe, who had lived alone since he was Carl's age, and he was finding it a draining experience. It was a strange thing, this relationship with his godson; there were several threads interwoven. The strongest of these was Alex – for over twenty years Alex Cline had played a part in Joe's life. It all went back to the time when Joe was new in Pittsburgh and had been driven by loneliness, by longing for his own place and people, to dream about meeting up with Hywel descendants. It was common knowledge in the family that way back, a contingent from Taibach and Aberavan had sailed off to seek their fortunes in Pennsylvania, and that there had been Hywels among them. In the little time available to him while scratching a living in Pittsburgh, Joe had scoured old newspapers in libraries, rolls of war dead, even baseball team lists for signs of the family name.

After a couple of years, on the verge of giving up, there it suddenly was, jumping out at him from beneath a photograph of a smart, dark-haired woman at some charity jamboree. Madeleine Hywel Cline, wife of Luke Cline, head of Cline Steel Inc. Joe had at once applied for a job in the Cline mills and secured one, cleaning up in the stocktaking office. He then discovered by various means all available details of the family. Once he saw Mrs Cline in person and studied her features intently, set on finding a Hywel likeness. He learned of an only child, Alex, just about his own age and destined soon for Harvard. It became clear that Luke Cline had made his fortune from the same war that had killed Joe's father . . .

Aware of the slow turning of a strange circle of fortune, the newest immigrant from Taibach continued cleaning up in the stocktaking office and held his silence, wary of confidences, never for one moment forgetting Norman Madoc; never feeling completely safe. Joe embarked upon a deliberate, studied campaign to make his face known to Alex Cline whenever the youth came to the works or its environs. He might drop something in front of him and retrieve it with a cheery smile, or ask him the time of day . . . Eventually Alex would nod his way, then in time exchange a word or two, such was the power of Joe's determination. He cultivated the friendship of none other. His Italian-Jewish landlady prised constantly at his polite shell but failed to crack it. So did his workmates, and fellow lodgers in the tenement building crammed with every nationality on earth. Joe, alone as always, would gaze from his small window over the jumbled roofscape, where Pittsburgh's mills and furnaces stacked into a monstrous, smoking skyline and think of Alex Cline, whose mother was a Hywel.

Thoughts of Wales would from time to time ambush Joe's senses, shooting the longing to be home through every nerve. He *would* go home one day; of course he would. Meanwhile, to what end was not yet clear, he would keep track of Alex Cline until his purpose in so doing became apparent to him, or disappeared. He worked hard, had a pleasant, intelligent manner, was extremely personable, and was soon promoted from cleaning to general assistant in the stocktaking office. He bought a cart, a more sophisticated version of the one he had pushed round the streets of home as a child, and used it to buy and sell bric-à-brac outside working hours. He rented a small section of a reasonably secure old warehouse to store pieces awaiting repairs or attention. Joe was on the first rung.

For the last Sunday of Joe's visit, Matthew and Ursula Mallow offered to take Carl and Liza to Greenwich, on the river. 'We can make a day of it – take a picnic.' Matthew looked quite enthusiastic. 'Jake and Nick will be back by then so with five of us to monitor Liza, even she will have difficulty falling in the river. And it will give you and Joe a few hours' peace together before you wave goodbye for another year.'

'That *would* be lovely.' Hannah looked up from writing to Florence and Harry in Taibach. 'The time has gone so quickly this August, with Carl to show around and Joe going to auctions. He has a mountain of stuff to ship back. If it fetches what he hopes, he'll have paid his expenses for the trip and a bit over. Oh – did you mean it about the boys sleeping in the summerhouse? Otherwise I'll ask Joe to have Carl in with him again, I'm sure he wouldn't mind. How d'you think they'll react to Carl, by the way?'

Matthew looked absent-minded; this was the expression he adopted when considering his answer to a serious enquiry. His blue eyes in his long, summer-browned face looked to far horizons. Then his slightly lugubrious features cracked and he showed big, even teeth in a wide smile. He really did look absurdly unlike a solicitor to Hannah, in an old shirt and slacks, grey hair blown untidily and strands of sticky goose-grass clinging to his shoelaces. He liked to change from the formal dark suit immediately on arrival home from his office and potter outside for a while – 'blowing the dust away' was his term – and today had been summer-pruning an elderly apple tree that might well have preferred to be left alone. Hannah's heart warmed to this untidy, often comical man who brought companionship, warmth and shared laughter to her life in such generous measure.

'What I think,' he said now, 'is that these young male animals will sniff carefully round each other, take a view from all angles, then decide who is top of the pecking order. My two have an advantage in that they're on home territory, but Master Carl may have his own tactics for counterbalancing. He has a powerful personality for a twelve-year-old.'

'Joe says he's had that from a baby. I'm sorry he and Liza can't find common ground somewhere. She's just too young to try . . .'

'They'd have made a formidable team pulling together. Maybe it's as well for the rest of us that they don't – we'd have been putty in their hands! So – will you and Joe have a quiet day here, do you think?'

Matthew lifted up a wave of hair to kiss Hannah's

temple. She drew his head down and kissed him back.

'Probably. He is tired, I can tell by the way he goes quiet. We may cook you all something nice for supper. Seven of us altogether, is it? No, eight, we'll ask Ursula to come back for a meal. She'll need pampering if she's to be O.C. Liza on the river!'

Nick and Jake Stourton were indeed wary of the young New Yorker. They had been well grounded in standards of civilised behaviour; by their mother, a meticulously raised Scotswoman, by their father who had a deep-rooted, built-in courtesy unaffected by distinctions of class, and later by the careful standards of their public school. They were dissimilar in temperament. Jake, fourteen, was slight and dark as his mother had been, also possessing her Celtic intensity of spirit. Twelve-year-old Nick was rangy, lighter of colouring and easygoing, more obviously following his father. But neither recognised in Carl Cline the make-up familiar in their contemporaries. They discussed this, camped out in the summerhouse – luxury, compared with the rigours of school camp – but boys rarely attempt to analyse the subtleties of human nature. Both knew simply that here was an alien creature, to be approached with caution. Young Liza was alien by virtue of her sex, yet they comprehended at least some of her reactions and stratagems, and could even deal with a number, which helped lessen the sense of frustrated helplessness she could engender in them. Occasionally they just wanted to hit her; at the same time they saw how feminine, beguiling and delicate she was. Carl Cline was a guest, and as such was also inviolate. They both hoped he would behave himself and not make life difficult.

Sunday began grey, still and chilly, but the sun strengthened to burn off the cloud blanket by mid-morning. Matthew decided to do the thing in style, petrol ration be damned, and everyone piled into the Wolseley, loading a hamper of food and drink, a rug, cricket bat, ball and stumps, a cushion for Ursula's back which she'd hurt digging up ground elder in her garden, a skipping rope for Liza – she was learning – her second-best doll and her sunhat, plus a change of clothes and a towel just in case. Nick and Jake were squeezed into the back with Carl, and Ursula sat by Matthew with Liza on her lap, and Liza's doll on *her* lap. Hannah waved them off with a silent prayer that proximity would not cause the boys to erupt into violence.

Joe let out his breath and said quietly: 'Rather him than me.' Hannah chuckled, linked her arm through his and they wandered back up the drive. The house looked friendly, the windows open and the curtains moving a little in the breeze that was fast dispatching the cloud. A Virginia creeper was taking on the first hint of autumnal copper, and a yellow climbing rose echoed the stonework's ochre tint.

'You're lucky, Han. This place beats an apartment in Manhattan, even one handy for Central Park.'

They walked round the side of the house, where stonecrop, saxifrage and close-matted thyme overgrew the mellowed flagstones. So unlike Morfa Cottage and its setting; but Hannah was fast establishing an affectionate relationship with this roomy, square house that was well born but a touch shabby, the garden crowded with old-fashioned plants that knew how to look after themselves. The rustic pergolas heavy with roses and honeysuckle leaned at daring angles, rockeries were cheerfully overgrown, shrubs stood in need of judicious clipping but thrived. Paths became minimal at points where exuberant perennials burst over them. But this added to the charm of the winding little byways that might open into a circle of daisy-strewn lawn, or tunnel through a dark arch of laurel and rhododendron.

They circled the house to the stepped terrace with its urns of tumbling geraniums. Here Joe subsided into a cane chair whose red cushions were faded by many summers to uneven pink, and put up his feet on the low wall of warm crumbly bricks. Hannah removed the remnants of breakfast and made fresh tea, which she brought out with a plate of shortbread and the papers. These remained unread. Both were aware of their imminent separation looming, and felt a need to focus on one another. They chatted companionably of cousins, uncles and aunts seen or missed, of plans and hopes for the months until they would meet again. To Hannah, Joe seemed less tired now as he relaxed, sipping his tea. This year neither had mentioned the heart condition, discovered when Joe had volunteered for military service after Pearl Harbor. It was nothing, he had reassured her last year – a little breathlessness just occasionally but he carried pills around and they settled it right away. Hannah had nodded; she had to trust him not to be lying. Joe being ill seemed impossible anyway . . . he had been tall and strong from a child and had never ailed.

'D'you ever think of coming home, Joe? To live?' She asked the question suddenly. Joe set down his cup then lay back against the cushion, his brown eyes following the flight of a red admiral from one purple spear of buddleia to another.

'At first I used to think of nothing else. It kept me going, believing that one day I'd be back in Wales. I never wanted to do anything but follow Da into the mill, you know – when I was young that is.' Hannah nodded.

'Every year I'd think – another year closer to going home. First I had to earn money. The depression was real hard, Han; but you'd know about that yourself.'

Hannah had known first hand about the depression; she and Joe had been forced to survive it on opposite sides of the Atlantic.

'Then when I'd got on my feet there was the war . . . years when no one could go anywhere. Now, I don't know. I've not closed my mind to it, not by a long chalk. I guess I'll know when it's time to move back across the pond.'

'You've made friends? Real friends?' she pressed, attempting to find what kept him there in New York. No wife, no family . . . there had to be something, surely. Was his business enough?

Joe was quiet for a moment. Then he said slowly: 'I suppose there's only Alex, if I'm honest. And his family. I've a good lad works for me, Gus, but I only see him in the showroom. Thanks again for making Carl welcome, Han, he's had a real decent trip I reckon, though he may not always make it obvious. I'm aware he's never been the easiest . . . but, well, a godson's not to be shuffled off.'

'I'm glad you wanted to bring him.' But why no son of your *own*, she wanted to cry. Why no wife? She said instead: 'Joe – you said you'd tell me about you and Alex when you'd time. Well, there's time now if you like. You told me he was the works owner's son. You said you had this idea that he could even share an ancestor with us. His mother had been a Hywel, you told me. So fill me in . . . I should love to know more. How you and Alex became so close, for one thing –'

Joe stared at the flower-filled middle distance. Hannah knew he was somewhere she could not follow, and waited. There would be months ahead when she would take out her stored images of Joe here and now; see again the set of the dark head, the tanned forearms and the backs of his strong-fingered hands lying along the faded cane arms of the chair. She recalled her thirteenth birthday . . . Joe had been five; had given her a bag of aniseed balls that had taken him weeks to save for, and the very best pebble from his treasured collection. Hannah still had the pebble . . . Through the long years of their separation she had only to hold it, close her fingers over its smooth coolness, and it became warm as a loving touch, full of comfort for her.

'It goes back – the very start of it – over twenty years.' Joe turned to look at her, then. 'His mother's name being Madeleine Hywel Cline made him – well, special, me being without family or friends. I thought of *him* as family – even searched for a likeness! Then I decided to have a shot at cultivating him. Seemed pretty hopeless, I know, me being a nothing guy at the time and him the boss's son and heir. But over quite a while I got him to notice me by any means I could drum up, some of them pretty odd, no kidding. Then the Wall Street crash of '29 came and everything changed; for him more than me since at that time I'd not climbed *that* far from the bottom of the heap anyway. But Alex . . . he'd been born way up, and had further to fall. Not so far as his father, though; he fell fast and hard. I'll tell you . . .'

When steel stocks dropped from ninety cents to twelve, Luke Cline wrote a note of apology to his wife and shot himself. Alex, just started on his sophomore year at Harvard, was summoned home to be told bluntly by his still practical mother that the bank owned everything but the clothes on their backs, and that he must find work or starve. After Black Friday on Wall Street, suicides were as commonplace as shut-downs. Luke Cline had been a big fish in Pittsburgh, but now big fish cadged dimes on its streets alongside the minnows.

Joe was just surviving. The loss of his job gave him the whole day to search out pieces to give the fastest profit turnover; often the smaller finds, a finely enamelled buckle or a brass bowl glowing mellow with age. He gave a fair price to women desperate to feed their families, and squeezed every last cent from dealers stocking up against happier times to come. As bells rang out the 1920s and welcomed in the new decade, men crouched over scrap-wood fires in abandoned warehouses and prayed to get through the winter; none but the lucky few thought further ahead.

It was on his way to offer old Nathan Finegold a little pair of lustre jugs winkled out of a German *hausfrau* in downtown Forbes that Joe saw Alex Cline. He was with a woman of late middle age; face fashionably thin between luxuriant silver foxes, with a saucy red hat clinging to precisely waved dyed hair. One of the lucky few . . . Joe heard her brittle laugh when she leaned towards Alex, resting a hand on his arm in a gesture of casual intimacy as they left Clarke's hotel. He also noted the expression on Alex's face, staring after her as her cab faded into the smoky murk of the autumn afternoon.

Poor Alex . . . so that was how he earned his meal ticket. Joe grimaced. Still, men were taking on worse than a stint of gigolo service to survive the crash – and at least Cline had the classy suit for the job, not to mention the all-important social graces. He hesitated, wanting to make contact. But before he could cross the road a second cab was hailed, and all he glimpsed was a pale blur of features that never failed to strike a tantalising chord of memory. Couldn't be making out too badly then, if there were dollars to spare for cabs. Although if you'd been raised to see cabs as basic essentials . . . Shrugging deeper into his jacket, Joe hurried on toward Allegheny Bridge and Nathan's shop. He would think about Alex later – adding up the dimes took precedence.

It was late spring before their paths crossed again. Joe had learned that the bank had sold the Cline mansion to a Sicilian from Chicago, rumoured to operate in the illegal liquor trade from behind his front of grocery stores, and that Madeleine Hywel Cline had left town. The family steel mill was just another petrified victim of the Wall Street volcano, silent behind its padlocked gates; squinting up at the familiar silhouettes of the blast furnaces on his way downtown, Joe suddenly thought of Hannah. The long-buried memory of running to meet his da when the whistle shrieked for end of shift rose to stop him in his tracks; the feel of his sister's reassuring handclasp was, for a second, unbearably real. And the smell of grease and heat on his father . . . the pleasure of being swung into those sinewy arms . . .

Swamped by unmanly longings this cold May morning, it was a while before Joe noticed the man standing alone by the great gates, head bent to light a cigarette. He glanced up as Joe approached, thin, wary in his expensive blue pinstripe. Brown eyes and grey met; held.

'Joe. Joe Hywel? Well, damn me . . . long time, Joe.'

'Must be a while,' agreed Joe. He moved to extend a hand, then stuffed it instead into his pocket. Times had changed but he was not certain yet how much. 'How're things, then?'

'Oh – up and down, Joe.' Alex Cline offered a cigarette and took a long pull on his own. 'And you? Beating the crap?'

'Just about.' Joe grinned then, realising for the first time that they spoke as equals. Their moulds of silver spoon top dog and low-grade employee were broken for good. He also saw that of the two, he was the better equipped for present survival; Alex Cline's eyes were pale with fatigue and a nervous tic twitched the skin of the sharp-boned cheek. His light brown hair, which used to dip over his high brow in an elegantly casual wave, looked stringy. On impulse, Joe touched his elbow.

'Time for a cup of coffee?'

The one-time heir to the Cline steel fortune stared through his smoke ring; nodded, pulled up his coat collar. 'Sure. Why not? Bertolli's?'

Joe had never been in Bertolli's but he hoped Alex would be paying. Something was up though – maybe he should stay clear. Since leaving Taibach, Joe's cardinal rule had been always to mind his own business, and never to enquire after anyone else's. Blast. Well; he was committed now, though only to listening.

'Are you certain? It couldn't be some other guy they're hanging around for?'

An hour later Alex lit his fourth cigarette, dropping the match casually into the elegantly fluted ashtray. 'It's me they're after, absolutely no doubt.' He turned the card of matches labelled "Clarke's Hotel" in nervous fingers. 'Outside my apartment. Saw 'em in time, thank God. Tricky, though . . .'

Bertolli's ornate wall clock agreed with Joe's stomach that it was time to eat. He could use a sandwich and more coffee but after what he'd just heard he might have to foot the bill. A mess, if Alex had told it right. Briskly he collated the facts in the hope that a solution might present itself and save him from further involvement. He'd quite enough problems of his own. Like staying alive.

'Right – so let's just check this out a final time, shall we? You had this key cut before the bank took possession?'

'Right.'

'You told this woman that you could lay hands on a Ferrago watercolour?'

'Right. She'd droned on about her collection, she was real crazy about Ferragos. Able to indulge herself too – she'd got out of the stock market before it folded, lucky bitch had a tip-off.'

'So you told her about this guy who you just might persuade to part with his Ferrago.'

'Right. I thought it might sound better than announcing I planned to burgle my own home. Correction, my one-time home.' Alex Cline gave a tired grin. 'Hard not to think of it as ours, Joe, you know? And that the bank takeover was just paperwork, not for real. None of it seemed in the least real.'

'So then, you said you could maybe persuade this man to sell.' Joe pushed him back on track; he couldn't afford to get soft about it, time was money. 'And she supplied you with "expenses" to set up the sale?'

'They did mount up.' Alex grinned again. 'I needed to settle my hotel bill for a start; and of course, the deal *could* have gone through like a dream. There was the Ferrago sitting in the empty house, *my* house as I still saw it, and here was a willing buyer with ready cash. Mutual benefit society.'

'Until the bank manager turned out to be a friend of hers.'

'And offered her a sneak preview of the auction catalogue,' Alex finished. 'You get the picture, Joe. Correction – no one got the bloody picture.'

Joe took a sugar lump and sucked it, considering.

'Stupid bitch had damn all to gain from splitting on me.' Alex blew a perfect smoke ring. 'Now she'll have to bid for the Ferrago and could well lose it. Hope she does!'

'Meanwhile the bank manager's put the cops on you.' Joe took more sugar. 'Can you be sure of this? No doubt?'

'She faced me with it – some cool lady! Saved me from walking into the arms of the law, at least – this pair of beauties busy hanging around my apartment. I bluffed it out with her of course, swore it was all a misunderstanding . . . promised to get right on down to the precinct and straighten it all out. Last night, that was.'

'Since when you've been . . . ?' Joe paused delicately, Alex shrugged.

'Let's say, I'd have preferred a bed at Clarke's to a corner of Towton's warehouse. The rats were as big as buffalo.'

'So; now? Any plans for tonight?'

'I'm open to ideas.' Alex lit another cigarette. 'And I'm bloody tired.'

'We jumped a box car for New York a couple of nights later,' Joe told Hannah. He reached for a packet of cigarettes on the table and lit one, bending close over the flame. 'I smuggled him up to my room while I got my own affairs sorted . . . sold off the bits and pieces I had in the warehouse, found a buyer for the cart . . .'

'What made you decide to go to New York though? Was there more chance of finding work there?'

Hannah had been riveted by the story.

Joe considered. 'I suppose part of it was wanting to stick with Alex. He was too nervous to stay around Pittsburgh, cop-dodging. And it may sound weird, but in a funny way I'd come almost to regard him as family – he was the nearest to it I had in the States, for sure! Anyway, Pittsburgh was real no-hope alley once the mills shut down. Oh yes . . . an odd thing, Han, I've been meaning to tell you. When we jumped the box cars that night making for New York we had to run fast. Alex hauled himself up first but then it really gathered a head of steam. I lunged for it and for a split second I was set to slide under the wheels. I grabbed for a hold and missed. Then – crazy thing – it was like a hand shot from nowhere to fasten on mine and connect it right up to the box-car door.'

He raised an eyebrow at her. 'Know anything about that, do you? One of your little miracles, was it?'

She laughed. 'Not that I can recall, from twenty years back. But you know things can happen when you want something badly enough, and it sounds like you needed a little miracle right then.' She paused. 'And how did you both survive in New York? I'd try so hard to picture it, when I'd get a letter.'

'Letter writing did fall off a bit around that time,' Joe admitted. 'There seemed only effort enough to make it through each day. And I guess there were a few things going on I couldn't mention anyway, not wanting to get you upset.'

'You could tell me now, it's far too late to get upset.' She laughed, and a glimpse of the young girl he'd remembered so vividly through those tough times broke the surface composure of the mature woman. Joe grinned back.

'Let it lie. We all did what was needed to stay alive;

it was pretty hard not to be on the wrong side of the law at some time or another. Alex was better at making a fast buck than I was . . . he could spin a yarn would charm the fur coat off a lady's back. Me, I was more of a plodder. But we both made it, by our different routes. We didn't go under.'

Looking at him, Hannah saw the years when 'making it' lay very much in the balance etched suddenly on Joe's face. 'Alex has made a good thing out of interior design,' he said abruptly. 'He's always had a good nose for the well-heeled and the willing.'

'It's certainly a far cry from Pittsburgh steel,' she observed.

'So's his wife. As far as you can get from Pittsburgh, is Delaney Cline . . .'

'You mean rich?'

'I mean rich. That is exactly it.'

'Nice for him. And doesn't he forget old friends?'

'No. But I'm ticking over fine on my own account these days with these premises I rent on 86th.'

'I'd love to see your place, Joe. I've promised myself I will.'

'You'd agree that it's a step or three from the cart I used to push around Taibach for old Jacobi,' Joe said modestly. 'I handle some decent pieces now – got my eye trained for a salesroom bargain. And more and more I'm nosing around outside of town. I'm building up selling contacts too – no use buying in right if you can't turn the stuff around. Found a peach of a violin table a few weeks back.'

Hannah sat back, watching him. Nicely put together, good to look at, dark eyes firing as he recounted recent successes. What held him back from having his own family rather than settling for being a surrogate member of Alex Cline's? Was he still crippled by the memory of Norman Madoc? That *had* to be it . . .

'Going back to "little miracles", Han.' Joe was watching her now. 'Do things still – well, happen around you? Has anything changed? It's not so simple to talk about that in a letter, is it?'

Hannah hesitated. 'It's not been easy, Joe – sorting out how I felt, what I should or should not do. After Darrow died . . .' She stopped; cleared her throat before trying again.

'After Darrow's death I was forced to take stock. I'd had a premonition about his fatal accident, you see – about what would happen to him that day. But I'd sworn to myself I would never act on one again, never again lay myself open to getting it wrong and being blamed. I was sure I could ignore this part of myself and simply be like everyone else. That was what I longed for: not to be different.'

She stopped, a hand curving at her throat.

'I might perhaps have saved my husband. By *making* him listen to me. But I was too cowardly. Unless – well, sometimes I wonder if I could have *forced* him to listen to me, not go to work that dreadful day . . . if I had really *cared* enough about keeping him alive . . .' She was silent again, reliving the agony of conscience for the husband who had mistreated her.

'So afterwards, that was very hard to come to terms with. It was later that I remembered what our father had said. About "being myself" . . . To accept what I am and not to fear.' Hannah raised an eyebrow at Joe. 'Not easy, is it – not fearing? You'd know that. But I have had some small success with healing these last few years; just now and again, though I try to keep it low profile. Sometimes it has worked and sometimes not – but that is usually the way with healing, at least for me.'

'And her?' Joe frowned. 'That woman – the one you told me you saw on the hill – whose records you traced? The same name as ours; Rachel Hywel. Has she reappeared? Or gone for good.'

Hannah picked up the cold teapot and started up from her chair, then changed her mind. Her face was serious now, the grey eyes big and dark. 'I saw her in April, Joe, on the same trip to Morfa Cottage that brought David Vaughan back into my life.'

'Some weekend; poor old Han. Two ghosts from the past, that's a bit thick! So, tell me.' Joe leaned forward. Hannah said tensely:

'I simply *saw* her. A vague shape in front of the old stones of the cottage. It wasn't pleasant; I'd really believed she might have gone, I hadn't thought about her at all in London.' Her hand reached for his, needing to make contact. Joe held on to it for a moment then took out two cigarettes, lit them and passed one over.

'If you see her again,' he said forcefully, 'tell her to drop dead.'

He watched her uncertain face nervously for a moment, then broke into a relieved grin as, suddenly, Hannah began to laugh.

They had salad sandwiches and another pot of tea then walked on the Common, sometimes talking and then silent for a while, but remaining linked by the comradeship that had been theirs always. There were parts of one another's lives that neither comprehended . . . Hannah could not bear to allow Joe into the trauma of her marriage to Darrow Bates, or give a coherent account of her love for David Vaughan that had spanned so many years. Joe had no way of conveying – nor did he wish to – the gut fear of a boy thrown into a world of strangers, who did not eat if he did not work; or the effect of the jungle that was New York in 1930 on one who had to survive on his wits. All this apart, there remained a rich legacy for them of shared childhood years, of love, pain, laughter, of fortitude and of continuing hope. So much of their lives had been lived apart, and might well continue to be; but nothing, they felt certain, could ever make them other than the closest of siblings.

Afterwards, they prepared together an outsize cottage pie, Hannah contributing the skill and Joe the slicing power.

'And pudding?' Hannah queried, as they picked runner beans.

'You know,' Joe told her, his smile wide. So they made a bread and butter pudding, with sultanas, eggs, milk, soft white buttered bread, with a sugar and cinnamon topping. Then they went back to the garden with a bowl to hunt for late raspberries to sit on top. This was Joe's farewell treat, and also their goodbye to one another until summer came again.

Chapter Four

October 1949

'So; how was the old country this year?'

Alex Cline handed Joe a bourbon and poured one himself. Smiling, he had the air of a cherubic small boy about to confess to an outrageous piece of villainy and confident of getting away with it. Only in repose did the taut lines of his face register the tensions of the past two decades. He was thin, long-backed and graceful, with bony nervous fingers and a way of throwing back his head when he spoke to regard his audience from under lowered eyelids. Joe had watched this mannerism develop with a mixture of indulgence and irritation – emotions not infrequently provoked in him by his one-time employer's son. He took a swig of the bourbon and rolled it appreciatively down his throat; as usual it was the best that money could buy.

'Smaller than I recalled. Still exceedingly shabby; post-war, bombed-out shabby, you'd find it hard to imagine. And my sister was more beautiful – that is one classy lady now. Marriage suits her.'

Joe drained his glass and absently held it out for Alex to refill, remembering how Hannah's eyes had been, saying goodbye.

'Here.' Alex rifled through a document case and passed a paper to Joe. 'These guys are in the market for a few decent pieces for the lobby of their new place on Central Park South. I'm doing the décor; I'll brief you on the details you'll need.' He smiled his cherubic smile. 'Nothing outrageous; the average of the boardroom's hitting ninety and strictly kosher.'

'OK – thanks. I've a few pieces of large and fairly boring Victorian mahogany might suit. I'll send photos. God, Alex – I could have filled that bloody liner with stuff a saint would kill for. The UK's the only place in Europe the Nazis didn't empty right out. It's bulging with superb antiques.'

'Then go to it, man, now you've your import licence. Get stuff over here pronto, you know the market's panting for it.'

'Yeah . . .' Joe reached for his hat. 'But I've not been through the mill these twenty years without learning something, y'know . . . which is never to overreach.'

'Credit's the thing, boy.' Alex waved an outrageous tortoiseshell cigarette holder, his new toy. 'Why use your own funds when you can utilise others'? I got the hang of all that way back.'

'I did notice,' Joe said. 'So – I have to leave you, Alex, for now. Love to the twins, and to Madame.'

'Come over on Sunday and tell them in person. The boy has a new bike, the two of you can try it out in Central Park.'

Joe groaned. 'God, you ruin him.'

'His nose was put out of joint, to be honest. The terrible twins, it transpired, got end of term reports better than ten of his joined up. Madame is feeling seedy with this heat, and making life uncomfortable for us all as a result. And *I'm* in the doghouse for an inopportune comment about her new autumn *chapeau*.' Alex grinned again. 'See you on Sunday. I'll be gasping for a little light relief.'

'Light relief from what? Do tell, darling.'

Delaney Cline stood in the doorway. Dark and

Junoesque, she just failed to be conventionally beautiful but succeeded wonderfully in attracting instant notice for being so much more. Her eyes were a lively black, big and lustrous, her skin creamy against dense, heavy hair and her long legs curved deliciously down to fine-boned ankles and narrow feet. Joe always enjoyed looking at Delaney Cline, intrigued by the slightly outrageous mix of jungle voluptuousness and patrician breeding. She stood now with perfectly arched eyebrows raised, confident as ever of who she was and where she belonged, dressed in an expensively simple housegown of burgundy velvet that Joe suddenly saw as giving her the ripe look of a plum exactly right for picking.

Delaney now offered Joe a slow smile. Joe smiled back, lowering his lids lest Alex should see how badly he wished at this moment to take his friend's wife upstairs, remove her clothes and make extremely passionate love to her.

'Simply light relief from the cares of the week, my love.' Alex enjoyed sparring with his wife; she had sufficient intelligence to lend a sparkle to the contest, while he was usually ensured top points at the end of the bout. But today she had a dangerous scent. He felt he did not absolutely have the measure of her and judged it best not to enter the arena.

'Are you able to provide light relief, Joe dear?' Delaney, still with the small enigmatic smile moving to the corners of her delectable lips, probed his face with dark eyes shiny with forbidden suggestions. Joe looked modest.

'I shall do my small best. But now I have to leave you.' Joe too scented danger and knew he had to make good his escape before Delaney's hormones got out of hand. 'I look forward to eating with you all, Sunday.'

Joe thought about Delaney, making his way home from the light, thickly carpeted apartment expensively adjacent to Fifth Avenue. It was impossible, he reasoned, for any normally sexed man not to think about Delaney for a while after leaving her presence. He also thought about Carl as he negotiated the chasms of Manhattan to his apartment . . . the first child he'd had truck with since his brother Tom. No real yardstick, that – little Tom had never bothered anyone, bless him. But Alex's boy seemed a force out of all proportion to the area he took up. No way of missing him – his impact was full scale; Joe swore he could feel the blue eyes skewering into his back from across the room if the boy was after his attention. He smiled; Carl rarely wanted something without finding a way of getting it. Interesting to see how his twin siblings would make out; certainly their school reports got more enthusiastic each term. Maybe it wouldn't be such a bad thing all round, for him to see that he wasn't alone in having a brain in his head. He'd most likely recognised that young Liza was also possessed of the odd grey cell, which may have helped foster the primitive atmosphere between them. Well; he'd done his best to make it a good trip for Carl . . . but the boy *could* be his own worst enemy if he didn't keep himself in hand as he grew to manhood.

Joe let himself into his apartment and slipped the lock behind him. He tipped the steak he'd brought in for his meal on to a plate, hung his business suit tidily in the bedroom and put on slacks and a polo shirt. He carried his expensive leather shoes into the kitchen to be cleaned, and dropped his shirt in the laundry bin. He grilled the steak with pepper as he liked it. For dessert he had a hunk of banana pie from the corner delicatessen with a wedge of blue cheese, followed by two cups of the creamy coffee which he so enjoyed. He lit a cigarette with a contented sigh after carrying his supper dishes to the sink.

He slid a pile of accounts from his briefcase on to the table, but stood for a while at the window, blowing smoke rings as he looked down at the traffic and up at the apartment blocks rearing about him. Above those, small jigsaw pieces of sky fitted into the man-made concrete and glass silhouettes.

He turned to survey the room. It was neat, functional, comfortable enough. It did the job and he felt safe here, but he could use a bit more space. Turning his radio to dance music, Joe's foot tapped to the beat and he began to hum, moving through to the bedroom. A double bed with a single pillow dead centre gave the impression of virginal space, and his book on furniture restoration lay beside the pillow. The impression was accurate, in that Joe never slept here with a girl. Or anywhere. He had sex, but always took care never to sleep afterwards; it had always been thank you, and good-night.

The danger was, Joe was aware that he could talk in his sleep. Alex had picked up on it when they had shared a room in the early days of New York. Mumbling gibberish he'd called it; but after that Joe would take no chances, you never knew what could slip out when your subconscious took over. There were still times when he woke sweating, staring into the night to watch Hannah and himself dragging Norman Madoc through the undergrowth. So, no wife; no regular woman, with whom his guard might slip. Concentrate on the business, that was the thing.

He went back to settle himself at the table with his accounts. But the figures blurred on the paper, he found himself doodling in the margins. The truth was that Joe had been unsettled by Hannah's new marriage. He had for the first time seen her in another man's house, in what was clearly a close relationship that promised much. Although they had corresponded throughout the seven years of her marriage to Darrow Bates, and although she had at some point in her letters disclosed her love for David Vaughan, Joe had never visualised his sister as half of a pair; as actually sharing her life with a man not previously known to him. As he took his regular evening exercise in Central Park, Joe was forced to ask himself if he was pleased about the marriage, and concluded that he might be just a touch jealous. He watched the leaves crisp and fall through autumn and became painfully aware of time passing, of another year, his fortieth, disappearing.

Hannah certainly seemed content with the new path she was travelling . . . This caused Joe to see his own path, by contrast, as pretty boringly straight and predictable. Well, he had made his choice not to find a partner, for reasons valid enough for him. So what options did he have to cheer himself up? Moving to a more spacious apartment appeared a step he could reasonably handle. His lifestyle had changed little over the last years while his income certainly had, and he now felt pleasantly secure enough to let out his belt a notch. A new apartment and a housekeeper . . . provided, of course, the housekeeper impinged in no way whatever on his private space. Joe nodded to himself, began to feel better. No wife – but fewer takeaways at least if he could find a competent housekeeper not averse to putting together the odd meal.

Joe did not move at once on the matter of the apartment change and the housekeeper; for the moment it was enough that he had decided to do so when ready.

He was busy that autumn, his business expanding continually, and his emotional unrest subsided under day-to-day challenges. Something he insisted on, however busy, was a daily walk – or rather a nightly one, when the city was relatively peaceful.

One night in late November he had worked late on notes he had made for Alex, on pieces he had that might be suitable for the Aspenfields hotel suite contract, and decided to drop it into the Cline mailbox on his late-night walk.

Manhattan was briefly clean and virginal under an early season cloak of snow, lent magic by the floating silver moon. Joe stood still in the park to savour it, the more lovely for its transience; an hour after dawn the white purity would be trampled as the city went to work.

This was the best time . . . the traffic stilled, the last boisterous party-goers finally gone to ground. The cold was the sort he enjoyed, dry and crisp and just tipping freezing. He walked briskly past the elegant little gazebo on the lakeside and towards the Terrace, his boots printing first marks on the pristine surface. He should have been tired, but instead was plagued by a restless, undirected energy, and Joe was keen on his energy being usefully channelled.

Thoughts of Hannah had been surfacing all evening – could account for the restlessness . . . She'd been on his mind since her last letter, he must try to get a reply out tomorrow night. She had asked him how he was, if he was still on the same medication, and he had had a sense that there was true concern behind the enquiry. His gloved fingers closed about the small pillbox in his coat pocket . . . yes, still on medication, Han . . .

He kicked at a cigarette pack humped under the

light snow and increased his pace: thinking of himself as a sick man filled him with self-hatred. Even Tom had gone through the war with the fittest and best, bless him. He recalled the small boy sitting under the kitchen table in Incline Row with bare feet and a runny nose, amusing himself with a couple of Joe's pebbles. It had been so good finally meeting up with Tom the young man, and knowing how strong were the bonds still binding the three of them. Really, there was no one in the US who would give a damn for his dicky heart. Han and Tom, though; they cared. He'd go back there one day, Joe knew that in his guts. Go back to Wales . . .

He smiled a little then, striding along towards West End Avenue.

Rounding the corner of West 83rd he saw a cab pulling up outside the Cline apartment block. A woman got out, and was still searching in her bag for change when he recognised Delaney. She wore a long skirt that glinted, and a mink jacket was thrown over her shoulders.

'Can I help?'

She turned to him with a relieved smile.

'Joe – what a surprise! You certainly can, I'm three-fifty short.'

When the cab was gone she laughed, her beautiful dark eyes reflecting the snow and the moonlight, and laid her hand on his arm.

'What on earth brings you here in the small hours anyway? Don't tell me you had this dream that I'd be stuck for cab change after the opera and a meal with cousin Louise?'

'Not exactly,' Joe admitted as he walked her to the lift. 'But I was out late myself, and wanted to drop this stuff into Alex's pigeon-hole.'

The lift doors opened and she went in then turned, smiling. 'Come in for a drink before you go back out into the cold, now you're here.'

He hesitated for only a second before stepping forward; a brandy would go down well before the walk home. And the scent of Delaney Cline in the enclosed space was even more inviting.

A lamp was on in the sitting room with a tray alongside, and the fire was still in. Joe warmed his hands at it while Delaney checked on the children, and struggled to ignore a bubble of excitement tracing a fast path around his guts . . . no sign of Alex.

'Where's himself?' he asked when she reappeared, this time without the jacket.

'He had a business dinner in Newark and is staying over,' she said casually, and then, 'So what will you have?'

When she bent towards the tray the deep vee of her midnight blue chiffon bodice revealed the sensational curve of her breast. 'There's coffee and sandwiches here if you prefer that to the hard stuff? I'm tempted myself, it seems ages since dinner . . . Alex says I shall end up a porker if I don't watch out. He's terribly cruel, you know –' She looked at him and laughed. 'Do *you* think I'm losing my figure, Joe?'

Joe looked at the voluptuous curve of hip, breast and shoulder, and the finely turned ankle and calf emerging from the narrow wrap of sequined skirt.

'No, Delaney. I do not think that. And I'll share those sandwiches with you.'

Joe turned from the fire and moved to her as though drawn by an invisible wire, warmth continuing to spread through his stomach. She put sandwiches on a plate and when she handed them over, their fingers touched, causing his hand to jerk with a tiny spasmodic reaction. She indicated the chesterfield.

'Make yourself comfortable. Coffee, whiskey, brandy?' She was bending towards him still, smiling and relaxed, and Joe struggled to remove his gaze from her loosely draped neckline.

'Brandy, thanks.' He stared at his sandwiches until she set his drink on the low table and sank on the sofa beside him. Joe stiffened; he had never been alone with Delaney before and he was unprepared for the effect she was having . . . their relationship had been strictly arm's-length with an element of wary speculation on both sides. Now she touched his elbow with a playful finger.

'So, offer me one, if we're sharing sandwiches.'

Her face was no more than inches away and she was warm, and scented, and more desirable than he had imagined possible. Furthermore, her eyes were sending signals that would have been clear to Joe had he been blind, deaf and dumb, and her lips parted in a smile that revealed the tip of her tongue between gleaming teeth.

He held out the plate and she took a sandwich, which she ate slowly and in silence. Then she took several sips of brandy, watching him over the rim of the glass. Joe finished his own sandwich and drank his brandy, and the alcohol added to the warmth in his belly that was already less than comfortable.

'Are the children well?' he asked weakly. Delaney nodded and her smile widened. She put down her glass and sat back against the cushions, and Joe saw the pulse beat under the white skin of her throat. He recalled dimly as he relinquished his plate and glass that this was the wife of his best friend; but the fact slid from his mind almost as it appeared, for Delaney's hand was now lying lightly but with sure intent upon his thigh.

Joe never had looked a gift horse in the mouth and this did not seem a sensible time to start. When his hand closed over the ripely inviting breast, his mouth over the curved lips, he was simply doing what came naturally. She was as pliant as a sapling to his touch, her tongue as sweet as he had imagined. His lips moved down but when he began to ease the chiffon folds from her shoulder she stayed his hand.

'Wait, Joe.'

Delaney was on her feet then, holding out her hands. She pulled him close, her body moulding to his as they kissed before she led him through the hallway and into her bedroom where a low lamp burned. She closed the door and turned the key. When she faced him she put up a hand to stroke his cheek, and she was smiling again.

'Now, Joe. Now . . .'

Joe walked home by the shortest route and climbed wearily into his bed to fall into oblivion in the black, icy pre-dawn. The problem, when he turned himself out of bed again a couple of hours later, remained.

He had blown it in a big way. Cuckolded his best friend. Joe downed a big cup of coffee and poured another, taking it over to the sofa and lighting a cigarette, staring into space.

The heat generated between himself and Delaney had been, to say the least, surprising. There had been nothing like it to date in his sex life. He sipped his coffee and blew a meditative smoke ring, reflecting seriously on the obvious benefits of an affair with Delaney. That was one whole woman . . .

Despite the fact that he should be showering and dressing by now, Joe poured a third cup of coffee. He was at a crossroads and needed to make the right decision; right for him. He had made such decisions since the age of twelve, had learned the tricky art of survival the hard way, and could not afford to mess things up now. By the time his last coffee had been downed, he had been forced to admit that the benefits of Delaney, great as they were, could not outweigh the danger.

There was a strong possibility that the liaison would be rumbled by Alex. Joe knew that discovery would not come through him – he was far too practised in the art of total caution – but Delaney was another matter, Delaney could not be trusted.

That settled, Joe laid the problem aside while he geared himself up for the day. He must put nothing in writing: that would be fatal. And he must make no move to meet her secretly: that was open to discovery. A phone call; not what he would have chosen, but the safest method. He chose mid-morning, from a callbox near his showrooms.

'Delaney? Honey, are you alone?'

'Apart from Freda, yes. Why darling – d'you want to come round?' Her voice was bubbly, inviting; Joe's spirits sank. This would not be easy.

'Delaney, you know I can't do that. Look; you have to understand . . . last night should not have happened. You must see that.'

'But it did, Joe.' She was smiling, he could tell. 'And it was wonderful.'

'Yes. But I cannot allow you to take the risk, Delaney. I think far too much of you to have your whole life and reputation jeopardised through my selfishness. You know how nothing gets past Alex . . . and all hell would break out –'

'Joe. Forget it. I do not in the least want an affair, I assure you.'

He winced as her controlled fury bit into the wire. Of course; this was where breeding told. He waited for her to take revenge, the least he could do.

'Nothing was further from my mind than to carry things further,' the cool voice resumed. 'Simply a weak moment on my part, already forgotten. Now you must excuse me, I have a luncheon date.'

Joe stood by the phone, silent with admiration. There would be effort to be made for a while now, massaging Delaney's ego. He guessed she would definitely sulk, but he would grit his teeth, be resolutely charming, and take his medicine like a man.

But now he felt more unsettled than ever, and it took his iron will to rationalise. Life, he decided, must move on, and this seemed the ideal moment for it to do so. He started the hunt for a more spacious apartment, found one, and busied himself with the move. The next step would be a housekeeper.

'It's a wife you want, not a housekeeper,' Alex told him bluntly when Joe got round to mentioning his intention (Delaney was tactfully absent). Joe did not, of course, explain why a sleep-in wife would not fill his particular bill; he simply smiled and said a housekeeper would do fine, they were easier to get rid of than a wife if you found you'd made a bad choice. Alex had been forced to concede the point . . . The concession seemed unusually heartfelt, which made Joe suspect that Delaney was meting out punishment all round.

Immediately she knew what was afoot, Delaney announced that she would find Joe the very housekeeper he needed. Now Joe knew without doubt that if Delaney had her way, the lady would be, as a first requirement, deeply unattractive. And while Joe had no intention of sleeping with the hired help he did prefer someone living in such proximity to be personable. So he was in the doghouse with Delaney again for refusing the offer. But he bore this with fortitude and composed his own advertisement, which ran in the *New York Times* in November, a few weeks after he was settled in his new apartment on 75th.

He interviewed five applicants from a total of nineteen replies. Some of the letters were just plain sad, from women needing home and security, mostly war widows. Aware that his heart must not be allowed to rule his head, Joe ticked off details against his carefully considered short-list of five. One he was not too certain about ... younger than he wanted, for one thing. But he liked the handwriting a lot: active and muscular, and the signature 'Sal Prochek' was attractive, with a cheerful flourish to the 'S'.

Interviewing two women each day left one for the final morning, which was Sal Prochek. There was really little wrong with any of the short-listed applicants – Joe reckoned any of them could do the job adequately. He pored over his notes the second evening, and was prepared to settle for one Ellen Gamber from Queens, a pleasant dark-haired widow of forty-five, unless Sal Prochek impressed more than a little. Twenty-eight *was* on the young side ... Well; he'd have to see her now.

She was one minute early and rang once, a positive peal. Joe's immediate impression was one of surprise. When he opened the door he could not pin down the reason for this, unless it was simply that she did not look in the least, well ... *ordinary*. Small, her round face and brown eyes were haloed by a mass of dark frothy curls, kept barely under control by a tortoiseshell comb pushed deep into either side. She had on a cardinal red coat and a little red beret that was being lifted steadily to the crown of her head by the thick hair, and sturdy brown fur-lined boots. There was also a quality of – merriment? – about Sal Prochek that made Joe smile. This he did, and her answering smile was wide and warm, showing strong white teeth. She put out a hand, having first removed a red and grey striped knitted mitt, and when Joe took it he found her grip firm without being aggressive.

'Mr Hywel? Good morning. I am Sal Prochek.'

Her voice was clear and crisp with an East European turn, not marked but enough to be a pleasant change. When Joe invited her in she moved with a brisk bouncing step that was absolutely in character with the rest of her, and looked about with unconcealed interest.

'Yellow is such a good colour. The colour of sunshine, is it not?' She gave a little nod to herself.

'Shall we have coffee while we talk?' Joe suggested.

'That would be most kind – thank you.' Sal Prochek smiled again and unbuttoned her coat. 'May I take this off? It is cold today but now I am glowing.' She fanned herself with a comical flick of the hand then peeled off the striped mitts and stuffed them into her coat pockets. Joe put the coat on a chair and led the way through the sitting room, handsome with muted copper velvets and two big sofas covered with an Aztec print, and into the kitchen; Sal Prochek followed close on his heels. The initial element of surprise had grown rather than lessened. She inspected the square, workmanlike kitchen with its good-sized windows on whose sill sat plants enduring a little healthy neglect, while Joe busied himself fixing coffee.

When he handed her the drink she thanked him again and perched on one of the two bar stools, cradling the cup in both hands. She wore a dress of small black and white checks with a demure fitted bodice, a black patent belt and a pleated skirt. Her shape was curvingly female; Joe told himself that she could perhaps run to fat in later life but she certainly had not done so yet. Now she looked at Joe with eyes that had become completely serious.

'Please. Before we talk of things, there is a fact you must know of me. The reason why it is not in my letter will unfold.'

'Go ahead.' Joe felt a prickle of unease.

'I have a brother, Mr Hywel. He is nine years of age and his home is with me. I came from Poland with my uncle just before our country was invaded. My mother escaped later, was smuggled out carrying her child.' She laid her hand on her stomach. 'He was born in New York. But our mother died when Marek was two. I believe of a broken heart, for my father, who is never heard of. So, my brother is for me to care for. You will understand that.'

'I do, Miss Prochek.' Joe was bowled over by the direct simplicity of the approach. 'Only, the room's not . . . I don't know . . .'

Sal Prochek held up her hand and his voice trailed off.

'I only ask that you consider this. Marek is no noise – no trouble. He is deaf; we speak with sign language. The school for him is nearby. I know it; it is good. We share a room with pleasure. But this is for you to decide, Mr Hywel. I understand if you do not wish for two people. *My* wish was to tell you this in person.'

Sal Prochek took a drink of coffee and smiled again, and waited, the small bright face composed, for whatever fate would now have in store for her.

'What about the work, Miss Prochek – have you done housekeeping before?' Joe struggled now for a point of reference. The Polish girl nodded vigorously and her beret almost bounced off her curls.

'I am presently working in a home for old people. But it is not so happy for Marek. Before, I worked as interpreter and translator. But the hours were not good for Marek, and I will not have him home alone.'

Joe went through the routine of the previous four interviews but it had a hollow feel. He was aware of being pushed into a corner. Yet he could not easily blame this young woman, who had simply wanted to explain her circumstances in person. She was no fool, and may have lost many an interview by revealing her nine-year-old dependant first off.

But Joe did not want any complications. He had avoided them since the age of twelve, and a child – and deaf, to boot – wandering around the apartment sounded like a complication of some magnitude. He began to wish he'd never had the idea of a housekeeper; the whole thing would be an intrusion on his hard-fought privacy. He had simply not thought through the full implications.

'Thank you, Miss Prochek.' He ushered her to the door. 'I'll be in touch with you – I think we've covered everything for now.'

He held out her coat. She buttoned it, then held out her hand to shake his.

'Thank you, Mr Hywel.' Her eyes met his with total directness, transmitting that she judged he would not be hiring her because of her brother Marek, age nine and deaf.

When she had gone Joe poured himself a large scotch, though he had a rule never to drink before midday. He carried it over to one of his big sofas, sank back and shut his eyes. Damn. Damn. He required only for life to be simple. He'd scrub the whole bloody lot and carry on as before . . . he must have softening of the brain even *considering* taking a housekeeper. They could spell only trouble, disruption to an orderly existence.

Joe drifted; dazed. He thought, or maybe dreamed, of Hannah, and she had a shock of dark hair and a rosy face. She held a small boy by each hand, and the toddler looked like Tom and the bigger one looked like himself.

Joe groaned. He knew he was beaten. A month's trial; and she'd better be good or she would be out on her ear, pronto.

Hannah had eventually written to Jonet, to break a month's mutual silence; as casual and friendly a note as could be engineered after three rough drafts and much pencil chewing.

> I am sorry that I spoke out of turn and soured your visit – do please put it down to too many people around me for a while, coupled with a resultant temporary shortage of sleep! None of this is offered as an excuse; merely mentioned as a probable reason. It was lovely to see you and I do hope you will come again soon. Joe was delighted by your interest in a possible visit to New York, and asked to be remembered to you as he left.

A nothing note really, she had thought, sticking down the envelope with a thump. The worst pain had subsided as of course she had known it would; work, and the demands of loved ones always were the greatest antidotes to hurt. Compassion for her daughter had resurfaced . . . but remaining like an uncleansed wound was the thought that Jonet had carried with her, since childhood, the secret misery of hearing her mother called a witch.

As she worked, Hannah at first ran through a list of possible culprits, but soon abandoned the exercise as it must include any ignorant female in the district. The 1930s had been bitter times, with women anguished to feed their children and menfolk on next to nothing; Hannah well remembered feuds and fights caused by nothing but desperation. But might there have been a seed of truth in the slander? She worked this over endlessly . . . Darrow Bates had once called her a witch, thrown it at her like a knife with intent to draw blood. Had she wished her husband, Jonet's father, dead? And possessed the powers to implement the wish? Had the nightmare premonition of his death been wish-fulfilment of a most hideous nature?

Now, Hannah regretted not talking the problem over with Matthew earlier; to allow it to assume this importance was futile. But there might be someone else who could help . . . Florence might know something.

Dialling Flo's number, Hannah saw the broad handsome face of her lifelong intimate, and smiled. Flo at five years old had held hands with her in the yard that first fearsome day at school . . . had shared Hannah's love for her bright-eyed, blond-haired cousin Harry; had watched with Hannah as Harry had struggled to beat the debilitating pain that was a legacy of his head wound. When Hannah's healing hands had eased that, Florence had waited still for Harry to feel ready to declare his love for her. The eventual marriage of two of the people she loved most in the world had been a joyful day for Hannah. She had attended Florence, dark hair knotted back with lilies of the valley and dark eyes full of love, as matron of honour, and they had prepared together the simple wedding breakfast, as they had cooked together since the early days. Now that both had reached calm waters, neither forgot the other's strength and comfort in the bad times.

'Flo?' Hannah's smile broke into a delighted laugh. 'It's good to hear you. No – nothing's wrong . . . just a chat. How're things your end?'

'Fine. If we discount my arthritic thumb. And Harry's knee that clicks like Mam's false teeth when he goes upstairs.' The honey-rich voice with its melodious accent made Hannah laugh again.

'That's all classified under advancing years, Flo. Standard wear and tear. How's trade?'

'No problems there, saving the Men from the Ministry. And like the poor, *they're* always with us, aren't they?'

'For the present. But one day in the bright new decade about to dawn they'll eat their bowler hats and disappear back into their holes. It has to happen. Then what will we moan about?'

'We'll find something – but I grant you they'll leave a biggish gap. Come on then, *cariad*; what's your problem?'

'Flo . . . How d'you know there's a problem?'

'My big toe itches when you've a problem. 'Scuse me a tic while I scratch it. There – now fire away.'

'Well . . .'

Hannah told of August's blow-up with Jonet *en route* to Paddington. There was of course no need to tell Florence how Jonet felt about David Vaughan's daughter, and her mother's lapse from grace; she had lived through it all with Hannah at first hand. She listened in silence, and Hannah saw with her mind's eye the humorous mouth drawn firm now, the warm brown eyes serious.

'The thing is, Flo, I can't seem to feel absolutely certain if Jonet actually did hear that said of me . . . or if she could possibly have made it up on the instant, to score a point. Or . . . if she heard it, believed it, and *does* hold me responsible for Darrow's death.'

Hannah stopped suddenly, swallowing back the final awful possibility: that what Jonet heard was true. Then she added in a little rush: 'Did you ever hear such a thing said of me, Flo?'

In the tiny silence, the second of emptiness on the line connecting them, Hannah had her answer. 'Who was it?' she asked quickly, aware while forming the words that it mattered not in the least; the only fact germane to anything was that Jonet *had* heard the slander.

Well, no. There was a more relevant issue, which was: was it true?

'It was that ignorant old biddy in Forth Street, as I recall,' Florence was saying calmly. 'You know – the one whose pinny was always messed up? She was forever blathering bits of nonsense around.'

It didn't matter in the least who had said it. Hannah chatted amiably to Florence for a while longer, assured her that no, she was *not* upset, that yes, Jonet would probably be regretting the whole thing by now and would realise what an idiot she had been about everything once she had a husband, children, and more important things with which to occupy her head.

'I'll be down to see you all for a weekend soon, Flo dear. We need to decide on redecorating the restaurant, don't we? Give Harry a hug from me . . . 'Bye now.'

She felt unusually tired. The receiver was too heavy for her to hold. Hannah put it down, then remained where she was, in the comfortable chair angled towards the french windows.

Was that it? Perhaps she was a witch. Her powers might be from a source of inherited evil rather than a force for good. Had she wished her husband dead? Might Rachel Hywel, the woman on the hill, have invested her with evil power? Hannah bowed her head. Dada . . . can you help me now? Accept what you are, you said. Must I accept *this* possibility?

She looked into the garden, where in the sharp autumn light Jake, Nick, Matthew and Liza were raking leaves; or rather, Matthew and the boys were, and Liza was jumping into the assembled drifts with shrieks of pleasure. It was half-term weekend . . . she *was* very tired, her eyelids were almost too heavy to remain unsupported. But now she would start supper.

Hannah pushed herself to her feet and went into the kitchen.

'Could I have a word, Mrs Stourton?'

In the lull between late lunches and early teas, Hannah was trying a new variation on strudel. 'What is it, Shirley?'

Shirley hugged her thin arms nervously and Hannah gave a smile of encouragement. She prized Shirley Foster more each day, a more willing, cheerful waitress would not be found, and had raised her wages two weeks ago in recognition of good work. She even managed to stay on the right side of Rose Chalker; no mean feat.

'Well . . . you know when I had that bad wrist?'

'Mm-mm. Is it troubling you again?'

'Oh no – it's absolutely fine, thanks. Only, Mum's back's giving her gyp. It's just never been this bad before. And you got this wrist right in a flash, with no more'n a rub, really.'

Shirley paused, lowered her voice. 'I only wondered if there was any chance you might give Mum's back a rub? I wouldn't think of asking, but she's gone nights now without proper rest.'

Shirley's eyes filled with tears and her face went red. Hannah touched her quickly with a floured hand.

'All right – don't worry about it. I'll come round tonight if you like, and see . . . Though I must tell you, I may not be able to help.'

Shirley's face broke into a tremulous smile. 'Thanks ever so much.'

She pushed through the swing door and started clearing. Hannah stared at her strudel mix, uneasy. It had been a gesture of pure instinct simply to hold Shirley's wrist, back in the summer. Hannah recalled its fragile structure, as she had encircled it with her fingers. Cold too, it had been; she had cupped both hands about it to warm it, nothing more.

Almost at once it had happened. She had felt herself joined to it, had felt the heat begin to pass on a glowing river through her fingers into the small cold core that was the damaged wrist, until the sinews had warmed and softened, and were healed. It had been instantaneous.

She had passed it off casually, saying that Shirley should wrap up the wrist overnight and that it might well improve. But next day it was perfectly better, Shirley insisted – all the miserable aching gone. She had waved the wrist happily at Hannah, had offered it up to Miss Chalker and to Thelma doing the washing-up. Hannah had repeated that she had done nothing, the wrist had simply got better as injuries do. She herself had been surprised; it had been a long time since such a thing had happened. She had intended telling Matthew, but in a busy summer the opportunity had not arrived, and soon the incident faded from her memory.

Now things were different . . . weren't they? She could have no confidence in her healing powers when she now had such serious fears for their source. Shirley's wrist had been an involuntary gesture to help, and the happy outcome had been fine. But to give a middle-aged woman who was quite seriously disabled any cause for hope? Yes; that was different.

When Shirley came through again she said, 'Look, I forgot we have something fixed for tonight, Shirley. Shall I let you know when I might manage it?'

Shirley's face appeared to crumple, then she managed a weak smile. 'Oh – right, Mrs Stourton. I'll wait to hear.'

Hannah prevaricated for two days while Shirley's face grew more pinched, her eyes more anxious. I am *not* a witch, Hannah would argue to herself, walking to and from work. Why should such drivel affect me? I simply want to see if I can alleviate a woman's pain. Does that make me evil? But if I try and fail . . . if Jonet came to hear . . .

But she had to try. In the end, for good or evil, she *had* to try.

Matthew had fetched Jake and Nick from school for the start of the Christmas holidays and chaos reigned. After a noisy supper Liza, querulous with excitement, had been persuaded into bed only if the boys came up to read to her.

'I need a drink,' Matthew said weakly, his hair stuck on end after a tussle with all three on the floor. 'When's next term start?'

'There's Christmas and New Year to get through

first,' Hannah pointed out ruthlessly and passed him the decanter. 'Darling – I've to slip round to Shirley's for a bit. Her mother's not well.'

'Is that usual? Do you know the woman?'

'Not actually. But Shirley's devoted to her – and I'm fond of Shirley. Tell you more later.' She dropped a kiss on his head. 'Stand no nonsense from Liza if she tries any tricks.'

Jake and Nick were creeping downstairs. 'She fell asleep,' Jake said with a relieved grin, his voice breaking on the last syllable. Jake usually established his authority by force of will, being no taller than his younger brother. That worked on easygoing Nick, but Liza being prone to mutiny, had the edge in the power struggle. Hannah grinned at him; she liked this dark, serious boy and was well on the way to respecting him for his industry and mature directness of manner.

'Just the luck of your first night home – you won't always get off so lightly. Now look, boys, I'll be back soon. If you don't want me to read your end-of-term reports you've got an hour at most to persuade your dad to burn them. Of course, they may be so splendid that you can't wait to show them off.'

Shirley opened the door of the ground-floor flat before Hannah had rung the bell.

'I was on the lookout. Come in, do.' She stood nervously as Hannah took off her coat, restraining the mongrel Ben who wished to lick her face. 'Oh dear . . . I'd better put him in the kitchen.'

'Not on my account.' Hannah bent to fuss Ben while Shirley hovered.

'Mum's in the lounge,' she whispered. 'She got a bit worried. I kept telling her you wouldn't hurt her . . .'

Mrs Foster was sitting stiff and upright by the fire; a thin woman prematurely aged with pain, with frightened blue eyes that once would have been as pretty as her daughter's. She wore a red jumper that accentuated her pallor, and above it her neck was rigid as her head swivelled to look at Hannah.

'Mum, this is Mrs Stourton to see you.' As Hannah was ushered into Mrs Foster's orbit she was overwhelmed by a wave of pity for the woman, almost helpless and entirely vulnerable to whatever this stranger might be planning for her. Her gaze met Hannah's briefly, then shifted to her daughter.

'Shirley, why don't you make a cup of tea for Mrs Stourton?' Her voice was stronger than Hannah expected, as though she was determined that this at least about her would be normal.

'That would be lovely.' Not in the least wanting a cup of tea, Hannah smiled warmly and sat opposite Shirley's mother. 'It's cold tonight.'

'Shirley shouldn't have bothered you,' Mrs Foster said quickly.

'But I've wanted to meet you. I asked Shirley to bring you to the restaurant for tea, but she said you couldn't walk there. That was when I realised you had this wretched problem.'

Mrs Foster was silent, looking at Ben's head pushed against her knee. It seemed to Hannah that her illness was too omnipotent a force in her life to be discussed in casual conversation with a stranger. She said gently: 'I should like to help you, if I possibly can.'

Mrs Foster cleared her throat. 'The doctor says to take these tablets. For the pain.' She nodded at a bottle on the low table by her chair. 'He doesn't seem to be able to do much else.'

'Maybe I shan't either,' said Hannah candidly. 'A healer can only be passive, a channel through which healing *may* come. But I'll try.'

'Here we are.' Shirley put down a tray set with the best china, and a plate of chocolate biscuits. Her eyes were nervous as she handed the cups; Hannah was painfully aware how important her visit was, how much hope was pinned on the outcome. She made a conscious effort to relax, aware that tension or nerves on her part could block a flow of healing energy. She drank her tea, ate a biscuit, chatted about Christmas, the restaurant. Tension gradually eased; Mrs Foster's neck became slightly less stiff and her thin lips more relaxed, and Hannah put down her cup.

'I enjoyed that. Now, could you just show me where the worst of the pain is? Around your shoulders or lower down?'

Mrs Foster moved her shoulders a little. 'They're stiff, of course. But the worst is lower, at my waist.'

'Let me locate it.' Hannah knelt by the chair. 'No need to move, just ease forward slightly. Then try to relax; I'm not going to do a thing.'

Her hand moved slowly, skimming the red jumper. The body beneath it was as rigid as a steel cage. Shirley disappeared with the tray and Ben sat with his eyes fixed on Hannah.

'D'you mind if I take your hand? It may help you to relax.'

Mrs Foster held it up as an awkward puppy might hold up a paw. Hannah lowered it again to the woman's lap; it was cold, and as rigid as the back. Her other hand touched the small of the back gently. Mrs Foster flinched, but after a moment leaned slightly against it.

'That's better. Fine . . .'

She let her hand rest. Through her fingertips came an impression of pain, the size and density of a cricket ball. Eyes closed, Hannah strove to empty her mind but an image remained that would not be dismissed. It was that of an old brick wall. Such a wall was purposeless, and she increased her effort to replace it with clean white space. It remained. At one point her hand became warm; then it cooled, and the wall, whose chipped discoloured bricks had gone slightly out of focus, steadied again.

Hannah opened her eyes, and saw Dorothea. The shock was invigorating as cold water splashed on hot skin. Dorothea had first come to Hannah in childhood, often at times of stress or difficulty. Hannah had accepted the spirit girl as a natural part of her life, unaware at first that not all children had such companions. Her long fair hair was, as always, tied with a lilac ribbon, blue dress flounced at the hem, light eyes calm. She smiled at Hannah from the far end of the room, and the familiar dimple creased her cheek. Hannah smiled back, feeling a surge of confidence. It had been a long time . . . but something good must be happening here if her old friend had returned. When she looked up again Dorothea had gone, but the confidence remained. She massaged Mrs Foster's back with light circular movements, and it seemed a shade less rigid.

Hannah withdrew her hand and clasped the bony fingers, which had become warmer. 'I don't think I've helped much tonight. But I believe I might if I came, say, twice a week for a while.'

Mrs Foster gave an embarrassed smile. 'I think it's a bit easier.'

'It would be lovely if that were so,' Hannah told her gently. 'But you've been in pain a long time.'

Shirley put her head round the door then came in, trying not to look as though she had been waiting outside. 'Mrs Stourton has kindly offered to come again,

Shirley. To do a bit more.' Mrs Foster was clearly uncertain what 'doing' entailed. Hannah got to her feet.

'We would know quite soon if I could help, Shirley. So how about if I come again, perhaps the night after next?'

Walking back through the lamplit streets, Hannah looked into a shop window and saw that she was smiling. Wipe that off for a start, stupid woman. Had she forgotten what Jonet had said, what Florence had admitted; what damage *she* might do, if what she feared was so? No fool like an old fool? Not at all; she was nowhere near old, still the right side of fifty. Never too late for a challenge – and Mrs Foster's back was a challenge, no mistake.

She dribbled a pebble along the pavement with her toe as she walked. All that might be fine in theory, but what if she failed? If she raised the poor woman's expectations then left her more hopeless than before? Well, she would warn her – as she already had – that nothing was certain. Then she would do her absolute utmost, and trust herself. After all, her friend Dorothea had come, and looked as though she approved. That had been marvellous, and could well be an omen for good.

It was, she knew, time to talk to Matthew. He was reading papers in the sitting room and making notes from them on the back of an envelope, brow creased in concentration. Hannah was continually surprised by how successful a solicitor he was, bearing in mind his unorthodox work methods and unlikely persona. He looked up now, took off his spectacles with obvious relief and cleared a space for her on the sofa.

'How about a drink?'

'I had a very indifferent cup of tea not long ago, that

I felt obliged to drink – I'll pass on anything else thanks, darling. Can we talk when you've finished what you are doing?'

'We can now,' he said promptly. 'I'm only sorting the wheat from the chaff. I've winnowed out a list of slow account settlers who won't get Christmas cards this year. So: what about Shirley's mum?'

Hannah told him. Afterwards she stood by the fire, stroking the back of his hand.

'So that's how it is, darling. She needs help so much, and I'd like to offer it if it's in my power. I'd love you to say – that's fine. Go ahead and I'll support you all the way.'

She looked at him. He had been listening closely, his gaze not leaving her face as she talked. She went on slowly: 'But if you tell me I'm a fool to meddle, I shall still have to try, I think. I just wish so much that I'd talked about it more with you – all of it – ages ago. I suppose I waited for the ideal time; and it never came.'

Matthew watched her fingers slide over his. 'I wouldn't dream of telling you you're a fool, sweetheart, because you're not. I know next to nothing about these "powers" you tell me of – never come across it before, you see. I've staggered through life to this point believing only what I could see with my own eyes.'

'Men do, mostly.' She knelt on the rug, hands on his knees. He smiled, and covered her hands with his large ones.

'Well then, why don't we settle for that first option for the present? Where I say "that's fine, go ahead and I'll support you all the way"?'

Hannah laid her cheek on his hand and they were quiet, watching the flames flare about the settling coals. She wanted this moment of closeness between them to be perfect, but knew it was not, because she still felt unable to tell him the rest of the story . . . The part where she had been accused by her daughter of being a witch, and could not say for sure that it was not so. What sort of a fool would he call her then?

'Oh – I forgot. Sorry, darling.' Matthew scrabbled among his papers on the carpet. 'This came second post.'

It was from Jonet. Hannah read it quickly, aware of the tension always engendered by her daughter. No acknowledgement of Hannah's apology, no mention of one from her. An impersonal page and a bit . . . She had been very busy at work, it had become cold quite suddenly in Bristol and she had had to buy an oil heater for her room. And she had become engaged to Mark Shapiro, newly qualified as a civil engineer. They hoped to marry in about a year, if they could find anywhere to live and Mark was settled in a good job.

She handed it to Matthew, a lump of tears in her chest making speech difficult. When he'd read it she said with stiff lips, 'She doesn't mention anything about my meeting him. I suppose that's because she's ashamed of me.'

Matthew drew her close and stroked her hair, while Hannah struggled with her emotion. Then she pulled her head back and gave him a watery smile.

'Come on, darling, let's go to bed. Have you ever made love with a mother-in-law to be?'

'Not that I recall,' he admitted. 'But I'm always open to new experiences.'

Chapter Five

Spring 1950

It was February before Mrs Foster began to relax. March, when Hannah detected a change in the consistency of the ball of pain. Heat flowed through her hands with greater freedom now, and she concentrated on being a clear and passive channel for the work. Mrs Foster repeated often what a 'bother' she was; as often, Hannah assured her that she would continue to come unless actually forbidden. The now weekly visit to the little flat became integrated into her life, the mongrel Ben welcomed her as a valued friend and she learned to drink the strangely unpleasant tea with a good grace. Each week she talked over the session with Matthew, who accepted Mrs Foster's small improvements without cynicism, for which Hannah was devoutly grateful. She tried hard to tell him exactly how it was ... the sensation of healing warmth flowing from her fingers into the pores of Mrs Foster's skin.

'That tallies with something I read.'

'Where was that, darling?'

'I got it from a book in the library.' He gave a self-conscious grin.

'You did?' She kissed his ear. 'It's lovely to know you went to that trouble. D'you think I should be doing that? You know, reading it up? I never have.'

'Maybe it's better to work instinctively, if you get results. They're what matter in the end.'

For Hannah it was not so simple. Sometimes she had an urge to stop what she was doing at this point, before it got out of control – a genie escaped from the lamp. Years ago, perhaps, she should have given a more wholesale commitment to her gift. But how could she have, fighting for the survival of herself and her family? And had she been too nervous of opening herself to these powers, of finding if their meaning in her life was more important than she wished them to be? Now, she wanted to be careful of herself; careful of her family.

It was also February before she came to grips with explaining to Liza the whereabouts of her father. A beautiful and expensive doll's house had arrived shortly before Christmas; panic-stricken, Hannah had rewrapped it and hidden it in the boxroom. 'She's loads of gifts already,' she had excused herself to Matthew. 'I don't need this problem right now; the situation is lying doggo and I'm happy with that.'

He had looked dubious; Matthew believed that complications invariably arose from devious behaviour. The ploy failed anyway because only two days afterwards, Liza had suddenly demanded to know what was a 'dad' and did she have one. So Hannah had told her that yes, she did have one, but that he lived across the sea in another country.

'Why?' Liza had asked, in the no-nonsense way of a four-year-old, and 'Why not?' her mother had countered brilliantly. 'People can live wherever they want, you know.' Liza had mulled this over; when presented with the doll's house and accompanying note she had sent him a somewhat obscure painting on blue sugar paper by way of thanks. There the relationship rested until April, when David Vaughan wrote to ask if he might visit Liza on her fifth birthday.

'It's too soon.' Hannah looked at the letter in her hand as if it might attack her. 'I don't want it; I absolutely do not.' She spoke to no one, she had taken the letter into the garden to read alone. Matthew had left for the office, Mrs Bridges had just started cleaning Liza's bedroom and Hannah could hear Liza talking to her, explaining what she would do at kindergarten this morning.

She felt the expensive vellum between her fingers. She recalled exactly when she had first read a letter from David Vaughan, first marvelled at the thick creaminess of the notepaper covered with his bold sprawling sentences. She had been twenty-four, in the summer of the General Strike, the summer before her marriage to Darrow Bates. She and Vaughan had met again by accident after a lapse of eight years, to find their youthful ardour undiminished, though he was now married. Hannah had told him of her agreement to buy a small shop in Taibach; he had quizzed her about the capital needed to get her business under way, and had looked dubious when told of the tiny amount she had. Next day had come a letter, delivered by hand. It requested Hannah to do him the honour of accepting the enclosed five £50 notes, if only to help pay the rent on the property until her trade settled down. That way, he wrote, he could feel part of her courageous venture. He had ended by saying he would never forget the time they had spent together, and that on his next visit to Wales he would hope to hear of her success and happiness.

Hannah sat down on a bench by the rose pergola, the letter feeling almost alive in her hand, so vivid were the memories it resurrected. God, how she had loved him . . . the letter, and the £50 notes had touched her so deeply as proof of his concern, his love, that finally she had found it impossible to throw that back at him. So she had answered that his motive appeared to be honest concern for her security and happiness, and because of that she would accept the money; but only as a loan, to be returned when trading became stable. She had added candidly that she *had* felt uncertain how things might work out with so little capital.

She had returned the money after about three years, with her grateful thanks, and in the belief that they would never meet again, for she was now married. Hannah sat for a moment in the warmth of the April sun, recalling the desolation of severing the final link with the man she had not ceased to love. As her marriage crumbled, she had drawn comfort from her memory of that love; strength and self-respect from the fact that David Vaughan, born to wealth and advantage, had loved her, Hannah Hywel from Incline Row.

Hannah read the present letter again then looked about her at the pushing, vigorous spring growth . . . at daffodils and late crocus, at primroses and straight green spires of embryo bluebells forcing a path into the sunlight. The roses put out tender, plum-coloured shoots that would quickly strengthen to bear their summer weight of blooms; a robin sat on a pergola strut and watched her silently, while sparrows in the budding apple tree fought with noisy energy.

Just a year, since they had last met at Morfa Cottage, since she had made her choice. Now that he was in the role of supplicant, Hannah recalled how much David Vaughan had given to *her*, in the fearful aftermath of Serena's death . . . how, fiddling a day's leave, he had taken his place unobtrusively at the back of the church for the funeral service; had later stood silent and apart by the yew tree for the committal. Some of the Hywel aunts had been outraged by the cheek of Hannah's 'fancy man', but Hannah had taken courage from his presence.

She got up, restless, and walked down the path to where she and Matthew had planted onion sets last weekend. What could she do now for David? Give him access to his daughter, of course; but where? She could scarcely invite him to stay in Matthew's house while he spent time with Liza, and he was not used to small children, or competent to look after one in a hotel. The alternative, of his taking her to Canada, Hannah did not entertain. In the end she composed not a rejection but a careful, friendly plea for a delay. Of course she understood his desire to see Liza. But she was rather young for him to take sole charge for an extended period. In a while perhaps he would find it simpler. Meanwhile he could write when he wished and Hannah would read the letter to Liza, and talk to her about David, the groundwork for a later relationship.

'Sounds perfectly reasonable, sweetheart.' Matthew read the letter with due attention. Hannah folded the single sheet into an airmail envelope, feeling depressed about the messy and unsatisfactory situation.

'It's the best I can offer, but he's not going to like it,' she said soberly. 'It *is* a mess. Darling –' Hannah turned and grasped his arms – 'How *could* you have taken up with a woman who had her life in less than good order by some standards?'

He thought for a moment, blue eyes serious, and Hannah watched his face with a sudden loss of confidence. The brass ship's clock on the wall of the dining room was ticking unusually loud and she had a stupid wish for it to stop, for time to stop before things went downhill.

'You're not "a woman", Hannah. You're the woman I love. Now, that means all of you, your past included.'

Matthew bent his head and brushed her cheek with his. 'The situation *can* be messy, I agree. People and their lives aren't neat, tidy little packages; you've only to read some of my clients' case papers to know that. Liza's relationship with her father, or the lack of it as it may fall out, might well give all three of you occasional grief. But take it a step at a time, eh?'

She nodded, reassured.

'I do love you,' she said, and meant it with all her heart. 'Tell me, Matthew . . . how would you feel about changing Liza's name to ours? I'm no longer a Bates. Jonet won't be a Bates after this year. Liza never was a Bates anyway. So it might be nice to drop it.'

'Fine by me. But with the entry on the stage of her father maybe you should let it simmer a while? It does occur to me that in the not too distant future she may want to call herself Liza Vaughan.'

Liza Vaughan . . . With a *frisson* of foreboding, Hannah guessed this situation might be messier than she or Matthew anticipated, and a cold core of uncertainty settled in her chest.

She congratulated Jonet warmly on her engagement.

> I should certainly like to meet Mark. Do please say when it is convenient for me to come down – or of course we should love you to bring him up here for a weekend any time you both are free. Where does he live? Where do you plan to be married? I shall need to talk over arrangements with Mark's parents in good time. I know you like to have things cut and

dried. Housing is so difficult right now isn't it – they just can't build fast enough! We wish you luck in your house-hunting. What do you think to wear? Oh dear; so many things to ask! I shall make a list of what I absolutely need to know and tick them off as you tell me.

Hannah was tentatively hopeful that Jonet might see her wedding as a time for reconciliation, forgiveness, whatever was appropriate, but it was high summer before she eventually met Mark Shapiro at Jonet's flatlet in Bristol. Liza had not been invited; Hannah had a defiant thought to take her anyway and be damned, but discretion overruled, with a fresh start in mind.

Jonet's intended was a tall, dark young man with horn-rimmed spectacles that contributed to his air of taking life seriously; Hannah had hoped for a more casual personality, to counterbalance Jonet's tendency to rigidity. Somewhat short on humour . . . ? not fond of animals . . . ? But hard-working and ambitious. Well, that would suit her daughter, and that, after all, was whom he was marrying.

They took the short bus ride to the hotel where Mark's parents were already waiting in the foyer. Seeing them rise, Hannah was grateful for Matthew's tip to put on her 'best bib and tucker' – in this case a long-skirted navy linen suit and apple green blouse, and a navy bowler hat trimmed with green petersham. Mrs Shapiro passed a discreet word to her husband, but Hannah was confident it could not possibly be a remark about her appearance. Her hair, cut shorter this summer, waved back prettily beneath the understated little hat; her navy kid gloves were hand-stitched and her slingback court shoes of softest leather. Pearls, a wedding gift from Matthew, glowed about her throat and earlobes; she looked an assured and beautiful woman and was grateful for it.

Introductions over, Hannah took stock of Jonet's in-laws as they took stock of her. Mr Shapiro was even taller than his son, hooked over at shoulder and nose, and with a small round stomach over which the buttons of his waistcoat marched like ants over a hillock. His eyes were pale and resigned, his mouth strangely at odds with them, hard edged and snappy; sparse hair was combed with precision over a bald crown. He leaned slightly towards his wife when she spoke as though hard of hearing, but she, perversely, leaned back a little as though to allow no advantage. Mrs Shapiro was much shorter, robust and ruddy cheeked, with lively dark eyes under heavy brows and a big mouth emphasised with red lipstick. Although the day was warm, a silver fox fur lay over the shoulder of her black and white checked dress and jacket which, though obviously expensive, did little to flatter her sturdy build.

Hannah sensed early on that there was small chance of striking up friendships here, but that must not prevent effort from being made. Small talk with the soup progressed to wedding talk with the roast chicken. Hannah, used to eating lightly at midday and already tired from the effects an early start, tension, and an over-sweet sherry pressed upon her, was alarmed at the increasing heaviness of her eyelids.

'The village church is really sweet,' Jonet was telling her with a degree of enthusiasm in her voice unfamiliar to Hannah. Mrs Shapiro smiled as if personally responsible for the sweetness of the church, which was in their village outside Bristol.

'You don't feel it would be nice to be married in our

own church then, darling?' Hannah fastened on that; unwise maybe, but a little sparring would at least keep her awake. The warmth of Mrs Shapiro's smile cooled a degree or two.

'Ah, but Mrs Stourton . . . there are just so many from our side we absolutely *must* invite . . . and Port – er – where was it? Well . . . We are *so* central in this area, are we not? And it is the sweetest church, a Norman tower of course.'

'I had no idea church architecture was so important an aspect of the marriage service to Jonet.' Hannah felt more alert now, smiling at her daughter. 'But she may have a completely free hand in her wedding arrangements. A choir, bells. A first-class sit-down meal at the hotel of her choice, whatever she wishes regarding gowns and flowers; I have already stressed that I do not intend to count pennies.' She cut a piece of chicken breast in two with a flourish, satisfied that she was holding her own.

'We did think, Mrs Stourton . . .' Mr Shapiro cleared his throat. His position as manager of a Bristol bank was perhaps responsible for his deliberate manner of speech, but Hannah found it a shade trying. 'In view of what may well be our superior numbers at the reception, that you might consider our contributing in some small way –'

'I could not hear of that.' Hannah held up an authoritative hand. She noted the large diamond cluster on Mrs Shapiro's perfectly manicured finger, the gold watch below her husband's immaculate shirt cuff, the quality of the fur draped over the back of the chair. She had a brief, glass-clear vision of the kitchen at Incline Row, and her mother taking down the blue toffee tin where the insurance money was kept, with hands scarred and calloused from her job cutting panels of tin; and of herself at fourteen turning the cuffs of her father's frayed flannel shirt. She laid down her knife and fork with a decisive click.

'It is the prerogative of the bride's family to play host to that of the groom's. Jonet's father died when she was seven, but I have worked to provide for her and she has wanted for nothing. I am now a woman of comfortable means, and they are at my daughter's disposal on this occasion,' she finished grandly. A sudden lump in her throat threatened to crack her voice so she smiled brilliantly at the party and picked up the dessert menu to study with close attention. This did not prevent her seeing Mark and Jonet exchange glances, and Mark's eyebrows lift a fraction, at which Jonet looked hard at her plate, dark hair swinging forward to mask her expression. Mr Shapiro cleared his throat again.

'In that case . . . splendid . . .' He dabbed his mouth with his napkin.

'Flowers in December are limited. I know –' Mrs Shapiro seemed to sound a conciliatory note now. 'But the church is quite tiny – a little will go a long way.'

'Whatever Jonet wants,' repeated Hannah with a hint of doggedness. 'Thank you, I shall have the *crème caramel.* Jonet . . . bridesmaids?' She wished desperately for Liza to be one, but hope faded as she saw the discomfort on Jonet's face. Suddenly, she wanted very much for this conversation to take place in private; too late now.

'It *is* a bit awkward, Mother . . . Mark wants his sister Angela to be matron of honour and she has these twins; they'll just be four years old. And Angela had rather thought of them being an identical little pair – you know, to walk in front of her and just behind me? Now, if you are absolutely set on Liza . . .

well, she would have to come in behind me as a single, then the twins, then their mother as another single. Which would make for a slightly ungainly diamond shape. What do you think?'

What Hannah thought was that Jonet was never going to come to terms with having an illegitimate half-sister. Or a mother who had a child out of wedlock. What had she told Mark? His parents? Sister?

Poor Jonet. At that moment Hannah would have given her life to make everything right for her daughter; she looked at her now with a troubled expression. Yet bitter disappointment made her unable to meet the lustrous eyes that could still remind her of Darrow Bates. He had had impressive eyes . . . Jonet now was all that was left of those years; and she, with Serena and Tom, had been the force to pull Hannah through them into better times.

'I think you should have your wedding exactly the way you want it, my dear. Liza may be disappointed – but she must learn that other people's wishes must be catered for besides her own. And this *is* your day.' She realised as she spoke that no one else at the table might even know who Liza was.

'Thank you, Mother.' Jonet put out her hand then, in a small blind gesture. Hannah took it, and smiled, guessing that this was the nearest her daughter could possibly come to an explanation, or an apology. Well, it must suffice.

'So who will give you away? Either Uncle Tom or Cousin Harry would do perfectly – Tom of course would be very honoured.'

Now she did indeed wish this conversation might have been private.

'You see, Mother – it's my boss, the head librarian. He's awfully keen to do it, knowing that my father . . .

well, you know, he would have been –'

'And in the absence of a father, the closest male next of kin usually takes over, in this case your Uncle Tom.' Hannah forced her voice into a low, well-modulated mould rather than the scream of sheer fury she felt pushing through her chest. Poor Tom; rejected she could only suppose as being sub-standard, Harry too on the same grounds . . . war wounds are rarely in fashion.

'Yes. Of course.' Jonet sounded just a shade ashamed. 'But you know, my boss and all that . . . it may be better to –'

'Of course.' Hannah looked at her untouched *crème caramel*. 'That all sounds fine, then.'

'He's a terribly nice chap,' Mark put in helpfully. 'Marvellous golfer – won cups by the dozen.' His parents spooned up their puddings; this was not their fight. Hannah nodded and started to button her jacket, wishing only for immediate flight.

'Oh well then; that sounds fine,' she repeated stupidly. 'Now I simply must dash –'

'You've not touched your pudding, Mother,' Jonet said accusingly.

'Will you not take coffee?' asked Mrs Shapiro in a concerned voice.

'May I offer you a lift to the station? My car is outside.' Mr Shapiro half rose from his chair. Hannah gave a firm shake of her head.

'Goodness no, thank you.' She gathered up her battered wits and rose, picking up her gloves. 'Oh – my contribution –' Pulling a pound note from her purse she laid it on the table, holding up her hand to check Mr Shapiro's protest. Time was running out on this scene and Hannah, aware that her behaviour might have been a touch wanting, had no wish to compound the damage.

'So nice to have met you. We shall see one another again soon, I hope. And Mark –' Hannah bestowed a frosted smile on Jonet's bemused fiancé and leaned to shake his hand, which was in the act of transporting a forkful of lemon sponge towards his mouth. 'Jonet, we must speak again soon about your dress. I know a very good woman in Clapham – but of course you may have plans made here. Have whatever you want; ivory velvet would be lovely for a winter wedding.'

Hannah bestowed a final smile upon the general company and left the restaurant at such a spanking pace that she all but collided with a waiter balancing a tray of drinks. In the foyer she stood irresolute. The cloakroom perhaps, to wash her hands and face; to cool down. Find a drink of water; her mouth was quite dry. Then a taxi to the station.

'Mother?'

Swivelling, Hannah was face to face with Jonet. Her mouth dried completely now; her voice could make no progress through it.

'Let's sit for a moment. Over there would do –' Jonet indicated a couple of easy chairs in a recess, partially screened by an oversized tub plant. Hannah followed her, though instinct urged her to make her escape, lowered herself into one of the chairs and gazed mute at her daughter.

'Mother.' Jonet paused. Hannah thought how pretty she looked; not the sunny loveliness of the young Serena but fragile, her small regular features and pale skin intensified by the backdrop of dark hair.

'I wish to say that I am really grateful for the things you gave me; and for the money you are prepared to spend on my wedding.' She swallowed, and Hannah wondered if her mouth too was dry and if so, why. 'I know you wanted Liza to be a bridesmaid; and Uncle

Tom to give me away. But thank you for not going on about it. All the same . . .'

She began to pleat her cotton skirt with her fingers, small neat pleats with small fine fingers. 'I don't think you understand, you see; you just think I'm being difficult. Don't you? You don't seem to appreciate in the least how horrible it was, knowing you'd gone ahead and done exactly what *you* wanted, with no thought at all for its effect on me!'

'I did my best to help you.' Hannah spoke slowly and heavily as though the words weighed too much for her tongue. 'I did know how upset you were –'

'You didn't *care* though, did you, Mother? Didn't care that I was *terrified* that what you'd done would get back to my friends at school, and even the staff. It was no fun, wondering what people were thinking and saying –'

'I did care. *I did care.*' Hannah repeated.

'Not enough to do something about it . . . No – you went on behaving like a – a floozie!'

The word struck Hannah like a blow in the face; staring at Jonet, she felt the bruise spread, fan outward, flow through her limbs. Jonet continued, her voice just one tone louder now as though the floodgates had opened and the strength of her pent-up resentment was forcing it out. 'Like all those cheap little factory girls who let themselves be got round by all the Yanks over here. But you were even worse . . .' Jonet's cheeks glistened now, with the effort she was making to express herself.

'At least *they* mostly had their babies adopted; they didn't saddle their families with the disgrace of them! They tried to put things as right as they could. And you were worse for another reason – you should have known better! You were middle-aged, and should have known right from wrong. But you were too selfish to worry about right and wrong, or *anything*, as long as you were doing what you wanted. Can't you see it's no use to keep pushing Liza at me, calling me her "sister"? She's nothing to do with me; she is a little bastard you had with David Vaughan!'

Jonet stopped herself suddenly. She was breathing hard, eyes dilated as she stared at her mother. Hannah felt her mouth pinched in, and the little navy hat seemed a shade too heavy now. But when Jonet opened her mouth to continue, she was checked.

'If you think, Jonet, that I could ever have given away one of my children you just cannot know me. I was capable of looking after her; I worked for her, as I had worked for you and Serry. I loved her as much; she was as truly mine as you were, even if I had not been married to her father.' Hannah's voice was stronger now.

'Yes: I may well have been wrong, to love a married man. But we aren't perfect – we all do wrong or stupid things at times. And I really loved him very much, you know . . . very much indeed, for a very long time.'

'You didn't love my father, then?' Jonet regarded her squarely.

'That was a different thing –'

'Either you did or you didn't. Did you wish him out of the way? Could that have been why you were called a witch? Because that is what you *are*? Margery Cooper heard her mother say so. All those visions and things . . . it used to upset me terribly. No one else's mother behaved like that.'

Hannah stood her ground there, deeply stung by the jibe. 'I thought you would have the intelligence to perceive that I had no choice in my inheritance, any more than *you* had a choice of light or dark hair, or of having brown eyes. Many Hywel women have over generations been passed down the gift of second sight and of healing; it was pure chance that I became one of their number. Before me, it was my great-grandmother . . . and *she* was loved, not reviled for the powers of her healing.' Hannah sighed. 'You are so lacking in compassion Jonet. Serena –'

'Ah: Serena.' Jonet fastened on the name with an eager snap. 'Always your favourite; don't think I didn't know that. You would have see me dead ten times over to have saved her.'

'That is a lie.' Hannah stood up, her eyes dark with anger. 'I have loved you deeply. If I had not loved you so much you could not possibly have hurt me so much.'

Jonet was quiet for a moment as they faced each other. Then she said with some reluctance: 'You do love me after a fashion, I suppose. I just always felt it was only a leftover sort of love, after those more important to you had had first call.'

'Not the case.' Hannah's voice was flat. 'There never was a question of "more" or "less".'

'You may wish to believe that, Mother. But your love for me was not enough to make you give up David Vaughan, was it? Or his daughter? I suppose I have to accept that, and perhaps you should too. That might help us rub along.'

'Why did you come after me?' Hannah asked. 'What did you really want to say?'

'I think I really intended to say thank you for what you are offering . . . and maybe try to explain why that is about all I *can* do for you. I am sorry, Mother. I wish as much as you that things were different.'

'Right . . . Well, Jonet; thank you for telling me how you feel. Goodbye now.'

She turned quickly and was out of the hotel and on the hot pavement, blinking in the sun and feeling as though she might be sick. And why not; all that lunch . . . then, all that . . . that . . . To her consternation, hot tears wet Hannah's eyes and she signalled a taxi disembarking its load; it would be dreadful to cry on the pavement.

One and a quarter hours to train time. She watched Bristol slide past the taxi window. A small gathering was protesting against British troops being sent to the Korean war, its placards waving at passing traffic. Hannah waved back assent, nodding. 'We should never have to fight again,' she told the taxi driver. 'I lost my father in the Great War and my daughter in the last.' He grunted, having no feelings either way so long as he was not called to go himself.

Despite the warm afternoon, Hannah felt cold. Jonet's voice repeated round in her brain endlessly now, echoing far back until it merged with itself coming again. She *had* been wrong; of course she had. Selfish – that accusation must stand. Why had she not been able to halt it all? She remembered how after Serena's death she had clung to David as a drowning man to a raft. She had been in too deep by then; needed him too much to turn away. And all the time she had been doing *that* to Jonet.

At the station she bought a newspaper and retired to the buffet. The coffee she ordered was undrinkable but provided a reason for being there. Hannah sat behind the newspaper and reflected upon options; it required no great brain to assess that she had just two. She could suggest Jonet stay away until such time as she could bear less ill will towards Hannah and her family generally. Or she could continue to turn the other cheek, while she was reviled and Tom, Harry and Liza were soundly snubbed.

No choice to make, in the event. She had set out this scenario years back by loving David Vaughan; had sown the wind, and must, it seemed, continue to reap the whirlwind. All she could do was try to ensure that neither Jonet nor Liza were too much blown about.

Hannah came out from behind the newspaper and found a phone box by the station entrance.

'Matthew? Hello darling. Just to confirm I'll be in on the 5.20 as arranged. What are you doing? And is Liza behaving? Oh, good – look, I've really no more change, must go – yes, everything is fine. 'Bye now.'

She waited a moment before pushing open the door. She had Matthew, and that was a huge plus. Just speaking with him for a few seconds made her feel more optimistic. She also had Liza. And dear Tom; and Joe would be here again soon, the year was shooting by. And maybe one day Jonet would see her mother's sins in a more forgiving light.

Hannah adjusted her hat and sat down to wait for the London train.

David Vaughan accepted, albeit reluctantly, the verdict on his proposed visit, and instead sent off another expensive gift to his daughter, this time an exquisitely made doll's pram complete with embroidered quilt and pillow and little grey storm apron to snap on. Hannah would have sent it back as being entirely too much, but the return carriage to Canada was beyond reason. It served instead to soften the blow to Liza of not being a bridesmaid, and Hannah wrote again to David, specifying gifts for birthday and Christmas only in the future.

By August, Jonet still had said nothing about wedding gowns or receptions, or referred to their last meeting. But Hannah bided her time; if Jonet wanted financial help she would be in contact, no matter how painful for her pride. The days were anyway over-full, with Joe's annual visit, Liza's school holidays, the restaurant, and Mrs Foster's back.

Mrs Foster and Hannah were together making a voyage of discovery. There was no set time scale for it, only an ultimate hoped-for destination. For a week, while at Morfa Cottage, Hannah made no physical contact but instead went to her room at ten o'clock each evening and sat quietly for ten minutes, emptying her mind of all but an image of Mrs Foster. Once during this week, the spirit girl Dorothea materialised, sitting on the bed and smiling at Hannah, which seemed to indicate that the right lines were being followed. By September the pain had eased sufficiently for Mrs Foster to walk with Shirley as far as the Common, movement was more natural in the neck, and sleep was usually possible without painkillers. Hannah would smile with delight at each milestone on this path they trod. Surely, if she was healing, she could not be a witch? She longed to tell Jonet what was happening; but now she realised that Jonet would not wish to know.

Jonet finally wrote in October. A nearby dressmaker was working on a dress design for her, she had seen some suitable material in Bristol and would it be possible for her to buy it, also material for the bridesmaids' dresses? Hannah read the brief letter several times, hoping to find nourishment for a hungry heart. Jonet apologised for the brevity; the standard excuse of being very busy, staff holidays this time, but said she would write again soon about the reception details, and that they had booked the church for the second Saturday in December. Hannah sent a generous cheque by return, more than sufficient for material, chewing her pen over the precise amount.

'She can put what's left over for the reception deposit . . . and she'll probably need money for church flowers and bouquets too.' She looked at Matthew for approval. 'Then there'll be her going-away outfit.'

'What did you do, sweetheart, for your wedding?' Matthew looked up from his macaroni cheese to catch a shadow darkening Hannah's eyes. She pushed her food around her plate for a moment then passed him the bread basket and took a drink of water herself.

'Oh . . . not much, actually. Strictly a no-frills function.'

Taking another forkful of macaroni, Hannah knew there was absolutely no point in going into detail; there was anyway no detail worth the mention in a wedding as stark as hers to Darrow Bates on a murky November day. She had worn a plain blue dress and jacket with a navy hat, and Florence had been her only attendant at St Mary's church. Sam Warburton, who had been her father's closest friend, had given her away, and cousin Harry's mother, Aunt Maggie, had asked the small assembly back to her house afterwards for refreshments. There was no need for a going-away outfit as Hannah was going nowhere save back to her house in Incline Row on the arm of her new husband, though Florence took young Tom in for the first night to give them some privacy. 'There was no spare money, you see,' she added simply, knowing that it would be difficult for Matthew to appreciate the sensation of being without the price of a pair of shoes for Tom, let alone so inessential an item as wedding flowers. 'I was just getting the business started.'

'Ah.' He smiled. 'That's why you intend showering upon this young lady every good thing a bride could wish for.'

'Darling, don't ever set up as a clairvoyant, you're quite unsuited.' She laughed at him. 'I'm doing it because I'm frantic to compensate her for causing so much hurt – I think.'

'It would be lovely if Jonet wanted to compensate *you*.' Matthew was suddenly serious. 'She's made you bleed a time or two, even in the past few years.'

Hannah gazed out of the window, where the garden lay dim, autumnal and silent. She had said nothing to him about the scene in the foyer. She felt too ashamed; not of Jonet, who had done no more than state truthfully how she felt, but of her own culpability as seen by her daughter. Having seen herself through those eyes she was too ashamed to pass on the vision of herself to Matthew, whose good opinion she valued so highly. She said quietly: 'After the wedding, perhaps. You know, when she's feeling secure – then she may find it easier to forget that I made her bleed too.'

Mrs Foster continued to improve through the autumn. She looked years younger, could take Ben for short walks, do light shopping and a little housework. But she was uncertain how to relate to Hannah; this stranger who had done something – she had no idea what – to take her from a living hell to somewhere miraculously within sight of normality. Hannah herself was so delighted at the clear progress that she had to remind herself firmly that it was not her doing; that she was no more than a conduit through which the healing force was able to flow. But each time she thought of it she found herself smiling broadly . . . it could not be evil, surely, to have relieved Mrs Foster's pain. The situation had, for Mrs Foster, no known rules of social conduct; playing for safety, she offered Hannah a glass of dark sticky-sweet sherry bought on

VE Day and kept for special occasions. Such occasions had been rare, for the bottle was still almost full. Conscious of the honour Hannah had sipped the sherry, smiling bravely over the brim of the glass and narrowly avoiding a refill.

'She does so want to know where I learned to "do it",' Hannah told Matthew. 'And when I say I don't actually "do" anything, that healing is simply channelled through me, she says "I see", and looks so worried that I have to divert her. 'Oh – ' she reached over to the sideboard for her bag. 'A letter from Joe. I was beginning to think he'd abandoned me.' She passed it across.

'There's something . . . I can't define it. But I sense a difference. I thought in August he seemed a shade more relaxed, but we didn't see enough of him to quiz him, did we – all those salesrooms and auctions?' Hannah frowned. 'I hope he's not overworking with that heart problem; I don't think he can be though, this highly unfamiliar aspect of him I noticed this trip didn't seem in the least like fatigue.'

'Could it be success?' Matthew spread out Joe's letter. 'He does seem to be doing quite well now. Or could it possibly be a lady? Might he finally have succumbed?'

'Good Lord. You know, for years I'd think, why on earth doesn't Joe *marry*. But this year I didn't give it a thought.' She spooned out dessert and handed it to him. 'Now I may have to wait till next year.'

'By then he may have owned up.'

Hannah's smile widened. 'How exciting. But you're probably wrong; after all you're only a solicitor.'

'Not a clairvoyant, certainly,' Matthew agreed, and grinned widely himself.

The wedding took place shortly before Christmas in the Shapiro village church, as arranged. Jonet was exquisite in a sculpted gown of ivory moiré, with crystal beading at the high neck and on the pointed wrists of narrow sleeves, and a long train. A small crown of shimmering beads caught and held her veil, and she carried delicate cream roses and lilies. The small bridesmaids were in ivory velvet trimmed with seasonal holly red, and carried baskets of Christmas roses. Their mother walked behind them in a New Look dress and fitted jacket of icicle blue bordered with midnight blue velvet, the full skirt belling almost to her ankles. Her matching velvet pillbox was swathed with veiling in which nestled more Christmas roses. Everything perfect, tasteful, just as Jonet had planned.

Watching them from the bride's family pew – herself, Harry and Florence, and Tom – Hannah had to admit that it was a charming little procession. But her heart ached to see Liza walking between the twins . . . or behind . . . or anywhere! And of course; no Serena either. She blew her nose, and wished very hard to have had Matthew there. But he was at home with Liza, who was in the late itchy stages of measles.

'She will be much better to stay here with me,' he had said. 'The journey's long and it's very cold. I shall write a note of regrets for myself . . . the main thing is for you to go to be there for Jonet.'

'I suppose so. But Liza had so looked forward to it, even though she couldn't be a bridesmaid. At least she has the Nativity play to come – she'll be fine by then. Oh dear . . . Nativity plays *again*!'

Matthew pulled a wry face. 'There's no way she'll miss that, particularly now she has that fetching blue curtain you found her to wear. Now that's strange, didn't you think –' He looked serious then. 'She saw at once that it was the exact colour of her eyes?' They had laughed together; but Hannah had long since noted in Liza an unusual awareness both of herself, and of her effect on others. Hannah lived with the possibility of this daughter inheriting her gifts, and was watchful, but hoped this trait was no more than an outsize dose of female vanity . . . hoped that no one, ever, would have cause to brand Liza a witch.

Harry and Tom loomed stoically at her side in the pew . . . the least they could do, they'd said; represent the family and back up Han. She'd booked them into a Bristol hotel for the night so they might travel back tomorrow in comfort. She glanced at Tom and stifled a smile; he looked as though he was about to have a tooth out. Soon be over, Tom; she'd be into the vestry shortly with the Shapiros, just across the aisle from her. All very correct . . . very middle-class. Mrs Shapiro's clothes were on this occasion both tasteful and expensive. Hannah was grateful to Matthew for persuading her to wear his advance Christmas gift: a detachable mink collar for her coat with a matching muff, that had made her gasp. 'You wear them,' he had advised. 'There's nothing like a touch of mink if there's a touch of one-upmanship about, as there just could be on this happy occasion.'

Jonet had been impressed. 'Wonderful' . . . She had stroked the luxurious fur with half-shut eyes. 'Mark will buy mink for you in a few years,' Hannah had told her, and believed it. Mark Shapiro was clearly on his way up as a civil engineer at a good time, when much of Europe's houses, bridges, public buildings, dams and road systems were still to be rebuilt. He stood with his long lean back to Hannah, putting a ring on the finger of her daughter. His dark head was turned to Jonet so that the December sun filtering weakly into the little church sparked off his horn-rimmed spectacles. Be good to her, Hannah told him in her head. It hasn't been easy for her. She is very proud, and we were so poor. She was ashamed that her mother had to work. Ashamed, I think, that her father was killed in the steelworks . . . though that seems a strange cause for shame, doesn't it? And she's so ambitious, which is always hard, particularly without a father. And I have hurt her deeply. I know that and I am sorry.

'Today must have cost you a packet,' said Harry, when they had repaired to their hotel for a meal and bed, tired after the day's early start and all the emotion engendered by the occasion.

'Like the price of refitting the *Queen Mary*,' said Florence with a wide smile, and winked at Hannah. Florence looked handsome in a no-expense-spared outfit of copper and oatmeal wool dress with a three-quarter copper coat deeply flared from the back yoke, and a wide-brimmed oatmeal hat that sat elegantly on the streaked dark hair. Hannah had always envied Florence her hair; the thick glossy braids had been the first thing she had noticed when they had stood together in the school hall as nervous five-year-olds. Hannah winked back at her then said seriously, 'It wasn't cheap. But I know you're all aware that Jonet has suffered quite a bit on my account. So I gave her a free hand; and you know how she likes things done properly.'

Buying love again? She stirred her coffee and smiled at these three people so very dear to her: a brother, a cousin, a beloved friend. Maybe she had gone a degree overboard on the wedding; but with no Serry . . . and Liza's wedding years off . . . and outward appearances had always meant so much to Jonet. Well, she had certainly had a stylish send-off with all the trimmings . . . a long way from Incline Row.

Hannah suddenly felt extremely sad, sad enough to want to put down her head on the table and howl. Stupid; she was just tired. It certainly had been a long day. She held up her glass to Tom.

'You've no plans in this direction, young man? No lady tempting you out of your comfortable little rut?'

Tom fidgeted, ducked his head in the shy way he had, and she regretted teasing him. 'I'm fine, Han.'

'You certainly are.' Harry leaned back, relaxed after the stresses of the day and the anxiety that one of his headaches might be triggered. 'You've got it made, Tom Hywel – a cosy little place with no one to tell you what to do – except when Han comes at a weekend of course! I bet Mark Shapiro doesn't get things all his own way with Jonet, Han.'

'I think he can probably hold his own, Harry.' Hannah poured more brandy. 'They're both high flyers. Jonet intends being top dog at the British Library one day, and Mark's set on building the most advanced bridge ever designed. If they pull together the world's their oyster.'

Harry was quiet, thinking of the oysters he had maybe missed owing to a second's bad timing on the Somme. After a minute he looked at his wife, smiled and said: 'Flo's got enough get-up-and-go for both of *us*.' Florence smiled back and blew him a kiss.

'Let's drink to that,' said Hannah, and buried her nose in her brandy glass to hide the tears that threatened again.

'So in the end I just let go and had a good howl when I got to my room,' she told Matthew on the way home from Paddington. He squeezed her hand.

'Every mother should cry on her daughter's wedding day. I'd have worried if you hadn't.'

'And Liza wasn't a lot of trouble?'

'There were no big dramas. She's getting excited about the boys coming home for the hols. Oh, and she's started hunting for Christmas parcels. Seems someone at school told her that Father Christmas isn't real, and that presents are hidden by parents.' Matthew glanced across and grinned.

Hannah groaned. 'That's what comes of lying to children. What did you do when yours were little?'

'Oh . . . Myra let them put out mince pies and a glass of beer for the visitor of the night, the Big Man himself. By the time they rumbled that I was scoffing the lot, they were only interested in what they had, not who gave it to them.' Matthew went quiet and she knew he was recalling other Christmases.

'The first one alone must have been dreadful.' She put her hand over his on the steering wheel.

'Not easy, certainly. It was the – suddenness. Those V2s . . . one minute she was there; the next –'

'So hard for the boys too, darling – your being away some of the time.'

'I asked to be kept in London where possible.'

'There's lots more I'd like to hear about your war, you know. "Military Intelligence" sounds, well . . . slightly mysterious, even romantic.'

Matthew snorted. 'Quite the contrary! It could be stultifying; paperwork, legal to-dos, endless meetings with desperately boring types. Now, and here, is a big improvement. I really hope it's better for you too, darling.'

Hannah nodded. 'Oh yes. Now is certainly better for me.'

Her war . . . no, not especially good. A child lost to her; quite the worst. The best, snatched moments with David Vaughan, but even those guilt-ridden, full of tension. And on VE Day, the war had ended for her with the birth of Liza; with the coming of new life. Alone in the Clapham hospital, Hannah had wept for the losses of the past six years, and had prayed for the rebuilding of so many millions of lives besides her own. Yes; now was without doubt better for her too.

'OK, sweetheart?' He turned for a moment in the dull December light as they sped home, where Liza would be waiting with Ursula Mallow, both wanting to be told about Jonet's wedding and expecting a piece of cake. She would tell all the good bits; but not about wanting to cry. Or about missing Serena so badly . . . or wondering if she ever would feel at ease with her firstborn again . . . ever feel certain she was not regarded as a witch, a murderer of her husband . . .

'Yes, dear. I'm OK.'

Chapter Six

May 1952

It was not until Liza was just seven that Hannah finally agreed for David to meet his daughter, on the May half-term holiday. She had asked if he would come mid-morning, when the house was otherwise empty; it was hard to judge who was the more nervous, daughter or mother, and she wanted no interested bystanders. David intended staying overnight at the Savoy and would arrive by taxi at eleven prompt. Liza had been sick with excitement during the night; now her bag was in the hall and she at the window, watching for a first glimpse of the man himself.

'D'you think this is really all right, Mummy?' She stroked the sleeve of the new maize-coloured, double-breasted coat with printed corduroy collar and pocket flaps. 'And the shoes? I really like the straps, d'you think Daddy will?' Pointing a toe as she bent to consider the pretty tan sandals, Liza pirouetted before her mother. 'Should I wear my hat? Yes, I will.' She put on her straw hat with turned-up brim and examined her reflection in the long looking-glass in the hall. 'Does that suit me?'

Hannah was desperate to reassure the child, who for the first time in her short, confident life hungered for approbation from a man she had never seen.

'Sweetheart; your daddy will like whatever you have on, I promise. It's *you* he wants to see and he may not even notice your clothes, although they really are beautiful. You just do not have to think about them, truly.'

'Shall I take my coat off when we sit down for lunch?' Liza pulled back her coat to examine the full skirt of the maize and rust checked dress, still anxious.

'Daddy will see to that, darling.' Hannah hoped devoutly at this point that David would be equal to all a very young girl's needs; he had not, after all, ever before been in charge of a child. So many small services were performed routinely during a day . . . really, this could be a terrible mistake she was making. Liza would be on the sticky end, miles away from her mother with someone who had not a single clue.

Too late now. And she must *not* undermine the confidence of either Liza or David by even suggesting they might not cope. How long now . . . Ten to eleven.

'My dad is coming from Canada soon to take me on holiday,' she had heard Liza tell schoolfriends, teachers, tradesmen, bus conductors. She had drawn a carefully coloured picture of the house to post to David, 'So he will know where to come.' She had spent a whole Saturday morning getting it exactly right, even to the tree in the front hedge and the parrot tulips, and had printed the address beneath, tongue out in fierce concentration. Liza loved Matthew, of that there seemed little doubt. But it was a casual, confident love, growing steadily from everyday contact and good-natured care on Matthew's part. He was a secure feature of her life; simply there, as her mother was there. This stranger from across the sea was an unknown quantity. Liza had no idea what to expect, except that they would love each other, for that was what fathers and daughters did.

Hannah was nervous for quite a different reason.

She had not seen David Vaughan since just before Liza's fourth birthday, when he had discovered his daughter. Then both atmosphere and dialogue had been, to say the least, tense. Three years on, Hannah wanted only to be pleasant, friendly and hand over Liza to his temporary care with a minimum of fuss and never a recrimination in sight on either side. Whether this could be achieved in so emotional a climate was uncertain, and she did her own share of skirt twitching, checking of stocking seams and hair patting as eleven o'clock approached. She had changed twice in an effort to strike exactly the right, relaxed note. Linen trousers had been first choice; they had been jettisoned for a flared navy and cream coin-dot skirt, and a navy cotton blouse with a mandarin collar and roll-back sleeves. When suddenly he was there, instructing the driver to wait and striding up the drive to the front door in the decisive fashion she recalled so well, Hannah caught her breath and a nervous drumbeat of a pulse started up at the back of her skull.

She seemed to take for ever to reach the front door and pull it open.

'Hello.' A stupid greeting.

'Hello, Hannah.' What an attractive, charismatic man he still was. The once auburn hair was grey but still curly, the deep-set aquamarine eyes that were echoed so potently in his daughter's, magnetic as they had ever been. The lantern jaw remained taut, brows met with a deeper but familiar fold over the narrow bridge of his nose. And he looked fit; fitter than during the harsh middle years of the war, when he had patrolled North Atlantic convoy routes in a Sunderland, searching for U-boats with cruelly little respite.

'Do come in, David.' She stepped back and trod on Liza's foot; the rest of Liza was right behind her and there came a loud wail from that direction. Hannah swung round and hugged the child, hoping to suffocate the noise before it took firm hold. 'Liza – I'm sorry. Don't cry now . . . please.'

Liza took a moment to decide whether a good cry would be worth the attention, but judged that she should be due for full attention anyway, so there was no particular point in getting herself red and hot. Anyway, she wanted to see this man, and couldn't if her eyes were all screwed up.

'Oh dear.' David Vaughan looked down at his daughter. Hannah tried not to watch, but it was impossible. They would not often be together thus, parents and child. This was the first time, and she would have been less than human had she not been riveted by David's reaction.

'Are you better now?' he asked Liza seriously. His gaze was fiercely intent as he studied the small, creamy-skinned face with freckles across the nose and cheekbones. Liza studied him in turn, her eyes so like his, checking every detail. Then she said equally seriously:

'Yes thank you.'

'Good.' He took her hand and briefly held it between his own, then bent to embrace her in a gentle salute. Over his daughter's shoulder he looked up at Hannah and smiled, and she smiled back, struggling with a torrent of emotions. David, she had guessed, had himself on a tight rein, as had she. Liza, the initial drama over, was *not* on a tight rein; she bubbled, jumped and squeaked with excitement at this amazing find of a father, allowing her parents to laugh companionably at her and so ease their passage through the meeting.

'Will you have coffee?' Hannah was apprehensive about this. Liza, impatient to be off, might get fractious, and their own fragile situation could deteriorate. Vaughan hesitated.

'May I take up that offer when I bring her back? We have to pick up a hire car, then get to the Savoy for a celebratory lunch before we set off for the coast.'

'Of course.'

'Now –' He hesitated again. 'Is there a list of things I should know about her routine? Don't think I'm not aware of them – routines. Give me as many instructions as you wish.'

Hannah laughed at his apprehension. 'I think Liza will tell you if you're not on track. Teeth cleaning, of course. There's a rag of pink wool she takes to bed – the remains of her first cot blanket. I have pinned it to her nightie. If she calls in the night just answer, and she should go straight off to sleep again.'

'Fine. Here's our hotel address, and the phone number. We will call you each evening, and post a card every day, shall we?' Vaughan smiled at Liza, who nodded vigorously.

'That sounds perfect. I hope you have a lovely holiday. I've put in plenty of clothes, and books and crayons for quiet times.' As Hannah bent for Liza's goodbye kiss she wondered briefly if the little girl actually *would* walk away with this as yet unknown man, leaving all familiarity behind. And if David would bring her home again as promised, saying goodbye for anther long year of her childhood.

David took her hand just before she opened the door. He kissed her softly on the cheek, perhaps reading the fear in her eyes. 'Don't have a single worry, Hannah. I shall deliver her back on time and in first-class condition, just as I have found her. You've done a great job on her . . . thanks.'

Hannah watched from the doorstep as they walked hand in hand to the taxi; David carrying the bag, and Liza her teddy bear and her hat, swinging it by the elastic and chatting to her father, who bent his head to listen. As they climbed into the car and David slammed the door they both waved, and she waved back, swallowing hard on the lump in her throat.

'That's a very pretty dress,' observed David Vaughan. 'Shall I give you a hand to tie the sash?'

'Yes please.' Liza stood with her back to him while he arranged the narrow, burgundy velvet bow of the sash. 'I had this new for my birthday party,' she told him, craning her neck to see if he was making a job of it. 'Mummy said it was rather a lot of money, but that she would make an exception. What is an exception? I didn't get one, are they hard to make? She was probably too busy. Thanks, that's right.'

She went to look at herself, and gave a satisfied nod. The frock was of dusky pink silk with a simple, dropped-waist bodice above a bias-cut circle of skirt. Now she went to the lid compartment of her case for a hair ribbon of the same burgundy velvet as the sash, and handed it to her father.

'You haven't said what an exception is. Can you do my hair right?'

'I'm not altogether certain . . . I hope so.' Vaughan had no idea if every small girl was as exacting as this one, and hoped that Liza's toilette would be complete before the hotel dining room closed for the night. He had been hungry an hour ago but felt he might be getting past it now; he saw he would have been wise to have had afternoon tea when Liza had had her bread and butter and bramble jelly with a glass of milk on arriving. 'An exception?' He rooted about in his brain. 'It isn't an actual *thing*, Liza . . .'

'How could Mummy make one, then?' she asked reasonably. She had slept for an hour in the car coming down, and now seemed fearsomely alert, whilehe was definitely on the wane. Vaughan drew a deep breath.

'What she meant was, she would spend a lot on the dress for you just this once. An exception means just this once.' He was rather pleased with that, and went on quickly before Liza could demolish it with her seven-year-old brand of deadly logic: 'How does the hair ribbon go, then?'

'Oh, dear . . .' Liza sighed patiently at his ignorance. 'Like *this*. Daddy. No – *behind* my ears. And you forgot to brush it first.'

Eventually the hair was passed fit, cascading in polished copper over the muted pink bodice to show-stopping effect. Her pink socks were each turned over exactly the same amount, and the black patent shoes buttoned across just so.

'Now I must find my bracelet.' Liza finally located that in a velvet drawstring bag and David fastened the small shells about her wrist after several failed attempts.

'I'm ready now. Do I look nice?' She stood before him, and did indeed look very nice; though her father sensed he would have been wise to say so whatever the end result of their labours.

'Liza – you look beautiful. So shall we go down to dinner, then?' He held out a hand.

'Daddy, aren't *you* changing?'

Vaughan forbore to point out that there were simply not the hours available for them both to change. 'I've freshened up; and this is a very nice suit, I thought it would do perfectly well with the change of tie. Tell you what – I'll change tomorrow night, when I'm not so tired, eh?' He guided her firmly through the door of the suite and shut it behind them before he remembered that his money and keys were on the dressing table in his room.

When they finally attained the dining room it was full, and couples were foxtrotting on the little floor. They were shown to their table against the wall, but Liza told the *maître d'* she would like to be near the band. Here David put his foot down hard. 'We won't be able to talk, Liza!' He practically carried her back to the quietly agreeable wall table. Liza looked mutinous but he chatted pleasantly and fast, giving her no opening to rebel. By the time they had studied the menu her pique had subsided; she asked for dandelion and burdock, and Vaughan ordered a single malt whisky.

'I don't want soup, thanks.'

'Fair enough. You can talk to me while I have my oxtail.'

'Oxtail? What is that?' She raised her eyebrows at him over her straw.

'Oh – well actually, it's just what it says. The soup is made from the tail of an ox.'

'A *tail*?' Her perfect nose wrinkled in distaste. 'How awful! Daddy, how can you eat a tail!'

They eventually progressed to the main course. David allowed her to wrestle with chicken for a while before realising that she needed help to cut it, and was not anyway high enough to the table. A cushion was fetched, he cut the chicken into bite sizes and then attacked his own meal. But Liza had lost interest now and idly speared the occasional pea.

'What I'd really like is jelly and custard, Daddy.'

Vaughan smiled, his mood turned benevolent by good food.

'Both together, sweetheart?' Liza pushed a pea into a cave of duchesse potatoes and rolled up a circle of carrot to block the entrance.

'Yes. You put the custard on top of the jelly with your spoon. I had it at Jeremy's party, it was super. Mummy keeps saying she'll do some, but then she brings home another pie from the restaurant. Pie's not bad with loads of custard, but I'd rather the jelly. Red jelly.'

'Mm-mm. Look, try a bit more chicken first, eh?'

'Do you love Mummy?' Liza manipulated eight peas into an upturned semicircle and placed two peas above them for nostrils.

'Yes, I do.' Her father served himself one more spoon of carrots.

'You can come and live at our house if you want,' Liza offered. 'Jake's room is often empty, even when Uncle Joe comes to stay. Or you could have the camp-bed in my room. That would be lovely.'

Vaughan put his knife and fork together. 'Honey, that's a really kind offer, and I'd love to accept it. Only, I have this really big airfreight business in Canada, you see. I may well sell out in a few years; but for now, I have to stick to it. So I can't leave Canada for too long a time.'

'Oh.' She sounded deflated. Vaughan summoned the waiter, and quite soon a red jelly rabbit arrived sitting in the middle of a plate, also a big jugful of custard.

'That fills the bill, does it?' He lifted the jug. 'Shall I pour for you, honey?'

'Yes please. Oh, listen . . . that's a waltz, Daddy. Can you do it? I do it at dancing class. Come on –' She wriggled off the cushion. Vaughan, fork poised over his dessert, set it down and pushed back his chair.

'Am I lucky! A waltz with the prettiest girl in the room.' He bent to take her about the waist but after a few steps gave up, and lifted her into his arms. They circled the floor slowly under the coloured revolving lights. He hummed the tune then sang it softly by Liza's ear, causing her to smile with delight.

The lights went up at the end of the song. Diners at the edge of the dance floor applauded as Vaughan set Liza down and swept her a low bow. She responded with an immaculate curtsy, and they were applauded again as they returned to their table.

'Oh dear.' The hot custard had melted the rabbit, which was now a raft of red liquid on a yellow sea. Liza waved her hand at it, flushed with public acclaim.

'Never mind. I can eat it anyway if you help me back on the cushion.' The lights had gone down again for a tango. When that was over, Liza was found to be asleep, face down on the table, with a lock of hair floating in the red and yellow pudding.

He carried her up to their rooms, wiped her hair in the bathroom and eased her out of her clothes and into her nightdress without a sign of consciousness. He considered trying to clean her teeth, thought better of it and eased her into one of the twin beds in her room, covering her securely with pale green sheets and blankets. Vaughan sat on the other bed and watched her for a while, then picked up the phone on the table between.

'Hannah?' He swung up his legs and lay back, kicking off his shoes. 'I'm sorry it's rather late. No, everything is fine. Only, it took so much longer than I'd thought to get organised to go to dinner . . . then that took ages too. Then Liza fell asleep at the table and so can't say good-night to you – I've just popped her into her bed and she's out for the count, no kidding. So I'll get some shut-eye myself now. Yes, the hotel's fine, accommodation A1. 'Night then, Hannah. I'll call you again tomorrow.'

He was still for a long time, too tired to get up, watching his daughter. Eventually he left the bed and perched on the side of hers, examining her face, her hand thrown across the pillow, a strand of copper hair draped over the sheet. When finally he went through to his room and got into bed himself he was too tired even to read the paper. He put out the bedside lamp and lay in the dark, listening to Liza's light, regular breathing through the open door.

Hannah took a letter from her bag and climbed into bed. 'From Jonet – I thought I would save it for last thing, and today's been such a bunfight . . .'

'Mm-mm.' Matthew yawned. 'That was a long session you had with Liza's teacher. Everything in order in that department?'

'Oh . . . a bit of naughtiness maybe. Inattention, talking too much, that sort of thing. There's usually a bit of adjusting at the start of a new school year, and more is expected of children in this class, they're not just babies any more. We shall see how Liza copes with a more responsible regime.'

Matthew took one of her hands and began to work on it, kneading and massaging. Hannah felt like purring. 'Where did you learn this, darling? It's lovely.'

'A by-product of my misspent youth. Good job I salvaged one small talent from it.'

'Was your youth dreadfully misspent? Strange;

there's so much I'll never know about you . . . I shall enjoy speculating on where, and with whom you became so proficient a masseur.'

'When one is articled to as boring an old toad as I was, it's absolutely essential to break out sometimes. These fingers are quite tense, actually.'

'Mm-mm.' Hannah was reading Jonet's letter. When she had finished she stared across the room.

'Is there a problem?' Matthew bent to intercept her gaze.

'I suppose not. Jonet's pregnant, a baby due in December.'

'That doesn't sound like a problem; unless you don't like the idea of grandmotherhood?' He laid down one hand and picked up the other.

'Silly. But this is the first I've heard, and she's due in three months, it's already October.'

He took the letter and put it on the bedside table. 'I dare say lots of women keep it to themselves for a while; it may not seem such an interminable time, then.'

'I wouldn't know. My mother was dead when I was pregnant.' She looked away. 'Jonet could easily have said something in June when we saw her.'

'She might not have wanted you to start fussing.' He stroked her wrist with firm fingers.

'I would not have. I'd just have been very pleased . . . there's surely nothing wrong with that. And I'd have offered to buy the pram, or cot, or something. That's a grandparent's prerogative, isn't it?'

'Sure. But you still can. You could drive down to Bristol at the weekend.'

Hannah said softly: 'She would say if she wanted that. But I'll reply tomorrow of course. And offer to buy anything she hasn't already got lined up.

Knowing Jonet, it will be highly organised by now, though.' She turned to him. 'Thank you, darling – that feels really good, lovely and relaxed.' She shook her hands, then kissed him. 'I hope you don't mind sharing a bed with a grandmother?'

She did go to Bristol, later on in October when Jonet had started her maternity leave. Pregnancy suited her, softening her sharp brittleness. She wore a pencil skirt with a football-sized hole cut out and tapes across the waist, under a paisley-patterned, fine wool top cut on the cross, and she looked extremely pretty. Hannah wanted to ask if she was happy; but she found it difficult to put such spontaneously personal questions to Jonet. The parameters of their relationship had, she believed, been well and truly set out the day of the engagement lunch, and did not include confidences.

They ate their meal at the little square Utility table at one end of the sitting room, with a vase of orange chrysanthemums in the centre of the green checked tablecloth. The flat was one of four in a converted Edwardian villa, which meant big windows and airy but cold rooms. The window by the dining table overlooked an overgrown, crazy-paved terrace and a stretch of uneven lawn bordered with mildewed Michaelmas daisies, gangling and sparsely flowered.

'It will be lovely next summer, when you can put the baby on a rug out there.' Hannah nodded at the terrace. 'And there's a park quite near for walks, isn't there? What about a pram? I need to know what you have and what you might still need.'

'Thanks, but Mark's parents have a pram already ordered; a lovely grey Osnath, the top of the range and a joy to push. My sister-in-law offered me one of the twins' cots, and Mark has painted it yellow to match the other things. If you've had enough lunch I'll show you . . .'

The small second bedroom had been painted in yellow and white. It had yellow striped curtains and a frieze of yellow teddy bears playing trumpets marching across the white walls. The cot was already installed, with stencils of teddies dancing on the head and base, and a yellow, blue and pink eiderdown. A chest of drawers had been freshly painted white with big yellow knobs, and a shaggy white cotton mat laid over the elderly piece of natural carpet.

'That is very pretty and fresh, Jonet . . . lovely.' Hannah gave an appreciative nod. 'Do you have a nursing chair? I saw a Lloyd Loom one, nice and low, with a drawer in the seat for all the stuff. And do you have a bath yet?' Balked of a pram and a cot, there was plenty left in the second league. A carry-cot: they must have a carry-cot to put on the back seat of the car for trips out; to Clapham perhaps?

In the train going home, Hannah summed up her small victories. She had won the carry-cot. The bath, Jonet believed, might also be coming from sister-in-law Angela. But she would *think* about the nursing chair, talk to Mark.

Hannah's face ran down in tired lines . . . terrible, to have to fight for a place in the most favoured grandparent stakes. Swallowing her pride, her disappointment, her feeling of exclusion from this momentous occasion of Jonet's – and indeed her own – life, she knew she must continue to visit Bristol, staying overnight in a hotel if necessary. Anger too must be swallowed sometimes, it having no verifiable target; and anyway, this *was* her grandchild, her stake in a loving future. She must fight any way she was able, to form a relationship with this new member of her family on whatever terms Jonet would allow. But another fight was not what she had looked for . . .

It had been obvious that Mark's family had known about the baby for months; Angela's cot already repainted, the pram ordered well in advance. Do not dwell on this . . . Hannah hammered in the message to the rhythm of the train, going home to London. Jonet told you clearly how she felt, how she read past actions, how she saw you. Take it from there . . . expect nothing.

She wrote Joe that he was to be a great-uncle and he posted a supply of kitten-soft, thick towels, the like of which had not been seen in Britain since before the war. They were dazzle white, with a border either end of jolly green dolphins; Jonet was delighted with them both for their superior quality and because they possessed the – for her – desirable cachet of having arrived from New York. Sal Prochek had chosen them, Joe wrote, using the yardstick of what she herself would most like to receive.

A nursing chair would be welcome, Jonet admitted after a decent interval. A delighted Hannah bought the Lloyd Loom one she had admired, and filled the drawer with baby powder, Vaseline, safety pins and cotton wool, and a dozen soft Harrington's squares. The carry-cot was installed, and Hannah began to knit bootees, while Florence crocheted a creamy wool shawl, having signalled firmly that one would be coming.

Mark at last telephoned with the news that a six and a half pound son had arrived, just after Hannah and Matthew had gone to bed one windy night in early December. All Hannah could think of to ask was were they both safe, at which Mark seemed a touch put out, as though anyone in his charge must be by definition 'safe'. Hannah, breathless with shock and delight, hugged Matthew.

'Isn't it wonderful? And I can see him tomorrow! Oh – darling!'

'Oh, Grandma!' he teased her. 'Would you like a drink to celebrate?'

'Well . . .' she screwed up her eyes, considering. 'Would Horlicks be in order? And chocolate biscuits? I suddenly feel ravenous!'

He raised his eyes to heaven. 'Horlicks she says – Grandma wants her Horlicks!' She threw a pillow at him.

'Right then – have we champagne?'

'It so happens we have one bottle, yes. That's more like it.' He hopped out of bed, looking pleased. They sat against the pillows with a tray of champagne and chocolate biscuits. She was awake for hours, imagining the child she would see tomorrow . . . her first grandchild, the first of a new generation; wondering if Jonet would take kindly to motherhood, determined as she was that it should mean no more than a temporary break in her career. Hannah herself had worked through two pregnancies, and directly after both, but not from choice . . .

Travelling down she was elated and apprehensive by turn, defining her role and rehearsing suitable lines; happy, but in no way proprietorial of either mother or baby was how the script must go. She had with her a teddy bear, and from the baby shop near her restaurant, an expensive blue knitted pram outfit: coat, leggings, a hat with a perky bobble and a chin-strap finished with a pearl button, and mitts to match. For Jonet she had roses, dark chocolates, and a phial of Chanel No. 5. She hoped it would pass unnoticed that she had been slightly excessive, and insisted to herself that she was *not* attempting to buy love again . . .

Beechwood Maternity Home was a florid Victorian villa, once the home of a Bristol shipping magnate and now extended at the back into its handsomely landscaped garden. Jonet was not sharing one of the spacious main rooms; she had a pleasant single at the back, looking over lawns and a shrubbery to a tracery of beeches, with smoky distant views of the city beyond. She was writing a letter in bed, and smiled at Hannah, putting down her pen.

'Hello. You found us, then.'

'The taxi did.' Hannah kissed her cheek, suddenly choked. Jonet looked terribly young and vulnerable, her black hair freshly shaped in a smooth petal cut round her head. She nodded towards a canvas hospital cot at the bottom of the bed.

'He's in there. They've just brought him in, it's almost feed time. I haven't much to offer him yet so he has a bottle to make up weight.'

'May I take a peep?' Hannah set down her packages, slid off her coat and approached the cot quietly. Behind a mound of blankets was a small round head with a fuzz of dark hair and pink, folded-over ears. Her grandson's eyes were open, ranging unfocused, blue and very new. His nose was small and well shaped, resembling Jonet's. His mouth could not be seen as he was stuffing a minute fist into it.

Hannah stared at the first of the new generation of her family, overwhelmed. What would he be like? Would she love him, would he love her? He turned his head a fraction and seemed to look straight at her. Of course; she loved him already, ridiculous as it might seem.

'He's sweet, Jonet. Beautiful. Have you a name yet?'

'Laurence Mark.'

'Laurie . . . is Laurie in order? Laurie Shapiro . . . nice.'

'You can pick him up if you like,' said Jonet casually. 'It's his feed time any minute. He has whatever I've got, then tops up with the bottle.'

'Oh . . . may I?' Hannah peeled back the blankets and the small cocoon was found to be wrapped in Florence's lovely cream shawl. The moment she lifted him she was immersed, feeling the heavy little head against her neck, smelling the new baby scent of him, baby powder and milk and downy skin. Then, conscious that Jonet was watching her, she dropped a kiss on the end of his nose and handed him over.

'He's a perfect darling. Looks a little as I remember you.' Jonet had downed a glass of water with the air of a tennis player topping up before the final hard set, and now unbuttoned her nightdress.

Hannah had a sudden catastrophic desire to cuddle her, to give her a smacking great kiss and tell her how utterly knocked out she was with this wonderful, amazing baby, and how very much she loved and cherished them both.

She picked up the flowers she had brought. 'I'll see if there's a vase for these,' she said, and hurried away with her bunch of exquisite yellow rosebuds before she could disgrace herself.

When Hannah came back the small room looked crowded. She stood in the doorway with the heavy vase. Mr and Mrs Shapiro and Mark entirely surrounded the bed, and Mr Shapiro's beautifully polished shoe had pushed under it her parcels containing the teddy bear and the pram suit.

'What a clever boy,' applauded Mrs Shapiro. 'He knows exactly how to manage that bottle, doesn't he?' The bodies parted to reveal Laurie securely fastened to the business end of his supplementary bottle, making contented slurping sounds and with milk trickling down from the corner of his mouth.

Hannah moved inside, and the trio turned towards her. 'Hello, everyone,' she said pleasantly. 'Shall I put them over here, Jonet?' She set the vase on a small table by the window, edging aside Mrs Shapiro's coat laid over it.

'Thank you, Mother, they're lovely.'

'Lovely,' echoed Mark, and adjusting his spectacles turned back to admire his son once more.

'What do you think of him then, Mrs Stourton?' Mrs Shapiro beamed in the baby's direction. Hannah moved to join the Laurie Shapiro fan club; although she sensed that she was well and truly outnumbered she would not give up easily.

'He's a beauty,' she agreed. 'There's a definite resemblance to Jonet.'

'Oh . . . I thought how like Mark he looked. Don't you think so, Edwin?' Mr Shapiro looked vague.

'Probably. Perhaps; I suppose . . .' He glanced round as if for an escape route. Jonet began to look very slightly harassed and asked Mark to pour her more water.

'Is it rather hot in here?' she asked him. Her meaning – there are too many visitors – was lost on him in his exacting new role of father, and Hannah came to her daughter's aid.

'Jonet – I have to get to my bank, and a couple of shops. I'll go while you are busy, and be back within the hour. That will give us just a little while before I have to go for my train. Oh; I'll relieve you of these –' she pulled out the baby gifts from under the bed. 'They're for Laurie. Those –' pointing to the chocolates and the Chanel – 'are for you. Goodbye, everyone.'

She sat in a nearby café with buttered toast and coffee. No point in crying; in fuming; in devising cutting remarks she might have made but of course would not. Jonet *must* have told Mark she was coming . . . had he no more sensitivity – or sensibility – than to arrange for his parents to double up on the visit?

It would always be this way, or at least as long as they lived so close to the Shapiros. She would be the odd one out, whatever the function. The christening, next . . . best thing would be to bring her own family in force – meet might with might!

Hannah ordered another round of toast and looked at her watch. Twenty-five minutes to go. And look out someone, if they were still there. Laurie . . . I have a grandchild. She smiled, and poured more of the tepid, bitter coffee. That was what she must hang on to. The family renewed . . . whatever happened, the family was a constant, the nucleus of life itself. And when had families ever been easy?

Chapter Seven

June 1956

'Liza, will you turn that *down*!'

Hannah called upstairs, with little hope of competing with Bill Haley and the Comets at full strength. The house continued to shudder.

'Did you not *hear* me?' She stood at the bedroom door, hands on hips. Liza, in half-mast cotton dungarees, ankle socks and pumps was hopping about in a demented fashion, auburn hair flying round her hot laughing face. Hannah's grandson Laurie stood transfixed, sucking his thumb, eyes huge below the silky dark fringe that was so like his mother's had been at his age. But now his knees were starting to bend to the rhythm and his head began to nod up and down.

Watching them, Hannah was swept by sudden laughter; she grasped Laurie's hands and bent to partner him. Soon he was jigging back and forth with shrieks of pleasure, his fringe bouncing to the beat and ears pink with excitement.

When the record stopped Hannah caught him up and twirled him round.

'There's a dancer for you! I shall have to buy you a gramophone, I can see.'

'I rockin' round clock, Nana,' he told her, and wiggled his behind.

'We'll have it again, shall we?' Liza energetically wound up her gramophone. Hannah put out a restraining hand.

'Tomorrow, love – remember, I'm going to the theatre tonight. And there's Laurie to get bathed and all . . . you won't play it later on will you, and wake him? Promise?'

'I'll read to him if he wakes.' Liza cleverly avoided the issue.

'No loud records while we are out. Promise.'

'Can I stay up late then? It's your birthday, after all.' Liza's mind swept round fast for concessions.

'Sorry, I don't see the connection.' Hannah was used to sparring bouts. 'We had a tea party, cake and ice-cream, the lot, to cover that. And don't try wheedling Aunt Ursula – she always tells me.'

She regarded her daughter with a wary eye. Liza had clearly been over-indulged on this last holiday with her father. Difficult to rein in at the best of times, she was now increasingly trying her hand at manipulation to get her own way, and not infrequently succeeding. Her undoubted personal charm was turned upon Matthew's sons in particular. It seemed to Hannah almost as if Liza honed her embryo woman's skills on them, two handy young males in a supposedly male-dominated world who would serve to cut her teeth on. And she would almost certainly have spent her Easter holiday dominating David Vaughan.

They appeared to have had a high old time this year, at an expensive hotel in Eastbourne. Folders of snapshots showing Liza on the beach, in the sea, climbing rocks, on piers or running across fields turned up on their return. Liza had come back loaded with whatever had taken her fancy and looking like the cat that got the cream. Now she was insisting that next time, she would be full old enough to make the trip to Canada on her own. Hannah, though, was prepared to say no until she was fourteen, and foresaw battles ahead. Matthew stayed neutral, but she could count at least on his moral support.

'How old is your birfday, Nana? How many candles . . .' Laurie's brow wrinkled, numbers not coming easily to him yet.

'She's fifty-four,' Liza told him helpfully. Laurie looked bewildered: it was beyond his small powers to imagine such an age. He inspected Hannah closely as though for signs of imminent disintegration.

'Oh. I free an' half.'

'I know, Laurie. I never could forget how old *you* are.'

Hannah picked him up for a cuddle. The carry-cot had not been used for visits to London . . . Mark was too often away on construction sites, or busy decorating the flat, or organising the garden, or catching up with the paperwork. Laurie had been almost two before Jonet had asked if she might like to take him for a couple of nights. Hannah had despaired of her standing invitation ever being taken up; it might not have been, had Jonet and Mark not bought a house on the outskirts of Reading and this was the weekend of the move. Hannah forbore to ask where Mark's parents were . . . it came out later that Mrs Shapiro had gone down with shingles. She was just grateful; that the weekend passed without drama or injury (save to herself, she had not dared close her eyes in case Laurie should stop breathing), and that Mark's firm had moved their base in her direction. She had taken Laurie for a few weekends since then and they had each gone well; Liza enjoyed mothering a toddler, Matthew still remembered enough about little boys not to be too devastated by this one, and Hannah herself was hugely entertained by the unfolding personality of the small individual who would carry her blood into the next century. Different facets of Laurie presented themselves constantly. Sometimes she would glimpse a look, a turn of head, a phrase that would cause memory to stir; the traits Hannah prayed would not emerge were those she still could recall only too well in Darrow Bates.

They had booked to see *Look Back in Anger* for Hannah's birthday treat; Matthew had left the choice to her and she was intrigued to know what all the fuss was about. They were subdued, coming home from Sloane Square, and were on their way to St Martin's Lane for a drink when Hannah suddenly laughed.

'What strange things we do . . . actually paying to sit in a public place and be bludgeoned verbally for a whole evening.' She leaned across to kiss Matthew's cheek. 'Thanks just the same, darling. I do hope you didn't suffer too much?'

'The worst part was restraining myself from standing up and shouting back at the young idiot. I had to remind myself that he was only an actor doing a job of work.'

'D'you think Nick or Jake would have appreciated Jimmy Porter's point of view?'

'God knows . . . Not that I could sort out a lucid point of view in that load of bearish bellyaching. Your usual, darling? No – let's have champagne for your birthday.'

They tucked into a corner of the busy room and he raised his glass. 'To my beautiful wife. You know, I could sit equably through Jimmy Porter's worst tirades this evening in the sure knowledge that you and I would go home together afterwards and climb into the same bed.' He took a drink, not taking his eyes off her face. 'What's even better, I'd lay odds that you'll be every bit as beautiful when we do this again a decade on.'

'I can't guarantee that.' Hannah looked modest. 'But it's a lovely thought. I've a feeling myself that so much – so terribly much – will have changed a decade on. Almost more than it's possible to envisage, from here and now . . .'

'Is that a generalisation or have you been having visions?' He smiled then, and Hannah thought she could have loved him for his smile if for nothing else. She shook her head.

'Not visions; but an awareness of ground moving under our feet. Maybe the play tonight – what was it poor Alison said? I can hear it still in my head . . . "*You're* hurt because everything's changed. Jimmy's hurt because everything's the same." Yet I have an idea that *now*, if the young don't any longer want things to be the same, they will shortly set about changing them! And the older generation that likes things the same will hate that!'

Matthew said thoughtfully, 'Maybe it wouldn't be a bad thing to ring in a few changes ourselves. We've been married seven years and one month. D'you really want to keep the restaurant much longer? And the Taibach business? I know you have them running like clockwork –' he covered her hand with his – 'but darling; you *can* feel safe now. You mustn't still feel compelled to work for yourself and Liza. The bad days are gone for good, I promise you. Even if you hadn't made a first-class living by your own efforts you have all *my* worldly goods bestowed into the bargain!'

He sat back, smiling at her. 'So, why not just relax a little? Maybe join one of those healing circles you hunted out? I have an idea the thought of giving up your businesses terrifies you, but that's no reason for pushing it all into a corner 'until you have more time'. Look what you did for Shirley's mother a while back. I'd have never believed it – I still try to think of believable reasons why she should have got better! Would you not enjoy exploring that avenue further?'

Hannah looked hard at her glass. The old tug-of-war . . . fear could paralyse the best of intentions. Fear of the unknown? For a moment the busy room faded and she was in the well of the Albert Hall, two years ago; one of six thousand packed in to witness Harry Edwards's triumphant demonstration of spiritual healing. She had gone alone, telling no one – reading about this man had not been enough; she had to *see*. And she had. Supremely confident, the healer had asked in particular for those pronounced incurable by conventional medicine. They had come – in wheelchairs, on sticks, or children in their mothers' arms – to be touched by the charismatic, silver-haired man. His powers had stirred his audience to deafening applause. But at one point he had raised his hand to say what he firmly believed to be true: that the work done that day was simply 'the continuation of the work of the Master'.

Hannah had been so deeply affected by the demonstration that she had not been able to speak of it. But she thought of it often. Might *she* have become an equally powerful channel, if . . . ? Useless to speculate.

She had not made the move. Except for Ben. When the Fosters' black mongrel went lame in the winter before last, she had held the haunch between her hands, as she had done long ago for their own little terrier, Fly, and after a couple of days Ben had ceased to be troubled by it. Then she had thought deeply. She *should* go further . . . But days, months slipped by, and still the maggot of doubt ate into her resolve.

She smiled at Matthew now. 'I will give it thought. I suppose old habits are hard to break. I worked because I needed to for so many years, and it is quite difficult to believe there will never be the necessity to do that again. I suppose that you'd have preferred me to be at home from the start, like the wives of your friends, and it's so nice that you haven't gone on about it. But you know, I do actually *enjoy* the work; I have good helpers, and am never forced to grind away for hours at a time. And the Taibach bakery runs like clockwork. You've said so yourself.' She looked at him with sudden anxiety. 'You don't want to retire, do you, darling? You're not tired or anything?'

'Not anything,' he assured her. 'Not even overworked any more now I've gone in with Fitzgerald and I'm able to pick and choose my cases.' He paused. 'It's more . . . well, that I think it would be so good to have time to spend together. You know, we've both had bad times, both worked hard, gone through two wars; all that. I love you, and I should enjoy our relaxing together – maybe doing some travelling if we fancied that.' He finished his drink. 'That's the way I'd like it to be. But the choice has to be yours.'

'Thank you, Matthew.' She looked pensive as they left . . . the very thought of giving up her businesses filled her with dismay; but how difficult to explain this to herself, even . . .

'I wish Marek was still small enough to take to the zoo,' said Joe. Sal gave a snort of laughter.

'If you had had children of your own, you could take *them*.'

'They'd be too old now, same as Marek. Years back I used to take Carl . . . hard to believe that now, with that grand young man up at Harvard an' all.'

'He gives me discomfort. Here –' Sal pressed her diaphragm, frowning. Now it was Joe's turn to laugh.

'That's not Carl, that's indigestion!'

'You can make fun.' Sal wagged her finger at him. 'One day you will remember. There is about Carl, something . . . I cannot say. But I fear. It is strange . . .'

'It is most strange,' Joe teased. 'He's a pain in the neck now and again, I'd be the first to admit. And he's passing good at getting his own way. He'd have done better with his ears boxed years back, whenever he got out of line. But fear? I dunno about that.'

'You shall remember what I say,' Sal repeated firmly. 'As to the zoo; I am not too old.' She regarded Joe with serious brown eyes, but her cheeks were verging on dimples. 'At fifteen yes, it is too old; at thirty-four certainly not.'

'Then will you do me the honour to accompany me?' Joe swept her a passable courtly bow, bringing her dimples into full play. 'This is very definitely a zoo day. I only ever went twice, once when Carl was so high, then with Marek, and I've been trying to get back ever since.'

'We shall take bread for the ducks.' Sal tidied away the breakfast at lightning speed, dark hair bouncing about her bright face. 'And I also shall eat ice-cream; chocolate mint chip.'

'You'll get fat. Polaks always get fat if they eat chocolate mint chip ice-cream.' Sal flicked her wiping-up cloth at him and disappeared to change, humming one of her interminable Polish folk songs under her breath.

Joe went to shave. He had no idea he was smiling until he saw his reflection. Sal had that effect on him. It was Sunday, and they were going out together into Central Park, to the zoo . . . life was good.

He suddenly thought of Hannah. Strange, how often he thought of Hannah in conjunction with Sal. There was something . . . the quick light movements maybe; or the way she would look very earnest, then laugh unexpectedly, infectiously. No – it had to be more than any mannerism in common. He studied his reflection. A lot of thought, he'd given to this unlikely bonding he had with Sal Prochek . . . it could only be that he saw himself and Hannah mirrored in Sal and Marek. That was probably the simple truth and he was stuck with it.

Joe grimaced, turned one cheek then the other to inspect his work. The grey hairs were definitely taking over now; not in bad shape otherwise, though. Alex would say with his astringent smile that was because he had never married and had a family – never had a soul to worry about but himself. Could be . . . but Alex didn't know it all. No denying that his life usually sailed along pleasantly enough, but that was down to taking great care that no one was allowed to mess it up. Plenty of hard work, concentrating on the business was, he felt sure, also a factor. And Alex certainly had no clue as to why Joe's relationship with Sal gelled so solid. How could he? He knew nothing of how it had been . . .

He rinsed off, brushed his teeth and opened his wardrobe to find a sport shirt and flannels. His clothes were kept beautifully, as was the whole apartment. He had found a bigger one the second year, when he saw that Sal and Marek were no temporary arrangement and would need a bedroom each. Marek's was one up from a broom cupboard but he had been as thrilled as if it were a suite at the Plaza. Still small for his age, dark and round-faced like Sal only the hair short and tamed back, he had thanked Joe in his low, strange-sounding voice that had improved enormously over the time at the special school. He conversed in sign language with Sal, but lip-read so readily that Joe had trouble remembering he was deaf, and might turn as he was speaking, forcing Marek to bob round him with an apologetic smile.

Sal had been right: no one could have accused the child of being in the way. After the initial sorting out of awkwardness they had slotted into one another's lives amazingly painlessly. Marek did an extra tuition class Sunday afternoons, and Sunday evenings they'd latterly dropped into the habit of a chess game, with Sal at the table putting together her weekly letter to the few members of the Prochek family to have survived the war. Joe knew she was saving to go back for a visit. Sometimes he felt he should offer the cash for a ticket but somehow hadn't managed to yet . . . he supposed he wasn't too keen on the thought of her going so far away. It just might cause things to change, when they were fine the way they were – he was a selfish old creep, no doubt about it.

He brushed his hair and put loose change in his pocket. The last months, he had tried to stand back and examine the situation. Nothing could stay still. Things had to evolve – he wasn't so much of a fool not to know that. And he hated the idea of the comfortable set-up he had, evolving. Earlier on, he'd guessed that he might be happy to give Sal and Marek security, a safe haven, because he knew only too painfully how it had been for himself through the years when he had none. But he wanted everything on a simple material level; no emotions engaged. A straight deal, in a way repaying his debt – repaying Sal for what he had had from Hannah, but this at no personal cost.

What had disturbed him was finding that imperceptibly, over the years and despite strenuous efforts, his emotions *had* been engaged. For the first time since he was twelve, Joe cared deeply about what became of someone – apart from Hannah of course, and Tom – and he still could not think how it could have happened. Certainly, it needed serious thinking space in his head. He wished he could talk it over with Hannah, but could not bring himself to do this. It had been too many years since Joe had revealed himself to anyone. Well . . . he would work all this out in the near future and find the sensible conclusion; but for now, they would enjoy today. He put a clean handkerchief in his pocket and called to see if Sal was ready.

They went into the park at 77th, and Sal said tragically:

'Always it is the same. I look, and I wish to go in all directions.' She made a comical little face under the straw hat with yellow ribbons. Her dress was sleeveless, with a wide scoop neck and fitted bodice that showed off her neat waist and round pretty breasts. She raised an arm to adjust her hat and in doing so exposed its soft underside. It was whiter than the rest of the arm, unreasonably defenceless, and Joe wanted suddenly to stroke it, cover it with his large, protective hand. He stepped forward and took the arm in a purposeful manner, surprised at himself and wishing to control the situation at once.

'We already decided on the zoo this time, didn't we?' He turned towards the lake, along West Park Drive. 'We can take our time, though . . . drop around the boat pond, maybe, then cut across East Green.'

'Lovely. Anywhere is good on a day such as this.'

They left the road and strolled between trees whose greens were still early summer fresh, skirting the boating lake where they sat on a rocky bluff for a while. A pair of unskilled rowers were attempting to balance their craft as their large and enthusiastic dog peered overboard at his reflection, and their laughter was a happy counterpoint to the lower, rhythmic swish of the oars and the distant drone of traffic. On the far shore a scattering of bright cottons blurred the sculptured balustrades of the Terrace, and the children gathered below the fountain that glinted and gleamed to animate the formal stonework. Behind that, massed foliage appeared dark against the haze-blue city skyline.

'There may be time for a boat, after the zoo.' Sal was a deep-dyed optimist. 'But is good just to look, I think.' She turned, smiling; the sun had brought out her freckles the last weeks, and now it lit sparks of amber in her dark expressive eyes.

'Sure is . . .' Joe put out a hand to help her up and they threaded back under the trees and over the shade-chequered grass. A Chinese woman was seated at her easel, oblivious to a couple of rubbernecks easing up behind her as she concentrated on putting paint on her canvas in some satisfactory order. Further on, when they were nearing the shimmer of the boat pond a child struggled to get his kite airborne, running furiously with it bumping along behind him, but never taking off.

'My dad made me a kite, once.' Joe watched the boy's efforts, hands on hips; it could have been himself way back, running up the big arc of Aberavan beach with the newspaper kite on its length of cotton failing miserably to perform. Thomas would usually make it in the end, tying extra bits on the tail or taking them off as conditions dictated. Then he would pass over the cotton to Joe who would set off with a whoop, bare feet flying over the sand, neck craned as he imagined that he was up there, circling with the gulls on air currents gusting in from the sea.

He sighed. Carl had been given a kite around the age of seven, and Joe recalled that he'd had it up once. But 'it doesn't *do* anything, Uncle Joe', Carl had protested. 'Just flops around up there on the end of the string.' Joe had heard no more of it. He sighed again, and turned to Sal, but she was running to the boy and was quickly head to head with him over the kite.

'Now we try again.' She laughed as Joe reached them. 'Here I risk my reputation as a kite expert.'

'Rather you than me.' It worked; after one false start the kite was up, weaving, dipping, swooping. Sal tugged gently and it responded, and the boy jumped up and down, waving his arms.

'Fantastic! Now me! No – tell you what, you hang on while I get my dad, he's at the pond. He said I'd never get it up!' he called back, running for the boat pond.

'You didn't,' yelled Sal after him. 'I did!' She appealed to Joe. 'Now what do I do?'

'You stay there like the boy said, keep going till you're relieved. Serves you right for meddling.' Joe was laughing. 'OK, give me a turn . . .'

He pulled on it a little, getting his hand in, then ran a few yards to get the air in it.

'It's wonderful – really good now,' Sal called, and enjoying himself Joe ran again. Not as good as Aberavan beach, but not bad . . .

'Stop!'

He pulled up at Sal's call and looked round. The kite was caught in the branch of a tree he'd not noticed, and the string was pulling. He stood there feeling stupid.

'I can do it –' Sal looked up into the tree, a spreading beech with a seat under it. 'You wind in.' She was already balanced on the bench, reaching for a grip to pull herself into a fork.

'Sal – hold on now, I'll do that. You take the string.' Joe was coming closer, winding in. She smiled back at him over her shoulder, her skirt billowing out to reveal a round thigh as she stretched.

'I'm almost there. See?' She found a toehold and hoisted herself into the tree. The next steps were easy, on two solid lateral branches. Reaching over to shake free the kite, her dress caught and impeded progress. Sal twisted back to free it and Joe heard her swearing quietly in Polish.

'Sal?' He was suddenly alarmed at how high she was. 'Stay where you are – d'you hear me now?' He laid down the kite string and made for the bench. 'Don't move a muscle till I've got you, OK?'

'For goodness sake . . . I am good always in trees.' She twitched again at her skirt as she spoke, laughing at her predicament. Bending round a fraction too far she lost her balance, and at once was gone, crashing on to the metal arm of the bench a second before Joe reached it.

'Christ – Sal!'

She lay on her back across the strong raised roots of the tree, staring at him. Joe dropped beside her and, for a moment hoped she might simply be winded. Then he saw the unnatural angle of her right leg under the pretty yellow and white spotted skirt . . . he saw bone sticking through the skin below the knee. Her fingers stretched towards him, then dropped back on to the grass. When the boy ran back from the boat pond with his father following, Joe was rubbing frantically at the limp fingers, ashen-faced.

'You take it easy now . . . we'll soon have you fixed up. There's someone coming, Sal.'

She opened her eyes and Joe saw that she was trying to smile, before they fluttered shut again.

'Rotten news . . .' Hannah handed the cable to Matthew. 'Sal's broken her leg. Joe's had to cancel their next month's sailing. I might have known something would happen – just as I thought I'd finally get to meet Sal and Marek.'

'Sorry about that . . . a bad deal all round.' Matthew looked through the cable. 'He actually sounds pretty upset about it.'

Hannah took it back and read it again. 'More upset than Joe would expect to get . . . I've an idea Sal might mean more to him than he bargained for.'

'I've often wondered –'

'Why he never married?' Hannah examined the strips of words on the cable again. 'So have I ,' she added, so softly that Matthew, switching on the nine o'clock news, failed to hear.

The cable made her restless. It had been nice, making plans for August . . . Morfa Cottage, with Joe and Sal nearby in the house she'd booked to rent. Have to cancel that right away. She hoped Jonet wouldn't change her mind about Laurie having a week with them. Tom had seemed pleased about that, wanting to take the little boy fishing. Matthew intended to paint. He seldom came to Morfa Cottage, not liking the encroaching industrialisation of the district, but he had lately begun a love-hate relationship with the steelworks; struggling to set down in watercolours his own interpretation of their endlessly variable shapes in the landscape. So far he had failed, but intended returning to the fray with renewed determination.

And there was Florence's son Raymond's new baby, Liza would be impatient to wheel the pram. Maybe she should get plans drawn up for an extra room built out from the kitchen, with a bedroom above, ready for next year. Maybe Jonet and Mark ... and little Laurie ...

Hannah stared at the television screen, with the strange sensation of a grey blanket settling over her world. Getting depressed about it would do no good. She was just a bit down about Joe; only natural, she looked forward all year ... Dear Joe; she never stopped missing him.

But there was something else – something off key. Hannah slipped from the room, stood irresolute in the hall for the moment. Was it Liza? Upstairs, she listened for the regular breathing by Liza's door – she should be out for the count after two hours' tennis on top of the afternoon's school games.

Hannah stood at the dressing table and watched her reflection in the triple mirrors with wary eyes. There was something wrong. It was not only Joe's letter. . . Someone else –

When she saw Dorothea sitting on the little chair by the bed, the gold of the July evening lighting her hair, Hannah caught her breath. The reflected eyes met, and Dorothea's held the gentle compassion in their blue depths that Hannah had come to love over the years. She smiled at her friend, her heart becoming calmer. Then another figure – or was it the strong golden light causing her eyes to imagine ... The figure, that of a man, seemed almost to be composed of glittering dust motes as he sat on the bed, swinging his legs and laughing. His eyes were the blue of summer skies and his thick hair the colour of ripe corn, and he brought up his hand in a debonair salute to her.

'Harry!'

Hannah sprang up, knocking over her stool. The figure was merging into the rays of the setting sun that poured through the open window; making it difficult for Hannah to see.

'Harry . . .' She moved towards the bed. But she was alone; Harry was gone, and Dorothea. Hannah sank to her knees beside the bed. She was still there, her face buried in the sprigged cotton coverlet when the phone on the bedside table began to ring.

'Hello?' But she knew who it would be, and she knew what would be said.

'Han?' Florence's voice was thick with unshed tears. 'Oh, Han – it's Harry . . .'

'Dear Flo . . . Look, I'll be there on the first train tomorrow, I'll be with you by midday. Phone Raymond right away now, he'll stay with you –'

'Han – how did you know? It only happened a few minutes ago . . . He'd just brought the washing in for me –' Florence broke off.

'I knew, Flo; I've just seen him. And I'd felt really depressed all day, I knew something was wrong. Harry and I, we've always been so close. But you know that.'

'Yes.' Florence choked back tears now. 'Maybe that's why I dialled you. He just collapsed, Han . . . over the basket of washing. He always . . .' Florence stopped again. 'He always gave me a hand with the washing.'

Hannah could hear the weeping begin then, and said urgently: 'Phone Raymond now, love. I'll be there tomorrow.'

She sat on the bed for a while before going to tell Matthew. Where Harry had sat, moments earlier . . . the young Harry, her adored cousin as she had remembered him in her childhood; lively, vibrant, always ready for a laugh. The golden boy, before the trenches, before the Somme. She could hear his laughter now, and stayed quiet for a while listening to its echoes.

A massive brain haemorrhage was the doctor's verdict. Florence and Hannah walked in the Memorial Park after the funeral, when Harry had been laid to rest near his father and his young brother Trevor.

'Thanks a million for helping with the food, *cariad*,' Florence said for the third time. Handsome as always, dignified in her grief, she squeezed Hannah's hand.

'I wanted to. If *we* can't put on a decent buffet, who can? Aunt Maggie looks very frail now . . . this will have hit her hard. At least she has all cousin Daisy's tribe around her, I've quite lost count of the great-grandchildren!'

'She did say something about Frank bringing his grandchildren over from Patagonia this summer. He'll be too late if he doesn't make the effort soon – she's past eighty now. Let's sit here a minute, Han, my legs feel a bit odd.'

'Your hands are cold, Flo. Here –' Hannah sat close and chafed Florence's hands between her own, sitting on a bench near the memorial plaque to the Fallen of the Second World War. Florence said suddenly:

'Did you see him again, Han? David Vaughan? This Easter, when he came for Liza?'

'Well – yes; I had to, didn't I?'

'Of course. Does Matthew mind? I mean . . . you know, men can be a bit funny.'

Hannah smiled drily. 'You're right there. But no, he seemed perfectly OK.'

'Ah. Does he – does he change much? David Vaughan? You know, is he paunchy, or has he lost his hair or anything?'

Hannah laughed, giving Flo a hug. 'You are a hoot, Flo. He gets older every year, as do we all. He's not got a paunch; no. And he hasn't lost much hair, though it's grey now of course.'

'That hair used to be lovely; those crispy, short auburn curls.'

'He used to hate it – he'd say he would like to cut it all off. Once he said he would shave his head! But I told him it would be an awful chore to re-shave it every couple of days; I think that stopped him.'

'It's nice that Liza has it – the Vaughan hair. Most girls would give their eye teeth to have that gorgeous colour; and wavy too. D'you ever – well, think you would have been really happy? If you'd married him?'

Hannah was quiet, looking at the memorial plaque. 'It brings it all back for a little while when I see him, Flo. But I made my choice, and I've certainly not regretted it.' She turned to Florence. 'He remarried last winter, actually. He told me when he came for Liza this Easter.'

'Good Lord!'

Hannah said reasonably: 'It has taken him six years.'

'So what did you say? Not that it's any business of mine –'

'Silly . . . I think I just wished him every happiness; which I do, of course.'

'No "of course" about it.' Florence was blunt as always. 'He could have behaved better towards you in my opinion.'

'His choices weren't so easy, Flo – I thought about that quite a bit.' Hannah hesitated. 'What we had between us – it was beautiful, when it happened. But there were always too many things that weren't right;

too many people . . . I never could forget that he had a wife, however hard I tried. And now, Jonet. I don't think she will ever forgive me, Flo. Too much wrong . . . I really did too much damage.'

Florence put her hand over Hannah's. They sat quietly, each with her own thoughts. Then Hannah saw that Florence's eyes were brimming with tears again, and got up, still holding the square, capable hand.

'Come to Morfa Cottage for a cup of tea, Flo dear. Just you and me. Then I'll walk you back home; Raymond will want to be with you tonight . . . and that lovely baby of his, she will do you good. And I'll be round in the morning.'

'Yes, Han.' Florence blinked hard. 'That will do me good. *You* do me good.'

Later, Hannah wandered in the garden, restless. Tom brought out more tea and they sat out on the little lawn to drink it, the pads of thyme spreading over the path, fragrant in the warm wind.

'That's lovely, Tom.' She reached for a leaf of eau-de-cologne mint to rub on her palm and inhale.

'It's always here, Han.' Hannah nodded, loving him for being exactly what he was.

'I do hope to come back one day. Matthew may well decide to retire quite soon, and then I probably shall, too. There'd be plenty of space, wouldn't there, once we've built on that extra room?'

'Plenty. And we could always grow more vegetables.' Tom smiled at the thought. They sat in quiet companionship before going in to make supper together; Tom always went directly to bed afterwards, setting off on his cycle for the bakery at 4.30 every morning but Sunday, but Hannah sat on in the warm little sitting room, thinking of Harry.

Raymond would be a willing prop now for Florence, who had, with Harry, cared for him since he had first been billeted on them as a nervous, bed-wetting little evacuee from Plymouth. After Raymond's whole family was wiped out in one of the worst raids of the war in the winter of '41, he had been invited to stay on, and had become their adopted son. When Hannah went round to Incline Row next morning he was already there with his busy young wife and fat little infant daughter, who was being cuddled by Florence.

'She'll be fine – no cause for you to worry there.' Raymond, now an elongated version of the bony little boy she well remembered, pressed upon Hannah the statutory cup of strong sweet tea. 'Me and Marion'll see after everythin'. She'll not be left.'

'I know . . . Thanks, Raymond.' Hannah gave him a hug. Florence might have missed out on babies of her own, but Raymond certainly compensated, and to spare. Cycling back to Morfa Cottage at midday, Hannah decided when next she came down to suggest that Flo might like to buy her out of the Swansea restaurant. It would give her a greater interest, a greater return; she might perhaps take Raymond in as a partner.

Back to Clapham tomorrow. She cut a sandwich and took it into the garden. The day was mild and overcast, smoke rising in vertical brushmarks to the sky. The great Abbey Works below were now operational, their hot strip mill the widest in Europe and among the most sophisticated anywhere . . . a far cry from the time when men like Dada had laboured in the foundry, soaked sweat rags tied round their brows.

Hannah was aware of a sense of foreboding. Change was fast overtaking the place where generations of Hywels had lived and died, and where most of her memories lay. Out of sight but just the other side of the river, a vast housing estate had been under construction for some years, to house new workers flooding into the steel mills. To make room for progress, the great rolling dunes and coarse grasslands behind Aberavan beach had been sacrificed; two million tons of sandhills, some of them eighty feet high, had been levelled. Necessary, she was told, if the town were to expand in the years ahead. But to Hannah, and to the many who could recall playing hide and seek in those wild blowing dunes fronting Swansea Bay, the achievement spelt irreparable loss. Lost too were the lonely, lovely beaches of Morfa Mawr, dredged to mud now in the cause of advancing industry.

Perhaps worst of all was the inexorable build-up of heavy industrial traffic through Taibach. Short of demolishing every building on one side or the other to widen the coast road, now one of the most vital trunk routes in Wales, the only alternative was a bypass . . . and trapped between mountain and sea, this was being investigated. The effect on the townspeople was one of growing nervousness . . . whatever the outcome, homes and businesses would be lost, the face of Taibach changed for ever.

She got up, staring across the rooftops to the giant-sized gasometer near the end of Incline Row, for so many years a daily, taken-for-granted sight. Was this the place to which she should retire? Or might it soon be little more than a grimy, noisy steel town smelling of coke dust and chemicals?

Hannah left the little garden and was soon on the familiar track. She had no fixed objective. Her feet, though, took her inexorably up and across the shoulder of the hill towards the tumbled, overgrown ruins of Rachel Hywel's cottage.

Ten years since last she had been here . . . On Joe's first visit home she had told him of Rachel, the spirit woman, and he had asked to see where she materialised. Hannah had seen her that day, standing before the ruined cottage that once had been her home, but Joe of course had not. She had confronted Rachel after Serena's death, hoping in her anguish to find some sense, somewhere in the tragedy. Again, shortly before her marriage to Matthew, she had begged Rachel to leave the place; leave *her*, and go on her journey in peace.

She had no idea what she would find today; really, no idea why she was even thinking of the wretched, troubled spirit. She went on, walking with long rhythmic strides, head down and struggling with disturbing reflections of past and future. She pulled up suddenly to find she was there, out of breath after the long climb.

Only this time it was different. Someone – most likely a hill farmer looking to repair a barn or a drystone wall – had taken away a load of stones. The gaps that once had been sturdy walls were being closed by bramble and nettle, bracken and dock. Also, in the decade since Hannah had last been here, two of the scrubby old pines behind the cottage site had fallen and lay rotting in the sparse upland grasses.

The deeply fissured boulder where she had always rested was still there, heavy and permanently embedded. Hannah sat on it now, pushing up the sleeves of her blue checked shirt and unbuttoning the collar after the exertions of the climb. A shock, to see this site disturbed by anything other than the passing of time. Taking the big, rough-hewn stones of Rachel's home seemed uncomfortably akin to grave-robbing. She waited, not having been here before without sight of the spirit woman. Had the destruction of her home removed her presence? Hannah gradually relaxed as the afternoon light took on a hint of pearl, and the hill-top breeze stilled.

There was nothing . . . nothing to disturb the ancient peace of this place. Grasshoppers whirred, bees foraged noisily in the yellow trefoil, an unseen lark rose singing. But Rachel did not come; the shadow, so unforgettable, did not this time take the shape of a woman with a long skirt, and with dark blowing hair about the narrow face.

Hannah got up, stretched, took a couple of steps forward. Why? Had the troubled spirit finally found its peace? Had it heeded Hannah's plea to go on its way, to seek tranquillity, not vengeance for some old wrong? Or did it hover now in some other place, disturbed here by the robbing of the stones?

She was hesitant to leave without discovering what was different; even felt a degree of concern for the lonely spirit who had vanished. Was the change in *her*? Had she lost her power to see and communicate with Rachel Hywel? Her new, easier life, or possibly advancing age, might have robbed her of her deepest perceptions of the unseen world, so clear from infancy, and in all her early years of struggle.

Frowning, she turned at last from the tumbled stones and began the walk back.

'So that's how it is.' She handed Matthew his coffee and subsided into the depths of the elderly sofa. 'I suppose I should start looking for another cottage.'

'It may not be so bad.' Matthew offered a lop-sided relieved smile. 'I know the steelworks are absolutely fascinating – I'm with you there. They're also pretty toxic . . . then there's the traffic!'

'I thought you enjoyed painting there.' Hannah was not certain whether she was disappointed or relieved.

'It's a pleasure I could forgo.'

'But I was *born* there . . . all my roots –'

'Maybe you're not too long in the tooth to transplant just a few miles? What will happen about the bakery? And Tom?'

'I shall have to think it all out carefully; what's best for everyone. No need to jump, it can simmer a while.' She frowned. 'Don't *you* have roots anywhere? You never talk about your family – I mean, I know your parents are dead, and that you are an only child. But –'

'That's about it.' He pushed fingers through his hair, making it even more untidy than usual. 'Maybe Home Counties people don't have roots like you Celts. I had the odd grandparent but no one I saw regularly. With the old man being army, just popping home now and again for a spot of leave, we hardly seemed to be a family at all.'

He balanced his coffee cup on the edge of the bookcase where it looked almost certain to fall to the floor, and poured himself a whisky. 'I sometimes think I may have married you to get myself a family! All those Welsh relatives . . . quite a clan.'

'That's how it used to be. There were dozens of us when I was young.' She looked so bereft that Matthew reached across to pat her knee.

'No looking back, eh? There's still enough of us. And here's another of us now –' The crunch of footsteps on the gravel was followed by the banged front door. 'Sounds like Jake . . . plans must have gone awry.'

His elder son put his head around the door. 'Hi. Any food left?'

'What went wrong, old man? Shouldn't you be *en route* to measure up the Pyramids?' Matthew waved his whisky glass. Jake came into the room with his quick light gait but did not join Hannah on the sofa, perching instead on the arm of an empty chair. Hannah smiled at him. She never had known him to share the sofa with her. Her twenty-year-old stepson's relationship with her was rarely more than one of passive detachment. That with Nick was more relaxed, perhaps because he had been only ten when she had joined the household. This had made it easier for her to offer simple affection along with the food, friendliness and general support clearly needed from the mother-figure of an all-male family. Nick was by character easier than his brother, inheriting Matthew's good-natured, casual and slightly simplified outlook. He was happy to give his stepmother a hearty kiss on the cheek, or a hug, and had soon dropped the 'Auntie' to call her Hannah. And that was absolutely fine, she assured Matthew; she was *not* their auntie anyway. To Jake also she was 'Hannah' most of the time; just occasionally he would revert to 'Aunt', with an overtone calculated to establish a distance between them.

Jake acknowledged her smile with a small salute. Nothing like his father or brother; all his mother's side, Matthew had explained. He was clever, studious, with two years of his mathematics degree course at Oxford behind him. Hannah was convinced that Jake was a little uneasy about his father having remarried into a working-class background, though this, of course, was mentioned by no one. Jake stretched now and yawned.

'It's this damn Suez thing that's blowing up. We were all nicely loaded, tickets and things at the ready when Percy's father got a strong signal from a chum at the Foreign Office. Absolutely no possibility of proceeding to Cairo, was the word. A balloon of some proportions may well blow sky-high before we could hope to get our work done and get out again. Piggish luck. All those weeks of slog – everything set up.' He shrugged.

'There's a decent piece of boiled ham left over,' Hannah told him. 'And some potatoes. Plenty of tomatoes of course. Shall I put a plate together for you?'

'Thanks –' Jake held up his hand. 'I'll hunt that up for myself – it sounds fine. Had a card from Nick yet, Dad?'

'Yesterday, actually. He's down near Naples; they're quite hopeful about this dig, apparently. Work's due to start tomorrow.' Jake nodded.

'Well, Percy and I thought that with Cairo off the agenda we'd go instead to plot out some ley lines around the Avebury area. He's just laid his hands on a first-class book by some chap who seems quite an authority. Anyway – food.'

Matthew followed him into the kitchen, muttering something about a ham sandwich before it all vanished. Hannah sat on, feeling unusually lethargic, watching dusk creep up to the windows. A pity about Jake . . . Nice, if Matthew could possibly have eased Jake's thinking round to the idea that working class was not a bad thing to be; that 'in trade' was not inferior in any way to being in a profession; that to work hard and honestly, and in the end to have earned a substantial amount of money, was something of which she was proud. Certainly, she had no difficulty coping socially at the level she had attained. So what was Jake's problem? And did it matter?

Hannah wondered then if one day Liza might learn to be ashamed of her. Well: so be it. Jonet already was!

One thing she knew for certain . . . Dada would have been proud.

Chapter Eight

Spring 1957

It was spring before Joe came over with Sal. Liza had gone off with David for their Easter holiday, and Jake and Nick were not due for a few days, so there was a brief island of privacy in which the visitors could adjust. Then, Hannah hoped they would go with her to Morfa Cottage. No decision had been made yet about the bypass through Taibach and she really wanted to talk to Joe about it.

Watching them filter through airport customs it was immediately plain to her that Joe loved the small dark-haired girl with the walking stick. He was unobtrusively matching his pace to hers and had allowed her to carry nothing but a light shoulder-bag. He inclined his head to listen to a remark, then threw it back to laugh. He looked less than his forty-seven years; fit and attractive, dark hair streaked with grey but eyes bright with life. Love you, Joe . . . That love welled up and threatened to engulf Hannah as she caught his eye and in a few strides he was to the barrier, catching her to him.

Always the same, and would be, until death parted them. Hannah, haunted constantly by the fear that one day it would become dreadfully apparent why he had been turned down by the wartime draft board, clung to Joe for a moment.

'Well then –' As he drew her back to look at her she saw his own eyes were moist. 'Hey, give me a minute to get out of here . . . we'll be right with you.'

Sal moved then, her eyes on Hannah and a smile widening the generous mouth. Hannah reached over the barrier with outstretched arms; her love for Joe swelled to encompass this woman, on whose face both pain and courage were stamped to lend a beauty she might not otherwise have owned.

'My dear; welcome to Britain. I've looked forward so long . . .'

Hannah kissed Sal's cheek, the dark tumble of hair under her hand soft and scented faintly with flowers. Sal kissed her back as though she had waited with as much hope and willing love as had Hannah; they exchanged one deep smiling look and the bond was formed.

'I too am happy.' Sal laughed suddenly, and Hannah laughed with her as her cup ran full. Her beloved Joe at last had a love of his own.

Sal and Joe slept late and Matthew had gone when they came down to linger over coffee and scrambled eggs. Sal looked tired, but better than when Joe had helped her upstairs last night.

'Strange, that it is so quiet.' She gazed about the sunny room whose long windows looked over drifts of sun-splashed daffodils. 'In New York we hear only the traffic.'

'When my daughter and Matthew's sons are at home we hear only the loud records.' Hannah poured them coffee. 'Can't say which is worse. But we've peace right now. I need only to be in the restaurant for a couple of hours around the middle of the day . . . you could join me there for lunch.'

'Marek would have wished to be here with us. But *I* say – *I* am enough for this time! And ticket money is so high.' Sal raised her eyes to the ceiling. 'You know that Joe has bought my ticket?' she added with a direct honesty that Hannah admired. Joe shrugged.

'In my own interest . . . I want to see that stick put out with the garbage.' He finished his coffee, and when he looked at Hannah his eyes were serious.

'I guess you know what's next, Han. Will you really work on that damn leg? We'll be back again in August – you could have more sessions then, maybe?'

'You know I will. Provided you understand what I said in my letters, Sal. That I can promise nothing? I can only be an open channel?'

Sal put out her hand. 'Joe has spoken of this to me. I trust you. I accept what you say. I wish very much to walk well again – it is slow, a housekeeper with a poor leg!' She smiled at Joe, teasing; but Hannah saw the love in her bright face.

'That's what we'll do, then. Will you come down to Morfa Cottage for Easter?'

'Will there be room?'

'Plenty. Tom decided to move into Incline Row with Flo a few weeks ago. A great idea; company for both of them. She misses Harry dreadfully, as you can imagine. Tom still keeps an eye on the cottage, keeps up the garden, his pride and joy, and Mrs Lloyd's daughter and son-in-law always see the place in reasonable order inside and out.' She decided not to start a discussion at this point on whether Morfa Cottage was going to survive the bypass route.

'Oh, right. Well . . . that OK by you Sal?' Hannah watched them; she had no idea if Sal knew Joe's past, but thought it unlikely. Joe's habit of self-containment would take some breaking, but Sal would do it if anyone could.

'I should like that. Thank you.' Sal looked from one

to the other and Hannah could see she was aware of the tension. For herself she felt only huge relief, that Joe had joined the land of the living and fallen in love at last.

They walked slowly along the hill, April sunshine pleasant on their backs. Sal's headband sprang free of her bouncing hair and she paused while Joe picked it out of the grass and fitted it on again.

'That right?'

'Fine, thanks. Would this be a good place to take a break?' She looked at where a stream cut across the slope between a tumble of rocks.

'Sure. Sorry if I've come too far for you . . .' Joe took her elbow and helped her down the rock. 'Your leg seems in much better shape.'

'Oh it is, Joe.' Sal sat, stretched her legs before her. 'Less pain; also stronger. Last week I could not possibly have walked here. Your sister has magic in her hands.'

'The first thing I recall about that, she made our little dog's leg well. Old Fly . . . on Han's thirteenth birthday. God, I couldn't have been more than five at the time . . . way back in the First World War.'

He lowered himself on to a small rock shelf and was silent, gazing at the foaming water. Sal sat quietly nearby, stroking the golden-bronze lichen covering the north side of the rock. She had absorbed a good deal in these few days at Morfa Cottage. She had met Tom, and Florence; had noted the affection between the brothers despite their once having been separated for so many years. She had also become aware of the strength of the bond between Joe and Hannah. Sal knew well of sibling loyalties . . . she loved Marek with a deep protective fervour and indeed, held his life in greater esteem than she did her own. Hannah, she thought, would understand this.

Less clear was the tension she felt in Joe. Sal loved Joe differently, but no less than her younger brother. She asked for nothing other than to go on living in his apartment and making his life comfortable. True, some nights she would lie in the dark, quite close to him and yet impossibly far, and imagine how it would be to share the warmth of his bed, his body. But Sal Prochek had learned to be grateful for what she had, and what she had now was good. All the children with whom she had played in childhood were almost certainly dead. She had survived, and so had Marek, and life was sweet. One day Joe might move, or marry, and give her notice; Sal looked into this abyss and drew back sick and shivering, and learned to live in the present. But loving Joe, she was aware of a shadow in his life; felt it fall across him now, watching his immobile figure by the water.

He raised his head in a sudden movement: their eyes met and his were haunted. Alarmed, Sal said the first thing that came into her head.

'You love her very much, Joe.'

'She saved my life.'

He picked up a stone and tossed it into the water.

'When my dad died she took over – Mam was expecting Tom. Then when Mam died she was all that stood between Tom and me and the orphanage.'

He stopped, dabbled his finger in the ice-cold mountain stream. 'She worked every hour God gave to keep us fed and sheltered. But it was more . . . for me at any rate. She gave me a sense of security; of being, well, valued I suppose. And I think that gave me the confidence to make my own way in the world. I was strong enough because of Han.'

Joe frowned, threw another pebble into the stream then added so quietly that Sal was not certain she had heard him aright: 'I would have killed for Han.'

After a moment she said: 'It is good, Joe, that you tell me this. But I think there is more.' She stopped, fearful of overstepping Joe's private territory as she saw his face darken. In the silence between them she heard lambs calling and the almost imperceptible rustle of life springing up about them.

'You need say nothing,' she said quickly. 'It is not for me to know unless you wish.'

He looked at her then. 'One day. I'll tell you about it one day. I'll know when I'm ready, Sal.'

'Whatever you want, Joe.'

He came to sit by her. Sal kept very still, afraid that if she moved the moment would pass. He took her hand.

'Being here with you this week has been good. I shouldn't have left it so long.'

'You must have had your reasons, Joe.'

'Yes . . .' When Sal looked up she saw his eyes were fixed on an unseen point of memory so painful that instinctively she put out a hand to comfort him. At once he pulled her close and buried his face in her shoulder.

'Stay with me.'

He had said it. As he held the small rounded body close, Joe wished only that it had not been so long in the saying. And yet . . . how could trust have come even now? What had changed, what had he learned to make the chance worth taking?

'I do love you, Sal.' Was that what had changed; when love becomes strong enough, has trust no option but to follow? When he had seen her fallen on the grass in Central Park, the surge of his love had winded him. Nothing other than that was different; yet it was sufficient to change the tenet by which he had lived these many years. Maybe he *would* talk in his sleep one night . . . but right now, Joe counted that a chance he had to take. And trust, miraculously, was there . . . trust that he was safe in Sal's care, as she would be safe in his.

'I love you so much,' he repeated.

His voice was muffled. Sal stroked his hair . . . how often over these last years had she resisted the urge to do that.

'My love too is very great, Joe dear.'

There was still – something . . . an unspoken fear in Joe's life that she could not love away. Perhaps the reason why he had not married many years before? But Sal wanted him so badly, had waited so long. Now, she must take the risk and hope that one day the fear would surface, and be seen to fade in the light of day. Her arms tightened about him.

'All will be well.' Her voice was a murmur against his cheek. 'Now we are together, no harm can come.'

They were married in August, at Blackheath register office. Marek had come over with them and stayed with Hannah when Joe and Sal went to Wales for a few days. Matthew gave Sal away and Liza was her attendant, in a cornflower blue dress with a misty mauve sash, and a posy of mixed sweet peas. Sal's limp had gone; pain was reduced to a slight ache after standing for a while. In a cream silk suit and a straw boater wreathed in cream roses she had exuded joy like a personal fragrance, the perfect foil for Joe's handsome gravity of bearing. Watching them, Hannah's joy was palpable; yet shadowed by the melancholy idea that now, with his heart's desire by his side, Joe might lose his dream to return to Wales, to his roots.

The happy tableau before her melted, merged into the child Joe's white face staring up at her that July day. *He said awful things about you, Han. I wouldn't have it – I just hit him. And he went down into the quarry.*

She stared at him, turning to Sal now to repeat his vows of marriage. He had done that for her; killed for her, bringing his world, his life about his ears, changing the entire course of it. She thought of the lonely hardships to which he had been, as a result, exposed. Please God, her own children would never face so harsh a fate – and please God, Joe would not pay all his life on her account.

The following August they missed coming to England because their son, Paul Harry, was born in September, the day before Joe's birthday.

May 1959
On Liza's fourteenth birthday, she finally won the battle to fly to Canada on her own in the summer holidays. Hannah fought a valiant rearguard action but was no match for her daughter's wily determination. Seeing her off at the airport with Laurie, who was visiting for the first week of the holidays, Hannah watched the tall, strikingly beautiful adolescent calmly select a book for the journey and was sick with apprehension. Thousands of miles alone . . . and she was taking it as casually as a bus trip into town.

'They may let you have a look in the cockpit, Liza.' Six-and-a-half-year-old Laurie was restless with excitement, the closest he'd yet come to flying.

'I wouldn't bother. My father will let me fly when I get to Canada if I want. He's lots of planes.' Liza shook back her mane of auburn curls. 'I'll buy you a comic to read going home if you like – I've loads of cash.'

Hannah swallowed. David *would* take her up if she asked – he was putty in her hands. Nothing she could do though, but trust him not to ruin his daughter. After all, he had made it clear that Liza was the most precious thing he had, not even excepting his newish wife who though young enough had given him no further children. David; so rich . . . so poor. Hannah had been unusually ambivalent in her thoughts on his wife. The news had been a shock. But she had no idea why, since it was a perfectly normal thing to happen. Even so, it had to be admitted that she did not greatly take to the idea. She was quite disgusted with this dog-in-the-manger attitude, and worked on it until she told herself she was actually very happy and relieved that he was no longer alone . . . she, after all, had turned him down in favour of Matthew. There remained, however, a certain curiosity to know what his wife was like, and she hoped very much that Liza would bring back a holiday snap of her, or failing that would at least offer a full description.

She sat by the baggage as the children pored over the comics stand. No – Liza was not a child and Hannah must cease thinking of her as one. Fourteen years, since that letter from David Vaughan had cast them both adrift to make their own way; since she had wheeled an illegitimate baby round Clapham Common and pondered their future. Now the baby was a rapidly maturing young person with a formidable will of her own, and to offer guidance was becoming a delicate business requiring endless patience and much tact.

Take this passionate desire to train for the stage. Theatre school . . . she absolutely *must* go to theatre school in September, Liza had announced. A battle royal had begun, with Hannah coming down heavily on the side of covering all options, taking O levels at least where she was, at Berrington's in Wimbledon, before narrowing her choices. But Liza's choices were already made – she *would* be an actress, she had declaimed in an undoubtedly resonant voice that had lately possessed a small and irresistibly throaty break in its clear flow. Hannah had dug in; a good general education was first on any sensible list and Berrington's could provide that.

The weak point in this stance was that David might well be swayed should Liza press him. Hannah had so far resisted all his attempts to finance Liza, aware that it could weaken her position as sole parental authority. He had insisted his daughter be educated privately, offering the fees. Hannah had declined, and paid them herself, fearing he might use that as a springboard for more say in Liza's upbringing. Now, she had written to tell him of the theatre school confrontation, and asked for his support. Whether he would give it she could not judge . . . there was so much of David Vaughan about which she had never learned.

The flight was called; she watched Liza stroll confidently to the departure gate, turn to wave, and disappear. What *was* it about her . . . indisputably, she had a marked ability to command attention. And now there was another dimension, of which Hannah had become aware as a terrifying fact since the end-of-term play last week. She had struggled with the little that had been confided, afraid that more questioning would lend the incident an importance in her daughter's mind that Hannah was desperate it should not assume.

'It was a bit weird, Mummy, I was about to go on in Act III – you know, where there's a storm? – when I saw this really odd-looking woman staring at me. It was pretty dark in the wings of course, it's such a pathetic arrangement and we're falling over each other constantly. And I *was* a bit frantic at that point, that first patch of dialogue with everyone rushing about the stage like demented rabbits is almost impossible to remember. Anyway, when I came off into the wings again she wasn't there . . . but she had been, I could swear. And she *had* stared. Dark eyes – they were really dark.'

'Surely it was one of the cast, darling? There were quite a lot, weren't there?' Hannah had moved back to judge the length of the skirt she was letting down for Liza. 'Just turn to the front again, will you?' Liza swung round impatiently, almost falling off the stool.

'Of *course* it wasn't. D'you think I don't know the cast inside out and back to front?' She breathed a dramatically heavy sigh. 'After all those weeks of rehearsals? This was a *woman* anyway – I *told* you. And her clothes weren't right . . . a long heavy sort of skirt. And a greyish shawl. And her hair was rather bushy looking, I think; dark and long . . . She vanished anyway, whoever she was.' Liza jumped down and unbuttoned the skirt, which billowed to the floor in a bright rainbow pool; she loved vivid colours.

'Thanks, Mummy, that's super. Must impress Pa and the new wife, mustn't we?' Liza's grin indicated that she knew perfectly well she would impress whomsoever was on her list to impress. 'That'll be a wow with the starched petticoat and the ponytail.' She shook the bright mass of hair, currently restrained with a turquoise ribbon pulled in high at the back to expose a slender neck, and was gone.

Hannah had stood motionless, staring after her. The woman had been Rachel Hywel; she knew it as she knew night followed day.

'Dear God . . .' She sank on to the stool vacated by her daughter and shut her eyes tight. So; Rachel was no longer confined to her homestead environs. But why in heaven's name was she with *Liza* – how did these things work? What could Liza possibly do for her? She should tell Matthew – ask his advice. How could Matthew possibly believe her, though . . . what sane, reasonable, logical man would?

Hannah got up from the stool, feeling stiff and quite old. She had called goodbye to Liza, told her daily to expect the groceries to be delivered, and that the ironing was in the basket. Now she let herself out into the blustery morning, already late for work.

She had said, done, nothing about it. Liza had always been reluctant to show interest in her mother's gift. She knew that Hannah had finally become a member of a small local healing circle some months ago, but had asked no questions. And for herself, Hannah had waited, watched and hoped . . . not that this last child had inherited her gifts, but that she had not, and would so be able to lead a normal life.

Now that hope was gone. Whether she was yet aware of it or not, Liza must have inherited at least something of the Hywel powers. No matter how reluctant both might be, they would have to talk when the visit to David Vaughan was out of the way.

'God knows it's a strange time for me to be celebrating . . .' Alex Cline regarded Joe glumly. 'With the best contract since all-get-out just fallen through my fingers. I wouldn't care – no, that's a lie! – if I knew what the devil had gone wrong! I'd have staked my life on being the only outfit able actually to cost the damn tender, let alone get under the price I had put in!' He downed his brandy at a gulp and poured another. 'There'd have been good business in it for you too, old son – maybe enough to have put that young Paul Harry of yours through Harvard.'

'Plenty of time to worry about that.' Joe grinned at Sal's expression. 'Right now we're celebrating the fact that your young Carl just has his auspicious first step on the ladder with the venerable and revered Holman Stiltzberg, Wall Street Inc. So, it's too bad a lost deal has soured the cream. Who the devil outbid you?'

'The name's Belman; J. Arthur Belman.' Alex spat it out.

'Surely he's in construction, darling? Don't I see him on billboards?'

Delaney, voluptuous as ever in black velvet that followed faithfully every curved inch of torso, sidled in by Joe to refill his glass. Joe got the message that she would never quite forgive him for marrying his housekeeper, the very thing she had warned him against, but that she was nevertheless doing her utmost to make the quaint little East European welcome in her select circle of New York blue-bloods. Sal bore this with characteristic good humour and was scrupulous about never taking a rise out of Delaney, whose own sense of humour was not overly sharp.

'Who's that you see on billboards, Mama?'

Carl detached himself from the shifting scatter of guests to lay an arm about his mother's handsome shoulders. At twenty-two he was something as Joe recalled Alex had been; whipcord lean, with a cleft in his chin that Joe understood to be devastating to women. The blue eyes of the exuberant toddler could in adulthood turn chipped-ice cold in seconds; the fair hair had tamed to light brown, while retaining sufficient wave to fall engagingly over the high forehead when Carl became animated. Joe moved aside to make room for his godson – the guest of honour, through with Harvard and starting out now like a fresh-faced young Spartan on the modern game of trading slips of paper on Wall Street. Alex regarded his wife and son with incipient irritation; this was not a matter for flippancy.

'J. Arthur Belman. He's construction, sure – there can't be many townships in the US of A who don't know that. What I also know, to my great cost, is that J. Arthur Belman had picked up an ailing, second-rate interior design outfit to add to his list of companies. Possibly he thought it might be compatible with certain areas of construction. Or then again he may have bought it as a toy for his ewe lamb, daughter Gayle. She's due down from Vassar any time now, and may fancy trying her hand at design. Some idiots, of course, think there's nothing much to it but a knack of selecting a pretty pair of drapes.'

Alex lit a cigarette with the controlled violence Joe knew of old. He had without doubt taken a direct hit and was shipping water. This had happened from time to time in his volatile career, points at which Joe usually disappeared until repairs had been effected. But this time he was curious, as it would seem he too had lost out here.

'What went wrong? I've never known you not win a tender you'd set your heart on. I've even thought at times that costing was the most inspired department of Cline's.' He chafed with gentle caution, aware of Alex's low flashpoint.

'You'd be right there,' Alex said unexpectedly. 'And I know I was dead on the nail in this Holt tender. I'd have sworn no one but Cline's had the know-how to cost a job of this size with any degree of accuracy.'

'This deal's got to you, Dad.' Carl was paying attention now. Joe knew he could appear to pay loyalty to none but Carl Cline; yet he was fiercely clannish – who injured his family, injured him. Alex gave a curt nod.

'Not only my pride but my pocket, boy. Nobody in their right mind wants to kiss a two-million-dollar contract goodbye.'

He was called away to take a phone call and Carl was summoned to a newly arrived guest. Delaney looked uncomfortable; she hated discussions involving money, which in her book was no more than the means of living comfortably. 'And how is your little boy?' she asked Sal, hoping that soon she would be rescued. Sal was about to tell her when Alex came back with red patches of shock on his thin cheeks.

'You're not going to believe this. I don't myself yet.' He reached for a cigarette with a fumbling hand. 'If you saw it in a bad movie you'd laugh at the corny dialogue.'

'Try us, Alex,' Sal said with her usual directness.

'Who was that call from? Belman, to say he's got cold feet?' Joe tried.

'You're warmer than the feet. Some guy who wouldn't give a name ... wouldn't say any damn thing, but the one sentence, which he repeated once when I asked, then hung up on me.'

'Which was?'

'That I had a leak at Cline's. Exactly that; no more, no less.'

In the silence, a woman came up to claim Delaney. She moved off willingly, bored now with the whole business. Joe said:

'What you're chewing on now is that this leak must be why Belman was able to get under your tender?'

'Just so.'

'And the caller was the leak himself?'

'Why? I'd say he was more likely an employee of Belman's with a grudge to pay.'

Alex's entire face had coloured now as all the implications hit him. He struck the table with his fist and their drinks rattled. A knot of Carl's Harvard friends glanced round, then averted their eyes with inbred good manners; if their host was throwing a tantrum it was no concern of theirs. But Alex pulled himself up at once, and shrugged.

'Let's forget it now. This is not the time . . . I'll work out later who the leak was. The important thing is that Belman was prepared to go that far; it must have cost a packet to finance that sort of leak. Have another drink, Joe, and let it drop for now, eh? Maybe we'll know more in a while.'

Carl came out of the marquee and looked about for a spare table place in a shady spot, next to a pretty girl. He found one, and made tracks for it, balancing his plate of buffet food in one hand and champagne glass in the other. The girl looked up, inspected him and smiled. Carl passed the test – but he knew that he always would do that.

'In that case . . .' She moved aside her purse. She was undeniably pretty, soft dark brown hair, big grey eyes, delicate white skin – the way Carl imagined an Irish girl would look, raised under damp mild skies. Her neck appeared too slender to support the large, wedding-guest hat of peachy straw and apricot roses, which shadowed her eyes to more mysterious depths than they probably possessed. Carl smiled with satisfaction at his luck. He'd almost not come, weddings being as a rule not that rewarding; but it had turned out a beautiful day. A client had backed off, and he had decided to opt for the alternative to an afternoon in the overheated offices of Holman Stiltzberg, having been there three months now, which he judged long enough to take small liberties.

'Carl Cline at your service. Can I get you dessert yet? The strawberry shortcake looks good enough to eat.'

'No hurry. I'm taking a while to recover from the lobster mayonnaise. I'm Gayle Belman. I was at school with the bride.' She smiled again and he located a dimple in one cheek.

'I was ditto with the groom.' Carl began to work on his lobster. 'I'd say twenty-two is a touch soon to marry, don't you agree?'

Gayle Belman gave a charming pout as she considered. Carl was grateful for the interval in which to digest that this must be *the* Gayle Belman, only daughter of J. Arthur Belman of Belman Construction. Which must be trying to tell him something. He chewed at his lobster, thinking hard, for Carl believed that everything happened for a purpose.

'I think it would depend.' Gayle turned the expensive diamond and sapphire circlet on her wrist in a pensive manner. It looked new, and Carl guessed it could be a down-from-college gift from an adoring and indulgent father. 'I mean, everyone is different.'

Carl agreed that certainly everyone was different, and a good thing too. He finished his lobster which had been splendid, fetched them portions of strawberry shortcake and more champagne, and continued to think as the pleasantly undemanding dialogue progressed. By the time the speeches and toasts began, he had asked, and was to be allowed, to take Gayle Belman to dinner the night after next. This would leave ample time to decide what he thought should be done.

Carl knew that Alex was pretty certain who the leak was. A young man from costing had left last month on a fairly lame excuse. He would undoubtedly have had sight of the Holt job prices, and would have the know-how to advise on a complete breakdown of costing.

He must have been well paid. Belman had dealt Alex a severe blow – not just for now, but for the future. He was big money, made in the war years and built on steadily since. To break into this new field successfully he could afford to buy the best ideas men; the only thing lacking was experience, and he could get with that this whacking great contract to revamp a chain of nineteen hotels countrywide.

Short of being able to force Belman to give up the contract, Carl wished to do him a bad turn. He owed this to his father. It occurred to him then that he was actually in a position to do exactly that. It became clear in the time he spent in conversation with Gayle Belman that she was indeed the apple of her father's eye. Sole heiress to his empire, nothing was too good for her. And no one. Discreet enquiries had elicited that J. Arthur Belman was a social climber, and who knew what pretensions he had *vis-à-vis* a husband for Gayle?

'Carl . . . we mustn't.'

'But we want. Don't we?'

'Oh . . . oh-h-h . . . '

'Easy does it . . . God, Gayle – Oh, come on now –'

'Darling . . . oh Carl. Oh God! No, don't stop!'

'Jesus . . . what a girl . . . Beautiful girl . . .'

'Oh . . . *darling*! I can't – oh-h-h . . . Carl . . .'

'You can't be sure, can you? Not this early?'

'I'm sure. Haven't you heard of morning sickness? And my breasts –'

Gayle pulled up her shirt and lifted her breast from its bra cup. It was incredibly but unmistakably fuller than when he had kissed it recently, pulling gently on the nipple with his lips. The nipple too was bigger, standing up darkly against the white, blue-veined heaviness of its globe.

Gayle eased it back into the bra and buttoned her shirt. 'It's very tender.' Her eyes were enormous with concern. 'Carl . . . what am I to do?'

The huge eyes were filled with tears as she stood stiffly hugging the tell-tale breasts. Carl lit cigarettes for them but she shook her head.

'I feel too sick, Carl, for God's sake – this is your *baby*!'

'We can't be one hundred per cent certain of that, can we, sweetheart? I mean, how do I know?'

Gayle lunged at him and he held her off, beginning to smile. 'Steady on!'

'How could you say such a wicked thing! You must *know* –' Tears spilled over now, marking her silk shirt. Carl took out his handkerchief and wiped her cheeks.

'Not serious – OK? Stop panicking. So what happens now?'

'I *can't* tell Daddy . . . he'd have an absolute heart attack. You'll have to.'

'What, go up cold, just like that to the guy and say – your daughter's in the club?' Carl's eyes narrowed to veil the pleasure of the idea.

'What a horrible way of putting it – honestly Carl, you sound almost amused! You haven't said . . . well . . . if you want to . . .'

'Want to what?' He watched her through his smoke rings.

'I'm having your *baby*, Carl. I mean; about getting married.'

'Ah. Marriage.'

Carl gazed into the distance. Then he turned his blue eyes on Gayle and smiled.

'Right. I'll see your father as soon as you like. Tomorrow night – can you fix that d'you think, honey?'

Carl and Gayle were married within three weeks. It was a low-key function, not in the least what J. Arthur Belman had planned in the years when he had watched his daughter grow and blossom. He had intended that failing an English aristocrat she would marry into the top strata of American Old Money. He had planned for a ceremony to overshadow all ceremonies in its brilliance, and its five-star guest list, second only perhaps to Grace Kelly's. He would have Harry Belafonte's 'Island in the Sun' and Pat Boone's 'April Love' played at the Plaza reception, and his angel's gown would be a Dior from Paris.

Carl played his cards well. The interview had been enjoyable as he had put a great deal of careful thinking into the preparation, and J. Arthur Belman none at all, which more than made up for J. Arthur having the advantage of home ground. Carl had appeared a mite reluctant to take on such responsibilities at his tender age, murmuring about tight budgets at the outset of his career, and the cost of a home in New York and so on. Purple-faced with ire, his prospective father-in-law had come up with the offer of an apartment in Upper East Side and a lump sum to invest. He would in addition settle a dowry on Gayle, the details of which were hammered out within a week and proved most favourable to Carl.

Carl looked splendidly handsome and at peace with the world as bride and groom were toasted in Krug. In a remarkably short space of time he had acquired a sexy little wife who would be the envy of his peers – and bring a most gratifying dowry with her – a luxury home, and a sum that with his know-how should quickly grow. He had also taken most satisfactory revenge upon J. Arthur Belman; perhaps the sweetest part of the whole deal. It did no harm to give his luck a gentle push when the occasion warranted . . . 'I sure am a lucky guy,' he told the assembly in response to the toast, blue eyes glinting with satisfaction.

'Lucky Carl Cline, that's me!'

Chapter Nine

March 1960

'I have to tell you, Jonet,' said Hannah painfully, sure as she spoke of laying herself open to the charge of interference, 'that I believe Laurie will lose more than he could possibly gain by being sent away to school so young. He won't even be eight until almost the end of his first term.'

Jonet set down her coffee cup. Signs of a small struggle passed across her lovely face like a breeze over long grass. Hannah wanted to go right on and say forget it, it was no business of hers. But it was said; and she felt anyway that it *was* her business if her grandchild was to be made unhappy.

'Don't you think Mark and I can be trusted to do our best for Laurie, Mother? I was perfectly happy myself at boarding-school, and –'

'Heavens Jonet – you were approaching twice his age when you went! And you were an *evacuee,* for heaven's sake!' Hannah's voice was sharp and Jonet's lips tightened. 'Furthermore you welcomed going away for reasons that Laurie certainly doesn't have – you saw it as a way of bettering yourself socially.'

That too was said now; Hannah, flushed and frustrated, knew she would regret it. 'A teenager already confident in her abilities is not a rather nervous and unconfident child of seven years old – you do see that?' she added in hope of calming the waters.

'If you didn't have a persecution complex about

Laurie you wouldn't think of him as nervous and unconfident. That is a highly personal view and, I believe, a warped one.'

Jonet's pale skin had coloured a touch. Her gaze met Hannah's and swung away; Hannah realised with surprise that her daughter was not being aggressive, but defensive about Laurie. She considered for the first time that it might be Mark who was insisting Laurie go to boarding-school . . . that it might not be a joint decision. She sat down opposite her daughter.

'If it *is* warped, that might be because I love Laurie very dearly and do worry a little that . . . Well, you work long hours . . . and Mark is often away.'

'And Laurie is neglected, and is to be sent to school out of the way?' Jonet finished for her. 'Do you recall the hours you used to work when we were small? Were *we* neglected? I think you'd have a short answer for anyone who dared suggest that!'

She got to her feet and stared down at Hannah. Why did she invariably become choked by so many conflicting emotions when talking with her mother? Whatever the issue, it became a divisive one . . . and always she found herself fighting the old sour resentments. 'I love my job, I've worked hard to get this far and I refuse to take your inference in the least seriously. But I am hurt that you feel compelled to voice it. Mark – we – happen to believe we've done what is best for Laurie. Going away will teach him self-sufficiency, and confidence when dealing with strangers. He has to learn to fight his own battles –'

'He has plenty of time to do that, Jonet.' Hannah's voice was gentle. 'I still think he would make a better job of it just a little later on, and with people who love him nearby to offer support. But please don't be upset – as long as you're both in full agreement –'

'Certainly we are.' Jonet jumped hard on that. 'And I would be grateful if you'd do nothing to undermine our decision. Now, I must be going. Are Laurie's things ready? Thank you for having him.' She ran a comb through her hair and put on her hat. 'It was awkward, this local history course falling at half-term.'

'He's been no trouble. When we're at the restaurant he sits down and draws, or watches what is going on in the kitchen. I shall miss his company.'

When they had gone Hannah went up to her room, past Liza's open door from which floated the strains of the latest Paul Anka ballad. She felt tired now, and depressed . . . she had an unpleasant feeling that she would see less of Laurie, at least for a while. When her record had finished Liza came in and sat on her bed, watching her mother in the dressing-table mirror.

'Shouldn't you be getting ready for Guides?' Hannah flicked up her newly cut hair with a brush and put on lipstick.

'I may not go tonight . . . I'm not interested in getting a housewifery badge. What colour is that?'

'Honey Rose. Means nothing, it's just a name.'

'Can I try it?' Liza picked it up and Hannah saw how neatly she outlined her perfectly curved lips, blotting them, then standing back to see the effect in the mirror.

'You've had practice, I see.'

'Oh, well –' Liza tried a slightly fuller bow on her upper lip. 'Dad's wife bought me one. She said, if I'd started my periods I was old enough.' She dropped Honey Rose into Hannah's lap.

'Thanks, Mummy. Actually, I'd already bought one for myself last spring.' She stretched and yawned, small breasts pushing against the tight sweater.

Hannah, realising here was a rare opportunity for a one-to-one chat, struggled to find exactly the right tone for what she had in mind, halfway between casual and interested.

'D'you recall after the end-of-term play last summer, telling me about that rather strange woman you'd seen in the wings? We were so busy then, getting your things organised for Canada – but I thought about it quite a bit. And I've been meaning to ask you; only time flies so alarmingly –'

'Mummy – for heaven's sake stop *waffling*.' Liza wandered towards the door.

'No darling – do listen. Please.' Hannah put out a hand. Liza hesitated at the door, and when her mother indicated the bed, turned with a show of reluctance and perched at the foot of it, frowning and twisting a tendril of hair. 'I was only wondering if you'd thought about it again yourself?'

'Why should I?' the girl countered. The fact that she did not look up as she spoke emboldened Hannah.

'Because, I suppose, you might have tried to work out who the woman actually was. You insisted that she was not a pupil, not staff. But she was *someone*, wasn't she? She was *there*?'

'She certainly was,' Liza said, but Hannah detected a shade of hesitancy. Her finger traced the pattern of a flower on the quilted eiderdown.

'And her clothes were strange; I recall you told me she had a long skirt and a grey shawl. And lots of dark hair?'

'Goodness, Mummy – how on earth can you remember that!' Liza's finger pressed hard into the quilt. 'I'm sure *I* can't remember anything like so much. I think now I may actually just have *thought* I saw her. You know; I was pretty het up at the time after all, trying to remember all those lines and everything.'

She looked up now, and Hannah caught a glimpse of – could it be pleading? – in the brilliant eyes. Liza was frightened. Of what? The mysterious woman? Of Hannah knowing of her fear? Of being told she had seen a ghost? Liza knew nothing of Rachel Hywel so far as Hannah knew. Perhaps she had pushed the incident away with characteristic determination as both insoluble and meaningless, a second in time best forgotten.

Hannah moved over to lay a friendly arm across Liza's shoulders, and was disturbed to find them trembling a little. 'You could be right, darling. Perhaps you glimpsed an odd-looking shadow and your well-known imagination worked it up. As you say, you were in a bit of a state at the time.'

She stroked back the mane of hair. 'I'm here if you should want to talk about it, anyway. Or if anything like it should happen again. Has this year's play been decided yet?'

'Oh . . . I'm not certain. Look; there's a load of geography homework I should be doing.' Liza extricated herself, smiling vaguely and Paul Anka was soon heard throbbing again behind the closed door of her bedroom.

Hannah picked up the lipstick from where it had rolled, and set it back in its place on the glass-topped dressing table. All she had learned was that Liza could not talk of what she had seen without experiencing fear; why she was afraid was not so certain.

She stared at the shiny lipstick case. She could do little more unless she was approached, other than wait, and watch. There was no way to make even an uninformed guess at why Rachel Hywel had materialised for Liza; unless of course that had been happening for some time and Liza had only last summer acquired the power to see her. Perhaps because she was entering womanhood? But how could the tragic spirit believe help was possible, from a fourteen-year-old who had no interest in the theory of second sight? If only Liza would talk to her . . . Little could be served by pressing for this, though, without Liza's willingness.

She *must* wait; and hope. In the end, Hannah had also refrained from asking for any details of David Vaughan's wife . . . Liza had not seemed inclined to speak to her on that subject either. So what if she *had* bought Liza a lipstick? A few weeks a year was scarcely enough to influence a girl in any direction; more important was that her daughter should not be influenced by Rachel Hywel.

By the end of the decade, memories of the long, lean years of shortage and privation were fading. There were still nowhere near enough houses; but goods finally had flooded back into the shops, and full employment with sharply rising wages gave families a new and heady purchasing power. There seemed no reason either to strike, or to be concerned about the future. True, the world had broadly divided into two hostile camps of capitalist and communist; racial passions were stirring, as was youthful rebellion against the self-satisfied status quo; mind-boggling new weapons of war were leading to protest marches by those fearing for mankind's survival, and American troops were already being sent to Vietnam as 'advisers'. But . . . a Russian dog had orbited the earth, an anti-polio vaccine had been developed, there were ten million cars on Britain's roads, and synthetic diamonds and non-stick frying pans had burst upon the market. With rock 'n' roll and skiffle groups thrown in, the country had been told by the highest authority that Britain had 'never had it so good'.

Hannah stood outside her restaurant and surveyed the knitting wool shop next door. Perhaps one-third the size of her own premises, it was in good structural order, with the door on the near side and a big, pleasantly proportioned window. The lease was running out. She eyed the FOR SALE notice; she knew Miss Jephson wished to retire with a friend to Bournemouth, and Hannah was seriously contemplating offering not to buy, but to rent it . . . provided the terms were right, and provided the plan to expand did not cause division with Matthew. The premises would, she believed, be perfect for a coffee bar.

Increasingly aware that the average age of her regular customers matched her own, Hannah deduced that younger age groups must have requirements other than those for which she catered. Young people now had jobs and money in their pockets; she had noted milk bars in a few suburbs, then, as a logical extension, coffee bars. These were less formal venues for meeting friends than her restaurant, with snacks or simply drinks in place of meals, and one of the new jukeboxes for the music the young had made their own. Could the little wool shop adapt?

Hannah smiled, and turned for home, raising a hand to Mrs Cheverley who was just going in for a pot of tea and a wedge of Victoria sandwich. It was a blowy April afternoon, full of agitated daffodils and small, busy white clouds; the sort of day when energy levels run high. Hannah walked briskly; she carried her years lightly, hair brushed back from a still clean jawline and waistline only an inch or so thicker than in youth. She wore a soft, dove grey twin-set with a wool skirt that swung attractively from her hips, and court shoes that became her pretty legs. She would be sixty in two years and two months, which would, she thought, be time enough to think of retiring. It was the first spring of the decade, of the unwritten, clean-sheet 1960s, and Hannah wanted to accept its new challenges.

She slowed in a moment. Did she really want to tell Matthew that she was thinking not of retiring, but of expanding? Why did she *want* to do that, particularly against the grain of his wishes for her to start winding down?

Hannah came to the Common and stood for a moment. What drove her to keep working? *She* knew . . . of her deep fears of insecurity, of hard times never forgotten, of the need always to consolidate, to secure defences against ill-luck. David might die without providing for Liza. Matthew might die and his sons inherit. She, Hannah, could stave off what dangers might come for her family, as her parents never could for her, for Joe, for Tom. Tom had been her responsibility since Betsy's death, and she would never let *him* down.

So . . . she would hope for Matthew to understand. Work was so deeply ingrained in her whole being; since fourteen. Was she unable to envisage life without it? Perhaps she did not want to.

She walked across the Common, thinking as she so often did of time spent here with Liza in babyhood, of her first meeting here with Matthew, of walking here with Joe. Joe, a father at last . . . Hannah was smiling at the thought as she turned into the drive of Greystones. Paul Harry Hywel – eighteen months old now; and recent news that a second baby was due at

Christmas. Going over to see them might almost be worth retiring for.

The kitchen door was open. She walked in, and at once saw Liza through the window. At the edge of the lawn under the willow tree, her daughter, still in her school gym-slip, was closely engaged in a passionate embrace with a tall young man in a blue sweater and flannels; Matthew's younger son, Nick.

Hannah watched them for a moment frozen in time. Then she heard the kitchen clock continue to tick, the April wind continue to blow through sappy young tree branches and stiffly creaking old ones, the resident pair of wood pigeons continue to coo gently and foolishly. Nick lifted his head, so that Liza could be seen smiling at him, her arms raised to wrap around his neck. He said something to her, then bent over her again. Hannah looked at Liza's long, slim black-stockinged legs below the short gymslip and wondered if she still had on her school tie. Then she turned and walked fast and soundlessly back into the drive, the quiet road, where the evening paper delivery boy, whistling, rode his bike along the pavement with both hands on his hips.

At the corner of the road she stopped. Better to have stayed there. What if . . . No; surely not, with her expected home, and Matthew shortly after. She looked back. How could she behave naturally? What could she possibly say? How *could* he – he was twenty-one and Liza not fifteen until next month. Nick had always been so easy, pleasant, no problems.

She would meet Matthew, he'd said he would be home in good time today. Still Hannah hesitated, her cheeks hot as though she had been caught in a shameful act. Matthew would have to do something, if only tell Nick there must never be a repeat . . .

'You *must* do something, Matthew.'

Hannah gripped his arm as they faced one another on the pavement. She had met him leaving the Common, and her relief at seeing the familiar figure, hat and briefcase in hand and hair blowing untidily in the wind, was such that she wanted to burst into tears. Instead she was walking home with him, explaining as calmly as possible the situation they must confront.

'You will talk to Nick? He's so much older than Liza, it's dreadful for him to take advantage –'

'My dear Hannah.' There was a small but distinct edge to his voice. 'I'd lay odds that if anyone has been taken advantage of it is Nick.'

'*What?*' Hannah's voice flared. He shook his head at her.

'Come on, now . . . you know your own daughter! I expect she's led poor old Nick on, to get a reaction. Well, he's only human so she's got one!'

'That's a horrible thing to say! She's just a *child*, Matthew!'

He frowned, and looked at her with concern in his blue eyes, then gave a wry smile. 'That, sweetheart, is some child.'

She stood still. Her first instinct was to hit out at him, to assuage her wrath. But as she scrutinised the eyes regarding her so openly she was calmed, as always, by the nature of this man she loved. He was right, of course. Who could gainsay Liza if she was set on a course of her choice? And what man would even think of resisting her charms once caught in the intense beam of her charisma. Liza was entering womanhood and testing its boundaries – and heaven help anyone involved!

'What shall I do?' she asked him quietly.

He took her arm and they began walking again. 'A

joint effort is the thing, I should say. Of course I'll speak to Nick; he's behaved badly and I shall say so, depend on it. Your task, dear Hannah, is more difficult . . . easier to deal with ten Nicks than one Liza! You can only do your best to point out the danger of playing with people's emotions; the big difficulty is that Madame has become aware of the effect she can have on the opposite sex, and finds it rather enjoyable.'

'I shall certainly talk to her.' Hannah was still subdued.

'Good girl. Now, we're almost there. Chin up, stomach in, or whatever will set you in good order. She'll probably be beavering away at her homework by now, butter not melting in her mouth.'

Liza was not doing her homework. She was walking up and down the one-brick-wide wall of the terrace in her stockinged feet, balancing the copper coal scuttle from the sitting room on her head. She explained that they were doing a Chinese play this term, *Lady Precious Stream*, and that she had to practise the very particular walk. She still had on her school uniform but had removed her tie and used it to pull back her hair. She had also fallen off the wall, with a resultant tear in the knee of her black stocking. Having agreed reluctantly to change before further acrobatics she went upstairs. Carrying the cup of tea now needed badly, Hannah followed.

'Liza; a word.' She edged into her daughter's room before the door could be shut and took a long, revitalising draught of tea.

'Sure. Say, what do you think of this?' Liza was already bent over her gramophone.

'No – Liza –' Hannah put out a restraining hand. 'Just give me your undivided attention for a moment, will you?' Liza frowned, then shrugged, leaned against the windowsill and examined the jagged hole in her stocking, glued to her knee with blood from the scraped skin.

'I came home earlier, then went out again to give myself time to think, because I'd seen you and Nick on the lawn, kissing.' The words rushed out, leaving Hannah a little breathless. She put down the teacup on the tallboy as it was clinking against its saucer. 'Have you done that before?'

Liza waited for a moment, still examining her knee. 'No, not actually.' Then she looked up and met her mother's gaze and smiled, the seraphic Liza special. 'But I wouldn't mind a repeat performance, Mummy. It was really rather nice. How old were you when you started kissing boys?'

'Older than you are, certainly.' Hannah sounded grim. 'But we're talking about *you*. Liza; Nick's a man, not a boy.'

'I think I prefer men,' her daughter confided. 'Boys are mostly absolute dregs, aren't they? Not a brain to their names, a total bore. Nick's quite nice when he's not trying to be clever. D'you think I should bathe this knee? I can't get the stocking off it.'

'Liza.' Hannah, sensing the interview sliding out of her control, took another gulp of tea. 'I do not think it a good idea for you to be kissing Nick. Why on earth *did* you?'

'To see if I'd like it,' Liza said in a reasonable way. 'And I did.'

'Well you should *not* have.'

'Liked it?' Liza sounded puzzled.

'Done it in the first place.' Hannah began to feel dizzy with the effort of keeping the dialogue on track. Liza sat on the floor, undid the suspenders of her stocking and peeled it down to the knee.

'You see, I can't get it any further.'

Hannah knelt by Liza and took her shoulders. She had a desire to shake them hard, but resisted, knowing that violence would mean she had failed utterly. 'Liza, you need to understand that I am serious. And quite worried about this. You simply cannot play with a man like that ... experimenting with your own sensations regardless of how *he* may feel.'

'He said it was great, Mummy. So honestly, where's the harm? It's only Nick, for heaven's sake!' Liza looked up and smiled again; a reasonable, friendly smile. Hannah stared back at her.

'There is no such thing as "only" anyone, Liza.' She spoke with quiet deliberation. 'Never forget that. And for your own sake as well as others', you *have* to think carefully of what you may want to do, before you do it. Do you understand this?'

Now she was aware of being in deep water; and knew that Liza had it in her gift to push her under if she chose. Mother and daughter faced one another across more than forty years but the gap seemed uncannily narrow suddenly, to both.

'I have no intention of becoming pregnant,' Liza said. 'I do realise that's what you're afraid of. But you don't need to be; you'll just have to trust me on that, Mummy.'

'Oh Liza. Liza.' Hannah spoke so softly that it seemed no more than a sigh. But the girl heard, and answered.

'I don't *mean* to hurt you, you know. You mustn't let me.'

'No ...' Hannah managed a crooked smile. 'I mustn't, must I?'

'Han ...' Florence sounded anxious. 'We've got it in

print, official at long last. I can tell you, it's goin' to be one almighty upheaval. And the thing is, *cariad* . . . the line of the bypass goes bang through Morfa Cottage. I thought I'd better give you a ring right away.'

'Through my house?' Hannah put a hand to her free ear as Liza's music bounced down the stairs.

'That's it. You had to know, I thought. Tom's upset, I can tell you. Keeps on about the garden, and the wall he built.'

'Flo, are you saying Morfa Cottage is to be *pulled down*?'

'Seems so. You'll get a compulsory purchase order. This road's called a bypass but it sounds more like an overpass – it will go on enormous pylons over Taibach. After all, there's no room for a bypass, is there? We're already all squeezed in without an inch to spare between the hill and the steelworks!'

'Oh, Flo . . . I suppose I'd realised what might happen. But when it actually *does* –'

'I know. It's goin' clean across the top end of Incline Row, Han. So all the houses on the slope above will be blitzed – you know, Balaclava Road, Inkerman . . . I tell you, we won't know the old place soon. And the dirt, the mess, for years on end it'll be. I feel like gettin' out, I really do. Raymond doesn't know for sure yet about his house, but it doesn't look hopeful. I mean, it's not just an ordinary road, is it? It's going to be a *Motorway*! When it's all done and joined up at both ends, that is. A Motorway, through – or over – Taibach!'

'Oh, Flo.' Hannah could think of nothing else to say. 'Look. I'll be down in a couple of weeks, we'll talk then. Thanks for phoning – best I should know. Give my love to Tom, won't you? 'Bye now, Flo dear.'

She leaned against the wall, winded and nauseous

with shock. Her home; for so long, the stone-solid symbol of all she had attained for herself and her dependants. Morfa Cottage . . . God no, they couldn't actually bulldoze down those strong, safe walls that had sheltered them through the war? Where could she remember Serry, if not sitting at the kitchen table chewing her pen over her composition, or running after the cat along the little garden paths, laughing? There must be a way to stop them; explain that it wasn't any old cottage but represented a generation of struggle to succeed, to build a sanctuary for those she loved. After a while she stood up straight, blowing her nose hard, and went to put on the kettle for a cup of tea.

In the end it was August before she made it, just after Liza had departed on her annual trip to Toronto, and she had Joe with her, over for two weeks but with a heavy auction schedule. Sal had stayed at home with toddler Paul Harry, and when Joe returned they were going to the coast for two weeks to escape the New York heat. Matthew was with Nick on a weekend dig in Wiltshire, before Nick left to join a big excavation in Turkey. When Hannah had broached the idea of the coffee bar he had seemed puzzled, but made no objection and in the end they had worked together amicably on preliminary figures. As a result she had been busy these last weeks supervising alterations, and planned to be ready for a September opening.

She was unsettled, apprehensive as the train drew clear of Cardiff on the last stretch. Nothing stayed the same, she accepted; but the whole face of her home town would be torn apart during the next few years. No one had told Hannah this, but her knowledge of it was gut deep inside her. No fancy 'premonition', but something that *must* come.

'Penny for them, Han.' Joe offered her a cigarette but she shook her head. 'You had a shock about Morfa Cottage sure enough.'

'It represents all I had worked for, Joe . . . it was stone-built proof that I had succeeded. I can't explain the glow, when I unlocked the door for the first time, knowing it was mine, and that I personally had earned every penny of the asking price. I wished very much that you could have been there,' she added. 'I do recall wishing that. Tom was with me – and the girls were running from room to room, they loved it all. But I stood in the hall, and wanted you there too.'

'I'm sorry I wasn't,' Joe said, and meant it.

'It is hard to accept that in a year or so a huge tarmacked road will be laid where we used to sit round the table having breakfast . . . and cars will be driving over the place where we gathered round that lovely stone hearth, listening to the wireless. And the garden; poor Tom cannot come to terms with the garden being bulldozed flat.'

'Will you look for somewhere else?'

Hannah frowned, staring out at the land streaming past the carriage window. 'I can't seem to think constructively about that.'

'I think you should at least *look*, Han. It may be stupid of me, but I just can't imagine you – how you'd be – cut off entirely from the place. You know . . . it's where your roots are.'

She stared at him. How had *he* managed, a boy of twelve torn away from all he had ever known, ever had?

'I never stopped being homesick,' he said as though she had spoken. 'It was pretty rough. Never a night for years, but what I didn't give it thought. Remember the time you gave me a penny to see the seals that man was travelling round with in a big tank? And when Da would go with us to Aber beach in that farm cart with the two horses big as elephants? Twenty or more that cart used to hold didn't it, at a penny each? Off across the bridge and us chattering and laughing and wanting to eat our bits of food before we even got there. Then it picked us up late afternoon, and we had to shake all the sand off ourselves first?'

'I told you what happened to all that.' Hannah sounded grim. 'It's buried under a new town of 3,500 houses. And more are still going up wherever there's a square inch of land – Flo says there's well over 18,000 men at the steelworks now, and they've all to live somewhere.'

'So you'd have a job replacing Morfa Cottage anyway.'

'I would look further east, probably . . . perhaps in the Ogmore Vale. The air around Treasure Island is a bit toxic to attract a buyer who's no longer *forced* to live there!'

'Treasure Island?' Joe raised an eyebrow.

'That's what they're calling the steelworks now – the area fenced off by the sea, the docks and the railway. It is a sort of island, I suppose.'

Joe looked depressed. 'Poor old Taibach. This Morfa Cottage thing may be a blessing in disguise then, if it's forced the decision you'd been agonising over for a while. What do you think you might do about the bakery?'

'I have to weigh it up; if it's worth keeping on. I believe the whole town is in a melting pot. But Tom's future must be assured if I *do* sell. So . . .' Hannah stretched, and reached for her jacket as the train rounded the bend that brought them into sight of Swansea Bay and the blue hills of the Gower beyond.

'Home again, Joe-boy.' She smiled at her brother, feeling not in the least like it. 'I bet Tom's at the station.'

He was. At forty-two, Tom had a bald patch, but his skin was unlined and he looked fit. For a man living in a toxic environment, Hannah thought as they hugged one another, he looked surprisingly well. When he had greeted Joe, Tom stepped back a pace to examine him.

'You look tired,' he said with his own brand of quiet simplicity. Joe assumed a hang-dog expression.

'That's because I am now a husband *and* a father. Wait till it happens to you, little brother.'

Watching, Hannah wished with all her heart that it might indeed happen to Tom. But it was not a realistic hope; Tom was content within the narrow confines of his life, and to step beyond them would be to have too high an expectation of his powers.

'Tom has more sense than you, Joe. I see he also has a taxi waiting for us, so let's make for home, and a pot of tea and Flo's scones, which I am absolutely certain she has waiting for us.'

'We'll do a little tour of the district tomorrow, *cariad*; just a look round, get an idea of what's on the market.' Florence kissed Hannah's cheek as she and Joe left after supper at Incline Row. 'Sure you don't want me to run you home?'

'Thanks Flo, but it's a lovely evening. And we need a walk after all that food! Of course I'll come with you tomorrow; though remember I've not been kicked out of Morfa Cottage yet.'

She and Joe walked along Margam Road arm in arm in the mild cloudy night, their heads full of memories. Hannah was grateful for his being there, she would not have relished letting herself into Morfa Cottage alone tonight. On their left, the mountain was a massive black hump; on their right the miles of coke ovens, strip mills and blast furnaces of the Steel Company of Wales were a brilliantly lit wonderland, noisily illuminating their very own Treasure Island.

'Is New York noisy at night, Joe?'

'Sure. But different sounds to those.' He nodded at the works. 'Traffic, and music from bars and places . . . and people; I tell you, Han, so many people! They make a sort of collective hum of their own.'

'And you're chalking up one more soon!'

'Yeah, well . . . that sure will add to the noise problem!' Joe laughed as they turned up the dimly lit lane towards Morfa Cottage.

It all looked perfectly normal inside, clean and polished, with a vase of phlox and scabious freshly picked from the garden glowing on the small corner table in the sitting room. Tom had refreshed the walls last autumn with a pale apricot wash, echoed in the chintzy curtains at the windows, and in the covers of the deep chairs. Hannah remembered the pleasure of finding the velvety old square of Turkey carpet at auction, and the dark oak bible-box that sat under the side window. The cottage had grown beautiful in her twenty-six-year occupancy; slowly, from the shabby, botched-up and unloved dwelling it had been, a confidently loved home had emerged. She ran a hand along the deep patina of the arched beam above the inglenook, and her mind closed off against its possible fate.

'Want a night-cap?' Joe appeared with the decanter.

'Thanks, Joe.' He handed her a glass and Tom had been right, he did look tired. 'Are you working too hard?' she asked suddenly, always aware of the phial of pills in his breast pocket. He smiled, shrugged.

'I may have been, a little . . . A growing family; you know only too well that has a definite effect on the breadwinner.'

'Indeed.' How could those eighteen-hour work-days ever be forgotten . . . 'But Joe, you'll be no use to anyone if you get ill.'

'You're not to fret about me, Han – I'm OK, I promise. There'd just been a flurry of activity before I could get here this time. But with Marek starting with me next month, I should see a benefit in a while. That boy may be deaf but he's one great little worker. And bright as they make 'em: being deaf seems to have been an obstacle put right there for him to overcome. He organises the paperwork like a wizard, and that's a weak point of mine – and his maths is quicksilver.'

'A good day for you all round when Sal read your advert, then?' Hannah teased him gently. She put out the lamp in the sitting room and they made their way up the narrow stairs, the fifth and ninth treads creaking as they always had.

'Guess so . . . though I recall not thinking that at the time. If she'd let on earlier about the kid brother she'd not have got past the door.' Joe grinned. 'Not too sure what that tells us about predestination, Han. Maybe you know how it all works? Damned if I do, specially when I'm half asleep like now.'

'Before you collapse entirely, there's something I want to show you –' Hannah pulled open the door of the cupboard on the landing. On the top shelf was an ungainly object folded into a large brown paper bag. 'See what I have here.'

She drew out a bugle, old, but polished so that the overhead light was thrown brilliantly from its curved surfaces. Joe looked at it, put out a hand and touched it with his forefinger, and his eyes grew darker.

'Da's bugle.' He took the instrument from Hannah and laid it across his palms. 'It's our Da's bugle,' he repeated quietly.

For a moment brother and sister were still in the pool of light, the bugle between them the jewel-bright focus of their rapt attention.

'I meant to show you each time you came, Joe, but I never remembered. I took it to Clapham when I married Matthew. But it never seemed right, somehow, to have it there. Sounds silly – but London was not its natural home. So I brought it back here. I played it once for Liza, out on the hill. That's where I learned to play it . . . for Dada. Can you remember?'

'Sure.' Joe still cradled the bugle; the only thing he had known to be his father's personal property, inherited from his grandfather who had played it at the battle of Balaclava. Mam had disliked it as being too noisy, and of no practical value. But Joe recalled, dug from a shadowy collection of childhood images, an air of expectancy, even reverence, when Thomas Hywel would take it out from the cupboard under the stairs. Occasionally he played it to them, up on the hill where they disturbed no one but the sheep. Then, when he went away to training camp in the bitter winter of 1916, Hannah had, with enormous effort, learned to play a few notes of a simple Welsh air on it. This was her farewell gift to him before he went to France. They had gone out on the hill on his last day at home, and the heartbroken girl had poured out her love through the old bugle.

'I remember,' he said. 'I never would forget that bugle. So you'll take it back to Clapham – when this place goes?'

She nodded, and kissed his cheek. 'For the time

being. Sleep well now, Joe.'

Hannah took the bugle into her room, and held its strangely comforting bulk against her under the sheet while she slept.

Chapter Ten

February 1962

'What I believe,' Miss Watkins told Hannah in her well-modulated voice, 'is that your daughter has no real interest in anything – any single thing – but acting.'

In the small but impressive silence that followed this pronouncement, Hannah looked attentively at Miss Watkins, then at the portrait above her on the light green wall, which was of the headmistress who had preceded her at Berrington's.

'Such single-mindedness may not be wholly bad,' she ventured at last. 'It cannot be easy to succeed in so hazardous a profession unless one's entire attention is brought to bear.'

Miss Watkins digested that in further silence, not afraid to take her time. She was a woman of around fifty, with smooth brown hair drawn into an admirably managed bun, alert eyes of an identical brown and a mouth whose mobility suggested humour when allowed. Her Prince of Wales checked suit was a perfect fit over broad shoulders, and softened by an oatmeal blouse with a neat bow.

'Liza does of course show considerable promise. Berrington's being so strong in the field of drama has meant that she has already had several opportunities to tackle major parts. The problem is that in other subjects she can become bored, restless, and a disruptive influence. Hard work in the Lower Sixth is crucial to good A-level results; pupils who leave the two-year course to be packed into a few months in Upper Sixth make a grave mistake, often costing them the grades necessary for their choice of university. Now, what is happening is that not only is Liza neglecting her own work, but she is on occasion the cause of other girls neglecting theirs. She is a dominant personality, a leader rather than a follower. Sadly she has yet to learn that with that should go a sense of responsibility.'

Hannah let out her breath gently. She had realised this interview was not set up to congratulate her on her daughter's academic progress, and was in fact as disturbed as the headmistress. 'How can I help, Miss Watkins?'

'Have you considered allowing her to apply for a place at RADA in September of next year?' Miss Watkins became more congenial as she sensed co-operation rather than confrontation in the air.

'It's a possibility I'd been aware of. Liza had badly wanted to go to a theatre school after O levels, but I persuaded her that a good general education was the soundest start she could possibly have, particularly combined with Berrington's interest in drama. I'm extremely sorry to hear that she has not taken our agreement seriously.'

'Agreement?'

'I said that I would back her stage ambitions any way I could, once she had taken A levels.'

'I see.' Miss Watkins rolled her fountain pen back and forth in her fingers. 'Well; you may not know, but RADA's fees are around £100 per term. They do have a few scholarships and half-scholarships available, but insist that first the local authority be approached for grants. And of course, their scholarships are offered only to candidates of outstanding promise. Now, what I could do is use what influence I have to sway our own Authority to offer a grant, should Liza succeed in being offered a place next year. Our record in drama may count for something; but RADA auditions – especially for females – are exacting and Liza will stand or fall by them.'

'Why should it be harder for females?' Hannah sounded a touch incensed.

'RADA's intake is probably about twice as many males as females. This is because there are far more male than female parts available to play in the theatre.'

'D'you know, I had not actually been aware . . .' Hannah frowned.

'A Shakespeare play might have twenty male characters and no more than three female.' Miss Watkins clearly knew what she was talking about. 'So . . . a female student must have every possible quality to offer. Acting ability alone will not suffice. Personality, beauty, iron determination to withstand repeated rejections and total faith in oneself are all essential.'

Hannah said simply, 'I believe Liza may well have what is needed. But I will certainly tell her what you say; she should know what the odds are. If she still wants to go ahead could she apply soon? I realise her A levels are over a year off, but it may help concentrate her mind on them.'

'She should ask for an application form in the first instance, explaining she would be available after A levels. We may get more effort towards her A levels if she knows that the Authority Grants Committee is more likely to look favourably upon her if they have a report from this school that Liza can apply herself to *whatever* course she is studying.'

Miss Watkins laid down her pen, and rose. 'Is, er Mr Bates – Liza's father – likely to offer any objection to Liza's trying for RADA, Mrs Stourton?'

'None at all,' said Hannah pleasantly. She held out her hand. 'Good afternoon, Miss Watkins – thank you for asking me in to talk. I shall speak to Liza of course, and I sincerely hope you will soon note a change in her attitude.'

'Now, I've no idea whether she thinks I am divorced, or worse, the mother of a by-blow,' Hannah told Matthew that evening. 'I suspect she knows the truth; it has an uncanny way of getting out.'

Matthew sighed; Liza's illegitimacy never would go away, it was like a burr under their collective shirt. 'I suppose if you've coped with it for going on seventeen years, you've managed to grow a protective skin. But attitudes are changing, you must know that . . . So much is changing. Another drink?'

'No thanks, darling.' Hannah pushed a hand through her hair 'Actually, there's no protective skin that I'm aware of. It never has been less than dreadfully awkward, though I'd admit that to no one but you. And now I'm bound to beard my dear daughter in her den. Subject: both her work and her general behaviour. But at least one good thing resulted – she has their support in a bid for RADA, *provided* she improves herself. Tit for tat, reasonable enough. Is she in her room, d'you know?'

'Not till later. She said she was taking some homework round to Audrey's place. Back by nine at latest she thought.' Matthew grinned. 'You've time to prepare notes. You know full well that otherwise she'll stand you on your head.'

'Not this time.' Hannah sounded grim. 'I can hold

the RADA gun to her head. What time is Nick expected?'

'Not till tomorrow now. He phoned to say he's spending the night with a friend somewhere in Hammersmith.'

'I'll get steak for him, then – he's always ravenous after a dig.' Hannah started a list for bringing in. 'Seems ages since he was last home – it'll be nice to have him.'

'So long as he doesn't stay longer than three days,' said Matthew, and grinned again.

'What if Hannah checks out that you're at Audrey's?' asked Nick. He pulled the blankets up over his buttocks, which were feeling chilly. Den's flat was inadequately heated for a night as cold as this.

'She won't as long as I'm back by nine.' Liza shifted under him, very warm herself after their strenuous exercise. She could still feel him inside her when she moved, and closed her legs, liking the sensation of trapping him. 'Are you going to manage it again, d'you think?'

'I might, if you give me a few minutes. Only I'll need another French letter.'

'I *hate* those beastly things,' she said vehemently. 'I'm going to see if I can get these pills – they sound a brilliant idea.'

'They'll never sell them to you, silly girl. You're not married . . . and not even seventeen yet.'

'I'll find a way.' She sounded so confident that Nick did not doubt but that she would. He hoped so; making love to Liza was mind-blowing. They lay quiet, thinking about their bodies and how enjoyable it all was. Then she made a small experimental movement . . . if they were going to do it again they'd have to get on with it, she could see the bedside clock. She felt an answering response, and pressed his buttocks closer.

'Come on then . . . show me. I think you can.'

'It was this rotten geography,' she told Hannah, sighing as she shed the navy duffel coat and shook her hair free of the woolly hat. 'South America is ghastly – who wants to *know* about it anyway! I mean, Mummy, *you* knew nothing much about Chile and the Andes and all that – and look how well *you* did!'

'I was not as lucky as you, Liza. I was working in a shell factory at your age, with my skin turning yellow from chemicals. D'you understand any of it better for having gone over it with Audrey, though?'

Liza's brow wrinkled. 'I think so. I tried, anyway.'

'That's not something you've been doing too much of lately, if I am to believe Miss Watkins,' Hannah said briskly. 'She requested my presence in her office today and it was not to congratulate me on my daughter's aptitude for hard work. You've been playing around, haven't you? And *I've* been taken to task for it.'

'I can't think why she should say that.' Liza looked bewildered. 'Mind you, it's all pretty boring so it's hard to produce the results they want.'

'If it's boring, that may well be because you are paying no attention. And much worse, in my book, is that you're distracting girls who may actually want to pay attention.'

'She's a crazy old bat, that's all I can say,' snapped Liza. 'How can you take her seriously?'

'Easily.' Hannah was unrelenting. 'I believe her. Also, I know she has your best interests at heart – which is rather more than you deserve. No –' she held up a hand at once as Liza opened her mouth to retort. 'Listen to me now, Liza. Sit down. This is important.'

'Mummy – I'm *tired*! I've slaved all evening on that wretched geography.' Liza turned on a wan expression and looked longingly at the door.

'Sit here.' Hannah pointed, and sat herself nearby. 'Miss Watkins has offered to help get a grant for you to go to RADA after A levels. It will not be easy, but I feel strongly that being answerable for a council grant, you might feel more responsible about making an effort. Provided, of course, you did successful auditions, and RADA wanted you. And provided you stop messing about right away, and apply yourself to something other than the current drama production, and interfering with other pupils' concentration. Now, that's the offer, and what you do about it is up to you. I was actually quite ashamed to hear of your present attitude from Miss Watkins, and I tell you now, I am only prepared to help you myself if I find it has changed.'

Liza, who had been studying her stockinged feet during this speech, looked up now and mother's and daughter's eyes engaged. Hannah took the strain of attempting to bend the will of this beautiful, powerful and charismatic adolescent who was her daughter. It felt as though she held tight to a rope, straining to keep her balance when losing could mean being pulled over a cliff to the rocks below. The kitchen was quiet but for the clock, and the murmur of the television Matthew had on in the sitting room. Liza's eyes seemed to reach her very soul . . . Hannah struggled to rid herself of a sense of danger.

'Well; that sounds quite good.' When Liza spoke her voice struck such a reasonable, normal note that Hannah wanted to laugh with absurd relief. 'How do we set about RADA – did she tell you that?'

'We send for an application form.' Hannah felt very

tired now. 'So why don't you go to bed and we'll do that tomorrow. It will be a start at least.'

Three months later, Hannah stood on the bridge across the Avan and looked east, collar turned up against a May wind that was cold enough to peel the skin off her face. Indeed she felt numb both inside and out. Not far from the docks, the old melting shop where Dada had worked had ceased operating. Just beyond, the Rhondda and Swansea Bay Railway had already been closed to passenger traffic, and would fall victim to Dr Beeching's axe in the near future. Inland, massive pylons were rising from a grey wasteland of demolition to take the new road over Pentyla and the river. And today, her home was being emptied and its contents taken into store. Soon now, machines would claw and tear at Morfa Cottage; would reduce it to a level site.

She shivered. Must get back ... Fill the car with things to take up to Clapham. For the present, her foothold here was gone. Florence had tried, spent time she could ill afford following up the unlikeliest bet, but no Morfa Cottage Mark II had appeared. So; she was lucky to have a home in London and not in Incline Row, where Florence fought a daily war on grit and dust that did indeed now seem to cover the whole town.

Get on with it, then. Afterwards, she would see Tom at the bakery before starting the drive to Clapham in a car loaded to the gunwales. They would have tea together, and she would take away a bag of spiced buns; she never had found spiced buns to match Tom's. Tomorrow, back to work; business was brisk, and she had a chef to interview at eleven. She had decided to apply for a liquor licence, and have the restaurant open five evenings a week under the management of a chef, and this one sounded promising. It was to be her final business enterprise, and she wanted it to work. She would be sixty next month . . . She felt nothing like sixty, but the fact remained. Soon, she would sell the Taibach bakery and shop to its manager, who was a willing buyer and would keep Tom on as master baker.

Perhaps she should finish now. Why *did* she go on – she had all the money she could ever need, and plenty for Tom's secure future. And Liza would probably inherit more than was good for her from David. Hannah and he had not met since Liza was thirteen, but they spoke occasionally on the phone, and he had talked of coming over later this year. Whether alone or with Ella, his wife, he had not said. Liza seemed to like Ella well enough, but Hannah had no real wish to meet her.

Yes – she would definitely sell up in a year or so, then she and Matthew would have time together. They could visit Joe and his family in New York; she longed to see her toddler nephew, small Thomas, and Paul Harry. Thomas was a few months younger than Brad, Carl Cline's son, and Joe spoke of high jinks when they met at Alex's. So . . . a couple of years, no more, and she would retire gracefully; perhaps clearing her mind for the possibility of opening channels to heal again. Her attendance at the local healing circle had lapsed . . . the time, perhaps, was not right.

She looked inland, towards the hills. Where was Rachel Hywel's shade now? Had Liza seen her again? She often wanted to ask, but the words failed to come. Leave well alone, perhaps. Yet part of her longed to climb the track one more time to stand by the rough old stones that once had been a home, and to wait. No;

leave well alone; Hannah went back to her car. A hot drink and breakfast, before the removal van arrived.

By midday it was all done. The men had gone with a last joke, thanking her for the generous tip, driving away a load that meant nothing to them, but so much to her. Hannah had known she should take this occasion to let Serena's things go; yet finally she had failed to make her head rule her heart, and had marked the case full of personal belongings for storage. The teddy bear, the scarf and the slippers Serry had just been given for her fourteenth birthday; her recorder, favourite books, and the little stool Tom had made for her . . . in the end, Hannah could not bear to obliterate these tangible mementoes of a beloved life. And Tom had dug up his niece's yellow rose for Hannah to replant in Greystones' garden. 'No bulldozer's goin' to flatten *that*,' he had said in his soft flat voice. This summer it would bloom in Clapham, along with the cuttings she and Tom had taken from their most precious plants, and a few Welsh foxgloves. Tom had asked if he should stay off work to help her today, but she had said no. He had felt bad enough about the fate of his home, without being forced to see it emptied out.

Hannah locked the back door for the last time, and put the key under the flowerpot at the side of the step. May was a terrible time to leave; the day had finally warmed up and plants were growing almost visibly, throwing out leaf, shoot and bud at a great rate. Pads of thyme were creeping over the path again, violets forcing a way between cracks, ivy reaching over stone in intricate, elegant patterns. Blossom on the sharply angled old apple tree forecast a heavy cropping, and the scent of may blossom was headily sweet as she walked slowly past the gnarled and sinuous little hawthorn.

At the gate she turned, and tears fell unchecked down her face and on to her jacket. Aware of someone standing by the apple tree, Hannah knocked the tears away to see clearly. Not one . . . two girls, hands linked, smiling at her. Dorothea, her spirit companion, not seen since the day of Harry's death; and Serena, bright hair dappled under the new foliage, the yellow gingham frock short above bare brown knees. The girls laughed and waved at her, and her daughter blew a kiss.

'Serry!' Hannah took a step forward, then halted. Waving back, she smiled as she wept. Serena stooped to pick up a little cat; it was Wedgewood, whom she had adored. Fondling him now, she and Dorothea moved along the path together, and suddenly were gone.

Hannah put down her head on the old wall and cried with fierce abandon, oblivious to any who might hear. It seemed now to be Serry she was leaving behind, not only their home, and for a moment she could absolutely not bear it. When she had finished she blew her nose hard, closed the gate behind her and got into the car.

That evening she wrote to Joe, desperate for contact. Tired as she was after the drive home she could not rest, or consider anything but her vision of Serena. Matthew was away in Brighton at a two-day conference; Liza, playing a moderately plausible part as a reformed character, shut in her room revising for her 'mock' A levels. Hannah, curled on the sofa with Joe's last letter, wondered how many hours of her life had been so spent since he had left home . . . it felt like a whole lifetime of waiting for Joe. Yet now, what to say? That she had seen the spirit of her daughter? Joe might talk that over with Sal, and decide that Han was a bit over-tired with the job of packing up at the cottage, and that her imagination had played tricks. They would not laugh; but would perhaps feel disturbed at what she had written.

She sighed.

Dear Joe and Sal

Back from a final sort-out at Morfa Cottage – all is packed and stored now, and the next task is to find another place. Not easy; but if anyone can succeed, Flo will. Meanwhile, I try not to think about what happens next. It is called progress – I am sure you have lots of it in New York! The road *must* happen; traffic has ground to a standstill practically, for want of it. And yet, should so much be destroyed, for progress? Port Talbot has the feel of a frontier town now – rough and tough, half-built, full of 'foreigners'. Booming. Lethal. So farewell, Morfa Cottage. And much more.

She stared into the May dusk. In a moment she would get herself a drink. No point really, mentioning Serena. She knew, and it had no importance for anyone but her.

Liza is swotting for exams; rather late in the day for it, but – ! Now she is fully fired up re. her RADA application, which went into the post two weeks ago after a great delay while she searched for *exactly* the right photo to include. She tells me she is being an *angel* at school, to give both headmistress and English mistress the incentive to press for a grant should she gain a place. I shall persuade her, if at all possible, also to try for a university place rather than have all her eggs in RADA's basket. But she is so set on RADA and threatens to DIE if denied a place there. Oh dear . . . Do enjoy your boys while they are tiny, it is much the easiest phase!

*

'Poor old Han.' Joe passed the letter to Sal. 'I'm sure sorry she had to go through that on her own. Twenty-nine years, I calculate she'd had Morfa Cottage. And I can still recall her writing to tell me she'd bought it! Her pride fairly set the paper alight. Ho there, young fella – no sticky fingers on your pa's suit, eh?'

Young Thomas Hywel, released from his high chair, propelled himself round the table with the wide-apart, lurching gait of a toddler. Sal caught him up just short of his father and mopped at him, relieving him of various bits of cereal, apple and toast stuck about his round little person. He could have been no one but Sal's offspring with his halo of dark, stand-away curls and bright cheeks, but his eyes were Joe's, brown as a peaty mountain pool. Paul Harry, about to be taken by Sal to his kindergarten, had lighter, straighter hair, nearer Hannah's in colour, and a paler skin. 'Like my Da,' Joe would say proudly, then Sal would say certainly not, their elder son was the living image of his maternal grandfather. Marek, who adored his nephews, would give his expressionless little laugh and say they were truly like no one but themselves. He had a small apartment of his own a few blocks away but came to supper twice a week, always arriving in good time for a romp with the boys then a read, with both on his knee while Sal stirred pans and sang snatches of Polish folk airs to herself.

Joe pushed back his chair and swung Thomas shoulder-high. 'My, you eat breakfasts like that every day an' pretty soon you'll pick *me* up!'

Alex Cline had told him he was crazy, he should give kids a miss at his age, but Joe had taken on new life in his middle years with his little sons. His fear remained; that fear which had kept him isolated through so many years, of talking in his sleep. Now, he believed he actually *wanted* Sal to know about Norman Madoc, but had not the wherewithal to make his confession from a cold start – 'Oh by the way, I killed a guy once, Sal.'

The phone rang, and it was Carl.

'How's tricks then, Joe?' Sometimes it was hard to tell Carl's voice from his father's on the phone; the same light fast delivery, unmistakable in clarity of syllable, and of intent.

'Fine, Carl – and you?' Joe looked at his watch. 'What can I do for you?'

'It may be the other way around . . . would you be in tonight around seven if I drop by?'

'Sure. Seven, then. My best to Gayle and the boy; see you.'

Sal came back from taking Paul Harry to school as Joe was almost ready to leave. Thomas was sitting on the floor transferring dried butter beans from a jar to a bag and back, currently his favourite occupation.

'I reckon he's all set for a career in grocery.' Joe gave his son's head a pat, and his wife a robust kiss on her laughing mouth. 'Honey, Carl just phoned, he wants to call in tonight. Around seven, not a long visit I think.'

'*I* hope,' Sal said honestly. 'What does he want?'

'No idea. I know you're never comfortable with him, sweetheart, I'll keep it as brief as I can. Maybe I'm due for more investment advice.' Thomas staggered over to offer him a butter bean and Joe took it, thanking him. 'I'm always happy to listen to that; he was right on the nose about last Christmas after all, selling off our shares and holding cash. The Dow Jones has been drifting down ever since. Look at today's news – down another twenty points. He's been right all along for us, if you consider; he's definitely put money in our pockets throughout the Kennedy administration. Alex was saying he's about to leave Stiltzberg for some new venture, so maybe I'll hear about that tonight.'

'He is so – *clever*, so sure of himself.' Sal pulled a face. 'He frightens me because of that perhaps.'

'He has that effect on a lot of people. Not me I guess, because I used to walk him in the park in his baby buggy. And tapped his backside once or twice. Don't fret, I'll not let him eat you. 'Bye now, young Thomas. You be good for your mam, eh?'

Joe always walked to work: the heart consultant stressed at each check-up that walking was good. Joe liked walking anyway and enjoyed stepping out across a sliver of Central Park to his business, whatever the weather. Today was perfect; the warmth of early summer had not yet turned breathless, and New Yorkers loitered a while under the trees. Youngsters pedalled bikes along paths, fed ducks, and a trio of Puerto Rican teenagers played a Mozart sonata, grouped about a bench by one of the bridges. Joe listened for a while to the timeless melody; this was one of the days when living in New York was more than just about bearable and it became the place to be, the hub of the world. When he dropped a dollar into the violin case lined with faded red satin and walked on, he began to calculate what business Carl might have with him to make it worth the while of this high flyer to devote x amount of time to him tonight. They'd eat later; with Carl, a man needed the full oxygen quota for his brain, not pumping around his digestive system.

Sal knew this too. 'Have a cookie now,' she offered when he got in that evening. 'I will have dinner waiting for when the business is over.'

Carl was late, it was 7.20 when Joe opened the door for him, but his ethic of 'never explain, never apologise' had long been familiar to Joe, being a hand-me-down from Alex. Carl at twenty-five had a look of his father in the lean build, in the clever, sharp planes of the face. The dark blond hair was layered immaculately, the grey barathea suit and soft pigskin shoes a triumph of expensive understatement. Most remarkable were Carl Cline's eyes: blue-grey, long, and perfectly placed in his head, they had a keen clear focus that could intimidate or entrap, and the brain behind them missed nothing.

'Carl – hi there. C'mon in.'

'Hello there, Joe.' Carl walked briskly through to the sitting room, put down his briefcase and smiled at Sal, who was coming through from the kitchen. 'Aunt Sal . . .' He leaned to kiss her cheek. 'Those little Turks tucked away for the night, are they?'

'It was them or me, Carl.' Sal smiled, patting his arm. She never understood, face to face, her nervousness of Joe's godchild, who was unfailingly charming and considerate in her company. Only when he had gone did she recall the hint of . . . not menace? How could it possibly be menace?

To give herself confidence, recalling how Carl's mother and wife both were invariably so faultlessly turned out, she had changed into a dress of midnight blue crêpe that had cost a deal of money but simply was not her style. A minute before seven o'clock she had rushed into the bedroom, stripped it off and thrown on a cotton frock in a warm peasant print, with a skirt that swirled about her pretty knees. This was a favourite garment in which she felt entirely comfortable, not being forced to hold in her stomach the whole time as the blue crêpe dictated. She had pulled a comb through her unruly curls, outlined her lips in warm red and decided that *nothing* would make her nervous of this young man tonight.

'So, what will you drink? Your usual?' Joe held up the decanter, and on the nod poured a generous measure of bourbon into two tumblers and a spritzer for Sal.

'Here's to us, then.' Carl lifted his glass and drank half, then sat down with a satisfied sigh, put his head back on the cushions and closed his eyes. Sal looked uncertainly at Joe then perched on a chair arm, while Joe sat opposite Carl, who opened his eyes and drank the rest of his bourbon.

'I'm leaving Stiltzberg at the end of the month,' he said without preamble, and smiled as if the fact gave him great pleasure.

'Your dad told me. I thought you were doing pretty well there – Alex said so anyway; though he did add you really put the hours in.' Joe poured more bourbon.

'Oh, I've done well as an analyst, sure enough. And I've no objection to working round the clock if there's a good return for the labour. The thing is, I can do better on my own now I've learned the ropes, and three years is plenty of time to do that even if you're stupid, which I'm not. I've made clients a lot of money in three years. Now I want to make real money for myself.'

Sal had finished her drink and shook her head at Joe's offer of a refill. She got up and adjusted a row of books that were already straight, clearly wanting to be gone. Joe wondered with a tinge of unease what 'real money' constituted.

'Now you're a businessman, Joe, and successful at

what you do. So you know without me telling you that you have to make your money *work*.'

'Yes,' Joe said, wondering what the hell Carl could be after. Sal twitched the velvet drapes and peered down into the street three floors below, more certain by the minute now that Carl must want to borrow a large sum of money.

'I really should be getting Paul Harry's things sorted for morning,' she said suddenly. 'I shall be back in good time.' For what, Sal did not say; only hurried into the sanctuary of the kitchen and turned on the radio so she should not be tempted to eavesdrop.

Carl, who had got to his feet as Sal departed, subsided again now, smiling the clever smile that always worried her.

'You're family so far as I'm concerned, Joe. You've been a good friend of Dad's since way back, and you're my godfather. So there are no strings here.'

He offered Joe a chased gold cigarette case and took out a cigarette for himself. Blowing a superior smoke ring he stared through it at his godfather. 'Now this is the picture. I have identified a company whose assets far exceed its market value. I intend putting every cent I can raise into a bid for a controlling stake. I won't fail because I have contacts who are already dissatisfied shareholders, and others who will follow me. Once I'm in the driving seat I *know* I can triple the share price in no time. The very fact that I've moved in will double it overnight. But that will only be the beginning; I see endless similar situations around all the time and I intend to set up my own investment company which will manage all the holdings. I'm inviting you in on the ground floor –' now the smile was seraphic – 'where the sky's the limit. Raise all you can and invest in *me*. Dad is.' Carl sat back, crossed his legs in a relaxed fashion and smiled.

Joe looked sceptical. 'But what about the slide in the market? All this talk of another 1929 in the offing?'

'It's gone down as far as it can go.' Carl spoke with supreme confidence. 'There are too many rules around now to let that happen again. In any case, this fall's been all about Kennedy getting tough with the steelmen – not allowing them to raise prices – and that's just about burned out now. What's left is a whole weight of money that just has to find a home. I tell you, the fall has almost touched bottom. Take a look . . .' He reached for his briefcase, snapped it open and pulled out papers to spread them on the coffee table.

He reeled off assets, ripe to be peeled off the targeted company; listed men he had ready lined up to take over key positions. A clockwork operation, he told Joe, and the model of more to come. Finally he mapped out how money could be raised by Joe to invest in the venture.

'Time is of the essence now, Joe. Some other smart guy could decide to beat me to it. First in wins, that's the game. You can come in now – that's the offer.'

Joe looked back at the young man who was, as he knew from the financial press, collecting devoted followers. Alex had shown him cuttings of the progress of 'Lucky' Carl Cline, and mentioned dizzy salary figures. But Carl's ideas of raising money would leave *him* completely exposed, for if things did not go right he would lose everything. And of course, being Joe Hywel, how could he trust anyone but himself? He never had, since the age of twelve.

He got up to stand by the fireplace. Sometimes in winter, Joe would have given anything for a coal fire, like the ones that would in memory blaze up in the black-leaded range in the little house in Incline Row . . . where you could stretch out your toes and wriggle them in the rosy heat. Here of course there was central heating. A fireplace; no fire.

For all that, a good comfortable room – Sal had seen to that. Warmth, cheer, an air of relaxed ease. What he had worked for.

'The truth is, Carl, I'll have to think about this. I understand what you say about timing, but this isn't really my scene. I don't doubt you have the Midas touch, and it's hard for you to understand that life has taught me to be this cautious. It would come pretty hard for me to raise a bank loan on my business, mortgage every stick I own, all that crap, to realise the sort of money you're talking about.'

Carl ground his cigarette into an ashtray and faced Joe squarely.

'I don't need to come here cap in hand, Joe. I'm here because of you and my dad – you've been buddies since way back, I know. Well, this would be my way of saying thanks, much appreciated. So there's really nothing in it for me. Of course –' he grinned, but his eyes were cold now – 'I know what a cautious old critter you are. Maybe you're not that bright either, to turn down a fortune.'

Joe regarded his godson for a moment, before his reply came bullet-straight. 'Maybe I'm not. But you're not qualified to judge how a man might feel about things he's fought for as I have. There's always been a silver spoon to pop into your mouth any time you got peckish.'

He held up a hand as Carl began to speak, his own voice cutting loud and clear. 'I don't take risks, too damn right. And you can't understand because *you* didn't push a screwy little wooden cart around back streets when you were eight, conning bits and pieces out of women in the hope that you'd make a few coppers by the end of the week. Those coppers could make the difference between having bread, and going empty – though my sister saw to it that I didn't go empty too often by working round the clock.'

Joe drew a breath, pulled his voice down. 'You see me as a cautious old critter. I won't deny I am – it's what life has taught me to be, but that's an area you're not familiar with. So how if you stick to what you know, boy, and I'll abide by what *I* know.'

'I'm with you.' Carl repacked his briefcase, face showing nothing. 'But you should realise that this deal could set you up for the rest of your life. You have those boys to educate . . . Anyway, I must push on now, I've two more calls to make this evening.' After a second's hesitation he extended his hand and Joe took it. 'My best to Sal – see you both around?'

When he had shut the door on Carl, Joe went to find Sal, who was ready to serve up. He felt stirred up, combative, and made an effort to steady down for her.

'So?' She raised her eyebrows and he saw apprehension. He laughed and dropped an arm about her shoulders to squeeze them.

'It's OK, funnybun. He just wanted to make money for us. Maybe we should let him . . .' He explained Carl's proposition.

'I don't understand. I heard you shouting, Joe.' Sal helped herself to fish pie and bean shoots. 'Is it honest to do these things he talks of?'

'Can't say. Though I doubt if Carl would get up to anything actually illegal. His conscience might not say no but his brain would; he knows he has to stay clean. In any case, there's this set-up called the Securities Exchange Commission which is supposed to police any sharp dealing. No; I don't think that's the issue. The question is more, is Carl overstepping himself. He is known around Wall Street as 'Lucky' Carl Cline, and has an almost frightening capacity for getting it right . . . makes me wonder sometimes if he knows something the rest of us don't! Maybe he just believes in his own luck? It seems Alex is putting money into it anyway, and Delaney; and they're not keen on taking too many chances with their funds.'

He sighed. 'But for us . . . I don't reckon it. Do you? I didn't go over the top when I invested in his share recommendations and that was fine, but I'd have to go *way* over the top for this one.'

Joe poured himself a beer, feeling calmer, and another spritzer for Sal. 'No, I don't think so. Unless you insist, hon, I might just take a raincheck on making a million right now.'

'I'm happy to hear you say that, Joe.' Sal squeezed his arm. 'We do not *need* the millions, like Carl does. He needs the millions to live in such a way. The fabulous apartment, the Long Island summer place, the big sailing boat. Not to mention the wife.' Sal raised her eye comically, Gayle Cline's essential lifestyle long being a cause for her amused wonderment. Joe grinned back. The temptation had been there, no doubt . . . but maybe, just maybe, he'd have lost his all . . . He offered up his plate for more fish pie.

When she was finally called to RADA for audition, Liza was all but past hope. Hannah had told her continually through the long weeks there was no need to panic, but in vain. Mock A-level results had been fairly disastrous, her report commenting that 'effort had been made, sadly at a date rather late for success'. So frantic was Liza to hear news of an audition that she at first insisted she could not possibly visit her father as usual in August. Only when assured that there were positively no auditions called in that month did she agree to venture so far from reach of Gower Street. Hannah sent with her a letter to David detailing the scene so far, not so much mistrusting her daughter, as recognising her propensity to fantasise and embroider. The reply came back, that should Liza be offered a place, but not a grant, David must be allowed to pay the fees in full rather than the RADA offer be lost. This was exactly what Hannah had hoped to avoid. But not wishing to shout before being bitten, she waited; there were two hurdles to clear before fees became an issue.

While Liza was in Canada Hannah had Laurie for two weeks, so Jonet and Mark might take a holiday. Hannah cared nothing about who was doing who a favour, the important thing was having time with her grandson. He was a lightly built child still, not a noisy, football-kicking nine-year-old but quiet, somewhat hesitant. He and Matthew were perfectly at ease with one another and Laurie slipped into calling him Grandad Matthew, initially in fun but then as an endearment. They played draughts together, and Matthew set him up with paints and paper to make what marks he pleased. He liked to stand at Matthew's shoulder, watching watercolours being laid on paper with apparent unconcern for the end result, which was usually delightful. 'You don't need to *worry* about it, old man,' Matthew would say, giving him an affectionate dab of paint on the nose. 'You simply enjoy it – have fun.' With Hannah, Laurie discovered the magic of seeing seeds he planted send up shoots. He had a tray of herbs, and one of lettuce, and he stared at them constantly in an effort to see them growing – it was a mystery to him that he never could catch them at it. But grow they did, and he went home with them potted on, and with instructions on their further care written in his round painstaking hand in a red-covered notebook. He talked little of school, or of friends there, and seemed to prefer to forget about it between terms.

The Reading house was a neat semi in a good area, but furnished strictly on budget as Laurie's school fees gobbled up a large chunk of the family income. The curtains were expensive damask to make a brave show, the exterior was perfectly maintained, and Mark drove an upmarket Rover, but corners were cut indoors. Laurie's room was a small, cream-washed utilitarian box, kept scrupulously tidy. His possessions were stacked into cupboards, his clothes folded in rigid layers in their correct drawers, and little of him seeped into the rest of the house. When Hannah took him back she asked if Jonet would help him bring the herbs and lettuce to full term, more in hope than expectation . . . nothing more was seen or heard of them.

Jonet worked in the university library during term-time, and seemed impatient for Laurie to reach an age when she might resume her full-time career. He was clearly to be the only child; Hannah concluded that his conception might well have been accidental, but expected that Jonet would be too proud to admit to this, so did not overstep the mark by attempting to bring up the subject. She remembered the younger Jonet, flushed and pretty with her new baby in the Bristol nursing home, and was sad for the family that would never be. Laurie's father remained a polite stranger to her, often working away from home and openly ambitious. For Hannah, Mark Shapiro never came to life. He may well have been warm, witty, even good company, but never when she could witness it. That left her able only to hope that Laurie and Jonet found, and returned, affection in the privacy of their little house in Bell Drive.

On the November day the letter with the audition date finally arrived, Liza was late home as there had been a first full rehearsal for the Christmas term play. She came in drained and tired, satchel pulling down her shoulder with a weight of homework still to be done. Jake had come to dinner with his new girlfriend Samantha, and the meal was half through. He had applied for the Fleet Air Arm after a good maths and physics degree, but failed on eyesight. He had, on the rebound, opted to go for a doctorate in applied mathematics, and was at present slogging through an incomprehensible thesis. Compactly built, darkly rugged, with nose a little hooked and a sensual, squared-off mouth, Jake had an air of detached indifference that run-of-the-mill souls found alienating. This trait may have been developed as a ploy, for Jake did not enjoy being involved with situations or people not of his choosing, and laid a roll of emotional barbed wire about his person for the purposes of privacy. Samantha was only the second girl known to his family, the first being Lucy, dating back to his undergraduate days and lasting longer than Hannah and Matthew had believed she would, owing to a colourless personality. 'Maybe he *likes* women who lead intense inner lives without external signs.' Matthew had offered his opinion. 'And she does have fantastic breasts.' Samantha was rake-thin with no breasts worth mentioning.

Liza stood in the doorway of the dining room, looking wan, and allowed her satchel to slide to the floor.

Hannah said quietly, 'There's a letter from RADA in your room.'

She was gone, taking the stairs in threes despite apparently terminal exhaustion. A moment later she was back in the doorway, even whiter, but now with excitement.

'The fourteenth of December.' Her voice had a sepulchral ring. 'The day after the play. I shall be *exhausted* . . .'

'Not if you get an early night,' Hannah said bracingly. 'You know how resilient you are. Liza, this is Samantha. And your supper's on the hotplate.'

Both remarks were ignored. 'Maybe I could ask for another date. When I'm fresher, in the New Year.'

'A bird in hand,' warned Matthew. 'They may change their minds if you prevaricate.'

'Hello, Liza,' said Jake pointedly. Liza appeared to notice him for the first time.

'Oh – hi, Jake.' Her gaze moved to the blonde, doe-eyed Samantha. 'Hi. Mummy, I can't possibly present myself to advantage the morning after a performance.'

'Nonsense.' Hannah gathered up the plates. 'Get your supper now – have you much prep?'

'*Acres* of it,' Liza said bitterly. 'It's going to be impossible to do all this ghastly A-level *work* and the new play *and* learn something for the audition. I mean, I'm only human!'

'Really?' asked Jake, *sotto voce*, but Liza heard him. She directed his way a withering shaft from her brilliant eyes.

'Samantha, I would advise you to drop this immature egghead right away, and hitch up with someone who doesn't behave like dog droppings. I'll take my food up if that's OK, Mummy, and have it while I do my prep. 'Night, sweet man. Sorry you fell so unlucky with your misery of a son.' She dropped a kiss on the top of Matthew's head, nodded at Samantha and swept out, picking up her satchel and shutting the door behind her. Jake clapped slowly with an air of bored weariness.

'Is that all, or are we to be treated to an encore?'

There was silence for a second as Liza finished her audition. She looked just above the heads of the half-dozen figures in RADA's dark auditorium, and remained still. About to incline her head before turning to leave, as she had for the morning audition, she froze. A lone figure could be seen dimly now, standing further back in the side-stalls gangway.

'Thank you. We'll be in touch quite soon,' one of the seated judges called up to her. But Liza did not move; her eyes were fixed on the woman. She could discern little detail but the silhouette was unmistakable . . . the long, heavy skirt; the shawl pulled about narrow shoulders. A cloud of black hair.

It was Rachel Hywel.

'Liza? Are you OK?' The man who had heard her first audition came forward into the footlights, looking up at her. Liza did not take her eyes off the dark figure beyond until he repeated her name in a firmer voice, when she stumbled forward a pace.

'Yes . . . Thank you.' Her gaze focused behind him again. Now there was nothing, no one; just rows of empty seats.

She turned abruptly, hurried into the wings and leaned against the passage wall. She thought she might be sick, and looked wildly about for a lavatory, swallowing and clutching her throat.

'Ghastly, isn't it? Mega-ordeal!' The young man

who had auditioned before her looked sympathetic, while the face of the girl who was waiting to be called next became greenish white with terror.

Liza croaked: 'My bag – anyone seen . . .' The young man dived for her brightly woven duffel bag hanging from a chair back. Liza took it and walked unsteadily down the passage to the outer door, looking over her shoulder a couple of times to see if she was being followed. A couple of auditionees talking by the door parted to let her through, but she bumped into one as if drunk.

'Wow – was it really that bad?' The girl laughed. 'We blew ours too! Come and have a coffee with us and get it off your chest.'

'I can't.' Liza gripped the bar and pushed open the door, almost toppling outside and gulping the cold air that slapped at her throat. She huddled against the street wall, trying to clear her mind, to think constructively. A ghost in the auditorium . . . was she hallucinating? Going mad? Possessed? It *was* the woman though, she would not be denied. The same woman . . . Rachel, her mother had called her; an ancestor. God; what was she *doing* there . . .

She was so cold, bone-cold. Her jaw stiffened with cold. Her eyeballs were tight with cold. When the car drew up she ignored it, staring up the street, hair twisted into ragged copper scarves by the chipped-ice wind.

'Liza? Wake up at the back there!'

She jumped. Matthew was leaning from the driver's window, his long humorous face anxious. Pushing herself away from the wall, Liza ran across the pavement, almost knocking down a passing elderly couple hunched together against the wind.

'Matthew! Oh!' She plunged into the passenger

seat, threw herself at the surprised man.

'I can't go, Matthew – not if *she's* there! Not her – not her!'

'What the devil do you mean?' Matthew gripped her arm. 'Good God, Liza – you look as if you've seen a ghost.'

'I have,' she said, and drew a shaking breath before bursting into a flood of tears.

'So that's all I know, sweetheart. This damn woman suddenly appeared as she finished her piece.' He stood with his back to the fire. 'I've never seen her in a bigger state, though. Madame can cope with most things, I'd have said. But when she tottered across that pavement one thing she was not doing was coping. And she hung on to me all the way home . . . first time I've seen her scared in all these years.'

Hannah stared at him, her brow creased. 'I have to do, say, *something* now . . . she *must* talk, whether she wants to or not.' She closed the sitting-room door and came to stand facing him, and he saw how tired she looked now, deeply shadowed eyes pale with tension and the corners of her mouth drooping. He, everyone, thought of Hannah as invincible. Suddenly he saw that she might not be; that she might long at times for the easy ride she had failed to get from life.

'Poor old thing.' He drew her to him. She stood in the circle of his arms, eyes closed, savouring his warm proximity. Then she opened her eyes and smiled at him, smoothing back a strand of hair from his temple.

'Not poor.' She drew down his head and rubbed her cheek against his. 'Not ever poor, with you. Come and sit for a minute . . . then I must go up to Liza.'

Matthew subsided into his chair and she sat on the rug by him, knees drawn up under the red woollen circular skirt that was her long-time favourite for winter evenings. She turned her wedding ring slowly, a habit when she needed to sort out a situation.

'You recall – oh, a while back now, a year maybe – when I talked to her last about this?'

'She didn't want to know.'

Hannah nodded. 'I tried; it's important for her not to be afraid. I told her – remember? – that I believed I knew who this woman was. That I saw her too; an ancestor of ours, Rachel Hywel, who was still here in spirit. And that she must not be afraid.'

'And she didn't want to know,' Matthew repeated with quiet emphasis.

'No. I'll just have to give it another try, now. She may even refuse to take up a place at RADA if one is offered . . . that would be sad. It's not helpful of course, that Rachel appears when Liza's on stage. Oh Matthew; why can nothing be simple!' He lifted a quizzical eyebrow.

'What *could* be simple for a family who sees ghosts?'

'You know it's true, though?' She looked anxious, and he smiled.

'Sweetheart, how could anyone make up such a story? Look, go and see if you can get her settled now, then we'll have a drink, eh?'

When Hannah tapped on the bathroom door, Liza called for her to go in.

'Just want a word.'

'That's OK.' Liza was immersed up to the chin in hot foam, hair bundled on top of her head with a green chiffon scarf. She looked with wary eyes at her mother, then shut them. Her transistor radio, balanced on the rim of the bath, was playing Marilyn Monroe's version of 'Diamonds are a Girl's Best Friend'. 'Why d'you think she killed herself, Mummy? She seemed to have everything.'

'"Everything" is very subjective, surely?' Hannah sat on the laundry basket. 'From where she stood it may have looked like she had nothing. She had no husband. No children. No parents.'

'Oh – people,' Liza murmured dismissively.

'It can be awfully lonely without them, Liza. Marilyn might well have hung on in there if she'd had someone close who really cared about what happened to her. That's actually why *I'm* sitting on this prickly basket right now. I care about you and I want to understand why you're so afraid of what you saw today. Then I can help you, I hope.'

Hannah thought Liza might be going to ignore this. But she remained on the laundry basket, gazing at her steamed-up reflection in the mirror on the opposite wall. Eventually Liza said sullenly:

'All I want is to be left out of *that* business.'

'I'm afraid I don't know how to arrange that; I didn't ever ask to be involved myself. But we *are* and –'

'*I'm* not going to be.' Liza fixed her with a glare of sudden antagonism. 'When are you going to catch on – this is absolutely not my scene! That – *thing* may have loused up any chance of my going to RADA – the judges must have thought I was completely weird, stuck there like a half-wit with eyes popping out of my head. D'you think they want students around who – who *hallucinate*, for God's sake?'

She sank down and caused a tidal wave to slop over the head of the bath and absorb darkly into the carpet. Hannah said carefully:

'There was no hallucinating. You saw the spirit of Rachel Hywel, if I must spell it out to you. I saw her for the first time when I was twelve. The next time I was twenty-four. I didn't like it; but I knew my great-grandma had second sight, and when I asked my father about it he said I had that, too. He said I should accept it and not be afraid.'

'Well *I* shan't accept it!' Liza shouted above the radio. 'I tell you straight – if you *knew* there was a curse like that in the family, you should never have had children! Didn't you *think* of that? Maybe it's given you some warped sense of pleasure in your own importance, but me, I refute it! I truly do!' Liza stared at Hannah, her eyes brilliant now with unshed tears. 'Leave me alone now, will you? I'm really terribly tired.'

'How can I leave you, when I haven't made you understand?' Hannah was herself almost crying with frustration and concern. Liza shook her head violently.

'You think all you have to do is explain carefully enough, speak slowly and clearly, and the penny will drop for stupid old me. Well, it's not like that. *Nothing* you say will change how I feel. Spell it out with sign language, burn it into my skin with a poker – no go. Now, will you please *drop it*?'

Hannah opened the kitchen door and stood on the step, looking up at the sky. It was icy, sparkling with stars, remote and dreadfully indifferent. She wanted very much to talk to her father . . . ask him what more she could do to help Liza. Ask him if, in truth, she had been right to have perpetuated the inheritance of second sight.

Liza need not have doubted the effect she had on the panel of judges. Four days later she was offered a place on the course, to start the September after her eighteenth birthday.

Chapter Eleven

April 1965

The morning David Vaughan's letter arrived, Hannah was feeling good. Not only because it was spring again and showing it, which was always an occasion for tossing hats in the air, but because her business figures were up for the first quarter, more than vindicating her efforts to get the restaurant trends on track for the rapidly changing times. The evening menus seemed to be well targeted, reasonably priced and with a certain flair now demanded by an ever more sophisticated clientele, but with steady favourites not abandoned. More young women were coming in for light lunches, not leisurely shoppers but working girls, who a handful of years ago would have been at home waiting for children to return home from school, and husbands from work. Now they took their washing into the recently opened launderette and came into Hannah's Place for a simple pasta or rice dish rather than the one-time meat and two veg, before hurrying on to shop for a couple of bags of food. Teenagers were rendezvousing in the coffee bar, where sandwiches were included, with fruit juices and milk shakes; nothing there to make a vast fortune but creating goodwill, filling a need and paying its way.

The past two and a half years had brought changes in other ways. The Taibach bakery, shop and snack bar had been sold to the manageress, with Tom's situation there secure. He and Florence had agreed that when she gave up the Swansea restaurant to sell it by instalments to Raymond in a year or two, they would move to a bungalow in Porthcawl, about ten minutes by road from Taibach and in the area where Hannah was now determinedly hunting for a cottage. The road through (and over) Taibach was due to be completed by the end of the year, towering now over the hillside with concrete legs straddling a chaos of rubble, rusting girders, twisted cables; the detritus of an embryo motorway on stilts under which huddled the little homes of Taibach.

Morfa Cottage had vanished. Hannah had so far felt unable to visit the spot where her home had stood, but Florence and Tom had been drawn to the scene one evening. Florence saw at once that it was a mistake. Tom had become at first agitated, and afterwards withdrawn, unable to respond to her comfort, or to a visit to Raymond's youngsters which usually delighted him. To divert him, she set about looking for a place for Hannah with renewed vigour and as the spring evenings lengthened, took him on expeditions to the east. 'Somewhere near the river,' she would tell him. 'The Vale of Ogmore, that's what would suit Han.'

This was true. Hannah was, in fact, increasingly aware of a need to draw near to her roots again; to re-establish a foothold in her own land. She was fond of their home in Clapham, with its big wild garden, but it could not satisfy her longing for *her* place; for Wales. This house was quiet these days, whispering of times past rather than of the future, for Matthew's boys made increasingly sporadic stopovers, and Liza had lived in a bedsit this past year.

'Everyone's in bedsits, Mummy.' She had waved an

expansive arm. 'All the second-year people anyway. And it takes for ever to get to Gower Street from Clapham.' Depressed, Hannah had viewed all that was available – a poky room with use of bath and kitchen at the end of a dim, narrow passage off which three further doors stood firmly shut and locked. Afterwards, she had stood in Liza's big light bedroom overlooking Greystones' garden, and made a determined effort to disperse the depression. Sooner or later all fledgelings must fly the nest . . . and at least they would now be spared the pop music. Liza's departure did, even so, leave a hole in Hannah's life that closed over painfully slowly, to be reopened after weekend visits ignited the house to vivid life again.

Liza had blossomed, burst into exotic flower during her time at RADA. From the moment she entered Gower Street's famous portals she embraced the environment and it became her own. Her passage was not unmarked by incident; Liza's high-profile personality picked up incident as a radio did static. Harnessed to her increasingly startling beauty, her charisma quickly lit RADA's rehearsal rooms and stages, collecting disciples and enemies in roughly equal proportions. To some she responded; others were scorched by her fire and retreated to lick wounds.

Hannah had attended all the public performances over Liza's two years, and was aware of the steadily developing talent and its power to hook the attention. Whatever the meaning of Rachel Hywel's appearance at her audition, it had not been to put a blight on Liza's potential. Could the gift of second sight actually be adding to Liza's dynamic abilities? Now the RADA course was drawing to a close, Hannah could only trust that Liza could handle what the future might hold.

She had a second cup of tea as she read David Vaughan's letter. He was coming over next month to see Liza's end-of-course production, and hoped to see Hannah too. He would be staying at the Savoy; only for a couple of days as he had business in Scotland and Northern Ireland before going back. He would call when he had checked in, and looked forward very much to seeing her and Liza.

The same expensive vellum, the bold scrawl. She smiled. At last, pain had drained from the memory of their long relationship. It was still possible to recall the agony of handling his notepaper when a rare letter would come ... the misery of wanting so much to have his physical presence and knowing she could not ... The final pain of rejection, and facing life without him. David; David. Hannah doubted he had ever for one moment contemplated the hurt done her ... nor, did she believe, could his mind have encompassed it. But still, she felt that he had loved her.

She put the sheet of paper back in its envelope. Now, wonderfully, she could look forward to meeting him as an old and valued friend, with whom happiness, love and pain had long ago been shared, and with whom a child was shared. Inextricably bound up with the pleasure of their child was the pain caused to Hannah by the loss of Jonet's goodwill and good opinion. Yet illogical though it now appeared, she just *had* to hope that, in time, Jonet might begin to comprehend that the huge forces released by love must write their own laws.

Florence phoned her the same evening. Hannah and Matthew were out on the terrace, enjoying the show of daffodils in the last of the evening sun and she ran to take the call, thinking it might be Liza.

'Han?' Florence sounded excited. 'Listen, *cariad,*

Tom and I have just been to look at a house – and I do believe this might be the one for you at long last. When can you come down?'

'Oh – er – Flo, you've taken me by surprise! Well, would Sunday do? Could you fix that?'

'No problem.' Florence was emphatic. 'I've wasted no time because I don't think this one will hang about waiting for a buyer. What I shall do is call the estate agent first thing tomorrow and see if we can have a viewing Sunday. Around midday?'

'Fine. Thanks so much, Flo. Where is it?' Hannah added as an afterthought, for Florence's excitement was infectious.

'Don't you trust me?' Hannah heard a giggle. 'Well then, it's near the Ewenny river – not far from the coast either. And there's a garden all round it,' Florence finished triumphantly. 'That's what you wanted, isn't it?'

'Provided a few other needs had fallen into line.' Hannah had to laugh at Florence's satisfaction with what she had discovered.

'Now – if you don't hear from me tomorrow you'll know to view Sunday, right?'

'Right,' said Hannah obediently. 'Flo, is Tom OK?'

'He feels fine now we may have found a place, Han. I think he's been fretting about it since Morfa Cottage went. Will Matthew be coming with you?'

'Hope so – I'll ask him now. Thanks a million, Flo dear.'

'So . . .' Hannah hooked her arm through Matthew's as they walked indoors. 'You'll come, won't you?'

'You *can't* decide anything on a first viewing.' Matthew was stern. 'But of course I'll come. We can go down Saturday afternoon, give ourselves plenty of time that way.'

That Sunday they drove along a quiet road parallel to the river, having picked up Florence and Tom in Taibach. The day had been grey early, but cloud was breaking and thinning now as a breeze picked up. Hannah felt the palpable, familiar sense of homecoming, a soul-stirring cocktail of joy and excitement. When Florence leaned forward and said, 'It's there, Han, on the left. See – side on to the road?' she craned her head to see over the tall hedge and shrubs.

Matthew slowed as they approached a stone house with a high-pitched slate roof, on rising ground set back from the road. First a small wooden gate and a footpath led up to the back entrance, partly shielded by trees and shrubs on sloping lawn. The north side of the house then, with a stone-built chimney breast, two windows up and one down. Finally the drive gates, open for Matthew to swing in and round to the front elevation, which faced west towards the coast. A red car was parked on the weedy gravel and the estate agent climbed from it to welcome them.

'We'd be better seein' it on our own,' Florence grumbled. 'They only witter on all the time and distract you.'

'They do it deliberately so you won't notice the dry rot and that funny smell around the drains,' Matthew told her. Florence snorted and heaved herself out of the back seat of the new Triumph. Tom, who had been quiet even for him, shifted uncertainly.

'Shall I stay here, Han?'

'Only if you'd rather, Tom dear.' Hannah ducked her head to see his anxious eyes, and was reminded of trying to get him to the dentist as a small boy. 'But I'd really like you to come in with us and tell us what you think.' She gave him an encouraging smile. After a second he nodded, and seemed to relax a little.

'OK . . . if you like.'

They stood outside the house in the balmy air, looking at it. The agent was droning on about local stone, features of special interest, the rarity of such a property coming on to the market in a sparsely populated district of scenic beauty. Hannah saw a sturdy building, perhaps a hundred and fifty years old; a little shabby. A bit needed doing to it, the agent admitted, jingling the door keys confidently. The owner, an elderly widow, had had a nasty fall and had gone to live with her daughter in Cardiff. It seemed a friendly house to Hannah, with a serene ambience, as if as certain as its agent that the right people would shortly turn up to provide the care lacking in recent years. An open front porch, bearing a tangle of budding clematis interwoven with an old climbing rose, shielded the oak door from prevailing westerlies. On the left side of the door were two windows on either floor and on the right, larger single windows. The stones were subtly tinted with ochre, moss green and peachy rose, and webbed with a variety of established climbers. A second chimney appeared to rise centrally through the house, with two tall pots in which jackdaws were industriously building nests.

They walked round to the south side, which had two pairs of prettily latticed windows. 'The devil to clean, those,' observed Florence. 'Break every nail you have.' Here a rose pergola leaned perilously after the winter's gales, with perennial flowerbeds in a lawn overdue for its first cut of the spring.

The garden sloped gently up the hill to a little orchard bordered by a low wall, then came downland dotted with gorse, and ewes with their lambs. At the edge of the orchard a summerhouse was sited for maximum sun and views, a vintage structure charming in its idiosyncrasy, nothing as it should have been but all the better for that. Matthew strolled up to take a closer look and came back with an unusual expression on his face.

'There's a big pot of brushes in there,' he told Hannah quietly. 'And a wooden easel. She must have been a painter.'

At the back of the house, which faced east, inland, a big covered porch surrounded the back door. At the south-east corner was a conservatory, whose inner door opened into the sitting room occupying the entire south end of the house. Hannah, becoming involved now, wanted to see inside and moved purposefully to the back door.

'It's slightly back to front, in that the hall is here.' The agent ushered them into a spacious hall, with stairs running up from it and turning round to a galleried landing. To the right, a big kitchen had west and north windows, with a walk-in larder. In the centre was the dining room, and to the left, the entrance to the big, light sitting room, with windows on three sides, and on the inner wall an inglenook fireplace. The layout was simple, the rooms airy and attractively proportioned. Upstairs were four good bedrooms, a bathroom and a boxroom.

'Big for a weekend cottage,' was Matthew's comment as they returned outside. Hannah nodded, and heavy disappointment hit like a physical blow. It *was* bigger than she had imagined.

They wandered up the hill next, turning often to look back at the house and environs. Trees were misting into tender leaf, the river ran gently pale. Tom and Florence looked at Hannah and smiled, as if certain already that she would buy Bracken House, the name written on the front gate. Hannah said yes, certainly she liked it, but no more . . . It *was* too big for a weekend cottage.

'A survey could find all manner of things wrong,' Matthew warned her, when they had made their goodbyes and headed east again. 'Some window-frames are rotten. It probably needs rewiring. And the roof tiles look dubious in a few places.'

'Yes . . .' Hannah thought of the sweet soft air, the subtle tones of changing seasons, the distant whisper of sea breaking over flat rocks. 'But what did you actually *feel* about it?

'I suppose –' He paused, frowning. 'I suppose I liked it.' She waited for him to add that of course it was too big; perversely, he did not.

They returned a week later. Hannah loved it more, and was more certain that she could not have it. For heaven's sake this was a family home, not a weekend cottage. The agent looked irritated that no offer was made and told them there was another very interested party now, and more people due that weekend from Bristol.

'Just as well, if I'm to be practical.' Back home, Hannah was white with disappointment. 'After all, it's clearly too big for a weekend cottage, as you said.'

They were quiet, Hannah staring hard at the wall, Matthew lighting his pipe with slow deliberation.

'We could buy it jointly if you want,' he said suddenly. 'I know I've said I'd quite like to retire to Sussex when I'm ready. But I'd no idea about that lovely corner of Wales . . . why should I, being a Home Counties man? I must say now that I'm knocked out by it. There's endless scope for a painter, and whichever way you look the walking is splendid. And it's big enough for anyone in either family to come for the hols.'

He grinned, and seemed for a moment no different from the day she'd first met him on Clapham Common, playing football with his young sons. 'You know, grandchildren on the beach with French cricket and sand sandwiches and all that ghastly business?'

Hannah laughed. 'And kites on the hill, and Pooh-sticks in the river by those stepping-stones?' She was serious then. 'Would you really be prepared for us to make an offer? I do have a quite strong feeling that it might be the place for us . . . and we may lose it if we sit on the idea for a while.'

There was a real danger of this, the agent reported. Matthew said not to panic but even so put in an immediate offer which was closer to the asking price than he liked. The vendor, wanting only a quick settlement, accepted. The survey revealed all they had feared and some adjustment was made to the final figure. 'We shall look on it as a long-term project – fixing up Bracken House,' Matthew said. 'Don't you think?'

'So long as we're not still at it when we fall off our respective twigs.' Hannah smiled. 'That would have made it all rather self-defeating.' But Matthew was confident; it would give them a good excuse for keeping fit and active for years to come. Hannah was content for the future to sort itself out; she was for now buoyant with a recognisable sense of joy, for she had a toehold in Wales once more.

Some things she had lost . . . her first bakery shop, that in her youth had seemed an unattainable dream, had gone now, passed into another's ownership. Hannah had stood across the road and looked at it, and the whole row of little shops dwarfed these days by the huge structure of the new road soaring behind. She recalled how agonising had been the choice of name for it, the choice of colours, the enormous burden of having to spend more money than she had handled in her entire twenty-four years; the awareness of disgrace and penury should her gamble fail. She had taken Tom to look when the workmen had finished . . . blue and white had been her final choice, crisp and clean, with lettering in gold.

'What does it say, Han?' Tom had tilted his head to stare up, his hand in hers as he always liked it. Being a little slow, Tom had mastered only a few words at that age, though Hannah was helping him every evening.

'It says "Hannah's", sweetheart,' she had told him, and her heart had all but burst with pride. Her one sadness then had been that Joe was not there to share her triumph. That night, with Tom in bed and the kitchen fragrant with an ovenful of fruit pies, she had made a few minutes to write to Joe in Pittsburgh, and tell him that her shop was a reality and ready to start trading.

So, doors close, others open. Now a new home – and a shared one. Morfa Cottage had been hers, while Greystones was above all Matthew's family home. Bracken House would be theirs; and the resonance of that word sounded good to Hannah.

She dressed with care for her meeting with David Vaughan; she might be sixty-three but that was no reason for anything save perhaps to be relaxed and fully herself. Time was, Hannah had thought herself inferior in some way to this man from a higher social class. His father had owned Vaughan Tinplate; he had lived in a big house, one of her cousins had been a housemaid there; he had been expensively educated, had served as an officer in two world wars. Now she knew for certain that she was not inferior; her own endeavours had made her classless.

She chose a simple print dress of harebell blue and black, with pearls given her by Matthew to warm the round neck. No one wore hats now – rather a loss was her feeling on this – but her loosely waved bob shone with health, and pearl ear-drops intensified the luminous quality of her grey eyes. Hannah's beauty was independent of unlined skin and youthful curves. It was elusive, ageless, blooming from a source not governed by the calendar.

He was already there when she reached the Savoy, smoking and leafing through a copy of the *Financial Times*.

'Hannah – my dear.' He got to his feet, smiling and holding out his hands, and she saw the nervous muscle jump in his cheek, as when he had been overstressed by too many missions over the Atlantic without a break. Filled by a sudden warm concern, Hannah leaned to kiss that cheek and they embraced, the past like a soft cloak about them.

'Sure is good to see you.' He moved back to look at her. 'You look great. As always . . . D'you know something we lesser mortals don't?'

'Can't think of anything offhand.' She smiled. 'It's lovely to see you too, David.' She did not say how well *he* looked; in fact he looked quite tired, and was probably working too hard for a man approaching seventy. 'Liza said to tell you she'll be along soon – she's up to her eyebrows in end-of-course productions, not least *Othello*. And endless writing round for jobs . . . But she's looking forward to seeing you – and to you seeing *her* on stage for the first time.'

'Who d'you think will be the more nervous?' He gave a wry grin.

'Oh that's easy; you! Liza has no stage nerves, that's

one of her great strengths. Though I believe her fellow students may often hate her for it. The good news this week is that she may already have found an agent. Also ... but no, let her tell you herself, she'll enjoy that.'

He groaned. 'That's cruel of you. Shall we order coffee?'

She watched him as he found and signalled a waiter with a skill born of long practice. Then she said impulsively, 'David – why do you still work so hard? What drives you?'

He lit a cigarette, drew on it with a small reflective smile. He remained an attractive man, lean and straight in a dark suit which proved that Toronto had an equivalent to Savile Row. His eyes were penetrating, direct as Hannah always recalled. 'Can't say for certain. There may be a variety of reasons ... some days one is in the ascendant ... at another time, a different aspect could be the motivating one.'

'Tell me.' They sat, not speaking as their coffee was served. Then he said: 'Restlessness is part of it; and I only recognised this in the past couple of years – I fear I have a chronic case of restlessness. I am also guilty of a low boredom threshold ... what the devil would I do were I not fully involved in my business?'

She nodded. 'I did think of that. Don't you like just pottering sometimes? Spending time relaxing with your wife? Gardening?'

David Vaughan blew a small perfect smoke ring. 'My wife is a career woman, Hannah. She has a garden design firm. Did Liza not tell you?'

'Well – no, she didn't ... that's strange, isn't it? I mean her not telling me, not your wife being a garden designer!' she added hastily.

He laughed. 'I guess anything not connected with

acting is too supremely unimportant to merit a mention.'

'Oh dear; so you've perceived that your daughter is a complete egoist?'

'I had noticed . . . I also realise that it must come from my side, as no one in their right mind could call you an egoist.' He paused. 'Why do *you* still work, Hannah? You don't need to, any more than I . . . You *are* happy?'

He pulled himself up then, embarrassed. 'I've no right to ask you that – forget the question. I just tried to imagine what might keep you in business, but forget it . . . More coffee?'

'Thanks. I've no objection to your asking me, because I am happy. I would only wish not to answer it if I were not. At least, I am most of the time. Only a half-wit would be happy continually, don't you think?'

'I guess so. So – why aren't *you* pottering in happy retirement?'

'Oh . . .' Hannah took a draught of the delectable, fragrant coffee. 'Probably I enjoy my work. Now I don't *have* to do it!' She smiled at him. 'What perverse creatures we are. But regarding egoism,' she added suddenly. 'My daughter Jonet believes I am both egotistical and thoroughly selfish.'

Now she was the one to look embarrassed, staring into her coffee cup.

'Can you say why she should think that?' David asked, serious now.

'Because I shamed her with an illegitimate half-sister twenty years ago,' Hannah said simply. 'She has a good case, you see.'

'Ah.' He stared at his hand; the long, bony hand she had always thought so beautiful. 'I am very sorry, dear Hannah.'

She shrugged. 'I've learned to accept her judgement. She is entitled to it.'

'That can't make it any easier.'

'No. But forget it now . . . it's just another fact of life. And I was out of order bringing it up.'

'I'm glad you did . . . it is right for me to know. I can't tell you –'

He was visibly upset; Hannah made an effort to lift the deteriorating atmosphere.

'Don't feel badly about it, David.' She gave him a warm smile. 'And Liza has more than compensated by being a joy to have around. You're due to be knocked out by her stage work, by the way – or she hopes you are! She seems to have made huge strides these last three terms.'

He nodded. 'And this bedsit – is that OK? I was sad to hear she had left home.'

'She couldn't wait,' Hannah said drily. 'It's the aim of every swinging chick now to have their own pad.' She laughed. 'I hope you know the jargon?'

'I've been struggling. But say, Hannah: one thing I wanted to ask personally . . . I couldn't find a way to write it in a letter . . . Liza hasn't any of this – of your – well, you know –?'

'Second sight?' she asked helpfully. Then turned her empty cup in her hands, smiling no longer. 'Poor David – it used to upset you so, didn't it?'

'Only because it upset *you* so,' he retorted. 'I hated what it did to you sometimes and that's no mistake. So, how is it for Liza? I never quite get around to asking her. I just hoped there'd be nothing I needed to know.'

'David –' She frowned, searching for words. 'I'd like to tell you there's nothing. But I can't. She doesn't want to talk about it – she won't – but I know she sees, well, something.'

'Something?' His brows came together. 'What the devil's *something*?'

'The woman I saw when I was with you that time on the hill . . . you remember?'

'Would I ever forget? God, Hannah, I was there when you had the nightmare! I damn well *do* remember! And I remember the night in the London Blitz.'

'Liza sees her.' Hannah spoke calmly to steady him. 'Nothing but a momentary vision, nothing to hurt her.'

'Christ, I should hope not.' He lit another cigarette with nervous movements. 'This is damned bad news, Hannah. Why? Can you say why?'

'I can't. I only wish I could, then maybe it would stop happening. I haven't seen Rachel Hywel myself for years now. But Liza has. At least twice, but it may be more, she doesn't talk about it unless I make her.'

'We needed this like a hole in the head.' Vaughan slumped, looking defeated. Then he looked beyond her and his face changed, alight with pleasure. 'Here she is –'

Liza Vaughan, as she had been for eighteen months now, walked towards them through the room and every eye was drawn, all heads turned. At just twenty, no one could miss the willowy young woman with hair the colour of conkers in sunlight, and large turquoise eyes. She wore her hair in a sizzling cascade, held back with tortoiseshell clips, and a miniskirt of emerald leather with a black skinny sweater that hugged full, beautiful breasts and a small waist. Long curvy legs were encased in diamond-patterned emerald and black tights and her shoes were flat black patent pumps. She swung a big multi-coloured bag on a plaited ribbon drawstring over her shoulder and carried a copy of the *Stage*. Liza looked devastatingly female, outrageously sensual and unforgivably beautiful.

'Pa!' She hugged him tight, laughing with pleasure, and every male in the vicinity looked on with envy. She smelled deliciously of cinnamon and ripe peaches; her voice was clear, with a husky undertone that took away from its pristine purity and added to its sexuality. 'And Mummy –' She bent to kiss Hannah. 'So glad you could get here. Wow – I could use a coffee. I've flown across London at the speed of sound.'

She collapsed into the third chair and stuck out her superb green and black legs. 'Poppa dear, I crave refreshment. Shortly after the coffee, may we have a stupendously over-the-top lunch with an unspecified amount of wine? After that you could post me by taxi to my dosshouse where I will recover, I hope, in time for tonight's dress rehearsal.' She closed her eyes and sighed heavily. Hannah looked at David Vaughan and laughed outright at his apparent bemusement.

'Take no account, David, of this display of theatricals. Liza, collect yourself up now there's a dear, and tell David the news; you know, the Big News.'

Liza screwed up her face. 'What news would that be now?' She paused, opened her eyes to make certain she had her father's attention. 'Oh – do you mean about the job? About the part I've been offered in a television play – is that the news you mean?'

She opened her mouth and affected a ladylike yawn behind her hand. She was still laughing at her father's delighted surprise, head thrown back in enjoyment, when Hannah quietly took her leave.

The next night, Liza entered the world she would encompass entirely, and that she would make her own. Her Desdemona possessed a quality of stillness that riveted upon her the attention of the audience in RADA's Vanbrugh Theatre. It lent weight to her every word. The honest dignity of her appeal to Iago, 'What shall I do to win my lord again?' struck an answering chord from the auditorium, where not a movement, a breath could be detected. Concentration beamed from every angle of the dark still rows on to the figure who stood with hands quietly folded, light playing on the austerely modelled face, long pearl-white throat and braids of autumn-warm hair. The fine balance between youth and maturity was perfect.

Spellbound, Hannah would not have known her daughter. She *was* Desdemona, doomed innocent wife of the demented Moor. Liza, the sometime wild, difficult girl, the egoist who demanded her own way and who usually got it, was simply not there. Hannah had lately recognised the seeds of a great talent; a charisma that inevitably would develop to wield power over others. Desdemona was led forward at curtain call and stood quietly with a tiny smile hovering, one hand laid with consummate grace on the proffered wrist of her murderous lord and the other, curved, relaxed, in the folds of her pale lilac gown. The audience, released from tension at last, found voice to record their appreciation as Hannah reached for Matthew's hand and gripped it hard. He caught her gaze, nodded and smiled broadly. Turning, she looked at David Vaughan on her other side. A tear tracked down his tanned cheek as he applauded with an unrestrained velocity. Returning his warm smile, a mist crept across the clear sky of Hannah's pleasure. Such power as their daughter had demonstrated here could do damage if not handled with care . . . and Liza was not a careful person.

It was when Hannah looked round at the audience,

still applauding, that she glimpsed the shadow standing well back in the side aisle. A few seconds, and it melted in the warm fuggy air as more lights came on; but for Hannah, it had a terrible identity. She strained to see Liza's face, turning from side to side in smiling acceptance of applause – thank God she appeared not to have seen. But no matter . . . Rachel Hywel *was* there.

The house was quiet next morning; quieter perhaps than she would have wished, for her own reflections were poor company. A dreadful sense of helplessness pervaded her mind. For all her experience, maturity, determination to protect Liza, she *was* helpless in the face of this unquiet spirit, straying so far from its home. How to fight a woman dead these two centuries? She stared through the window open to the colours and scents of early summer . . . Could Liza's undoubted power over her work, her audiences, perhaps stem from the spirit wandering lost through the years? Or were these two strands of Liza's life quite disconnected? No one could say . . . Rachel Hywel seemed to have no power herself to communicate, only to materialise. Whether she or Liza chose the times, who knew?

It was with a sense of relief that Hannah finally went upstairs to put on her jacket. She brushed her hair and applied lipstick with care, never heavy-handed now. Old . . . sixty-three could not even pass for late middle age, could it? Strange, how she could see this reflected face and know with her brain that it was hers, yet feel inside her ageing skin no different than she had felt for years. She pulled a face, smiled at this ageless woman imprisoned in the body of a sixty-three-year-old, and was aware that every older human being must share the same sense of unbelief.

She looked into Liza's room, little used these two years; a charming girl's room, unusually tidy now and bearing little impact of its owner's chaotic habits. The blue and lemon spread was smooth, the midnight blue patterned rugs straight on the gleaming oak boards. Dolls and shabby, big stuffed bears and dogs sat in a row on the white-painted shelf, butterfly mobiles hung motionless from the ceiling. Yellow and blue checked curtains were drawn back just so from the windows that had once been bright with stuck-on stars and moons and comic faces. Anyone's room, now.

She had locked the house and started up the drive when the slightly built boy in grey flannels and green blazer moved from the cover of the rhododendrons.

'Laurie!'

'Hello, Gran.' Laurie stopped in front of her then said in a breathy rush, 'I've run away.'

'Oh.' Hannah considered. 'Well, you can go in if you like, you know where the food is. Or you can come with me. I'll be about two and a half hours at the restaurant.'

'I'll come. Thanks.' He fell in step, snapping off a twig of privet and demolishing it leaf by leaf. 'I hope you don't mind,' he added politely in his uncertain voice.

'What do you think I should mind? That you've run away from school? Or that you've chosen me to run to?'

He thought for a while before saying slowly, 'Both, I suppose.'

'Tell me *why*, though, Laurie. Has something special happened?' Hannah recalled how they had first used to walk hand-in-hand when he was small, and later, she would rest a hand companionably on his shoulder. Now he was too tall for that, and of course too self-conscious to hold hands. Barely three inches shorter than she, he matched strides with her and occasionally brushed arms, but studiously remained separate.

He walked on for a moment, clearly struggling to marshal his words into coherence. The fresh May wind blew the dark hair off his brow to expose vulnerable white skin above freckled nose and cheeks. He frowned in concentration.

'It's nothing so bad that you can't tell me, Laurie,' Hannah prompted.

'It's not really one thing, Gran. But mostly . . . well, there's this boy Hurst . . . And then last night . . . Anyway I just bunked off right after breakfast, I didn't want . . . well, I wanted to get out.'

He stopped then and looked directly at Hannah for the first time. 'I don't want to go back, Gran.'

They faced each other on the pavement and Hannah saw the strain in her grandson's eyes. She had never loved him more than now; never found him more vulnerable. 'What *about* last night, Laurie? Tell me.'

She started to walk again and Laurie moved to catch up. 'I always think it's easier to talk when I'm walking, don't you? Why not tell me about Hurst for a start? What he does that upsets you, for instance.'

Laurie plucked a fresh privet stalk from a hedge and examined it minutely. 'Will Mum and Dad make me go back?'

'That may depend on why you ran away,' Hannah said gently. 'But I'll certainly have to phone the school the minute we get to the restaurant to say you're OK, and with me.'

'Oh, *Gran*!' Laurie dropped the privet stalk in his distress, and Hannah put out a friendly hand.

'I have to, dear. Surely you can see, it won't help a bit to have the school in a tizzy, thinking all manner of dreadful things may have befallen you. They will have already phoned Mum, and she'll be in a state too.'

'She's at work.'

'Even so, they're certain to have her number there. Did you come here by train? Where did you get the cash?'

'I said I wanted my pocket money out to buy a present.' Laurie put his head down and muttered, beginning to sound mulish.

'Look . . . we're almost there.' She put a restraining hand on his arm as they reached the main road. '*Please*, Laurie – tell me about Hurst.'

'When we get back home, Gran – honest, I'll tell you then. There's not time now. I say, can I have lunch at your place? I'm starving.'

Hannah sighed. 'Come on then. But I just can't think what to say if I don't know . . .'

She could get no more from him. She phoned the school, who seemed to believe she was covering up. Then Jonet, who sounded furious once she knew her runaway son was safe.

'What an unspeakable nuisance he's making of himself! How *could* he!'

'I don't think he's done it to be a nuisance, Jonet,' Hannah said reasonably. 'He must have been very upset, whatever happened.'

'He can't be more upset than I am, Mother. And d'you mean he hasn't told you what got into him?'

'Not everything . . . he was too tired; he'll tell me soon, he says.'

'He'll tell *me* soon.' Jonet sounded ominous. 'And his father. And I have already made an appointment for us to see his housemaster on Saturday. Well . . . now I suppose I must leave my work and get up to Clapham to take him back to school.'

'Jonet – aren't you anxious to know why he did this? Before you rush him right back into whatever situation he tried to escape?'

'Certainly I want to know. And I expect to find out directly I get there.'

Hannah heard the militant ring to her daughter's voice, and tried again. 'Jonet; look, it's such a hike for you . . . coming here, going down to Kent and back, then on again to Reading. Would you consider allowing him to sleep here tonight, and I would drive him back to school first thing in the morning? Then you and Mark could sort it all out on Saturday?' She made an effort to strike the right note of neutral reasonableness.

'Oh . . . well, I don't know. You do spoil him rather.' Jonet was not convinced. 'And I would hate him to think he had done something clever.'

'Oh absolutely. But he really does seem quite tired now; it seems to me that he's under quite a bit of stress. But after a night's sleep he may be prepared to go back and try again. And you would have been saved all that running around.'

There was a pause; a heavy sigh. 'Oh – very well. If you're *sure* you won't make a silly fuss of him? Please tell him I am terribly upset by his incredibly thoughtless behaviour, and only hope there is a good reason – though I cannot for the life of me think of one.'

'No. Yes. Right. I will call directly I get back tomorrow.'

Laurie continued to prevaricate. He ate a reasonable lunch, walked back with her discussing every possible topic but the one Hannah was determined he should, then finally said that he was actually awfully tired, and could he just go up for a nap first?

'Oh, *Laurie*.' But he did look undeniably peaky now. 'I shall have to hear your explanation soon. I have undertaken to get you back to school first thing tomorrow.'

He looked at her with trapped eyes. 'Oh. Well – I really need to sleep for a bit now, Gran.' She saw the beginnings of panic.

'Do that then, dear.' She gave him a friendly hug and for a moment he clung to her like a small child. 'Liza's bed is made up.'

He nodded, and his eyes filled with tears before he ran up the stairs.

'I'll talk to him,' Matthew volunteered when he came in and heard the story. 'Man to man . . . it might just be easier for him.'

'This boy Hurst is quite likely bullying him, wouldn't you say? Laurie did say he was older – in the Sixth Form.' They strolled in the garden, Matthew sipping his pre-dinner whisky.

'I shall see if he's awake when I go up to shed my glad rags.' He pulled at his dark, formal jacket, grimacing. 'The light is so splendid now, I thought I might do a spot of painting when we've eaten. The lad can sit with me and watch if he likes; might take his mind off his problems for an hour.'

He finished his drink and hooked an arm in hers as they made for the house. Hannah brushed a rose petal off his cuff. She would never, she hoped, cease to appreciate how talking problems through with Matthew eased the pressure of them. It had taken a while to learn the art of sharing problems as well as pleasures; now, she rated it a valuable bonus.

She hovered in the hall, hearing voices from Liza's

room. Scenarios presented themselves, each one more disturbing than the last, before she forced herself back to the kitchen to dress the salad and steam the first tiny new potatoes. When Matthew's tread was heard on the stairs, he was at once herded into the privacy of the kitchen.

'How is he? What did he say?'

'That he's hungry,' Matthew told her. 'Can he have supper?'

'Of *course* he can have supper.' She shook his arm. 'Matthew, don't be maddening. What did he *say*?'

'Well.' He helped himself to a grape from the fruit bowl. 'It would seem that Hurst nurses something of a passion for young Laurie. I imagine he was just too embarrassed to tell you himself.'

Hannah stared at him. 'Matthew! That is terrible! What on earth is to be done?'

'Not absolutely first-degree terrible, darling. It happens quite often at boarding-schools, when large numbers of single sex youngsters are corralled together. Well, boys get crushes on other boys for sure, and it's doubtless the same for females.'

'I never heard it so, from either Jonet or Serry.' Hannah was firm. 'What wretches . . . So, what will happen, d'you think? Will they expel Hurst?'

Matthew pursed his lips. 'Depends on the school. And how gravely they view the absconding.'

'He's a right to abscond if he's being molested!' Hannah looked indignant. 'No wonder he's upset. Should I phone Jonet . . . so she can talk it over with Mark before Saturday? They may want to take Laurie away. He should never have gone off to school so young, he isn't the –' She heard footsteps in the hall and attended busily to her salad.

'Come in, old man.' Matthew smiled as the boy put

his head round the door. 'Food's almost ready. D'you like salmon steaks?'

'Of *course* we're not taking him away, Mother. It would seem to him then that if he ran from another situation he could get out of that too.'

Hannah shifted the receiver into her other hand but it made the conversation no easier. 'But Jonet – he is patently not happy –'

'For goodness sake – being "happy" is not the be-all and end-all of life. He will come up against much worse situations than this. Boarding-school will give him the wherewithal to cope. He needs to get on, work towards a suitable career, meet a circle of decent people –'

'By decent people do you mean wealthy and influential?' A bubble of angry helplessness began to rise in Hannah's gullet.

'Mother – that is totally uncalled for!' Jonet's voice rose a tone. 'What a ridiculous thing to say. And what's wrong anyway with being ambitious for Laurie?'

'Absolutely nothing, provided you are aware of where his interests lie. In growing things, for instance. He –'

'*Growing* things?' Jonet's voice rose further. 'Well if you think we should encourage our son to set up as a gardener . . . Mother, this conversation is going nowhere; Laurie is staying. Boarding-school gives a boy the best possible start – makes him self-reliant, able to cope.'

'It didn't help you to cope with my having Liza,' Hannah said quietly.

Once said, it could not be stuffed back into the dark hole where it usually lay. The bubble of helplessness burst in her throat and left her feeling sick. An electric silence reached her from Jonet's end of the line.

'No.' When it came, the voice was clipped, precise. 'But thankfully, Laurie will never be called upon to cope with his mother's disgracing him by behaving like a cheap tart. Goodbye.'

Jonet cut off with a sharp click.

Hannah continued to hold the receiver, hanging on to it as though Jonet might come back and say none of that had been true, or that another woman had butted in to speak the last sentence. But she had gone.

A cheap tart . . . She sat in her quiet bedroom in the early summer evening. In the garden below, a murmur of voices reached her from the summerhouse where Matthew and Laurie were painting on the little veranda.

She had so much. Useless, to try for the unattainable. Jonet had been honest with her once, that day of the Bristol lunch party. It seemed a long time ago now but she should have remembered Jonet's bitterness, the depths of her hurt. That would not just disappear, uncomfortable as it was to live with. It might well be too deep to fade in a whole lifetime . . .

A cheap tart. Hannah caught sight of her reflection, and thought she looked rather old to be any kind of tart. She smiled grimly at herself, and combed her hair before going down to Matthew and Laurie.

'Hi, Mummy. What d'you think I have here?'

Liza pushed open the kitchen door and pirouetted inside, waving a letter at Hannah, who laid down her own mail, her daughter being clearly in need of an audience.

'I'll bite. What is it?'

'Oh –' Liza dropped gracefully on to a chair. 'Just a

job I've been offered. Birmingham Rep – £20 a week.' She jumped up to execute a second pirouette, her hair – which she had lately tried in vain to straighten – flying about her face.

'Marvellous! May I see?' It still gave her a jolt to read 'Liza Vaughan'. But it *was* a good stage name; and David had been delighted.

'It's for six months initially, which is fine.' Liza lit a cigarette with long nervous fingers. They liked my Desdemona, it seems – they had a scout there. Though I preferred my Eva.'

'The Brecht? I loved that too – Eva was such a wonderful spoiled tomboy. I suppose you'll be stuck making the tea for a while?'

'Guess so. They're doing *Separate Tables* soon; I already know it, we did it last term. It would be super if I could nab the Jean Stratton part.'

'I remember. No harm in hoping. Even asking.'

Liza crossed her elegant legs. 'It'll be a bore if I have to sleep with the Big Man to get on stage in any capacity but tea lady.'

Hannah refused to look shocked, the reaction Liza wanted. When the pill was marketed Liza had grinned, and said lucky for her it hadn't been on sale in '44. Hannah had retorted that it would have made no odds, she'd been a welcome pregnancy. Afterwards, she was angry for having lied . . . but it had seemed too cruel to admit the truth, however obvious. Yet Liza had grown up with the fact of her illegitimacy. She appeared to be unconcerned, had even joked about it; but that was no proof of how she saw herself. Ostensibly she had lacked for nothing – two devoted parents, if not married to one another; a secure home, and Matthew, to provide a first-rate father-figure. More than Serry had had, with a father dead in infancy and a mother responsible for providing everything from new shoes to love.

Serry . . . twenty-two years since Serry had gone . . . yet still Hannah could turn suddenly, certain she had glimpsed her. Then, pain would cut sharp and raw as new. Last year, another image of Serena and Dorothea had appeared to Hannah: the two girls had stood smiling in summer sunshine, holding hands, and Hannah had simply smiled back, tears blurring the beloved image. She had been crossing the Common, on her way to help the arthritic shoulder of a customer of many years. She had been aware that day of a deeper power, an extra depth to the charge flowing through her fingers. For days afterwards, a great serenity of mind had rolled away problems like rocks downhill, and she had begun treatment on the painful hip of a neighbour's spaniel.

She looked at Liza now and said crisply, 'If you will insist on wearing your skirt up around your bottom, you must expect to be treated as fair game.'

'*Mummy* . . .' Liza heaved a dramatic sigh and blew a smoke ring at Hannah. 'You can't help being old but you *can* help *talking* like you are. If I went to Brum with my skirt tied round my ankles it'd make no odds to the way the Big Man arranges his casting. Anyway, it doesn't happen all that much in rep I understand, so you can stop palpitating!'

'I'm not,' Hannah said coolly. 'I'm fully aware of the permissive society even if I don't belong to it. I just think *that* mini is . . . very mini. D'you want me to come up with you to look for digs in Birmingham?'

'Oh – thanks, but Phil's coming to give me a hand. His folks have their place a few miles south of there, we may stay with them for a night or two.'

'Fine.' Hannah filled the kettle for coffee. She had

absolutely no right to feel cut out. Liza was twenty . . . why should she want her mother along to vet her lodgings? She wondered suddenly if in fact the accommodation, when found, would be shared with Phil Spenceley. Liza would say so if asked, she could be painfully truthful; as when she had told poor Jake, who Hannah had long suspected was secretly besotted with her, that he was a boring egghead. Even so, she had seemed put out on hearing at Christmas that Jake had been quietly married at a register office in Carlisle to a hitherto unknown young lady, name of Rose Hamilton, a fellow mathematician. Hannah reasoned that though Liza might not covet Jake herself, she did not wish him to pass into other hands lest he should at some future time divert her. Phil Spenceley possibly fell into this same category.

'Has Phil found work?' She slid a mug of coffee across the table.

'Nothing firm yet. He thought he was in with a chance at Bristol Old Vic but nothing came of it. He has a contact at Butlin's – he might fill in as a redcoat till autumn.' Liza giggled. 'Can't see it myself, Phil rising and shining at the crack of dawn. His biological clock is simply not set for it.'

'No.' Hannah stopped herself from saying more. Phil Spenceley, she hoped, would soon fade from the scene. He got on by his undoubted charm, a capacity to turn a soft answer to awkward questions, and far more than his fair share of this world's goods, donated by his industrious father.

'Actually, I'd give him a couple of years before he throws it in and joins Papa's firm. He's not built for roughing it and there's usually some of that in this business.'

'Are you? Built for roughing it?' Hannah watched

her daughter's arrestingly beautiful face. Liza's eyes, so like David's, met hers and held, and both women recognised the moment for one that would stay in bright memory.

'Do you doubt it?'

What was it? That nerve-tingling, inexplicable *something* that set Liza apart. A unique quality of voice? An expression? More ... or perhaps altogether less definable. An aura.

'No, my dear. I do not for one moment doubt it. You will do, or survive, whatever you must, to succeed.'

'You were the same.' Liza touched the back of her mother's hand with a finger. 'Uncle Joe told me a few things about you. How *you* roughed it for years and years, in order to succeed. Which of course you did. So you see, Mummy darling, I get it from you.'

Their smiles faded then and they looked steadily into one another's eyes until Hannah seemed to be drowning in those aquamarine depths.

'What of that other thing you get from me, Liza?'

There it was, drifting between them like dangerous smoke. Liza looked away, though her body remained still. Her hands were linked loosely over the Birmingham letter but Hannah saw tension in her immobility and leaned forward in sudden anxiety.

'Please ... won't you talk to me?'

Liza got up in a fluid graceful movement and went to stand by the window with her back to Hannah. Her sandalled feet and bare legs were braced strongly beneath a body-skimming shift in a pink and purple concentric print. Her hair was tethered by a purple ribbon and from her earlobes swung hoops of fine carved bone. She looked powerful, barbaric almost.

'I've seen her several times.' Her voice had a dream-like quality. 'But she won't get anywhere with me.'

She turned, bending back against the cupboard and her eyes were bright, dark-ringed orbs against her creamy skin.

Hannah said carefully, 'I saw her myself. At the end of the *Othello* performance; just a glimpse, a shadow in the aisle. I've no idea why she has left her cottage unless it was because a farmer had taken away a load of stones from it – disturbed it pretty much.'

They were quiet for a moment. Then Liza said in a low voice, 'I hate her.'

'Don't do that,' Hannah said at once. 'She means no harm, I believe, and is to be pitied, unable to rest, or to move on. Please don't hate her.'

'She had her life,' Liza said harshly. 'Now I have mine and I shall not allow her to disrupt it.' She gathered up the letter and stuffed it into her bag. 'I must go now – I'm seeing this agent who wants to take me on, and we've to sort out the TV play details.' She smiled suddenly. 'Will you watch me, Mummy? Could lead to big things . . .'

She was the child again, wanting attention, appreciation. Hannah kissed her goodbye. 'Of course I shall watch you. When have I not?'

Chapter Twelve

Winter 1965

Liza could not take her eyes off Edward Anderssen. He leaned over the table set up on the stage, discussing with the producer, Don, a poster-sized rough of a butterfly for the Christmas production, a fantasy enacted in a haunted wood. Anderssen was tall and lissom with an angular, ravaged face that reminded Liza of Leslie Howard, as did the darkish blond hair that fell across his high forehead as he bent over the sketch.

She had first seen him three days ago when he had called to take Don, who appeared to be a friend of long standing, for some lunch. Don had a sets crisis in full bloom and had instead sent out for sandwiches; these they had eaten sitting in the stalls, struggling to resolve the difficulties of an on-stage wood and its flora and fauna. Liza, who was to play the butterfly, rehearsed with a dozen others and watched Edward covertly. He then disappeared; she thought about him a great deal for some days, and made what she hoped were discreet enquiries. 'He was here before, about a year ago,' Henrietta Starkey in Wardrobes told her. 'Brilliant wildlife artist – you'd probably recognise his work. Anyway – forget him; he lives in Northumberland, and he likely won't turn up again for another year!'

She could not believe that. As she left the stage door that night after her stint as Lady Plyant in Congreve's

The Double Dealer she had half expected to see him walking out of Station Road to meet her. Hunching into her duffel coat, Liza was reluctant to leave the vicinity of the theatre just yet; she had walked to the nearby bus station but instead of queuing for a number nine, had turned and walked back again. By then the theatre was looking empty . . . if he *had* come she had missed him. Angry with herself for delaying, Liza had run back to the bus station and had a fifteen-minute wait for her pains.

Miraculously, he had come back after about a week, and now was once again on the stage with Don, no more than six feet from her. Liza looked at him and concentrated. All her energies gathered for one single purpose: to make him look in her direction. She knew perfectly well she was capable of doing it . . . she simply had to concentrate.

Edward Anderssen raised his head to see a young woman looking at him intently from the near wing. She had on black ski pants and a loose black sweater, over which flowed a bright fountain of Pre-Raphaelite hair. Her skin was sheened with a faint lustre and her eyes under strong arched brows were an intense aquamarine. She wore no make-up but for a vivid lipstick on the curving mouth with deeply cut cupid's bow, which widened now into a faint smile. Her head tilted back a little and Edward Anderssen stared at the pale column of her neck, where copper shadows reflected the rich tumble of hair. She stood motionless, poised like an exquisite, exotic bird caught for a second in his camera lens. His fingers jerked in their need to start mixing paint to capture the subtle, sensual tones heightened by the dark bulk of the sweater. He thought how she would be, divested of that, and of the narrow casing of the ski pants, and experienced a warm crawling sensation in his loins.

She turned suddenly and melted into the darkness of the wings. Anderssen, whose mouth had dried out, swallowed. The butterfly chalked out on the paper faded in brilliance after the impact of that bright image carved from the gloom of the stage wings.

'Who's the new girl? The one with the hair.' He hoped his voice was not giving him away.

'Liza Vaughan.' Don looked up and grinned. 'She can act, too! She got a small but juicy part in a play for Granada straight out of RADA, and two agents were chasing her like crazy. And Tennants are interested – but I'm not sure she is; says she wants rep experience first. She's no fool. Has to be shot down occasionally for her own good but it's all there. Come tonight; I've given her Jackie Coryton in *Hay Fever* and I've been surprised. I think everyone may be.'

'I'll see.' Anderssen was casual. 'Now what about this damn robin? If you want to pick my brains for any more of your creatures we shall have to talk expenses at least.'

He thought it unwise to see the performance that night, aware that his reason for doing so would be to watch Liza Vaughan on stage. He had anyway seen *Hay Fever* at the Old Vic last year, directed by Coward himself, and that would last him. Curtain-up nevertheless found him in the stalls, irritable with himself for behaving like a fool. She was just a kid with a paintable face and spectacular hair and it was time he got back to his own place, his world of windswept dunes and huge fast skies, of silent hours in the cold north light of his studio. He was oppressed by the crowded theatre, the fuggy heat, the waves of chatter. On the verge of leaving, he was trapped by the lights dimming and a sudden silence, and settled back prepared to be judgemental.

The pace of Don's production was fast, and funny as Coward intended. But for Edward Anderssen there was only the giggling Jackie Coryton, cleverly dumb, engagingly shy. The hair had disappeared, unbelievably crammed under a blonde 1920s bob, turning the girl he had seen this morning into a different person. But as the evening progressed he saw that it was more than the wig . . . she was another girl altogether, not Liza Vaughan wearing false hair and acting. Each time she appeared his gaze fastened on her. When other characters were speaking he scrutinised her for a trace of the sculpted figure he had first seen in the wings; but not by the slightest movement did she relinquish her hold on Jackie Coryton. At curtain-call he watched the leggy grace with which she ran across the stage, the bashful, pretty bob of acknowledgement, the generous smile. Then he went round to the stage door and waited, turning up his collar against the sleeting rain.

She was one of the first out, wearing boots and a headscarf and shrugging into a transparent raincoat. A few wet autograph-hunters pushed their books at her and she signed, with a smile and a few words. Then she turned towards the bus station and Anderssen stepped from the shadows.

'Good evening. My car's parked quite close, may I give you a lift?'

She recognised him at once and did not prevaricate. 'Lovely. Thanks.'

They might have known each other for years but for the electric excitement sparking between them. Under her instructions he drove steadily up Broad Street, over Five Ways and left towards Harborne, the dark rain, the rhythmic windscreen wipers creating a world quite separate from the one they usually inhabited. Liza took off her headscarf, sighed and shook out her hair.

'That blonde wig must have been a tight fit.' He smiled, glancing sideways as they halted at the traffic lights.

'Scratchy . . . terribly scratchy.' She rubbed her head. 'Strange, the ways people find to earn a living, isn't it?'

'You made a great job of the dumb blonde, though. I suspect it may be more than just a way of earning a living?'

'I can't recall ever wanting to do anything else, certainly. What do you do?' She knew of course, but did not wish to tell him this.

'Oh; paint, draw. Wildlife and nature studies mostly.' They chatted idly as their intimate metal box rolled into the suburbs, their ease and their excitement at odds to generate total awareness. When he drew up outside her rooms in Harborne he turned towards her and smiled. She looked tired now, with shadowed eyes, and her gloved hands lay still in her lap.

'Have you eaten?'

'I'll have hot milk and a sandwich while I learn next week's lines.' She pulled a wry face. 'That's why I can't ask you in, I've at least a couple of hours' work to do.'

'Of course.' He picked up one of her hands and it lay lightly in his. 'May we meet tomorrow?' The day he'd intended to drive north. God, what was happening here?

She considered. 'Is four any use? Till six? That is absolutely my only free time.'

'Four it is.' He got out and opened the door for her, walked her to the neat Edwardian villa, waited while she fished for the key in her shoulder-bag. He felt peaceful; unhurried. Liza turned from the door and gave him her hand.

'Thank you. I shall see you tomorrow.' She closed the door and in a moment he saw the light go on in the room above. Anderssen got into his car and lit a cigarette. The peaceful sensation was good, akin to the way he felt after he'd completed a piece of work to his satisfaction. He would take her to the Grand for tea in the two hours available. Some time, sooner rather than later, he knew they would make love; the thought wrapped him with pleasure as he drove away, for he wanted Liza Vaughan more than he remembered wanting any woman in his thirty-five years.

He had to get home soon though . . . this newly commissioned book represented months of work. Nothing was ever simple.

Liza switched on the light then stood still, waiting for the sound of his car driving away. When she heard it, she wanted to cry with disappointment.

'Silly cow,' she told her reflection in the dressing-table mirror. 'Did you think he'd camp out there all night?' She put out her tongue at her reflection then pulled herself together, got out of her clothes and ran a bath in the big draughty bathroom along the corridor. The linoleum was icy, the sash window would not quite close and what comforting steam there was quickly disappeared in the spidery cavern of the ceiling. Liza slid down as far as she was able into the water that was as hot as she could get it (which was not very) and considered Edward Anderssen. He was quite old. But she cared little for boys her own age, they were mostly boring, vain and utterly involved with themselves and their egos. She wanted nothing more at that moment than to climb into bed with

Edward Anderssen when she was dry again. Or before . . . She thought of him lying here in the bath with her, skin to gleaming wet skin.

She sighed, took a deep breath and reaching for the shampoo slid under to wet her hair. She knew they would make love soon, and waiting was part of the pleasure.

Hannah said to Florence: 'I doubt if Laurie will be allowed to come for the usual few days around Christmas; I've heard nothing. My own fault – I should have kept my mouth shut. I never learn, do I?'

They were sitting in Florence's Swansea restaurant, drinking coffee. Florence drew tramlines on the pristine tablecloth with a fork. 'I have to say, there are more forgiving ladies around than your eldest, Han.'

'And yet – it may in the end have a cleansing effect . . . like the opening of a wound to get rid of the unpleasant stuff that has accumulated since the last time she let off steam. That must have been – what, fifteen years ago? But really, it's high time Jonet got rid of this bile for good. I sinned against her, that is irrefutable, but God knows I've paid my dues. Anyway –' Hannah tipped back the rest of her coffee – 'I simply cannot crawl for it any longer; I've waited patiently for five months this time. I just hope like mad that I'm not forbidden Laurie permanently for my bad behaviour.'

'She'll be punishing him too if she does that . . . From where I sit, he looks on you as something of a refuge. You don't expect things of him and don't regiment him; you just love him for free and he finds that very nice.'

Hannah pulled a face. 'That's exactly what grandmothers are always blamed for is it not? Spoiling, parents call it.'

'Here's to it then.' Florence finished her own coffee. 'Thank God I'm *allowed* to spoil Raymond's two. Though I do insist on brushing teeth after sweeties. You haven't said what you think of Raymond's ideas here –' She waved a hand at their attractively comfortable surroundings. 'And a few of mine thrown in of course.'

'I thoroughly approve, Flo. As you say, eating habits are changing so fast, we must change with them or quit. D'you recall the time these windows were blasted out when Swansea was blitzed? 'Forty-one, was it?' Hannah touched the arm of the handsome woman across the table; her lifelong friend and confidante.

'Do I not! And the day the MOF threatened to close us down because they were sure we'd served black market meat? I never did get the hang of those damn forms.' Florence grinned. 'Now of course we have an altogether different set of problems. But we usually manage to solve 'em after a fashion.'

'True.' Hannah got up and wandered around the room, quiet now and set ready for tomorrow's meals. Full of memories. They had been here, cashing up after closing time when she had told Florence about the baby . . . about Liza. The first person to know; she had not seen a doctor, even.

'Things are looking good here, Flo.' A small bar had been built across a corner, and through glass doors, a self-service coffee shop was fitted in warm honey pine, and dotted with healthy-looking plants. Times certainly had changed since the war years, and the austerity decade of the 1950s. Florence looked pleased.

'It may not be Harrods, but it suits this town's needs

and that's why we're still doing good business. I did think of finding a chef to open up evenings, as you have – Raymond, Tom and I talked it over lots. Then Tom said, I don't need the money so why give myself the extra worry? He'd like to see me taking things easier now, bless him. So I shall.'

She smiled, the broad honest smile at which Hannah had warmed herself in the bad times. 'It's lovely you know, Han – having Tom. When I lost Harry, I felt so lonely I thought sometimes I could scream out loud. But with Tom around . . . he's quiet, but we're *comfortable* together. He really seems to care how things are for me. And he brings *you* closer, somehow, and Harry, you all being cousins. That's often why I phone you – when Tom's said or done something to bring you to mind.'

'I'm really glad it's worked so well for you both, Flo,' Hannah said gently. 'I always worried about him being on his own, you know.'

'You did so much for him, Han. You gave him what he needed for a good life. He remembers the hours you spent teaching him to read and write – and how to respect who and what he is. You did a good job there, *cariad*.'

Hannah took Florence's hand, feeling the small single diamond of the ring Harry had given Flo on their betrothal. 'Thanks, Flo dear. And who knows, maybe Jonet will feel better about it all one day; we can always hope! I do miss Laurie. Liza may not be home for Christmas this year, either; we thought we might come down to Bracken House, see how it's shaping up for winter living. It's quite habitable there this weekend. Then we could meet up, play silly card games as we used to.'

They put on their coats and Florence turned down

the lights, leaving one glowing in the window. 'Let's get a taxi, eh?'

Hannah adjusted Florence's fur collar. 'Let's. The days have gone when we need to queue in the cold for a bus! You know, by far the nicest part of coming home is seeing you and Tom.'

'And here's me thinkin' it was this posh motorway we have up and running through the place.' Florence shook her head. 'I tell you, Tom and I are lookin' pretty hard for a place ourselves now. We may ask to rent out a couple of rooms at Bracken House if we don't find somewhere quieter soon!'

It was certainly quiet as Hannah let herself into Bracken House. Newly made curtains were drawn, lamps lit; outside the winter landscape slept. Matthew was reading the paper and listening to a Bach concert on the radio, tired after the drive down and the list of ongoing jobs to be checked. The list seemed to be truly endless, but the major work had been done and the house was perfectly habitable. All it lacked now were refinements for which there was no hurry . . . already the house lived up to its promise of approachability and was assuming a feel of quiet warmth. After six months, it felt like *their* house.

He came into the hall, smiling sleepily. 'Hi darling. Flo all right?'

'Fine.' Hannah took off her coat, eased off her boots, looking about her. 'This place *is* good, isn't it? Good to come into, to have for ourselves? I feel it strongly tonight.'

'That's good, because there was a phone call from Liza confirming she can't come home for Christmas. Apologies and all that . . . she seemed a shade cagey about the actual reason so I didn't press. In touch again soon, she said. Sorry, sweetheart, that's a disappointment for you.'

'So – we'll come here anyway, shall we?' After the first sharp hurt, the first Christmas away for the last child, she made an effort. 'We shall enjoy it, I think. Loads to do, and Tom and Flo, and good walks provided it doesn't pour down non-stop.'

'OK by me. I wondered if Nick might turn up . . .'

'He can come here if he does, and welcome. Even if Jake and his lady did too, there's still room.'

'I doubt they will.' Matthew had become philosophical about the wandering habits of his sons. 'But sure, we're here if they want us.'

But not Laurie . . . Hannah thought she would leave it just a few more days, before calling Jonet. She knew she would though, in the end . . .

'This is heaven. Quite the best way to spend Christmas.'

Liza curled her toes in pleasure, tucked into a cavernous, cushiony sofa before a leaping fire. Edward Anderssen, stirring the contents of a pan in the galley kitchen off the square, white-walled room, smiled, bending to sniff the fragrant mixture.

'A brief idyll – one and a half days! Just as well; any longer and I doubt you would squeeze into your butterfly costume.'

'I always eat like a pig when I'm happy.' Liza took a Turkish delight from a box on the arm of the sofa. 'I shan't eat a thing tomorrow with that ghastly journey and a performance at the end of it.'

'You know you'll love it once you're on the stage. Up there in the spotlight . . . that's what you are about.' He put the lid on the pan and came to lean over the sofa back and caress the nape of her neck, pushing his fingers up through the luxuriant hair.

'You know that, don't you?'

Liza leaned into his hands like a cat, eyes closed. 'Aren't you the same? With this?' She waved a hand to where six of his wildlife paintings were grouped on the wall. 'Bet you can't wait to be rid of me so you can hotfoot it back to that *freezing* studio.'

'You may be right,' he said calmly. 'I'd say we're both fairly committed. Which leaves us – where?'

Liza turned her head and reached to pull his down. 'Let's not be boringly practical, darling. We have the rest of today. And all night.' She kissed his neck then reached further to his mouth. 'We could go to bed now if you like . . . have a really long night.'

'Not when I've been slaving over a hot stove to get this meal. And no more Turkish delight – I'm producing the full menu in around half an hour.'

Anderssen extricated himself from her arms and poured them champagne. He gave a glass to Liza and sat on the rug, stretching his long legs out to the fire and resting his head against her knee. She picked up strands of his hair and let them drop again, idly.

'That was a marvellous walk this morning. All that beach . . . that amazing threatening sea . . . and the castle reared up like a great protective monster above everything. And the islands . . . Can we cross to them when summer comes? I could watch you paint.'

'You've no idea where you'll be when summer comes. You may be on the south coast.'

'You know, you can be quite depressing when you try.' She gave his head a little smack. 'I shan't go to the south coast if I don't want.'

'You will want, if you get an offer that appeals.' He captured her hand and nibbled a finger. 'You will go wherever you must – and why not? These first years are crucial. I couldn't afford to play around when I was your age – it was work work work. Actually, it still is.'

Liza jerked her hand out of his. 'Edward – you sound like my grandad! Only I never had one. If you can't be nice go back to your stove.' She pushed him with her knee. 'Go on!'

'I'm sixteen years your senior, Liza.' Anderssen turned and gripped her thighs. 'Your parents' generation.'

'Not mine, darling. Mummy's a young and beautiful sixty-three and Pa's moving towards his seventies.' She enjoyed the surprise in his face. 'And I'm a bastard; a wartime love-child, born on VE Day with a flag up my nose.' She giggled, sipping her champagne.

Edward Anderssen said calmly, 'You enjoy that, I think. But it doesn't have the shock value of a few years ago, does it? Bastards, love-children, whatever, thicker on the ground post-war, as women begin to feel free to choose.'

'My mother didn't choose. I was thrust upon her by a married man, which was Pa. Poor old Mummy.' She put her arms round him suddenly and held him tight. The Bob Dylan LP ended and in the silence the east wind could be heard whipping round the eaves.

'I want a smoke.' Liza released him and reached in her bag to roll one from a little tin while Anderssen went back to the stove. She followed him and after a few puffs offered him the joint. 'Want some? That chicken smells ace.'

He took a draw. 'How long have you been on this?'

'I'm not "on" it, silly man. You can't be "on" grass, it's non-addictive. As you well know. Where did you learn to make bread sauce? – God, *chestnuts* . . . dreamy!'

'Stand clear now or it'll all be on the floor. Go and put on another record, there's only room for one adult or two children in here.'

They ate sitting on the sheepskin rug before the fire, pulling crackers. Liza put on a yellow crêpe crown at a rakish angle and Anderssen chose a purple wizard's hat, consigned to the flames after it twice fell into his dinner. They read one another joke slips and Liza had a plastic whistle which blew alarmingly loud. Anderssen won a ring with a yellow piece of glass. He turned it over in his palm and Liza watched him under her lashes. When he lifted her left hand and put the ring on her third finger he grinned, and raised his glass.

'There. Now I've made an honest woman of you.'

She warned, 'Don't torment me, Edward.'

He reached out a hand, his face serious now. 'Darling Liza; don't be hurt. I'd absolutely no intention –'

'Don't I know! Which is why I said don't torment me.' She looked down at the ring, flexing her fingers, turning her hand to see if the little chip of glass would catch the firelight. It remained opaque, leaden. Liza caught her breath as a child will, recovering from a crying bout.

'Sweetheart; don't take on,' Anderssen said carefully. 'I don't need to tell you how I feel about you . . . Good God, you're *here*, aren't you, that must tell you something? But – my base is here too, where I spend countless hours and weeks and months at a stretch, alone, working. Then there's fieldwork, and that's done in isolation too. Sometimes abroad. It's a life that's damn difficult to share, darling. It's *my* life . . . and the life you've chosen would be just as tough on a partner.'

Liza was staring at the ring. When she lifted her

head she smiled brilliantly at him and nodded, and firelight sparked her long, lovely eyes as it had failed to illuminate the ring.

'Stupid of me. Forget it, Teddy. I wouldn't want to be tied anyway.'

He smiled. 'No one's called me that since I was five. Come here . . .'

He pushed away the debris of the meal, the crackers. Liza closed her eyes and her head fell back as he kissed her throat, unbuttoned her black silk shirt. Against it, her skin was pearly pale over her breasts, and mauve shadowed in the scented hollow between.

Not speaking, they took off one another's clothes with a leisurely eroticism fuelled by the warmth of the fire. They stretched out together, skin to skin on the deep rug, Liza's copper hair pouring over him when he bent his head to her nipples and she curled about him.

'Jesus Christ!' Anderssen groaned and covered his face.

'Liza Vaughan, darling,' she corrected him. They lay untidily, damply by the now dying fire. 'Did you enjoy that? Not too much for an elderly gentleman? I should hate to do you an injury.'

Anderssen groaned. 'I'm not certain you haven't.'

Liza, laughing, smoothed her crumpled paper crown and set it on his head.

'I crown thee king of Liza's temple of Venus.' She reached for a witch's hat and perched it on her tangled curls. He traced the curve of her cheek with a finger.

'I think you may be a witch. Could that be so?'

'Mummy is.' Liza looked thoughtful. 'I'm not certain yet about myself.'

They drove to the beach around midnight, reluctant

for the day to end. It was intensely cold but the wind had eased and a three-quarter moon rode high and fast, ducking in and out through tumbling, silver-edged cloud. Anderssen had kitted out Liza, who had ignored his warning to bring warm clothing. She had a woollen hat pulled over her ears and a broadly striped knitted muffler wound about her neck. Under her duffel coat was a thick sweater, knitted, as was the muffler, by Edward's elder sister in an excess of zeal but with no sartorial taste. She had pulled his fisherman's socks over her tights, and an old pair of wellingtons left by the same sister over those. As they were two sizes too big she held fast to his arm to avoid tripping as they scrambled over the dunes.

They could have been alone on the planet. Moonlight cut a path across icy waves to the islands offshore, and touched the dunes behind them with light. Marram grass danced and rippled in it, creating a fantasy choreographed by the elements. Above all, the castle towered on its cliff, ancient and indestructible.

They walked to the frothing wavelets and threw pebbles along the moonpath, skimming them to bounce like the dam-busters' bombs. Then, shivering, they jogged along the sea's edge before turning back up the ridged, shining wet sand. Liza was tucked into his sheltering arm now and matched pace to pace, thigh against thigh.

'You said your mother was a witch,' Anderssen said suddenly. 'What exactly did you mean?'

'She is a good witch,' Liza assured him. 'If she's ever cast evil spells over anyone I've yet to learn about it. But she sees spirits, has premonitions of future happenings . . . that sort of thing. That's what witches do, isn't it?'

'Possibly. But I speak purely from hearsay.' Anderssen was uncertain, not knowing this girl well enough to judge exactly when she was teasing.

'She can heal too. But she doesn't do that much now, though I'm told she was a dab hand.' Liza bent to the task of negotiating the dunes in the overlarge wellingtons.

'So what about you?' Anderssen, intrigued, persisted. He had cooked Christmas dinner, eaten and drunk not wisely but well, made energetic and prolonged love and pulled Liza over the dunes and back, and was justifiably tired. But he wanted to get to the bottom of the witch business before he flaked out for the day. Liza stood still, panting, on the crest of the dune, hands on hips and the woollen hat sinking over her eyes.

'Well, I've not actually tried healing anyone. Nor yet had a premonition. But I do see – something . . . Last one down's a sissy. Geronimo!'

She plunged down, arms flailing, wellingtons going in all directions. He followed her and together they rolled in an untidy heap to the tough grass and stones of level ground.

'What sort of "something" d'you see?' He lay across her, peeling back the woollen hat the better to see her eyes. 'Are you serious?'

'Yes. Cross my heart. Well; maybe. Wait and see.'

Liza pulled down his face and kissed his cold cheek, then his warm mouth. 'Now shut up. Let's go home and make love again. Then how about a turkey sandwich?'

He groaned, collapsing on her. After a moment he began to shake with silent laughter.

He drove her as far as York to put her on the train there. She leaned from the carriage window, all tumbled curls and big tired eyes. The station was dreadfully noisy and the train crowded; Edward Anderssen badly wanted to delay it, or remove Liza from it and take her home again.

'Don't sit on those sandwiches, now.'

'Would I be likely to? On your own meticulously prepared turkey and chestnut stuffing sandwiches?' she teased him. 'Tell me again what time this thing is due in?'

'Five-fifteen . . . sorry, it's dreadfully slow.'

'God! Will I make the performance?' she moaned to herself and pulled at her hair. Three young men in khaki and loaded with rucksacks flooded into her carriage, filling it but for Liza's corner. Anderssen swore quietly. One of the soldiers stared at her neat bottom and delicious legs and winked at his companions, giving a thumbs up. Edward Anderssen jerked suddenly at the door handle.

'Come out of there.' He swung her down. 'I'm driving you the whole way. Don't argue –' as she opened her mouth. He reached for her bag. 'We can do it comfortably if we don't muck about; Boxing Day is no time to be riding about on bloody trains.'

Stowing her bag in the boot, he thought briefly of the book of paintings he had been due to make a start on today, and of the long drive back from Birmingham.

'This is wonderful, darling!' Liza looked up, laughing as she slid into the passenger seat of his Volvo. 'But I hate to think of your having to come all this way back on your own.'

'No problem, dear lady!' He turned on the ignition and leaned over to kiss her nose. 'Absolutely no problem.'

Matthew found Hannah in the greenhouse, which was bathed in early spring sunshine. 'They're a bit late going in' – she nodded at the packet of herb seeds – 'but they usually catch up.' She kissed his cheek, a tendril of hair straying across her warm face. Matthew perched on the high stool to watch, and to allow the tensions of a difficult day to loosen their grip on his head. Hannah shook out the seeds on the smoothed surface of the compost with infinite care, her fingers gentle as they would have been in healing. Chives, parsley, marjoram, thyme, basil . . .

'I wish you had more time for this –' he said suddenly, gesturing around the greenhouse.

She looked across. 'Your head hurts.' He gave a wry smile.

'Is that an accusation? If so, I need time to consult.'

'Disallowed – sorry.' She wiped her hands and came to stand behind him. 'Relax now . . .'

She placed her hand on either temple and Matthew could smell faintly the earthy, greenhousy scent of them. He closed his eyes, sagged slightly against her warm body and gave himself up.

'What reminded me that I must put in my seeds, was a letter I've had from Laurie today.' Her fingers moved with a firm tenderness about his head and Matthew felt tight membranes ease almost at once. He sighed, and allowed his shoulders to drop.

'He wrote that he's started pottering in the school kitchen garden a bit, now the evenings are drawing out. And that he has some herb seeds in.'

'Oh, good.' Matthew sounded far off. Hannah smiled, and moved on to his neck. 'Funny thing for a young chap to be interested in . . . growing things.'

'It's more usually some sport or other,' Hannah agreed. 'Or girls, once his voice has broken.'

'His dad would feel more comfortable about football or girls, I'd say.'

'His dad wants him to be a civil engineer like him,' said Hannah. 'Anything less – or more – will be frowned upon.' She gave his neck a final firm stroke. 'How does that feel?'

'Superb.' Matthew stretched, rolled his head. 'What's the charge?'

'Not mentioning our retirement for six months, from –' she looked closely at her watch – '*now*.'

'Sorry. It slipped out – I just see so much else that you want to do – like going over to see Joe and Sal and the boys. And this –' he pointed to the seed trays. 'And more healing. In fact, it was rather on my mind because I decided something myself today.' He stopped, and examined a little beetle climbing laboriously up the pot of a geranium. Hannah sprinkled compost over the seeds and patted it.

'When?' she asked. Then smiled as though she'd learned a naughty secret. Matthew looked slightly sheepish.

'I thought, next Christmas? It was quite sudden, really. The perfect spring day; and a dreadful client whose case I saw little hope of winning. I simply knew I'd had enough. Christmas will give me loads of time to run Whittaker in gently. I shall be sixty-eight,' he finished defensively. 'And I want to go to Wales and mess up these marvellous tubes of paint you gave me for Christmas while I can still wield a brush.'

Hannah lifted a tiny fly from his hair and blew it off her finger, her smile broadening. 'You don't need explanations for me, darling – I've been hoping you'd call it quits for months. I could see you were ready . . . you're so tired some evenings, and you don't leave after breakfast with the same *élan* any more. It's becoming more of a reluctant crawl.'

'Didn't realise it showed.'

'Just sometimes.' She closed up her seed packets, watered the trays. They strolled across the lawn already starry with daisies, the hum of the rush hour faint through the baffle of mature trees and shrubs. 'Well . . . if you've made *your* decision I believe I shall look for a buyer myself in the New Year. For one thing, I couldn't bear to have you idle at home without me! Right now I'm enjoying the business – that's the truth. There's still lots of other things I love to do, but somehow they get fitted in without too much fuss. But yes . . . Let's agree on a more leisurely life as of next year.'

She bent to pull grass from the rosebed. 'If I'd time on my hands right now I might fret more about Laurie; and that's pretty pointless. And of course I still miss Liza skipping in and out.' She paused, looking pensive. 'She's terribly tied up with someone, you know. Don't ask me how *I* know, the wretch doesn't say a thing in those frantically brief phone calls. But she did spend Christmas somewhere, with someone, even if she only had two days off. And I just don't think it's working . . . she was all knotted up last time she called. She won't say who it is, where he is – *anything*.'

'She can't afford to get knotted up about anyone right now.' Matthew followed her into the kitchen, took off his tie and undid the top button of his shirt. 'Not if she's moving to Nottingham Playhouse in a few weeks, and with the *Z Cars* episode to do, and the film test. Tell you what – let's go and have a meal at Richmond – you know the place? To celebrate my retirement in eight months' time? And yours, with any luck.'

He was smiling, looking better than he had for some

time and Hannah laughed at his eagerness. 'Give me an hour for phone calls and a bath and I'm yours.'

It was 11.30 when Liza phoned.

'Not woken you have I, Mummy? Just want to say hello. Are you in bed?'

'On our way, darling. We've been to Richmond for dinner. Is everything all right?' A tiny pause.

'Fine . . . well, a long day – matinée and evening. *And* a morning rehearsal. I'd hoped for a week off, but it's not materialised. Still . . . I've got Bellamira in *The Jew of Malta*. Lots of work.'

'Oh. Well, that's a good part, I know. But I'm sorry you can't get down. If your work's going so well though, that's everything.' Another pause.

'Yes. Of course. Everything.'

'So get some sleep now, Liza dear. We shall come up to see *The Jew of Malta* if we may. And do let us know when you're coming down to do the *Z Cars*.'

'OK, Mummy, fine. You get your sleep too. Love to Matthew. 'Bye.'

Hannah lay by Matthew's side, staring at the rectangle of night sky. Something *was* wrong. But at least thank God it didn't seem to involve Rachel Hywel. Flesh and blood men were difficult enough, but better by a mile than a woman dead these last two hundred years.

Liza stood alone on the Birmingham Rep stage, savouring one last time the special feel of this place. It was right to move on, she believed . . . and Nottingham Playhouse was the best possible destination. But the slightly shabby, utilitarian premises of this illustrious little theatre had been a nursery beyond price for her, as for so many alumnae passing through before her.

She smiled at the drab browns and beiges of the auditorium, so great a disappointment to the young RADA hopeful but regarded now with uncritical affection. Her gaze idled up over the alarmingly raked seating – for only four hundred or so, another early disappointment – to the tiny balcony tacked with a distinct air of danger up at ceiling height. 'Make the kids in the balcony hear you and you're home and dry,' Don had told her last autumn, and by some unimagined expertise she had done that. Her reward had come as week by week her circle of fans grew, more autograph books were thrust into her hands outside the stage door, more letters waited in her pigeonhole in the uncarpeted dressing-room on the first floor.

The television play transmitted last October had been a godsend, the invaluable exposure coming just as she had started here. It could have been counterproductive for the most junior member of the closely interwoven team but Liza, aware of the danger, deliberately played herself down, working across the grain of her innate showmanship. Her physical attributes were not easy to minimise, but the total commitment to her job, and to a willingness to learn from mistakes – and from any member of the company – turned aside envy. She had learned more in these six months, and at a greater cost, than at any time in her twenty years. Her agent, Penelope Fine, a crisp American brunette, was ambitious for her and clear-eyed as to the path she should take. The television play straight out of drama school had been a gamble. But the part, of a rebellious youngster who steals a car to visit her boyfriend in jail, and crashes it, was so tempting; Penelope Fine put the dangers to Liza without mincing words and Liza took up the challenge.

Her notices were splendid. 'We're on our way,' Penelope told her, and Liza knew it.

She walked down to the auditorium, sat in the front row and looked up at the stage. So small . . . yet encompassing so much of tears, laughter, tragedy, farce, good and evil; every human emotion was played out on these boards. She was tired now, after a draining matinée and evening as Elvira in another Coward revival, *Blithe Spirit*. Also, she felt ridiculously depressed for a lovely and talented young actress doing all the right things. Liza knew of course what was the matter, what was wrong with her life. She was in love up to her eyebrows, and was being denied sight of the love object.

She stared at the stage, empty of all but that memory of Edward Anderssen bending over the table discussing designs with Don. Why the devil could he not come here to work – he could paint anywhere, damn him; paint all day if he must. They could at least sleep together. April already, and they had met once since Christmas and that for under twenty-four hours in a less than satisfactory hotel in Derby where they had heard people having a row through the bedroom wall. The situation was initially comic but quickly became tedious and then downright awful. Anderssen had finally rung down to reception. As he explained their complaint at length to an unusually dense receptionist, Liza heard the noises on the other side of the wall change from those of anger to those of amour . . . loud and uninhibited amour. By the time the phone rang in the next bedroom Liza and Edward, choking with suppressed mirth, had thrown on their clothes and escaped to the bar. They returned later; all was quiet with their neighbours but their own ardour had found expression only in careful whispers and sighs, taking the edge off a reunion that should have been joyful as church bells on Easter morning.

Now they were apart again. Liza phoned him regularly, reversing the charges as asked, but plans to meet were made and broken as work schedules won the day over desire.

'*Why* can't you paint down here? Give me one reason.'

'Because – and I do repeat myself – my studio is *here*, dear girl.'

'What's wrong with a hotel bedroom?'

'Not a thing, for sleeping in. For painting you have to take my word it does not make the grade. Now, when do you have a day off?'

'I don't, till probably some time after I've moved to Nottingham. That will be a different set-up entirely I suppose, so I've no idea. Anyway, Penelope has a *Z Cars* episode lined up for me soon, and that's such a super series I'd kill for it. But it will mean going down to London for rehearsals, then recording and fitting that in with whatever I'm to do at Nottingham. So . . . days off disappear over the horizon for a bit, I should imagine. If you can come down to London you could watch us do the episode then we could go somewhere nice and civilised together, like the Dorchester. How about that?'

'Liza, I'd need at least two days off for that – three really, since it's a day either way down and back.'

'You clearly don't love me. Just be honest enough to say so and we'll both know where we are.'

'Oh, do grow up, for God's sake. If you want to be treated like an adult try behaving like one.'

'Right. Adults exercise choice of action, don't they? That's what I am now doing. Goodbye.'

That had been last night, from the phone booth on

the corner of Liza's road. She had run up to her room afterwards and leaned against the door, tears of frustration flooding her eyes. Damn. Damn.

Tears gathered again now. Through the blur she saw a shadow to the right of the stage, near the backdrop. She wiped the tears with a hasty hand, and looked hard. Rachel Hywel stood motionless before the gauzy curtain, facing towards her. Over-tired, over-stressed, control snapped; Liza yelled, a hoarse maddened shout, and with every ounce of her strength she flung her bag hard across the stage at the tormenting image.

'What do *you* want, you disgusting object! How dare you show yourself? Get *away*!'

Footsteps hurrying, and Steve the caretaker pushed through the wings of the stage. He saw Liza and peered down, wiping his hands on his blue overalls before picking up her bag.

'Blimey – I thought the place was clear this last 'arf hour, Miss. What a bleedin' fright you gi' me wi' that row. What's up for Chrissake? Why've you not gone 'ome? I was abart to lock up!'

Liza let herself out of the stage door and ran for the bus station. No buses, no queue, she'd clearly just missed one. Panting and exhausted she ran back to the phone box on the pavement outside. A two-shilling piece and two sixpences . . . she picked them out of her purse with clumsy, shaking fingers and put them on the top of the dusty coin box by an old piece of chewing gum. With an eye open for the appearance of her bus she began to dial. Twice she botched it as buses followed one another into the concourse.

'Teddy?' She began to cry with relief. 'Oh Teddy, it's so wonderful to hear you. Look darling – I've only a scrap of money, can you call me – I'm in the bus station? It's the same number as the theatre, but the last three digits are 472. So I'll hang up. Please call right now. I need you so.'

Sobbing, Liza put her forehead down on the cold plastic of the telephone. When it rang she grabbed and dropped it; grabbed again.

'Now, what on earth's going on, darling?' Edward Anderssen's voice was reassuring in its wonderful normality. Liza swallowed more tears and grasped the receiver hard to her ear.

'Teddy . . . Darling. I want to apologise for yesterday's ghastly call – I behaved quite unreasonably.'

'OK. So now, what's the problem?'

'Oh . . .' She breathed deeply for control of her tears. It was better already, just having him on the other end of the line, ready to listen. 'Teddy – I really am awfully tired. *The Jew of Malta* and *Blithe Spirit* was a bit much, one on top of the other! That's why I'm so stupidly *weepy*. I just want terribly much to see you.'

'Yes.' He paused. 'OK, I'll come down. Tomorrow?'

Taken aback by his capitulation, Liza thought quickly. 'What a wonderful offer, darling. But your work . . . and there's only hotels down here. Look, if I can hold off starting at Nottingham for a few days maybe I could come to you?'

'You know you can. That's what I suggested! So, tomorrow?'

'I'd have to square it with Penelope. Can I call you when I've phoned her in the morning?'

'Fine. Right then, we'll speak tomorrow. Go and get some sleep now. 'Night, darling.'

Simple; Liza went back to wait for the bus, almost light-hearted. Penelope must tell Nottingham the truth – that she was exhausted, needed a few days before starting her contract. She had the *Z Cars* script, she could start work on that on the train. Time to themselves ... marvellous. The image of Rachel Hywel was fading by the time the bus came.

'Teddy!' She flew up the platform to him at York, hair flying, pulled sideways by her bag. Anderssen picked her up and held her tight, their lips meeting hungrily.

'Well then. Let me see you.' He observed the thinner cheeks, the khaki smudges round the eyes. He picked up the bag and took her hand. 'Come on. Lunch, then we'll be on our way. Lovely day for the drive.'

She fell asleep soon after they started north, in mid-sentence almost, sated with fillet of beef with wild mushrooms and a wonderful damp Brie with a pile of sweet grapes. Anderssen made the A1 and settled down, his face expressionless, hand and foot movements automatic. He was north of Newcastle when she stirred.

'Thank God. I'm dying for a pee.' He smiled and touched her knee. 'Now we can stop – how about a pot of tea?'

'Brilliant.' She stretched, smiled back. 'Have I slept long? Where are we?'

'Going up the bloody A1, where else? I'll pull in soon for a bit.'

'Darling, I did offer to do it all on the puffer. You should have agreed and got in a day's painting. And after all the effort, I go to sleep on you!'

'You were flaked out, it's OK. Sit back and relax for now.'

She watched the grey little town of Morpeth fall away and the landscape open up again. Colours intensified over the fields, copses, hills, as spring worked up the pale palette of ochres and duns. He forked left into a lane that became a village street, and pulled up by a low stone house with a 'Refreshments' sign by the door. He smiled across at her.

'End of first leg. Hop out.'

The land became wilder, the road quieter as they drove further north. He travelled fast in the powerful estate car, his driving economical and unshowy; Liza was dozing again as they finally left the main road for a minor one that wound towards the coast. In this northernmost corner of England spring was later, and wind raked the clumps of tough grass and trees that bent landward. The skies were huge, filled with light, the towering steely cloud massed against thin blue.

'No more snoring, wakey wakey.' He drove past a ribbon of mellow stone houses, a pub, a burly little church with daffodils blowing under a glowering old yew. The last house, after a rough bit of pasture, was back from the lane and attached to a long, one-storey barn with skylights in the stone-tiled roof. Anderssen parked on gravel before the house, a four-square dwelling of solid dignity with a central door flanked by two windows, repeated above.

They sat for a moment. Liza gave a great sigh and put her head against his arm. 'Marvellous . . . It's so *good* to have made it here. We have three whole, complete days now – doesn't that sound fantastic?'

'Not bad at all.' He dropped a kiss on her hair. 'Meanwhile, more tea, gallons of it. Driving always turns me into a tea freak. We can eat at the pub later on, it's not half bad.'

She eased herself out, flexing her legs and arching her back, staring at the house. 'It's nicer than I remembered, you know. Does all that stuff come into leaf?' She gestured at the faces of the house and barn, criss-crossed with budding clematis, a wistaria and a huge climbing rose.

'It surely does. Come on; inside with you. There should be time for a quick walk before dark.'

The walls of the little front hall were a pale wash to set off Anderssen's paintings and sketches . . . of birds, insects, wildflowers, boats drawn up on a shingle beach before a luminous grey-green sea. His sepia and sienna tones had a translucent clarity, greens usually muted and shadows with a mysterious purple core. The skies ran tone into tone, each blooming towards and into the other yet the whole with a clear, fresh immediacy.

'I do love them,' Liza said softly. 'I do love *you*.' She turned into his arms and stood still as he stroked her back.

'Let's both get into a big hot bath.' He spoke into the windblown hair. 'Full to overflowing. We can have tea afterwards.'

He pushed the front door shut with his foot and still entwined, they climbed the stairs.

The sun was well up when he woke her, pushing gently at her shoulder. 'There's coffee here – can't you smell it? God, you could sleep on a clothes line . . .'

Liza stirred, grizzled for a moment like a bad-tempered cat, opened an eye and screwed up her face as he pulled back the printed cotton curtains. 'Not tried sleeping on a clothes line; wouldn't know.' She stretched out her arms luxuriously. 'So where's the coffee?' Pushing herself up against the pillows she smiled at him, shook back a tumble of hair and accepted the steaming mug, taking an appreciative sniff. 'Mm-mm.'

He sat by her, an arm about her bare shoulders. 'Think we may be in for a good day. We shouldn't waste it.'

She twisted to look in his face, and laughed. 'You

didn't rate time spent in bed as wasted last night. What changed things?'

'Oh, nothing has changed, believe me.' His eyes were serious. 'But variety is the spice of life, we are told.' His hand slid to cup Liza's creamy breast, shadowed with delicate veining. 'Shall we go to the islands?'

She looked at him over the rim of the mug. 'In a boat?'

'I know of no other way unless you can walk on water.'

'Idiot.' She pushed his leg off the bed with her foot.

'I only wondered, you coming from a long line of witches an' all.'

They sat contentedly for the time it took to drink the coffee, Liza gazing about the bedroom that bore no imprint of a woman's touch. The walls were a paled-down terracotta, giving a luminous quality against which pieces of well-used old pine looked golden. Wall recesses either side of the chimney breast were shelved, with lamps, books, relics of Anderssen's life. The boards were uncarpeted but brightly patterned rugs splashed colour at the bedside and under the open window. Again, a group of paintings dominated the inner wall.

'Did you love your wife?' Liza asked suddenly. He frowned.

'I did, certainly. At one time.' He stood up and took her coffee mug. 'You get your shower while I fix breakfast, OK?'

She looked at him intently. 'Do you mind me asking about her?'

'Not at all. It just seems irrelevant. We parted five years ago, in another life.'

'Yes. Of course.' She stood up, the sun casting warm

shadows on her skin. He had a strong inclination to place her back on the bed and push deep into her curved little belly as he had last night, groaning with the delight of it. But then he knew they would not get up for hours, and he had plans.

They hoped to slow the day, make the hours appear longer by attempting to do very little with them. They agreed on the islands, Liza with a touch of apprehension for she neither liked water, nor swam. The truth was that she was afraid of water, but reluctant to admit to it.

'This is what I use when the weather's right.' They had strolled round to the back of the house to where a sailing dinghy was parked stem down on its trailer. 'I draw and photograph quite a bit on the islands, and this is invaluable.'

'It looks quite small.' She sounded doubtful. 'Is it actually safe – you know, on the sea?'

'Sure it is. It's a Wayfarer, a guy's sailed to Iceland in one. But I do cheat when I'm pressed for time – there's an outboard motor. My objective is after all work, not hobby sailing.'

'And is the weather right today?' Liza squinted up at the skyful of blossoming cloud changing shape fast in a lively breeze.

'For me, probably. For you . . . I rather think, darling, that you may be a fair-weather sailor. We'd be wiser to go the tourist way, there's a service out of Seahouses.'

'Can we lunch on these islands?'

He gave a shout of laughter. 'Not unless you enjoy raw eider, tern or kittiwake! And can catch 'em first. You should not anyway be considering food after the size of that breakfast – gluttony is one of the seven deadly sins I would remind you.'

'Don't be unpleasant. I always eat well when I'm on holiday.' She flounced off to stare in at the window running almost the length of what had been the attached barn. He drew her away.

'We'll go in the studio this evening if you'd like. *Now* we're going to the islands. And you must change those ridiculously thin trousers, or add a second pair.' He sighed with fine drama. 'And woman, *where* is your thick sweater?'

The tourist boat trip was just a few days into the season, and ill-attended. Anderssen and Liza had only to share with three elderly ladies in plastic macs and headscarves, a burly cleric with excessive facial hair and a small wife wearing a thick woolly bobble hat and carrying a vacuum flask, and three student-type young men with one pair of binoculars between them and a bottomless supply of chocolate bars and hand-rolled cigarettes. As they eased away from the wall of the little harbour, stacked high with empty lobster pots, Liza was assailed by oily engine fumes mixed with the pungent aroma of fish from boats unloading their night catches into metal containers. When further out they met the first slap of the swell and spray smacked her face, she looked at him and her cheeks paled.

'Come on.' He led her down to the covered seats and they sat in the front row. 'That better?' Liza nodded.

'Much. The fish was the worst . . . sickening.'

'Living near the sea it becomes familiar enough not to notice it. Now, look back and you'll get a view of the castle.'

'Wonderful. Darling – is it always this rough?'

'Rough?' He peered out at the steely, sloping sea. 'This is *smooth*; scarcely a white horse in sight. Look around for a sight of seals any time now. That's Inner Farne in front of us, with the cliffs and the lighthouse. And see all those puffins?'

Gradually she settled down, though never feeling safe. They ploughed past rocky protuberances low in the water to east and west of them. Interested now, Liza turned and turned again as Anderssen reeled off the species of birds flying about them between the islands. 'A razorbill. They're fulmars. And they are cormorants, see? Ah yes, *they're* Arctic terns – thousands of them. Here's Staple Island coming up, we should land here for a few minutes. See the Pinnacles?'

She gazed at the line of tall dark needles of rock, powerfully inaccessible, and topped with shoulder-to-shoulder guillemots. The boat chugged past and veered in towards a small haven, where it manoeuvred sufficiently close for them to scramble ashore. Liza stumbled, missing her balance on firm rock after the movement of the boat then stood with feet braced, laughing.

'You were right, I'm not a born sailor. *Terra firma* feels wonderful!'

'Well, you're only on it briefly this time.' He held out a hand to her. 'Welcome to my world.'

Bare, fissured rock, to Liza the ultimate inhospitable environment, hosted colonies of nesting seabirds in every crevice. Anderssen used his camera sparingly, knowing exactly what might be of use to him in his work, with one shot of Liza silhouetted against the Pinnacles, snuggled in her sweater with hair whipping across her face.

'That's Brownsman.' He indicated the island just north of them. 'See, it's covered with nesting terns. I've been over there to draw them sheltering about that old tower. It used to be a lighthouse early last century but it killed more mariners than it saved, it was wrongly sited. There's another now, built further out.'

Liza nodded, wishing for hot coffee. The uncompromising aspect of nature presented today daunted her, and had until now been outside her experience. But she absorbed it into a storehouse of the subconscious, perhaps to draw on for her craft at some time in the future.

Back on board, they headed out to circle Longstone with its powerful red and white lighthouse. Liza was mastering her nerves now, and watched with delight a group of seal pups at play in an adjacent nursery. Coming back, Anderssen told her the story of Grace Darling and her father, the lighthouse keeper.

'Liza you *can't* not have heard about Grace Darling at school?' He raised his eyebrows to heaven. 'She helped save five mariners in a shipwreck; became a national heroine. Now, we're heading down to Staple Sound, see? Sit tight, there's a bit of a swell here.'

Liza watched the heaving water laced over with foam and suppressed a tinge of nausea; she simply would not disgrace herself at this point. Past the lighthouse and ruined chapel of St Cuthbert on Inner Farne and she knew she could make it, the coast was definitely closer. Fifteen minutes? She could do that; she renewed interest in the nesting puffins and eider ducks, and cliffs full of kittiwakes like statues as they passed.

'Wonderful, darling – amazing.' Safely ashore, her enthusiasm for the sights of the morning was boundless. Off the water it was reasonably warm as they strolled about the little harbour; the sea gleamed silver where the sun touched it, and slapped good-temperedly at the sides of the boats freshly painted for the spring. They drove the few miles along the coast to Bamburgh for lunch and Liza bought a box of fudge in the post office that was also the birthplace of Grace Darling. They walked round the castle, then over humpy grasses to the huge empty beach. Barefoot in the shallows, Liza shouted with delight as icy wavelets caught her ankles, jumping to avoid them as a child would. The islands sat remotely on the horizon now; she stared at them, quite intimidated by having been out there among them in the forbidding North Sea.

'I've only been to the south coast,' she confided to Anderssen. 'Pa used to come to see me once a year and we'd to go to Bournemouth or somewhere. It was nothing like this.'

'The south coast isn't so *real* –' he gestured at the blowing salty emptiness. 'Except occasional bits of Cornwall; I've been there to do some fieldwork.'

'There *are* lovely places further south,' she insisted. 'Wildflowers, butterflies, heathlands, birds . . . rivers, lakes?' He frowned into the distance.

'Nothing speaks to me like this place,' he said quietly. 'I cannot truly say why.'

They faced each other on the running wet sand, their rolled-up trousers damp where the sea had caught at them. They looked small, isolated and of no importance in the landscape. Then Anderssen took her hand.

'Let's go home, sweetheart. Let's go to bed and make love.'

Hands linked, they meandered back towards the dunes.

Time slid like sand through their fingers. Next day they drove north to Berwick, walked round the Elizabethan town walls; then up the coast . . .

Eyemouth, the deserted rock-bound sweep of Coldingham; St Abbs where they pottered about the dour grey little harbour. Inland then to Coldstream, and they crossed the Tweed again here, back into England. The sun became warm by the river and they idled on the grassy bank while Anderssen sketched her, eating apples and bananas and reading leaflets collected from the tourist information centre. The sky was gentle, milky, the water echoed its calm and swans slipped through it silently.

On their last day Liza wanted to spend time about the property. When it began to rain, not hard but with a quiet persistence, they were in the studio, Anderssen explaining the layout of his book in progress. The room was the full length of the former barn, with a big wood-burner at the end furthest from the house and a capacious old coffer by it stacked with logs. The ceiling was unboarded, with skylights allowing a north light to flow into the room. The wall overlooking the back garden carried a huge window to the floor, double-glazed, with heavy linen curtains to swish across the length of it.

Along the house wall, an oversize sofa was draped with woollen tartan rugs, and the cushions were big, deep, inviting. Before the window, a table, a desk, an easel and a draughtsman's drawing board were each loaded with papers, sketch-pads, boards of varying thickness, tubes of paints, jars of brushes or pencils. On the table was a typewriter, with reference books; files of photographs, and more books were stacked around the boarded floor. Photographs and drawings were pinned to chipboard along the front garden wall, and there was a sink, kettle, toaster and a small refrigerator. They had tinned lobster soup and toast for lunch with great mugs of coffee, and oatcakes with a local cheese, and a melon they had bought in Berwick-upon-Tweed, as they lounged on the sofa to pore over photographs and rough layouts.

'You get on with a bit of painting, darling,' Liza instructed him after he had taken their dishes to the sink. 'I'll stretch out on this gorgeous piece and do nothing more than watch you, or look at some of these books of paintings. Later we can take a walk if it clears up; or even if it doesn't, I suppose. I intended learning my *Z Cars*, but I can do it on the train tomorrow.'

'Don't know about painting . . .' He sounded dubious. 'But there are photos that need editing and filing, and a few sketches to organise against copy.'

He started to work, and turning to show her a sketch a few minutes later found she was asleep, curled on the sofa with her head on her arm. Anderssen smiled, laid a rug lightly over her and returned to work, switching on a Mozart tape turned down low.

'I shall never forgive myself,' Liza repeated yet again, hugging his arm as they paced the southbound platform at York station next morning. 'Falling asleep on my last afternoon . . . darling, how could I?'

'It seemed easy,' Anderssen said, teasing. 'I've known for a while that I was not the most exciting chap. Even so . . .'

'Shut up about it now.' She shook his arm. 'Oh God, here's my train. Darling, I shall miss you so much.'

'And I you.' He was serious now. 'And promise me you will never get that tired again?'

She felt tears constrict her throat as she slammed shut her carriage door. 'Teddy . . . thank you for having me.'

'That, sweetheart, was my pleasure.' He grinned

broadly, then reached up to kiss her sweetly on her drooping lips. 'Call me when you arrive.'

Liza concentrated on smiling as the train moved out so she should not cry. She must think positively. It was not written in concrete that he would not come south; not if he loved her. OK, it was a pretty good studio, but not the only one in England. She would give it her concentrated wishful thought.

She was getting out the *Z Cars* script when a strange fact occurred. What had instigated her desperate phone call to him – the need for him to know her fears about Rachel Hywel – had in fact entirely escaped her memory . . .

Well. That could only mean that it was not important; that seeing him, their being together, was all she needed.

Chapter Thirteen

March 1967

Joe and Sal, with Thomas on Joe's shoulders and Paul Harry firmly anchored to his mother's hand, walked slowly in Central Park. Spring seemed late, trees just thickening with budded leaves now and the wind still cold enough for jackets.

'Say again what it is, Pop?' Thomas patted the side of his father's head, cheeks pink with excitement and nose pink with cold, as the crowds milled about them in East Drive.

'It's called "An Expression of Love for all Mankind",' Joe said, and winked at Sal. A small girl in a pink jumper stood in their path, looking up at them with serious blue eyes. She had freckles across the bridge of her nose, a ribbon about her head into which white flowers had been tucked, and a small round of white paper was stuck to her brow bearing the instruction LOVE NOW. Thomas stared down at her, struggling to decipher the message, but the girl was suddenly whisked off by a young woman in jeans and a brilliantly patterned shawl, over which streamed pale hair decorated with an assortment of beads.

They edged along, under one tree bubbling with multi-coloured balloons on streamers, and another inhabited by an excited bunch of teenagers lodged precariously in its slender branches. A circle of others, cross-legged on the grass, were burning paper ignited by a candle, and chanting something unintelligible, passing round paper cups of coffee and cigarettes as they did. Both males and females had entwined flowers and leaves in their hair, others carried a single flower, and baby buggies were decorated with them.

'How much nicer than that Vietnam protest we saw here last weekend.' Sal stopped to read two banners whose owners were taking a break on a bench. "Hare Krishna – Hare Krishna". Well, that harms no one, does it? Ah . . .'

Led by the sound of bells, they moved on to a crush of spectators round a blonde girl beating a tambourine with the flat of her hand, another playing a flute, and a barefoot young man with bells on a leather thong about his neck, gyrating happily to the rhythm. Thomas bobbed up and down on his father's shoulders, clapping to the beat, but Paul Harry, too self-conscious for such uninhibited goings-on, frowned and pulled on his lip.

'Hey!' Joe pulled Thomas's leg. 'Come down from there if you want to dance.' They passed slowly along the path, each moved in his own way by witnessing the love-in, if only as onlookers rather than participators. Something was being communicated, though too nebulous to pin down and dissect. Both Joe and Sal felt aliens here; no matter that their European origins were distant now, or that their sons were New Yorkers born and bred. One day, Sal dreamed of spending time again in her native Poland; one day, Joe hoped for a home in Wales. But now they breathed in this strange, comical counter-culture of a young white middle class, a campus revolution against the materialism of their generation, against the pass to which *they* had brought civilisation. Both wished devoutly that these flower children might indeed change the old order . . . both feared it was unlikely. The cold war, the nuclear arms race, the horror of Vietnam, racial stresses that might soon become sufficiently powerful to tear apart their adopted land . . . quite a task for flower power to accomplish.

A little before they turned for home they passed a hippie wedding party. A couple stood with daisies painted on their cheeks and entwined in their long hair, while a circle of friends clasped hands and danced barefoot round them, singing. Sal paused to watch, then turned a smiling face up to Joe.

'I wish them happy,' she told him, and pressed his hand. 'I wish them happy as we two, dear Joe.'

Joe smiled back, and kissed her cheek.

The day he saw Delaney was a little warmer, though mist was slow to clear; spring making a definite move, with blossom trees on the verge of covering themselves with glory. Joe had not felt up to par for a couple of days; breathless now and again, more tired than was warranted . . . days when his hand was poised to dive into his pocket for his pills. But today the bad patch seemed on the wane. Spring had come, and he was grateful to be here yet again to greet it.

What had slipped his mind was that today around 100,000 Vietnam protesters were expected to end their parade through New York with a rally in Central Park. Long wooden trestles were in place reading POLICE LINE DO NOT CROSS. The press of citizens was already more dense than at the hippie happening a few days earlier, and the scene was thick with banners waiting to be added to those of the marchers.

Joe took it all in, to describe in his next letter to Han. She'd said they had an increasing number of hippies in London, and regular CND marches protesting against nuclear armament. But Vietnam . . . that was the American trauma, Uncle Sam's one-way ticket to hell for those families whose loved ones' bodies were being returned daily. Carl's brother Toby had had his draft papers, and was working his way through the tricks in the book for a get-out. Who could blame him ... who could believe that Vietnam was *their* fight?

Joe turned away from the hopelessness of yet one more protest march. And yet ... maybe if enough Americans said loud and clear – Halt, enough? And how would he be feeling if it were his sons having to go? Maybe he should be marching through the city with his boys, adding his own voice. Was not that how democracy worked in practice?

But Joe had found it politic to turn aside for too many years; and old habits do die hard. He hurried on, leaving the park by the next gate and making for East 57th off Madison Avenue. He didn't often go in on a Saturday these days, but today was the end-of-spring stocktaking and he was needed.

He loved approaching his shop, eyeing it as a stranger might, and then turning in at the impressively expensive door, knowing it was his. He looked about as he walked down the long room towards his office at the back. He checked that every spotlight flattered its targeted piece exactly as intended; that every vaseful of flowers was spanking fresh; that no speck of dust sullied the gleaming surfaces of the seventeenth- and eighteenth-century furniture in which he specialised. Joe was good to his staff, but expected the highest of standards in return. Gus was second to none in his fine attention to detail and painstaking goodwill towards the most wayward customer. Young Ellie had matured way beyond the initial hopes he had had of her, and was a joy in her eagerness to learn, doing well now in a diploma course in antiques she attended twice weekly. And Marek was impressive in his ability to set at naught his handicap, and to do business on an equal footing with the best. The cleaner, William, was fond of the drink; but only after he had worked on the show-rooms on both floors to his own and Joe's complete satisfaction, adding lustre to the smallest strut of the smallest stool in the dimmest corner. It had taken Joe years to orchestrate this happy state of affairs. He knew that Ellie could at any time fall pregnant by her husband, who played oboe in an up-town jazz group, or that William might take his liver one double whiskey too far. But for now, today, things had come good.

He was immersed in paperwork when Ellie came to say a lady was asking if he was in. Joe hesitated; the sooner his work was finished the sooner he could go home. But natural curiosity prevailed and he went to the door of his office. The woman had her back to him, a beautiful, expensively clad back, the whole shape very pleasing, topped by a head of luxuriant, glossy dark hair. He knew her by that alone. He walked towards the figure and was close before the woman turned.

'Joe . . . how good to see you.' She extended her hand, drew him in and offered her smooth fragrant cheek for his kiss. Joe obliged; kissing Delaney Cline had ever been a pleasure and was no less for her now being – what – fifty-three? She remained a sensually attractive, voluptuous woman who was defeating the passage of time with an unusual degree of success.

'Delaney. Well now –' Joe continued to hold her soft fingers. Fifty-eight he might be, but the memory of holding the whole of Delaney, skin to silken skin, was still sufficiently vivid to make him breathless. 'It's been a long time.'

'Too long.' Her mellow voice was regretful. 'And not of my choosing, Joe.' It was Alex, her expressive dark eyes were telling him. Alex, who was angry when you turned down Carl's offer, when you had not sufficient faith in our son's business acumen to mortgage your life and follow where Carl had gone – with everything. It was Alex who decided to drop you, to punish you for failing his son when he needed everyone's money. Not my choosing.

'What the hell, anyway,' Joe told her gallantly. 'It's great to see you. Is there something I can do for you?'

Delaney pursed her lips. 'I'm hunting for a gift for Gayle's birthday. Something rather nice. Like this?' She indicated the Ming vase she had been studying when he approached. 'It really is enchanting.'

'I shall ask you to accept the vase if you will have lunch with me.' Delaney laughed outright, showing perfect teeth.

'Joe Hywel – I could not possibly accept that! The vase, that is. The offer of lunch I am happy to accept. Sadly we cannot linger over it – I have to be back soon.'

'Then we shall go to a quiet little Hungarian place very close, where I eat the very lightest, fluffiest omelettes on the planet.' Joe got up and reached for his hat.

They smiled like conspirators, their elegantly set table in a discreet alcove, and raised champagne glasses before attacking a pair of truly royal omelettes with a beautiful salad.

'You know –' Delaney paused delicately to sip her champagne. 'You did make a mistake, Joe dear, not investing with Carl. We have done terribly well out of it ourselves; it bought our Long Island place.'

'I did not doubt Carl had the Midas touch,' Joe assured her. 'It was simply against my nature to gamble everything I possessed on one throw. There seemed to be nothing Sal and I needed that bad. I'd thought Alex knew me that well. I'm real glad Carl got it right, though.'

He poured her more champagne. 'It did sting, I admit, when I wasn't welcome at your place as a result, Alex being way and above my best and oldest friend.'

Delaney leaned over to touch his arm, smiling. 'Sure, Joe darling. And I could not be more sorry about the rift – Alex has missed you lots. He was always hoping you'd come marching round of your own accord and set things right. Anyway –' she lowered her voice. 'The company is being taken to the market very shortly, I understand, and is expected to do really well. Alex is over the moon about this. The dividends have been great, but now we'll be able to realise some profits on our investment. He said I was to ask you all down to Long Island next weekend for a celebration.'

Joe was quiet, finishing the last of his omelette. He could tell Alex to go jump in the lake. But they *did* go back one helluva long way. And Alex *had* put many good clients his way.

He looked at Delaney watching him over the rim of her glass. God, that was one woman between the sheets, it had been damn hard to say no to a full-blown affair. But what of Alex then? He'd not just have gone cool on him; he'd have bloody knifed him. No, Delaney was *not* on the menu now . . . and not only because of Alex. Now, there was Sal . . .

'OK,' he said. 'I'll see what Sal's doing next week-end. If you're certain Alex is ready to kiss and make up. Though he's an ornery critter.'

They were working out in the garden at Bracken House when the phone rang in the late afternoon. Hannah let fall the timber she had been holding and hurried indoors, kicking off her muddy slip-ons.

'Mummy?'

'Liza – hello darling. How's things?' Hannah stretched on the carpet for a few moments' relaxation; she, Matthew and Laurie were putting up a pergola and she seemed to be doing the bulk of the navvying.

'Oh . . . OK, I guess. I really am sorry I couldn't manage Easter in the end – I'd looked forward to going to Wales. I'll see you when I've finished my stint in *Earnest*, though.'

'It doesn't seem like a penance, does it? You know, when we saw it the company seemed to be having a ball. So the audience had one too, it was that infectious.'

'No – it's a great company, and an ace producer – he's made us all give our best. I'm enjoying Gwendolen, and the costumes are wonderful, the classiest ever. But there's a lot going on, simmering, right now . . . the film contract, my contract here, the incredibly long-drawn-out negotiations with the BBC for a part in a new series. And I suppose it all unsettles me . . . I think I may actually be terrified of committing myself to things.'

'Surely you can trust Penelope to work things out in your best interests?'

'Well . . . She's not *me* though, Mummy. She can't get into my head to see how one thing or another might affect *me*.'

Hannah heard what sounded suspiciously like a sob strangled at birth. She said carefully, 'Liza. Can't you tell me about him? Don't tell me to mind my own business – you *are* that . . . And only a love affair could be screwing you up when everything's taking off for you like magic.'

There was a long silence. 'Liza?'

'Mummy – I hate it when you're so horribly perceptive.'

'Wouldn't it help to talk? Have you told *anyone*? You can't bottle it up for ever and I'm certain this has been going on for ages.'

'It won't help to talk, honestly. It's an insoluble situation.'

'He's married.' Hannah sighed.

'Funnily enough, no. He was, but not any more. He's just totally inaccessible. Practically in Scotland, actually. So . . . all slightly unsatisfactory, I fear.'

'I *am* sorry, Liza. How miserable for you both, not being able to be together.'

'I'm not certain if *he's* miserable.' Liza sounded choked. 'Maybe it's only me.'

'You should know about that, darling – any perceptive woman would. Perhaps you *do* know, but don't want to believe what you know? In which case you're heading straight up a blind alley.'

'Well . . . some people are terribly hard to read, aren't they? Anyway, you're not to concern yourself – it will be resolved one way or t'other. Oh – my flat's been redecorated at long last – hope you'll approve.'

'That sounds as if you don't think I will.' Hannah laughed. 'Is it psychedelic?'

'Not at all; quite restrained, really.'

'Liza – I find that hard to believe! You, restrained?'

'I shall hang up if you're going to be horrible to me. Must go anyway – time I was heading for the theatre.'

''Bye then, dear. Thanks for the call. Let me know

when we can meet.'

Hannah lay on the carpet for a moment longer, staring at the ceiling. She had of course known there was a problem. And really, that was about all she knew now . . . that Liza was in the throes – had been for more than a year – of a love affair that was not going right. Natural curiosity wished to know much more; but instinct warned not to press. It all seemed the more odd because Liza, caring little for outside opinion, rarely felt the need for subterfuge.

She put the phone back on the side table and rejoined Matthew and Laurie, feeling thoroughly unsettled: an effect at which her daughter excelled.

They had come to Bracken House with Laurie to celebrate the first weekend of Matthew's retirement, the planned Christmas deadline having passed due to a flood of unexpected work. Yesterday he had arrived home somewhat the worse for an affectionate and exuberant send-off by the entire staff and other well-wishers, and had still been under the weather this morning, so Hannah had driven them down. Tonight was to be Matthew's retirement celebration meal, with candles, crackers, champagne, and his favourite dishes. He thoroughly recommended the move to Hannah, though moaning good-temperedly that he was now certain to be busier than he had ever been. Hannah had indeed put her own business in the hands of an estate agent as promised, and any regret was finally giving way to happy anticipation.

They were spending an increasing amount of time in Wales, and Matthew's rapport with the district strengthened with each visit. He had adopted the summerhouse for painting projects, moving into the smallest bedroom for winter work. His style was changing with changing subjects; he was now embarked upon a struggle to master seascapes and coastal scenery, working in oils and pastels to achieve bolder effects. He was also framing his work, which entailed at this stage much banging, heaving of sighs, occasional swearing and consigning to the flames of unsuccessful efforts.

Another project in progress this weekend was a garden pond on the south side where the land rose. This, Matthew assured Hannah, was to be a masterpiece of landscape engineering and necessitated countless diagrams and scale plans; water was (one day) to run from one level to another, and return by means of a small electric pump. With completion far along the road, Matthew was enjoying the journey.

Laurie was today busily excavating good-sized holes for the pergola posts, throwing aside bigger stones and flints for use in a little wall he was set on building soon to shelter his herb garden from the east wind. He wore a frayed shirt left behind by Jake, and jeans bought by Hannah for him on a shopping trip to Swansea; he was looking more relaxed than Hannah had remembered him for a long time, clearly much enjoying his second visit to his grandmother's new home. He said suddenly, collapsing on the grass beside her, 'I wish Mother was here. She works too hard, you know.'

'I wish she would come too, Laurie.' Surprised, Hannah felt her way. 'Do you think you might persuade her?'

He pushed his fingers into the springy grass. At fourteen, Laurie was slightly built, small-boned like his mother, with a neat round head under hair silky-fine as Jonet's. His features were regular but his ears stuck out slightly, which Hannah knew he hated, but which gave him an endearingly vulnerable quality.

She believed he was teased at school about the set of those ears; once, he had asked if it might help to stick them back with Sellotape, at night. Pointing out that young Prince Charles's ears grew much more away from his head, Hannah had said to try Sellotape by all means, and offered some. He had applied it (she was not allowed to see) but abandoned it at the end of the visit as too painful.

Now he considered, watching blackbirds upending for food under the shrubs. 'She's not an easy person to persuade.'

'That's true.' Hannah spoke with some feeling. 'D'you think your father might? Would he enjoy a weekend break here?'

'I could try . . .' Laurie did not sound hopeful. 'But he's away quite a bit. And he does paperwork at weekends – and the garden of course, and washes the car.'

'Well look; why don't I send a special letter of invitation to them both for you to take back? To come for half-term, with you?'

Laurie nodded. Hannah felt, for a moment, close to disliking them both for hurting their son, not deliberately but by default. But that would serve no purpose. She had been delighted when last year Jonet had relented and Laurie's visits had eased their way back on to the agenda; she must do or say nothing to rock the boat again. She was always aware of old resentments lying beneath the surface, and needing only an extra shot of tension – such as Laurie's running away from school, or an unwise remark – to bring them bubbling up again. For now, she was grateful for another reprieve for all their sakes, but particularly for Laurie's. She longed so much for security for her family; for each of them to trust that their well-being was important in the scheme of things. To Hannah, each and all were loved.

Liza's career was, as Hannah had observed, taking off like a bird in flight. Her season with Nottingham Playhouse had been successful, hard work and application paying off. The *Z Cars* episode had led to a second television play, involving logistical problems while in Nottingham; Liza though had uncovered a steely toughness not apparent in other areas of her life, and problems appeared to her as no more than stepping-stones to fulfilment of ambition. Just short of her twenty-second birthday, she aimed in the near future for at least one season at Stratford; Penelope had approved, and decided to work towards arranging a Royal Shakespeare Company audition in the New Year. Liza would be prepared to take anything; a play-as-cast contract, understudying, anything that would take her into the company where she might watch and learn from the very best. Parts in Shakespeare were, she knew, horribly few for women. Young men could often manage to get on stage as spear-carriers or attendants, but now Liza remembered the dire figures quoted by her practical-minded headmistress to her mother, and prepared for a struggle.

The end of her run in Wilde's *The Importance of Being Earnest* was in sight at the Queen's. This was the first time she had performed in the same part for more than a week at a stretch, and repertory experience had not prepared her for the difficulties of bringing freshness to a character's words and thoughts six days a week for an indefinite period. She quickly learned that a fine line must be trodden between achieving that freshness, and putting the rest of the company off its stride by introducing innovations. Once she gave

Gwendolen a fit of sneezing – it seemed a good idea for some reason that quickly escaped her – and earned the wrath of the director for surprising Lady Bracknell off her cue.

In the late winter she had secured the part of Celia in *As You Like It* on the Third Programme, a prestigious production with a star cast and her first part in radio. The technique for this medium, specific in its intimacy and close teamwork, had been both nerve-racking and enthralling. That the producer had become beguiled by her charms had given the work added zest. She had been dined by him at Claridge's, taken to a sought-after midnight film première, and had almost finished up in his bed. She had left it very late to make up her mind about whether she wanted to sleep with him. He was attractive in a forty-ish, untidy, intellectual way and had likeable, sad grey eyes. But when he so patently expected that she would, after sharing a reefer and a bottle with him, be accompanying him into his cold black and white bedroom she had suddenly decided no, not tonight, and had extricated herself with consummate skill.

A seven-year film contract with ABC had yielded nothing yet but a series of poor scripts of stereotypical air-head parts, but Liza was in no hurry; theatre experience was more valuable at this stage. And a tempting offer had just been garnered by the vigilant Penelope, of the part of Masha in Chekhov's *Three Sisters*, to open in Bournemouth in July and tour six theatres before a probable West End run in the autumn.

So; her life was moving smoothly along lines that Liza did not doubt were leading her to the top of the professional tree. Her stage presence was powerful. Eliciting attention by silence at exactly the right second in speech, and by an intuitive hoarding of movement, when she even lifted a finger it had impact. And when she turned her beautiful, tapered back on an audience they watched that too; her entire persona generated close interest.

The area filled by Edward Anderssen, though, was generating turmoil. Liza, on the Sunday after her conversation with Hannah, ran a hot bath, slipped out of her robe and into the silken foam of her expensive bath oil. Sunday was the day when she did as she pleased, ruled not by the clock but by her whim. She needed to think, and did that best immersed in steaming luxury.

She loved Edward Anderssen, and was finding it hugely inconvenient and quite uncomfortable. It was a see-saw business; for a few days she would feel all-powerful, believing he would in the end find it impossible to continue his stubborn fight to remain in the north when she was in the south. She had only to wait a little longer . . . She did so, and nothing happened. Then came doubt again – was he going to ignore her siren call? – and she would plummet into a black hole. She had been in one for two days now, it was affecting her work adversely and she must stop it. Liza stared at the ceiling.

When the phone rang she pulled herself from her deep reverie with difficulty, frowning. She had a mind to let it ring; then rose suddenly, water and foam streaming down her body, and reached for a towel.

'Hello?' Clutching the huge towel, she pushed the receiver under tendrils of damp hair.

'Liza darling. So pleased to find you in.' Anderssen's voice was warm. Liza hooked the instrument under her chin and began to rub herself dry, perching on the sofa arm.

'You also find me wet, I was in the bath.'

'Oh – my apologies. D'you want me to call you back?'

'It's OK, the worst is over now.'

'This is an unusual time for a tub, surely?'

'Anything goes on a Sunday – nothing is unusual.'

'Ah . . . So how are things apart from the wet?'

'They're up to standard, thanks.' She began to dry her legs and feet.

'I wondered if you would care to put up a guest for a night or two next week?'

'Anyone in mind?'

'Me. I have an exhibition at the Fareham Gallery, starting Monday week.'

'You are a pig! You must have known *ages* ago!' She dropped the receiver as she stood up in agitation. 'Edward Anderssen, what is to be done with you?'

'I shall make a suggestion when the time is propitious. Meanwhile, please say if it is convenient,' he said in a prim voice. 'I kept it to myself for a while in case there was a cock-up.'

'You may come. Convenience has nothing to do with it. *Come*.'

'Fine. Now, go and get dry. I'll call you midweek, around 11.30. 'Bye, darling.'

Liza rewrapped herself in a dry towel and reached on the mantelpiece for a cigarette, which she took to the window. She turned to examine the room, her brilliant eyes reflective. She was pleased with the Notting Hill flat; not cheap, but worth the rent . . . half a well-built villa in a quiet road close to the tube and bus routes – though Liza rarely used either now. This room had pale walls, with two long sofas covered in heavy oatmeal linen. A broad sweep of oatmeal curtaining had a frieze of appliquéd flowers and fruits which was startlingly beautiful when drawn across. She had found a heavily ornate coffer to stand along the wall, and a long, low table with a top into which jewel-toned Victorian tiles had been sunk. There was a workmanlike desk, plenty of bookshelves, a giant art nouveau vase filled with stately iris with their spear-like leaves; lamps where they were needed.

Liza nodded, satisfied. Then she appeared almost to ignite with joy, dropping her towel as she whirled naked round the furniture, singing.

He was coming. Coming here, to her. She could do the rest, she was certain of it.

Still singing, she stepped back into the bath and turned on the hot tap again.

They came together like two halves of a whole. On stage, Liza became incandescent, glowing like an exotic flower so that the other actors appeared just a touch drab. Her voice took on a stronger, sweeter timbre; her timing was matchless. The power contained in her brain and spirit ratcheted up several notches due to Anderssen's proximity. She felt it swell within, felt there was nothing she might not accomplish under such conditions. He came twice to see her performance, and during the day she went twice to see his work at the gallery. Both were impressed, both were aware of the other's talent, both were proud of it. Their love was intrinsically threaded into this pride and nourished by it. Anderssen's second visit to her play was on the night of the final performance; there were enthusiastic standing ovations from the entire house and he could feel his pride and love increasing as he joined in. Liza accepted her own share of the applause with enormous grace and modesty, turned always towards the principal actor, and the redoubtable Lady Bracknell in her magnificent bonnet and beaded black taffetas. As the demure young Gwendolen, Liza had kept her fire under control. Now she curtsyed deeply, eyes down, but at the third curtain-call allowed her eyes to gleam with laughter and brought her dimples into play.

She had demanded he go backstage afterwards to join the cast and guests thronging the dressing-rooms, where champagne flowed. The revival of Wilde's classic had been a success. The final night had been filmed, and plans were afoot to sell it to the BBC. Cheeks were pink, eyes shone, adrenalin flowed as copiously as did the drink. Anderssen watched as actors projected themselves according to their natures and their adrenalin levels, none more positively than Liza. She swayed laughing towards one guest, then another, white shoulders and breasts glowing like pearls above her tiny waist, hair tumbling about her graceful neck and flushed peachy cheeks. When finally she climbed into their taxi she was as high as a kite, strung tight as a violin. He tucked her coat about her, as he would a vulnerable child.

'Quite a night, sweetheart.' He lifted her hand and sandwiched it between his own. She looked up with glittering eyes, laughing, and the pearls in her ears glimmered like milky stars.

'Mm-mm.' She kissed his neck and Anderssen felt the warmth of her breath. 'Did you enjoy it, darling?'

'I did. Will you sleep late tomorrow?' He pushed his hand under her hair and her head fell back on it. When he kissed her parted lips there was the warmth again, like a stoked fire at her core. Her lips closed, clung; Anderssen felt himself travelling, drawn inexorably through a hot dark tunnel, and he hardened with wanting her as he guessed she intended he should.

The taxi ground into the kerbside. He extricated Liza and they turned for the door, close as a single shadow.

'Liza. Liza.'

She leaned against the hall door, laughing again.

'Teddy. Edward. Would you like a drink?' she said, and moved to the kitchen. 'I bought this for us to celebrate.' She waved a magnum of champagne at him.

'Why don't we take it to bed? I made us some chicken sandwiches after you left for the theatre – we'll take those too.' He took the bottle from her to put on the table and circled her waist with his arms. Liza kissed his neck again, then his ear, and gave a husky little laugh.

'Let's go to bed anyway.'

They were almost angry at first in their passion, in their need to express so urgent a desire. They bruised one another's arms, holding so fast; only when Liza winced did Anderssen pull himself up. He began to cover her body with kisses, murmuring endearments. Clothes were fast discarded as they fell on the bed and strained tight against one another, unwilling to be separate by a hair's breadth. He would have waited but Liza refused, pushing hard against him, so that when with a groan of pleasure he entered her Liza groaned too, for it seemed he had reached her very heart.

'Darling . . . darling.' She was breathless, as though he had entered and possessed every pore of her body. 'Oh, I love you so. Never leave me. Never!'

'Never – never – never.' Each word stoked the rhythm of their passion, consuming them now as that rhythm quickened with unstoppable inevitability. Both were conscious of nothing but the other's body, pushing them on and up until they reached the crest and tumbled, shaking and crying back to reality.

They clung together, exhausted and speechless. After a while, neither knowing when, Edward Anderssen rolled off the bed and away, to return with a tumbler and the champagne. Liza opened an eye.

'We'll have to share . . .' He climbed back into bed and struggled with the cork. Finally it shot off and they were sprayed with champagne foam.

'Fantastic!' Liza wiped it across her over-warm skin. They drank thirstily from the tumbler, smiling at one another over the rim. 'Now the sandwiches?'

He pulled a face and made a second trip to the kitchen. They ate and drank in contented silence. Then Liza said in a pause between bites:

'Darling – shall we look for a place in the country? Not too far out but somewhere right for all needs? I could alert estate agents, and view on Sundays.' She leaned across him for the refilled tumbler and another sandwich.

Anderssen pursed his lips. She saw it and paused mid-bite.

'You did say we were going to be together? Just now?'

He sighed. 'Liza – you know it's not that easy.'

'So you didn't mean it? When you said you'd never leave me?'

Anderssen sighed again. 'I didn't *not* mean it. But there's no use being simplistic about this.'

'Ah. So you *don't* want me to look for a place for us? For us to be married? You just lied, because you were enjoying sex so much and didn't want it spoiled? You wanted to have that amazing orgasm uninterrupted by boring practicalities. Yes; I see.' Liza put down the remains of the sandwich.

'For God's sake, darling – do stop being childish. You know –'

'Childish?' Liza sat up straight. 'Oh it's *childish* to expect the man who professes to love you, who is at that moment making love to you, to tell the truth?' Her eyes began to spark. 'Goodness, what a stupid childish idiot . . .'

Her chest suddenly gave a great heaving shudder and she burst into tears. Before Anderssen could make a move she flung the tumbler hard at his head. It glanced off him just above the ear, splattered him with the remaining champagne and smashed to the floor beyond the bed.

'Christ!' He rubbed his head, dazed. Liza shot out of bed, dived for his travel-bag and swung that at him, hitting his shoulder.

'You take that and get out!' she shouted between sobs. 'Don't ever come *near* me! You're just a common liar, a vile cheat – you've *never* cared about me!'

She turned to the wall and buried her face, weeping with a hopeless, alarming sound. Anderssen was standing now at the other side of the bed, rubbing his head, watching her. Then he walked round and stood at her shoulder.

'Liza. Look – it is not in the least like that. I do love you –'

'But you don't want to make a home with me – what sense does that make?' She turned a red-eyed, tear-wet face to him. 'Just go – you've done enough damage. Liars can do terrible harm to people who trust them – didn't you know that?' Shivering now, she dived back into bed and pulled the covers over her head, her sobs muffled and hoarse.

He stared at the hump under the duvet. Then he lifted the edge of a curtain and looked down into the deserted road where cars were parked nose to tail along the kerbside. On one, a black and white cat sat washing its face under the lamp. He dropped the curtain and knelt by the bed.

'Liza, can you forget all that crap? Forgive me? I didn't get it right.'

There was silence under the bedclothes. He turned up a corner. 'I was wrong; I do see that. It *is* inconvenient for me to leave my place up north . . . but of course you're right, love should not be chucked away because it's inconvenient. I do value you, you know . . . more than you can imagine.'

After further silence there was movement; Liza's hand emerged, then her flushed, miserable face, with swollen red eyes.

'Do you mean the lie – about never leaving me – was *not* a lie?'

'I mean I am prepared to give it a shot if you can still face it. And I'll try like the devil to make it work. I'm just a bloody coward, that's the problem.'

After a pause Liza said in a tight little voice, 'Most men are. Can we go to sleep now? I'm tired enough to die.'

He watched her as she curled up and closed her eyes, and his eyes held for a moment a pale, bleak emptiness.

Three Sisters played to excellent notices in Brighton, their second venue. 'Liza Vaughan is fast developing into an actress of unusual presence' . . . 'Liza Vaughan commands attention for a freshly seen portrayal of Masha, victim of a dull marriage and a tragic infatuation', were among the reviews. When the company transferred to Bournemouth, before Cambridge and finally Sheffield, they had already melded first-class individual performances into an attractive whole. Liza developed a good working rapport with Olga, the eldest sister, but had more difficulty with the girl playing the younger sister Irena. Complete understanding of the character of Masha was also hard for her to find; but she mined and burrowed through the text to reveal it finally with touching conviction.

Hannah, who had seen the play in Brighton with Matthew, was hesitant when Laurie told her he and his parents were going to Bournemouth for a week at the start of the school holidays ... it might be presumptuous to suggest that Jonet might wish to see her half-sister in a performance. In the end she said nothing; if they saw the billboards they could make up their own minds.

Laurie was the first to see a handbill in the reception area of their hotel. He read it with concentration then pointed it out to his parents, wandering past for an after-dinner stroll on their second evening.

'Shall we go? It would be great to see her – it's been ages. And we've *never* seen her on the stage.'

Jonet said nothing, examining the notice. Mark jingled the door keys.

'Why not ... What d'you think, Jonet? If we could get tickets ...'

Jonet seemed unable to commit herself. 'We might walk along and look at the photos outside,' she said reluctantly. So they strolled towards the theatre, Jonet walking between her husband on the outside, and Laurie on the inside, no one quite touching.

Jonet was two weeks off her fortieth birthday. She was trim, good to look at in tailored navy slacks, a blue and green checked shirt and with a chunky, light blue sweater embroidered with pastel flowers draped over her shoulders. Her dark hair was cut to fall in a soft fringe, then comb back and turn under, slightly backcombed to give height to the crown and to show her pretty, pearl-studded ears. A few hair-fine lines about her eyes and mouth betrayed constant tension; her thin hand wore an expensive emerald and diamond ring that looked too heavy for it. Her brown eyes were serious, watchful as the family crossed the road and approached the Winter Gardens, where her half-sister's photograph would be displayed.

She had seen so little of Liza . . . a relationship had never been formed and it was unlikely now that one would be. Twenty-two years ago she had stood by Liza's cot, looking down at the two-month old baby girl, and recalled now the sensation of choked and breathless antagonism. Her mother had, she knew, wished her to pick up the baby, or at least touch her. But Jonet had remained frozen, unable to put out a finger, and desolate that her mother could not understand why this was . . . why she felt so wounded and betrayed.

She did not recall ever meeting Liza without Hannah being there too; tense, alert for signs of difficulty . . . struggling to accept that this situation was unlikely to change for the better but always hoping that it might, that Jonet would begin to love her young half-sister. Poor Mother; she really had tried over the years. But she was waiting, hoping for the impossible. Jonet had no idea how to change her attitude, and perhaps saw no need to. She moved towards the theatre now and studied the publicity photographs outside.

'There she is –' Laurie pointed. They stood in a row before the studio print, Mark peering close because he was not wearing his spectacles. He was a good-looking man, dark hair showing its first grey, tall and distinguished. Successful now in his career, he had decided last year that they should move further up the property ladder into a detached house in a small estate of 'executive' homes on Reading's outskirts. He enjoyed his work and rarely felt the need for a holiday, but was anxious for them occasionally to take a break as a family, conscious this year that, quite soon, his son might prefer not to accompany them.

'Shall we see if they have tickets?' Laurie looked at his mother, knowing she would have the deciding vote. Mark nodded his agreement.

'Why not? It has excellent notices. If she's as good as they say and her career's set to take off she may soon disappear to Hollywood.'

Jonet's mouth tightened. Her own career, planned and worked for since so early an age, had been blighted by Laurie's birth . . . Women who can work only in term-time are passed over in the climb to the top librarianships. Two years ago she had been invited to apply for a supervisory post that would have entailed full hours. She had discussed it with the woman who cleaned for her twice weekly, and found her willing to come in weekday mornings in school holidays, making lunch for twelve-year-old Laurie before leaving. Mark, though, had vetoed the plan; they did not need the money, he had pointed out, and it was unnecessarily cruel to leave the boy in a stranger's care all morning *and* on his own all afternoon.

The fight had been bitter. Jonet had seen it as Laurie's temporary comfort taking precedence over her desired full-time career. By the time he was eighteen he would have no need of her, but by then her chance would have gone. Mark had wilted under her frustrated fury, while clinging to his point. She should not have had a child without being prepared to face the sacrifices that meant for a woman. Neither had been 'latchkey' children themselves, and should not inflict that on their own son.

Jonet had capitulated with smouldering bad grace, and a rift had opened between man and wife that had left its tensions. She had not, to her credit, blamed Laurie, who hearing of the arrangement had been more than willing to fit in – it might indeed have worked to his advantage, as he might have spent extra time at Hannah and Matthew's place, which was just fine for him. Dreams of a senior post at the British Library finally crumbled for Jonet; she saw herself now as a might-have-been, and Mark's talk of her bastard sister's career served only to rub her nose in her own disappointments.

Mark, seeing a refusal coming, took the plunge. He was of course aware of the long-running trauma and thought it long overdue that it should peter out.

'I shall see what they have – box office is still open –' He dived inside, followed closely by Laurie. Jonet stared at the publicity board. She was part angry at being hustled and part relieved for having been, for against her will she actually wanted to see Liza's play. Well; she wanted to . . . but knew she would hate to witness a triumph by Liza. What she probably hoped to see was that Liza was nothing special after all, only a jobbing actress.

'Thursday evening.' Mark waved the tickets, smiling. 'Just got there as they were ready to shut up shop for the night. Stalls . . . close enough to catch the spit if they get carried away!'

'Dad!' Laurie shouted with laughter. 'We'll bring our plastic macs!'

Jonet suddenly smiled; the beasts were delighted that they'd out-manoeuvred her. 'OK – you win. Come on, let's walk along the beach as far as the Chine then go up and around. Then a drink . . . all right?' She linked arms with them, savouring the momentary unity of her family.

On Wednesday morning, on his way back to lunch from the swimming pool, Laurie went up to the theatre box office. He pushed a folded sheet of paper from his drawing book under the grille.

'Please will you give this to Liza Vaughan? She's my auntie.' He hurried away through the gardens, smiling and swinging his damp towel. They were getting cleaned up for dinner that evening when the phone rang and Mark took the call, pushing an arm into his clean shirt.

'Liza?' His eyebrows shot up. 'Good grief, what a surprise! Yes – hang on a minute, I'll get him for you. Oh – no, of course you are. Yes . . . yes, tomorrow night. Oh well . . . that would be great. Yes – sure we'll do that. We're looking forward to it; we saw the advert in the hotel. Right, thanks a lot. See you tomorrow. 'Bye.'

He looked at Jonet. 'Liza. Laurie left a note saying we had tickets for tomorrow night, and that he would like to see her, and this number. She says would we like to go backstage to say hello afterwards.'

'All I did was say *I'd* like to see her if she'd time,' Laurie protested. 'Of *course* I'd like to see her. We used to play together. I remember it – and she used to play her records for me. What's wrong with wanting to see her? She's my aunt after all!'

'You should have said,' repeated Jonet tightly. 'Now you've landed us *all* in for it.'

'Well, what's wrong with that? She's family, isn't she?' Laurie defended himself. He exchanged glances with his father; both knew why Jonet was angry but neither intended talking about it. Family skeletons were uncomfortable out in the air, better off locked in cupboards.

*

Jonet was still angry as they waited for the lights to dim. She had been painted into a corner and would be blamed if she messed up the paint jumping out of it. Both Mark and Laurie expected that she would now bow to the inevitable and go and be polite to Liza, making friendly noises. And she had no reason to believe that Laurie was lying when he insisted he had only written that *he* would like to see Liza, which meant that his only crime lay in not telling them he had contacted her. So: if she did not bow to circumstances, Jonet saw that she would be deemed an unfriendly troublemaker.

She sighed. The house lights dimmed.

When they went up for the last time as the curtain dropped, the applause was unequivocally enthusiastic. Laurie leaned across his father and nodded, bright-eyed.

'Good eh, Mum?' It had definitely not been his sort of meat; people hanging around talking, not much action except for the fire, and that guy had even been killed in the duel well off-stage, all they'd heard was one shot from a distance. But it had been strangely interesting, even so. And most of all because of Liza. He'd hardly known her at first, dressed all in black. But as the play advanced he actually forgot it was his youthful aunt up there. It was Masha, who was pretty bored at first then falls heavily for Vershinin. And goes somewhat off her trolley when he's posted away and she's stuck with her boring old schoolmaster husband again. When she had said 'I think a human being has got to have some faith, or at least he's got to *seek* faith. Otherwise his life will be empty, empty . . . How can you live, and not know why cranes fly? Why children are born, why the stars shine in the sky! You must either know why you live, or else . . . nothing matters . . . everything's just wild grass . . .' Laurie felt his eyes warm with tears.

'Great, wasn't it, Dad?' Everyone was still clapping. Now the three came on alone, Liza in the middle, holding hands and bowing. Her extraordinary eyes shone out at the audience, she smiled her amazing smile and everyone responded. Sitting quite still now, Laurie found he had a definite lump in his throat.

'Laurie!' Liza held out her arms and he dived into them. 'It's been *ages* – much too long. I'm so glad you sent the note.' Over his dark head she smiled at his parents. 'It's really nice to see you all, thanks for popping round. Well – goodness Laurie, you're not far off as tall as your poor old aunt!' She held his shoulders to inspect him and Laurie gave a sheepish grin.

'You were super,' he told her. 'Great.'

'It was a really enjoyable evening.' Mark added his own more restrained plaudits. Jonet, cheeks pale with effort, nodded agreement.

'We thoroughly enjoyed it, Liza. The production was first-rate.'

'It will need to be if it's to transfer to the West End.' Liza smiled. 'There's a lot of hot competition. Mummy said she enjoyed it when she and Matthew came to see it in Brighton. Look – do have a quick drink – I must, I'm so dry I could disintegrate! Sorry there aren't enough chairs . . . there's never enough *anything* backstage!'

She pulled a bottle from a small fridge in the corner. The room was cramped, lit by harsh bulbs with a long table along one side littered with tubs and tubes of make-up and with a wig-stand on which draped Masha's dark curls. Liza's own hair was scraped back under a tight gauze scarf. Her face had not been cleansed yet of her stage make-up and in this light the accentuated skin tones and dark khol eye pencil gave her an air of unreality. This hyped-up, exotic creature in the cluttered room seemed to have no connection with them; with their quiet orderly lives. The black taffeta dress she had worn in the final scene was flung over a tall screen of woven cane, and an elaborate Edwardian hat was hung on either corner. There was only one easy chair, piled with garments, and an upright chair on whose tapestry seat was curled a black and white cat, sleeping soundly.

'Now; glasses . . .' They were located on a tray on the floor behind the open door. Liza smiled at Mark. 'Would you?' She handed him the bottle of white wine. 'The opener can't be far away –' He found it in the corner of her make-up counter and got to work. Liza meanwhile peeled off the head gauze, shook her hair with a huge sigh of relief and began to brush it hard.

'God, that's better!' She took her glass from Mark with a brilliant smile which failed to hide her utter exhaustion, and pulled her multi-coloured silk robe further across her throat. 'Well now; shall we drink to the family?'

There was a small sharp silence. Laurie's father had given him a glass of wine too and all four stood in a circle, glasses held out. Then Mark Shapiro lifted his.

'To the family. Good health.'

They drank; Laurie coughed awkwardly, and apologised, blushing, and Liza laughed. 'Oh Laurie, is it not to your taste? Never mind, it will help you sleep.'

'What d'you do now?' Mark asked her. 'A meal? Might we –'

'Oh, thank you, Mark.' She shook her head, laughing again. 'But it's back to the hotel for a bath now, then something on a tray while I make phone calls and things, and a colleague is popping in to discuss some problem.' She finished her wine in a gulp, long throat arched. 'And I have to go through a batch of brochures from estate agents – I'm house-hunting, and it's a pretty exhausting job!'

She passed her smile around the three of them, kissed Laurie's cheek. 'I'm so very pleased to have seen you all. And that you enjoyed the evening. Maybe I'll see you around Christmas time? Come, I'll show you the quickest way out.'

As the stage door shut behind them they stood silent for a moment in the warm evening. Then Mark Shapiro said quietly:

'Shall we take a few minutes' stroll on the beach? I'd like to cool down, I think. Then how about coffee and doughnuts before bed?'

Jonet seemed to be carved from stone in the summer moonlight, her face expressionless. He took her arm, then that of his son. 'Come on – let's go.'

When Edward Anderssen phoned on a Sunday morning in late November to say he was in London unexpectedly and could he call in, Liza searched out the latest folder of house brochures that had arrived, and notes on a riverside house she had viewed last Sunday. She had been able to do very little while on tour, but since *Three Sisters* had come to the West End in early October she had recontacted several agents. She was, in fact, depressed by their failure to come up with a range of suitable properties; it seemed her specification of somewhere close to London but also close to specialised wildlife areas was an impossible one. She was mostly getting details of large country houses with acres of parkland, maybe a lake or some other appendage, all hopelessly unsuitable.

Anderssen had come down to Sheffield for a weekend while she was playing there. They had walked on the moors, and stayed the night in a secluded hotel on the pleasant upper reaches of the Loxley, to the west of the city. There had been a flare-up, Liza now recalled with a degree of guilt. He had brought down his satchel of sketching materials and she had fired from the hip, saying she had hoped they might have given complete attention to each other on what was such a brief reunion. Afterwards she was contrite, explaining that it was simply because she so valued their time together. But the damage was done.

This time she was determined to be undemanding, to demonstrate that she was not the supreme egoist he had accused her of being. Hair-washing and bathing were done in – for her – record time. Humming, she put fresh sheets on the bed, then shot round to a first-class delicatessen in her new red Austin. She had not actually passed her test yet . . . but with typical confidence – arrogance? – had applied for it, almost at once. She had intended writing to her father today, a letter long overdue . . . maybe she would phone him instead, he loved them to chat and insisted she make reverse-charge calls whenever she wanted. She would invite him over in early spring; she might have found a house by then and he and Edward could meet.

He arrived before she was quite ready. Liza checked on her reflection a last time and, smiling, hurried to the door; she knew she looked good anyway in a flowing velvet caftan, printed in jewel colours that perfectly complemented her vivid hair and eyes.

'Darling.' She went into his arms with a radiant smile. They remained close for a moment; then he pushed the door closed and, seeing his face, Liza was suddenly afraid.

'Teddy? What's wrong?' She caught at his hand. He held it, gave it a small squeeze, then relinquished it to shrug off his coat and drop it on a hall chair.

'Can we have a drink, Liza?'

'Well – of course.' She went into the sitting room, struggling to stifle the fear that rose to choke her. Reaching the drinks cupboard she stared at him. 'Teddy; tell me *now*. What's happened?'

He looked drawn, older. His hair needed cutting: it flopped across his forehead and he pushed it away with an impatient hand.

'Liza . . . there's no easy way to say this. So all I can do is tell you that I have been offered a commission to do a book on Malawi wildlife. I've thought about it very carefully indeed, and now I've accepted.'

Liza looked blank. 'Malawi? Where's that?' Anderssen gave her a tiny grin.

'Didn't I always say your geography was as full of holes as a colander? It's in Africa. I'm flying out tomorrow week.'

'Tomorrow week,' she repeated. She examined his face with close attention. 'How long will you be gone?'

'At least six months.' His voice was flat. 'Are you going to get us that drink?'

'Probably not. Look, will you be clear about this? Are you asking me to put everything on hold for six months? Or –' Liza hesitated.

'I think a clean break is far better for both of us.' He paused before adding: 'Though I realise it's almost impossible for you to see it that way right now.'

Liza stared at him, her eyes like blue ice. 'Since when did you know what was best for *me*?'

He sighed. 'Well probably only lately, darling –'

'Don't darling me,' she spat, wrapping her arms about her body as if to protect herself. 'You tell me after two years together –'

'Together! That's rich!' His laugh held no humour. 'Liza, I would have no problem counting the *hours* in those two years we actually spent together. We have, I grant you, spent plenty chasing up and down the country after one another, and on the telephone trying to work out ways and means, and getting ourselves het up and stressed out and bloody *nowhere*.'

He stopped, making an obvious effort to collect himself, loathing anything approaching a scene. 'Liza, *please* will you make an honest attempt to understand what I am feeling here, and how impossibly difficult it has been to come to the conclusion I have finally reached? I just cannot live my life on the edge of a volcano. And that's how it's been feeling for a while now –'

'A volcano?' she interrupted. 'Is that how you see me? Interesting.'

'That's how you are sometimes,' he said bluntly. 'Like last time I was here. Hyped up with adrenalin and alcohol, beside yourself. So to calm you, to please you, I agreed with what you want. Not because I believed that it was wise, a good move, but simply to *please* you.'

He put up his hand as Liza drew a sharp breath. 'For both our sakes, hear me. When I really thought about how it might be, Liza, I began to fear for us. If you moved right into the centre of my life I believe you'd take it over. My own identity would be swallowed in your needs, your plans, your career, your emotional crises. I'd end up running hard just to keep you reasonably content, while *my* life slid out of control. When we've managed time together lately it's been pretty fraught, you going up and down like a yo-yo and resenting me for not being there when you want me.'

He held out a hand, then it fell to his side in a hopeless gesture. 'Maybe you could live this way, Liza, but it's killing me. I cannot work under such conditions and I have to call quits. That's the bottom line.'

'Is it really?' Liza's eyes shone with fury. 'Well, the bottom line for *me* is that I regret every moment I've wasted in your company. You're nothing but an empty shell, d'you know that? You don't want to *live*! You just want to sit hunched over your wretched work day after day, nice and safe. You're a deceiver, a cheat, a liar! God – to think I believed that you actually *loved* me.' She laughed and her eyes shone more brightly, this time with tears.

'I do,' he said quietly. 'At least, I almost certainly still do. But right now all I feel is bone-weary. We're just too opposite, Liza. We want such utterly different things out of life that our lines never meet at any point – probably never could. And you would destroy me.'

'Get out while you can, then!' She flung the words at him like darts. 'Run off and hide in – where is it? *Malawi*? God in heaven, Malawi! Just what you deserve, a year in Malawi. I'll try to remember to buy the book when it comes out – though I may not have time to look at the pretty pictures – I'm booked up for some time ahead now. I'm a success, you know. A runaway success!'

With a sudden whooping uncontrollable sob Liza ran past him into the hall. He reached her and pinned her against the wall, breathing hard.

'Not like this, Liza. You'll regret it, I swear. For Christ's sake try to be civilised about it!'

She struggled, freed an arm and hit him hard across the face. 'Yes, Edward; like *this*. Because this is how I *feel*! Now get right away, and never come back. And I wish you no luck at all!'

He stepped back then; stood motionless for a moment, looking at her as the imprint of her palm reddened his thin cheek. Then he picked up his coat and went out.

Liza remained still until she heard the engine of his car start up. When it had faded along the road she turned and walked unsteadily back to the sitting room, hair swinging about her white face, and reached for the decanter of brandy.

Liza had phoned, and when Hannah heard the taxi turning in the drive she hurried to the door, but there was a look about her daughter that silenced her cheerful greeting. She kissed an icy cheek.

'I'm pleased we were here today, dear. We might have gone to Wales, but for the man who's bought the restaurant coming to see me. We'll be having a bite of supper soon. Would you like to go up and rest for a while?' she added softly. 'You're very tired . . .'

'Yes. But I should like a brandy.' Liza walked into the warm sitting room, its curtains closed against the winter night, and lamps splashing soft light in pools. She dropped into a chair and said in a flat, unfamiliar tone: 'I am so cold. I simply cannot get warm.'

It was mild for November but Hannah poked the fire into life, poured Liza a brandy then hurried upstairs to switch on the electric blanket. When she returned, Liza was clutching the glass with both hands and staring into it.

'Liza, would it help to talk? Matthew's doing some letters. Or do you just want to sleep? I can bring you a tray up later?'

Hannah stood by the fireplace, looking down at the girl's bent head. Then she sat down and waited. Whatever had brought Liza home on a Sunday night in this state was surely better out in the open than left to fester.

Liza tipped back her head and swallowed the brandy at a gulp. She shuddered, grinned and held out the empty glass. 'Thanks. That's better. You are looking, Mother dear, at a rejected lady. *I* have been *rejected* – cast off –' she threw out her arm in an extravagant gesture. 'Another brandy would be nice. I feel like an old sock that's been thrown in a bin.'

'That won't last long.' Hannah handed her more brandy. 'Leave it at two, darling, or you'll muff your lines tomorrow. Who is he?'

'What does it matter who he is now? He has gone to Malawi.' Liza giggled, and Hannah realised that the last drink had not been the first. 'Malawi is a silly name for a country, don't you think?'

'What will he do there?' Hannah asked politely. Liza frowned.

'Why, paint of course. That's all he ever does.'

'And is that the problem?'

Liza's face became blank momentarily; a slate wiped clean. She stood up then, a lean silhouette of checked flannel shift, black legs, black pumps.

'The problem is that I actually loved him quite a lot.'

Hannah moved up the room to see Liza's face clearly. It was full of pain, and also of anger spilling over from some boiling, invisible core.

'I'm learning the lessons, though. It won't happen again, Mummy dear. No man will *ever* hurt me again – that is my firm promise to myself. And one day I may even settle the score.'

When Liza had gone up Hannah stood irresolute, twisting her wedding ring. Hurt was never pleasant to witness, least of all to one's child. But the vengeful quality of Liza's answering anger was even less pleasant; not a quality she had passed down, nor one she could recall in David Vaughan.

So strange the mixes families were capable of producing . . . and none more strange than Liza.

Chapter Fourteen

Laurie was struggling with his O-level syllabus. His mocks, done in January, had shown up his weaknesses and he was depressingly certain that short of a miracle, he would be in trouble when the time came to sit the actual papers. A feeling of resentment was growing towards his parents for throwing him to the lions, then leaving him to climb out of the cage as best he might. They expected great things of him because they were paying for a better education, and demanded value for money. As Laurie saw it, *he* got nothing extra for the money. He disliked the masters (with the exception of the English master who was a fanatical gardener and had loaned Laurie a piece of garden for him to plant out) and felt he was merely being crammed with facts, the majority of which it was impossible for him to retain, or make use of in the foreseeable future.

He hated academic subjects, which both alarmed and occasionally cowed him. Practical work was more appealing, projects he could pursue with his hands working in harmony with his brain. Non-competitive, non-aggressive, he was slow but thorough in whatever he did, and had a charmingly quirky imagination. When asked to write an essay about flight, his contemporaries had listed the history of man's efforts to become airborne and after. Laurie had handed in an imaginative and well-researched probe into the various means of flight in the insect, bird and animal world, ending with a humorous glimpse into the possibilities of elephants flying.

Laurie's mind was not mainstream but gently eccentric, needing understanding and confidence-building to fulfil his potential. He was not given this by his parents, who simply wanted him to produce the requisite number of O and A levels to justify their outlay and see him to university to study for a respectable profession. This, Laurie was incapable of delivering.

Hannah understood his nature better than any, which was why he enjoyed being with her. She and Matthew encouraged him to make things grow, and in this he took a delight. Matthew pored over natural history books with him, and together they explored life in ponds, under stones, across fields and up trees. Matthew was the natural grandfather for him that Darrow Bates the steelman never could have been. Hannah saw this and was grateful.

Now she was finally retired, Hannah enjoyed her life so much she could not understand why she had fought so long against selling up. Fear had been in imagining long days impossible to fill; reality was that her days were – or seemed to be – as full as ever. The last week in business had been an emotional one, with a seriously extravagant party in the restaurant one evening attended by staff past and present and almost the entire local Chamber of Commerce. Tears were narrowly avoided; when reminded that she had had the restaurant for twenty years, Hannah was shocked to realise that was two years longer than she had run the Taibach shop and bakery. Over half a century of work ... She was sobered, thinking back over the span. The First World War came into focus; the first job up at Madoc's farm, the closest she could get to war work at fourteen. The job in the shell factory, face and hands yellow with chemicals; one of the 'canaries'. So long ago – as were her first attempts at cooking for the Taibach better-off, progressing slowly to her bakery stall in the market. Now, finis . . . A new page to turn.

After the party she and Matthew were free to escape to Wales for a quiet Christmas. Or rather a Christmas that had been planned as quiet; it turned out the opposite. Jake, his wife Rose and new baby daughter arrived at short notice. At even shorter notice came Liza, complete with a desire to wreak vengeance on any man – excepting Matthew, whom she regarded as special – for the wrong done her by Anderssen. Her father was also exempt; she would have flown to see him but had only a couple of free days.

Hannah and Matthew loaded up with supplies and hoped for the best, which was not what they got. Rose was entirely taken over by the baby, Ruth, who was demanding to be fed two-hourly or else. In the intervals between the traumatic routine of the milk bar Rose slept or ate; she had neither time nor energy to spare for Jake.

This left Jake feeling a degree of neglect, and suitable prey for Liza. She began a crash programme of infiltration, which bore fruit with remarkable speed, as she intended it should. She and Jake talked quietly in corners, exchanging slow smiles, sat close enough for shoulders to touch. Rose noticed nothing, being in turn asleep, eating, or feeding her child; Matthew did, and was not pleased.

'I know *why* she's doing it,' he told Hannah tersely. 'She's doing it to get her own back on men, exactly as you say. But I want her to *stop* doing it, at least in our house. Will you tell her or shall I?'

'She has to go tomorrow,' Hannah pleaded. 'She

can't do much damage in the time left, surely? Not enough to warrant a showdown?'

'Can she not?' Matthew laughed unkindly. 'Hannah; I have never ceased to be *thunderstruck* by the amount of damage your daughter can do in no time at all when she puts her mind to it.'

'And can you back that unpleasant remark with evidence?' Hannah bridled at the insult. 'Why not ask your son to stop being an idiot instead? It takes two, you know.'

'Not when one of them is Liza,' Matthew snapped. 'I give fair warning, let her cause trouble between Jake and Rose and she won't be welcome here again.'

'You may have forgotten.' Hannah was icy now. 'But this house is half mine.' Bested, Matthew became childish.

'Then you'd better confine her to your half, and more civilised guests can stay in my half!' He marched out of their bedroom, slamming the door and leaving Hannah amazed. The first time they had ever had so unpleasant a slanging match . . . and caused entirely by Liza.

She combed her hair slowly to give herself time to settle down. One had to wonder, on the Edward Anderssen front, what percentage of Liza's apparent devastation was rejected love, and what percentage pique . . .

Jake took Liza for a walk on Boxing Day, just before dark. Rose, feeding and nappy changing, appeared not to notice, but Matthew simmered.

'Jake can't come to any harm out there,' Hannah said soothingly. 'It's far too cold for passion.'

'Well, I'm warning you,' Matthew told her darkly. 'So you'd better warn her.'

Hannah did nothing, fearing that a complaint might

provoke defiance, but tailed Liza closely for the remainder of the visit. Jake insisted on taking her to the train next morning, piling cases and packages into his car before Hannah could object and leaving his wife bathing their child, Matthew simmering again on the doorstep, and Hannah greatly relieved to see the back of her daughter. Soon afterwards she heard that Liza had been offered a contract for a season with the Royal Shakespeare Company on leaving the cast of *Three Sisters*, and would be looking for accommodation in or near Stratford-upon-Avon.

Other moves were being made. An offer arrived for Greystones, at the time when Hannah and Matthew, with memories of Christmas at Bracken House still fresh, felt ready to take the next step into the future – 'lock stock and barrel', as Matthew said wryly as they rolled up their sleeves for the effort. They decided to rent a flat in Clapham for the present – a toehold there, to be near to Laurie, and to Liza when she had a London run. The furniture would divide between that and Bracken House, and Hannah would at last have her possessions from Morfa Cottage out of store.

Excitement mounted. Matthew masterminded the intricacies of vans going hither and yon while Hannah turned out cupboards into 'keep' and 'throw' piles. Her own excitement became difficult to contain as the Day approached . . . she was going home, to Wales. Back where her heart and spirit belonged, where hills and sea would welcome one of their own.

Matthew's painstaking efforts ended in chaos, with vans taking their contents to the wrong destinations and mayhem reigning for a few hours. Only Hannah kept smiling; the small serene smile of one who knows that the important things are on track. And by evening, they were indeed installed at Bracken House.

Nothing in the right room . . . but what is perfect?

Their first Sunday in residence Tom and Florence came, bringing 'standbys' in the form of an outsize steak and kidney pie, an apple pie, and three dozen Welshcakes. They all strolled out to inspect the garden, where bulbs pushed strongly through the detritus of winter under a mild March sun.

The two-level pond of Matthew's was slowly evolving on site rather than solely in the head of the inventor, and soon, green shoots would make their various journeys up the new pergola. The vegetable garden was Tom's special interest; he and Matthew wandered towards the greenhouse to compare seed packets as the women moved further up the slope.

'I've a bit of movin' news too,' Florence admitted, looking arch.

'Flo – you've found somewhere?' Hannah gave her arm a shake. 'And you've been here an hour and said *nothing*! Tom neither.'

'Well, you wouldn't expect your Tom to broadcast his news, bless him. If you want a secret kept, tell Tom!' Florence lowered her matronly backside on to the wooden garden bench Hannah had bought Matthew for his last birthday. 'Anyway; yes, we're movin' at last. And not before time . . . the District Council's just unveiled plans for the wholesale redevelopment of the town, and all hell is due to be let loose.'

'I thought it already had – with the bypass-cum-motorway.'

'Worse is to follow,' said Florence darkly. 'Half Aberavan is to fall to a shopping mall and car park, bus station, you name it. Some of St Mary's churchyard is to go. And Water Street . . .'

Hannah gazed over the land that fell gently to the

river. Her family lay in St Mary's churchyard. And she had been born in Water Street. The past, it seemed, was crumbling behind her. But for now, she would not think of that; certainly she could do nothing to change it.

'I'll go and take a look at the plans, Flo. Maybe you'd like to come? Anyway – what about moving? Where? When?'

'In around three months if things pan out. Now Raymond seems quite confident to handle everything in the restaurant I've just about bowed out of Swansea, so I've been looking hard. Last week, Tom and I offered for a really decent bungalow in Porthcawl. And Tom seems to have fallen on his feet with a job there too, saving the daily journey into Taibach. Drew's Bakers were on the lookout for someone, their man is keen to retire and *his* daughter's friendly with my nephew Hughie, so it came on the grapevine. Anyway, Tom went along to Drew's, told them where he'd been and for how long, and about our movin' to Porthcawl an' everything. And they are happy to have him – so that's great, don't you think? This bungalow's in Clarence Avenue, nice and light, good garden, central heating . . .' Florence grinned. 'So now we're both ladies of leisure, Han . . . I never thought we'd see the day, did you?'

'I never actually thought we'd *want* to!' Hannah grinned back. 'D'you remember the way it used to be? Right through to the fifties, when women weren't supposed to work if they didn't actually *have* to?'

'When Harry died, I'd have gone off my head without a hard day's work to get me through the daylight hours and tired enough to sleep nights,' Florence said soberly. 'Anyway, the money was there to be earned, and I wanted to earn it – it's given me the security and peace of mind I have now. And I tell you, Han; things have been good through the last years, no one had to be poor unless they were work-shy. But it's beginning to change again . . . Men are being laid off at the steel-works. I reckon the slide started when the Dyffryn and Rhondda railway closed. Then, Dyffryn colliery closed, soon after that outsize Avan Lido complex was opened by the Queen an' all, no expense spared. Now there's this twenty-million-pound tidal harbour being built, she'll be back in a couple of years to open that! Maybe they'll see the money back and maybe they won't . . . maybe they were wrong to nationalise steel and maybe not . . . all I know is that 3,000 jobs have gone in the last few years. And how can families use that Lido if their men aren't in work?'

They looked at one another, remembering the 1920s and '30s. Hannah put her hand on Florence's knee.

'Flo . . . we can't *do* anything. Whatever happens, boom or bust, we can't do anything to influence events. I used to think that we could – that meetings, marches, strikes, could turn back clocks to the good times, or forward to new good times. Now I don't believe that. I think ordinary people can only hang on to the edge as best they can in bad years, and enjoy the good years when they come. Maybe the cycles of good, then bad are inevitable – that whoever's in power can't halt the tide any more than could Canute. Like the seasons of the year, almost – and whether we like winter or not, it comes, and we endure it to get through to spring again.'

'You could be right, Han.' Florence laid her hand on Hannah's. 'Could be, there've been enough good years for now, with jobs for all and money in folks' pockets. But we never do like winter when it comes . . .'

Matthew agreed there were signs of a downturn. 'But we won't lose our jobs because we haven't any,' he pointed out. 'So why don't we do something nice instead; like going to see Joe?'

When Liza heard of her mother's departure for America she experienced a curious stab of abandonment. Edward Anderssen; now her mother . . . those she had counted on being to hand when needed, were gone. Anderssen's rejection had cut deep and, as Hannah suspected, wounded not only heart but ego. If anyone should have ended their relationship, *she* should. If she chose to endure its shortcomings, *he* had no place giving up on it. Liza could not in fact understand how he could have done this, if he had loved her; so the conclusion she came to, however reluctantly, was that he had felt only physical desire. The bitter conclusion that she had been duped provoked both deep disquiet and rage, and Liza craved revenge.

Meanwhile, she had presented a good enough audition to be offered a Stratford season, and the stamina and staying power required for this feat of endurance left no time for mooning over wrongs done her by Edward Anderssen. Competition among actresses for acceptance on any terms by the RSC was fierce; Liza knew this was a good break and not one to be squandered. She had signed a play-as-cast contract, so could be asked to do anything. Every hour she could snatch was spent reading the plays, poring over criticisms of, essays on, interpretations of each one. Of course she wanted to be the definitive Juliet – one drawback being that it was not in this season's repertoire – the Desdemona everyone would remember; and one day, Lady Macbeth. For now, she would be content with the part of someone's maidservant, or a tavern wench so long as she could be on the stage, in there with the action, absorbing.

What happened was that the season opened with *Richard II* and Liza miraculously had the part of his Queen. This had not been the plan; only when the Queen went down with glandular fever was there a hasty shuffle through the small pack of available cards and Liza came out on top. How might she approach the part? What was her capacity to learn the lines quickly? How well did she know the play? Had she studied *Richard II* at RADA? Liza, bone-weary due to having been up all night reading *Richard II* plus footnotes, said she knew that Isabella was very miserably depressed because her new husband was going through a really bad patch, and that she simply hated seeing him rubbished by cousin Henry Bolingbroke, and in the end usurped, and killed. She said that she completely empathised with the young queen and would love the opportunity to do a read-through. The director, lulled if not completely mesmerised by the wonderful turquoise eyes, asked Liza to read the garden scene. Liza gathered up every sinew and launched forth, with the director's PA reading gardener and servant.

> 'Come, ladies, go
> To meet at London, London's king in woe.
> What! Was I born to this, that my sad look
> Should grace the triumph of great Bolingbroke?'

The director scribbled a note on his hand, stroked his beard, and asked if she would attend a cast read-through at 10 a.m. Liza said certainly she would, if he could supply a substitute for her own part, that of one of Isabella's attendants.

There followed four weeks of the toughest and most

concentrated work she had ever done. Movement, lighting and sound, costume changes, exits, were beginning to dominate the true heart of the play: the text, and how to speak it. Liza had endless sessions with a voice coach, and when she stood facing the empty 1,500 seat auditorium and knew she had to project to the back row of the balcony she had a moment's doubt of her sanity. What was she *doing* here? She did not need the money; she could have been her father's PA in Toronto, naming her own figure.

It somehow happened: it came and went. The previews, the first night, in a miasma of nervous energy blended with terror that her voice could not remain pitched exactly right, and that in her anxiety she would forget the lines to be spoken. The cast supported her with their goodwill, being themselves further on in the development of their own parts, and so more secure. The camaraderie was not on the level of repertory, but a diverse collection of artists were struggling to bring together a performance of power and meaning to audiences who had come from the four corners of the world to hear it, and so were to a degree interlocked, each needing others in order to function at full stretch.

Notices were satisfying: 'Liza Vaughan brings a deeply felt, penetrating sadness to the young Queen, drowning in fear for her doomed husband' . . . 'The Queen conveys in her classically perfect silences, all she feels of grief.'

A few weeks into the season, rehearsals started for *As You Like It*. The glandular fever unimproved, Liza was called in for the part of Celia. She was an obvious choice for this as she had already played Celia in the radio production of the play, and had read one of the speeches as part of her Stratford audition. Now her workload doubled. Edward Anderssen, her mother, all was submerged in the tide. She managed a weekly phone call to her father, and when *As You Like It* opened he came over to see that, as well as *Richard II* which remained in the repertoire. She found herself at one frenetic point in five different productions and far from being – as she should have been – exhausted, Liza was exhilarated and fully charged. This was what had been her intention, though she'd had no idea how it might come about. She began to believe that she was under a benevolent star, that would ultimately take her to the moon. For Liza Vaughan, anything was possible . . .

Hannah found New York, and indeed America, a city and country seemingly riven by violence. The day they arrived, Martin Luther King had been murdered. The airport was subdued, groups talked together with serious faces. As Joe drove them into the city they listened quietly to radio reports of civil unrest in many states.

'Just chatting to Jesse Jackson, he was,' Joe said for the third time. 'Standing talking to a friend and some devil comes up and pulls a gun on him. I'm real sorry to give you both such a poor welcome. Who would have *thought*? It's been brewing and boiling for years, this racial problem . . . So many have died – and no doubt more will now. Over Vietnam too; if we don't pull out from that crazy scene God knows where we'll end up.'

They passed a demonstration against the Vietnam draft, young men with placards stating 'Hell NO, We Won't Go'. Hannah, disorientated after the journey and time shift, began to feel depressed. In Wales, there were no assassinations, no riots, no tear gas; no placards, even. She held Matthew's hand in the back of Joe's car, which drove disconcertingly on the wrong side of the road, and looked forward determinedly to meeting the children and Sal.

It did not improve – or perhaps she got used to it: to the crowds, the marches and the placards, the police with guns and an apparent willingness to use them, and their lethal-looking batons. They went to Washington and that was worse, anger everywhere. Civil rights and Vietnam protesters camped around the White House, hiding the daffodils and all signs of spring. They would sit around Joe's table after dinner, the boys in bed, and always the talk turned to the violence permeating daily life. Joe made an effort, telling of plans he and Sal had to move out of town, where it would be quieter, and schooling better for Paul Harry and Thomas. They were looking for a property, and felt sure they'd drop on the right place soon enough. They caught one another's eye and smiled; Hannah smiled too, content with *their* content. It had taken Joe so long to reach harbour ... Sometimes, she longed to ask him if Sal knew; if he had told her of Norman Madoc, and the tragedy that had driven a twelve-year-old from home, and from his country. One day it might be right to speak of it, but meanwhile she was happy to see that life in this household was good. It was after Sal's young brother, Marek, had been to see them that Hannah thought of Carl Cline, last seen aged twelve but never forgotten.

'Oh, Carl ...' Joe pulled a wry face. 'Well, Carl's quite a big fish now, Han, and we don't see a lot of him. He offered to make me a millionaire a while back, but I chickened out as it entailed mortgaging every last stick. Small sums were of no use, Carl operates on a heroic scale. Things have been a mite cool since then . . . but I read of his doings in the financial columns, his firm forever buying or selling some business. His friends call him Lucky Carl Cline. Everything he touches succeeds. Enemies call him a corporate raider, so take your pick. He and his wife are also in the social news, great party throwers and goers. And you'll maybe find him in the sports pages; he's taken to yacht racing, a rich man's sport if ever I knew one.'

'So we won't see *him* this visit. Why did he want your money?'

'To help start up his company, Cline Investments. Both Alex and Delaney put a load in and took a real big profit, as did Carl's wife Gayle. The other guy was a former colleague. Anyway, eventually they went public . . . floated shares on the market. They made millions, but they still have enough shares between them to control things.'

Hannah raised her eyebrows. 'So you really missed out. But Alex took the plunge?'

'Yeah. Well, he's more of a gambler than me!' Joe hesitated. 'A shame we drifted apart though . . . we used to be real buddies.'

'But now?' Hannah sensed the regret, felt it herself.

'Fact is, he was put out that I didn't raise the wind to help Carl out when he suggested. It's smoothed over now, we spent a weekend at his Long Island place a while back. Even so, he's in a whole different league, Han.' Thoughtful, Joe pushed at the rug with his toe. 'They have this superb place up in Long Island, and another in California. And they travel around, lots, right now they're in Florida. I do miss seeing him regularly, it's true; but I do pretty well myself.' After a moment he added: 'If I'm to level with you, there's the odd occasion when things foul up in the business, and I catch myself thinking. If I'd mortgaged our lives at the time Carl asked me to, Sal and I would've been sunning ourselves in Florida now like Alex and Delaney, super-wealthy, top of the range! But I think back on my beginnings . . . and look at my life now. I'm damned lucky, Han; you know that.'

Her voice was soft. 'I know that, Joe.'

They were coming south through Connecticut on the final leg of a week's tour, when news came in of Robert Kennedy's assassination. The radio behind the bar of the roadside diner broke into its music for the bulletin. An initial shocked silence was followed by cries of disbelief, oaths, and a young woman about to leave turned and burst into tears.

'Christ . . . not again!' Joe's face had drained of colour. 'Not another Kennedy!' The bulletin droned on but was of little importance now; it had said all in that first sentence. They drove away, appetites gone, through a land plunged again into shadow. Two days later Hannah and Matthew left, with happy and terrible memories of their time in the New World. Matthew took her arm, leaving Joe and his family with tears and smiles and pledges to meet again soon.

'Back to Wales now, eh sweetheart?' The words sounded good.

Hannah nodded. 'Sure. Back to Wales.'

By November, Liza was extremely tired, and content to see the season close. She was also satisfied with the results of her labours. Penelope was sifting assiduously through offers of work, determined to plot this potential star's course for maximum success. She had the material; it was up to her to make the most of it.

Liza was right with her, ambition knowing no bounds. Bitter memories of her rejection resurfaced and part of her desire was to show Edward Anderssen what he had thrown away.

She had had a couple of pleasant liaisons at Stratford, but had bestowed no sexual favours. To any who pressed her she became graciously dismissive. She felt no need to please them. I have been here, was her attitude, and I have done that. I do not need it now, and I do not need to please you by pretending to desire you. You can take me as I am or leave me; either way is OK by me. This attitude caused a certain amount of grief, frustration and wounded vanity, which provided Liza with mild amusement.

Both Liza and Penelope jumped at the chance for her to read for the part of Sheila Birling in a production for Granada Television of Priestley's *An Inspector Calls*. Margaret Leighton had played Sheila in the first, much admired 1946 production, with Ralph Richardson as the Inspector. Sheila was a bright, pretty girl in her early twenties, who during the course of an evening has some lessons to learn. The part had scope; Liza was avid for it, and got it, and after a week off doing absolutely nothing at Bracken House was ready to start rehearsals. These were in an icy church hall, with everyone reading huddled about a primus stove. The cast list of only seven was further simplified by the play taking place over the course of only one evening. Spared expensive sets and outdoor shooting, the production could afford to concentrate on quality of performances; solid, first-rate theatre.

The polished end product deserved and won acclaim. Liza got a three-page interview in a leading glossy, and more importantly a contract to appear for six months in *Balcony View*. This was a new play by

Willard Singer, a playwright who had done no wrong for the last eight or nine years and whose work played to full houses. This new play was true to form, a multi-layered, subtle yet at the same time attractively simple plot with an emotional, bitter-sweet aftertaste. Liza had a central role as the daughter of a diplomat who gets into deep water with a distinguished foreign politician. Singer wrote superb dialogue that was a joy to deliver, and the play left thought-provoking echoes.

Balcony View opened in January to good reviews, and Liza began to develop an in-depth portrait of a girl of her time who becomes trapped by her nature. When John Foxley, the actor playing her father, indicated that he regarded her as more than just another member of the cast Liza was at first amused. Then she became nervous that his attitude could shake the delicate on-stage father/daughter balance the script demanded. As he was between marriages, she agreed to go out to dine with him after the performance to attempt to explain this in a relaxed environment.

'You *do* understand my nervousness here, John?' Liza turned on her most brilliant gaze, and smiled with just a touch of melancholy. 'You do understand that I would adore to sleep with you', was the intended interpretation of this smile. 'But might it not make a hash of our scenes?'

John Foxley covered her hand with his and leaned across the table. He was a seasoned veteran of thirty years' stage and film experience, rarely if ever out of work. His sexual powers may have been fading a touch but he retained charisma, and a strong presence. He prided himself on laying as many of the female cast as was possible and/or desirable in whatever production he was in, and had a pretty fair success rate. He was getting quite hot for Liza, due in part to the way she pressed her wonderful breasts against him when they hugged one another in the first act. He saw no reason why they should not copulate perfectly happily without feelings of incest; indeed, the thought of Liza Vaughan's warm body writhing with pleasure under his – or over his, he was happy either way – made his brown eyes glisten now. He held up her hand, bent his head to kiss it.

A figure in white glided into Liza's orbit, carrying a carafe of water. This, without warning, was tipped over John Loxley's handsomely greying head.

'That should cool you down, darling. I know how hot you can get at times like this.'

The figure in the clinging white crêpe Christian Dior tipped back her perfectly coiffed head and gave a delicious peal of laughter. At the same time a camera clicked; the resident personality-spotter in this restaurant currently favoured by the rich and famous was not about to pass up the coup of the month.

He did an excellent job of selling his shots to the tabloids. Next morning, Liza faced an unflattering likeness of herself with open mouth, staring in horror as John Loxley's glamorous wife (separated but not yet actually divorced) doused him with water. The fact that Lucinda Foxley had sadly been wined over-generously by her own escort at a nearby table did not detract from the punchiness of the shot, or its caption: 'JOHN FOXLEY COOLS OFF IN COUTTS WITH LIZA VAUGHAN'.

Penelope repaired the damage to the best of her ability. A friendly meeting to talk over small problems with their parts . . . no hint of any romance . . . Liza's hand was grasped merely to illustrate a stage move. Liza was asked in for a chat with the director, to whom she vehemently told the truth; that she had been pursued by Foxley and had met him only to tell him to back off.

Liza extricated herself from the publicity, comforted by Penelope, who said that bad publicity was preferable to no publicity. Liza could not agree; she felt demeaned, embarrassed and angry. None of these emotions helped make her scenes on stage with Foxley other than enormously difficult, but that was a problem she had to wrestle with and overcome. Foxley seemed to make nothing of it and from the high ground of his mountain of experience, laughed off the episode as one more illustration of his wretched wife making a spectacle of herself.

Lost ground was gradually recovered, though Liza never did cross the threshold of Coutts again. The play continued to prosper; perhaps some bookings were made purposely to inspect at close quarters two players in this triangular mini-drama. When Liza was told the production company was opening *Balcony View* on Broadway in June and that she was invited to join the cast there, she felt a great lurch of joyful triumph. She had got there. She had made it.

The night following this offer, Liza glimpsed the dim shadow she knew to be Rachel Hywel at the back of the stalls' side aisle. This time she felt neither fear nor anger, but a resurgence of triumph. The wretched shade no longer held terror for her; she, Liza Vaughan, could rob it of all power. Do your worst, she wanted to shout across the heads of the applauding audience. You cannot touch me; I am the stronger, I am inviolable.

The same night, Hannah took a last stroll round the garden at dusk to enjoy the beauty of another spring. Looking up at the summerhouse she thought she discerned a shadow standing near it. The figure was motionless, but dark hair lifted in the evening zephyr, and the folds of the skirt stirred.

Hannah remained stock-still, not breathing until the shadow faded, melted into the general twilight. Then she turned and, sick at heart, made for the house and the sanity of Matthew's presence. The first time in – how many years? A great many.

A shock, to find that Rachel Hywel had discovered her new home.

Chapter Fifteen

Summer 1969

When Liza flew into New York in late May, she – as had her mother a year ago – arrived in what seemed to be an angry country. The fatalities of Vietnam, now over 33,000, had overtaken the body count of the Korean war of the 1950s. That conflict had seemed to many a futile exercise; to repeat it, this time on the side clearly set to lose, made sense to few. The new President, Richard Nixon, had been voted into office promising to bring soldiers home and by March had withdrawn 25,000 troops of the upwards of half a million in Vietnam. Still protest marches, sit-ins, vigils; every possible means at the disposal of democracy was vigorously employed to redeem a hopeless venture with all speed.

Despite the pervading air of violence and confrontation, Liza's welcome was warm. On a personal level, she was taken into the bosom of Joe's family at once, and her father came down from Toronto to install himself at the Pierre. Professionally, New York seemed to be full of British artists doing well, on all levels up to the sublime Fonteyn practising her special magic at the Met, partnered by Nureyev and with never a seat unfilled.

Balcony View rehearsals got under way, to open at the Ethel Barrymore with a predominantly American cast apart from three London players in their original parts. Liza's main preoccupation, understandably, was with the actor who was to play her father, who turned out to be a (for now) happily married family man and looked unlikely to give her trouble. At first she tired quickly, adapting to a new continent, city, lifestyle, vernacular, and the speed and noise seemed hopelessly distracting. By concentrating hard on what had to be done *that* day, and by striving both to mark and remember everyone she met who would figure in her life, and note them in her diary, she slowly infiltrated Broadway theatre life. She allowed nothing to distract her, or take precedence over her performance, and declined most offers of nights out in order to conserve energy.

She went often to the theatre to learn all aspects of stage, auditorium, acoustics, wings and backstage layout. She would walk the short distance to and from her hotel, wanting to take in New York's vibrations. When they were finally able to rehearse at the Ethel Barrymore, every nerve was primed for maximum attention to detail; Liza wanted no mistakes.

None were made. Apart from a secretary offering the diplomat a glass of whisky that slipped from his fingers, they got through the first night unscathed. The cast took their bows to a highly appreciative audience; with some experience of applause rating, Liza smiled her angel's smile and recognised good signs. Now they had to wait for the morning papers. As the curtain fell the cast sighed, and relaxed.

The opening night party was next. Liza sat in her dressing-room, staring at her face in the unflattering light of the hooped bulbs. She had opened on Broadway. In a few moments her father would be here to congratulate her, and Joe and Sal; also Hannah and Matthew, who had wired to say they would be flying over and would she reserve two seats. She had seen them all clapping furiously as the lights went up.

She would have liked Edward Anderssen to have been here, to witness her success. Sipping mineral water, still looking at her reflection as she creamed off her make-up, Liza knew that he had been right; it never could have worked for them. But occasionally, alone in the night, she cried for him, and hated him roundly for having been right to say goodbye.

Her dresser came in with a hot, fluffy white towel as she was finishing her face, and Liza smiled at her.

'Right on time, Vera – thanks. A shower, and I'm as good as new. Oh – wonderful!' – as a messenger appeared loaded with three baskets full of flowers. 'Now I know I've arrived!'

The party was warming up when she arrived at the Plaza. Charged with adrenalin still, with a couple of hours before she would wind down, Liza prepared to enjoy her high. She came in on David Vaughan's proud arm, followed by her family.

Poised in the doorway of the ornate, high-ceilinged room she took in the scene. The freshly washed, burnished cascade of hair fell about the slender neck, touching the shoulders of a smoke-grey satin chong-sam cropped at the ankle and split either side to just above the knee. An exquisitely embroidered spray of exotic flowers crossed one hip, and her high-heeled slippers of matching dull grey satin were also embroidered. Her only jewellery was a pair of antique turquoise and gold ear-drops given by Hannah and Matthew for her twenty-first birthday, discovered by Joe at an estate auction. They were exactly the same colour as her eyes, looked wonderful, and Liza knew it. She looked at David Vaughan, and her smile broadened to an impudent grin.

'OK, Pa. Let's wow the company, eh?'

Carl Cline, who had arrived a few minutes back and was about to raise a laugh in a small group that included his wife and his father, looked across and saw Liza by the door. He had just taken two glasses of champagne off a waiter's tray and handed one to Gayle. He had been uncertain about coming when invited by Joe, theatrical parties rated low on his list of good (rewarding) ways to spend an evening, but Gayle had been keen. Alex had accepted Joe's invitation for old times' sake, interested to meet the sister who had played so vital a role in his friend's life, while being absent from it for its greater part.

Carl did not take his eyes off the most beautiful woman on view; assured, cool on Vaughan's arm. The room was becoming noisy; earlier, modulated tones were re-pitched by experienced actors to make themselves heard as the crowd thickened along with cigarette smoke and the babble of conversation. Carl identified Hannah and Matthew from that far-off August with Joe. Wales . . . damn queer place. His eyes went back to Liza. Then he moved.

'Remember me?'

He had reached her side. He smiled, and touched his chest. 'Me Carl. You Liza. Only the last time we said hello you were four and something and I was a sophisticated twelve. Twenty years . . .'

Liza looked at him closely. Slightly above average height, light brown hair slickly cut, narrow piercing eyes that you knew had the capacity to turn from warm straight down to deep freeze. Sharp cheekbones, sharp jaw. She had the sensation of a tennis ball hitting her hard in the solar plexus.

'Twenty years in August.' She put out a hand and he took it in a light cool clasp. 'You killed ants. I hated you.'

'How is it that some folk have this memory that goes way back?' He smiled again, the bottom lip drawn down a little at one side. 'I hated you too, you scratched like a wildcat. But I was twelve; I do not recall a damn thing about being four.'

They stared at one another for what felt like hours, but was seconds. Electricity leapt from fingertip to fingertip; they had omitted to unclasp hands.

'Just as well you don't.' Joe had edged up. 'You were an above-average unspeakable brat at that age. Hi Carl.'

'Hi there, Joe. Well, so I'm outnumbered two to one. Maybe I can get you on my side, Mrs Stourton?' Behind Joe, Hannah laughed and extended a hand.

'I'll stay neutral if I may. How are you, Carl? I would have known you I think, twenty years or no. Will you introduce me to your family?'

'My pleasure.' As they moved off he said over his shoulder to Liza: 'I don't kill ants these days. Am I forgiven?'

'I must consult the charge-sheet,' Liza told him coolly. 'I've a hazy idea there was more than ants on it. But it *was* a long time ago . . . and I *was* only four.' She looked after him, swallowing on a mouth that had unaccountably dried out.

'That is one stunning niece you have there –' Alex and Joe stood by an open window, smoking. Both had regretted the strain put on their forty-year relationship by Carl's business dealing, and were grateful to ease themselves back into mutual goodwill. Both had come far in their respective journeys. Joe had become comfortable by any scale, by virtue of his skills and intelligent capacity for effort, while Alex had regained the rank and privilege to which he had been born, and had progressed to become extremely wealthy.

Both would be sixty this year but Joe looked the fitter of the two now, despite his heart condition. Alex's face and demeanour bore signs of a stressful, restless nature responding to the pressures of the times, and those borne in on the tide of wealth. His twins Belinda and Toby had caused – and were causing – him angst; Belinda by joining the alternative culture in a San Francisco commune after an expensive Vassar education, Toby by successfully dodging the Vietnam draft only to tour first guitar with a fifth-rate pop group, putting in an appearance at the family home when he required further funds. To say that Alex Cline was bitter about the twins was no lie; conversely, he was proud of his firstborn and took comfort in Carl's meteoric rise.

He also took comfort in his grandson, Carl's Bradley. He believed Belinda also had a son, born out of wedlock in the hippie commune and so not for viewing or – in his book – taking to the family bosom. This niece of Joe's . . . now there would be a daughter to rate. Her father had done well too by the cut of his tuxedo; in aviation. He turned abruptly to Joe.

'Bring your folks to our place, Sunday. Sister, niece and father – the lot. Time we had a get-together. Delaney would like that, she's strong on theatre. See her now, hanging on Liza's every word?' He lit another cigarette; Delaney had been nagging him to ease up on them but he was impervious.

'I'd like that,' said Joe. 'I'm not sure how Liza's fixed, with the play just opening an' all, but I'll ask.'

'What do you make of Carl now?' Matthew asked Hannah, feeling irritable. He hated dos where everyone stood up, everyone shouted, and where there was no comfortable way to eat the food spread enticingly along a garlanded table.

'I would say he's the epitome of success, Manhattan style.' Hannah sipped her rapidly warming champagne. 'I think his pretty wife looks a mite lonely.'

'She's maybe fed up with being left while her husband romances other men's wives. He doesn't pay her that much attention,' Matthew observed. David Vaughan, looking hot, edged towards them as his daughter disappeared in a knot of attentive men. He and Matthew had developed a courteous rapport, despite one being the one-time lover of the other's wife; a curious situation, particularly as one of the stars of this gathering was the illegitimate offspring of the liaison.

'How soon d'you think we can go?' Vaughan pulled ruefully at his tie. 'I'm already fantasising over a cool shower.'

'And a steak. I'm ravenous.' Matthew took a tentative step towards the food and came up hard against a bunch of people all talking at once. 'Is our Liza worth the agony, I ask myself.'

'She *was* great though, you have to hand it to her.' Vaughan the father swelled with pride. Matthew nodded.

'Yes, she was. One only wishes the play had opened in December.'

'Or in Iceland.' Hannah smiled. 'But the least we can do is pay homage. She's done the work, we just have to endure the party. She should enjoy her hour of triumph.'

Her gaze returned to her daughter and Carl Cline staring at one another again, and the smile faded. She gave a tiny shiver . . . Liza and Carl . . .

Gayle Cline lay on a sunbed by her father-in-law's pool, watching her husband swim with Liza Vaughan.

Her son Bradley splashed about nearby with Joe's sons, and other family members and guests were scattered in the shade sipping long drinks.

Gayle foresaw the scenario but was powerless to change it. Over their years of marriage, Carl had almost certainly been unfaithful; how many times she had no idea and had no wish to count. She had married because she had been pregnant, and in love. That was true no longer, as love rarely can survive without a minimum of care. But she had a child, a family; and was not actively unhappy as Carl was not actively cruel. Rather, he was not there . . . a minus factor in the partnership, which thus became an empty word.

She shifted on to her stomach and closed her eyes, but still could hear the muted blur of Carl and Liza's conversation. Silly, for her to care. He would stray when tempted – and Gayle had to admit Liza was tempting – but she felt confident that he would not pitch her, Brad and his reputation into the pit. He would sleep with Liza for a while maybe; then she would return to England and he to his favourite pursuit of making money.

Sometimes, when she had allowed herself to be hurt by Carl's peccadilloes, Gayle had contemplated suing for divorce. But she enjoyed the social status of being not only the daughter of J. Arthur Belman, but the wife of Carl Cline. As a single woman she would be less acceptable; it was a fact of life that doubles fitted more neatly around the best dinner tables, and no one built single cabins into their yachts. So she averted her eyes and ears when the need arose.

Sitting up, she beckoned her son. 'Let me cream you darling, the sun's strong.' She watched, smiling, pretty, expensively maintained in her white bikini, as

Brad hauled himself from the sparkling water and shook it laughing from eyes resembling his father's. Towelling off the surplus from his sturdy, fair-skinned frame, she began to smooth suncream into his shoulders.

'I suppose Joe told you, he's certain we're related!' Alex came over with his plate of food to sit by Hannah and Joe under a poolside umbrella. Joe poured him fruit juice and refilled Hannah's glass.

'I've been looking for a resemblance.' She smiled at him over her drink. 'Two centuries can dilute features somewhat; but I do believe you have a hairline resembling our father's.'

Alex burst into laughter. 'A hairline, is it! Well now, would you believe that? You know, I do recall my mother took some pride in the Hywel name, in that she kept it after her marriage. I wonder . . .'

'Did your mother *know* anything?' Hannah said quickly. 'About where the family originated? Joe said –'

She broke off. Joe, she remembered, had never disclosed to Alex with what fervour he had pursued his interest in Alex's possible family connection, all those years back in Pittsburgh. Joe always played his cards close to his chest . . . 'Joe really gave me a thrill when he said he knew a Hywel Cline,' she corrected herself. 'You see, there'd always been talk in our family about some emigrating to Pennsylvania years and years ago. And we've always wanted to know more.'

'Well now –' Alex narrowed his eyes. 'My mother just might have a lead or two. Tell you what – I shall put it to her at the weekend, see if she knows where to start digging. She's in Florida now, eighty-three but sharp as a pin.'

'That would be wonderful.' Hannah was surprised

at how eager she felt now to prove or disprove the faint possibility that Joe had opened up long ago, and which had never left her consciousness.

'My pleasure. And you're from a steel town too?'

'Oh yes. Steel, coal, tinplate. On the coast, with big docks.'

'And is your place as God-awful messed up and filthy as Pittsburgh? Of course, they're doing something of a clean-up job now; but earlier on, when Joe and I were there it was a dump straight out of hell.'

'Pretty well messed up,' Joe answered for her. 'Han's not been to Pittsburgh yet, but so far as fallout went I doubt there'd be a lot to choose between them. Pittsburgh's just bigger! We couldn't go on expanding in Wales, we were crushed for space between the sea and the mountains.'

'Why don't you come over and look?' Hannah offered. 'There's more to Wales than steelworks. Most of it is beautiful, and unique. We have a house by the sea – not on this scale, but pleasant. You would be welcome; you might even get a sense of *déjà vu*!'

'I might just pick you up on that –' Alex got up with his plate. 'May I get you dessert? Ah – goddamn –' He frowned, rubbed at his knee.

'What's the problem?' Hannah bent to look. Alex frowned again.

'Oh . . . it's called old age, I guess. Damn knee's been doing it for a couple of years on and off. I sit down; get up, and it catches me like it's been put out. Well – I've not *put* a knee out, you understand, but that's the type of feeling I imagine it might be if I did!'

Delaney, Sal and Matthew came to join them after a stroll about the grounds, with their choice of food from the buffet spread out in the dining room opening on to the poolside terrace. Delaney pulled a face at Alex.

'Is it that stupid knee again, darling? Maybe you should have walked with us instead. Move over a teeny bit, there's an angel.'

'Why don't you sit here –' Hannah motioned Alex to the chair by her. 'I'll take a look at that knee.'

She touched the leg with the gentlest of pressure and Alex, after initial surprise, relaxed, took off his sunglasses and closed his eyes. Hannah covered the sunbrowned knee with her cupped hands, and was still; quite soon she felt warmth flood and tingle into them as they appeared momentarily to fuse to the knee.

Alex opened his eyes. 'Your hands are hot.'

'I know. All the better to heal you with,' she said calmly. 'Just keep still now.'

All eyes were on the knee now, forks laid aside. Joe's sons climbed from the water to come for food; Joe motioned them to be still and they stood dripping by their parents, watching Aunt Hannah's hands. For a moment all was silent . . . Liza and Carl were deep in conversation propped against a willow tree on the grass, and Gayle had gone indoors with Bradley.

'Now –' Hannah's hands moved slowly around the area of the knee, then she lifted them away and sat back. 'I hope that might feel a little easier.'

Alex looked down at the leg, bent and flexed it. 'What did you do?'

'I put my hands on it. You saw,' Hannah said. 'May I have some dessert now please?'

'Sure – I'll get it.' He got up and disappeared through the long open windows of the dining room. Delaney said:

'Well I never did,' in a shaky voice.

'I can't take her anywhere.' Matthew looked resigned. Joe grinned.

'Bully for you, Han.' Alex reappeared with a tray of lemon sorbets with chocolate shells, which he set down with a flourish before Hannah.

'Have as many as you want. Have all of them,' he said recklessly.

'One will be plenty I think, though they look very good. How's the knee?'

'OK.' Alex executed a series of skips and jumps. 'The knee's fine. Now, what can I do for you? Name it.'

'A big cup of hot tea, please,' said Hannah, and laughed at the expression on his face.

'Of course I damn well mean it,' Carl Cline told Liza sharply. 'When you know me better you'll know I do *not* say anything without meaning it.'

'That's exactly what *I* mean.' Liza was equally sharp. 'I don't know you and you certainly don't know me. So how the devil *can* you mean it when you talk about *loving* me? What you mean is, you'd like to sleep with me.'

'That too.' He lit two cigarettes and handed one to her. 'Yes, I want to sleep with you like hell.'

'Well, sorry about that,' she said with a hint of cruelty. 'Actually, I'd quite like to sleep with you, but I shan't.' She was disturbed at how much she wanted to sleep with him; she had thought of little else for days.

They were having a late theatre supper in a discreet Italian restaurant on West 51st; their fifth assignation in the eighteen days since their meeting. The risotto with pink champagne was sensational, but Carl had laid down his fork to smoke. Liza continued to eat. She needed the calories: her nightly role took up a great deal of energy and it was imperative to remain well nourished, but she had little appetite. The man sitting opposite had seen to that.

'I simply can't get the measure . . .' He checked himself, started again on a softer, more amenable note. 'Darling. Don't try to make things more difficult than they are, please.'

'Things *aren't* difficult, Carl. There's no problem, if you could but see. We live on different continents. I shall shortly return to mine, and that will mean cheerio, nice to have met you again after twenty years. Where's the angst?' She told this to herself, had been doing so for days. Why did she not believe it? She continued to eat but her hand shook a little.

His face darkened again. 'There you go. Hell, it's not possible I can be going through all this, and that you've caught none of it!'

Liza played with her risotto. She *had* caught some of it . . . for the first time since Edward Anderssen, she had caught a packet. Carl Cline had knocked her sideways. She had promised herself never to fall into the same trap twice; no use hurting like hell if you learned nothing but how much the wound bled. But the unpleasant truth was, the trap seemed to be already sprung.

She sipped her champagne, and looked at Carl Cline. Here he was, waiting and fully expecting her to lie back and say OK, take it if you want it. Hell, she *did* want him! But Liza, perhaps because she had fought illegitimacy all her life, had promised herself most solemnly that she was through with all that now. When she had told Edward Anderssen that she needed someone to put a value on her, she meant just that – that he should be prepared to go to some trouble to rearrange his life to accommodate her. He had failed to do that; he had failed *her*.

'Carl – please listen to this. I am not interested in a hole-and-corner affair, I neither need nor want one. If you want me so much, the relationship can only be a legitimate one. I believe I am good enough for anyone – why on earth should you rate me so low?'

'I *don't* –' She held up an imperious hand.

'But you *do*. You want me, but for nothing, for free, to toss aside when you've had me. Now, the only way you could attain me is publicly and legitimately. If that price is too high, and I would expect it to be, no one is asking you to pay it. Though I *am* attracted to you, I'm still fine as I am and need no man to survive.'

'Liza, I could buy us somewhere –'

'Spare yourself, Carl.' She dabbed angrily at her lips with her napkin. 'Don't shake a fistful of dollars at me, I'm not interested. I have enough money, and intend having much more soon, earned entirely by my own skills.'

She frowned at her plate. He caught at her hand on the table but she removed it quickly and picked up her bag.

'Will you take me back now? I'm tired and I've a matinée tomorrow. I don't think it's a good idea for us to meet again . . . pretty pointless, really. Just upsets us both.' She rose and he had no option but to do so too.

In her hotel room Liza turned on some music low, organised her clothes for tomorrow, made a few notes of things needing attention. In bed finally, she felt restless and emotional – she hoped he had the message now, she needed none of this. It was laughable really, the way men were ruled by their genitals . . . Maybe she would laugh tomorrow.

She was missing Pa of course; he had checked out yesterday, promising to come again before she flew back to London. And Hannah and Matthew had gone the day before. Nice to see if Pa was safely home – maybe she could get up there for a few days when the play closed.

Liza picked up the phone and asked reception for his number. He would be in bed probably, but she knew he would not mind if she woke him up. He never minded whatever she did, bless him. He just loved her . . .

Carl paid off the cab; hesitated before going to his apartment. No one there; Gayle and Brad were at Long Island, they only came here when Brad had broken for school, or if Gayle wanted to shop or do a theatre. He began to walk.

It was a fine midsummer night, warm, still and starry. He wandered west along 79th, crossed Madison and soon was in the park. There were plenty of youngsters about; groups spread under trees with someone strumming a guitar, a girl piping on a recorder; a juggler practised with coloured balls under a lamp, people were walking dogs, couples kissed on benches.

He was seething with half-formed thoughts, holding conversations with Liza in his head. He wanted to do *something*; positive action was indicated. He also knew, with the cool, logical part of his brain, that in this over-excited state positive action should be avoided as it could well bring disastrous consequences. Cool down, count ten . . . he wasn't a child, he was thirty-two, rich and successful. No good ever came of hasty decisions.

He wanted that woman as he had never wanted before. He left the Transverse and turned south along East Drive, pondering the reason. Of course she was stunning to look at . . . but he'd never had a problem with beautiful women. He was, moreover, married to one. There was some extra dimension . . . fire in the belly – that's what Liza Vaughan had. He thought of Liza's belly.

God, he had to be bloody careful here; so easy to get carried away. Gayle's father would explode. Belman had only kept an uneasy truce with the man who had pulled the dirtiest trick ever on him because his adored daughter was in the line of fire. With her out of the way, and clear space between them, bullets would fly. Anyway, life with Gayle was pleasant enough; she interfered with his freedom only minimally, and she had given him Brad, who meant a lot to him. Why didn't he just take on a new mistress, there were always plenty from which to choose; forget about Liza Vaughan? Why wouldn't the stupid cow *sleep* with him, maybe that's all there was?

Not true – no woman had done this, had this effect on him before. She was the biggest thing ever to hit him, and he could envisage no life that did not centre on her.

He passed Conservatory Water and swung towards East 72nd exit. He had a great deal at stake. He had seduced and married Gayle to take revenge on her father, not thinking of her. He had not come to know her well; had not considered how the deal had gone for her. They had rows, but over trivial matters usually – he seldom knew, cared, what she thought on bigger issues. Such as, was she happy, content; probably because for him they were *not* big issues. He had married her, possessed her, end of story.

It would be different with Liza; he knew instinctively she would not be slipped into a pocket of his life to stay there quietly. His hands would be full. But was that not what he wanted, for God's sake? To have hands, life, full to bursting with Liza Vaughan?

He phoned her next morning before she had time to leave her hotel.

'Carl – this is too bad, we agreed –'

'We did not. Absolutely not; *you* said what should happen. I do not agree.'

'So what can I say to convince you?'

'Tell me one thing. If I were free, would you marry me?'

'I do not answer hypothetical questions. You must do whatever you want to do. Anything I may want to do as a result of that is hypothetical. You would have to take a chance, Lucky Carl Cline! Now, I am putting this phone down. Sorry, but I have to leave right now anyway.'

J. Arthur Belman refused to meet in Carl's office; he said he would be in the boardroom at ten and Carl could join him there. As he took the elevator to the seventh floor Carl felt prepared; or as prepared as it was possible to be with as wily a bird as Belman. Over the last days he had thought through every angle so far as he was aware, consulting his lawyers on every likely point. His chest felt as if a steel band was encircling it . . . but he was ready.

He entered the boardroom promptly but Belman was before him, sitting at the far end of the huge mahogany table like a bulky, heavy-jowled bird of prey in his speckled grey suit. Next to him sat a middle-aged, powerfully built man with smoothed-back grey hair who was delving in an imposing leather briefcase, his eyes behind expensive horn-rims, pale and detached.

'Good morning, sir. How are you?'

Carl pulled out a chair a couple removed from the men and sat half facing them, smiling politely.

Belman ignored the salutation. 'This is Salinger, my legal expert.' No words were wasted on niceties. He laid square-tipped, meaty hands flat on the table.

'What exactly are you expecting of my daughter? She's called me every day this last week and she's in a fair state, for which I hold you entirely responsible.'

Carl gave a small, patient sigh; he had hoped all the crap had been gone through, it had been a tough enough week. But he'd known Belman would insist on his pound of flesh.

'We have already been through this,' he pointed out. 'You will know already that Gayle has agreed to divorce me.'

'She should have divorced *you* long ago –' Belman said unpleasantly. 'Now it will be on *her* terms.'

'On your terms, you mean.' Carl Cline, still polite, showed a row of well-cared-for teeth. 'That is what we're here for, is it not?'

'It sure is, so remember that.'

'I'll remember.' He showed a rough edge now. Carl had no wish to joust with his father-in-law, there were other things needing his energy. 'Gayle has her own stake in Cline Investments, which is worth many times over the settlement you made on her when we were married; you are on the board to represent her. She can have the Long Island house and I'm certainly not going to be unreasonable in providing for Brad. What else can you ask for?'

'More.' Belman was brutally blunt. 'If you expect Gayle to fly down to Vegas for six weeks' residency, then file, so you can lay some broad who's been keeping her legs crossed, there's a high price tag. We want our stake in the business upped to 15 per cent. How you go about that is up to you – but it has to be firmed up before Gayle goes ahead.'

He leaned back and lit one of his huge cigars, enjoying himself now. 'And I want your father off the board – you have his proxy anyway – to bring on my own nominee.'

Carl studied the close, beautiful grain of the table. The old shit . . . the clever old shit, pitching his demand exactly at the point where I can just about afford to agree. He knows that with Arney Bold's support, and Dad's, I can still hold him off. But God, he's not kidding about the price.

'Thirteen,' he countered, without hope.

'Seventeen.' Belman's mouth edged up in a satisfied grin. 'Think I'm a dope? You just don't have the cards of ten years back, do you, when you gambled with my daughter as chips? Sorry boy, but it's all downside this hand. Of course, she can just stay on here to divorce you and let New York State rules apply, if you prefer?'

Carl was silent. Belman's grin widened. 'You're the one to get the crap this time; how's it feel? Still can't wait to drop your pants for the lady? OK . . .' He motioned to Salinger, who drew out papers from his impressive briefcase. Belman pushed them down the table.

'It's all here, drawn up in detail. Run it across your people then get back to Salinger here. We can tie it up fast. That's all.' He pushed back his chair with a satisfied nod to his attorney, and marched from the room.

Carl stood slowly and walked to the window. He felt stiff, sore; as if he had been beaten. He lit a cigarette and drew deeply, staring into the cavern of the street below.

Well, he *had* been beaten . . . little wonder he was sore. He had known of course that Belman would extract what vengeance was possible; *he* had, after all, deflowered the man's ewe lamb! More, gone on to bargain for her honour . . . not the action of a gentleman.

He rested his hot brow against the glass, closing his eyes. So; he could not beat the pay-off. But he had not expected Belman to take his pound of flesh in the form of Cline Investments shares. There could only be one reason for this – Belman was going for control of *his* business. But he, Carl, would prevent this. He would be smart; keep his powder dry, live to fight another day – all the clichés would apply!

He made for the elevator. What had Liza told him about wanting to be valued? Worth something? Carl gave a sudden snort of laughter. She'd be delighted then, wouldn't she, to know what a hell of a price he'd paid for her.

Chapter Sixteen

Summer 1969

Laurie sat on the grass in Hyde Park, smoking a reefer. He had very little room for his legs, there being around a quarter of a million other people in Hyde Park that weekend. The Rolling Stones had reappeared in public after more than a year's seclusion to give a free concert, and their welcome was rapturous. It had also become a requiem, as one of them had been found dead in his swimming pool three days earlier. There was much weeping by young girls, much swaying, shaking of long hair and rattling of beads for the dead idol.

Laurie's exeat had worked exactly to order that weekend. He had asked his parents if he might spend it with his grandmother at the Clapham flat as they wanted to do some things in London. This in itself was lucky, as his gran had only just got back from New York, seeing Liza's new play. No actual lies were told; Laurie simply forbore to mention that one of the 'things' was the Stones concert. He was well aware that parents were in the main dead against the Stones as inciters to rebellion in the young, a definite influence for bad all round. He loved them next only to the Beatles.

He took another pull on his joint. Dope was quite cheap here; he felt he could afford to roll a few. He liked the effect dope had on him . . . the skies were a more intense blue, leaves, a more intense green, a packet of crisps tasted better and his bed felt softer to lie on. He also felt perfectly relaxed and peaceful despite the crowds and the noise, so that was fine. He'd been talking with some really decent people down from Yorkshire for the concert. They had a minute tent between three, but no one seemed to be minding too much about the lack of privacy. Hannah had provided him with a stack of sandwiches and some fruit, and he'd shared everything out four ways. They had in return shared their cider with him, but it was what they called 'rough' and had made him quite sleepy. In fact, so sleepy that now he got to his feet with some difficulty, and began to pick his way through the crush to where it would be a bit quieter and he could maybe lie down. Though he must be careful not to go to sleep, he'd promised he would be back at the flat by 10.30.

He did, in fact, go directly to sleep, during which time someone picked his pocket. He woke with a fearful headache and no money, when the light was already fading. Fortunately he had his little packet of dope safe in the breast pocket of his shirt. He sold this for the price of the bus fare back to Clapham, and got there at almost eleven o'clock. As he drifted to sleep he thought of Liza ... He'd not much enjoyed Gran telling him all about that amazing food and drink at that huge wedding party she'd had. Seemed that Liza might be bypassing the things that mattered, these days; that mattered to him, at any rate. He'd been quite shocked at the waste ... that sort of money would have bought tons of ordinary food, to feed *hundreds* of people. He really liked Liza and hoped that hitting the big time wouldn't spoil her.

'You must be crazy.' Liza stared at Carl as though searching for outward signs of insanity. He ran a hand through his hair in a gesture of frustration.

'Oh well, thanks. You say you want to be worth something – no hole-and-corner affairs. I'm now arranging that, at the cost of a king's ransom; so you accuse me of being crazy.' He sat down on the dressing-room chair.

'You weren't supposed to do *this*,' she said slowly. 'You were supposed to walk away. From me – not from your wife and son.'

'Well I didn't. I don't turn my back on something I want as much as I want you. I go for it.' He grinned. 'This is all part of the getting to know you process, I guess. We don't interpret each other's signals too well yet.'

'We're practically complete strangers,' she corrected him. Turning away, she sorted over her make-up for the performance, her face serious. 'Carl; we're still at square one, you know. I mean, we still may or may not make it together – that's right, isn't it? The only thing different from how it first was is your being free to have a relationship. There's still all the usual hurdles. Some pretty high, like living 3,000 miles apart.'

'We can jump them if we're determined to.' He came to stand behind her, hands on her shoulders, watching her reflection. After a moment Liza reached up with her own hands to cover his and tipped back her head. He bent to kiss her eyes, then her lips, and dropped his hands to cup her breasts under the thin silk robe.

She felt a warm lurch of pleasure. Standing, she turned into his arms and they pressed fiercely against one another. She remembered thinking this was not a good idea; God help them both. After a moment she pulled away, leaning back to see his face. It was strangely, unaccountably dear to her, and she traced its sharp planes with her finger. His eyes weren't in the least cold, were they – not even cool, but warm and deeply alive.

'You may have to give me a hand over these hurdles, Carl.' Her voice held a certain hesitancy. 'Hurdling was a pet hate of mine at school and nothing's changed. Now go, please. I need a full hour and a half before curtain-up.'

'I still can't believe it's happened,' Hannah said to Matthew. She had brought out a tray of tea and set it on the low wall near where they were working. She rubbed her back before sitting down to pour; there had been too much spadework today for a sixty-seven-year-old . . . or a seventy-one-year-old, judging by Matthew's face.

'What can't you believe? That we're actually almost at the end of this damn wall?' He took his tea from her. 'Is there whisky in it?'

'Would I dare offer it if there were not? I have over the years come to recognise the signs of Matthew being in dire need of whisky in his tea. I mean, they're based on different continents, for one thing . . .'

'That's not what's got to you though, is it? It's a personal thing?'

'A personal thing,' she echoed. 'Of course you're right. How could a man simply junk his wife and child without *reason*? And according to Liza, she's made absolutely no commitment anyway, so he may end up with neither. But she's certain to feel pressure, even so . . .' Hannah frowned into her teacup. 'I just hope she can think clearly when the time comes. She seems to have made one mistake already, and it's cost her some self-esteem . . . she needs to be certain she can handle this. You know, the ex-wife, the child . . .

maybe some public antagonism.'

They stood for a moment before going indoors, Matthew's arm slung across her shoulders in the way she loved. The August afternoon had thickened and there was the vague bulk of a thundercloud building far out to sea. About them were the results of their labours; the pond was a winner, with a small cascade of water falling over rocks into it from a tiny pond above, and vegetation trailing about it in happy profusion. Roses were in their second flush of the summer, and a group of sapphire-blue delphiniums lorded it magnificently over lesser species. Bracken House and gardens now had an unmistakable air of being loved; as do people, the place responded by giving of its best. Nick had been for a visit this summer though he was currently based in Italy, and Jake had come with Rose and delicious small daughter Ruth. Even Jonet and Mark had been dragooned by Laurie into making an overnight visit, and all had gone well, while Laurie had stayed a fortnight and made great strides with his herb garden.

The house was becoming what Hannah had hoped for: a warm and welcoming place for them, and for anyone in the family needing peace to draw breath, somewhere to draw her difficult, fragmented family together. Hannah only wished her own present unease would dissolve in the peaceful ambience.

There was a letter for her from Alex in the next morning's mail.

'Shall I read it to you?'

'Sure.' Matthew looked up from his paper and saw the lines of concern pulling down her face.

'East Hampton
Long Island

Dear Hannah,

Thought you might like to know that the knee has given me no more trouble to date. It sure was an experience; long may it last! Thanks again for the great job on it. One of my partners says he has a hip out, and asks would you like to pop back over and fix that too!

This business with Carl has rocked us all. I guess it's had the same effect on you – though we're aware no blame rests with Liza. Carl has at least been up front about that, it is clearly all his doing.

Delaney is upset for Gayle, her having no mother. She went down to Vegas to see what help she might be, but Gayle's holding up well, all in all. And of course young Brad is with her, it being his long vacation, so they've been out on trips. When they come back to NY – only a couple of weeks or so now – Delaney is insisting she comes here for a while at least. If nothing else she will be suffering with heat exhaustion – Vegas is a cauldron this time of year.

It's going to be tough on Brad, of course. But sadly, marriage break-up becomes more common each year; and he does have us as family still. Joe seems pretty upset, but you will doubtless have heard from him. I believe he is concerned for the possible bad publicity for Liza too. In case you would rather be in the know about newspaper reports, I send you a couple from the NY papers. Of course, it's of no interest to *them* that Liza has had no say in all this.

So there it is; we shall have to see what happens when Gayle has her decree. Children surely never do cease to surprise us! Toby and Belinda are at Woodstock, up in the Catskills, some big music party going on there around now. At least we finally put a man on the moon, so it can't all be bad!

Oh, and I've a lead on a possibility of tracing our lines back further – my mother's cousin, in Oregon, seems to know quite a bit, has an old family bible, stuff like that. Useful, maybe?

We send our best to you and hope things are good right now, it was great meeting up with you.

Regards from Delaney and myself to you both.

Alex Cline'

Hannah picked up the two cuttings and passed them across, her eyes alarmed. 'Liza would not be best pleased . . .' Matthew looked them over and pulled down his mouth. One was headed 'BRITISH ACTRESS BIDS FOR CLINE TAKEOVER'. Both were on the theme that for an emerging actress to hook a millionaire entrepreneur was a good career move.

'No . . . but one always takes press reports with a pinch of salt. Maybe it's true that any publicity is good in the acting world. She must just face it down; she should manage that.' He picked up Alex's letter. 'She may feel badly about the boy . . . even though it wasn't her doing.'

'Such a mess –' Hannah stared at the letter on her knee. Concern ballooned across her brain like a grey fog, obscuring all else; yet why? Of course Carl had behaved badly, of course Liza should steer clear of such a man. But it went beyond that . . . there was something *about* Carl. If she went to New York herself right now, made an effort to point out to Liza . . . ?

She looked up to find Matthew watching her. 'She would not accept anything I might say,' she observed, her voice flat.

'Probably not, sweetheart.' He put a hand over hers. 'I think they're both set on it. And when did Liza ever take advice? But this bit about the Hywels' – he sought to divert her – 'That's interesting, don't you think?'

Penelope called New York at the end of August to say that Liza had been invited to read for the part of Lady Plyant in a top-flight BBC TV production of Congreve's *The Double Dealer* scheduled for January. Restoration comedy . . . Liza's eyes gleamed. She was due a few days off in early September; yes, of course she would get there – and get the part. Penelope then said she would arrange interviews at the same time for a possible film. This was provisionally pencilled in for March, pending negotiations with the final member of the backers. An adaptation of the award-winning Australian novel *Stars in Milk* . . . the script was excellent after several years' work, and budgets looking good enough. She would send out a copy of the script and Liza would agree, she felt sure, that the part of Edie was tailor-made.

Liza, too excited to eat, phoned Joe and Sal, who said wonderful, come to supper on Sunday and tell more. She bought a copy of *The Double Dealer*, and prepared to dissect it. After much hesitation she called Carl.

'All that sounds fantastic. What a clever girl.'

'What a clever agent!'

'That too. So may I take you out to celebrate?'

She hesitated. 'We did agree, Carl. Not before –'

'No. Not before.' He sounded dispirited. Liza said suddenly:

'Look: can you get away around lunchtime? I've some shopping to do, we could meet in Central Park, buy a sandwich. Not your usual style. I would prefer it, though, to a heavy date at a top feeding trough.'

'I have never bought a sandwich in Central Park,'

he admitted. 'You see it as more anonymous than my usual haunts?'

'I suppose. Particularly if you take off your tie.'

'Will do. And my jacket?'

'Absolutely no jacket – not in this temperature. See you one-ish? I'm coming in from Bergdorf Goodman so I'll walk through Army Plaza. How if we find each other by that next path off to the left?'

'I'll be there. With lunch. Thanks, darling.'

Putting the phone down, Liza felt a small rush of tenderness. She had no idea where this would end; where *they* would end. But it seemed nothing would stop them from beginning . . .

He looked happy when she caught sight of him at the turn-off, and quite different from the business persona he could present, or the expensively dressed socialite. His white shirt was open at the neck, his hair disordered by the warm breeze. He waved and hurried over, swinging a small carrier bag.

'Food and drink. Hi, darling.' He kissed her cheek. 'You look marvellous. Success agrees with you.'

'Does it not agree with everyone?' Liza laughed, because she was happy. Her eyes sparkled with it, it crackled through her lovely flying hair and shone on her luminous skin. She wore a snow-white cotton top with a deep square neckline, a pair of faultlessly cut cobalt blue Bermuda shorts, and white sandals. Her earrings were simple white hoops, and on her slender brown arm were pushed white bracelets. 'What do we eat?' She peeped into the bag.

'Never mind about that right now. First we must find a tree for shade.' He took her hand and they walked along the path. There were not too many people around, it not being a weekend and with offices closed for vacations. Liza gave herself over to the pleasures of the hour. She had a sense of wrong-doing, but on a small harmless scale, nothing that need do other than add a tingle of excitement to a stroll in Central Park. It was necessary, of course, to block thoughts of Brad, or of his mother. She, Liza, having done nothing to bring about this family break-up, could not be held responsible for their situation. *She* had made no move, given neither encouragement nor promises. When Carl was a single man again she would reflect; sound out her own emotions. Logic did urge her to cut and run while she was still uncommitted; Liza felt his hand holding hers in a strong confident grip, and knew that this was unlikely.

They settled under a willow, with the pond before them and the soaring white Plaza topped by its green gables glimpsed through the trees. A couple of small boys were pulling boats through the water, watched by their mothers, and an old man threw bread to a trio of lethargic ducks. Liza sat down on the daisy-strewn grass.

'Now may we eat? I'm starving.'

'You always are. OK – we eat.' Carl shook out a small cream linen cloth and set two translucent china plates on it, and two matching napkins. Liza looked interested as he produced a carton of ice-packed prawns, another of green salad, crusty rolls, a wedge of perfect Camembert, fragrant peaches and a flask.

'Wonderful. Oh, marvellous –' She fell on the food. 'What's in the flask?'

'A small refresher.' He delved into the bag for two glasses each rolled in a napkin and poured ice-cold champagne from the flask into each.

'Mm–mm.' Liza picked up her glass, raised it to Carl. 'Thank you for a perfect picnic.'

'Thank you for coming.' As they drank they

watched each other. Sometimes she was wary of this man, unsure of his true motives, but now she fell in with his present relaxed mood and they chatted amicably as they ate. New Yorkers strolled past, a few settled nearby to rest under trees, and children called at their play; Carl and Liza, though, were untroubled by the surrounding city and its denizens. When a toddler's ball rolled towards him, Carl toed it gently back with a wave to the child.

'You'll miss your son,' Liza said suddenly. He looked up, wiping his fingers on the napkin before finishing his champagne.

'Yes.' He made no attempt to prevaricate. 'My lawyer's negotiated access of course, but it won't be the same. I understand the divorce will be through in about eight days. May I call you when that happens?'

'Surely.' She hesitated. 'But I have to make a quick trip to London – Penelope's arranging a play reading, and a first discussion about a film. I've three days off, part of the contract here is a mid-run break – so I must go then.'

'Tell them to come to you.' He spoke forcibly. 'Don't wear yourself out tearing 3,000 miles and back in three days. Penelope must tell them that if they want you, they'll find you here.'

'Carl – if I want the parts I must –'

'You must recognise your worth!' he interrupted harshly. 'You're a rare and talented actress – they know that, and will come. You try and you'll see I'm right.' He smiled slowly. 'Then we might use a couple of those days to get to the coast for a breather. I could take you sailing.'

'I don't like boats.' She was forceful now, recalling with sudden pain the day she and Edward Anderssen had taken the boat trip round the Farne islands . . . the crisp, clean, grey and white world of tumbling breakers and sea-birds and huge intimidating skies. Edward . . . where was he? Did he think of her? He had hurt her so . . . 'I shan't ever come sailing with you,' she said cruelly, and jumped to her feet. 'Now I have to go.'

Carl Cline looked up at her, squinting in the hot brassy sunlight. 'Ouch,' he drawled. 'What was that about? And there I was thinking I might finally get to seduce you next week, in the privacy of my sexy little black leather cabin.'

She stared at him, taken aback by his cool effrontery. He stared back but now she saw the glint of laughter. 'Seductions are out,' she told him, unsmiling. 'I hoped that had been sorted. I have satisfied my need for sexual indulgence, it's on the have-done list.'

As she bent to pick up her bag, Liza found her wrist circled by his fingers and Carl said quietly: 'We are talking human beings here, Liza Vaughan. They don't always stay sorted out – don't forget that, will you?'

'You mean I can't trust you?' She looked intently at him. 'No, I suppose I can't . . . thanks for reminding me you're no different from the rest.'

He got quickly to his feet and his face was serious. 'You will find I am different. I'm sorry that whatever I said hit a raw nerve. Will you forgive me, and forget the last few minutes?'

'It comes from your not knowing me,' she told him flatly. 'Not knowing things that have happened. It's the same for me – I don't know you.'

'You will. And I'll learn about you. Only give us both a chance; you *have* to do that or we can't make headway.'

'No.' She picked a bit of grass off her shorts. 'Thank you for the picnic, Carl. Why are you in town, anyway? Why aren't you taking your vacation – surely Wall Street's out of school? Uncle Joe's away; don't New Yorkers leave the city to the tourists, come August?'

'I shan't go anywhere while you're here.' He spoke with evident sincerity. 'I've plenty to do, anyway. But yes, this is usually vacation time. We'd take Brad –' He broke off, and looked hard into the distance.

'Carl . . .' She touched his hand as they began to walk. 'I'm so afraid you've made a terrible mistake, taken a step you will regret. Is it too late to go back?'

'Going back never works. If you will come with me, going forward will be wonderful.'

'Not necessarily.' Liza found she wanted to be honest. 'I am attracted to you, as you are to me. But nothing else augurs well – you can't help but have noticed! Your home life, for a start. I don't know how you felt personally about Gayle, and I've no wish to know, it is simply nothing to do with me. But she obviously ran your home, probably entertained your business friends . . . provided for your personal comforts. And cared for your son.'

'Sure. All of those things.' Carl's face was expressionless.

'Well –' she spread a hand helplessly. 'I can't. My life is a close-lapped schedule of work, hard, energy-sapping work into the foreseeable future. And for the moment anyway, mostly on the far side of the Atlantic. You work all hours yourself, I know that. When would we even meet up?'

They walked in silence for a few moments. Then Carl said, 'I can't off the cuff say how we would work out our lives, Liza. And I can't understand how or why I feel this colossal pull towards you. But I haven't gone to these lengths simply to get you into bed –

appealing though the idea is.' He smiled then. 'Maybe I even *need* your inaccessibility; the challenge such a lifestyle could bring. Each reunion could be another honeymoon. You see? We'd have no chance to go stale on each other for sure!'

They slowed as they joined the main road, with a reluctance to part. He said slowly, 'Liza; I only feel certain we *could* make it work. Hell, I'm a wealthy man . . . I could provide a home here *and* in London, or anywhere else you want . . . maybe help make funds available for any special vehicle for your special talents.' He paused. 'But there is one thing –'

He faced her. 'You're right about Brad. His loss – and I have lost him, his mother will see to that – can't be minimised. He was my only child. If you and I were to succeed in building a life together, an essential brick would be a child of our own. The biggest thing two people can share, the most unifying element, is a child they've made together from their love.'

Liza was silent, watching his face. He put out a finger and touched her cheek. 'Don't say you've no time to have children, that you're too busy building your career. You can't honestly envisage going through life without that experience? Sure, it'd mess up the schedule for a year maybe, but actresses have kids all the time and survive professionally. Anyway –' He gave a shrug. 'I have to lay that on the line.'

'Yes. I see that.' Liza pulled back a lock of hair as the heat of the city hit her afresh. 'I shall think all this over . . .'

She lay on the bed in her room for a while after showering, naked to catch the relief of cooled air blowing in through the ducts. She wanted to sleep, the most satisfactory route out of thinking, but knew she had not long enough before leaving for the theatre. She put a call through to Penelope Fine, lips pursed in a soundless whistle. Nothing ventured . . . After they had spoken she lay back with a little smile. Penelope had taken it in her stride, not thought the idea absolutely outrageous . . . it might just work.

An extraordinary man . . . a potent mix of power, audacity, perception, with dangerously endearing glimpses of tenderness. Not that she knew him at all, of course; when – if – she ever did, she might discover all this to be a cynically constructed image. No; don't be a half-wit – no one, however clever, could successfully present a completely false persona. Could they? *Some* of it must be the actual Carl Cline. Maybe she should have a serious talk with Uncle Joe; he had known his godson since birth. But then she would have shown her hand . . . admitted her deep interest; that she was actually contemplating marriage with this man who had just cast off with single-minded ruthlessness his wife and child. Why had he married Gayle in the first place; had he not loved her? If he had, how could everything evaporate in ten short years? How could he let his son go?

Liza turned and buried her face in the pillow. The skin of her back was touched by cool, faintly moving air and it was pleasurable as the caress of cool fingers. She thought of Carl Cline; of their making a child together . . . felt her cheeks warm with desire for him, her stomach crawl with anticipated delight. Don't make another mistake . . . they are too damaging.

For the first time in a couple of years, she wanted her mother. Hannah would be calm, would reassure her. Yet think of Hannah's mistakes – *she'd* made her share, God knows, she could scarcely be trusted! No, she, Liza, must be the sole arbiter of her own actions.

After a while she got off the bed and took another shower before setting off for the theatre.

'Liza? Oh, it's lovely to hear from you, dear. Are you well? . . . Good . . . Yes, we're OK, thanks. Well, I knew you'd be busy of course. Joe wrote when they came back from holiday, he said he'd seen you . . . Oh, we pottered around Brittany for a week, September's a good month and we enjoyed that. We took Laurie – I think he liked it too. He's back at school now, which is not nearly as much fun, according to him . . . Oh . . . Well, yes, of course I knew he was divorcing, and Joe said it was through when he wrote . . . Oh Liza – are you really? . . . No, I'm not upset. Surprised, rather . . . Well, I do wish you both all happiness, Liza dear – so will Matthew of course. You've thought it all through I'm sure – so when would this be? . . . Heavens – that doesn't give me much time to make arrangements . . . In New York? . . . Oh has he? – well that's in order, I suppose . . . Well, yes of course we'll be there.'

Hannah sat down, still listening, a despairing frown creasing her brow. Matthew got up to pour her a drink, he had a feeling she might shortly appreciate one. When finally she bade Liza good-night she looked at him, still gripping the receiver.

'She's really going ahead, then.' He took the phone from her and cradled it, then gave her the drink.

'Going ahead. I suppose I knew she would . . . It had to happen. I said I was surprised, but that wasn't true.'

'Did she sound confident?'

'Perfectly. I just wish *I* could be . . . I just have this . . .'

'Premonition?' He smiled, but Hannah failed to respond.

'No. A heavy idea that it's not the thing to be doing. Carl worried me – silly word, but you understand – when he was twelve. David's paying for the wedding, by the way.'

'He'll enjoy that – are they making a splash?' She nodded, finished her drink and got up, restless.

'A classy country hotel. No honeymoon as she's working. She comes back to London in early December, seems there's a play lined up and also a film in the offing. Anyway, darling –' she looked apologetic. 'Can you face another trip to New York?'

'I can if you can.' Matthew wrapped an arm about her shoulder and together they looked out at the early autumn evening, mellow light spilling on to the garden. Evan Griffith from along the road had taken the mowing and heavy work off their hands, leaving them with the pottering they so enjoyed. 'You may not recall, it being a long while ago,' he added with a grin. 'But it was thanks to Liza that we met. I wouldn't want to miss her wedding.'

Laurie sat on the front doorstep with his friends, who were squatting in one of a terrace of houses in Weir Street, behind King's Cross. Tomorrow he would be in the Lower Sixth, starting his two-year A-level grind. His O-level results had been indifferent, to put it mildly . . . 'Considerable under-achieving' in the words of his housemaster's report. 'Lacking effort and concentration'.

He took a joint from Rich and drew on it deeply before passing it to Lou.

'Thanks, man.' Lou parted her curtain of long, not absolutely clean hair and the joint disappeared temporarily before being handed on to Vernie, who was cuddling the stray puppy they had taken to feeding lately. Laurie spent time here increasingly when not with his grandmother; it was easy to give his parents plausible reasons for his absence from Reading. His father had a commission in the north of Scotland and had only managed two weekends home during August. His mother had worked through at the library, happy that he had been invited to Bracken House, so relieving her of the necessity of going on holiday with him. His parents planned a holiday in Sicily together when work finished in Scotland in late October.

Laurie had enjoyed joining the protest marches of the homeless this summer, and of being accepted by them as an OK guy. While not homeless himself, he identified increasingly with the underdog, the disempowered in society. He had smuggled a spare blanket out of his parents' house last month to help with bedding in the Weir Street squat. And when battle had been joined with the police up west a couple of weeks ago, over a place in Piccadilly due for demolition where 300 squatters had set up home, Laurie had been there, holding up placards with his friends. Squats were now being cleared as a police policy, though Weir Street had so far escaped. He hoped the homeless young he had come to care about might winter there rather than be evicted on to the streets; but Laurie was learning fast that people of no importance materially were treated as of no importance, full stop.

He had a vague idea of attempting to form a protest group at school; after all, protests were the thing now, from the London School of Economics down to Eton, where he'd read that a branch of the Schools Action Union had been formed. The New Left ... Che Guevara ... Laurie read of students worldwide rising in protest, fired by the horror of Vietnam where (according to the communists) the most powerful capitalist power in the world was striving to crush a small Asian country.

Laurie could not be quite certain if he was a communist; but he knew for sure that he was for all men being equal and he certainly knew he was not a Tory like his father. Last October, he had witnessed the massive anti-USA demonstration here in London, and had his first glimpse of people-power ranged against the Establishment. Over this year he had formed opinions, some naïve, some woolly, but sincerely felt, and had come to believe that sides must be taken in the struggle.

When Liza actually went to America to work he had felt outraged, for America – save for her disadvantaged blacks – had come to be the big bad wolf of the world. If she had done something worthwhile like going to the Woodstock festival he'd have understood; he would have given his own eye teeth to have been there. He hoped devoutly that his young aunt was not intending to sell her soul to the gods of capitalism. If she did, as his parents had, he would not.

He had wanted to talk all this over with his grandmother, and with Matthew, for whom he had a lot of time, but Laurie had not so far found the words. He felt though, as he sat in Weir Street with his shabby *aficionados*, that one day soon he would . . . and that he might even hope to be understood by them.

Chapter Seventeen

Autumn 1969

'It's going to rain,' said Hannah. 'I just know it is.'

'What does it matter, darling?' Matthew said for the third time, concentrating on keeping her calm. 'If it's fine the wedding is in the garden, if it rains it's indoors. Either will be beautiful. All will be decided in the morning, so take your bath now, then get a good night's sleep. It's wonderful, don't you think,' he added to make her feel better, 'that you've been spared all the expense and worse, the ghastly trauma, of arranging your daughter's wedding?'

'If you recall,' Hannah said distantly, 'I had only the expense of Jonet's wedding, none of the arranging. What I should have loved, this time, is actually to have had a *hand* in the occasion.'

'Ah . . .' Matthew sighed. 'Well, that didn't work out, so why not accept the status quo and enjoy it? It's so unlike you not to make the best of things; really, I'm quite out of ideas on how to cheer you up.'

Hannah laughed then and put her arms around his waist, which was only slightly broader than it had been when she had first done so. 'Darling. You deserve a medal for even trying. I'm a neurotic, ungrateful old hag and shall complain no more. The Cedars is a beautiful place for a wedding, and rain or shine, tomorrow will come and go as days do. I only wish I felt just a mite warmer towards my future son-in-law, particularly as his father has made us such welcome guests here. What a place . . .'

The wedding ceremony was to be at the Cedars, the discreetly luxurious hotel not far from Alex Cline's Long Island home – or for that matter from Carl's, though this was not being mentioned. Hannah and Matthew had been invited with Joe and his family to stay at Alex's, and all available accommodation at the Cedars had been booked for other wedding guests. Those not here already would come by car for the three o'clock ceremony. David Vaughan was expected by private aircraft around breakfast time, and Liza had already retired to one of the guest rooms, close by that of Hannah and Matthew, having been flown the hundred miles after the night's performance. She appeared calm, and in no way awed by the formidable arrangements in train. Most of the cast of *Balcony View* were being brought from New York by coach in the morning, to be returned in time for the evening performance; Liza's part would be played by her understudy for one night.

'Don't tell me you can't get longer!' Carl had exploded. 'Anyone is entitled to get married, surely!'

'Perfectly,' Liza had retorted. 'But not to break their contract by disrupting a production, and the public's enjoyment of it. People have bought tickets expecting to see me, unless I'm actually ill; I'm lucky to have one night off. That's the way of it in my profession . . . it is not too late to back out if you think it's too tough,' she had added with some bravado.

'But Liza – this wedding's superb publicity for the play – our guest list's awash with heavy names!'

'If you think it merits special treatment you must take that up with the management. I certainly can't – my day's full enough doing the job I'm paid for. As for publicity; we play mostly to full houses anyway so maybe we don't need it.' Carl had taken her in his arms then and held her quietly, stroking her hair until she relaxed again.

She woke early on her wedding morning. It was fine. Pulling open the curtains she saw dew like diamonds on the grass and a pale, peerless sky, the sky she recalled on fine October mornings at home. Liza at that moment, and uncharacteristically, yearned for home with the powerful yearning of the Welsh. Well, she *was* Welsh, was she not; and so entitled to a bout of *hiraeth* so far from home on her wedding day. She had wanted more of her family here; Laurie and Jonet; dear Tom. And Florence, who was as good as an aunt. She had sent Jonet an invitation, but with little hope of it being accepted. It was not *her* fault, Hannah had hastened to reassure her; Jonet's hurt stemmed from *her*, Hannah's actions, so long ago that it should have ceased to be an issue. When Liza came home in December she could have a post-wedding party for those not here today, and Jonet and Mark might come to that.

Liza curled on the window-seat in the lovely room, enjoying the quiet before the day got under way. Below, landscaped gardens unfolded through copses and shrubberies taking on the first touches of autumn splendour, to a path winding to the beach, and the heady tang of the ocean. Carl's own place must be as gracious as this, a jewel in a perfect setting. But she might never see it . . . It was at present Gayle's territory, until such time as she chose to vacate it. And Brad's home . . .

For a moment it was all quite difficult to believe. The time since they had met could still be counted in weeks, for heaven's sake; and yet, it was sometimes hard to remember back to when Carl had no place in her life. Now he filled it, to the exclusion of everything but her work. His attraction was like a powerful tide, giving her no recourse but to be drawn in, submerged. One should fight a strong tide, when strong is dangerous . . . but she *wanted* to go with this one, she loved its danger. She was not happy about Brad, nor, if she were honest, about Gayle. But he *had* gone ahead with absolutely no encouragement from her, she had seen no way to prevent his divorce. Now she must concentrate on the future.

Hannah opened the doors on to the balcony, and laughed with pleasure. 'Beautiful! It's a perfect day, all we could want! Come and see –'

Matthew followed her out, tying his robe. 'Not bad . . . So, our bride will be wed in the rose arbour after all. Shall we need galoshes with our morning suits after yesterday's rain?'

'We'll have a breakfast tray, then I'll go along to see how Liza slept. I hope Carl gets in from New York in good time – I think she was a fraction jittery that he might go on a bender.'

She found Liza drying her hair. 'Delaney wants her stylist to do it, but I'm better at it myself. So I'm beating her to it. Mummy, d'you want yours done?'

Hannah declined. 'I've been doing my own hair for enough years to cope with its idiosyncrasies, thanks. How is Delaney bearing up?'

'Seems fine.' Liza added candidly, 'Of course, it's not easy for her, entertaining what amounts to the enemy camp . . . you know, she also has this supportive role with Gayle. It was good of her to invite us here . . . but she may feel pretty sore underneath.'

Hannah had hoped that the spectre of Carl's first wife would not invade today. 'She may blame Carl for his actions, but I don't see how she could lay any of Gayle's problems at your door,' she said.

'We shall see.' Liza was quickly creating order from chaos with blow-drier and brush. 'She's going to be my mother-in-law but probably still thinks of herself as Gayle's . . . nothing's easy.'

'It was perhaps provoking that your courtship was so brief. You might have been wise to wait; allow one daughter-in-law to quit the scene before offering another.'

'True. But I'm leaving New York in December and we wanted some time together to get to know one another better.'

'Even so . . .' Hannah strove for a tactful note. 'Maybe if you'd done the "getting to know you" bit *before* the wedding?'

'Mummy. I'm aware that you neither fully trust nor particularly like Carl. But I have thought lots about this. So has Carl, believe me . . . we've discussed it all often. He's laid his cards out for me, and I have no feeling of being manipulated for his purpose. For instance, he's happy to take a change of lifestyle to allow for mine, which I've made plain to him.'

Liza paused. 'He's honest about wanting a child. Not to entrap me, but for us to share, something precious. And I like that idea, too. You know, he does care – he suggested I did not wear myself out hopping over to London last month to read for that TV play. I put it to Penelope, and got the part without the trip! So, I must simply ask you to trust *me*, because I trust *him*. You were running your own life pretty competently at my age after all, weren't you?'

'I had to,' Hannah said quietly. 'Both my parents were dead. I was actually just making my first shaky steps into business . . . baking pies by the dozen, endlessly. I was also about to make a huge mistake by marrying a man who could not have been more wrong for me.'

After a little silence Liza said, 'I'm not doing that, you have my word.' She stretched out her hand. 'So, please Mummy, put your fears on that score away. I know I've been so lucky to have you, and Pa, both so ready to support and cherish. And dear Matthew as an added bonus. Lucky old me . . . I'll try not to let you all down.'

As Liza hugged her Hannah felt tears hot under her lids, then on her cheeks; for she was thinking of Jonet, whom *she* had let down by having Liza. A knock on the door brought Matthew, who surveyed them with a pained look.

'Now why should you be crying on such a lovely morning? I never will understand women.'

'I am crying because it's Liza's wedding day,' said Hannah with dignity. 'All mothers cry on their daughters' wedding day, it's traditional. Any man should know that.'

'It's also traditional for daughters to cry,' said Liza, and blew her nose hard. 'Now I vote we have more fresh coffee.'

Liza was indeed married in the rose arbour, the day having turned warm and benignly sunny. Small gilt chairs were set in rows on the wide terrace of the Cedars, to the side of which a pianist, a violinist and a cellist made Schubert sound like angel music from heaven. The roses were still in exquisite second bloom. Behind them, the house basked in golden light, its walls cloaked in brilliant creeper. Before, and to either side, three acres of exquisitely nurtured gardens gave of their best, with every shape and hue and texture to delight the eye and calm the soul.

If she cannot be happy having been married here, Hannah thought as they waited, she cannot be happy at all. Please God, let her be happy. She gripped Matthew's hand.

'You look wonderfully handsome,' she whispered. He smiled modestly, the slightly comic smile that had always charmed her.

'I do rather, don't I? You don't look half bad yourself.'

Hannah looked down at her becoming dress of buttermilk fine wool crêpe, with a pleated skirt and a deep collar of antique lace. A small beret of the same lace sat on her short, wavy hair, and her earrings were opal drops set in antique filigree gold. A single perfect, creamy rosebud was pinned to her collar. Hannah had learned to triumph over the vagaries of fashion to point up her highly personal, indestructible beauty, seemingly fragile as a shaft of sunlight but with an enduring core of honest warmth.

Carl, waiting by his father and his brother Toby for his bride to appear, looked at Hannah and recalled her calm approachability of twenty years ago, when as a wayward, prickly twelve-year-old he had been pitchforked into an unknown country, and the alien family of Joe, his godfather. He had never admitted it, but this woman seemed to him to possess every quality he most admired; qualities neither encountered nor allowed for in his day-to-day dealings, where no quarter was given and no quality other than a ruthless expediency expected. Most valuable in his eyes was her trustworthy brand of strength. If Carl ever needed to trust totally in one person, it would be Hannah Stourton to whom he would turn. He sighed, and hoped again that Hannah's genes prospered in her daughter.

The music broke, changed to the Wedding March, and Liza came slowly into view, framed in the open doors that had been decorated with trailing ivy and roses. A bronze carpet ran along the terrace down the steps to the arbour, where the clergyman waited with Carl and Toby. As Liza, on the arm of a smiling and immensely proud father and followed by Carl's sister Belinda, paused for a moment, the assembled guests rose as one. With superb grace she moved pace for pace with David Vaughan along the flower-strewn carpet, looking to right and left and smiling at the company. They smiled back, with a warmth they had not been prepared to feel for this usurping English actress.

It was indeed impossible for the most prejudiced and cynical New Yorker to dislike Liza today. She exuded not only happiness, but pleasure at finding herself among them so they might share that happiness. This may well have been a clever projection by a now experienced actress, but her demeanour achieved the desired end.

She wore an ankle-length champagne-coloured gown of finely lined silk organza, with a long toning veil caught by a halo of small cream and apricot roses, and silk slippers embroidered with roses. The gown was cut in Empire style, its scooped round neck and long tight sleeves puffed at the head. The airy skirt was lent weight by appliqué at the hem, about which drifted the gauzy veil. Liza's hair was drawn back and up to fall gracefully about the nape of her neck, and turquoise ear-drops echoed the colour of her eyes. A spray of pale roses and freesias trailed from one hand; the other was laid lightly on David Vaughan's elegantly tail-coated arm. These two were followed in the British fashion by fair-headed Belinda Cline, beaming in chiffon toned from biscuit to orange – no one who knew her had any idea how she had been persuaded away from her out-at-the-knee jeans and crumpled tie-dyed T-shirt.

The seats of family guests flanked the arbour. As she approached, Liza smiled at Hannah and Matthew and dipped in a small curtsy that said plainly 'thanks for everything'. Hannah flashed an answering smile; saw the love on Carl's face as he turned to greet his bride, the pride on David Vaughan's. It *will* work . . . it has to, please God.

The Wedding March ended, the clergyman cleared his throat. In a young redwood nearby, a blackbird began to sing.

'Dearly beloved . . .'

Hannah looked into the shade under the redwood. *She* would not be here, surely . . . not today. She scanned the garden as the service got under way, but no shadow materialised as Rachel Hywel. Of course not – this was 3,000 miles from Wales . . . Rachel was the past; this, the future.

'Just twenty-four hours then back to work; heigh-ho!' Liza grimaced at her mother in the looking-glass as she brushed out her hair with vigorous strokes. Hannah had hung up the wedding dress and veil to await transport to Carl's apartment, and was assembling Liza's travelling outfit. To where it would travel was known only to Carl; Liza had said she cared not where they went for their one-night honeymoon, and that Carl's preference would do fine. She accepted that work came first, that the shortest of breaks was a bonus and that they could take a longer honeymoon when commitments allowed. Carl already planned to spend Christmas with her in England, and Hannah had agreed to look for somewhere attractive in London that could be taken on a short lease.

'It *was* a beautiful wedding,' she said suddenly, laying the green crêpe shift across the bed alongside its matching coat. 'And darling . . . I *do* believe, as you said, that Carl will pull his weight in the marriage.'

'He'd better,' Liza said darkly. 'When I'm ready, I'll tell him I'm a witch, and will stick pins in his effigy if he doesn't rate ten out of ten for effort.'

Hannah's memory flashed to the days after Serena's birth, and her cheeks blanched. She had, in fury and frustration after a particularly unpleasant row with Darrow Bates, done exactly that . . . running wildly out of Incline Row on to the hill, she had made a little figure from mud scooped off the track and had stabbed it repeatedly with her neckpin.

'Mummy? What's the matter – what have I said?' Liza stared at her, hairbrush in mid-air.

'Just a memory . . . it's nothing.' Hannah sat on the bed, examining the long suede boots Liza would wear with her maxi-coat.

'Did you see her too, Mummy?' Liza asked softly. Hannah looked up, and it was impossible to misunderstand.

'No –' her voice cracked, and she cleared her throat.

'She was over by the lily pond, by that big dark shrub.'

'A bay tree,' Hannah said automatically.

'Whatever. I saw her as I turned, after the clergyman had finished.' Liza looked down at her hand, with the fine solitaire given her a month ago by Carl overlying the slim new wedding band.

'Liza, I am sorry.'

Liza laughed. 'Mummy – it doesn't *matter*. Not a hoot; honestly. I know she's upset you for years . . .

but you *allowed* her to. She's just some sad projection of a nutter stuck out of her time, and trespassing on ours. How can she harm us, anyone, for Pete's sake! She isn't real, she's only a vague imprint on the air, probably seen by us because there's a faulty gene somewhere in the Hywel family!'

Liza pushed back her hair, satisfied with its healthy sheen, and stood up to slip off her robe. 'I think I see her when I'm a bit hyped up – like taking curtain-calls; or on my wedding day! I get this faulty vision, if you like. But please believe me, I don't give a fig for silly old Rachel Hywel, and neither must you. OK?' She gripped Hannah's shoulders and smiled confidently into her eyes.

'That may be so for you.' Hannah turned from her, troubled. 'I've given a fig since the first time I saw her . . . aged twelve, the first night of the Great War. We had had a fire in the bedroom I shared with Joe. You could say I was also a little hyped up as you describe it: my hand had been burned!'

She examined the faint scar remaining from the distant past, still terrifyingly vivid. 'I did not see her so often, Liza.' She gazed over the manicured garden, where Rachel had stood as Liza made her vows. 'Less and less, over the years. But I *do* believe there is reason to this somewhere – I cannot think she is just some accident of time and space. She is an ancestor, remember . . . it does surprise me that you've no curiosity about that.'

'Ancestors are dead.' Liza was dismissive.

'You're wrong; I'm certain,' Hannah replied firmly. 'I suppose my great-grandmother Hywel is just an ancestor to you? And my father? But to me they are both close, a real part of my life . . . sort of joined up in a line. You're at the end for the moment, that's all – but one day there'll be a longer line beyond you.'

She frowned with the effort of explaining. Then laughed and turned back to touch her daughter's bright hair. 'Now, get into your glad rags. Everyone's waiting to see you off – and I know your father would love a last word with you before you go. It's meant a lot to him; you know, being here today. He may be feeling just a touch bereft now.'

'Poor lamb.' Liza slid the shift over her hips and pulled up the zip. 'I wonder why step-Ma cried off at the last moment – that was a shame.'

'A cough and cold, he said.' Hannah eased Liza's feet into the mushroom-coloured boots and laced them up. 'But maybe she just decided against it at the last moment.'

'Chickened out?' Liza shrugged her shoulders deeper into her dress; put on a touch of soft bronze lipstick and Hannah held out the elegant sleeveless coat. 'Mummy, you don't have to baby me, I can do quick-changes standing on my head, you know!'

'Of course I know. I just want to baby you one last time . . . any objection?'

'Absolutely none.' Liza gave her a sudden hug that winded her. 'I hope it won't be the last time you baby me, though. I'm still going to be around! And Mummy –' She hugged her again – 'Can I just say this once: I'm very pleased that you didn't decide to abort me . . . being alive is too good to have missed.'

Hannah gave a choked little gasp. 'Never entered my mind,' she whispered back when she had control of her voice. 'No possibility.'

The late November wind off East River whistled about the apartment block, to lose its puff soon after Lexington and peter out entirely before the park. It was scarcely heard in Carl's elegant sitting room, muffled by the glazing and lined brocade curtains, and by thick wool twist-pile carpet laid wall to wall. Liza was curled on the deep-cushioned sofa in a jewel-green velvet robe; this was their precious time for relaxation between theatre and bed. She sipped hot milk and brandy and Carl a bourbon; he was tucked into the other end of the sofa with legs stretched out and ankles comfortably crossed.

They had shaken down into a tentative routine, soon to be disrupted when Liza flew back to London in mid-December. Carl had hoped she might stay on for Christmas but the television play would not wait; neither would the projected film. Their honeymoon was still to be taken at some indeterminate date; possibly even next August now, as Carl would find it hard to be too far from Cline Investments at other times. He had become more determined than ever to be seriously rich; and knew that did not happen lying on a beach in Bermuda, or yachting lazily around the Caribbean. He smiled at his wife.

'So, tell me what your mother said about the house?'

'Oh . . .' Liza screwed up her face. 'Should have written it down . . . but I was only minutes off my entrance. She's sending on the agent's details, of course; sounded promising though – she was very excited about it. In Holland Park, I remember that. One of the white, double-fronted houses you find around there with steps to the door; four floors including basement. Oh and a garden – that would be lovely, wouldn't it?'

'Sure. But in a park? That's unusual isn't it?'

'Ah, well. Holland Park itself is in Kensington. But this Holland Park is actually a road outside the park.'

'Ah; what about furniture?'

'No problems there. Mummy says everything is just perfect. Not a thing needed. But the rent is extremely high.'

'Would you be happy to spend Christmas there, instead of in a hotel?'

'Oh yes.' Liza stretched herself luxuriously and settled deeper into the cushions. 'If Mummy says it's OK it'll be fine. And if you're staying on through January it will be loads better than a hotel suite.'

'Look, your mother will be in bed and asleep now. But don't waste time waiting for details. Ring her first thing in the morning and tell her to clinch it; no matter what it costs; anything extra good never hangs around.'

'OK, darling.'

'While we're talking property, do you want to look at something else here in New York? Or maybe another place out of town?'

'Heavens, no – this is fine for now. And you won't feel strange, alone here when I'm away . . . you've lived here during the week for a while, haven't you?'

'Four years.' Carl looked around the graceful, understated room. 'But it will be lonely here without you. No talc on the bedroom carpet, no scent of Liza.'

'Oh, I'll leave talc for you to toss around – and perfume on my dressing table. And how about a nightgown folded on my pillow, just to remind you?' She laughed. 'But no one else is to wear it, mind. I shall know, being a witch, and that will be *finito*, Carl Cline!'

He traced a finger over her bare foot. 'I haven't found gold only to throw it away. Although the bit about being a witch is a mite unnerving.'

'Don't fret about that, darling. I keep it up my

sleeve for a rainy day, nothing more.' She yawned. 'Shall we hit the hay?'

'Suits me.'

'I thought it might.' She gave him a demure smile and Carl tweaked her toe, smiling back. Both admitted to the pleasure their love-making gave, and were happy to joke about it; both knew how they would miss lying together in the big bed when they were separated by the Atlantic Ocean.

Liza missed her period in early April and knew at once that she was pregnant. Carl had come over for a week in mid-March and they had made love with total absorption, and without contraception. She had decided that this was as good a time as any to have a child, and was at first rather pleased with herself and excited, then as she quickly became nauseous, afraid. The commitment was so huge, so permanent; how could she jettison it if she found it all too demanding? Really, things had been going wonderfully well . . . it seemed ridiculous to fracture the cycle of luck. But it was done; a new life was growing inside her, the die was cast.

The Double Dealer had gone down extremely well with both television critics and viewing public, and Liza had hugely enjoyed her part. Lady Plyant is the young wife of an aged gentleman, who is manipulated mercilessly in private by means of her conditional bestowal of sexual favours. The part was a joy to play and Liza did so with both wit and clever understatement. The result was that other offers, scripts and vehicle ideas tumbled via Penelope Fine on to the mat of the pretty house in Holland Park. Then the film, long projected, scripted, scheduled and rescheduled, rescripted, cast and recast, became a reality one day in early January. Liza, up to her eyes in Restoration comedy, must now read and digest again and again the part of Nancy, the girl whose mother is drowned in a flash-flood and who ceases to speak after witnessing this. There was a series of meetings with varying permutations of director, casting director, producer, co-producer, and the few actors already settled upon; on shooting times, budgets, interpretations, costume, climatic conditions and the possibility of getting a cat trained well enough to pat a woman's cheek and to jump on the back of a horse in motion. At one point, the whole production team seriously considered moving to Australia to obtain an authentic background.

Shooting was due to start with indoor scenes at Elstree at the end of March. By early April Liza was feeling very slightly queasy on rising, and by the end of the month, sick enough to lie down and die. This being impossible, she carried on, her diet being mainly dry crackers and lemonade with occasional tiny portions of macaroni cheese. She told no one of the child; not Hannah, not even Carl, feeling that the less she spoke or even thought about it, the less ill she would feel. When location work started in Wales, a spot having been found in Merioneth that corresponded well enough with the description in the novel, life became harder. The hotel was comfortable, with log fires and lashings of tasty food. But as Liza was repelled by food and was rarely given time to sit by the fires, her only interest lay in the bed. This was an outsize four-poster, and the high spot of her day was the moment of climbing into it; heaving a vast sigh of relief, she would reach for her Jacob's Cream Crackers and the radio.

The actor who was playing her cousin Alfred was

kindness itself. Ken Warner, a wiry little man approaching forty, from Queensland, was of course not told of the pregnancy but, even so, clearly knew what ailed her. He showed her photos of his three children and their pretty mother, dropping broad hints about the satisfactions of family life. Liza still admitted nothing, but Ken Warner did his best to ease her path over what was becoming pretty rough ground. She was grateful, and they established a good rapport over the fifty-seven days of shooting.

Her biggest difficulty lay in the accent. Easy as pie, Ken insisted. Just say 'pin' not 'pen' and 'tint' not 'tent' and you're home and dry. Liza was not; Judy, the voice coach, spent hour after frustrating hour on one-to-one tuition; Liza could say 'pin' and 'tint' but nothing else that rang true. One night she called Carl and decided to blow his mind by coming on Australian, and the effort finally cracked it for her – he could not *believe* this amazing accent. She was so thrilled at having got it right at last that she told him about the baby. There was a small silence.

'You're not kidding?' He spoke cautiously.

'Certainly not. I couldn't kid *anyone*, the way I'm feeling!'

'God, that's amazing . . .'

'Not really,' she said reasonably. 'Unless one of us is barren it was a cert. We were scarcely out of bed for the entire week of your visit.'

'I had jet lag,' Carl said with dignity.

'Not so I noticed.' Liza laughed. 'Anyway, can I take it you approve?'

'Do I not!' Then he said: 'Hey, what was that about riding a mule?'

'That was wild,' she admitted. 'The mule was –'

'Never mind the bloody mule!' he roared. 'Don't

you *dare* get on the damned beast one more time – understand?'

She smiled, mulling that over in bed as she nibbled her crackers. Quite pleasant, a chance to be seriously fussed over. Maybe she would tell Hannah . . . go and see her, to be made a fuss of there too. A few days at Bracken House . . . lovely. She turned over and slept, still smiling.

It was a disastrous spell of weather, cold, wet and windy. The costume people were tearing their hair, make-up was ruined, hats were bowling about like poltergeists at a party. Liza's skirts seemed to pull her down; she had a continual urge to sleep *right now*, wherever she was. And yet . . . the accent at last was effortless for the relatively brief script she had; and somehow, by some inexplicable alchemy, she was in the mind and body of this character with whom she could have had nothing in common save their shared humanity.

May was almost over and the land smelled powerfully of hawthorn blossom and cow parsley, Liza was two and a half months gone and the company reached fever pitch, it being the final shot. It had become very hot and Liza discovered that Catering had no lemonade left.

'You load of shits!' she yelled, sticky with sweat and angst. 'Why don't you do your sodding job! Christ – out of lemonade on a day like this!' She went behind a tree and an assistant director came with a glass of champagne for her, which everyone else was drinking to celebrate the finish. In desperation Liza gulped it down, and after a moment vomited into the grass. When Ken gave her some cold water she sobbed on his chest and felt better.

'So sorry –' she wiped her nose on her neckscarf.

'I'm pregnant – that's the trouble.'

'Of course you are, idiot sheila. Thought you'd never admit to it. Now we can pass you your g'bye pressies, so mop up and come on, do.'

The end-of-film gifts, she discovered, were, for her, all baby things. Intensely embarrassed, Liza even so could see the joke was on her for being stupid enough to believe she'd kept her secret. She was waved off with hugs and good wishes.

There would be odds and ends of studio work to finish up, but for now, she made for Bracken House. She wanted to tell Hannah about the baby. And wanted to see Carl; she would ask him to fly over at the weekend if possible.

It was unbelievably peaceful, lying under the new, tender green beech leaves. Liza stared up at the deep blue sky through their pastel softness. She had lain here for what seemed a blissful infinity, hearing birds busy about their work of feeding their young. Thank God she would have no such hassle feeding hers! She sipped lemonade, wondering how long it would be until she could eat and drink like a human being again.

Hannah had been absolutely delighted to hear of the baby, her second grandchild after so long an interval, though was concerned that Liza had not seen a doctor yet. Where would she like to have it? London? New York? Or here at Bracken House, where Hannah could help out? When? Mid-December, if Liza had her dates right; a Christmas baby, like Tom had been, and Laurie. Christmas was a wonderful time to have a new baby in the house . . . Hannah's face had glowed. They would invite Jonet and family. And Tom and Florence would be delighted at the news. Joe – would Liza phone Joe, to tell them? Liza had laughed, and said of course she would tell Joe.

She had called Penelope Fine a couple of weeks ago on location, asking that offers be held now until the new year. When Penelope called that afternoon to ask how the final location work had gone, Liza was aware that there was a sub-text to this conversation, and waited.

'By the way, Liza . . . are you putting on weight yet?'

'I've lost a little, as it happens. Due to semi-starvation, due in turn to feeling sick all day. Why?'

A pause; Penelope feeling her way. 'It's Max Butterfield. A six-part mini-series, BBC prime-time Sunday-night slot. Georgian; a classic. Liza – look, I've said nothing, except that I will tell you about it and get back to them a.s.a.p. I don't see quite how you can . . . December, isn't it?'

'Yes. And they're casting now?'

'They are. It's the lead part . . . What I'll do anyway is put the presentation and estimated schedule in the post tonight, you should have it tomorrow. Only you can decide if you might manage it, and would like to talk to Max. I do see . . . but I felt it only right to tell you. We'll talk in a day or two. You have my home number for the weekend, I'm not away.'

Liza's mouth was dried out. She went for more lemonade, ideas chasing round her head like bats on a summer night. If she had known, if it had come up earlier. Or later. But now . . . if they were casting now, shooting would be unlikely to start before September.

She had virtually no sleep and her head was banging unpleasantly when she took Penelope's envelope from the postman early next morning. She went straight back to her room with it, shook it out on to the bed and began to read. Almost an hour later she lay back and reached for the lemonade, staring at the wall.

It was perfect. The dream come true for any actress who needs one last big boost to the top, where she could remain, growing in stature decade after decade. She wanted it. *Wanted* it.

Getting off the bed, Liza dropped her robe and examined the profile of her nude body in the long corner looking-glass . . . drew in her breath; let it out again slowly. Finally she sank down on the floor, and leaning against the end of her bed, closed her eyes. She was still there when Hannah knocked and put her head around the door.

'Liza?'

Liza's head appeared above the end of the bed. 'Darling, what *are* you doing down there? I've brought you tea, very fresh, very weak. And some Melba toast, that's so good first thing.' She put the tray down on the bed, avoiding the scattered papers. 'Are you all right?'

Liza pulled herself to her feet. 'Not really.' Her voice was low and flat.

'Are you ill?' Hannah started forward but Liza shook her head. 'What then? Tell me, please, what's wrong?'

Liza moved to the window and opened it to lean out and inspect the morning, which was all that a late spring morning ideally should be. She said, not looking at Hannah: 'I don't really want the baby.'

Hannah sat down on the edge of the bed, not even noticing that she had knocked the tray and crumbled the Melba toast. 'Liza – you're tired. You feel sick. You're nervous about whether you can actually cope with a baby. This will change quite soon, and it has nothing to do with *wanting* your baby. Truly.'

'I don't want the baby,' Liza repeated. 'It will stop me working.'

'Only for a short time. In the length of your whole career, a *very* short time.' Hannah went to the window and touched her daughter's shoulder. 'Liza; Carl's flying over tomorrow, all this way and back to spend a couple of days with you. You told me how pleased he is . . . when you and he talk, I feel certain your fears will go, and you'll look forward to December. Six and a half months – no time, really.'

Liza said tiredly, 'Probably. Thanks for the tray, Mummy. I will try the toast. I'm actually thinking of having an abortion,' she added.

'I can't believe I am hearing this!' After a moment of stunned silence Hannah withdrew her hand as if it had met hot coals. 'There's no *possible* reason – Liza are you quite mad?'

'Is it mad to recognise that a mistake has been made, and to want to put it right? Am I wicked to want to put my professional career first?' She turned to face her mother. 'Any woman with the right physical equipment can give birth. How many can hold an audience in the palm of their hand for three hours? If I want to do what I was *born* to do, am I then mad?'

'What did you say to me just before you left to go away with Carl after the wedding?' Hannah asked sharply. 'I seem to recollect your thanking me for having you! I could have had *you* aborted, as you said; but I chose not to. Now it seems you can't offer the same chance of life to *your* child – and in ideal conditions, compared to those *I* faced! Good God, Liza – I am so ashamed of you. You are *bone selfish*.'

She stared at her daughter a moment longer then turned and hurried from the room.

Liza moved back to where she had been, looking

out of the window. Her face was white in the May sunshine and her eyes the darkest aquamarine. She remained for some time, watching the garden where sparrows and blackbirds quartered the beds after food for their young. Then she fetched the Melba toast, crumbled it and threw it down to them, and watched as it quickly disappeared.

'Are you out of your mind?'

Carl stopped walking and stood facing her on the beach. The light was just beginning to fade, a subtle lack of definition in shape and clarity, though the hills grew sharper against the faint lemon in the low sky. They had had a meal soon after Carl had arrived from Heathrow in the hired BMW; an unmistakably strained atmosphere had militated against lingering at the table and Carl anyway felt the need to walk after the flight and then the drive into Wales.

Liza would have preferred not to have had this conversation until morning, when he was rested. But the atmosphere had been impossible to disguise and now she stood at bay. Wearing cotton trousers rolled up to her calves, and a long cotton sweater embroidered with huge daisies, she had been walking in the shallows, carrying her sandals. The sand still bore the warm print of the sun and the sea frothed creamily over it. She waited just for a moment now, wishing with all her strength for Carl not to be angry; to take her hand, so they might walk back up the cliff path to the car together. Then she bent to push her feet into her sandals, rolled back down the trousers over damp legs. When she looked at Carl again, she thought how much she preferred him dressed casually like this, in open-necked shirt and cotton drill trousers. But his face was hostile, the lips a thin furious line. She straightened her back.

'Not at all, Carl – I really think you should try to see this from my side. The lead in this mini-series is by far the most important thing I've had come up.'

'Oh?' His voice sliced the air like a butcher's knife. 'As I see it, my baby's life is the most important thing he or she has had come up. And I am not about to see you take that away for your own self-advancement. Christ!'

He turned from her in disgust and Liza's face flamed with unexpected anger. She opened her mouth to retaliate but he was in front.

'D'you know, I think I must be dreaming, still up there in space over the ocean. I cannot credit that you'd even *consider* killing your child because of a fucking *mini-series*!'

'It's not a child! It's just a collection of cells. Carl, I can have another baby in a few months –'

'But not this one. This one would be dead; a bit of blood and tissue chucked into an incinerator so its mother can preen herself in a mini-series. Is that what you want – to be a murderer?'

'I'm *not* – I'm *not*!' she yelled. 'Don't I have a choice over my own body?'

'You made a free choice to have a child. I said I would like one, certainly, but I did not say when. That was down to you. And you chose now. So that's when you'll have it: *this* baby, *now*. End of conversation.'

'Is it?' She ran in front of him as he started to walk. 'You can't make me!'

He stopped. His face was inches away and Liza, accustomed only to finding love, was shocked to encounter the fury in her husband's eyes.

'I tell you this; and mark it well, Liza. If you abort this child you will regret it. I shall see the story is spread over the *New York Times* as well as all the papers here. And I think you may lose your adoring audiences when they see you as a cold-blooded child-killer. You've said yourself that an image is important . . . so think on that. And don't think I wouldn't. I have never been more serious.'

He walked past her and began to climb to where they had left the car. Liza stood still, watching him through a red blur of frustration. She willed him to turn, to come back to her and say he understood, that she had a right to make the best choices available, that it was her life.

When he was out of sight she sat down on a rock and began to throw stones at a chunk of driftwood. She threw them for so long, and so hard that her shoulders ached and it became difficult to aim in the dusk.

She would stay here; force him to come back to look for her. Was he concerned already? He had not gone, she would have heard the car engine. But Liza was cold, feeling sick, and wanted to go home. No other soul was about and the sea, as it came closer, had an air of menace. She hated it, it was treacherous and cruel.

Darker still. He should have come back long since. She got up, stiff with cold, and began to walk up the path, not knowing what else to do.

He was in the car, head back and eyes closed, asleep. She hesitated, hand on the door. She had decided nothing; felt only tired, cold and in need of a warm bath and bed. The miserable business appeared unresolvable. Tears of self-pity gathered and fell, and Carl moved, yawned and saw her by the passenger window.

They stared at one another in the dark, each

wrapped tightly in their own misery, hugging it and powerless to release it. Then he leaned over and opened the door for her. She got in and sat stiffly silent, looking ahead.

'Shall we go now?' His voice was carefully expressionless.

'If you want.' Hers was small, impersonal. She added, 'You win.'

She had not intended to say that, had not known that she had decided anything: the remark appeared to have been involuntary. Afterwards, both experienced a cold emptiness of spirit, a knowledge of irretrievable loss.

'No one has won, Liza.'

'No. We may as well go, then.'

He turned the ignition key. Liza felt at that moment that she would not care if he had driven over the cliff. At the house they made the briefest of excuses to Hannah and Matthew and went upstairs, Liza disappearing into the bathroom. When finally she emerged, reluctant to rejoin Carl in their room, he was already asleep in the bed by the chimney breast; or feigning sleep, Liza could not say which.

She slid quietly into her own bed under the window and switched off the lamp by her pillow. Hot tears made their way down her face and neck and she allowed them to flow soundlessly, looking through the window at the stars, until, turning wearily on her side, she slept.

They went back in tandem next morning, Liza following Carl in her car with all her location luggage stowed neatly by Matthew. Hannah kissed Carl's cheek on an impulse, wanting to say something but knowing this was one time she must stand aside.

'Call me any time, Carl,' she said instead.

'Thanks, Hannah.' His handclasp was firm. 'You look after yourself now. This is a beautiful spot, I hope I'll see more of it.'

'Just let us know when –' Matthew touched his shoulder. Like Hannah, he was desperate to say something when there was absolutely nothing that could be said. He turned to Liza and embraced her. 'Take care. Come again soon.'

'Yes . . .' Liza could not trust her voice. She turned to Hannah then. 'I'll be in touch tomorrow, Mummy. And don't fret,' she added, so quietly that the men could not have heard. Hannah nodded, and they kissed.

They stopped once on the way back to London, for a drink and a sandwich in a Gloucestershire village pub. It was raining gently, darkening the golden stone of the buildings, but the clouds were thinning and showing streaks of clear sky. Liza stretched, rubbed her back . . . gazed about her at the incomparable mix of young foliage and old Cotswold dwellings. She looked directly at Carl then, for the first time since they had stood together on the beach. He seemed unfamiliar; pinched, with bleak, wounded eyes. She could not bear to be responsible for this, and put out her hand to touch his, but lightly, expecting a rebuff.

'Carl. I am so sorry. Please forgive me. I was terribly wrong.'

He looked at the back of his hand where she had touched it, then past her at the middle distance.

'Thank you.'

There was silence between them, so palpable that Liza felt she might knock it aside with her arm, and so reach him. But she judged it would not be that simple; both were so sore that time would need to pass. There would not be a short cut, an instant fix. She had learned that some wounds cannot be healed by an apology.

'Would you like to go in now?' she asked politely.

'Sure . . . if you like.' They walked shoulder to shoulder across the car park, careful not to touch, each aware that the other needed space about them if progress was now to be made.

They reached Holland Park wearied by stress and driving. Carl unloaded the cases into the hall, illuminated by a decorated fanlight and two door panels and given additional light from the double, patterned glass doors of the sitting room to the right and the study to the left. The house was airy and delicate and Liza was coming to love its feel of peaceful, gracious living. Not having chosen its contents, she still found them to her taste, elegant but not pretentious, with frankly pretty touches that showed clearly the hand of a woman.

'Would you mind if I rested for half an hour or so?' she asked him formally, hearing the awkwardness of the request as she made it.

'Go on up. Can I bring you anything?'

She smiled, just a small one but her first of the day. 'The cupboard may well be bare. I forgot to ask Jenny to provision up . . . I'd not actually planned when I was leaving Wales. I just fell into Bracken House, as it wasn't terribly far from where we'd been on location.'

'Would you like to eat out?'

She looked down at her toe on the edge of the first stair tread. 'Well . . . I suppose we'd better.' She added carefully: 'Only, not somewhere grand – where I'd feel I should dress up.' Another weak smile. 'I'm rather off food at the moment; feeling sick much of the time.'

'Oh. That's too bad.' He looked uncertain.

'There's a nice place in the Fulham Road we could

try. Not too many tables; quiet. We could phone them, I have the number.'

'I'll try them. You lie down for a while then.'

Liza made her way slowly upstairs. She wanted very much to weep, and weep; the weight of what had happened between them pressed on her, making it difficult to ascend the stairs. She drew over the stiffly lined taffeta curtains, kicked off her shoes and crawled under the covers, too exhausted to do more. She did not sleep but lay unmoving, drifting in and out of consciousness. Thinking of nothing, aware of nothing, until after an hour she pulled herself back to life and went to run a bath.

Carl sat outside, smoking and drinking black coffee. The garden was vastly superior to the majority in London, Liza had assured him. There was a terrace, and a path winding to a pretty gazebo. Further down, an ornamental pond was bordered by iris, and water lilies grouped themselves over the surface. A high wall of mellowed brick surrounded the garden, covered by climbing roses and clematis. A blackbird was taking a bath on a submerged stone, beating up the water with his wings. By the gazebo, two newly fledged starlings sat back and opened their mouths at their mother, who was doubtless hoping that they would forage for themselves.

Carl Cline did not know a starling or a blackbird from a bull's foot. He had no idea of the names of shrubs, flowers or trees in the garden he was renting for a great deal of money. He paid a man to see to it, and birds were expected to take care of themselves. Carl knew about how to make money; every man to his craft. He knew how businesses were – or should be – structured; how to add to their market value, how to assess their viable components and how to dispose of the dross. He knew much more, and turned that knowledge into increased assets for Cline Investments.

He did not, though, know what to do about his wife. He could go upstairs, strip her down and service her, as a mechanic would a car that was performing badly. Given the present atmosphere, that might be labelled rape; and anyway he had no urge in that direction. Liza had wounded him mightily in voicing her desire to destroy their child. From being the love object that he had taken enormous pains to possess, she had become at best a frightening enigma; at worst, a dangerous adversary.

He tipped the dregs of his coffee into a planter holding a riot of parrot tulips, and stubbed out his cigarette on the terrace stones. She had said she was sorry; that she had been wrong even to voice such a wish. But the retraction had not closed up the gaping wound. Also, he had no idea if she had retracted from expediency, having judged she could not possibly win from the ground on which she had taken her stance, or because she genuinely believed she had made a terrible mistake.

Carl walked down the path and stood by the pond, hands rammed into his trouser pockets, staring into the streaked green water. A schism of this nature might not destroy a long, deep-rooted marriage; but it might well destroy trust. What was certain was that both had discovered the other's power to fire deadly bullets. That should make for greater care in the future . . . a bonus that could prove valuable.

They were married, they were to have a child, and effort must be made; but carefully – no bull-at-gate tactics. He had shown his cruelly accurate weaponry should it be needed and she would remember the sight, he felt certain. Now weaponry must be locked away, and they would take time to lick their wounds . . . to learn to respect one another, be gentle again, in the hope that some at least of their mutual trust would re-establish. Carl sighed, and started back up the garden.

They were quiet, eating their meal at the Magpie. Carl had thought that this weekend he would be pushing the boat out in a big way, with the best London could offer to celebrate Liza's pregnancy. Instead he wanted no more than steak with a salad, while Liza struggled with grilled chicken before giving up and asking for biscuits and cheese with soda water.

'What time is your plane tomorrow?' She was struggling with conversation as well as food. Carl thought wryly that she would likely prefer his space to his person right now. Tough; he'd go when he was good and ready.

'Mid-morning.'

'I'll come,' she offered. He shook his head.

'No need, if you have to work again on Monday.'

'It's a short story to record for Radio Four's *Morning Story* slot. There's another to do later in the week.' Liza nibbled round a piece of biscuit. She wore a simple black shift with a white-banded square neck and her hair tied back with a white ribbon; she looked very young and distinctly peaky.

'So, you think you might come over to New York after that?'

'Well, there's just a couple more things . . . We have to record a radio play, due to go out late June. It's a good part, Bernard Shaw. Then there's still odd bits and pieces of studio work to be done on the film.' Liza broke off. 'Penelope wants to keep my name in credits where possible, so that next year –'

'Of course.' Carl was brisk. 'So, I'll phone you evenings, and you'll let me know when you see your way clear?'

'Yes – certainly I will. Maybe three weeks?' She knew it could be longer but once three had gone, another week would not sound too disagreeable.

'Right, three weeks then. Only there's a lot to be arranged; getting a doctor, booking a hospital – is your doctor here satisfied with things at this stage?'

'I haven't seen him yet. There's not –'

'Not seen him!' Carl's voice rose and Liza cut in fast.

'I simply have had no opportunity, Carl – I've been on location for weeks.'

'Jesus wept! Look, if –' He stopped, began again on a calmer note. 'Liza, you phone for an appointment Monday, first thing? OK?'

Liza sipped lemonade to give herself time. Concern for her? For the baby? Both? Whichever, she was perfectly competent to organise this department. She must not get stroppy, though . . . his baby too, he had a right.

'OK. Monday.' What she would have to wait to tell him now – she could not risk another explosion – was that she intended having her baby here, not in New York. Better, next month; things would have cooled a little. Enough, for now.

As they stepped back into the hall, Carl looked about him. 'Not a bad place, is it? Are you comfortable here?'

'I love it,' Liza said emphatically. 'It's just about perfect. If we could find anything similar to buy I'd be over the moon. But places like this seem hard to come across.'

They were painfully aware, preparing for bed, how different the day should have been, and their coming together this night. They watched the late news, looked at the papers ... When Liza put off her light and turned to sleep Carl read for another few moments then folded away the paper and switched off his own lamp.

'D'you want the curtains pulled back, Liza?'

'Thanks, that would be nice.'

They lay side by side, not touching. Liza could not decide what to do; what might be the right thing, what he might expect. She became increasingly sleepy as she wrestled with the problem. At last, on the verge of sleep now she felt quietly for Carl's hand. Finding it, she laid it across her waist, and allowed her own hand to cover it. Then she said softly:

'Good-night, Carl.'

Carl felt the warmth of her hand on his, and the warmth of her stomach beneath it. For the first time in over twenty-four hours he relaxed just a little, and was suddenly and blissfully on the verge of sleep himself.

'Good-night, Liza. Sleep well.'

Faint beginnings of healing easing them, the warmth of their close bodies lulling them, within moments they slept.

Florence and Hannah strolled along the promenade at Porthcawl. They had lunched together in the bungalow in Clarence Avenue, and were enjoying the sea and sun before Tom came home from work. Hannah had said nothing about Liza; after her phone call on Sunday afternoon apologising for upsetting all of them, and recanting any intention of an abortion, it seemed wiser to try to forget what had taken place. She had been over-tired, Liza explained; over-wrought. But she would be fine now, and hoped Hannah would be up to visit before she went to the States again next month.

'Has she said where she's having it?' Florence asked now. 'Has she booked in yet?'

'She hasn't said. That's not going to be an easy one, is it?'

'Not really . . . must be simpler when you both live in one place!' They paused to look over the rocks of Rest Bay towards Port Talbot. 'Funny . . . I've never really strayed from where I was born, have I? Not beyond Porthcawl anyway.'

'But you're content – you and Tom?' Hannah searched her friend's face.

'Bless you, yes. It all works beautifully – but I'm sure you know that from Tom.'

'Well, Tom doesn't say a lot. But I think I would know if he felt unsettled. He did enjoy your jaunt to see the Queen!'

Hannah herself had missed the big excitement of the spring, the official opening of Port Talbot's new tidal harbour earlier in the month. At a cost of twenty million pounds, the gigantic harbour could provide for ships in excess of 100,000 tons, with a mass production unit alongside able to handle the biggest bulk iron-ore carriers in service. Four years in the making, and the first harbour to be built in Britain this century, every flag in the district had been out for the monarch and her consort on a beautiful spring morning.

'I enjoyed it too, if I did get my hat knocked off in the crush! She looked so pretty, Han. I hope the harbour does all those good things it's supposed to for us all. What was it? "Part of the current success story of the South Wales Docks".'

Florence screwed up her eyes as if trying to see round the headland to the vast complex of harbour, docks and steelworks. 'We lived so close to that for so long . . . I suppose we'll always think of ourselves as part of it.'

'Dada would have a shock to see that harbour.' Hannah spoke almost to herself. 'He could never have imagined . . .' Nor could she, in the hard years; when she was struggling to feed herself, Joe and Tom in a tough world of strikes and lockouts, soup kitchens and dole queues and grey-faced men scrabbling on the tips for buckets of coal. Then the fight to feed and clothe Jonet and Serena too, and work eighteen hours a day to keep her business going and a roof over their heads.

She looked at Florence, who had worked side by side with her and shared most problems. Except for Joe; she had kept Joe's youthful tragedy even from this dearest friend. No one knew about Joe and Norman Madoc, nor ever would.

Florence was meeting her gaze now, and smiling. 'None of us can ever imagine the future, Han. But we can remember the past, and the road we've travelled to get where we are. I certainly remember well the day you told me you were expecting the baby who's having a baby of her own now. I thought I'd have a heart attack! And I *hated* that David Vaughan!'

Hannah smiled back. 'It had taken two of us, Flo. I recall the day too, we were in the Swansea restaurant and you were making me a sandwich. Always trying to coax food down me . . .'

'So why don't we get ourselves one of those smashing Italian ice-creams?' Florence took her arm and steered her back along the road. Hannah went obediently, thoughts turned from the past to the present now. She would see Liza before she took off again . . . and find out her plans for the baby.

If only she felt – well, *better* about the whole thing. Matthew would say, if she couldn't find something to worry about he'd worry about her. But still . . . there was an indefinable unease for Liza and her future. So far, good things had seemed to drop into Liza's lap; if they had not, her daughter had grabbed them with both hands, brooking no opposition. She had talent, beauty, and a charisma that commanded attention and adulation; though with that went the wilfulness to carve her way if necessary through others' needs.

Why then could she, Hannah, foresee any problem?

She could, though. But not its nature. An invisible tiger . . .

Chapter Eighteen

August 1970

'This is worse than anything I ever saw in London,' Liza said tartly to Carl as the hunter green Bentley convertible appeared to swim through the New York smog.

'It doesn't often happen . . . and I can't recall one worse than this. Once we hit the Interstate north it'll melt away. It's all the 'scrapers pinning in the fumes – a city thing. Not made you sick, has it?'

'Not really.' She was examining the convertible's beige hide interior. 'I haven't seen this before – is it new?'

'Dad and I got it this spring. We share it; it's better for a vacation than a city limo, don't you think?'

'It's certainly a serious car.' Liza ran a finger along the walnut facia.

'I reckon so. Driving this machine makes a statement, like "never explain, never apologise", as Dad put it.' Carl shot her an amused glance. 'No need to explain *anything* when you're at this wheel.'

Liza looked prim. 'Mummy would take issue with you on that.'

'I'm sure she would.' He grinned. 'But your mother doesn't have to survive in the New York jungle.'

'She would though. She would survive anywhere.' Liza watched the blur of yellow cabs about them . . . she would not in a hundred years agree to drive in Manhattan. She sighed. It was hateful not being able to work; thank God July was over. Penelope was lining things up for the new year already, there were some interesting options being chewed over. The difficulty was, which side of the Atlantic . . .

She looked at her husband, but he was concentrating on getting them intact on to Interstate 95. Which side of the Atlantic their child was to be born had been an issue which had threatened last month to tear down the earlier, careful fence-mending over the telephone. Liza had booked into the Cairns Maternity Home in Chelsea before flying to New York – a bird in hand she had reasoned; a *fait accompli*. Collecting her from the airport last month, Carl had remarked right away that the first priority must now be to see a doctor, then to book a bed.

'Carl . . .' Liza had summoned up her wits. 'Darling, I really want to have Mummy help me – it's awfully important to me. And to have the baby in England . . . I really do want to have it in England. *Please* don't put me under pressure over this.' She allowed her voice to tail off, indicating fragility.

'No pressure. I'm just saying we'll have the baby right here in NY, OK?' His voice had showed no fragility. 'American father, American baby, American medical care; the best there is.'

'Darling, I've made all the plans –'

'Unmake them.' He had sounded uncompromising.

'I don't want to,' she had said clearly. 'I want to have my baby in my country. Of course, with you there – that of *course*. You come and stay in England as you did last –'

'Why the hell did you marry me?' He had ice on his tongue now. 'Why?'

'Because I thought we could enjoy our relationship. Because I am greatly attracted to you. Because I guess,

I love you. Although I did say, you will recall, that you may not have thought it through when you were so certain we should marry. But you said you would enjoy the challenge! Ha!'

He had been silent then, approaching Queensboro Bridge into Manhattan. 'You are right.' He glanced at her, when they were over into 59th. 'I had not reckoned on it being so damn *difficult*. Or maybe, on finding so many points of conflict.'

'There need be none, if we talk things through quietly.'

He had laughed outright. 'You mean if you tell me when you've decided what you intend, and I make no fuss.'

'Now darling; we're not going to fight over semantics surely?' Liza had kissed his cheek lightly, sensing victory. That night they had made love gently, in the quiet apartment on Upper East Side. Liza had realised her pregnancy gave her bargaining strength, but that with the new year would come new jockeying for position in the partnership . . . a test, perhaps, of patterns for the future.

For now, she was the child carrier, perhaps to be indulged a little; and now they were taking a vacation so she must relax, take issue on as little as possible, and hope for them to enjoy their time together.

This was a strange time for Liza – a time out of her regular life. For over a decade she had thought of very little but being an actress. International incidents, changing governments, wars, issues serious enough to die for, passed without her being conscious of their hot breath. Her sense of world geography was abysmal, her sense of history nondescript. Liza knew surprisingly little about anything other than acting, and was sublimely unaware of her inadequacies. She was learning a great deal about the one thing of interest to her, was very good at it, and intended to be much better. She wished to be regarded as the finest performer of her day; nothing less than this would content her, and to earn it she would climb any mountain. She had even thought to sacrifice her unborn child on the altar of success. Now she waited, in limbo, until it was time to continue the journey to her ultimate goal.

Carl had not fully understood the extent of his wife's commitment. He was making strenuous efforts to incorporate her into his world, and did not yet dream how hard a task he had set himself. He was proud of her because she was successful, sought-after, talented and beautiful, but he had so far failed to connect up the results he so admired with the huge single-minded effort demanded to achieve and then sustain them. It was possible, he would tell himself firmly, for her to compartmentalise her life ... to spend a certain number of days each year working, and the rest doing other things. He was Lucky Carl Cline – he could do anything, he could not fail. So how could he not make his marriage to this superb, amazingly magnetic woman, whom he loved so ardently, as great a success as his business life? To this end he had sacrificed his son and his first wife, and could not countenance not balancing the books in so telling a transaction. Liza *had* to be worth that.

It had been a sickening blow to his pride to hear her first wish to abort their child, and then to insist it be born in London. He had at least won the day over the abortion, if only by fighting dirty. So he finally decided that it was perhaps politic to give way over the birthplace, tough as it was on his ego. She had come to him, she was pregnant, and so more vulnerable than usual . . . he would be wise to show a gentleness and generosity somewhat alien to his nature. This vacation now, a few weeks far from the world of work for both, would, Carl hoped, bring them closer and help heal the rift opened with such shocking unexpectedness in Wales.

So, with the first half of August theirs to do with as they pleased, they now sped along the Connecticut coastline, quickly leaving behind the smog that had caused chaos in Manhattan. They stopped for lunch at Stonington, a village on Fisher's Island sound; Liza lifted her face to the wind and laughed with delight at the beautiful old wooden houses and white-spired churches. They ate pan-roasted lobster in chervil butter near the harbour, and 'Mummy couldn't have managed this in Clapham,' she reported, wiping her chin on a crisp blue linen napkin. Sated, they meandered down to inspect the boats nodding at their moorings, then along Water Street to the Old Lighthouse Museum, where Liza insisted upon climbing to the top of the tower for the amazing ocean view.

'Wonderful . . .' She clung to his arm. 'This village is perfect, can we stay here?'

'How long for?' Carl laughed at her enthusiasm.

'Oh – ages.' They reached the bottom of the steps again and strolled back towards the harbour.

'Well – that would rather upset all my plans . . . I want you to see some of the places I went to as a kid.'

'You've been up this way with Brad, too?' Liza paused, then forbore to add 'and Gayle'. Carl nodded.

'Sure. He liked to come sailing with me.'

'I really hope you'll still take him, Carl,' she said seriously.

'Well, yes. Not easy to fix, though . . . not when he's free, and I am too.' He stared ahead as they walked.

'I can see that. Maybe when we get back? Before his autumn term?'

'If I can.' He looked at her. 'I'm sorry if – all that, causes you concern. You must not allow it to.'

They walked on; a handsome couple, arms linked. Liza's copper hair was looped back with a dark blue ribbon and her face was clear of make-up, her slightly thickening figure undetectable under a loose blue checked shirt and navy linen slacks. The only status giveaways were the superb solitaire ring, a top-of-the-range Rolex and a long, solid gold neck-chain given by Carl on her last birthday. He wore a casual shirt, slacks and sneakers, yet was firmly stamped with an air of authority and assurance. Now that he was thirty-three, the bridge of his nose was slashed by a vertical line and two more ran from nose to mouth; these served to add interest to well-constructed features, the narrowed blue eyes in a wide brow, a head of unfashionably close-cut dark blond hair.

'Naturally, I am concerned,' Liza said thoughtfully. 'Because Brad doesn't *live* with you now, he is no less than who he always was; no less your son. And I *should* feel badly, if any way we behave now makes for more unhappiness for him. Do you not see that?'

'Sure I do.' He loosed her arm and pushed his hands into his pockets. 'I want the best for him too, remember that.'

'Of course.' She slipped her hand through his arm again as they mingled with other couples and families. 'So, where are these places that are even better than *this* –'

'Well now, I didn't say that. But I've made a reservation for us at Newport tonight. Then I want to take you round to the Cape, where my boat's in harbour

. . . you just have to see her, Liza – she's a good-looker, I can tell you.'

'What is the name of this beauty?'

'*Jamboree*. Getting a touch long in the tooth now, but she's a great old girl, won me a few pots over the time we've been partners.' He hesitated. 'I'm not sure what to replace her with . . . a more competitive out-and-out racing machine, or something more comfortable if you should take an interest.'

'We'll see – I've only recently stopped feeling sick on *terra firma*, remember!' But time, she feared, would do little to allay her reluctance to leave the safety of shore for the hazards of the ocean. She had always feared water and Hannah admitted to the same weakness.

It was late afternoon when they drew into Narragansett, where they walked on glorious open beaches until Liza pronounced herself starving again. This became the pattern . . . a while on the road, long walks in the warm salty wind, wonderful food. That night they slept in a king-sized canopied bed, in an elegant old house where Carl's family had stayed years back. High windows opened to ocean views; in the garden, lawns sloped to the sea, and a long porch had rocking chairs from which they could admire a spectacular sunset. They dined on salmon with lime and ginger dressing, on mussels steamed with white wine, with rolls and desserts baked fresh in the kitchen and pots of fragrant coffee. Liza slept as her head touched the pillow and Carl lay for a while, watching her.

Newport was crowded but splendid. They spent three days here; at ease on their balcony watching the bay, pottering about the harbour, shopping and sightseeing. Liza was turning a delicious apricot gold when they set the Bentley north to Cape Cod; she had tied on a cotton scarf to prevent her hair knotting in the wind in the open convertible, and was poring over the map book when they stopped for lunch.

'This is ridiculous.' She snapped shut the guide-book. '*Everywhere* here has an English name!'

'Darling; this is New England. You know, where the Pilgrim Fathers landed?'

'Don't patronise me, Carl, I have learned of the Pilgrim Fathers. They must have been extremely homesick at once, that's all I can think. They would really have done better to have turned their boat straight round and sailed back home.'

Carl snorted. 'Liza – it took them over two months to *get* here!'

'Don't bother me with details.' She flapped a dis-dainful hand. 'I'm just fed up with reading all these lovely English names in a foreign country. We just drove through Wareham and it looks nothing *like* Wareham! You've never been to the *real* Wareham I know, but it's beautiful; I suppose we'll be driving on to Falmouth next and that'll be nothing like the real Falmouth either!'

Carl said after a moment: 'You think of America as a foreign country?'

Liza stared ahead for a few seconds. Then Carl saw a tear roll down her cheek under her expensive sun-glasses, followed by another. She gave a little heaving gulp and began to weep.

'Liza? What on earth!' He reached across, took off her sunglasses and examined her face. 'Are *you* home-sick for England?'

'I am *not* English,' she sobbed. 'I am Welsh! My mother is Welsh, my father is Welsh, *I* am Welsh!'

'So – tell me why you are crying, for God's sake.' Carl frowned.

Liza blew her nose on a tissue, wiped her eyes on another, then began to weep afresh. This bravura performance in the Bentley in the car park of the best hotel in town was not passing unnoticed.

'Because I do not like boats! But you're hoping I'm going to sail in one, aren't you? And I'm *afraid* of water! Mummy is too, and she said I was not to worry about it – it's quite a family failing she believes, goes back *years*.'

She was on the point of collapsing into tears again so Carl held her very tight, burying her face in his shirt.

'Liza, I will not insist you set foot on my boat. What we'll do is, we'll stand by it and you can just look at it. You may feel easier about it in time – if not, fine.' He paused. 'It wasn't the place names then – it was the boat?'

She nodded miserably. 'I feel better, now you know.'

Carl was forced to smile. 'We'll go to Hyannis after lunch and it'll be OK, I'm telling you.'

Liza had never imagined an expanse of water so densely populated by anchored boats of every shape and size. She did feel better now she had made a clean breast of her antipathy to them, but remained wary, though determined to be brave about it if at all possible.

'Which one is yours? How do we get to it?'

'She should be alongside now.' Carl drove with care along the busy waterfront. 'I had her brought here because I was certain of getting to a jetty.'

He parked in the members' area of the Yacht Club, guiding Liza through the bar and out to the waterside.

'I can see her already – there, at the end.' They negotiated trailers and dinghies and were on the jetty. Liza stared up at the gathering of slender masts spiking the blue sky and swaying in a slight but disconcerting manner. The planks beneath her feet swayed too; she grasped the jetty handrail but walked steadily on, with all the control her profession had taught her. Carl tightened his hold on her arm.

'Here she is.'

Had Liza not been preoccupied, she would have seen a beautifully presented fifty feet of racing yacht. She would have admired a perfectly laid teak deck, gleaming metalwork, every sheet neatly coiled and no sign anywhere of tarnish or corrosion. She would have noted the furled foresail and the mainsail stowed tidily along the boom, both ready for deployment, and recognised this as a well-run craft. But she saw only the narrow steps down which she must now descend. From below, Carl held out his hand with a smile of encouragement.

She was down on the shifting pontoon . . . then into *Jamboree*'s cockpit. Here a sinewy man of around forty with a weathered, hide-brown face under a denim cap touched its peak to her.

'This is Graham, darling. He looks after *Jamboree* for me.'

'Hello, Graham.' Liza nodded graciously. 'I'm afraid I'm not used to boats.' Graham smiled back in some disbelief, never having met anyone who was not used to boats. He indicated a pair of ridiculously strapping young men, ogling her from alongside the mast.

'Sam and Clancy – they gave me a hand to bring her from Long Island.'

Liza smiled again, but uncertainly, while Carl

regarded her with perplexity. He had had his boat brought here specifically to initiate her into his world. A warm eight or nine knots of breeze, clear blue sky – perfect. They would motor out, hoist sail, reach out of the bay on one tack, reach back on the other. Presto, Liza would be hooked. He had to admit now that things were not on course.

'Want to see below?'

'Oh . . . sure.' Following him down the hatchway, Liza was aware of her performance falling below standard, and renewed her efforts. She admired the galley, the navigation station, the three cabins . . . began to feel unmistakably nauseous. Oh God, seasick and still tied to a jetty!

She hurried up the steps in search of fresh air and leaned on the cockpit safety line, taking deep breaths. A launch was making its way out of the moorings and its wash reached *Jamboree* as Liza moved to sit on one of the teak laid cockpit seats. The boat rocked against the jetty piles; Liza missed the seat and, as Carl in the hatchway looked on in consternation, sat down hard in the cockpit well.

'Darling – are you absolutely certain there's no damage?' Carl leaned over her, still concerned three days after the mishap.

'For the umpteenth time, none at all. Truly.' Liza bestowed a serene smile on him. 'So, tomorrow you're taking me to Plymouth to look over the *Mayflower*?'

'Unless you'd prefer another day taking it quietly here?'

'Sweetheart, the last few days have been a joy and I'm fine now, Falmouth was so lovely . . . and Sandwich, and Barnstaple and Brewster, I adored them all. And Eastam; God, all those dunes, all that ocean! Yes, I'd surely love to come back every year. And I'm dying to see Boston.'

Liza gave no trouble for the rest of the vacation, relieved now of the fear of having to go sailing. Carl, contrite about the fall on *Jamboree*, made renewed efforts to accommodate her tastes. She would take a sail round the bay she assured him; next summer? That seemed far enough off to be no threat . . . she might be busy on a stage run by then, or doing a film. Her own world, understood and presently longed for. Her meat and drink. Her oxygen.

Joe and Sal were childishly excited about their first August vacation without the boys. 'They're more than ready for summer camp,' had been Sal's verdict, and Paul Harry and Thomas were in full agreement.

Joe and Sal's summer vacation was to be combined with a special project; Hannah's project, Joe called it but Sal smiled, knowing Joe's enthusiasm was no less. They were to visit Alex's elderly relative in Oregon who might – or might not, she had good days and bad days – offer information and/or anecdotes on the Hywel family tree. There was some talk of a family bible, causing Joe's eyes to gleam. They were to go to Chalmer's Rock, in the valley of the beautiful Columbia river, to meet Eugenie Manners, who lived there with her daughter and who was a Hywel. They had not been so far west before and were as excited as children setting off on a mystery tour.

Hannah had written months ago with the request to visit Mrs Manners 'should they ever feel like a trip west' and she now waited, deeply interested in any news of what might be uncovered. The possibility of an American family branch had intrigued her for years, since Joe had first talked of Alex's mother,

Madeleine Hywel Cline, and admitted even to seeking a family resemblance in Alex. She was ambivalent about what she wished; hoped simply to hear something, anything, about the Hywel family. She wondered if perhaps she should stop poking around in the past and forget it all. But she did not . . . Instead, she thought often of Joe and Sal as August approached and wished for a good outcome to their quest.

They hired a car and decided the town of Bend would be a good centre; adjacent to lakes and forests, with the Mount Hood area not too far, and the Hood River valley. The first week of the holiday idled deliciously by. Mount Hood, up and over the Santium Pass, down to Warm Springs Indian Reservation, around Waldo Lake . . . Sometimes they would take a picnic into the forest, revelling in doing very little but doing it together. No going where the boys would be amused, this trip; Joe and Sal used days according to their mutual tastes. They had a rock-firm relationship inside which their individual personalities flourished, nurtured by steady love and more than a little laughter. Joe remained an attractive man of relaxed, graceful stance and open friendliness of demeanour. The openness was not to be taken at face value, for Joe had never lost the habit formed in youth, of presenting only what he wished of himself to the world. When he had asked Sal to marry him, he had admitted to a past not open to the public. One day he would talk about it with her . . . one day, he had said. But years, full and fruitful, passed and still this one thing lay covered and indeterminate between them. Joe would from time to time attempt to formulate the words in his head but they never quite were heard.

Sal at forty-eight was still capable of making Joe

smile simply by looking at her. The thatch of dark curls was peppered with grey but the eyes were lively as ever, the wide mouth had the same ability to curve in a luscious smile. Sal loved Joe with all the fervent loyalty and passion of her Polish heart. She would have killed for him, for Marek, or for her sons. Joe's continuing to hold back from her a part of himself hurt more than Sal admitted; it must stem, she argued, from some sad lack in her. After thirteen years of marriage she had ceased to hope for Joe's secret to be shared, and instead thanked God for all His blessings. She and Marek had survived the war; had found happiness and comfort in the New World, had Joe's love and devotion, and all five of them were a close and self-supportive unit. More than so many had. Joe's heart condition made each day count for them, his return home after work a small occasion to rejoice. Now Sal had him to herself for two whole weeks, and wished no further than that.

Mrs Manners's address in Chalmer's Rock was in an affluent suburb whose houses stood behind mature trees and immaculate lawns. The maid who answered the doorbell took them through what appeared to be a granny-annexe, to double doors open to the garden. Here were more trees and lawns but with broad flowerbeds, and a sunken pond in the terrace. The woman sitting in one of several basket chairs under a cedar raised a hand, and the maid ushered them down to her.

'Glad we've our decent duds on,' Joe hissed at Sal, then offered his charming smile. The woman smiled back but did not rise; Joe, introducing Sal, noted the two sticks by her chair, and the fissured, papery skin of a thin face and gnarled, fragile hands.

'You've come a long way.' Mrs Manners's cadences

were unsteady but there was a pleasingly humorous look to her to which Joe and Sal warmed.

'Sit yourselves down and Ethel shall bring us tea – will that be what you would like?' She scrutinised them as they arranged themselves. Her gaze, pale but with a fierce core, centred on Joe.

'Tea would be just fine, Mrs Manners,' Joe told her amiably. 'And you could say I've come all the way from Wales – my sister there has a great interest in anything you may be able to tell us about the Hywel family.'

Mrs Manners transferred her gaze to the distance. Only bees, grasshoppers and distant car engines disturbed the tranquil afternoon. Then she said: 'No Hywels left now, y'know. No sons; that's why Madeleine, with me and my sister Bella, decided to hang on to the name after our marriages. There'd been Hywels going, oh, way back . . . seemed a pity to let the name just die off.'

'D'you have any idea about where your roots were as a family?' Joe pressed gently. The old woman pursed her lips, deepening the web of lines about them.

'Story goes, we were Pennsylvania bred. Before that . . ' Her eyes, red-rimmed, rested on blue distance. Ethel appeared with a tray, the teapot Georgian silver, with butter cookies warm from the oven. As Sal poured, Mrs Manners added, sounding stronger, 'Wales, before Pennsylvania, the southern part it is said. Many Welsh came to Pennsylvania you know, after work in the mines. Then there were the mills of course.' She bit into a cookie with clear enjoyment.

'My dad was a South Wales millman.' Joe sipped his tea, watching her. Sal, watching them both, willed Eugenie Hywel Manners to do more than use Joe as a diversion to while away a hot August afternoon. Family meant so much to him, and to Hannah . . . to her also, though Sal was content simply to know that one or two relatives of hers had survived the enemy occupation of their land. She saw that Joe was excited by the affirmation that Alex's family might have originated in his district. But 'the southern part of Wales' was vague; if that was as close as they could get, it would not be close enough.

'Who told you of Wales?' she asked now. 'Is anything written down?' Mrs Manners drank from the hand-painted china cup then dabbed at her lips with a napkin.

'There are some entries in a family bible.' She gestured towards the house. 'My daughter Katy Ann has it now. What I'll do is – when she and Clem return from their vacation I'll have her call you. My memory lets me down a little, that's the truth of it.'

She treated them to a smile of such sparkling charm then that it was plain to see that Eugenie had been a beautiful woman.

'But Katy Ann, now, she will do better for you. She's real keen on the idea of getting a family tree started. Just a question of settling down to it. She's so many irons in the fire; and now the grandchildren too . . . I have to make an appointment to see her myself, some days! But she will be delighted to hear of your interest . . . shouldn't be surprised if she hasn't questions she'll be asking you, too.'

After they had taken their leave and were heading back to Bend, Joe felt dispirited, increasingly enervated by frustration; edgy.

'I think we've wasted time there. Katy Ann sounds too busy by half and Han will be disappointed that there's nothing to report.' He stared at the road ahead.

Sal saw sweat on his forehead and said at once:

'Shall we stop for a break, stretch our legs? The trees here are lovely, and we have all the time we want.'

He coasted to a stop in a shady lay-by. 'Why not?' He wiped his face, breathless with a mix of sensations, none of which was pleasant. They followed a track through the trees, the canopy protecting them from the sun. Birds were everywhere, with small rustlings as the creatures of the forest floor went about their business. They skirted a lake where a family fished from a little boat, then climbed slightly. Joe felt strange; the afternoon had refocused his past to an uncomfortable degree and he walked quickly in an effort to leave it behind him, where the past should be.

'It is so – *big*.' Sal paused as they topped the rise to view a fresh panorama under a cobalt sky. Joe opened another button of his cotton shirt.

'I suppose that's what the West is, if we're to believe John Wayne. Big. Want to go on, or are you pooped?'

'I'm fine.'

As they trekked towards the next rise, Joe was overtaken by a disconcerting sense of *déjà vu*. Incredible . . . how many thousand miles west? Best part of six? And yet . . . he was back in summer 1921, on the hill track above Taibach, pushing his bike with its big front basket loaded with groceries. Up . . . up . . . Joe plodded on, his face beading again with sweat.

'You are well, Joe?' Sal caught him up as he paused, clutching a trail-side sapling.

'Fine, honey.' Actually he felt sick. It could be the same curved track, the same scrubby undergrowth. Bigger trees of course – look at the sky, fool, it was clearly not Wales. But there . . . *There*. That was the same.

A drop off the trail was quite steep on the left.

Ground fell away into a quarry-like indent, the sides rough with wild growth. Joe walked towards it, frantic to turn back but unable to do so. The scuffle, that drunken pig Madoc knocking him off his bike. The insults he'd mouthed about Han had been vile, maddening Joe sufficiently to lash out at his red, leering face.

Joe's chest tightened. He stared down the track into the dim foliage, where a bird scratched for grubs in the leaf mould. He fought for breath as the pain increased.

'Joe? You have pain?' Sal caught at his arm.

'Some . . .' He scrabbled in his trouser pocket for the pillbox but it fell from his stiff fingers. He recalled the feel of knuckle on flesh then, connecting with Norman Madoc's jaw in a sickening crunch.

'Foul-mouthed sod!' Joe was certain he yelled aloud, but Sal heard nothing as he stooped to retrieve the pillbox. He saw the man bump and slide down the quarry and end at the bottom with his head against a rock. Joe, with a little groan, keeled over.

'The pills.' His voice was a croak, his arm stretched vainly.

'I shall get –' Sal pulled him into a sitting position. 'I see it, Joe.'

She inched her way over the incline, clinging to any growth firm enough to bear her.

'Here –' Joe reached to grasp her outstretched hand. 'God, be careful now –' His shirt was drenched and sweat rolled off his chin. The pillbox was just within the reach of her other hand as she bent desperately to retrieve Joe's hope of life. Joe gasped for breath; saw Norman Madoc's eyes turned sightlessly up, and began to choke.

'I have it –' With a huge effort Sal forced herself

upward from the slope to Joe; to safety. 'Here, my darling –'

Joe gagged, then forced down two of the little pills, his face grey and wet as he slumped on the track. Sal crooned with distress, holding his head.

'He's dead, Sal. He's dead!' Joe gave a great sob. 'I killed him . . .'

'Not true, my love,' she said with conviction. 'My Joe would harm no one. Rest now.' But Joe began to weep with tearing, heart-rending spasms.

'I did kill him. All those years back. Strong for my age, I was. He said wicked things about Han, you see. Called her a whore, and a witch. More than I could take, that word. I hit him, *here*. Down the quarry he went –'

He shuddered, struggled to master his grief. Sal continued to hold him, kissing his damp hair, stroking his cheek. Gradually he quietened, and after a few moments took a shuddering breath.

'Feels better . . . pretty tired though.'

'Of course.' She continued to hold him. 'We can stay here a little while, there is time enough. Soon you will feel stronger.'

They sat together on the trail, backs against a tree, sun slanting through to them as it dropped in the sky. After a while Sal asked softly: 'Is that what you feared to tell me?'

Joe nodded.

'Easier for you, Joe, if you had.'

'Yes.'

'But now, is out. All is well, now.'

'You reckon?'

'Oh yes. I was unhappy about not knowing.'

'Sorry, sweetheart . . . not easy to get out, a thing like that.'

'Later . . . if you want, you tell me slowly, from the beginning.'

'OK, hon. I'll do that. In a while.'

Back in New York, Liza had become restless, enervated by the heat. She made long calls to Hannah, and almost as many to Penelope, discussing options for the following year. A high-profile part in a BBC TV play was read, and a deal was made for late February. Following soon after, a contract to play Paula in a revival of Pinero's *The Second Mrs Tanqueray*. The Old Vic . . . the company of the great. Liza did her exercises with renewed energy: she would need her figure back fast.

In September her father came down to take her back for a visit. 'We shall keep one another company while Ella visits with her sister in Vancouver.' David Vaughan was stooping slightly now, but still looking fit. He embraced her, then stepped back to admire her glowing face.

'I can still scarcely believe it . . . two of you soon. Twice the pleasure!'

'Silly old Pa.' Liza hugged him. 'One of me and one of someone else – maybe nothing *like* me.'

'Whatever; the more the merrier.' They flew to Toronto then on north to Vaughan's ranch outside Barrie. The air was so clear and sharp after Manhattan that Liza slept on late next morning before breakfasting on the long veranda of the handsome, low-slung timber house.

'It's so good to be back, Pa dear.' She stretched out to touch his forearm. He took her hand and gave it a gentle squeeze. They sat in contented silence, gazing over the fields grazed by young cattle, the mass of trees by the lake starting to colour into their autumn glory, his float plane riding calmly at its mooring. 'This *is* beautiful Pa. Your own private world. Is this why you came to Canada – to find such a place?'

'No. I have to say I came to Canada in the first place to escape from my father – or more precisely his business, Vaughan Tinplate. He expected me to take over his factory when I'd learned the ropes. But I hated it all. So . . . I had a small inheritance from my grandfather, which sufficed to give me independence. I came here partly because of what I learned from Canadians in the Great War.'

'You've never wanted to go back?'

'I guess not. Canada has given me everything I could wish for – these hundred and fifty acres especially.'

'I've always loved coming here. I recall how I looked forward to each August, those early years.'

He poured more coffee, peeled and quartered an orange and offered the plate. 'They were special times for both of us. I was always terrified you wouldn't get here till I actually met you off the plane at Toronto. And when I took you back . . . well –' He shrugged, emotions playing hide-and-seek across his features. 'But this time it won't be so long, will it – I'll be over to see my grandchild soon as you give the word. By then, my time should be my own – I've been in business quite long enough. You are happy?' he added suddenly, brows drawn over the aquamarine eyes that were less intense than she recalled in childhood. Liza swallowed the segment of orange, nodding.

'Sure, Pa. I know it must be strange, people being married and yet apart so much. But we did think about that. And we're both trying really hard to make it work. We reckon it might work even better, not living in each other's pockets!'

'Could be so.' He passed her a plate of honey pancakes she'd always loved.

She buttered one sparingly. 'I've always wanted to know, and maybe I can ask you now . . . why did you not marry my mother?'

'Because I was a fool,' he said, and buried his face in his coffee cup.

'Oh dear; should I not have asked?' She was contrite.

Vaughan set down his coffee and looked across to his lake. 'You've a right to know, haven't you? Well . . . I suppose it was all rather a mess, one way and another. But I should have married her; I saw that much later. I had married Julia, my first wife, for the wrong reasons. But I always thought, one day . . . one day . . .'

He stopped for a moment. 'I simply did not know about *you*, sweetheart. And Hannah had a right to do as she pleased about that; I have to admit, I'd let her down. When I did know about you, Julia had died and I was free. But your mother was set to marry Matthew by then. And I reckon he's probably made her a damn sight better husband than I could ever have done.'

Vaughan pulled himself up short. Liza waited, aware he was struggling to make sense of the relationship that had spanned so many years. 'None of that's going to mean much to you is it, honey? But I guess the simple truth is that there were two occasions when I could and should have asked your mother to marry me, and I failed on both.'

He looked at her, and Liza saw the pain of wasted years in his eyes.

'Was it because she came from a poor family and yours was wealthy?' she asked directly. Vaughan let out his breath, unaware that he had been holding it, and took more coffee to give himself time.

'For the first occasion I'm afraid that may have been so.' He spoke with heavy emphasis. 'At that time, you know, people thought it important to marry within their class. But the second opportunity – at the end of the last war – was crass neglect.' He looked at her then. 'I guess that's tough for you to make sense of, let alone condone.'

'I think I can see that years ago it would have been a problem . . . I guess I was really thinking about later on. You see, I just couldn't understand. I've always felt that Mummy was good enough for anybody. She seems, well, pretty special.'

'You're right there, honey.' He smiled wryly. 'And I should have recognised that right off. But you know, most of us make a fair mess of quite a few lifestyle decisions. It's much easier to judge the wrong turnings others are taking than to chart your own course straight.'

'Yes . . . Well, Pa – thanks for letting me talk. Men don't find these conversations easy, do they?' She laughed, wiped her hands and reached over to kiss him. 'Can we go out? D'you know where I want to go?'

Vaughan laughed back, tension gone. 'Let me guess. Bass Park?'

'Where else? You know, when I'd get back to school after I'd been here, my friends would ask where I went, and what did I do in Canada. And I'd say every year, oh, we went into Bass Park, and I suppose they thought how boring, a little old park with railings and footpaths and square flowerbeds! They didn't know Bass Park, did they? Will Geraldine pack us a picnic?' Liza looked down at her stomach. 'I may not get quite so far into the forest this time . . . But we can hunt for fossils by that little lake – and see if the beavers are still around.'

Jonet and Mark walked with Hannah along the river that ran below Bracken House. Laurie followed, in close conversation with Matthew. The day was calm, with pale high streamers of cloud, the year on the cusp . . . summer hovering, but starlings starting their autumn gatherings on telegraph poles, jostling noisily for precedence.

'If he doesn't work these next two terms he'll have messed up everything.' Jonet sounded despondent, pulling her cardigan closer about her trim body. Just forty-three, Jonet's smooth prettiness had sharpened. She still wore her dark hair stiffly backcombed, when a softer style would have better suited her small face, and her eyes in repose were brooding, her mouth tight. Hannah said, not wishing to prolong this conversation with Laurie almost within earshot, 'I've been trying to encourage him all I can: Matthew too, I know. Let's see how he settles down this term. Did you say you were going out to Bahrain next month, Mark? Does that mean you'll miss the winter?'

'Yes – wonderful, isn't it! My contract will take six months.' He laughed, and Jonet's mouth tightened further. Mark Shapiro was moving smoothly up the career ladder and two years earlier had become a director of his firm. The executive home in suburban Reading had been vacated for a detached, stonebuilt house in a satellite village; they had begun to collect antiques, and Coalport china. At this point, Jonet could well have become a housewife, occupied by fund-raising coffee mornings, afternoon art classes, conversational French evening classes or even flower arranging, ethnic cooking or keeping fit.

Jonet though was increasingly aware that her life was not in the least as she had envisaged it . . . that the plans drawn with such single-minded care over many years had not brought fulfilment. Mark Shapiro had seemed exactly the man to partner her: clever, ambitious, not of the working class she so despised. After an early childhood hated for its drab penny-pinching in a mean little house in a dirty town, she had sworn to marry as far as possible from her roots, and had done so. She had entered the profession planned for since schooldays, had the son she hoped would complete the image of success and family happiness. So why did she struggle daily now with the bitter taste of failure?

Plans, Jonet saw, do not always translate successfully into reality. Laurie had blocked the route to the top of her profession. And though his birth should at least have made them a complete family, each of them appeared to walk alone. Their son had inherited none of their traits, had turned increasingly from their values, their ambitions for his future. Overtly, she and Mark were perfectly compatible, yet a depressing sterility was clouding their relationship.

At times now Jonet struggled to remember her father, thinking he might be responsible for his grandson's nonconformist attitudes. But she could recall only the dark bulk of him, and the constant need she felt as a small girl to be picked up and cuddled, to be *noticed* by him. She sighed, depression clouding the day. She was working full-time again in the Reading main library, clawing her way back into the system at whatever cost it took in an effort to gain the satisfaction so clearly missing in her life. But her ambitions continued to extend to her son, no matter how he attempted to shake them off. He shrank from them; ran to hide with Hannah and Matthew, or with young protesters in London squats, with whom he could identify more easily than the boys at school who planned to be bankers, media moguls or research chemists for multinational drug firms. Laurie did not like the way the world was going; not any of it.

'It was rotten when Mick Jagger got that £200 fine for cannabis,' he confided glumly to Matthew as they strolled behind the others. 'Then when the *Beatles* broke up . . . well that was a fantastic blow. Now the Tories have got back in again.' He shook his head. 'An' Vietnam just goes on and on . . .'

'It's a lot of bad news,' Matthew acknowledged carefully, not wishing right now to debate politics with this gentle, slightly melancholy and unconfident step-grandson, of whom he was extremely fond. He judged there were few people Laurie could trust with his confidences, and certainly not his parents. Matthew missed his own sons, seeing little of them now, and was happy to give Laurie whatever attention he needed. 'We'll have a spell in the garden when we get back, shall we? That will cheer you up – the news is good there! Your lavender bushes are roaring ahead still, and the lemon thyme looks and smells a treat. And the rosemary hedge needs a light trim. Would your mother like some stuff to take back, d'you think?'

'I doubt it. She doesn't have much time to cook, you know. Has Gran got all she needs to dry for the winter?' Laurie was proud of his beautiful herb garden here, and grateful for Matthew's guidance.

'Loads, I think. Tell you what – why don't I ask around, put a notice in the village shop, maybe the pub too? You know: "Fresh herbs for sale at nominal prices"?'

Laurie brightened now. 'Matthew – would you? That'd be super. I don't like to see them wasted. Great – let me know what happens.'

'I'll drop you a note,' promised Matthew, and Laurie, knowing he had never been let down by this man, smiled again.

'And will you show me your new seascapes later on? Maybe you'd let *me* have a go?'

Hannah found it a strain when Jonet and Mark came, sometimes no more than once a year; paradoxical, since she was so keen to have them come, to keep the slender thread of their connection unbroken. She guessed they ran out of excuses to offer Laurie, to whom this family contact was clearly important, and for his sake she was happy to welcome them. Neither she nor Jonet talked of personal matters; conversation was usually general and controversy kept at a distance, but Hannah sensed that Jonet was not a happy woman. Her relationship with Mark appeared lifeless, even indifferent. Jonet, though, had never worn emotions on her sleeve . . . the state of their marriage would probably remain a secret between the two of them.

Since she had seen and spoken with Liza in Bournemouth three summers earlier, Jonet's half-sister had rarely come up as a topic of conversation. Hannah then, was surprised by Jonet's sudden question.

'Where is Liza having her baby, Mother?'

'Oh – in London so far as I know, dear. Around the middle of December. Carl is due to come about then, to stay over into New Year.'

'So will they all go back to New York then?'

'Well . . . Liza goes into rehearsal for a play fairly soon after that, so maybe she'll stay on in London.'

'So the baby will have a full-time nanny,' Jonet observed in a flat voice.

'I suppose so, yes. I know Liza's looking forward to things Penelope has already sorted out for her to do.'

'That's nice,' Jonet said in the same expressionless tone. 'I should have liked a nanny for Laurie. I would have been able to pursue my own career then, like Liza.'

Hannah slid a glance at Mark, who appeared to be concentrating on the close observation of a pair of mallards. 'I would infinitely prefer to have the care of my baby,' she said quietly to Jonet. 'I planned my own business to allow for that.'

'Sadly, I was unable to do the same.' Jonet dropped back to ask Matthew about the day's tides. Hannah walked on. She would like either to slap Jonet, or attempt to comfort her.

Liza looked down as the plane descended on its approach to Heathrow. Lights were everywhere as the short winter afternoon became dusk. Had she not known that Hannah would be down there, she would at that moment have felt lonely. Then her child threw her an energetic kick – she could now differentiate between fist and foot – and she laid a hand on her stomach.

'All right, all right. I know you're there. We're going down; you won't like that but for God's sake don't make a scene.'

Carl had actually felt the baby last night, he said, when they had made love, just a little and very gently.

'Sure I'm not hurting, honey? You must say . . .'

'It's OK, Carl. Honestly.' She didn't really care for

him inside her now, it all seemed too crowded. But it was a favour she could do him in return for him not creating an issue over her going back to Britain. Her body was public property anyway, until it opened to expel the new human it had grown, in around four weeks' time. Please don't be late. If you are, I shall bounce you around the district on the top deck of a London bus till you call quits.

Hannah beamed with delight as she identified the glamorous figure of her daughter emerging into the arrivals concourse; wrapped splendidly in mink, her glossy hair a bright banner in the winter gloom, two porters trailing her with piled luggage trolleys. The eyes of the large group of welcomers, previously fixed expectantly on the exit from customs, now followed this beautiful, elegant traveller. Where had they seen her before, this lady of such obvious consequence . . . the television? Wasn't she in that film about . . .

Hannah recalled the thin, tense figure of her older daughter as she had seen her in September, and her welcoming smile shadowed. Oh Jonet . . . Jonet. Cannot you be happy too?

'Mummy!' Liza sailed towards her, an eight-month pregnancy marring her grace not one whit. 'Mummy darling, how lovely! Home again . . .'

The house in Holland Park was warmly welcoming, lamps diffusing soft light upon vases of roses, from deep magenta through every hue to swan white. Mrs Roberts the agency housekeeper beamed her own welcome. Middle-aged and competent, she had cheerfully dyed hair and a big mouth that smiled and smiled. Liza slipped out of her mink and turned about, admiring the place afresh.

'It *is* nice, isn't it? . . . Don't you think, Mummy? Look, you find us a drink – it's over there – while I give Carl a call to say I'm home and dry.'

When she had done that, Liza went up to put on a comfortable housegown. She lay on the bed for a few minutes; she really was quite tired after the long flight. She put a hand on her stomach. Four weeks . . . she could get through that; she would go down to Wales with her mother for a few days. It simply was not fair to expect Hannah to stay here waiting for the baby, and leaving Matthew on his own. Then when she got back here it would be almost time, and Carl would be with her again.

'I hope this is going to work out,' Hannah said with an anxious frown as they neared Bracken House two days later.

'Mummy – I told you, the clinic has said it's a *good idea,*' Liza repeated patiently. 'No point moping around an empty house, they said. And the baby's absolutely on course – you *heard* them. Some sea air will be perfect. So don't fuss; oh, I'm terribly looking forward to seeing dear old Matthew.'

'Hello, Tug-boat Annie.' Matthew, warned of their imminent arrival, came out to meet them. Hannah climbed stiffly from the driving seat but Liza was already out and hugging him. 'So, a ship in full sail now, is it?'

'Don't be a pig. I'm relatively sylph-like. Agree with me or I'll pull out your fingernails.'

'You are relatively sylph-like,' Matthew agreed obediently.

'I am not. I'm like a ship in full sail.' Liza laughed with delight. 'Oh, it's good to be here!'

They struck a mild patch, with heavy night rain but calm days and even some watery sun. Liza, according to instructions, phoned the clinic matron every third day to report in, and her doctor at the end of six days.

He advised that it was about time now to get back to base; she agreed to do so, but somehow omitted to tell Hannah. The days were so pleasant . . . and she was aware of how little time she would spend here once she was working again. Carl phoned each evening and she promised him not to leave it too late; that she was incredibly well, and would probably go 'tomorrow'.

She was helping Matthew clear dead leaves from his pond when her stomach became as hard as a cannonball, causing her to straighten with surprise. When it happened again she got slowly up from her knees and stood still, looking out over the countryside to the distant dunes. A third tightening; this time in concert with a low backache.

'I'll go and see if Mummy's ready to make some tea, shall I?' she asked Matthew, and walked carefully back down the garden.

'The thing is not to panic,' Hannah told her. 'I've been ready to go back with you for some days. But when will you ever listen to me?'

'Don't lecture me now, Mummy, please.' Liza leaned over slightly into a contraction that seemed a shade stronger. 'I admit I've overstayed. It's all your fault, and Matthew's – you shouldn't be so nice to stay with. You don't reckon we can make it back to London, then?'

'No,' Hannah said bluntly. She got the directory and pursued hospital numbers while Liza drank her tea walking about the hall. Her mind was quickly becoming blank, save for the immediate business of how often the contractions were coming. They weren't pains; she could handle this perfectly well, stay in control. The backache was a bit miserable, but would probably soon go. Maybe if she took a nice warm bath . . .

'Is that Bridgend General?' Hannah was hot on the scent. 'Please put me through to your maternity wing.'

Matthew put his smiling face round the back door, and his hair was wet. 'Tea?' he enquired. 'It's started to throw it down.' Hannah beckoned him in.

'Take off your wellies,' she instructed. 'Liza's gone into labour.'

'God in heaven!' Matthew's smile fell straight off his face. Hannah concentrated again on the telephone.

'Maternity? Can you help us please? My daughter's visiting from London and has gone into labour, I believe. Could she come to you?' Liza came in from the hall and Matthew returned in his socks. Hannah shooed them both away and continued her dialogue with Maternity. When she joined them in the sitting room she regarded Liza with a keen eye.

'How often are they now?'

'I couldn't actually say.' Liza pulled a little face. 'I'd better time a couple. What did they say?'

'They've agreed to look at you. It may be a false alarm; first labours can appear to make a start then peter out. I'll go and put some overnight things together for you while you check.' Matthew poured himself a whisky though it was only 4.15. Outside, rain spat hard at the windows and the light had almost gone.

'Twelve minutes,' Liza told her when Hannah came down with a small case. She stood awkwardly by the fire, shifting from one foot to the other; sat down and almost immediately stood up again. Matthew watched her anxiously.

'Can I get you more tea, dear? How about a sandwich?'

Liza thought about Matthew's sandwiches, which

she knew from experience were never less than an inch in depth. 'I don't believe I will just now, thanks Matthew. I really am awfully sorry about this,' she added with honest contrition. It was, she knew, entirely down to her own wilfulness that she was not now safely in London.

The baby's clothes . . . she had not even a nappy here. And she had assembled a wonderful layette, purchased in New York with Carl. It was awaiting her baby in the room she had made into the nursery, along with the antique Welsh baby rocker bought by Hannah, with its hand-embroidered sheets of finest cotton. All she had here was the crocheted shawl Florence had brought over on Wednesday, and a lemon matinée jacket and matching bootees Tom had bought in the Porthcawl baby shop.

Her eyes filled with sudden tears. Perceiving them, Hannah got the ball rolling. Within half an hour they were on the way, Liza washed and changed and complaining that she had desperately wanted a bath, and clinging to the small bag containing the shawl, jacket and bootees. Matthew drove, peering into the sluicing rain, and Hannah sat in the back with Liza.

'Carl –' Liza suddenly yelled as they passed a roadside phone box. 'I have to call Carl!'

'After we get there. First things first, darling. If it's a false start and you can come back there'll have been no need anyway. Now, let Matthew concentrate on driving; these conditions aren't ideal.'

It was not a false start. 'We've not a bed in the place,' Sister told Liza with a touch of satisfaction. 'So we'll pop you up on the delivery bed in here –' The delivery room was all it need be: square, white, businesslike. 'You'll be nice and quiet in here tonight, an' if you're not busy yourself by mornin' we'll have an empty bed for you. If we need this room during the night we can always switch you over, like.' She paused, and looked at Liza with more interest. 'I've seen you somewhere, haven't I?' Liza hesitated; decided to milk the situation. 'It could have been on television, my new film's not out till February.' She winked at Hannah as the sister left to spread the news that they had a VIP in the delivery room.

She was finally taken into charge, leaving Matthew reading *Country Life* in the waiting room while Hannah called New York.

'It's rather a surprise, Carl. Liza is in labour . . . Yes, I know, a couple of weeks early – but that's nothing to worry about. The thing is, of course, she is still with us, so she's gone into our local hospital . . . Well, she was going back tomorrow . . . Carl, I can't make this a long call, it's a public phone . . . Yes, I've got that. Right. We'll either hear or see you then. But don't worry –'

'He blew his top.' She joined Matthew. 'Why was she not in London? How good is this hospital? He did not want his child delivered on *welfare*!'

'The chap's probably pretty much frustrated – Liza said, did she not, that he'd wanted her in America for the birth?' Matthew shrugged. 'And *welfare* . . . he doubtless thinks that in Wales that means she's lying on slatted boards in a room with flaking whitewash.'

Hannah burst into a laugh, leaning against the wall. 'Matthew, I love you, you restore my sanity. The upshot was, he's determined to catch an evening flight which he thinks gets to Heathrow quite early. He'll ring when he arrives, and his office will organise a car to bring him straight here. As for us; I shall go in search of news of Liza.'

'She has started, but nothing much is happenin'

yet,' was the news. 'We're hopin' she'll get some sleep, be fresh for tomorrow.'

Liza was now lying on the high, hard delivery bed, looking depressed. 'I'm allowed a bath, then horrid things are to be done, then they think I should sleep.' She clutched herself, grimacing. 'I couldn't possibly do that; the contractions are really quite, well, *strong* now.'

'Just try to let everything go, darling – just relax. The bath will help. I've phoned Carl, he should be here around lunchtime tomorrow.' Liza grimaced again.

'He's going to be furious about this. He said last night on the phone, do go back to London today . . . and now look what's happened!'

'He'll forget it all when he sees the baby tomorrow,' Hannah promised. She smoothed back Liza's heavy hair. 'Shall I brush this for you?'

A long night. 'Go home, make a sandwich, get into bed, go to sleep,' Hannah exhorted Matthew. 'You can come back fresh in the morning. I don't think myself she'll wait about, so I must stay.'

She was right. Liza decided to get on with the job in hand quite soon after her bath. 'Might as well,' she said tersely between contractions, as Hannah rubbed her back. 'Since I'm actually *here*.'

The baby was born at 6.15, with a gigantic push and a shout of triumph from her mother. Hannah's face was wet with tears as her new granddaughter was held up for her inspection, fists waving in healthy defiance of the rough world. Liza's hand, which had been gripping Hannah's wrist in a painful vice, relaxed as she reached for her daughter.

'Well now . . . just look at you.' She smiled at the small wrinkled creature, wrapped in a cream NHS blanket. 'Will she look more presentable by this afternoon, Mummy? Otherwise –' she gave a tired grin – 'we'll have Carl sending her back as sub-standard.'

Jessica Hywel Cline had become all but beautiful within the day. Her velvet skin smoothed out, her ears unfolded and her lips took on her mother's naughty curve. Her crowning glory was the light-brown fuzz with a hint of auburn on her neat round head. And 'oh my, looks like we might have a second redhead in the family,' were her father's first words.

'To us, honey. The three of us. A Happy Christmas.'

Carl raised his champagne glass. They stood by the tree, a splendid specimen loaded with lights and all things good. Jess's treasure cot was nearby, where she could see the shimmering baubles; now she slept, barely visible but for a miniature fist that had escaped from her shawl as usual.

Liza, in black silk velvet pants and a tunic patterned in vibrant, stained-glass-window colours, looked as beautiful as she ever had. All the fuss was behind her. Carl was charmed by his daughter, and was over his paddy about his child being born on the cheap, and in *Wales* of all places. Not allowing that slight to pass, Liza had retorted that she had not only been *born* in Wales, she was also to have a Welsh middle name. Carl had given in on that one only out of the deep respect he was fast developing for Hannah. And Hannah was so delighted to learn that her family name was continuing in this grandchild, that Carl allowed her to believe it had been his idea.

A highly recommended nurse was installed, and Mrs Roberts found a maid to help out with the extra work. They were to spend Christmas quietly, with Hannah and Matthew coming up for New Year, and

David Vaughan had promised to fly over to inspect his grandchild later in January. Liza felt well, was proud of the delicious baby tucked into the treasure cot, and knew she would be ready to start work again in February after Carl's return to New York. 'No hurry to get back' he had said. Things were pretty quiet on the corporate scene just now, and there were anyway a few contacts he would like to make here in the City. A breather then, for both of them.

'By the way, sweetheart –' he smiled, the secretive smile she recognised. 'I've a little something extra for you, apart from these –' nodding at the wrapped gifts piled under the tree. 'Not easy to wrap; so . . .'

Carl went to the walnut desk and drew out a largish buff envelope. 'For you, with my love and thanks.'

'Darling . . .' Liza sat down, eased open the flap and drew out a legal document. 'What *is* it? Oh, tell me! You know I have a block over legal-speak.'

'I do recall.' Carl came to lean over her shoulder. 'Well, cut out all the crap and it says that you are now the owner of this place.'

'This place? But Carl, we rent it!'

'Not any more.' Carl smiled that 'I-know-something-special' smile again. 'I made them an offer they couldn't refuse. It's yours, honey, lock stock and barrel. I've been working on it for months and it finally got settled a couple of weeks ago. Your signature on the dotted line completes the transfer. It's been a hard secret to keep, I tell you.'

'But didn't you want us to share it? I mean – why *mine*? Not that I'm not utterly thrilled of course – I've never owned property before!'

'Maybe a security for you? A nest-egg? Whichever, I thought you'd like the idea of it being *yours*. Hope I got it right.'

'You did!' She put her cheek against his. 'And you must have paid the earth . . . thank you a million times.'

'Every time you put your latch-key in the door, remember I love you. That's all I ask.'

Chapter Nineteen

January 1971

David Vaughan winged towards home in his Twin Otter. A long day; but a good one, completing the finalities of the sale. Well – good? Maybe not, as the sense of loss pressed on his consciousness; forty-six years was a helluva time to have one business, from raw new infancy to the sophisticated freight empire that had now been absorbed into a multinational organisation. Everything got bigger – businesses merging like drops of water joining to make a sizeable puddle.

He smiled sourly. Big puddles could get pretty murky. He had to believe he was well out of it. Since old Nev's death five years ago the game had been getting dirtier, pressure put on him to sell out Vaughan Air mounting relentlessly. As partners he and Nev had been invincible. Now . . . it had become pointless, a fight for nothing, fresh headaches at every turn.

Thinking of headaches made Vaughan aware of his head banging away now. The stress of the day, most likely. That would be why the engine noise was bugging him, though they were running as evenly and sweetly as ever, all indicators normal. Not long now, then a drink and dinner, feet up with the newspaper.

He sighed. Would the ranch be the next to go? Ella had voted to move into Toronto as their two closest friends had, last spring. Other old neighbours were going, leaving the district to be infiltrated by the young and youngish, as he had done forty-odd years ago. It had been a fine place, then . . . but maybe the time had come to move into the city; though the idea made him gag a little.

A grandfather . . . his mind had continued to circle around Jessica ever since he'd heard. Next week he would be off to see her, loaded down with a bag full of ridiculously cute soft toys. Jessica . . . Jess, they seemed to be calling her. That was nice, an old-fashioned name. He was old to have a first grandchild, but wasn't he just so damn pleased. He had missed Liza's babyhood . . . must see to it he didn't miss so much of Jess's.

Hell, they could all come out here come summer, to the ranch. They would take Jess to Bass Park, dandle her feet in the lake by the beaver run. Hannah, Matthew, Carl, Joe and Sal – the lot. Ella would be happy to have them; she'd love to show off her home. They'd plenty of room and they could get in extra help. The awkwardness had gone with Matthew; time mellows all. That was one genuine fellow and God bless him for making Hannah happy.

Hannah. He had thought so much about Hannah, this last week. Increasingly, since Liza had brought it all bubbling to the surface last September. How different, if he and Hannah . . . Liza, his legitimate daughter, and Hannah his wife. His own fault. But he could not feel more strongly that they were his family, bless them. More and more, his own folk. Yes, he'd set about organising a visit. Funny, he'd had Hannah at the back of his mind all day.

Vaughan eased back the throttles to commence descent. Losing height, his ears popped and he was aware of his headache increasing. Thudding. Hannah used to be able to cure headaches. Could she still?

Barrie, down below. Left a bit now, line up with the road. My head's splitting open, thank God I'm almost home . . .

Lower. Bank to starboard . . . over Gordon Fryer's place. Lower flaps . . . Christ, something's wrong . . . can't reach the flaps . . .

There's the trees, the lake . . . Christ Jesus, my head . . . *Concentrate*, clear the trees . . . get it down.

Oh God . . . can't . . .

Why – Hannah! Hannah? How come you're . . .

The Otter's skis hit the ice on the far side of David Vaughan's lake. The plane careered unchecked into the shore and torpedoed on into the trees.

There was no fire. After the crunching sound of tearing living wood and dead metal, there returned the deep silence of midwinter timberland.

'Let's go in the park,' Hannah said. 'This is the best bit of the day, the sun is out, and we can be back before Jess is hungry again. I've not seen Holland Park yet . . . and I want to blow away the remains of a snorter of a headache.'

'Poor Mummy.' Liza saw the blue sky through the window. 'I could do with a breather myself, actually. This script's not the easiest, I'm feeling quite depressed . . . I'll ask Lucy to get Jess wrapped up.' She was halfway up the stairs when the phone rang.

'Would you get that, Mummy?'

'Hello?' Hannah also had her eyes on the sky and now it looked cold; empty. She shivered, and last evening's headache pressed afresh against her temple.

'Is that Liza Vaughan?' The voice was Canadian, pleasant and low.

'No, this is her mother speaking.' Hannah was at once stiff with foreboding and the sun had gone. 'Liza is upstairs, shall I call her?'

'Well . . . that's Hannah, then?'

'Yes. You are Ella.' She knew; of course she knew.

'Yes . . . Hannah it's very bad news. I have to tell Liza her father is dead.'

Hannah took each word as a blow to the body. 'Oh . . . oh, I am so sorry, Ella.'

'A plane accident. He crashed on the edge of our lake late yesterday afternoon.' The police have been there all night . . . there is to be an inquiry.'

'I am so sorry,' Hannah repeated. 'Would you like me to tell Liza?'

'I would, obviously . . . But thanks, Hannah; I guess she has the right to be told this first hand. I must do it.'

'I'll call her, then. And Ella – please accept my deepest sympathy for your loss.'

'Many thanks, Hannah. And I hope you will come to the funeral . . . if you want to, that is. But I do hope anyway that one day we will meet. When this is over I will write to you.'

Hannah stood by the window in her room while Liza took the call. Her chest shook with tears asking to be shed as she stared at the winter trees laced over the pale sky. Her head had begun to ache violently after she had fallen quite unnecessarily down four stairs last evening, and she had not slept. Now she knew why.

David. She thought of the long years of their relationship. Clearest, was the terrible time after Serena's death, when his had been the hand to which she had clung for sanity in a world at war, gone mad; reason gone, for what reason had there been in Serena's death? Now she had to comfort David's daughter, as once David had comforted her.

She found Liza on her knees with face buried in the sofa cushion, her sobs muffled. Hannah went down beside her, embraced and rocked her, cheek against the rich copper hair inherited from David Vaughan.

'He won't see Jess now.' Liza's voice broke. 'He was coming *next week*.'

'I know . . . I know, dear.' The nurse came downstairs with Jess and Hannah signalled her to go away. She stayed by Liza, wishing Matthew would come back from the Old Bailey where he was following a trial in which he had a special interest. Not that he could do anything; no one could. She stroked Liza's hair and they wept, remembering the man they had loved.

Carl had only flown back to New York the previous day. When he made his regular call that night Liza was again in tears. He offered to come right back, but she insisted he stay with his business after the extended break. And they could meet at the funeral whenever that was to be, she would need him there.

'You can't go,' Carl said sharply. Then, more gently, 'Honey; our baby is not six weeks old. It isn't right to take her on a trip like that.'

'Of course it isn't. She will stay here. She'll be fine. That's what the nurse is for, Carl, to look after Jess when I can't be there. And I shall ask Mummy and Matthew to be here too, so absolutely *nothing* can go wrong.'

'No.' Carl sounded firm. 'She's too young yet. Now forget it, Liza. I shall go on your behalf, your representative.'

'If you think I'm not going to my own father's funeral you are crazy! Carl – have you *any* idea how I feel? Of course not! You had a father from birth, saw him always, still do, just fine for you. I didn't see mine till I was seven, then just a few weeks a year. Have you *any* idea how I feel now I've lost him for ever? So don't tell me one more time I cannot go to his funeral!'

'Maybe if you'd made more effort to see him the last few years you wouldn't feel so guilty now. Is that the problem? Going to his funeral won't make up for anything – the poor guy won't give a toss if you're there or not!'

'God, I really hate you,' Liza screamed. 'I'd go to his funeral if I had to walk across the Atlantic. And *I* don't give a toss if *you* go or not!'

She slammed down the receiver and fled to her room, leaving Hannah and Matthew exchanging uncomfortable signals. After a moment Hannah went to stand by the door into the garden, cheeks flaming with resentment. How *dare* Liza take her so for granted – not understand her own wish to pay her last respects to the man she had loved so long? Liza really could be horribly self-centred.

She pushed her fingers hard against her temples, which still felt tender. Liza . . . when *will* you see others' needs as equal to your own?

On Thursday morning of the following week Liza flew out of Heathrow for her father's funeral. Hannah had thought carefully, and come to the conclusion that it might well be more considerate to both Ella and Matthew if she stayed at home, and remembered David Vaughan in privacy, in her own way as he was laid to rest. Liza, in response to a certain coolness, had been apologetic.

'It will help placate Carl I'm sure, Mummy, if he knows you've both stayed on here until I return. You've had three babies, after all, and Matthew would be brilliant in any emergency, bless his blue eyes. I think Carl is being totally unreasonable anyway; but . . . well, you know . . . oil on troubled waters seems to be called for.' So Joe had volunteered to represent Hannah at the funeral, and Hannah herself, while ruing the unattractive heedlessness displayed by her daughter, made her own arrangements.

Liza was tired when she landed at Toronto. She was also sore at heart. So easy to feel guilty, without Carl being unnecessarily cruel at such a time. Pa had never missed being here to meet her before. God in heaven, don't cry, not in the bloody airport. Pa's friend and neighbour Gordon Fryer was to meet her, Ella had said. Well, she'd known Gordon since her first trip, so she could cope with that if he could. In September he had asked for her autograph! There he was now, waving. Liza waved back, swallowing her tears. Thank the Lord she had professional experience in putting her best face forward. And the mink coat helped . . . thanks, Carl, you miserable pig.

After the committal, they stood in silence for a further moment at the graveside before dispersing. A path had been cleared through the snow, on which brilliant sunlight alternated with purple shadows cast by headstones and bare trees. Beyond the church, trees were massed banks of purple against the indigo sky.

Carl and Joe stood on either side of Liza. Ella was flanked by her older brother and by Desmond Vaughan, David's younger brother who had flown in from Scotland. With Ella's sister was a cousin of theirs from Ottawa, and surrounding the principal mourners were friends and neighbours from the district, and business associates.

Carl put a protective arm about his wife. He had thought carefully about their abrasive difference of opinion. Perhaps he had unfairly taunted her about a guilty conscience, when really he had no idea what effort she had made to see her father in earlier years. David Vaughan's death was clearly a blow. She had agreed to come back to New York with him this evening, and they could have Saturday and Sunday together before she took the night flight back to London.

Joe had his hand supportively under Liza's elbow. He knew what David Vaughan had meant to his sister, through all those years when he had contact only by letter. She had truly loved him, of that he was certain. He only hoped that Vaughan had loved her too. Ella seemed to be a nice woman, warm and approachable . . . it could not be easy for her to accept the idea of Hannah and her illegitimate daughter, though she had not married Vaughan until later, of course. But she had welcomed Liza, helped her feel she had a place here. She had a kind heart and Joe hoped that Vaughan had treated her well in their time together.

Liza stared at the trees, her face stony with grief for the father whose name she had used, but on whom she had no real call. Yet they *had* loved, as father and daughter, and she would grieve always at the briefness of their time together.

Better though by far, than not to have known of his existence. Matthew had always been good to her, but a natural father was irreplaceable. Ella had gone with her just before sunset yesterday to see the spot where he had come down. The plane had been removed, but trees were broken and the land scarred. As the sun went down, an orange ball over the quiet lake, Liza thought that, given a summer's growth, little would remain to bear witness to her father's death there. She felt the warmth of Carl and Joe surrounding her now, and was grateful to them for coming.

Before she left, Ella drew her to one side. 'Liza, our solicitor will be in touch with you of course, but meanwhile I have a copy of your father's will here for you. Also a letter for your mother, it was in David's desk. Will you give it to her, please?'

Liza took the buff solicitor's envelope, and the thick vellum one with 'Hannah' scrawled across it in the easily recognisable, authoritative hand. It seemed oddly alive in her fingers, and the lump was in her throat again.

'Thank you, Ella. I'll see that she gets it.' She kissed David's widow on the cheek and the two women embraced for a quiet moment. 'I shall come back if I may, at a less sad time for both of us.'

'That would be good . . .' Ella smiled. 'I may have sold the ranch, but I shan't be too far away, and Canada will still be here.'

It was a silent, sober trip back in the hired car to Toronto, then by plane to New York. Joe hugged her before parting. 'Tell Han I hope to see her in the summer, eh?'

'Sure, Uncle Joe. I'll see you myself, later on. Love to the family.'

She and Carl sat without speaking in the cab; Liza's eyes were closed, her head back on the seat. Carl felt for her gloved hand and held it on his lap as Manhattan's lights flashed about them. When they reached the apartment he slipped off her coat, eased off her soft leather boots.

'You go and draw a hot bath, honey. I'll fix the drinks and bring one to you. Would a brandy suit?' Liza nodded, too weary to speak. She was lying motionless, submerged in fragrant suds when he came into the bathroom.

'What about food? Can Chita fix you something? She waited up.'

'Oh . . . thanks, I think not.' Liza took the brandy glass and stood it on the ledge by the oval, half-sunken bath. 'Perhaps you'd tell her we won't need her any more tonight? Oh, and Carl, maybe you should take a look at Pa's will? It's just inside the end pocket of my grip.'

When he returned with the buff envelope and his drink he sank into the white bamboo chair near the bath.

'OK, let's take a look . . .' He took a mouthful of brandy then eased open the envelope. 'Wouldn't you like to read it?' He offered up the document. Liza shook her head tiredly.

'You know I wouldn't understand a word. Can you précis it for me in plain English?'

She soaped herself slowly while Carl perused the pages. When he had finished he shuffled them back into order and looked at her, taking another drink.

'It seems that in 1949 he invested $75,000 in a fund for you. That has been added to from time to time. You can now do whatever you want with it – leave it invested, take an income from it or realise the whole amount. That in a nutshell is it.'

Liza was silent. Then she said in a quiet voice, 'Dear old Pa. He did think of my welfare, didn't he? Even though I was only his bastard.'

'Don't say damn fool things like that.' Carl was angry now. 'The fact of your parents not being married is irrelevant – you've had love and care in plenty from both of them and you know it!' He gulped down the rest of his drink. 'This fund will now be worth around a couple of million dollars, maybe more . . . so yes, he *did* think of your welfare.' He went out, closing the door behind him.

Liza stared blindly at the wall, then hurled her glass against it with sudden force. It shattered and fell to the floor, and brandy ran down the tiles like blood from an open wound. Her hurt at Carl's censure . . . her own growing guilt over failing to see her father as often as she might . . . her grief at his death . . . all combined to fill her impossibly full of violent boiling frustration. As she saw the shards of broken glass now, she felt the shattering of that potentially lethal cocktail of emotions. Wrung out, but calmer, Liza stepped out of the bath and began to towel herself dry.

They got back on an even keel over Saturday, Liza still too stupefied with reaction to both travelling and grief to be combative, and Carl preferring to call quits. They walked in the park after a late breakfast, arm in arm, subdued, wearing warm jogging-suits under ski jackets, and fur caps. The sun shone, but had no strength to temper the eight-below-zero chill and unforgiving wind.

'The last time we walked here it was hot enough to melt flesh,' Liza said. She hated being cold.

'And we picnicked.' Carl nodded towards the frozen pond, where ducks stood around disconsolate despite the bread with which a concerned army of small children showered them. 'I've been thinking about your father's fund, honey. D'you know what you want to do about it yet? I could take it on and make it work for you, I haven't a bad track record in these matters.'

'Could you, Carl? I wouldn't do anything but bung it into a bank account. I couldn't *think* what to do with it otherwise.'

'I can do far better than that,' Carl said emphatically. 'Now, how about we go see the Big Apple Museum? You'd maybe like to learn something about the city? They have a pretty amazing collection of dolls' houses there too – we can get ideas for Jess.'

'Carl – Jess is a bit young for a doll's house –' Liza laughed, the first time since the death of her father. 'But yes, I should like that.'

'And afterwards, Ferini's for a late lunch? Then take in a movie?' Carl tucked her arm through his, feeling better for Liza's laugh. 'We've had no time so far for museums and movies, had you noticed? So; let's go.'

They were sprawled next day on the sofa with Sunday papers when Carl said: 'I've been giving thought to a place for us for weekends. How do you feel about Long Island? Gayle's moved out of the one we had, but obviously you'd prefer to start fresh . . . Long Island's good though, in that it's reachable for short spells.'

Liza nodded. 'I see that . . . Well, yes, that would be fine. I think your father's place is wonderful.'

'They're not easy to find, of course; but they're there if you put enough people out on the job. Come spring we may have struck lucky.'

'Lucky Carl Cline.' Liza held out a hand. He came to her and they curled together, saying nothing . . . both aware that it was four hours to take-off, and another separation.

Hannah walked through the house in the lull between lunch and Jess's afternoon feed. It was a beautiful house; she was pleased to have discovered it for them, and even more pleased to hear that Liza now owned it. Carl had been generous in the extreme to make an outright gift of the deeds . . . it gave Liza complete security, and such a property could only appreciate with time.

It did seem to Hannah that her early fears of Carl's

nature – not fears; wariness – may have been ill-judged. He did not suffer fools gladly, nor condone self-delusion. Well; neither did she, though she might have a less abrasive approach. Liza would have to toe certain lines or expect fireworks . . . and it seemed inevitable that on occasion, antlers would lock. Not good, if Jess were to witness too much of that; but no outsider could protect a child from its parents' behaviour. Witness Laurie . . .

Fresh coffee was brewing when Liza's taxi drew up, and she opened one of the black outside doors. Hannah had swallowed her hurt, had grieved privately for David, and was prepared to put the unpleasant taste of Liza's behaviour behind her.

Liza smiled at the taxi diver and he immediately carried her bags in for her; still basking in the smile, he crashed his gears as he departed.

'Hello, Mummy . . . Matthew . . . that coffee smells divine.'

When cups of it had been emptied, refilled and emptied again, and the salient details of the last days exchanged, Liza got up. 'Can't wait another moment – I have to see Jess. I've really missed her, you know. Oh –' She pulled David Vaughan's cream vellum envelope from her bag. 'This is for you, Mummy. Will you come and see Jess with me?' she added from the doorway.

'In a moment.'

The shock of holding the letter in her hand, seeing her name in the familiar script, was such that Hannah was suddenly breathless. Liza could be cruelly careless – how *could* she be so insensitive as to hand her this in front of Matthew? She stood like an idiot, looking into space. Sensing the difficulty Matthew got to his feet.

'I'll see if the papers have come . . .'

Hannah threw him a ghost of a smile. Ghosts indeed were before her . . . shades of other letters she had had from David in the past, the first when she had been no more than sixteen, and never, she recalled, telling her what she hoped to hear. This was the last she would receive.

It needed an effort to steady her fingers sufficiently to pull open the envelope; even then, she did not extract the contents. She moved to the garden window of the drawing room and leaned against the leaded panes, finally drawing out two pages covered in his dark, purposeful scrawl.

My Dear Hannah,

I cannot date this letter because I have no idea when you will receive it; only that I shall be dead when you do. You will be sad I believe, because you allowed me to be a part of your life for so many years, and because I am Liza's father. I want you *not* to be sad, Hannah. I have led a privileged life, and have no complaints.

I must, though, tell you how you contributed to that life. Your love served actively to keep me alive in the last war. Even, I believe, in the final stage of the first one, when you were so very young. And no single thing has ever meant more to me than that love.

Inextricably tied with this is the joy you gave me by allowing me to share Liza. I am all too aware that this joy was entirely in your gift, not mine by right, and I am deeply grateful for it.

One thing more, Hannah. I must tell you now, when the chips are down, that I have loved you always. For years, there was nothing I could do about it. But finally I muffed my golden chance.

Forgive me please, for the pain I must have

caused. And believe me when I say I shall love you always, wherever 'always' is.

I wish you long and happy years still to come with that man of yours – he was a good choice. I know, and it comforts me greatly, that you will be on hand to pick up Liza when from time to time she falls.

God bless and keep you safe, my dearest Hannah

David.

Hannah drew a deep quivering breath, and tears that had been damned up since Ella Vaughan's phone call twelve days ago were released. As they coursed down her cheeks, Matthew walked into the drawing room with the morning papers. He saw her face, her shaking shoulders; they stared helplessly at one another. Then he turned for the door again in a blind, blundering gesture.

'Matthew!' Her cry stopped him. She ran across the room and caught his arm. 'Please darling – don't go. Don't leave me!'

He put an arm about her then but stared over her head, isolated in his own misery, for Matthew had long feared that David Vaughan had Hannah's heart. Now he felt helpless to comfort her; could only pat her shoulder as he would any friend in such straits.

Hannah raised her head and saw defeat dulling the kindly blue eyes. She put up her hands to draw down his head, her own grief forgotten in his. Her tears were not for herself now, or for David Vaughan, but for this man, her beloved husband.

'Darling . . . don't be sad. I was only weeping over the last letter of an old friend.' She touched his cheek, his lips. '*You* are my life. *You* have given me all I could ever want. David never could – never did – give so generously of total sharing, patience, laughter, constant undemanding love. Sweetheart . . . you've given me *so much* happiness. You *must* know that?'

Matthew cleared his throat, stroked back his dishevelled hair. 'Steady on. You'll be giving me a swollen head.'

Laurie scraped through his A levels that summer by virtue of a crammer's one-to-one attention, and as a result scraped into London University to read English. By the time his course started at the beginning of October he had grown his hair shoulder-length, torn interesting holes in his flared jeans and painted psychedelic whorls on his white pumps. He thought seriously about having an ear pierced, but when his nineteenth birthday came in December he had incurred debts that swallowed up the ten pounds sent by his father, and the earring went on the waiting list. He roomed in a depressing block behind the Kennington Oval, which became more grimly cold and forbiddingly unlovely as winter progressed. He bent over his table those chilling days and evenings, endeavouring to put together essays already overdue that held not the slightest interest for him, and became depressed. He attended lectures, and dozed by that lucky find, a radiator.

Why did he not *join* something, his father demanded to know. If he went to the Debating Society he would learn verbal skills – sadly lacking at present. If he joined the History Society he would learn valuable perspectives on the past. Or why not go and play a *game*, for God's sake – what was wrong with an afternoon's rowing or a spot of rugger? Laurie shivered at the idea. Amateur dramatics? Post-modernist poetry, Pre-Raphaelite art; *brass-rubbing*?

He found a job in Debenhams before Christmas and

quite enjoyed that, mainly because the store was warm and the canteen food was cheap and had bulk. He smuggled out rolls under his sweater and fed them to the starved-looking sparrows hopping around the shrubs outside his window. After Christmas at home the sparrows had disappeared; he had to assume they had died of hunger in his absence.

He struggled for a few weeks against increasing odds. His tutor became incomprehensible, perhaps because a shutter fell in Laurie's mind each time the man attempted a discussion. Laurie knew this was his own fault, but knowing that did not prevent it happening. He attended no lectures in February, but took to visiting acquaintances in Queensway. The friends from Weir Street of the summer before last had fragmented. Rich, though, had introduced him to Cassandra and Len, who had rooms in Newton Road, and last summer Laurie had gone to a few gigs with them. They had picked fruit together in Kent, taken by Dee, who possessed a Ford van of uncertain age and temperament. Dee was older than the others, around twenty-seven, Laurie believed; an educated man who had been turning his hand to a variety of projects during the last few years. Laurie had an idea that Dee had fallen foul of the Metropolitan Police prior to that, but friends did not discuss either a man's misfortune nor his shortcomings behind his back, so nothing was definite.

Laurie had tried once or twice to talk to his mother about this loss of contact with his degree course. He thought she had probably tried to understand . . . but as he scarcely understood himself what was amiss he could not blame her ultimate impatience.

'Laurie – if you make no *effort* you cannot expect results. Have you talked to your father?'

'Not really . . . I didn't want to bother him over Christmas. He kept saying how tiring this Hungarian contract was, and falling asleep.'

Jonet banged the iron down on her pyjamas. She was tired too, the in-fighting amongst library staff was quite wearing. Over Laurie and his education she was experiencing a definite sense of hopelessness and helplessness: the whole thing was becoming akin to pushing uphill a car with its brakes jammed on.

'What I really would like is to do a gardening course. Horticulture,' he added, as that sounded more upmarket. 'I'm actually interested in herb production, it's a coming thing.' That sounded even better and he looked expectantly at his mother. But she was frowning.

'That's a bandwagon on which any cheapjack can jump. No security – you've no land, for one thing.'

Laurie's spirits sank to boot level again. Of course he had no land. Where would he get land from? He had no money. He couldn't borrow money without collateral and he had none of that unless you counted his guitar. Matthew had a good big garden, and had given him a smashing patch for his herbs, they'd done brilliantly. But none of that was a basis for starting a business. He didn't know enough yet, anyway. And here *they* were trying to wring *essays* out of him. Laurie had at that point wanted something more pleasant to happen . . . had gone to lie on his bed, roll a joint and listen to the Bob Dylan he'd had from Hannah for Christmas.

It was April when he moved into a room rented from Dee. He simply told his parents that London University was not for him, that he was sorry he had been such a disappointment to them, that he would not leech on them, but look for a job. His father's face was somehow closed off, as though the person inside had gone away. This made Laurie sad, as he was fond of his father and missed the relationship that had slowly collapsed into empty space. His mother had reacted to the news by a tightening of lips, and anger, plain honest anger. Laurie understood this of course, but did not enjoy meeting it head on.

'We can do no more, then,' she had said finally. 'You will have to make your own way.' That meant removing his bits and pieces from London University premises and carting them over to his room at Dee's place, then going to sign on at the Unemployment Office.

There was not an exciting choice of work on offer. 'I should like something in the horticultural line,' he had told the clerk.

'Nothing going, sorry. Kitchen hand at the Great Wall, Finchley Road?'

'What about trying the Parks Department?'

'They'd let us know if there were vacancies. Hospital porter?'

'I have three A levels,' Laurie told him distantly. 'I'll try around.'

'There's Burtons if you have the suit.'

'I shall try around,' Laurie repeated, feeling certain that the interview was going nowhere. He went back to Dee's place, lay on his bed and thought.

Dee had a decent enough flat, the first floor of an end-of-terrace a stone's throw from Len and Cassandra, just north of Queensway. Laurie had the back room for £15 per week, use of bathroom, with his own gas ring. There was no electricity to pay as a friend of Dee's had arranged the meter in return for a favour done him by Dee. The back room looked out over a great many other back rooms, old sheds, yards where broken bikes, chairs and bedsteads proliferated, with washing strung about in dry weather and cats sleeping on anything that might catch the sun. Laurie liked to look out of this window, and learned to prop it open with a batten of wood Dee found for him in the yard below.

The room itself had a fireplace with alcoves either side, which were painted sun yellow. The remaining walls were clad in a particularly drab fawn trellis wallpaper. Dee had been going to 'do' the whole room, he explained, but did not explain what had halted the project. He had 'done' the door, painting yellow mountains on a purple background in brilliant gloss. Laurie, recalling Matthew's subtle watercolours, initially found the door slightly primitive but quickly became accustomed to it. His bed was along the window wall, a divan with a patterned cotton cover brought back from India by Dee two years ago. In the alcove near the foot of the divan an elderly armchair was in need of re-upholstering, but comfortable enough with a piece of Mexican blanket folded across. The other alcove housed his gas ring and kettle on a table with a square of green lino to protect it, and had two cupboards above. Between the door and the divan head had been squeezed a single wardrobe and a small chest of drawers. The drawers doubled as a bedside table, and above that and the divan, Dee had fixed two shelves to the wall. Against the wall opposite the window were a small square table and two upright chairs.

The cupboards and shelves were painted in the same purple as the door. Laurie had now completely filled the shelves with books, records and oddments, but the purple cupboards, suspended halfway up the wall, were unused as they seemed likely to fall at any time. Laurie discovered that Dee had a little yellow paint left, so with this he painted intricate scroll patterns over the cupboard doors and sides. He came to like this effect after the first shock, and would lie in bed tracing the scrolls with his eye.

The curtains, old brown chenille, were a disaster. Dee admitted this: they had been abandoned there by the previous tenant as not worth taking away. After many hours spent watching and waiting in Portobello Road, Laurie found a cut-price remnant of cheerful shadow-striped yellow cotton, the only problem then being to transform it into a pair of curtains. He folded it away into his suitcase which slid under the divan, and decided to ask his grandmother's help.

He was welcome in the kitchen any time he wanted to use the cooker, Dee told him, and might keep food in the fridge. He could also stick things on his walls. Laurie accordingly covered the fawn trellis with posters of Bob Dylan, Melanie, one of a superb Bengal tiger he had bought for his twelfth birthday and not been allowed to put up in his bedroom, and a fresh, clean seascape given him by Matthew and treasured.

Dee was a skilled carpenter. The shelves and cupboards he had made for his own room were dovetailed, aligned, rubbed down, well finished. Laurie would examine them often. He borrowed Dee's woodworking magazines one at a time, and decided he would learn how to work in wood himself. He needed money to buy tools, to buy wood, to buy space in which to work. Sometimes he watched Dee working in the yard below, and his fingers itched to try. What about going to classes, Dee suggested; to get the idea, see if he had the feel of it? That was fine, but first, money was needed. The DHSS was providing his bare necessities and for that Laurie was grateful . . . but he *must* find a job. But hearing on his radio that unemployment, at 800,000 now, had risen to the highest level since the end of the war, he saw he would have his work cut out. He also heard that Apollo 16 had landed on the moon; but somehow, this seemed to have little or no relevance to his life.

Arney Bold was developing an incipient ulcer, and carried antacid tablets in various pockets with a back-up pack in a drawer of his desk. He sucked on one now as he contemplated an interview with Carl Cline. Carl had done well by his senior aide; his share-out from Cline Investments had bought Arney and his wife Rosa an apartment within reach of Central Park, a Puerto Rican maid and a New Orleans Creole cook, and a place in the Catskills where he could fish weekends.

Now, he saw no alternative but to lay on the table, person to person, the fact that things were on the slide. The deals that Carl had put together with such *élan* in earlier years were scarcer; other corporate raiders were hard at it seeking out profitable situations. Market movements in stock were detected and pounced upon, driving up the share prices of targeted companies. For these and other reasons, Cline Investments had lately found it more difficult to create growth.

Arney reached for another antacid tablet. He held 7 per cent of Cline Investments shares. He had left Holman Stiltzberg with Carl, had been the minor partner in the original deal that had launched Cline Investments, and now knew he had Carl's complete confidence. He had marvelled at Carl's touch, at the audacity of the positions he could take, at the immaculate timing of decisions. He, more than most, knew how perfectly the 'Lucky Carl Cline' label fitted, being aware that none of the dramatic deals were made as a result of in-depth analysis. Carl Cline's decisions sprang from his guts . . . the intriguing thing being that later he could usually explain the logic behind the moves then sit back and enjoy the open-mouthed admiration.

Now, though, business was nearing stagnation. Cline Investments must continue to find profitable situations to exploit, or face decline. An additional complication was that J. Arthur Belman was gunning for Carl, and was powerful enough to be dangerous. To this end, Belman had been angling to enlist Arney's support, and continually issued invitations to lunch to discuss 'situations'; Arney fielded these with some dexterity.

But he was now prepared for a first-time-ever confrontation, and was sidelining the usual memos, graphs and charts invariably consigned to Carl's unread pile. Carl had never written a memo; detail was anathema to him, he worked with big brushes and left others to fill in the detail. For the imminent meeting, Arney had enlisted the support of the finance president, Earle Curtis, for whom Carl had a well-earned regard. Arney at forty-seven was looking mature in an industry getting younger every day; Curtis was thirty-one, and his dynamism was impressive.

Carl had not turned up at the meeting time of 11 a.m., which to both men was the norm as he rarely used his office, his style being to conduct business on the hoof. He did not dictate letters, telling his PA the bones of what was needed and the intended recipient. His office as a consequence was comfortable but spare, the desk a dignified one of carved mahogany, which Joe had refurbished and presented to him for his thirtieth birthday. All else was modern, including the two leather sofas, on one of which Carl, when he arrived, sat down facing Arney and Earle Curtis. His PA brought coffee, placing the tray on the glass-topped table between the sofas and as she exited Carl opened the meeting.

'What can I do for you, team?'

Carl had a lot of time for Arney. He had been a first-class retail sector analyst at Stiltzberg, but at Cline Investments he had gradually taken over administration, thus freeing up Carl, who trusted him completely. Now he could see from the solemn faces that unpleasant business was afoot. He was perfectly well aware that things could be better; now, though, was a time for optimism to come into play . . .

'Did you read my last report?' Arney made a start.

'No time yet; I've been too busy putting out fires. I guess it tells me we're going to under-perform the Dow?'

'Well, yes. Earle and I have been working on what we need to do to maintain the dividend.'

'Jesus. Arney, we're not terminal!' Carl's smile disappeared. 'OK, it's been a while since I came up with a killing. But you know my track record; we'll be fine. I just need a little time.'

'No, Carl.' Arney's face, pleasantly pink when things were good, had gone darkly mottled. 'There's more to it than that.' Clutching his sheaf of papers he looked Carl straight in the eye.

'Like what?' Those eyes were cold now.

Arney gulped air, then said with desperate abandon: 'It's your lifestyle, I'm afraid.'

Earle made a play of picking up the papers sliding from his knee. Adrenalin squirted unpleasantly into

Arney's stomach. The dull ache became a sharp pain and he dived into his trouser pocket for his tablets before recalling he had left them on his desk. Carl's face coloured now; Arney's had gone yellow-white.

'What the hell does that mean? Since when has my lifestyle been *your* business?'

'Since it started affecting *our* business.' Arney hung on. 'Cline Investments just doesn't command your full attention these days. It suffers as a result, and you know it, Carl. How many weeks have you spent in the UK this year? And we're only in the spring . . .'

He had finally said it. Arney was surprised to find his stomach pain easing.

'Is that *all* you want to say?' Carl asked thinly.

'It's what I *had* to say,' Arney said simply. 'Earle has a few ideas, too.'

Carl stared at Arney, and his anger evaporated. That must have taken some effort . . . and would have done the old guy's ulcer no good at all. Poor sod must have been psyching himself up for weeks. He reached for the coffee-pot.

'OK, OK. Let's drink this now. Fire away then, Earle.'

'You're not going to like it,' Curtis warned. 'First off, we're too much of a one-man band.'

'Meaning me.'

'It's no way to run an organisation of our size,' Curtis ploughed on. 'We need to re-evaluate people, positions, on a regular basis. In the past, Carl, what you've accomplished has been brilliant, amazing, and we've all been busy following up your ideas. But times get tougher. Now we need a more structured approach, more research and analysis; properly to quantify the value of each deal. You can still point us in the right direction, of course.'

He set a blue-bound folder on the table between them. 'If you'd look at that when you've an opportunity . . . I've set out how we should go about it.'

Carl looked at the folder. Then he stared down at the carpet between his spread knees. When he raised his head they knew he had made up his mind about something; but it was not for today.

'I hear what you say, both of you. I'll come back to you on it.'

In June, Hannah invited Laurie down to Bracken House. When he had moved to Dee's she had sent money for him to phone her once a week, and had been up to see him last month. Both his appearance and his accommodation had startled her, and left lingering unease. The way of life he had chosen was pointed up in dramatic fashion because she had come straight from Liza's house, which could scarcely have cost Carl less than a million pounds furnished. Laurie had still not been offered any work within his A-level qualification range, he told his grandmother, and if he accepted less he would be stuck in a downgrade job permanently. He had actually found one half-day a week gardening, from an advert in a shop door – an old lady in Pembridge Place. But that was strictly unofficial; he had shot her a bashful smile here, one Hannah recalled from his childhood when he was not certain if he had her full approval.

'I could well afford to pay his fees for a horticultural course,' she said to Matthew on her return. 'But Jonet would feel insulted. They could afford it too; so they must have taken a conscious decision to leave him to stew. Poor Laurie, there's a classic case of a round peg being forced into a square hole. And not fitting!'

'He may find his own level, sweetheart. He doesn't

fit the accepted mould, right enough. But things *can* happen if given time. Shall we ask him down for a break?

They did, and Laurie came by coach a couple of days later. He was thinner than ever, and rather spotty, but delighted to be there. For Hannah's birthday gift he had brought down a dragon, printed on gauzy Nepali paper, coloured in personally with skill, folded over a piece of card and glued. He had put fine gold thread through a little ring, for hanging. It was an immensely attractive labour of love and Hannah hung it in the dining room where the sun lent it brilliant life. He did some planting out, weeding and trimming for them, and took pleasure in the robust state of his herb garden. He potted up cuttings of the most popular ones, bunched a good selection, and went with Matthew into Bridgend, Porthcawl, and local villages, where to his joy greengrocers' shops took almost all he had. There were two wonderfully hot days spent on the beach, when Laurie and Matthew swam and Hannah paddled – she never had overcome her fear of water – and found a glorious convoluted shape of driftwood and three large shells, which she gave Laurie for his windowsill. He stretched out on his towel in the sun, holding each in turn to his ear with a smile of delight.

'Now I shall hear the sea in W11 . . . brilliant.'

After a lengthy struggle with herself, Hannah did call Jonet the evening of Laurie's departure. Matthew had suggested she play it low-key, which made sense but was hard; Hannah loved Laurie and what was happening now was what she had long feared. The usual niceties were exchanged before Hannah said pleasantly:

'Laurie has just left after a few days here.'

'Oh. He still has no job, then.'

'No. He's looking, though. He did some work in the garden for us, and sold some of his herbs and cuttings in the local shops.'

'That wouldn't pay his rent for long.' Jonet's voice was acid. 'Lucky he can sponge off the state, meaning you and me.'

Hannah said neutrally: 'I believe he's deeply interested in learning about horticulture. Had you thought about helping him get on to a course?'

'No. We helped him get into university. He threw that back in our faces.'

'But that was what *you* wanted, rather than him, wasn't it? That may have been the problem. Anyway, dear –' she pushed on before she could become bogged down in altercation – 'I just wondered how you both were. I do hope you'll get down some time this summer.'

When she replaced the receiver, Hannah took a breath to steady herself. She should hold her counsel . . . any conversation other than strictly general was suspect with Jonet. And she never asked about little Jess; of course, she had never asked about Liza at Jess's age . . . Liza had invited the three of them to the March première of her film. Laurie had gone with Hannah and Matthew in his good school suit, Mark was away on business and Jonet had pleaded flu. However, she had sent a card of congratulation. The truth, Hannah suspected, was that she could not bear to witness at close quarters her half-sister's undoubted success. She had also sent a card for Hannah's birthday last week. No mention that it was a milestone birthday, though . . .

Hannah pulled a wry face. Jonet possibly believed she might prefer to forget that her mother had now attained the great age of seventy.

Laurie found temporary work through into autumn: potting on in a nursery, fruit and vegetable picking, potato lifting, and Debenhams again for the summer sales. It was the end of October before things went slack. He found he smoked more joints when he was at a loose end, and that left him short of cash . . . When Dee had an occasional job to offer him, perhaps a delivery to make in the van that needed two pairs of hands, or a packet to take to a friend, Laurie was grateful. He liked Dee, a silent, peaceable man, small and wiry, whose straggly shoulder-length brown hair was balding from the front, and whose wispy moustache drooped comically into the mugs of coffee endlessly consumed. To Laurie, Dee's personal space was a wonderland of tat. Colourful and evocative detritus it may have appeared to others; to Dee it was the stuff of life. Even broken 78 records were not junked but arranged tastefully on a door lintel, and empty jars of Marmite were stacked in a pyramid balanced with great care on the kitchen windowsill.

It was on his way back from an errand for Dee that Laurie found himself outside the local library, and on an impulse went in and signed up for four tickets. That day he came out with four books on gardening. He had a barely used loose-leaf pad from university days and began to make notes in that on aspects of particular interest. Some days he would read in the library: it was warm and congenial in there and he had not the feeling of isolation he often felt in his room. The ugly brown curtains were drawn now for warmth; he asked Hannah's advice on the yellow material when she came up in November and she turned it into curtains, which cheered the room up enormously.

He went with her occasionally to see Liza's baby and was charmed by the beguiling, dainty toddler. Almost two, Jess Cline had an air of total femininity, whether dressed in frilly frock or denim dungarees. Her fine, acorn-brown curls were bouncing around her neck now, and took on a chestnut hint in sunlight. Her pearlised skin pointed up the blueness of huge calm eyes, black-lashed, and her forehead was high and deeply curved under a soft fringe of hair. She had a quick light walk and would run suddenly on tiptoe, holding out her arms and laughing to show tiny white teeth. Laurie enjoyed playing with her, and Jess would practise embryo female skills on him to the delight of both.

He had not seen her mother since the film première; Liza was rarely at home. She had recently completed another film, was now playing Portia in *The Merchant of Venice* at the Old Vic, and before that had taken a month's holiday with Carl and the baby in the south of France. Laurie was always somewhat intimidated by the opulence of his youthful aunt's lifestyle, and inclined to be depressed after a visit.

He accepted his first line of coke after the November visit, when he called to see Len and Cassandra. He had always refused cocaine before, the warnings of his parents hanging in the back of his mind. He had asked Dee if *he* was addicted, and Dee had had a good chuckle out of him. 'God no; it's just a social thing when a friend drops in, like giving them a mug of coffee, I suppose. I'm totally in control there, boy. You've been listening to the wrong people, the ones who know damn all about drug use!' Feeling strongly the need to unite with his peer group, Laurie decided to risk it.

'You just sniff up, using the straw,' Len explained,

tapping out a thin line of white powder on to his piece of mirror. 'Go on, it won't bite. You'll like it,' as Laurie gingerly lowered his straw. He did not like it; he felt jumpy, irritable afterwards, and believed it must be the coke. Was this how it usually affected people? He was not sure; it was too expensive anyway – what was the point of trying to like something he could never afford to buy? No, grass was best . . . When a few days later he asked if Len had any grass to spare, he was told that Dee could maybe get a bit if he asked – his quality was always reliable and he sometimes had a little for friends.

'I've a bit around somewhere.' Dee turned down his stereo.

'How much will it cost?'

'Well, I could let you have a bit to roll up if you help me load the van on Thursday.'

'Fine.' Laurie had smoked his cannabis with Dee. Afterwards they had listened to records for a while, had a laugh and beer out of the fridge, and Laurie had found the idea of Christmas with his parents less difficult.

In fact it was a fairly miserable experience, made bearable by his having the odd joint in his room. He made a couple of attempts to talk to them about his horticultural studies and how they might help him; it was tossed back that an English degree would have helped him even more. So he clammed up, watched television, ate, and lay on his bed playing his music.

One thing about which he had not tried to talk to his parents was his recent second fine for being caught in possession of cannabis. The first time had been £20; this last was £25, and it had hit him where it hurt. Caution was now indicated.

On a bitterly cold night in January, Dee asked if Laurie would help him deliver a double bed to a friend setting up a pad in Marylebone. There'd be no rush to get back afterwards, it would quite possibly develop into a pad-warming party. To get themselves in the mood they shared a reefer on starting out, and collected the bed from Leigh Road. They were three-quarters of the way to Marylebone when a police car passed them, signalling them to stop.

'May we see your current licence, sir?' The heavier of the two policemen put his hand on the window Dee had just wound down. The document was found and handed over. The other policeman checked the registration disc and compared it with the plate.

'Did you know you had an unsafe door at the back?'

'Really?' Dee asked politely. 'Sorry about that. I'll fix it.' He jumped out and inspected the swinging door. 'It's the lock. I've some twine about somewhere.' As he went up front to look, the officers peered into the rear of the van, flashing their torches.

'Who does the bed belong to, sir?'

'My friend. I'm delivering it to his house,' Dee called from the cab where he was delving for twine. One officer leaned right into the van; then spoke quietly to his companion before coming round to Dee.

'We'd like to take a look in the van. That all right?'

'Help yourself,' Dee said shortly. He located the twine and waited with it to secure the door while the officers eased their way around the bed.

'We believe we can smell recently smoked cannabis here. Do you have any in the vehicle?'

'Not that I am aware of.'

The policemen poked about the interior, moving sacking, a couple of piles of newspaper, a bag of tools. A black bin bag had clothes in it; the officer handed it to his partner.

'That's my laundry,' Dee protested. Feeling around

it, the man drew out a tobacco tin.

'This yours?'

'I don't recognise it.'

The tin was opened and sniffed at by both policemen. The officers then climbed back on to the road, one carrying the tin.

'We have reason to believe this is cannabis. We must ask you both to accompany us to the station and explain how it came to be in your laundry bag.'

As Laurie woke, a heavy sense of something bad fell on him like a dirty blanket. Last night re-ran itself, forcing a path through his somnolent mind. God . . . charged with possession again . . . He lay for a while until fully orientated, then went to the bathroom, put on his clothes, made a mug of tea. The drawn curtains revealed a day as grey and cold as his predicament. Laurie brushed his teeth and made an effort to pull himself together. He had books due back; he would go to the library, buy a currant bun on the way, then get warm, and interested in soil structures. He couldn't do better; help him forget the magistrates' court appearance now looming.

He was about to open the front door when bulky shadows appeared through the frosted glass and the bell rang. He opened the door; three policemen faced him on the step.

'Mr Dee Claygill?'

'I think he's out, I'm Laurie Shapiro. I was just going out too.' Laurie moved back, giving way to the first of the policemen, a sergeant.

'Perhaps you'd better hang on, sir. We've a warrant to search the premises. Why don't you sit down in here for a bit.'

'I'm returning my library books,' Laurie said inanely.

'Time enough, it's early yet. Any idea when Mr Claygill might be back?' The officer remained with him in Dee's room, the others were already making their way upstairs.

'Not really. His van's gone. I have the back upstairs room,' he added, hoping they would not mess that up. He heard Dee's bed being moved, and the lump of lead in his stomach became heavier. What the hell had Dee *done*? This was more than a bit of dope.

The officers came down and started on the kitchen; the man with Laurie stared out of the window, whistling under his breath, hands clasped behind him. When they began on the living room Laurie was invited into the hall where he leaned awkwardly against the wall, examining his pumps. At this point he asked to empty his bladder and was escorted to the bathroom. He was also hungry, having missed the currant bun.

The three now conferred, and the sergeant waved him back into the sitting room. 'Did I get your name right? Mr Laurie Shapiro?'

Laurie nodded and a wave of apprehension broke over him. 'Would you like to remove your jacket, Mr Shapiro? We need to check you're removing nothing from the premises.'

Laurie realised the futility of saying no, he would not like to remove his jacket. The officer moved expertly over the garment. He stopped at the inner breast pocket, and drew out two small waxed paper packets about one-and-a-half inches square, held together by two rubber bands.

'These *are* yours, sir?' Laurie dismissed his first idea of saying no, he knew nothing about them as being likely to provoke . . . He had heard it didn't pay to provoke the Metropolitan Police.

'Then would you like to tell me what's in them?'

As before, Laurie saw it to his disadvantage to play word games with the Met. After a small pause he said simply, 'Cocaine.' The officer nodded.

'You were just going out. Were you taking them somewhere?'

'No.'

'I'm wondering why you hadn't left them in your room then, son. Where'd you get them?'

Laurie tried to assess if the change from 'sir' to 'son' was good news or bad. 'From a friend.' He had almost said 'from Dee' but realised how that would be incriminating, turning Dee into a dealer. Laurie now suspected that in his own small way Dee *was* a dealer; but the fuzz wouldn't hear that from *him*. He really liked Dee.

'And you're going to tell us the name of that friend?'

'I'd rather not.' Laurie sighed. He was in it now, right enough.

Dee turned up, and things moved quickly then. A small pair of brass scales was produced, discovered, he was told, in a polythene bag beneath his bedroom floorboards. A small quantity of cocaine had been found in a Bird's Custard tin in his food cupboard. Laurie and Dee were then invited to accompany the officers back to the station.

Chapter Twenty

January 1973

Hannah was about to put on her coat and boots to go to see Florence in Porthcawl when the phone rang.

'Laurie – hello dear, how nice to hear from you. How are you?'

'Oh – all right I guess, Gran. But look . . . it's a bit awkward . . . I'm speaking from Marylebone police station. I've been charged, and they say it's OK to call you.'

'Charged? With what, Laurie?' Hannah was already signalling to attract the attention of Matthew, who was in the sitting room. Laurie cleared his throat.

'With being in possession of a grade-A drug, and intent to supply. Cocaine, they mean.'

'And have they got it right, Laurie?'

'Not the supply part, Gran. Definitely not that.'

'Glad to hear it. Now, have you a solicitor?'

'No . . . I suppose I need one?'

'I should think so. Look, can you give me the number of the station there? I'll have a quick word with Matthew and he'll call you as soon as possible. Don't make your statement till you hear back.'

'OK. Thanks, Gran. I say . . . could you possibly phone Mum for me?'

After a tiny silence Hannah said: 'Of course, I'll do that.'

'I have to go to Marylebone Magistrates' Court tomorrow. Ten o'clock.'

'Oh. Well, dear – sit tight, Matthew will call you in a few minutes. I'll be thinking of you. 'Bye now.'

'Can you help?' She searched Matthew's face. He nodded, folding his paper.

'There's one man in particular – but I can think of three or four who might help. Might take a while to find their numbers.'

'This is the station number.' Hannah passed him the slip of paper. Matthew got up, damped down the fire and made for the door, where he turned.

'What about his parents?'

'He's asked me to tell Jonet.'

He screwed up his nose. 'Rather you than me! Look darling, could you do that from Flo's? I may well be on the phone quite a while. See you later, then.' He was already busy when she left.

'So that's all I know,' she said to Florence, having imparted the news. The import of Laurie's call had hit now and Hannah felt slightly sick. 'Flo, may I use this phone to call Jonet? I'm really hoping she will decide to go for the hearing in the morning; so I can't leave it till she gets home, I must try to reach her at the library. I'd go myself, but I couldn't get to London tonight . . . and *someone* should be there.'

'I can't see Jonet doing it,' said Florence the realist. 'Appearances are everything to her, you know that better than anyone. And though of course she'd never tell anyone, she'd be terrified that somehow the story of her sitting in court with her son in the dock would get out.'

Hannah's jaw set. 'I shall ask her if she doesn't volunteer, even so.'

'I know you will, *cariad*.' Florence leaned across to kiss Hannah. 'You go ahead and phone now – I'll make us a pot of tea. And I baked Welshcakes, you can take some back for Matthew.'

Hannah sat for a moment before dialling. She almost wished the number she had would be redundant, that would spare her for a few hours at least. It would also mean that almost certainly Jonet would not go to court in the morning.

She mis-dialled twice. The third time she connected, and asked for Mrs Shapiro.

'Hello?'

'Jonet.' Hannah's voice shook; she coughed and tried again. 'Jonet, I'm sorry to disturb you at work, but it's Laurie ... I felt I shouldn't wait till this evening.'

'What about Laurie, Mother?' The voice was sharp with anxiety. 'Is he ill?'

'No. But he is in trouble with the police. He phoned me to say he's in custody on a charge of being in possession of cocaine and –' the hesitation was fleeting – 'of attempting to supply.'

'Supply? You mean *sell*?'

'He says that is absolutely not true,' Hannah said at once. 'Now, Matthew is ringing round to find him the best possible solicitor near enough to reach him quickly. And he has a court appearance at ten tomorrow morning in Marylebone.'

There was no sound from the Reading end of the connection. She added quietly: 'Will you go, Jonet? Someone belonging to him should be there.'

'Mother; he's made his own bed.' Jonet's voice was even quieter, Hannah could scarcely hear it.

'Most of us do ... That doesn't mean we don't sometimes long for someone who cares to help us climb out of it. Laurie's a lovely person, Jonet; gentle, kind. And he needs you now as he never did.'

'I'll have think about it, Mother ... It would mean a

half-day off, and what reason can I give? And Mark is in Birmingham. But I'll think about it.'

Jonet thought of very little else. That night, as she ate her scrambled eggs on toast, her orange and slice of fruit cake off a tray by the fire, logic told her that it would be a useless exercise to put herself through so traumatic an experience. Laurie might or might not see her; and if he did, it might or might not benefit him. Why anyway should she change her mind about how *she* felt – that he had done this to himself, and must not expect others to involve themselves in his folly?

But he *was* her child. Her responsibility?

She caught the 8.10 out of Reading still not understanding her motive for going. Mark had agreed on the phone last night that no useful purpose would be served. Now she stood in the crowded oblong room behind the court, and was told that shortly before ten o'clock she could go through the left-hand door, up the steps into the public seating, and that the first case was Clayhill and Shapiro. Her stomach churned with nerves. She had on a grey checked business suit over a cream polo-neck, and was carrying her cream trenchcoat. Her face was stiff from the walk from the tube in the searing wind, toes and fingers numb with cold. She ignored the babble about her from solicitors and offenders and their families, locked into her own lonely crisis that seemed to promise no bearable outcome.

She looked at her watch frequently. It was twenty minutes before an official opened the door to the public seating and with another lurch of anxiety, Jonet followed a knot of people up the steps to the courtroom. They filed into seats along the side of the room; she halted to get her bearings. The dock was quite close from here, on the back wall, so Jonet took the nearest seat . . . the objective of coming was after all to have Laurie see her. People conferred at tables in the well of the court, documents were arranged. When a door opened at the far end of the big, high-ceilinged room and three magistrates appeared on their platform, everyone stood while they settled themselves on chairs behind a long table. Jonet saw now that while she would be as close as possible to Laurie, she would hear little of what might pass between counsel and magistrates. She sighed, feeling nauseous; fixed her gaze intently on the steps at the back of the dock and waited for the appearance of her son.

When the dock door opened and she saw him, her breath caught on a tiny sob that took her entirely by surprise. He was followed by a smaller man, late twenties, and flanked by two policemen. Jonet recognised the good school suit and tie; his hair was brushed tidily back, showing a pale face with big dark eyes that looked straight ahead at the magistrates. Various people rose to speak to the three magistrates and sat again, papers were rustled; Jonet registered nothing but her son's slight figure and white, anxious face and stared at him, motionless. It was all-important that he should see her, know that she was there.

He continued, though, to fix his eyes straight ahead. She had a fearsome urge to stand up and call his name, but remained still and quiet. Her eyes did not move to see who was speaking, and since the officials at the tables below faced the magistrates she heard little of the proceedings. At some point the three magistrates retired briefly and Jonet became more anxious for Laurie to see her. But he stared resolutely at the floor until the reappearance of the trio, when once again he looked straight ahead.

Finally the court was standing again for the magistrates' exit . . . He was not going to look . . . Jonet scrambled to her feet: her agonised stare at last found Laurie's as he swung towards her to leave the dock. She smiled, and lifted her hand to him. Laurie halted for a second, thrown. Then as he reached the dock steps, he turned his head and smiled back at her.

She made for the door. She had heard nothing, seen nothing but Laurie. But a word echoed . . . Custody. It bounced about her brain. An official stood nearby and she asked in a small breathless voice:

'Sorry – I missed . . . What did he say?'

'The magistrate? Both remanded in custody, to appear one week from today.'

Jonet stumbled down the steps, through the anteroom and into the street. The wind hit her face with ugly force as she halted, dazed, on the pavement.

Laurie was in custody? That meant in a cell. In a prison. Laurie; for God's sake, how could they *do* this? Twenty last month, and anyone could *see* he was no criminal. There was *no way* he would sell cocaine. He was her son, and they were locking him up rather than bailing him.

She should go back in there, find his solicitor, discover who the other man in the dock was, ask why Laurie was not being bailed, ask where he was being taken. But now, on the busy London pavement, Jonet began to weep. This was her son and she could not bear what had become of him, could not begin to see what had gone so terribly wrong. Laurie . . . oh God . . .

Head down to hide her tears, Jonet pulled up the collar of her trenchcoat and made for Baker Street underground.

*

In early March Liza came out of *The Merchant of Venice* and having insisted that Penelope keep the space free, took Jess, at two years and two months, on her first trip to America. She went straight through the Heathrow VIP lounge, where Jess was made much of and presented with a flaxen-haired doll from the airport shop. She was carried aboard the 747 by the devoted Lucy and settled in one of the ample seats in first class. After some fussing with safety straps she was made comfortable with her current favourite toy donkey – her own size – and the new doll.

Liza reclined her own seat after take-off and relaxed. She smiled to herself, looking forward to a longer reunion with Carl this time. They had evolved a pattern during theatre runs which meant that Sundays were blissfully free and relaxed, and Mondays until early evening were spent together. Carl would fly in for them to have a light supper together late on Saturday night after her ten-hour stint, then they would have a tray in bed with the Sunday papers, Jess joining them for drinks of orange juice and titbits of toast. Later they might take her into Hyde Park, or by the river at Richmond, or simply laze in the garden where Jess had her play equipment and a tiny tricycle with which to roar along the paths. They might go for drinks on Sunday evening, perhaps an occasional party. One Sunday they flew to Paris to a theatrical gathering at Versailles, and stayed to shop on Monday before returning laden. They planned a trip to Italy when her run was over in early summer, taking Jess and Lucy.

He had been right about their frequent partings adding spice to their marriage. When they were apart, irritations, personal clashes, small vendettas had time to fade and their powerful mutual love would reassert itself. Each missed the stimulation of the other's presence, the charisma that, when withdrawn, took brightness from the sun. Each provided the oxygen on which the other thrived. Disputes – often over whose will should gain the upper hand in a particular power struggle – could be resolved either in quiet reflection upon priorities, or in the telling force of their physical desire for one another.

The very best times were those spent with Jess. They were inordinately proud of this small, perfect creature they had made together. They laughed at her audacious manipulation of her powers, at unfolding personality traits they could recognise as stemming from their own. They loved her quirky humour, her infant vulnerability, her need for their protection. Because they never saw enough of Jess, time shared with her was doubly precious.

Liza, who would be twenty-eight in May, was now in a commanding professional position. Her face was known everywhere through her work for television and through the success of her films, and she won critical applause for serious contributions to the theatre. Like Carl, she did not enjoy the separation caused by a long run. While she could be satisfied creatively by a character's emotional growth over a steady, night-by-night portrayal, she believed she could do enough in three months, and wanted contracts now that allowed her to be replaced at that point. Also, she felt she had now reached the stage when she need not work ceaselessly, but could take time to enjoy with Carl the fruits of her success. Carl might look doubtful, tell her that his dealings were not always easy to drop when one of Liza's 'rest' periods came up on the calendar. She would reply that he must sort his priorities: his business, or his wife.

She thought sometimes of Edward Anderssen. He had put her firmly behind his work. The cut had been cruel and she never would forget it. The sight of a new book of his in a window display, a review of work exhibited, would cause a fog of hurt anger to fall, behind which she would bleed again from scars reopened. It was obvious now that their work could not easily, if ever, have been reconciled; and that Carl, who must perform hugely clever business manipulations to clear time to spend with her, loved her far better . . . In this way Liza's hurt was salved, but it was stored in her memory, and did not mellow.

This trip, they were to see the results of work done on the Long Island house found and bought last summer, and would be introducing Jess to her paternal grandparents' home about six miles distant. Alex and Delaney had made a brief visit to London to see her at four months, but this would be their first opportunity to get to know her. Gayle had moved with Brad from Long Island when she had remarried a year ago. Liza, aware that Delaney and Alex's ex-daughter-in-law and grandson were still involved in their lives, hoped they would make room at least for Jess, if not yet accepting herself wholeheartedly. She saw so little of them . . . Carl was making moves at present to raise a consortium to finance a play for her on Broadway, but it was proving more difficult than he had dreamed. She had a feeling that *The Country Wife* was ripe for a new airing there, and wanted to play Margery. Meanwhile, she would make herself charming to them on this trip, ask Delaney's advice on furnishings, show herself as an acceptable wife, mother and family member. Joe and Sal would be certain to join them at some point and Liza was happily at ease with them; as Alex's oldest friend, Joe bridged the gap for her between the American family and the Welsh.

She closed her eyes as the great bird flew her from the old world to the new. Joe and Sal seemed intent on narrowing the gap between Carl's family and her own . . . her mother, she suspected, was at the bottom of it. Some woman in Oregon – her mind took leave of the boring details – a family tree, and a firm intention to turn Carl into a cousin of hers two hundred times or so removed, the facts to be squeezed into the required shape to fit the picture. It seemed all manner of people were now busily consulting old records, family histories, you name it. For herself, Liza retained a deep uninterest in the past, and was impatient with those who held the opposite view. The past and everyone in it was dead – what relevance could it have for lives lived in the here and now? If they carried on, they might even unearth Rachel Hywel as a terribly aged auntie. She had no idea if Joe knew of her existence; maybe he should be warned . . .

She recalled that she had last seen the shade of Rachel Hywel in the Long Island hotel garden at her wedding. Would she appear at the new house . . . or had she drifted off to attach herself to a victim who would react more satisfactorily? Was that her objective – to instil fear? Liza did not believe this; had no idea what motivated the poor wandering spirit, only believed she would be safe if *she* continued to demonstrate absolute indifference. One day – when there was time – she would talk to her mother again about Rachel, who lay over both their lives like a shadow who would not quite be mocked away. But for now, her busy life took precedence.

Hannah checked again that she had the day right on her visiting pass and folded it into her bag. March the eighth . . . Wormwood Scrubs.

She and Matthew had come up to the Holland Park house yesterday, and would return tomorrow. Liza liked them to stay there while she was away – 'Keeps Mrs Roberts on her toes' – and had indeed urged them to sell the Clapham flat. 'What do you *want* it for? You can stay whether or not I'm here, whenever you need a pad in London.' So they had parted with the flat. Increasingly content in Wales, Hannah and Matthew had found it surplus to their life.

'Of course I shan't let you take a cab.' Matthew had been firm. 'I shall drive you there, park somewhere with the newspaper for a bit and come back for you.' They discussed what Mark might have done when he had used last month's visiting slot; imagined the indignity of his queuing outside the gate. 'He'll have had a cab from Paddington and told it to come back for him,' was Matthew's opinion. Hannah disagreed; she believed he would have given instructions to be dropped on Westway then walked, and reversed the business afterwards.

'Poor Mark would never bring himself to direct a cabby to take him to Wormwood Scrubs. He'd walk miles in the rain to preserve his anonymity.' Indeed, Hannah was quite surprised that Mark had agreed to make the visit in any circumstances . . . he must have succumbed to pressure from Jonet.

As they drove up Wood Lane and crossed Westway, Hannah's own stomach was fluttering. It was disgraceful that someone convicted so far of no offence should already have been locked away for seven weeks, and still no date for the trial. Had the police prosecutor not been so adamant that there was a danger of re-offending, Laurie would have been bailed. It had appeared, so Laurie's solicitor had disclosed to them, that Dee's name had been on police records as being suspected of dealing, and had been under surveillance; that was the reason given for the flat being searched. He was himself furious that Laurie had been lumped in along with Dee in such a fashion, and continued to try for bail.

Matthew pulled to a halt. 'That's it, sweetheart.'

The imposing façade of the prison entrance was a dozen yards away. Outside, people queued by a small gate set in the massive one, each carrying a polythene bag. Hannah stared at the bag she herself clutched, carrying the maximum allowed a remand prisoner per visit, and did not want to join the queue. She would, though. She looked at Matthew for re-assurance. . . . He leaned across and put his warm hand across her cold one, and his eyes smiled at her with just that reassurance, so that she smiled back.

'No need to get out till they start moving. I'll be around here when you come back. Give Laurie my love, will you?'

'I certainly will.' They sat tense and watchful, until the personal gate was opened from the inside.

'Chin up, darling. Sock it to 'em.'

Hannah gave a sudden grin. 'I should like that.' She walked briskly to join the queue stepping through the gate. She had her pass examined, her bag searched, the carrier of things for Laurie was probed and taken away. She was directed to a light square room with tables and chairs spaced out, and chose one of the centre ones. In a moment or two, a trickle of men came in from the door opposite the one by which she had entered, and the third to appear was Laurie.

He saw her at once and came to sit at the table, smiling widely. Hannah leaned to kiss him, and when she sat back their hands remained clasped firmly across the surface between them.

'Great to see you, Gran. Thanks for coming.'

He looked fresh and clean in a blue shirt and denims. His hair was shorter and newly washed and he had put on a little weight.

'Couldn't wait, dear. This was the first date I could get, though. How are you feeling?'

'Quite good, thanks. Benefiting from regular hours and three meals a day.' Laurie raised a quizzical eyebrow and smiled again, as did Hannah.

'I brought a bag of apples for you anyway. And the other stuff you asked for, and a book on organic gardening.' They chatted for a few moments, then Hannah said quietly:

'Laurie – do *you* know why you weren't bailed? It makes no sense to us.'

'They found two little packets of coke in my jacket pocket, Gran. They'd like to prove that I was about to sell it. I was going out as they arrived.'

'Were you?' She watched his face with sharp eyes. 'About to sell it?'

After a second's hesitation he said: 'No. It was mine.'

'Why, Laurie? Why in heaven's name get into something as lethal as cocaine?'

He looked at their joined hands. 'I've only had the odd line with some friends, Gran. No quantity at all. I'm not a complete fool, I don't intend getting hooked. I'm not that keen on coke actually.'

'D'you suppose anyone ever intends getting hooked?' She sighed then. 'Laurie, love . . . I've not come here to read the riot act; I've come because I love you and I want to help. That's not to say that I don't think you've been an idiot. Anyway – your solicitor is still pushing hard for bail. He's trying to separate *your* case from Dee's.'

Laurie said slowly: 'That won't be easy. The morning they turned over the flat, they found a set of brass scales wrapped up under a floorboard under Dee's bed. And a bit of cocaine was hunted out of a tin in his food cupboard. *And* we'd both been picked up in Dee's van the night before with dope in it. Cannabis. So you can see why we're lumped together.'

Hannah groaned. 'I knew about the van episode. But not the scales and the extra coke. So . . . Did *you* know Dee was a dealer, Laurie?'

'I don't really think he is a *dealer*, Gran. But he does know where to get good-quality coke, not interfered with. And when he gets that, he likes to move it around his friends; that's all.'

'Your solicitor told Matthew that Dee's been to prison already because of drugs,' Hannah pointed out.

'That I didn't know.' His face creased nervously. 'Not good . . . though he's a really nice guy.'

Hannah thought it time to change tack. 'How was your father's visit?'

'Hairy. We couldn't find a lot to say. I've never seen Dad so seized up.'

'I'm not surprised,' Hannah said drily. 'Wormwood Scrubs is not his scene. Are you handling it, Laurie?' she added quietly. He squeezed her hand.

'It's manageable. The worst part is we're three in a cell, and one of 'em is barking mad. I've got work, which is great because it gets me out of the cell a bit more. I clean the church . . . it's quite something, really, Saint Francis of Assisi's Chapel it's called. And I clean the library, and a couple of other places. The exercise is good – and necessary 'cos the food's real stodge!'

A buzzer went; the seated warders stood up, looking businesslike. Laurie gripped her hand tight again.

'Gran, it's been fantastic seeing you. Now look – you're not to worry, OK? Tell Mum I'm fine, I have written to her. One thing . . . you won't come to court when the trial comes up, will you, please? I can handle it best if no one's there, honestly.'

'Right, *cariad*.' Hannah stood, and their lips met in warm affection. 'Matthew sends his love, sweetheart. He put a packet of Mintoes in for you. And we'll hope for the best. God bless . . .'

He turned and gave her a smiling salute at his door. When it shut, Hannah walked to the door which led to freedom. Tears were very close, but she stemmed them until she was in the car, when she went into Matthew's waiting arms and sobbed her heart out.

Three days later the solicitor Matthew had found for Laurie phoned him.

'Good news. Not bail, but we've been offered a court slot in eight days' time. We're ready, all gathered up quite well. So it appears are the prosecution, so that's excellent. Now, Helen Midwood is appearing for Laurie . . . she'll make a good job of it, they've already met a couple of times and are *simpatico*. She has persuaded Laurie that – although he insists he is not addicted – she should say that he is willing to attend a rehabilitation centre; and that this, with probation, would be vastly more appropriate an outcome than a custodial sentence in view of his age and experience. One thing . . . your wife giving evidence of good character on the boy's behalf . . . I wouldn't advise it, old man. They could take her apart and she simply may not be up to police prosecution rough stuff. What would serve equally well, with no risk attached, is a letter of character reference to the court – that's in order in situations like this. If she will let me have that a.s.a.p.?'

'I'm still happy to take the stand . . .' Hannah was unconvinced. 'I know Laurie had said he didn't want "anyone" there; but if this might actually help swing the case –'

Matthew was firm. 'If Ned says it would be counter-productive he'll be right. Look, sweetheart – have a stab at a letter. The prosecution can't play dirty with that, after all.'

Your Honour,

I am impelled to write to you, in the hope of the court taking into account what I know of my grandson, Laurie Shapiro, that might pertain to his case. Laurie has clearly, but I pray temporarily, lost his way. He is a good-natured boy, of a kind and non-competitive disposition. He has, I believe, been under some pressure to compete with his peers in areas in which he is unconfident, and this has caused him to become depressed about his own future. He has turned to drugs to alleviate this.

He does understand now that this course can have no happy outcome. If he could be helped at this point to restart his life in a constructive fashion, which is his wish and his need, there is time to salvage his undoubted potential as a giving and useful citizen.

Laurie has for a number of years wanted to work with his hands, growing plants. If he can be rehabilitated, I am prepared to fund him on an appropriate course, which will also serve to help him escape his former environment.

'What d'you think?' she asked, her face anxious.

Matthew handed back the letter. 'It's just fine. I reckon it could do the trick. We'll drink to that?'

*

On the day of the trial Hannah would not go out of earshot of the telephone.

'There's no chance of a thing before midday,' Matthew told her for the third time. 'We can at least walk around the garden and admire the daffodils.'

'Someone might phone to say *something*.' Hannah went halfway round the garden with him, but was so abstracted that he took pity on her and led her back indoors.

She settled down to write to Joe; or rather, did not settle down . . . Jonet had phoned yesterday and appeared utterly fazed by events; she simply could not believe what was happening to her son. 'How *could* he let us all down in this way? My son being tried at the Old Bailey, as a common criminal!'

'Some extremely *uncommon* criminals have been tried at the Bailey,' had been Matthew's observation. 'And our lad's appearing there for no other reason than that it is his local. The whole shooting-match is preposterous, though, I'm with Jonet there. If Laurie hadn't been coupled up with Dee he wouldn't have got past a fine at a magistrates' court.'

'Maybe this is what he needed,' Hannah said suddenly, and frowned. 'Would another piffling fine stop him throwing his future on the rubbish heap? Perhaps a few weeks in Wormwood Scrubs and the panoply of the Old Bailey will stop him in his tracks.'

Now she put down Joe's letter, barely begun, and went to stand at the back door of Bracken House. Beyond the riot of spring bulbs Laurie's herb garden was budding strongly again, sheltered by two hedges of box over which climbed a sturdy Albertine and a Dorothy Perkins. The garden was just as they liked it . . . a little unruly, plants growing happily into one another, nothing regimented.

They were so lucky; every day she knew it, was thankful for it. Beside them, Jonet's life was arid. Poor Jonet ... in striving to have everything she had grasped empty air. She had wanted a career so had not had a family – just a token child to say she had one. But because of that child, she had been unable to rise to the heights of ambition demanded in her career.

Serena would have done it another way. Hannah imagined Serena knee deep in babies, laughing and loving each one, each day. Now she would have been looking forward to grandchildren. Her hair would have lost its corn-gold glow, but the lines on her face would be laughter lines.

Hannah looked up the garden into the sun, and she believed she could see a slight, bright figure under the Japanese cherry, waving. Serry ... Love you, darling ...

The phone rang at five to three. If Laurie had been convicted it would be his solicitor's voice. If not, Laurie would make the call himself. She and Matthew looked at the phone; at each other. When Hannah's hand reached for the instrument, Matthew was at her shoulder.

'Hello?' she croaked.

'It's me, Gran. I'm free. Well; I'm going to a rehab centre in Kent for a few weeks. And I've been put on probation. I reckon your letter really helped swing things in my favour. They say I should come down to you for a while after rehab. Would that be OK? Gran? Are you still there?'

'Yes, I am. And yes – that would be OK.'

'What're you crying for then?'

'Because I'm so damn relieved, you idiot. Have you rung your mother?'

'Yes. At the library. She said "that's very good news".'

'Well, she couldn't say much more, could she, in front of a whole library? But I bet you a fiver she's crying too now, in the staff lavatory. What happened to Dee, Laurie?'

'He got six months, sadly. It seemed to be finding those scales; the police made a meal of them. I'm sorry, 'cos he's a nice guy.'

'Well, it was his second conviction. Will you call us from the rehab centre?'

'Surely. And thanks for everything. How're my herbs? Looking good?'

'Very good. They're looking great.' And then she was laughing.

It was early May when he left the rehabilitation centre and came down to Bracken House on the coach, with his few clothes, some books and his guitar. His hair had grown a little again and he looked reasonably well, his dark eyes more peaceful than for some time.

'There were some OK people there.' They sat on the warm grass with mugs of tea and a plate of Welshcakes that were disappearing fast. 'I had some really interesting conversations. It was an amazing house, old, with loads of trees everywhere. I worked in the gardens – there was quite a bit needed doing. And I got started with the greenhouse stuff a couple of weeks back. It's all a bit wild, I think you'd have liked it.'

'Was it entirely for people with drug problems?' Matthew was interested.

'I think there were other things too. I didn't ask people why they were there. They didn't ask me either.' He added in a moment: 'I wasn't in the least addicted, you know, I didn't form much of an affinity with coke. In fact, the packets they found on me weren't for my own use. I was going to deliver them to a friend of Dee's. The fuzz were right there. But it wouldn't have been useful to Dee's case for me to have admitted that I was delivering for him, would it? Though it was helpful to the case for me to go along with the idea that I was addicted and wanted to go to rehab.'

'Of course. Well, there's a bit of good news this end about some work. We've been getting our plants, greenhouse stuff and suchlike from a good nurseryman up near Bridgend. We were chatting about the possibility of your finding what you wanted, and he says he may take you on until September if you go up and see him right away. Only pocket money – but the important thing is you'd learn a lot between now and then. He also knows of a course run in Swansea for the autumn term that might suit you very well – on soil types and that sort of thing.'

Laurie ate his seventh Welshcake and drained his mug of tea. 'That sounds brilliant, Matthew.' He looked of a sudden peaky, vulnerable, as he plucked at a daisy head. 'It's fantastic of you to have sussed all that out. I'll go to see him tomorrow.'

Frank Coulter had a long talk with Laurie, showed him around greenhouses and growing beds, and seemed to approve. A second-hand bicycle was found from an advertisement in the local paper and Laurie began work right away. He left at 7.30, with sandwiches and a drink in his saddlebag, and worked from eight to five. His pale skin tanned and freckled, his skinny frame muscled up and he was happy. Each week he reported to a probation officer in Porthcawl. Every other weekend he took the coach to Reading to see his parents.

'It's hard going, Gran,' he reported to Hannah. 'Dad's unbelievably uptight, can't seem to find any point of contact there. And Mum . . . well, that's not much better.' The visits were soon altered to one a month . . . Hannah watched for an improvement from the Reading end but none came. There may have been resentment that Laurie had taken sanctuary with her; but there had been no offers to have him home again, and so everyone got on with the situation they were dealt.

'If we could find a smallholding with a cottage, I'd advance him the funds for it.'

Hannah and Matthew were walking on Kenfig Burrows, just inland from the coast, with Port Talbot's steel mills glinting to the north of them. Progress was slow because the day was pleasant and they had no cause to hurry. Hannah had walked these sandy paths for years; she knew well the history of the medieval borough, once a busy walled town, that had by the seventeenth century become submerged by sand dunes. She had enjoyed hunting out the sandy remnants of Kenfig Castle, just north of Kenfig Pool. That was another story again, no more than a legend . . . insubstantial but none the less evocative for that. The legend was of the pool's dark waters, and the drowned city, from the golden mists of the past, consigned to its cold depths. This city, more than the sand-covered borough of the latter-day Kenfig, had stiffened Hannah's spine with horror when she was a child. Wales echoed always with legends, none, for Hannah, more poignant than that of a mythical city left to the fish of Kenfig Pool, with nearby a factual town choked for three centuries under blowing greedy dunes. She felt the past so strongly here, she would tell Matthew, that she never failed to listen for the bells of sad, buried Kenfig church, silenced by sand. Now they walked arm in arm in June sunshine,

Matthew reluctantly using a stick to support a knee that had lately been misbehaving despite Hannah's best efforts.

'Would he have the know-how to set himself up? Remember, he's not twenty-one till the end of the year.' He swung his stick at a pebble and sent it bouncing over the coarse, rabbit-cropped grasses.

'He's inexperienced, I know. I've a feeling though that what he might need more than experience is the responsibility of having to commit himself, *having* to make the project work. In at the deep end, rather than wriggling toes in the shallows?'

'You may be right. It might take for ever to find the right place, of course . . . we should start reading adverts in the local press.'

It took not for ever, but five months, to find a cottage with slightly over two and a half acres of land, a few miles south-east of Bridgend. The cottage was a basic but sound two-up and two-downer, the land on a slope – 'but what land in Wales is *not* on a slope,' observed Matthew. The old man living there for years without number had lost his wife and wanted to live with his son in Cardiff. He'd run a few sheep on the land, made hay for them, grown vegetables for the family, lived his life.

'What d'you think?' Hannah asked Matthew after they had been shown round by the agent. 'Is it a close enough bet to sit Laurie down and talk to him?'

'I reckon so. But we'd have to be very certain he would take it seriously. Nothing else has come up that would be remotely suitable, and it's a good south-facing site, with trees for shelter to the north. It's on a decent road, and maybe ten miles from Cardiff and less from Bridgend, so he should have markets. Then there's Porthcawl and its holiday trade. We should make an offer; the owner might be prepared to deal.'

When Laurie had come in from college and eaten, Hannah made coffee and sat down opposite him, with Matthew as independent observer.

'Are you still serious about wanting to start up a nursery of your own?'

'Well, yes.' Laurie eyed her carefully, stirring his coffee.

'We may have found somewhere. Here –' she reached for the agent's leaflet. 'Would you like to take a look Saturday morning?'

He took the paper, scanned it intently. 'But Gran, let's be realistic. Where would I get a mortgage with no collateral?'

'From me. I could loan you the money. When I started in business at twenty-four, renting a little shop to sell my cooking I had two loans – one of £25 and one, from Liza's father, of £250. That was a lot of money, then. I couldn't have managed without either loan, and I repaid every penny as soon as I could. Would you do that, Laurie?'

He looked hard at her. The old, uncertain, abstracted and depressed Laurie was slowly being replaced by a firmed-up, more positive personality. He was continuing to report to his probation officer, but fortnightly now, and without fuss or complaint. He had done useful work at the nursery until the start of his course, and was apparently tackling that head on, with a considerable thirst for the knowledge available. Hannah looked hard at her grandson, assessing if she should take a gamble on him.

'Yes, I would,' he said after thinking time. 'I really would put my back into it. But no one's infallible . . .'

'True. Everyone can try, though. And we've enough trust in you to put it on the line.'

Matthew bargained adroitly after Laurie expressed himself content with what he saw, and the deal was made for an eminently realistic price, even allowing for what wanted doing. When Tom and Florence were taken to view, Tom's eyes shone in anticipation.

'I can help here, boyo; weekends, an' evenings too, come spring. Just up my street after a few hours in the bakery . . . an' our garden's done up to its eyebrows. There'll be a lot to do, mind.'

'I know. That's OK by me, Tom. And it would be fantastic if you'd give me a hand.'

Hannah looked at the patch of land under lowering skies, the elemental little cottage. It was a lot to ask . . . Too much? She felt nervous now; if she asked too much of Laurie he might disappear into his protective shell again, into a half-lit fantasy world, and she would have done him a bad turn. *She* had done it once, long ago . . . had taken the plunge into the business world, totally unequipped for it. But she had not been Laurie.

She felt for Matthew's hand. He took it, squeezed it. Hannah held on and made, with Laurie, another leap into the future.

Chapter Twenty-one

January 1974

Carl was in an aggressive mood; so was J. Arthur Belman. The scene was set for hand-to-hand combat and the venue was the board meeting convened at J. Arthur's insistence. His objective was to draw blood, in opposing openly and for the first time one of Carl's decisions.

It was two years since Arney Bold and Earle Curtis had blamed Carl for allowing Cline Investments to stagnate, and Carl had not addressed their specific criticisms. He had failed to devote more time to the affairs of the firm, as Arney had demanded . . . the reverse; he was spending more time than ever with Liza and Jess. Nor had he answered Earle Curtis's complaint that a more analytical approach was required to decision-making.

He had instead gone his own way to combat stagnation, by increasing the number of deals he personally set up. Arney and Earle, together with the entire organisation, rolled up their sleeves and worked at full stretch, doing what was needed to follow up and consolidate Carl's initiatives. Not one of them had questioned his decisions; why should they? Carl had the magic touch . . . the same profitable outcome must flow as it always had from his previous deals.

It had now become clear that this was not so. One acquisition was highly profitable, but the frenetically active period resulted in no more than marginal benefits to Cline Investments.

Carl had already realised that these deals were below his expected quality; what he could not assess was *why*. His success had until now been an automatic result of his hunting down a deal and deciding to pursue it . . . if Arney and Earle complained, he had no need to listen to their moans; need only find more deals to make. In the dark of the night, Carl now had to ask himself why he was losing the magic. Could it possibly be that Arney had got it right? Was he spending too much valuable work time in the UK? Was the downturn in his fortunes at Liza's door?

He quickly dismissed that notion and changed tack . . . tried the novel idea of weighing up pros and cons before acting. Some decisions he got right, some wrong. That, for Lucky Carl Cline, was not the way it worked; back as far as he could recall, situations had presented themselves out of the air almost, making decisions virtually redundant and resulting in total confidence, a sensation of all but clairvoyant vision on his part.

Now, a further complication. Due to an embargo on production by some Gulf countries, the price of oil had soared. Share prices were falling, and interest rates rising . . . and Cline Investments had borrowed heavily to fund Carl's spate of deals.

He had, though, a card to play now. Tasman Wilkins, an oil prospecting company, had for three years been working off the south coast of New Zealand. Carl had the word from one of his sailing friends that they would soon report on their survey, indicating vast reserves of oil. In fact, an oil rig had been towed from Indonesia and test drilling was about to start. Carl had his gut-deep good feeling about this set-up, and now of course was the time to buy into it. The western world was scrabbling frantically for every available drop of oil, and profits would be on a tremendous scale. At whatever cost, funds must be found for this venture.

J. Arthur Belman, through his daughter Gayle, controlled 15 per cent of Cline Investments, and was determined to resist this move of Carl's. More; it was his plan to use this opportunity to unseat his former son-in-law from the chair of the board that comprised Carl, Belman, Arney and Earle, two representatives of institutional shareholders, and one Belman yes-man: a total of seven.

'It's a hare-brained escapade.' Belman scowled now, his bright black eyes pushing out aggression round the table. 'Damned irresponsible on all counts. I'll not sanction the risking of shareholders' funds in an outright gamble.'

'The rewards would be tremendous,' Arney Bold pointed out reasonably. 'We have to take chances all the time to make profits.'

'Not chances like this one,' Belman snapped back. 'We'd need to dispose of some seed corn for this caper – safe quality assets would need liquidating and no fool wants that.'

Coffee was brought in and Belman picked his up as if tempted to fling it in Carl's face. The ding-dong battle was almost an hour old already, and Belman wanted done. Carl hung on; he had his earlier reputation to support his cause, and the 'Lucky Carl Cline' tag was still a powerful argument. Earle Curtis was wavering, though; Carl divined how the board might divide in Belman's favour and was now perturbed. Belman had his own nominee member, and one of the institutional members was leaning their way. Three to Belman . . .

Carl could count on Arney, and the second institutional man. He had to get Earle to clinch it, with his own casting vote.

Coffee was sipped and more information folders from Tasman Wilkins were handed round. While others stretched, wandering around the room, Carl sat down by Curtis, who was leafing through the new information.

'You know, Earle, I reckon I slipped up badly, not adopting your ideas right off for a more structured approach to decision-making ... in-depth analysis, that sort of thing. If we went that way now, could you set it up, make it your baby? For a consideration, naturally – you'd not be asked to take it on board for free.'

Earle turned his coffee cup with careful deliberation and Carl watched his long, strong fingers.

'Sure Carl ... I could handle that for you.'

'Fine. We'll set it up after this bun-fight folds, OK?'

Ten minutes after the coffee break, Carl asked for a vote. The hands went up; three for, three against ... Carl cast his deciding vote, and Cline Investments were going into the oil business.

Jonet went to pick up the post as she ate her toast. There were three letters: the telephone bill, an appeal from Cancer Research and a letter from Mark, postmarked Edinburgh. She dropped the phone bill into 'pending', a wooden letter rack made at school by Laurie when he was eleven, dropped Cancer Research into the bin and sat down again at the pine table in the kitchen with Mark's letter. She laid it down, looking at it as she ate the remainder of her toast and finished her coffee. She glanced at her watch; fifteen minutes before she had to leave the house for the bus stop, fifteen minutes' ride then to the stop in the middle of the town adjacent to the library. It was unusual that there should be a letter from Mark. He rarely wrote, phoning instead, and was anyway due home in three days' time. Jonet slit the envelope cleanly with a knife, glancing out of the window. It looked mild and fine, spring at last – she could skip the boots today and go in shoes. The letter was handwritten, on A4 paper with the business logo.

Edinburgh, 27 March 1974

Dear Jonet,

I have started this three times already. It is just incredibly difficult. But I feel you may have come yourself to the conclusion that our marriage has run its course. No big upheavals – with the exception of that dreadful business with Laurie – but a definite, depressing widening of a gap between us.

It is a sterile exercise to try to search out causes – if we had had more children, if you had not worked, if I had not been away so much. Whatever the cause, it has happened. There seems to be so little to come home to now.

A year ago a very nice young woman joined the staff here. We began to be friendly, and that friendship has gradually developed into love. Had there been love left in *our* relationship, that could not I think have happened.

I wish very much not to hurt you, Jonet, but see no way of avoiding doing so. I think the most humane course is to make a clean break. I will make no objections to a generous settlement for you, and hope very much that it can all be arranged without acrimony. I shall certainly try my best not to generate any.

I will phone you at the weekend to arrange a convenient time for me to come and pick up my clothes. I realise there is much more to talk over, possessions to be divided, legal steps taken, but the whole wretched business will have to be got through in due course, one thing at a time.

Again, believe me, I am extremely sorry to be the one to hurt you. I hope you will find happiness in the future.

With my best wishes,

Mark

Jonet folded the letter back into its franked business envelope and put it in the zipped compartment of her handbag. She cleaned her teeth, found her brown court shoes, slipped on her brown and beige jacket and tweaked at her fringe in the hall mirror. She felt a little dizzy, and discovered that she was holding her breath. Then she slammed the door of the handsome stone house behind her and hurried for the bus to go to work.

Laurie and Tom had repaired the boundary fencing now to make the plot sheep-proof, and had erected a good-sized shed. The lengthening days gave more time for work, but a law of diminishing returns seemed to be operating: the more was done, the more needed doing. As Matthew's contribution to the enterprise he had found a first-class jack of all trades, Dai Rainbow, who had a tractor. It was elderly and needed kind treatment and frequent rest periods, but had, under Dai's cheerful guidance, ploughed up as much of the land as was needed for the time being and had harrowed it to a decent tilth. Tom could do little during the week, but had worked weekends with energy and enterprise alongside his great-nephew. In middle age, Tom was a man at peace with himself and the world, knowing and accepting his limitations and not wishing to be what he was not. He was robust and healthy, his eyes were kind, calm as a child's, and what hair he had left was still light brown. He and Laurie were perfectly comfortable together, and worked side by side with great goodwill.

For his twenty-first birthday in early December, Mark and Jonet had given Laurie a cheque for £1,000; conscience money, Matthew had called it with humorous raised eyebrows. He believed that had they not pushed Laurie with such determination in a direction alien to his nature and deep inclinations, he would not have reached the pass he had the previous year. Hannah feared she might now have pushed too far and too fast in the direction of his choice. But it was done, and she concentrated now on bolstering his morale at every turn. Fit as she was for her age, she could not help actively in the labouring required on the smallholding. She did make curtains for the cottage, find pieces of furniture surplus to requirements at Bracken House for it, and, with Florence, hunted for floor coverings and a cooker, a fridge, and numberless other small domestic comforts for the rugged little dwelling.

Laurie was struggling to assemble his first polythene tunnel one morning in April, when a girl on a bicycle came around the bend in the lane. She had a haversack on her back and another strapped to her saddle-rack, and wore a floppy yellow hat with a brim that drooped at one side. Laurie stared . . . he recognised the hat. Then he gave a shout and, loosing his troublesome tunnel, ran for the lane.

'Primrose! Hey, Primmy!'

The girl saw him and waved. Wobbling dangerously, she fetched up at the gate. 'Laurie! God save us,

I thought I'd never find you! Put the kettle on the hob man, do.'

'Primrose, how the devil –' Laurie picked her up in an enthusiastic bear-hug, for Primrose was not above five foot two though nicely rounded in her tight, well-worn jeans, whose flared bottoms were folded into pink cotton socks. Her floppy hat fell off to reveal a ponytail of pale silky hair and a small, slightly weatherbeaten face with large hazel eyes and a wide smile.

'Hey, you – watch ma hat, will ye!' The voice was northern Scots, bubbly yet modulated. Laurie picked up the hat and stuck it back on Primrose's head with a courtly bow.

'My apologies – I know what the hat means to you, Primmy. It's *fantastic* to see you! A year, is it? C'mon in, tell me what's been happening.'

They sat on polythene bags outside the kitchen door, sipping tea and eating wedges of Tom's good bread with cheese, and Welsh perpetual onions, which thrived under the window along with mint, thyme and sage. Primrose had been at the rehabilitation centre at the time Laurie was there and the two had struck up a rapport. The senior by a year, Primrose was originally from the Isle of Mull, and had had a chequered childhood and adolescence. Her father had died and her mother remarried a sheep farmer who had abused her two daughters. Primrose had run away at thirteen, been fetched back and put into care. She had packed a bag and hitch-hiked to London at sixteen, living on her wits and sleeping in squats. Picked up and raped by a small-time drug dealer, she had after some months made her escape, taking with her what cash she could find. By this time she had become an addict herself. Caught shoplifting, she had like Laurie been put on probation, having volunteered for the centre in Kent. They had exchanged addresses before leaving there, Primrose giving that of a brother on Mull, and Laurie, Bracken House.

'So that was it –' Primrose bit contentedly on her onion. 'Your granny's fine, a lovely lady. And that nice man of hers took me round the garden, a great place they have. Then they drew me a wee map to get here . . . So what's going on here then? Going into business, are you?'

'On a small scale, when I have something ready to sell.' Laurie sounded uncertain, as indeed he often was; so uncertain sometimes that he had diarrhoea, thinking about what he was doing. He was even reluctant to give a name to his 'place' for fear of turning it into monstrous reality. But he hung on when doubts gnawed at him; narrowing his sights down to what must be done or decided that morning, that hour.

'I did a course at Swansea College,' he told Primrose. 'I understood it all pretty well really, and I've a correspondence course I'm doing evenings, too. Though what will happen to that when there's maximum daylight Lord knows, with all the outside work.'

'It's going to be a nursery, then? Selling plants, things like that? I love the sound of it.' Primrose took off her pink socks and waggled her toes in the intermittent sunshine, sighing with pleasure. She had bought the bike cheaply from a shop-window card and for want of a better idea, was cycling around the country on it. But the winter had been simply no fun, and hostels were not always to be found at the end of a wearying day. Primrose loved the outdoor life, but not for twenty-four hours at a stretch. And she would enjoy having just a little money, so she did not need to steal her knickers off market stalls. All else could be bought for a song in charity shops but she did prefer new knickers. 'Anything besides plants?'

'Vegetables, herbs, soft fruit . . . all organic, no poisons. Free range eggs if I can do that, or I may at first find a farmer who'd supply. And Matthew's giving me driving lessons, I'll need a small pick-up truck at some point. He's been helping lots, bringing stuff in his station-wagon so far. They've both been fantastic; can't think what I'd have done . . .' He stopped, chewing on his lip.

'So how's your ma and pa been?' Primrose's voice was even prettier when she dropped a tone, the vowels soft and precise. Laurie squinted along the lines laid by Dai Rainbow's idiosyncratic tractor.

'Mum came down to see me last Saturday, actually. She seemed a bit – well, as if her body had made the trip but her mind had said "count me out of this one". Thought I'd phone, maybe tomorrow – see if she's gone down with the flu or something. Just the fact that she came down was odd; she never does things like that on the spur of the moment . . . likes to work to a plan, my mum. Anyway . . .'

'And your dad?'

'Working away, Mum said. They were shaken rigid, you know. Dad said my Shapiro grandparents were never on pain of death to be told about the court case. Mum couldn't do much about Gran knowing, she gets to know everything! A witch, I've heard from someone who shall be nameless. She can do things other people can't . . .'

'You're kidding? She looked fine and normal to me.'

'They always do,' said Laurie with a ghoulish laugh. 'Now look, I've to get on. You'll stay for a bit, won't you? There's a lovely big sofa Gran found, and you've got your sleeping bag I can see.'

'Hoped you'd ask.' Primrose grinned at him. 'I'll help you with that polythene barrage balloon I caught you having a losing battle with. I can turn my hand to most things.'

This was true. Primrose Henderson was small but tough, and physically tireless. She dug, planted, painted, sawed, nailed up and sanded down, made compost compounds, fixed roof tiles, patched clothes, cooked . . . after four days Laurie could not imagine how anything had worked without her. She had also provided the name for 'the place' – The Primrose Plant Company.

Jonet had told no one at the library. No one in the urban village where she lived. Not Laurie, not Hannah. There had been no social congress with her in-laws. She had told Mark when he phoned that she did not want to see him, and that if he had to collect things from the house he must do so under the cover of darkness.

'Jonet – it will have to come out eventually . . .'

'When I am ready,' she had snapped, the heartbeats loud enough, she felt sure, to drown her words. Mark had said:

'We'll need to meet to discuss what each of us will keep.'

'I agree to *nothing* at present.' Her voice had risen. 'This was not my idea, I was not consulted, it is not a two-way agreement and I will not be pushed along by you. If you want a divorce you will do it my way or it will not be done.'

'Look, have you seen a solicitor yet?' There was no answer. 'You must do so. We have to have an agreement about the house. It should go on the market.'

'You will not sell this house from under me. You can

forget that. This is where I live until I choose to move, and you are to maintain it exactly as before until that time.'

'Jonet, for God's sake. Why can you possibly want to stay on in a family house?'

'That is for me to know and for you to guess. You may let yourself in next Saturday night at eight o'clock and stay no longer than an hour. And take only your *personal* effects. I have made a complete inventory.'

'And have you told Laurie about all this?'

'No. But you're not to – I intend telling him next week.'

After this phone call she had been sick down the eau-de-nil lavatory pan. On Saturday night she had vacated the house at 7.50 and sat in her car at the end of the road. She saw him sweep into the drive, and the dark shape of his car edge out again at 9.05. When his tail lights had vanished in the direction of the town centre, Jonet had crept in, garaged her car, and gone to have a hot bath. Then she went to bed, where she lay without moving with the lights off, listening to Radio Four, which was still on when she drifted into sleep some time in the small hours.

On Sunday she drove into London and walked through Hyde Park. Without conscious decision, Jonet found that she had walked through Kensington Gardens across Notting Hill Gate and into Holland Park Avenue. She walked steadily on, and past the house she knew to be Liza's; with sunglasses and a headscarf she felt invisible as she glanced up at the beautiful façade. She had been there once, when Laurie had persuaded his parents to attend Jess's christening . . . she had come away hurt and resentful that Liza, who had done nothing to merit it, had been so showered with benefits. David Vaughan had also, Jonet knew, left Liza a fortune. Her own father, Darrow Bates, had left *her* nothing but a legitimate birth certificate. That was the one thing no one had been able to give Liza – she had been forced to steal the name of Vaughan, it had never been hers by right.

Afterwards, Jonet had walked back to her car slowly, feeling tired. She had afternoon tea at the Dorchester, but the scones were a little dry and there was a leaf floating on the surface of the China tea. Also, she was painfully aware of being alone, a single woman with whom no one wanted to have tea this spring Sunday afternoon. She had on navy trousers with a white shirt, a navy double-breasted blazer from Jaeger, and a patterned silk scarf was loosely knotted around her shoulders. Sensible, suitable attire for walking in spring in London; appropriate clothing for a middle-aged woman out on her own and not wishing to be conspicuous. She gathered up bag and scarf and left quite soon, forgetting to leave a tip, and drove home unusually slowly to delay the time when she would close the door of the house again and be cut off from the rest of the world.

It had been the following Saturday that Jonet had gone to Wales to find Laurie. She had only been to the smallholding once, but dropped down on to the A48 from Cardiff and located it by asking. Laurie was clearly set back on his heels at the sight of her . . . she made no excuses, said only that she thought it would be nice to see how things were going with him. When he asked after Mark, she said 'oh, fine, but very busy you know'. Obviously at some point she would have to explain. Explain? How did she *explain* why Mark had left her? She had absolutely no idea.

It was doubly hard now, trying to find a means of

conversing with Laurie. She had never had much success. Now, after the court case and – everything, dialogue had become a minefield she could scarcely cross for fear of finding herself transfixed. Tom was with Laurie, beavering away quietly at one job after another; and it had never been easy to find things to say to Tom. Jonet recalled as a girl deriding Uncle Tom for being 'simple'. He did not come across as simple now; only quiet, self-contained, transparently kind.

She thought briefly of going on the few miles to Bracken House, asking if she might spend the night with her mother and Matthew. But she never had called unannounced, ever – they would suspect something was wrong, and she could not have borne to tell them. So when Laurie asked if she was going on to Gran's she shook her head; not this time, she had to be back tonight, she was busy tomorrow. As she drove away Jonet realised she had not told Laurie about Mark. Then she realised that she had not, at any time, had the least intention of telling him.

She was back in the house by 8.30, passing the local pub where the car park was packed as always on a Saturday night. They had eaten there a few times themselves, soon after they had moved. Jonet locked the front door and wandered around the garden in the spring twilight. Daffodils were over but the tulips were good; the doronicum's yellow petals had closed but she knew they would reopen with the morning light, standing strong and tall over the spread of primroses. The dahlia tubers needed to go in soon, didn't they ... Not worth bothering perhaps, this year ... but she could do a bit of weeding and dead-heading tomorrow if there was no rain. There was everything to be sorted, too; emptying out drawers and getting rid of the dross of, how long was it? Twenty-four years next December?

She went in, bolted the kitchen door. Mark had said she *must* talk to him soon, he could not arrange his finances if she would not say what she intended. Jonet, taking a cup of Horlicks upstairs, had no idea what she intended. When she attempted to think of the future and how she wished to arrange it, her mind froze, nothing happened in her head but a vein banging against her temple.

She switched on the bedside radio and listened to the last part of *Saturday Night Theatre*. It was incomprehensible, but it was voices, company.

Liza had been sent a complimentary copy of *Woman Today* which had her on the cover with an interview inside. The photograph was flattering and she was idly paging through with a warm feeling of satisfaction when she saw the picture of Edward Anderssen. He was standing beside the best-selling novelist Catherine Orville, who was the subject of the story. They were to be married later in the month, the honeymoon deferred until the last volume of Orville's historical trilogy was complete. She was still transfixed by the picture when the doorbell rang. It was the taxi to take her to a church hall in St John's Wood for the first rehearsal of a radio production of Pinero's *The Second Mrs Tanqueray*.

She found the rehearsal room dusty, draughty and too dim to see the script clearly. None of the assembled company but Liza appeared to mind this. 'It's pissing down with rain, of course it's dark': ugly fluorescent lighting was turned on. Liza still could not easily decipher her lines, which seemed to be jumpy and blurred.

'Could it be time for an eye test, darling?' suggested the director cattily. Liza had worked with her once before and they were not as compatible as they might have been. She thought for a moment about making a scene and leaving; she hadn't intended doing any more radio work anyway. But she was contracted . . . there would be words with Penelope and there had been too many of those lately, her agent objecting to the amount of work Liza was currently refusing. Besides, she had a great respect for the actor playing her husband, and it was a good part in a quality production . . . If this damn headache would clear she might settle down.

The day went steadily downhill. She lost her normally immaculate timing, and her voice had the wrong inflections for the character of the girl, Paula. When she read the line 'I believe the future is only the past again, entered by another gate' her eyes closed and a tear escaped on to her cheek. She blew her nose at once, mortified, but her disarray had not escaped notice and there was an uncomfortable rearranging of bottoms on chairs. Val the director drew an impatient breath and tapped her play copy with an unforgiving finger. Liza ground on until towards the climax when Paula commits suicide, and Val said suddenly, as though she were reprimanding a seven-year-old for inattention:

'Could you perhaps read this bit just a little less like a grocery list, Liza? I do appreciate that it's only a boring old read-through but we have to make a start somewhere, and today's it.' Then she flashed a smile in direct opposition to the barb.

Liza stood up, scraping back her chair with a tooth-jarring screech, bestowed upon Val a glare that would have shrivelled a Chieftain tank and stalked out. She walked several hundred yards down the road before she picked up a taxi and sat in her wet linen slacks and shirt, dabbing at her hair with the only tissue she had in her bag. She stared at the steamed-up windows, glowering, and on making her exit from the taxi, holed her tights by some means she could not begin to explain.

Running upstairs she pulled off her clothes, climbed into a black jogging suit and ran back downstairs, ignoring Mrs Roberts who had come to welcome her home. She picked up an umbrella from the hall-stand, pulled open the door again and jumped down the steps. She had to walk; get this out of her system. Edward Anderssen must *not* be permitted to make this sort of impact upon her present life. He was the past, long gone.

But that was not so. Liza walked rapidly about Holland Park, up and down the paths, back and forth, her umbrella held before her face like a shield. If he was the past, why did news of his marriage affect her so? She continued to walk, her efforts to think clearly helped by the movement of her body.

She had worked it out by the time she stopped, leaning against the trunk of a plane tree. Really, she was just unable to cope with the simple fact of rejection. He wanted another woman more than he wanted her; had made a fool of her in public, inescapably.

Liza looked across the empty park, whose midsummer foliage dripped and drooped about her now. She looked into the blue shadows and imagined she saw him there, waiting for her judgement on him for the damage she could neither forget nor forgive.

Now she recalled her research for a radio play about the supernatural: 'Thoughts are living things . . . psychic matter is created from strong desires and is the basic material of the universe.' Why not put this to the test . . .

'I hate you,' she said in a clear voice. 'I wish you and your wretched wife the worst luck in the world. I hope that you are hurt as you have hurt me.'

Feeling tired enough to crumple to the ground now, Liza walked stiffly home. She phoned to apologise to Val the next day, saying she had been unwell. The play was recorded successfully and won an award for the best radio play of the year.

In August, Jonet had two weeks' holiday due. She put it about that Mark was abroad and that she would join him there; Hannah, her neighbours – all were told this. Jonet herself almost believed it. The truth was that Mark was almost at the end of his tether, and by now demanding of his solicitor a solution that would force his wife to make the necessary moves.

Jonet's grip on reality loosened a fraction each day. She could handle the hours at work, there being no contact between them and her other life. It was as she walked down the library steps into the streets packed with home-going thousands that the now familiar stomach-clenching fear of her shame being discovered took over. Her small face became pinched, she would bend over a little as though with physical pain. To Jonet, status in the eyes of the world was paramount. She had lied to disguise her humble origins from her classmates at the boarding-school to which she and Serena had been dispatched as a safe haven from German bombs . . . had lied to prevent friends knowing of her mother's illegitimate child. These were not *proper* lies, she would rationalise. They were social lies, so she would not be looked down on; as was a mythical wealthy father she invented some time after the death of her own, the foundryman Darrow Bates. She had been uncomfortable about her mother being 'in trade' and furious that Uncle Tom was what some called 'nineteen and sixpence in the pound'.

To have one's husband leave the marital home for another, younger woman was the ultimate: deserted wives must be at the end of the pecking order in society. All Jonet had worked for, lived by since childhood, collapsed like paper in flames. The charred remnants blew away and nothing was left. Her body, even, felt cruelly exposed to public knowledge, so that she took to wearing several layers of disguising garments, and dark glasses, and grew her short hair so it would shield her face from scrutiny.

With August, time was running out for Jonet. Mark was placing the house on an estate agent's books, and demanding she give the man access to draw up a brochure. He also demanded she come to an agreement about house contents. She was losing the strength to fight free of this net as it was drawn about her; the terrifying sense of being trapped became inexorable.

She obtained sleeping pills from her doctor on grounds of pressure of work and an inability to clear her mind at night. These were not effective. By two or three o'clock she would be awake, traipsing up and down with a succession of drinks, the radio on permanently. When Laurie phoned she asked the stock questions, but could think of no more to say . . . if she could not speak of what occupied her whole mind, nothing was left. It was the same with Hannah, who had been aware of trouble for some time but had so far failed either to divine its nature, or coax Jonet into confiding anything other than that she was 'fine'. This, patently, she was not.

She left the library on the first Saturday of August to begin her summer leave. By the fact of her position as head librarian she was not on the rota for Saturday duty, but for some weeks had insisted upon volunteering. On Sunday she caught up with some gardening; the rustic pergola had partially collapsed and much wistaria had run amok, which was a ladder and secateurs job. And the shed roof was leaking. Here, Jonet ran out of expertise, and made do with a flattened fertiliser bag secured all round with sticky brown packaging tape. On Monday she weed-killed the terrace and path and cleaned and polished her car inside and out, and on Tuesday she washed all the curtains, dried, ironed and rehung them.

On Wednesday morning there was a phone call from the estate agent asking when it would be convenient for him to view and measure up. There was also a letter from Mark's solicitor that Jonet did not fully understand, but which resulted in a sleepless night for her. She pulled herself out of bed on Thursday in a nauseous state and fell over, head swimming horribly, when she bent to run her bath.

The effort of conscious decision seemed now to be beyond her. She walked round her home, seeing each room through eyes made dull by a hammering headache. After that she filled a flask with boiling water, and lodged a teabag inside the screw-on cup. It was neither hot nor cold, an unremarkable day with light high cloud and not too much wind. She combed her hair with its smattering of grey, observing her reflection impartially, and recalled that she would be forty-seven the following day.

'If I live,' she said to her reflection. 'A day is a long time . . . anything can happen.' She did not want to bother taking clothes wherever it was she was going –

though she had not until that moment thought to go anywhere – but she realised that she had made up a flask so put her bottle of sleeping pills in her bag in case she might need them.

Locking up the house she backed her car out of the garage, pointed it due west and began to drive. She had no conscious thoughts, only a vague jumble of recollections drifting about her mind like scarves of mist. As she drove steadily, the automatic gearbox of her vehicle smoothed her path; she had not *decided* to drive west, that was simply the way she went.

Jonet never enjoyed traversing the Bristol suspension bridge; she complained that it gave her vertigo. This time she was scarcely aware of it. A few miles into Wales she stopped to drink her tea and go to the lavatory, then continued west, passing caravans and family cars bound for the Gower peninsula. With Cardiff behind her she took to the road leading to Laurie's place. Approaching, she thought she saw him coming from the back door of the freshly whitewashed cottage, but drove on past the gate with the sign PRIMROSE PLANT COMPANY in big yellow lettering on a green board. That seemed just for a moment to be a strange thing to do . . . then Jonet realised that Laurie's could not be where she was going.

After Bridgend, the skyline of the giant conurbation that was the British Steel Corporation soon cut the seascape. Jonet ignored the major carriageway overflying Taibach and took the old coast road through Margam, driving more slowly now before stopping altogether. She sat unmoving . . . it was all so different. The steelworks stretched endlessly between road and sea, convoluted shapes of metal, harsh noise, acrid smell. This was another world from the one she had inhabited all her adult life; from quiet libraries, close-carpeted centrally heated homes, gardens with flowering cherries and stone birdbaths.

Jonet climbed stiffly from the car and began to walk back the way she had come . . . past the engineering shops, the stripping bay and soaking pits, the slabbing mill, hot strip mill. Her father had been killed in a strip mill, but these new works had not been built then . . . he had been in the older works alongside the docks. Seven, she had been, when he had been burned to death by a strip of molten metal about his neck. Someone had told her much later, she had forgotten who . . . Her mother had said simply that he had died in an accident. Jonet struggled to recall him now, but had only the impression of a big dark man, sitting on a wooden chair with a newspaper spread in his hands.

She was looking for the road that led up the hill towards Morfa Cottage. She knew of course that it had been demolished . . . she had driven here along the motorway for which it had been sacrificed, running now along the rim of the hill on pylons that dwarfed the houses of Margam and Taibach. There *must*, though, be something left of the past? Something to indicate where they had lived their lives?

She found the road, the name still on its metal plate. But it ended in nothing; in concrete and metal and cars and lorries roaring by above. Where Morfa Cottage had stood, she could not now be certain. Jonet stared, swaying slightly, at the progress that had wiped out her past, then, shaking, she made her way back to her car.

There was another house . . . in Incline Row, where she had been born, and lived for eight years. Jonet drove slowly on and in a couple of minutes was stopping again, seeing Incline Row running up on her right. At the top end, more pylons, more motorway.

Their house had been up there, with the school opposite.

She stood by the car, leaning against the wing for support, and looked about her. Her roots . . . a few little shops, some boarded up; a run-down garage, a fish and chip shop, terraced houses with thick lace curtains. She had lived here. Her father had walked down this road every day, had crossed over the railway line to the works, where blast furnaces and coke ovens roared day and night . . . until the day he had been carried home by his workmates to lie in the front parlour.

She felt too unwell now to go further, though she would have liked to see the sea from Aberavan beach again. She turned the car round in Incline Row and drove back the way she had come.

Instead of heading due east for her home, Jonet turned for the coast at Bridgend and crossed the bridge over the Ewenny river. She seemed now to be using the steering wheel for support, hanging over it with tightly clenched fists. Her mother's house was quite close; she was aware of that, but little else. When she caught sight of the chimneys of Bracken House in the trees she took her foot off the accelerator and coasted to a standstill.

Now she folded her hands in her lap and sat quietly, looking ahead. Cars came towards her and flashed by, carrying tired sandy families home from the beach, packed in with the flotsam of the day. Jonet saw them with her eyes but did not note them.

She guessed that this must be where she had meant to come . . . to her mother. Yet now she was so nearly here, she had no means to bridge the emotional chasm that had separated them since before Liza's birth. This, it seemed, was as far as she could reach. Too tired by far to go elsewhere, she remained. There was after all nowhere else to go.

Hannah and Matthew were returning from an afternoon at Laurie's place. Hannah had been picking and boxing tomatoes ready for delivery. Laurie was serving fresh produce to passing trade, and potting on hardy perennials. Primrose had picked a load of fit-looking runner beans and picked, washed and bunched up young beetroot. Matthew had dropped the produce off at Cowbridge where there was an eager market.

'Primrose must be the best thing ever to happen to that young man,' he observed, coasting downhill to the river.

'I tried to spy out their sleeping arrangements but have had no luck yet.' Hannah grinned. 'But I shall. What do you think?'

'I think you should not be a beaky old lady, sweetheart. What I say is, they're welcome to make whatever sleeping arrangements are, well, convenient.'

'Oh, I agree . . . I only *wondered*.'

'Well, wonder on. One day all will be revealed.'

'He's holding things together pretty well, don't you think? In view of . . . everything. But I think he's more than a little disappointed not to have heard from Mark. If he would just come once . . . take a look round, make a polite noise or two.' She turned suddenly as they passed a silver car parked on the verge near Bracken House. 'Matthew – can you stop?'

Hannah put an urgent hand on his arm as he braked and drew in. 'Thanks.' She turned again. 'I think it's Jonet – Hang on a minute, will you?'

Walking back, she saw her daughter staring blankly ahead. 'Jonet? What is it? Have you been trying to get into the house?'

'The house.' Jonet's voice was flat. Hannah leaned towards her through the open window.

'Move over,' she said gently. 'I'll drive us in.' She signalled to Matthew and waited for Jonet to ease herself over to the passenger seat. As she got in, Jonet said:

'I don't feel at all well . . . Sorry . . . So sorry –'

'No. I can see that. There's nothing to be sorry for, though.' Hannah put the car into drive and eased off the verge. 'Let's go home, shall we?'

Liza was packing to go to Italy when she heard about Edward Anderssen's accident on *News at Ten*. Looking up sharply midway between wardrobe and suitcase, she saw a shot of his wife walking quickly into a hospital, followed by a picture of them both outside Chelsea Register Office after their marriage. Catherine Orville was an attractive woman of perhaps forty, dark-haired and slender, and on her wedding day she was laughing. Now she was waiting at an intensive care ward in Scotland, after a climb during which a fall of rock had sent her new husband hurtling down a slope. A broken back . . . all possible had been done by paramedics helicoptered to the spot . . . fears now were of partial paralysis.

Liza sat on the bed, a pair of shorts across her arm. A surge of emotion so powerful it threatened to choke her, filled her throat.

Had *she* had done this? She had demanded retribution for harm done her, and retribution had been exacted. Did she, Liza Vaughan, have power over life and death?

Dropping the shorts on the bed with a pile of bikinis she went quietly downstairs, through the dining room and pushed open the doors to the terrace. She made her way through the rose arch, past the pool with the statue of a small girl beside it, past the summerhouse, down to the trees. She leaned against a pear tree, struggling to master her breathing, to comprehend the extraordinary power pulsing through her body.

It was Rachel . . . this *must* be what connected them. She knew there had to be a connection, Rachel would not be around for no reason. Hannah had not been able to explain the spirit's presence; now it was clear, at least to Liza.

'Where are you?' She peered into the night, velvet soft with a yellow moon hanging low so that leaves were printed across it like a lino cut. 'Do I have power over you, too?'

There . . . the shadow materialised; the silhouette familiar now, of long full skirt, shawl, ink-dark hair blowing slightly, though in this London garden the air was still. Liza thought she saw a pale flash of cheek, of hand across the heavy mass of skirt.

'Is this your gift to me – to give me power over others? Am I invincible now, Rachel Hywel? Is that why I hold an audience silent? Why they sit mesmerised like rabbits in headlights?'

They faced one another: the actress and the shade of the woman dead two centuries past. Then Liza gave a little laugh.

'You can go now . . . I don't need you again. But I shall make good use of what you have given me, I promise.'

She turned and ran lightly through the scented garden back to the house.

Thin and acquiescent, Jonet chewed obediently through small and beautifully presented meals. The sharpness had gone, replaced by polite exhaustion of spirit. She had told her mother that Mark was away, and she couldn't contact him, but none-the-less Hannah took to phoning the house at intervals in case he returned.

Hannah asked her doctor to call, and he had pronounced complete nervous and physical exhaustion.

'The remedy does not lie in tablets, but in restorative care from those who love her, which alone will provide an incentive to improve.' Hannah phoned the library, told them that it might be some weeks before Mrs Shapiro would be well enough to return and posted off the doctor's certificate.

'Her entire personality seems to have shut down.' She was walking in the garden with Matthew while Jonet slept. 'But she just will not give a clue as to what the problem is.' They decided to tell Laurie she was with them, but not to come until they gave the nod.

'It's to do with Dad, I know it is,' he said worriedly. 'I haven't heard from him in weeks. I can't work out where he is.'

Jonet lay back in a garden chair, watching her mother coming out with a tray. She had been at Bracken House five days; a spell of stormy weather had given way to a tranquil time of gold and blue with sharp nights, bringing heavy dews and magical, frosted spiders' webs in the hedgerows.

Hannah set down the tray with a translucent china dish of beef broth, a triangle of Melba toast, a small slice of Brie and a tiny bunch of sweet green grapes on a plate hand-painted with trailing ivy.

Jonet said very quietly, 'Mark has left, you know.'

'Oh.' Hannah moved the stool with the tray closer to Jonet. 'When was that, dear?'

'Quite a while ago . . . a long time, it seems.' Jonet began on the beef broth, taking minute sips. Hannah seated herself and was still, content to take this as slowly as need be. The broth took some time, then Jonet laid down her spoon, looking worn out with the effort.

'Has anything been done about it?' Hannah asked as though it was not of paramount importance either way. After a moment Jonet shook her head.

'What would Mark like to happen?' Hannah probed gently.

'He said I had to get myself a solicitor. And he said I had to tell Laurie. Or he would . . .' Jonet lifted her head as if it were too heavy to bear and stared across the garden.

Hannah laid her hand over the transparently thin one on the chair arm. 'Jonet . . . would you like me to help? I will of course in any way you ask. I love you. You're my daughter. Nothing changes that, or ever will.'

Jonet had been quiet then. Hannah waited, hearing the blackbird singing with heart-rending sweetness in a little apple tree behind her.

'Thank you, Mother.' The words came finally, and Hannah felt fingers press hers. 'Please help me, if you can. I do need your help . . .'

She began slowly to improve, though on some days slipped back into a painful trapped silence, staring at nothing. She would lie still for hours, and Hannah would often find her asleep, her bulk scarcely more than a child's. It may take time, but healing will take place, the doctor assured her again. Hannah would sit by her and allow her hands to hover over Jonet's, hoping to transfer her own energies into the depleted body of her daughter. When they at last made a slow tour of the garden she saw it as a landmark; a visit from Laurie was another. After several weeks Matthew took Jonet for a brief preliminary talk with a solicitor.

Most important, her bitterness towards Hannah seemed to have eased; or rather, was no longer discernible. With its demise Jonet showed a peacefulness to which Hannah responded carefully, but with joy after so many years of deep disappointment. She told herself to be wary; Jonet had a long road to tread to full recovery and when she was better, might recover her deep prejudices with her health. It was, though, a beginning . . .

Twelve months after Tasman Wilkins began drilling they had still not struck significant quantities of oil. Drilling had been abandoned in the southern midwinter, with impossibly heavy seas off the south coast of New Zealand. Work had restarted in November, but by New Year 1975 there was still no sign of oil.

Tasman Wilkins pointed out that it was early days yet, and this point was hammered home by Carl Cline to the board of Cline Investments.

'The oil is there.' He hit the table with a confident fist, facing down the bleak headshake of J. Arthur Belman. 'And in great quantities – all the indications show that. Drilling just needs to continue. It isn't that no oil is there, only that it has not yet been *found*. There's all the difference.'

'Not in my book,' Belman growled. 'No oil is no oil – *finito*.'

'Not so.' Carl was stubborn. 'Time will prove you wrong. But the kitty has run dry. They need us to provide more funding *now*: drilling is an expensive business.'

'You're going to tell us next just one more donation and they'll be home and dry,' Belman sneered.

'I wouldn't insult your intelligence by telling you that's all they need.' Carl's voice was icy. 'We're the majority stakeholder, other investors are looking to us for a lead. If we pull out they will lose confidence and we'll have lost everything. Is that good business policy?'

'I tell you it's *us* that have lost confidence in the whole blasted set-up.' Belman stuck out his jaw and Carl had a barely resistible desire to throw a punch at it. 'It was a damn-fool exercise from day one. If there'd been any hope of oil there, the multinationals would've fallen over themselves to get their mitts on our stake.'

The vote was unanimous, but for Carl and Arney Bold: not another cent for Tasman Wilkins. And this was not the first time he had been voted down . . . he had recommended buying into a construction company in the fall and that had died when Earle Curtis's new research team had been unconvinced by the figures. Now, it seemed that Lucky Carl Cline's luck might be getting a touch rusty.

Chapter Twenty-two

Winter 1976

Princess Anne opened the Aberavan Shopping Centre on 20 February. She stepped out of the helicopter on Aberavan seafront wearing a duck-egg blue outfit with a light brown fur hat. Her motorcade travelled along Princess Margaret Way, Victoria Road, and what remained of Water Street, the route thickly lined with cheering flag-wavers of all ages. The royal party then disappeared into the Centre, which had cost five and a half million pounds to build, tearing out in the process the heart of the ancient borough of Aberavan. The house where Hannah and Joe had been born in Water Street had gone. Also the familiar streets of their childhood, a score of pubs and clubs and many shops, including the one where in 1926 Hannah had with such intense pride – and trepidation – first displayed cakes, pies and breads baked by Florence and herself.

The two old friends stood silent now, collars pulled up against the chill of February. Then Florence said quietly, 'I hope it's been worth it.'

'That's hard to believe, Flo.' Hannah looked over to St Mary's church, standing uneasily by the new bus station and car park which had gobbled up a portion of its churchyard. Thankfully, the graves of Hannah's mother and daughter had been undisturbed.

'It can't be worth it,' she repeated stubbornly. 'To destroy a community to build a shopping centre and a tarmac car park. We know the steelworks are continually shedding jobs, and that other trades are faring no better. So why more shops? For men to wander round, bored and angry, on the dole? Why not spend the money cleaning up the air?'

Florence laughed. 'We survived it though, didn't we? And lots of others . . . But I do hate *that* monstrosity –' Her smile vanished as she gestured towards the motorway that seemed to skim the rooftops of Taibach. Hannah nodded; that 'brutal road' had destroyed her home . . . and the entire village of Groes, hard by it.

They walked soberly back to their car, with no stomach for more cheering. All different, now. The old railway bridge by the school gone; the railway gone, the once busy railway yard cleared for a private housing estate . . . Dyffryn Colliery closed, then all the others . . . The old docks closed, where as children they had watched the ships edge in, and had imagined the countries where they had loaded. Next year the motorway would be connected up and officially opened, as had the shopping centre been today . . . all in the name of progress. And constantly, jobs slipping away; in ones and twos, sometimes in great swaths as with the closure of the Abbey melting shop.

'We're lucky though, *cariad*.' Florence sighed as they settled themselves in the car. 'My Raymond's doing well, and look at your Liza, the sky's the limit. And Laurie coming good too . . . that's a sweetheart of a lady he has, never mind if they haven't the marriage lines! And that baby boy . . . an angel.'

Hannah grinned, starting up the motor. 'Even if he was almost the death of his poor grandma! You have to feel sorry for Jonet – a "natural" grandchild for her of all people . . .'

'Took it on the chin though; she seems a changed woman at times, wouldn't you say?'

Hannah was quiet as she negotiated the traffic through Taibach. Then she said: 'Sometimes, yes. It maybe had to happen that way. You know – a really fearsome knock to send you right down . . . to cause life to be evaluated afresh. I still fear for her now and then; she's not adept at bending with the wind. But at least we *talk* . . . and I think she's less angry about her own and others' inadequacies.'

Hannah set Florence down in Porthcawl and drove on to Laurie's before dropping back to Bracken House. She told herself that of course she needed vegetables – and Laurie's organically grown vegetables were extremely good – but knew also that she made every opportunity to see three-month-old Ben, her first great-grandchild and every gorgeous baby rolled in one. No doubt they should not have had him . . . not a practical move with their agenda. But happiness had transformed Laurie from the depressed, unconfident boy of yesterday, and Ben was the natural outcome of that happiness. Primrose had been exactly what Laurie needed to coax out his aims and ambitions, which had turned out to be wonderfully compatible with her own. Namely, to live simply, profiting modestly from their own labours; to grow the purest food, the healthiest plants they could, and to enjoy their lives in the process. They were making the narrowest of profits; but even so Laurie was paying the interest on his loan regularly to Hannah.

Ben's arrival had been a testing time for Jonet. She had only recently secured her transfer to Cardiff's main library, into the top administrative echelon. One of the points decided during her five weeks' stay with Hannah and Matthew had been the need for her to move promptly from the Reading district; a new start, Hannah had urged. A clean page. And where better than a first-class library in an important university city, and only a few miles from those who loved her – her son, her mother, her Uncle Tom. Her family.

She had taken her time making the move, and afterwards felt immediately better. Matthew guided her through her divorce and house sale with a gentle firmness that caused Hannah's heart to swell with love for him. He had also monitored her renting a flat in Reading while she was waiting for the Cardiff transfer. But only Jonet could have made the conscious decision to abandon her long dream of the British Library . . . to abandon her resentment towards Laurie for being the child standing between her and her ambition to reach the pinnacle of her profession. Hannah guessed the struggle it had been. Imperceptibly she had seen the change become clearer; the bridge finally crossed.

They had been gardening together at Bracken House one weekend. Jonet had taken to coming regularly, able at last to accept the help always available for her there. They had been talking of Laurie's successful marketing of his herb cuttings, his speciality.

'He knew all the time, didn't he?' Jonet sat back on her heels, the short fork poised for its attack on persistent oxalis. Hannah had nodded.

'What he wanted? Yes, he did.'

'I may have wanted to punish him on my own account, you know.'

'Don't be hard on yourself, Jonet,' Hannah said as she moved her kneeling pad further along the bed. 'I'm sure you knew in your heart that none of it was Laurie's fault . . .'

Jonet hesitated. 'Certainly he didn't ask to be born.'

Then she had looked across at Hannah, kneeling by a clump of heart's-ease. 'Liza didn't ask to be born either.'

'No.' Hannah met her gaze. 'Liza was down to me. I pick up that tab.'

'It was a mistake,' Jonet said heavily. 'You made a mistake, didn't you? Then I made another.'

'*Liza* was a mistake; yes. But I did not want to make a second, more terrible one. Do you see that?'

'I do now. I'm sorry, Mother . . .'

Liza's year was busy and triumphant, her path taking her far from family concerns, from the tranquillity of life in Wales. She made a film which was a departure into romantic, zany comedy and scored a hit with its delicious sureness of touch. 'Not certain if she needed to be slapped or cuddled, but I could not get enough of Liza Vaughan,' voted one critic, smacking his lips. And 'There's that about Liza Vaughan that rivets attention, set apart from her beauty.' Her unusual portrayal of a solicitor in a three-part TV thriller – 'turned out to be a triumph of casting' – and she played Desdemona in a stunning production of *Othello* for BBC TV. Watching that, Hannah recalled her Desdemona of RADA days, and saw how Liza had matured. This Desdemona was a strong, sensual woman, driven by physical passion for the black beautiful Moor, but displaying a piercingly moving dignity in her submission to him. Her voice took on an untypical bell-like clarity for the role . . . 'It echoed round the head into the small hours,' read one review, and Hannah found that to be true.

Liza, though, was demonstrating change in other ways than by a mature, gloriously spoken Desdemona. The crippling of Edward Anderssen had been a watershed. She had no doubt that she personally had been responsible for the rock-fall that had left him helpless in a wheelchair. 'Thought, if sufficiently forceful, can become matter' . . . So her thoughts had become rocks, which had dislodged other rocks to become a landslip, bringing to pass the ill-luck she had wished upon Anderssen. Knowing in her heart she was treading dangerous ground, she sensed even so that normal standards of behaviour need not apply to her.

Her sense of power grew, as with each performance she proved her ability to claim total audience attention. A unique 'listening' quality to her stillness, on stage or before camera, centred minds upon her and her alone, no matter how illustrious the company surrounding her. With the increased awareness of her gifts, Liza became more egocentric and less concerned with others' needs, problems or desires. This rebounded both on those with whom she worked, and on her close family. Jess was dispatched into the care of Lucy whenever she showed signs of disturbing Liza's plans, and Carl's business difficulties impinged on her now only when they prevented him being where he should be for her own comfort and enjoyment. In her work, she took to behaving as she wished, regardless of the difficulties in which she might land her colleagues. What was important for Liza was only Liza.

When she signed in late autumn for the following season with the Royal Shakespeare Company at Stratford, her sole concern was for the lustre it would bring to her career, with the offer of Rosalind in *As You Like It* and Katherina in *The Taming of the Shrew*.

'But we agreed some time back you would not work again through August,' Carl, furious, remonstrated. Liza shrugged her shoulders.

'Darling, Stratford is different. Audiences come from the four corners every summer – I shall get the best possible exposure in the classiest set-up. I'll take a house there and you and Jess can join me – the countryside is wonderful. And I'll have lots of days free once we're into the schedule.'

Carl shook his head, the blue eyes cold; he too was used to getting his own way. 'Thanks, but no. I'll take Jess to Long Island. We'll find better things to do there than get stuck in a time-warp in ye olde Bard's home town.'

'Carl – you're *not* to do that! I want her *here* in August – I've scarcely seen her for months now she's started school!' They glared at one another, neither powerful will prepared to bend to the other's.

That round was won by Carl. He came over for two weeks at Easter and saw both performances. The productions had corners to rub down and parts would develop over the weeks, but the reviews were encouraging. Six-year-old Jess, with Lucy, stayed at Liza's Stratford house through the school holidays and Carl took her – on promise of good behaviour – to the matinée of *As You Like It*. Jess was transfixed, scarcely moving a muscle . . . When Liza spoke Rosalind's epilogue, standing motionless with hands clasped quietly before her and her rich hair braided with flowers, Jess almost ceased to breathe. The small girl fixed her slate-grey, shimmering eyes on her mother's face, and listened with her heart.

> '. . . And, I am sure,
> as many as have good beards, or good faces,
> or sweet breaths, will, for my kind offer,
> when I make curtsy, bid me farewell.'

Liza curtsied, turned, light and full of grace, and

walked with smooth paces into the wings. The curtain came down; but before applause thundered out there was a momentary silence, as though none there wished to break the spell cast by the Forest of Arden, and by a magical Rosalind.

Carl looked at Jess as his daughter collapsed in a welter of sobs. He picked her up and carried her backstage, where the three of them laughed and cried together. That night, Carl and Liza had a quiet supper together after the performance then went to bed, attuned again, to make love. Carl knew he had no wish to break the silken web of the spell with which she bound him, and Liza had no wish to release him. When August came, with three other plays newly in the repertoire she found she had eight whole days without a performance and flew out to join him and Jess in Long Island.

That summer, Carl was forced to curtail his trips to London because of an increasingly turbulent situation at Cline Investments. To strengthen his own hand after Belman had blocked his intention to continue funding Tasman Wilkins, he had suggested to two institutional holders of Cline Investments stock who were personal friends that they should seek representation on the board. This ploy had worked in that the board now numbered nine, the two new members nominally appointed by Carl. He reasoned that now it would be harder for Belman to unseat him which was, he knew, the eventual aim.

His elevation of Earle Curtis with a bribe was backfiring, for Curtis was now providing a filter through which all Carl's decisions were channelled. This was not only frustrating, but dangerous. Because of the amount of time devoted to Liza rather than to the business, he could not search out and then manipulate deals as he had in earlier years. He still had gut feelings regarding certain moves he could make; but how to quantify these against Curtis's number-crunching department? As a consequence, relations between Carl and Curtis were souring fast. Curtis was now too powerful to be easily disposed of . . . and as Carl's core method of dealing was to have the final say, his frustration mounted.

Joe and Sal, with seventeen-year-old Thomas, came to Britain in August. Liza had invited them to make use of the Holland Park house while in London as she would be in either Stratford or Long Island; they spent a few days there then drove down to Bracken House, for Joe had made a decision.

'I'm sixty-eight next month,' he told Hannah and Matthew as they sat over their coffee the first evening. Matthew smiled wryly.

'Lucky old you. I'm going on seventy-nine!'

'And well you might remember that next time you clear out your pond.' Hannah's tone was brisk but her eyes smiled, and she briefly touched his hand. Matthew had an aspect of frailty some days that concerned her more than a little . . . his tall spare frame bent into a strong sou'westerly looked as if it might just snap. There was little she could do but watch him like a hawk while appearing not to, and encourage him to paint and potter rather than navvy over favourite garden projects.

'Shall I begin again?' Joe asked patiently. 'OK – I'm sixty-eight next month and I want to retire out of New York and into Wales.'

'Joe . . . that is wonderful!' Hannah gave him a radiant smile, which time had dimmed not one whit. Joe smiled back. Over fifty years since he had lived in

Wales . . . still, he felt it to be his place. He caught Sal's eye, and she was smiling too; he had needed to be certain this was right for her, and for young Thomas.

'We shall be near to my own country,' she had told him when they had first discussed the possibility. 'We can go to Poland once we have time to travel . . . I will show you where I was born. Oh Joe; it will be good. My people all were killed . . . now I shall belong to *your* people. That will satisfy me well.'

Thomas too had been enthusiastic. 'If I want to study forestry I'd as soon do it in the UK. A Yank will make it good with all those English chicks, eh?' He had grinned at his parents; an open-faced, friendly boy with Sal's merry eyes and Joe's clarity of reasoning. Thomas had long had an affinity with all things green and the summit of his ambition at present was not to make a million, but be warden to an area of historic woodland. Paul Harry had different dreams, which included a job at Christie's or Sotheby's after obtaining his degree in English and History of Art . . . and if he discovered an Old Master and made a packet at the same time, all to the good.

'So, what had you in mind?' Matthew poured more coffee. 'We have Flo and Tom in Porthcawl, Laurie a few miles off in his nursery, and Jonet in rather a nice ground-floor garden flat in Cardiff. I'm trying to persuade Nick to move back from boring old Italy; and Jake may well execute a sideways move to Swansea, he's become unhealthily addicted to marine engineering. Weird, for a professor of mathematics . . .'

'We're not pinned down to any one spot, are we Sal? Not too far from the coast perhaps. Or the mountains! We'll tour round for a week anyway – call in on agents, look around a few properties. We've become quite fond of mountain walking – just the lower slopes, you know – since that vacation in Oregon.'

'Does it help your heart problem – walking?' Hannah asked. She rarely enquired after Joe's health; she would know surely, if there was a deterioration.

Sal said happily: 'We do not hear of a heart problem for some years now, Hannah. He did have pain on that very trip to Oregon, now you speak of it. After that – nothing.' She waved her hand in an expressive gesture. 'Now we thank God, and have thrown away the medication. He looks well, does he not?'

'He does indeed.' Hannah smiled at Joe again. 'We thank God too.'

Liza had a severe attack of pleurisy in November, and Carl decided she must soak up some sun over Christmas, before filming Bergman's *Hedda Gabler* for BBC TV. They flew to Bermuda directly she had medical clearance, leaving Jess and Lucy in Holland Park with Hannah and Matthew. Jess was playing Mary in her school Nativity play; afterwards, they would spend a family Christmas in Wales, bringing Jess back for start of term at the American School in Kensington, and for her parents' return from the Caribbean.

Watching her in the final small tableau, in a long blue dress and white wimple, the doll representing her Babe cradled in her arms, Hannah had a strong sense of *déjà vu*. Yet Jess at just seven did not bear a particular resemblance to Liza. Her hair had turned from copper at birth to a fine, gently waving acorn brown as Hannah's had been; her eyes not aquamarine but a dreamy, translucent grey. She actually resembled Hannah as a child quite strongly, as Florence had pointed out. She had a delicate build, small-boned, and her almost transparent skin took on the pallor of a medieval portrait when she was cold. Neither did she resemble her mother in character – nor for that matter the wilful, manipulative child that Carl had been. Her nature was quieter, more reflective than either of her parents', and she would happily play alone, talking to herself as small dramas were acted out with dolls, soft toys, or sometimes bits of coloured paper or pretty pebbles. Then, watching this small granddaughter, Hannah would remember her own childhood . . . sitting on the rag mat before the fire in Water Street, talking quietly . . . not to herself, but to Dorothea, her spirit friend.

Hannah had begun to observe Jess more closely of late, for a strange certainty had come to her of the child's resemblance to other aspects of herself. She had spent autumn half-term at Bracken House, in gentle October weather that had been a joy. Taken for her first sight of the steelworks and harbour, she had been speechless with awe. The massive shapes, the chimneys throwing flames high in the air, the giant hoists and cranes . . . all had bewitched her with their unfamiliar power. In simple words, Hannah had told Jess something of her own childhood days here; how it had been then. Jess had sat with rapt attention, luminous eyes fixed on Hannah's face, silent but for an occasional question.

'And did you like that, Grandma?'

'So what did your dada say then?'

'Has Uncle Joe any of those pebbles left now?'

When they reached home again, Hannah took out the pebble Joe had given her on her thirteenth birthday, and showed it to Jess. She had picked it from Hannah's palm with her small fingers, and laid it on her own, curling her hand about it. After a moment she looked up, her face serious.

'It talks to me, Grandma. They're not words exactly . . . but it's a *kind* of talking.' She had unfolded her fingers then and the pebble had glowed softly against her small pink palm. 'How beautiful . . . beautiful.'

Then, for no reason she knew, Hannah had reached down her most valued possession from the top wardrobe shelf. Together, she and Jess had sat on the carpet and unwrapped from its soft cloth the bugle given Hannah by her father before he went into the army in 1916.

'How do you like that, sweetheart? Is that not beautiful too?'

Jess had lifted the instrument slowly, with gentle exploratory fingers. She balanced it in her hands, and her eyes glowed with pleasure.

'It is so lovely, Gran . . .'

'It was my dada's, Jess.'

'Yes.' Jess had lowered the bugle, shining with honourable age, back on to its cloth, then looked up. 'May I play it one day?'

'You may, dear. And it will sing the sweetest song for you.'

All this Hannah recalled as she applauded the children standing in a self-conscious row in their draped tablecloths, sandals and painted cardboard crowns, holding gifts for the Babe, or shepherds' crooks, or lanterns. She watched Liza's child, holding the close-wrapped doll in the crook of her arm, and she began to feel that the gift, the inheritance, might well have passed to her.

In early March 1978 Joe heard of a good house not far from the Mumbles, west of Swansea, just on the market. Hannah and Matthew went to look and voted it worth a trip over before it was snapped up as a holiday home. Another option appeared after he had booked a flight for himself and Sal, and this was special ... one of the houses in the small village of Merthyr Mawr across the river from Bracken House. When Joe and Sal saw that, they were lost. 'Perfect for our antiques,' was Joe's verdict, 'and perfect for *everything*,' Sal added. Only a mile from the main road which connected with the new motorway, yet with a footpath through trees in the direction of the sea to reach Merthyr Mawr dunes, stretching on to the coast ... 'Perfect,' Joe said again. 'Perfect,' echoed Tom, for Joe could reach his Porthcawl bungalow in maybe ten minutes.

Hannah was deeply content. She and Joe had been apart so much of their lives, and finally, unbelievably almost, he was coming home. Now all was bustle and organisation – young Thomas began a round of applications to British universities offering degrees in forestry, and tackled his final months in high school with enthusiastic effort. Marek and Gus prepared to take over the reins of Joe's business and Paul Harry, in the middle of his own degree course, wished them all well and said he would see them after his spring term ended. Joe put his New York home on the market and helped Paul Harry find a small place near Marek, with both Alex and Carl promising to keep an eye out for him.

Liza had come back fit from the Caribbean, to film a difficult but satisfying *Hedda Gabler*. She then went directly into a new production of Coward's *Hay Fever* at the Aldwych; not this time to play the Jackie Coryton part as at Birmingham Rep, but to take on the more challenging personality of Judith Bliss. The contract was for three months; Liza could earn more money by doing another film, or a range of television work, but the truth was that she was increasingly drawn to a live audience. The power, the control she could exercise over hundreds of strangers was addictive . . . a movement, an inflection of the voice, a moment of complete stillness or a pause between phrases could coax a reaction from these people she never had met and never would meet. It was heady, dangerous excitement, and Liza loved it. So much so, that when offered the part of Sally Bowles in *Cabaret*, she had not hesitated. A musical . . . new fields to conquer. It would be hard work, singing, dancing six days a week, and the company was insisting on a six-month option. Was it what she really wanted? It must have been, because Liza began rehearsals while still in *Hay Fever*, and only broke off at the start of May for ten days on Long Island with Carl.

Four days into her stay she had still not told Carl about *Cabaret*. He had not objected to the *Hay Fever* run, though his trips over at weekends had not been as regular as previously. All his energies were focused on securing new opportunities for Cline Investments, and a telex machine was installed in his study on the first floor of their light, attractive Long Island house. This buzzed away at intervals, spewing out messages which Carl would rip off and scrutinise. He spent hours on the telephone, and company reports were minutely examined. He carried a pad on which he constantly made notes.

'Sorry about all this –' he pulled a wry face, rejoining her at the poolside after another protracted absence. 'I could tell you what's happening, honey, if you're interested.'

'Oh . . .' She turned her face away, stretching on the lounger under sun just comfortably strong. 'I wouldn't understand, darling, you know I'm stupid about these things. It is a shame though, that when I come all this way for a little time together, you're in such a twist.' She closed her eyes. Carl watched her for a while, in two minds over whether to explain his predicament anyway, then shrugged, folded back the *Wall Street Journal* and made some more notes.

She waited until the last day before telling him about *Cabaret*. 'I *know* long runs are not good things as a rule, darling. But I've not attempted a musical so far. Noel's a great producer, if I can succeed with anyone it will be with Noel. And it has such a great feeling about it . . . I just *know* it's right for me.'

'That's OK then. If it's right for you.' Carl's back was to her now; his voice thin and uninvolved. 'Which flight are you leaving on tomorrow? It will be a while before I can get over myself . . . I'll have to phone . . .'

Jess spent May half-term at Bracken House. *Cabaret* was close to opening. Liza had neither sung nor danced since RADA and had undergone hours of extra coaching; she was now honing her performance for the dress rehearsal. Carl had finally decided that a suitable hotel group would offer the best potential for a deal, had followed one trail in Virginia but had reached a dead end. A second possibility took him to Las Vegas, but after weeks of checking and rechecking he was forced to concede that was a non-starter also. Family was for the moment not on his agenda, which was now professional survival.

Jess loved being at Bracken House. She adored her grandmother, and of course Matthew, whose charm for children did not dim with age. She enjoyed the walks at Ogmore, over downs that ran down to the rocks and sea, and on the bay at Dunravon a mile along the coast. She went to see the pretty thatched house Uncle Joe and Aunt Sal had bought, and walked across the stepping-stones over the river by the ruins of Ogmore Castle. To go to the Merthyr Mawr dunes was another treat . . . she would climb laboriously to the top of one, stand poised for a second, arms outflung, before throwing herself down, tumbling over and over like a small clown and shrieking with pleasure. She would bring back sand in polythene bags, which Hannah tipped on to a big tin tray for her. Then she would retreat into a world of her own and bother no one. With modelling clay, she would make huts and thatch them with a mixture of hay and sheep's wool gathered from barbed-wire fences. She would model small people to sit by the huts, and animals, and would build a fence around the compound with twigs. Or she might make a sand garden with shells gathered from the beach, and dried flowers and grasses. She would also talk to herself. Only sometimes, watching her, Hannah could not be certain if it was to herself or to a person invisible to anyone but Jess that she talked.

To visit Laurie, Primrose and Ben was another treat. Laurie and Primrose were perfect for her – informal, friendly, courteous in making time to answer her questions no matter how busy. They allowed her to 'help' with pricking out and planting, and showed her how to pick peas and beans without damaging the plants. She was able to take a bunch of blue borage flowers from the patch where the plant grew in profusion, to be cut down later for green mulch, and pull rhubarb to make rhubarb and ginger jam. Most of all she loved to play with fat little Ben, wheeling him up and down in a barrow with screams of delight, romping with him on the patch of grass before the cottage, showing him his picture books. With this small family, Jess established a rapport that would become a comforting permanency in her life.

On the last day before going back to London, Jess went with Hannah at her own request to Taibach, to see the great tidal harbour and steelworks again. There was little left now of the beach where Hannah and Joe had played as children; industry had encroached there, and across the *morfa* where they had picked wildflowers, and wynberries dripping with dark juice. Hannah shaded her eyes against the sun, searching for the spot where the *Amazon* had at one time lain. Its disintegrating ribs had stared naked at her . . . But worse had been the shadowy figures of mariners drowned in her, moving aimlessly over the bare timbers. Hannah had known, by what she saw on the *Amazon*, that she was different, for none of her companions saw the figures. Finally she had asked Dada, and he had said that yes, she was different; so was her great-grandmother, and other Hywels before her, and he stressed that she was not to be afraid. Second sight was a gift from God, and Hannah must accept it.

Now she moved as close as she could to the place where the *Amazon* had last rested, holding Jess's hand. She saw the girl focus on the spot; stiffen, then look up to meet Hannah's eyes with a questioning frown.

'What is it, Gran? Something . . . I don't know. But I feel –' she gave a self-conscious smile – 'I think I can see little shapes . . . yet not *quite* . . .'

Hannah bent to hug her. 'Darling Jess – it's nothing in the least to worry about. When I was small I saw them too, right here. I see them now. You and I share a special gift, you see . . . sometimes we can see things, people, extra to what most see. I rather thought you might have the gift too.'

'Really?' Jess frowned. 'Is that all right, Gran?'

Hannah told her gently: 'It's perfectly all right, sweetheart. We simply have the ability to see memories.'

They began to make their way back to the car. Hannah felt apprehensive, knowing finally how it was. It would be up to her to help Jess now, so there would be no fear, but acceptance of a natural state. As Dada had helped *her*. Easier though, if Jess had not been – like her?

'Did you have a special friend too, Gran? Who would sit on your bed sometimes?'

'Oh yes. I called her Dorothea. What is your friend's name?'

'I call her Daisy,' Jess confided. 'But you'll keep her a secret, won't you?'

'Yes, sweetheart . . . I'll certainly do that.'

By August, Carl had exhausted his hopes of finding a suitable candidate for Cline Investments in the North American hotel and catering scene. He had sent for information from a London-based analyst and as a result had focused on Willow Hotels, a chain of large hotels in central and greater London. He considered the share price low for so much potential . . . his fingers began to tingle, for he sensed that he had viewed his target. The next step would be to have it four-square in his sights, and to this end he flew into Heathrow. Willow Hotels was the most promising project he had turned up in the whole grim year, and his feeling about it was strong.

Liza was making a great success of her part in *Cabaret*. Her voice was not that of a professionally trained singer, but it did not need to be. It had exactly the whisky-and-cigarettes huskiness to capture the ambience of between-the-wars Berlin lowlife and night-club culture. With her long curvy legs encased in black fishnets, a top hat set at a naughty angle on her copper curls and brilliantly provocative eyes roving over the audience, Liza played them like fish on a line. Sometimes her voice sank to a smoky whisper, at others rose to a harsh, throbbing siren call . . . whichever way she played it, Liza was in control. Her dancing was a sinuous, seamless undulation of movement; a careless leg flung high over the chair, black patent toes pointing the way, all was wonderful theatre.

She was on a high, professionally. She could not put a foot wrong. With her thirty-third birthday now behind her, Liza took on a lustre rarely seen in the theatre; her beauty came to glorious maturity with the confidence given her by this success.

'Darling – welcome!' She kissed Carl enthusiastically when he arrived at dawn, rousing her from sleep. Carl's spirit was willing to respond but his body would not hear of it. After a few affectionate strokes and pats he subsided into slumber so profound that even Jess, creeping in to see if he had arrived as promised, could not arouse him. He slept till noon, spent the afternoon on the telephone, then saw *Cabaret*. He was immensely proud to be the husband of this scintillating woman casting her magic over the whole theatre. She was trouble, but so was anything worth having. They had a somewhat hilarious supper party afterwards, with Liza – and three other members of the cast – still full of post-performance adrenalin. The table sparkled and fizzed for over two hours, until ground level was gradually attained and taxis summoned. Even then Liza was too high to sleep, and they made love with creative imagination until just before dawn.

Things changed after that. Liza would rise at around ten and drift down in a wrap to find a meeting in progress in the drawing room, study, conservatory, terrace . . . wherever, it seemed, Liza herself had thought *she* would like to be at that moment. Strange men in suits, usually smoking, and invariably drinking quantities of coffee, spread themselves over unnecessarily large areas of her home to confer with Carl. The phone rang often, usually for Carl, occasionally for another member of the coffee party. Mrs Roberts developed an uncharacteristically stressed expression and even Jess looked mutinous when asked to 'go play in the garden like a good girl'.

'We'll have lunch out tomorrow, darling,' Liza told him on the fourth evening when he came in late from a meeting at the Savoy. 'Then we could go on to Harrods. It's ages since you last went shopping with me.'

'Not tomorrow, honey.' Carl looked up from a load of phone messages. 'I've another meeting – sorry.'

'At *my* house?' asked Liza pointedly. 'When is this place going to become more a private residence again and less a coffee bar on Paddington Station? Would you like to install some Muzak for the clients? Or maybe the odd call-girl waiting upstairs in case they need something a little extra to coffee and smokes?'

'Don't be unpleasant, Liza.' Carl sounded tired. 'I've had one helluva day, and I've another coming along in a few hours. I'm trying to do business to our mutual advantage and if it's no picnic for you it's hell for me. I just have to get this right.'

'Well maybe you should hire a suite or something, rather than disrupt my home. I've a job to do too, you know – and I need a modicum of tranquillity when I'm not in the theatre. If you weren't coming over to see me and Jess, you should have said. I'd made plans for us,' she added, playing for sympathy now.

The ruse failed; Carl sat down to study the latest market news in the *Evening Standard*. The following Sunday morning, Liza drove with Jess to Bracken House, returning in time for the theatre on Monday evening, having left her daughter with Hannah for a couple of weeks.

In early October, Carl flew back to New York with every scrap of information he believed necessary to convince his board that Willow Hotels was for them. He had spent a day and a night in each hotel, making copious notes on how it might be transformed for success with the minimum outlay. The asset value of Willow Hotels, he judged, was not reflected in the share price and the potential was there for a vastly improved performance. He lay back and sipped a glass of champagne, smiling a little, content . . . this had to be the deal with which he would wrest back control of Cline Investments; re-establish the reputation of Lucky Carl Cline. He broke into an outright grin – about time too, now he was an old guy gone into his forties!

He strode into the board meeting with confidence undiminished, even after a sticky session with Earle Curtis the day before.

'I know how we can pick up 20 per cent of Willow shares at a discount,' he had told Earle. 'Twenty would get me on the board – and I can tell you it's a sure-fire situation back there in London. I've found nothing so good here all year, and God knows I've looked hard enough.'

He stared at Curtis's hard square face, and was suddenly, bitterly angry. Hell – why did he have to justify himself to this ass-head? Curtis should be having to justify his mega-salary to *him*! He lit a cigarette to give himself a moment to steady down; an angry man can misjudge his opponent.

'Look, Earle; we have to move right now on this, I can't keep the lid on it while you take a month to go through the numbers. The managing director is a ball of fire, it's the rest of the board who've been fouling up the nest, family in-fighting, all that crap. But as I say – speed is of the essence now; I know another hotel group is looking at the situation.'

Earle's face was closed and stubborn. 'We've already got together a big proposition that fits neatly into our portfolio, Carl. We can't –'

'*Portfolio*!' Carl was on his feet, eyes hot with deepening frustration. 'For Christ's sake; its not a mutual fund we're running here, man! We're entrepreneurs! You know, Earle, the trouble with you is you think like a bloody accountant – no wonder our share price is stagnant –'

Curtis's face coloured to a dull red and his cold eyes become colder. 'Well, you're in the chair. The board will have to decide. Certainly we can't go ahead with both deals.'

Carl had miscalculated. The efforts of Earle's department, while not producing the spectacular results achieved by Carl in his heyday, were none the less giving Cline Investments a blue-chip, if dull rating. In striving to put together a once-for-all deal this year, Carl had not picked up the change of mood of the board. But on the issue of Willow Hotels he had firmly nailed his colours to the mast and must not – could not – retreat.

All board members were present, and Belman's

eyes were bright with malice. Curtis was the first to lay out his position, with quantified growth graphs, estimated returns for the first five years . . . an immaculate presentation by a careful man who allowed no element of risk. Carl took a long breath and opened his own briefcase.

He had a deal of material on London hotel occupancy rates, growth of tourism – all good convincing stuff. He had, however, no solid estimates for refurbishment to four-star standard, nor estimates for loss of revenue during work in progress. And one of his own nominees looked worried.

'I don't have a good feeling about London, Carl. Every time the IRA plants another bomb tourists stay away in droves. What are the insurance rates against loss of revenue?'

'I can tell you why he wants to get to London.' Belman smirked. 'What better way to keep his airline bill down?'

Carl ignored him. 'I started Cline Investments as an entrepreneurial business,' he said carefully. 'I brought it to the market, and some of you made a great deal of money out of it.' He looked at Arney Bold, who coughed.

'I see now that was all a mistake. I should have kept things under my own control, not floated it. But I felt I needed to make a quick return for those friends who had, at the start, the faith to support me with their own funds.' Again, a look in Arney's direction.

'Over the past couple of years I have located some first-rate propositions for us, only to have them talked out by Earle. I told him yesterday that he's turning this organisation into nothing more than a mutual fund. And that is not what it is supposed to be.'

Carl paused, looking either side of the table. An ice-cold calm had frozen his body so that not a muscle moved. It was crunch time; he knew it and met it head on.

'This deal is as good as any that could possibly be made.' He spoke slowly and forcefully now. 'I have complete faith in it . . . so much so that I am prepared to make it an issue of confidence. If the board turn this deal down, nothing I can do is viable. Therefore, if you do not go along with my present proposition I will have no option but to resign.'

'I move we accept what the chair says and put his deal to the vote right away,' said Belman, his voice shaking with excitement.

'I second that,' said his yes-man, who was sweating freely.

There was silence for a few moments. Events were moving faster than most were prepared for, or wished for.

'Go on then, put it to the vote.' Belman grinned. He too was sweating, and made no attempt to conceal his pleasure.

'The market won't like Carl leaving.' This was Arney, finally mustering the courage to look up from his papers.

'That's a matter of opinion.' Belman's eyes gleamed in anticipation.

'Perhaps we should take a break and think about all this.' One of Carl's placemen attempted to bring calm to the proceedings, which had clearly bolted out of control. Carl raised a hand, shaking his head with complete resolution.

'No. You all know now as much as you're ever going to know.' His voice was rock hard, as was his face. 'We'll do it now. All those in favour of going ahead with my deal?'

Arney's hand went up, followed by one of the institutional representatives. Carl looked each other member in the face. All averted their eyes, except Belman, who looked directly at him, his face a triumphant mask. No other hand was raised.

'OK, J. Arthur. It's taken some time, but I guess you've finally got your own back.' Carl pushed back his chair, picked up his briefcase and left the room in complete silence without a backward glance.

Could he have stayed there, he would shortly have seen Earle Curtis installed in his place as president of Cline Investments.

Chapter Twenty-three

October 1978

Carl flew back into Heathrow on the last Saturday of October. He had been holed up in his Manhattan apartment for four days. Although almost constantly on the telephone, he had during that time done a great deal of thinking. His mind had gradually cleared of choleric frustration, damaged pride and thoughts of vengeance. An eye for an eye, tooth for a tooth, had been extremely important to him at twenty-one. At forty-one, Carl needed to use his grey cells to more productive ends. It seemed, now, to be poetic justice for old Belman to have ousted him from his own firm, his personal baby. He had, after all, seduced Belman's daughter to take vengeance for Belman's cheating on his father over an important tender. Now Belman had evened the score.

The important thing he must work on was how to survive, and Carl was strong on that. The shares of Cline Investments had edged up on the news of his removal. That had wounded Carl's ego until he rationalised it . . . Wall Street had long been cognisant of boardroom warfare at Cline's. Now it was logical to expect that things would settle down and that there should be a gradual performance improvement with the coming of peace.

The share rise was a plus for him, of course. The value of his stake in Cline's would be higher, a bandage to his hurt ego. Carl had now to formulate how best to liquidate his holding in good order. While in New York he had taken the decision to bid for his own place on the board of Willow Hotels. To achieve this he had borrowed from a more readily available block of Liza's funds. There had been no time to consult her; he must gamble on being able to replace quite soon the million dollars needed to buy into the hotel group. He remained confident that his hunch about Willow was spot on, and that they would bring forth gold. And this way, though a risk, at least his share would be larger.

Realising this spell away would probably be a long one, his father had driven him to Kennedy Airport. Alex could be depended upon to look after his affairs. They had always been close, and would miss their regular contact and the easy relationship existing between them.

Carl chewed thoughtfully through his dinner, washed down by champagne, the only drink he would touch in flight. Liza would be pleased to learn that he would be basing himself in London for the foreseeable future. They would have a steadier life, an improvement perhaps on recent ups and downs. And he would see more of Jess, bless her. Food finished, Carl stretched out for a nap . . . thank God there'd also be less flying.

He was desperately tired on reaching Holland Park. His deliberate buoying up of future prospects had evaporated, to be followed by a deep low. The night was a vile one, heavy rain and gusting high winds – 'the first autumn gale of the year' the aircraft captain had advised before landing, and by the time he let himself into the house Carl had slipped back into a slight depression. He had made a pretty good job of scraping himself off the floor this last week, but it had all been something of an effort, and he had not been able to sleep or even relax on the flight.

There was a note scribbled by Liza propped up against the whisky decanter. 'Be in soon as poss, but it's *Last Night*! Do come along if you're able. Mrs Roberts off with flu, Jess in Wales till tomorrow (half-term). See you – L.'

Christ, he'd forgotten *Cabaret* closed tonight. No idea what was lined up next . . . his own affairs had for once taken precedence over Liza's. Carrying a generous tumbler of whisky Carl went slowly upstairs, his legs like lead now. A shower, a shave then to bed – God knows when Liza would extricate herself from the end-of-run knees-up but there was no way he would join her this time – he could only put a damper on the fun. A bath . . . he wanted a long, hot bath. Last night's evening paper was folded on Liza's bedside table and Carl took that through with the drink, shaved, then eased himself into deep foaming water.

He lay for a few minutes, savouring the quiet, the blessed peace, the coming reunion. They could go together to fetch Jess tomorrow, the damn gale would have blown itself out by then. He would tell her what had happened with Belman on the way down to Wales and hope, then, that she would understand his problems of the last months. A modicum of support would not come amiss. Carl sighed, reached for the paper and turned to the financial section . . . first things first. Afterwards he leafed through the other pages, finishing his whisky.

> Liza Vaughan, about to end her triumphant run in *Cabaret* at the Apollo, has been intriguing us this past month with the identity of her late-night supper companion. This diary can now reveal all. The dark

and handsome escort is her stepbrother, Professor Jake Stourton of Southampton University, currently on loan to the Ministry of Defence while working out the shape of ships to come. The glamorous Liza may well be comforting Professor Stourton on the recent quitting of the family home by his wife Rose, taking with her their children Ruth and Matt.

Carl lay for some time in the bath, staring at the gossip column. Then he dropped the paper to the floor and began to soap himself.

It was 12.40 when he heard Liza's key in the door, her foot on the stairs. He had on his pyjamas and robe and was in the easy chair in their bedroom, studying some papers and making notes.

'Darling –' Liza held out her arms, laughing. She had on a black, heavy silk lounging suit with an aubergine silk polo-neck underneath. Her face was flushed and her eyes brilliant, and the glorious hair tumbled about her shoulders, damp where she had run from the taxi. She looked extremely desirable, so full of life that it was almost an affront to the tired, jaded man observing her. She came to embrace him now and her fragrant hair fell across his cheek.

Unsmiling, Carl reached for the newspaper and handed it to her, folded at the piece he had read. Liza took it, and after a glance tossed it into the waste basket.

'Carl – really! How *can* you bother yourself with such twaddle! Why didn't you come to the theatre? Was *that* the reason?' – throwing a disdainful hand towards the paper.

'As a matter of fact, no. I was simply too tired. Maybe it was just as well though – was Jake at the party, or does he only enjoy *tête-à-têtes*?'

'I've told you – that's gossip column guff.' Liza frowned. 'My God, what a welcome home ... I'm sorry you came if all you can do is make ridiculous assumptions from some trash diarist.'

'*Is* it ridiculous?' he flared suddenly, too angry and too weary to care. 'Or is it *true*?'

'It is if you simply read the *words* –'

'Well *they're* what I've just read,' he snarled. 'And a few thousand others too. What will your adoring public make of their idol now, turning out to be just another whore? Quite an image-denter, I'd have thought.'

Liza's face turned to a stone-carved, ice-cold mask of fury, from which her magnificent eyes blazed. 'Take back that word.' She swung back her arm and smacked him hard across the face. 'Take it back.'

Carl stepped back a pace, rocked by the blow. He said quietly. 'If the cap fits ...'

'You wouldn't be interested in the truth if it jumped on you, so I shan't waste good breath.'

He took her shoulders in a painful grip, and for a moment saw fear in her eyes. 'You've never been anything but trouble, have you? You've wrecked my business, wrecked my life – but *this* is one aspect neither of us had troubled about before. Strange ... I never really expected you to lie back and open your legs for your stepbrother! Bored, were you? Thought it would be fun to wreck someone else's marriage?'

He released her suddenly and Liza, off balance, fell back on the bed. She regained her feet instantly and walked to the door, turning with a hand on the knob.

'You are pathetic.' Her voice was low and filled with contempt. Then she was gone. He heard her wrench open the front door, heard it slam. Moving to the window, Carl looked down to see her get into her car; the engine roared, and the vehicle shot away into the black night.

Liza turned on to the A4 and swerved into the forecourt of an all-night garage to fill up with petrol. She walked to the phone box a few yards on, then put in a ten-pence piece and dialled her mother's number.

'Mummy? . . . Yes, I'm fine – I'm terribly sorry to have dug you out from your beauty sleep. Look – I've just started down, is that OK? . . . Yes, it's a bit wet and blowy here too, but nothing too awful . . . No really, I'm fine, and I'll be careful, I promise. You go back to sleep, I'll let myself in and see you at breakfast, eh? There's the pips – 'bye now. Love you.'

She was wet, getting back into the car, but it did not seem to matter. She settled herself, switched on a tape of a Chopin piano concerto and set the nose of the powerful car due west. She would reach Bracken House in time to get at least a little sleep if nothing got in her way.

The traffic lights were unexpected. She was through them at red without noticing, but fortunately no other car was crossing her path. Must be careful though, the last thing she needed was a police siren howling after her. She took a few deep breaths and pushed her back hard into the seat; it ached a little with tension.

Quite a day. That bloody diary columnist had caused chaos, and not only with Carl; there'd been a call from Penelope and a number of snide remarks from the company. Liza automatically felt in the map compartment for a cigarette before remembering she no longer smoked. Hell. She roared into another garage and bought a pack, and a bar of chocolate. God knows why, she never ate it . . . she must feel the need for comfort food. Jess could have it tomorrow.

That had been a very ugly row. Unnecessary too. Rose had been going to leave him anyway . . . nothing to do with her, Jake had said that several times. He was quite sick about the children; he'd looked like death, telling her. He was a difficult man, yet could at times be charming. It had been a love–hate relationship for years, but she about had the measure of him now. Beautiful hands . . . very important, in a man.

Liza was driving fast, and very fast indeed on some stretches. She smoked three cigarettes and was going to light a fourth, but dropped the lighter as she snatched it from the facia. She was relieved about this as her mouth felt bad enough already, like a barn floor. She could do with a nice crisp apple. But in the middle of nowhere in the dead of night, apples were unlikely commodities.

She was at the Severn Bridge in no time, it seemed – this motorway certainly made a difference. The structure loomed huge, terrifyingly above her in the sodium lighting. The car, normally so reassuring in its solidity, now seemed no more than a fragile box, a toy to blow over into the estuary running deep and fast below. High-sided vehicles had been banned in the severe conditions obtaining . . . Liza had found the lighter at the toll plaza, and lit another cigarette because she was shaking after crossing the bridge.

Into Wales . . . better now. She was home. She frowned at that, then smiled; the first time she recalled thinking so. Mummy would be delighted to hear she thought of Wales as 'home' – was actually comforted by the idea. Maybe all this family roots nonsense had a grain of truth in it after all.

The road was quiet now save for the noisy lashing of the storm. Trees were stripped of their last leaves, they whirled like demented spirits before being beaten to the ground by the force of the rain. Branches, free of their summer burden, waved frantically in the beam of her headlights. At one point a tree had crashed across the road, a fearful tangle of timber. She was late seeing it and swerved violently, lucky to find room for the manoeuvre with small branches scraping the side of the car. Flattened corpses of hedgehogs and rabbits proliferated here, and a big dog fox freshly killed passed between her wheels. Liza's eyes blurred with fatigue and she punched buttons on her radio for something lively to buck her up.

Cardiff. Pay attention here; she gripped the steering wheel. How empty it all looked at this time in the morning . . . on this stormy night on the brink of winter, when everyone apparently slept but for Liza.

Not far now. She had been keeping Carl locked out of her mind, but now she allowed him in. He had behaved badly . . . but she did love him. She felt the anger, hugged closely for miles, seeping from her pores to leave her relaxed and boneless. She would phone him when she got to Bracken House – a quick call to say where she was, and that she would be back home tomorrow with Jess. They would smooth things over; they always had, because at heart, their desire was to stay married. They each knew there was no one else . . . he *must* know that, as she certainly did.

Liza pressed on now with a powerful sense of urgency; she badly needed to reach Bracken House, the danger of sleeping at the wheel worryingly real. She came to a downhill section she recognised and knew there was a river bridge at the bottom before a sharp left turn. Her headlights picked up the bridge and the boiling river. She negotiated the river but still at too high a speed and skewed the car awkwardly through the turn.

'Dear God –'

Straightening, Liza did not brake but sped on alongside the roaring waters, badly shaken. Vaguely aware of something in the driving mirror, she accelerated over the saturated road surface to draw away from it.

Still there. Her eyes almost impossibly heavy, she forced them to focus on the driving mirror. The glint was another pair of eyes. Expressionless, disembodied, they yet possessed an intensity that threatened to suck Liza into their fathomless depths.

Her body froze with fear so intense it stopped the breath in her throat. She stretched a hand through to the back, and touched a fold of heavy woollen cloth.

'No! Christ – not *you*!'

Liza twisted round to confront the shadow . . . dark glowing eyes in a narrow face; black, blowing hair. She screamed, a piercing, heart-stopping scream. Her foot jammed the accelerator to the floor. With steering unattended the car veered towards the river, as from high ground on the right, water poured across the road.

Frantic, Liza braked and wrenched the wheel to the right. The car careered sideways, spinning sickeningly. Its rear end smashed into a great tree that loomed from nowhere, catapulting the car over and over until it reached the flooding river in a ball of fire.

Liza had failed to digest an important factor in the research she had done for her play on the supernatural. Psychic matter created by strong desire will, if baleful, in the end return to its creator.

After the phone call Hannah had found it impossible to go back to sleep. She had lain still by Matthew's comfortable warmth, relaxing, thinking how good it would be to have both Jess and Liza here tomorrow if only for a few hours . . . what they would do if it was fine. No use; there was a disquiet in her that would not allow sleep.

Something – what? – had happened to decide Liza to rush down here, to make such a drive in these weather conditions. She lay now, listening to the gale battering Bracken House, and feared for any soul out in so distressful a night. The most likely scenario had to be a row with Carl, who had been expected tonight from New York. She had, it was true, had some reservations about Carl, but these had lessened over the years. What could have happened between them . . . it could equally have been an explosion from Liza and not down to Carl.

Hannah closed her eyes, but sleep evaded her. Her perceptions had alerted her a couple of times lately to a change for the worse in Liza. Difficult to pinpoint . . . but she sensed it might be to do with Liza's own powers, barely perceived by their owner and so possibly still lying dormant. Hannah knew well enough that power of any description may be corrupted; used for good, or evil. She could do nothing now but hope, for Liza had to take responsibility for her own actions.

After what seemed an eternity in the dark room she eased herself out of bed, trying not to disturb Matthew, who grunted and turned over. She settled herself on the living-room sofa with a rug, turned up the central heating and warmed milk to sip, hand folded about the cup for comfort. Only 2.30; no chance of Liza for two hours at least. She turned on the radio quietly for company and lay back against the cushions, unable to dispel her unease. Two hours . . .

She eventually dozed; then woke to shocking life.

Four-thirty. Some terrible event had taken place, a thing so dreadful that Hannah shook, and all her courage, which had carried her straight-backed through so many vicissitudes, deserted her.

With a moan she sank her head in her hands. At that moment a scream from Jess shattered the black quiet. Hannah hauled herself to her feet and made for the stairs, face drained of colour. Toiling upstairs, she looked her age for the first time in her life, bent and haggard with the anguish of knowing why Jess was screaming.

'Come, darling . . . Gran's here, don't be frightened now.'

She moved quickly across the room, to hold the small figure sitting stiffly upright, staring before her. Jess lay against her for a moment, vibrating, then asked in a whisper, 'Where's Mummy?'

Matthew put his head round the door, hair tousled and eyes heavy with sleep.

'Is there a problem?'

'I'm afraid so.' Hannah buried her face in Jess's hair, and the two clung together.

The half-submerged car was reported to the police soon after daylight. Matthew had phoned Carl, then the local constabulary, to give a description of the car and of Liza. Hannah was certain whatever had happened could not be far away. She was right; the car had plunged into the river about twelve miles from Bracken House.

Arrived impossibly quickly, Carl at first questioned the facts, face sharp with anger and eyes hostile. Only when he had been shown the car did reality pierce his guard and flood his anguished mind.

'Why did that happen?' He intoned the words like

a mantra, repeatedly. Hannah, herself stunned with grief, saw no point in responding, for Carl knew well enough there was no logic to such tragedies. Only when she had stayed with poor bewildered Jess, reading and singing softly until the child's eyes closed, and Carl had taken aboard sufficient whisky to climb the stairs to brief oblivion, did she cling for a moment in the warmth of Matthew's arms and ask on her own account, why . . .

Over a breakfast table where no one ate, Carl asked if Jess might stay there for a while. 'She is with those she loves, and who love her. This is the best place.' He looked at Hannah with eyes so full of pain that she touched his arm with a compassionate hand.

'It will help us too if she stays, Carl. You see to what has to be done, she will be safe.'

'I'll be back for the inquest.' His face worked then, and Hannah thought he might break down. 'I have to find a place in London for Jess and myself if this hotel deal works out; and there are so many things to be attended to. Thanks, Hannah.' He took her hand and gripped it tight. 'I'll ask the school to send some work down. It will be helpful if she is occupied, and not falling behind in class. Shall I ask Lucy to come?'

'No need; I have plenty of help for now – maybe Lucy can be of use to you up there.'

He was back in a week. Hannah stayed with Jess while Matthew and Carl went to the inquest in Bridgend. The police gave evidence that the car had swerved off the road in extremely hazardous driving conditions, the road at that point known to be covered with surface water after heavy rain. The car had crashed into a tree which had ruptured the fuel tank, and somersaulted in flames down the bank to the river, which was in flood that night. The doctor gave evidence that Liza had died immediately when her neck was broken by the impact of hitting the tree. The verdict was accidental death.

After Jess was in bed the three of them sat round the fire. There was a stunned, empty expression on Carl's face and he had aged five years. He looked at Hannah and wondered how she slept through the nights. The second daughter to be lost . . . She caught his eye, and signalled that if she could survive then so could he.

'I've found a house to rent for Jess and me and Lucy,' he said. 'Not far from her school – and with a decent garden for her. Things with Willow Hotels look hopeful and now I must realise my shares in my previous firm in good order. I'm acting as a consultant to them in the meanwhile, looking at refurbishment contractors.'

'Not quite the way you work as a rule, I understand.' Matthew passed him a tumbler of whisky and water.

'Thanks. No – my style was more freewheeling by half.' Carl's mouth stretched but failed to achieve a smile. 'I don't doubt the discipline will be good for me, though.'

'What will you do about the Holland Park house?' asked Hannah.

Carl's eyes glazed. 'Get as much as I can for it. Then create a trust fund for Jess. Added to what Liza was left by her father it will all amount to a very sizeable nest-egg. So, whether I sink or swim, Jess will be fine; what she has will be inviolate.'

He had made the vow that if he robbed for it, that inheritance *was* inviolate. Nothing would prevent the million dollars, now hers, being replaced with interest. Liza had trusted him to manage her fund –

their daughter's fund now – and that he would do.

'You'll swim, Carl. You must, for Jess. Money isn't enough, you know.'

Carl looked down at his hands, clasping the tumbler. 'Until now, I always thought it was.'

'And now?' Hannah prompted. He gave a tiny shrug.

'Oh . . . I guess this – what's happened – makes me see that it's the people in your life that are of greater value by far.' He coughed, embarrassed. After he had recovered he reached for his briefcase.

'Look; I'm not sure if you want to see this. But if you'd let me . . .' He pulled out a newspaper. 'This is why Liza ran down to you so fast that night. I exploded all over her, it was all my fault.'

He passed the paper to Hannah. She read it in silence then handed it to Matthew.

'I tore into her about this the moment she got in that night. I was flaked out, flat on the floor – just been kicked out of my business, faced with starting from scratch. This piece of copy seemed one thing I didn't need. And Liza walked straight into it – high as a kite on adrenalin from the last performance, the adulation, the lot. I cut her down like mowing a meadow and she wasn't looking for *that*. So we combusted. She –' He pulled himself up. 'That was the last time I saw her,' he said, very softly. She said something like "you're contemptible", and then she just walked out.'

'Carl –' He silenced her with a hand. His features were stone hard with misery.

'*My* fault, Hannah. Matthew, I don't know your Jake, but I'm real sorry if Liza broke up his marriage. Liza said the report was only crap mischief-making. I should have held my tongue; not pre-judged her. Had I not acted as I did, she would not have reacted as *she* did. And she would be here now.'

There was a silence. The three looked at one another, his words hanging in the air like foul smoke.

'Carl . . .' Hannah's voice was tentative with emotion. 'You have to look forward now, not back – not wallowing, not punishing yourself. Bring up Jess the very best you know how – we're all of us here to help – and *live yourself* the very best you know how. And we'll put *that* where it belongs.'

She screwed up the news-sheet fiercely and tossed it into the fire.

He left the next morning. The weather was calm now, crisp and pungent with autumn. There were leaves everywhere to be swept up, the garden to be put to bed for winter. Jess stood between Hannah and Matthew, and waved to Carl as he drove slowly away. She was sad, anxious and puzzled about what had happened to her mother. But it was not an irredeemable situation, Hannah could sense that. Her own sadness was different . . . but then, she was not rising eight.

'When I've seen to a couple of things, why don't we go to Laurie's to buy our wallflowers?' she suggested. 'Next spring the whole garden will be scented with them, and bright as spring gardens should be.'

They were almost ready when the phone rang and it was Joe. 'How're things now, Han? Pretty dreadful, I guess; we can't even take it in.'

'Well . . . we're through the night. Carl had to go, but I'm keeping Jess for now.'

'Sounds a good idea. We just thought you might like our bit of news. Some mail from the US today. And some surprise – one from Katy Ann in Oregon! We'd given up on her after all this time but she's come good, would you believe?'

'I scarcely would.' Hannah's eyes were on Jess, who was putting on her coat. 'Tell me, then.' Though she gave not a damn now for any news.

'Well, seems she's finally winkled out something from another cousin, who's been down in Texas for some years. She can say nothing concrete about what part of Wales the Hywels were from, only that it was south. But –' Joe paused for dramatic effect – 'she dropped out that her great-great-grandmother had been a healer of some renown.'

'Oh,' Hannah said weakly.

'She gained her reputation as a girl when her brother-in-law came home from the Civil War with a shattered arm and she got it working again. Seems she was acclaimed after that. So –'

'Thanks for telling me, Joe. Nothing proved, of course . . .'

'Not in black and white. But it seems pretty unlikely that *two* families of Hywels who could heal came from South Wales. Anyway, Han, think on it, eh? We'll be round to see you later, as promised.'

She cradled the phone: stared at Jess, who had just mastered the last coat button. For a moment she felt light-headed, and reached for the newel-post.

It had to be. Joe was right, the coincidence was too great; it had to be their own family.

'Gran?' Jess touched her sleeve. Han continued to stare at her, her mind a confused rag-bag of hopes, doubts, suppositions, fears. It seemed certain that Jess had inherited the gift of second sight, handed through the Hywels over generations. Now, if that had come through not only Liza, but Carl . . .

'Gran!' A firmer tug. 'We were going to Laurie's. Remember?'

Hannah looked at the small face upturned to hers.

What other powers, magnified perhaps; even distorted, lay behind the child's eyes . . . She patted the hand on her arm.

'Of course I do. We'll be off the minute I find my gloves.'

She could not dwell on this now, and should not, for she was able to change nothing. What powers Jess might possess were there, seeded and growing for the future.

Epilogue

June 1982

Hannah and Florence had a joint eightieth birthday party on the second Saturday in June. Trestle tables were set end to end on the lawn of Bracken House, and for once the weather was accommodating, with soft spun-sugar clouds idling around in a summer-blue sky. Skylarks sang their hearts out above the surrounding downland, where lambs tumbled in little gangs among harebells and cinquefoil and budding foxgloves.

The roses were glorious this year; bowls of them graced the tables. Hannah had hunted out the long, hand-embroidered cloth, one of her family treasures passed to her from grandmother Hywel. She recalled seeing the cloth each Christmas in childhood, when the Hywel clan gathered at the senior female's house for the festive meal. The practice had been discontinued long years ago; family, community, had lessened in importance in this second half of the century.

Hannah had rediscovered a further treasure laid in the lavender-scented folds of the tablecloth . . . On her twelfth Christmas, a small blue-covered book of healing remedies had been given her by her dear *Nain*, great-grandmother Hywel, who had died shortly afterwards. For years Hannah had kept the book under her pillow, but it had eventually been packed away in the tablecloth. Now she had it under her pillow again . . . *Nain* Hywel had possessed the gift;

had been aware that the child Hannah did also, and had wished her book, hand-written with infinite care, to go to the family member who would most value it.

Florence had come early to Bracken House, and the two friends had supervised the setting out of tea. It was to be an old-fashioned tea with the big copper tea-urn, and an even bigger cake with two circles each of eight candles, one for each decade. They worked happily side by side, as they had almost sixty years ago, filling the shelves of Hannah's small shop. It had been to Florence that Hannah had turned two summers ago, when Matthew had drawn a few quick breaths, clutched at his shoulder then collapsed on the lawn.

Hannah had knelt to support his head, talking quietly . . . she could not save him, but was able to cut through the pain of heart failure, feeling her hands channel it down through her arms, her body, and away into the earth. He had died peacefully then, his hand in hers, appearing so tranquil that she would not have tried to keep him. Now Matthew lay by Liza in the churchyard along the road. Then, as at Liza's death four years ago, Hannah had been supported with love from Florence, and from Joe and Tom, as long ago she had with such fierce tenacity supported them.

There were all ages at the tea party, from senior citizens down to Laurie's newborn daughter May Jonet. Her grandmother was inordinately proud of her namesake, not least because Laurie and Primrose had actually decided to get married last year, and had conceived May Jonet on the right side of the blanket.

Jonet's quality of life had improved over the last few years. Mark's liaison with his paramour had not stood the test of cohabitation and two years ago he had put out friendly feelers in Jonet's direction. By then, she had the confidence to say thank you but no; but the fact that he had approached her boosted her self-esteem and Jonet began to feel better. Top of the tree now at her library, she did a good job and knew it, and stress disappeared. She was on friendly terms with Laurie and Primrose, found young Ben a source of pleasure without anxiety and was now set fair to enjoy a relationship with little May Jonet. She also had an English professor in tow, a relaxed, urbane widower who had taken early retirement to write, and with whom she shared outings and holidays while retaining her independence. 'The best of both worlds,' Laurie had said to Hannah with a grin.

Laurie himself worked all hours and loved it. He and Primrose would never be wealthy, but would not starve either, and that suited them perfectly well. Their organic vegetables, their healthy plants and seedlings found a ready market for as many as they could produce. They paid Hannah the interest on her debt every quarter on the dot, which she quietly put into an account for their children. She had no need of the capital sum and had already willed it to them.

Hannah missed Matthew dreadfully, but was aware of her great good fortune in having her family about her, and in the continuing friendship of Florence. Her memories of the love she had shared with Matthew were all good, and Hannah had known enough of the bad to recognise her luck. These days, she would find herself laughing sometimes at the things he had said, at situations she recalled . . . Her lips curved in her still lovely face, and that was thanks to Matthew, who seemed always near.

Liza's death had been a bitterly cruel blow, one she had found hard to accept. Two daughters . . . where was the justice? Don't expect it, Matthew had said; there is no law that stipulates justice as being part of the natural course of life. Be grateful that you were allowed to love Serena for fourteen years, and Liza for thirty-three, but do not ask for justice . . . So Hannah had lived through her sadness one day at a time, and gradually it had eased sufficiently to become bearable, as is the way.

Eleven-year-old Jess had become a deepening consolation. When Hannah greeted her after each absence she loved her more. Not like Liza, nor Carl, nor any one person, she was inalienably herself, Jess Cline. Yet Hannah caught glimpses of so many loved ones in this thin young girl with the mane of nut-brown hair. Best were the times when she would square her jaw in the manner of Thomas Hywel, or regard Hannah from the slate-grey, luminous eyes that she recalled from him. She liked to tell Jess of Dada, and Jess could never hear enough.

'Tell about the old days, Gran,' she would beg, and Hannah would smile, and need no second asking. Jess had looked forward to this party, and when she and her father had arrived last evening had at once set to baking a trayful of chocolate cornflake cakes. 'We did them in cookery,' she told Hannah, licking the chocolate from her fingers. 'I'll make you jam tarts in the morning.' When Carl had attempted to steal one she had slapped his hand, then laughingly relented and handed him the plate. The relationship of father and daughter was good; each showed open and honest concern for the other. Carl would clearly have died for Jess, and Jess worried about Carl's welfare in a quite touching fashion.

Everyone had gone to bed early, and from breakfast on the Day, activity was non-stop. The birthdays were ten days apart, but this date suited everyone – even Laurie and Primrose had bought in extra help so they and Ben might come for tea, with baby May in her carry-cot. Carl, as temporary man of the house, had been doing the heavy work, leaving Joe and Tom to pay attention to the two birthday girls. They were allegedly to do nothing but look decorative; both had nevertheless been busy all week baking, which was in truth a pleasure for them.

'This is nothing to what we used to do, eh, *cariad*?' Florence handed Hannah a Bakewell tart to slide into the Aga.

'And we're nothing to what we used to *be*!' Hannah laughed, pointing to the stick Florence had used as an aid to get about the sloping garden.

'Nonsense. You're as old as you feel. And I feel fine – today, anyway. What are we giving everyone to drink?'

'Gallons of tea. Lemonade for the littles, and champagne for the toast. I think we're worth a drop of the best, aren't we? Carl has brought down a case, so he must think so.'

Jonet turned up early, and Joe and Sal followed soon after. Tom had to do his shop baking, but would be free by two and Joe went to pick him up from Porthcawl. Tom was due to retire in the autumn and was so full of plans for his 'spare' time that Florence swore he would have to continue to get up at four o'clock to fit everything in. Everyone set to, making sandwiches, mixing salads, carving ham, poaching salmon. Jess had made her tarts before breakfast so keen was she, using the last of Hannah's strawberry jam from last year as by next week there would be a fresh crop. Laurie's strawberries were superb. He and Primrose were to bring their first picking of the season for this celebration, also the cream, for now they had Mabel, the prettiest young Jersey cow on record, who had at once become a member of the family.

'This is a tea such as I have never seen.' Carl looked on in wonder at the food being prepared, then stowed under cloths, or 'fridged'. 'We don't seem to have this particular meal in the US . . . I regret to say.' He stole a loose shaving of ham off the joint and rolled his eyes in appreciation. 'Oh my –'

'Wait till you reach the raspberry and sherry trifle,' his daughter told him. Jonet, scrambling eggs for egg and cress sandwiches, laughed.

'He couldn't possibly have any of that, Jess – you know how Americans watch their weight.'

'I shall watch mine tomorrow. Today, the trifle.' Carl was firm.

Balloons were strung up to fruit trees, streamers were floated from shrubs, chairs were arranged. Carl carried out the great tea-urn, groaning that thank God they didn't have these back home either. A beaming Tom arrived, looking younger than sixty-four; lean and fit with a weather-tanned face which belied his trade, and a ready smile. Primrose had bound up her long hair in a scarlet ribbon to match the roses on a print dress bought for the occasion; the first time Hannah recalled seeing her in anything but jeans. Then came Florence's adopted son Raymond, his wife Marion and two daughters, one with toddler twins. People strolled about the garden, admired the newest baby, laughed with the pleasure of meeting together. The sun continued to shine; flowers, trees and shrubs made their own contribution to the occasion.

Everyone was finally arranged to their satisfaction about the feast, which was a sight to set any taste bud back on its heels.

'I must have a record of this for my folks –' Carl brought out his cine-camera. Raymond had one too, and the party table was saved for posterity with Hannah at one end and Flo at the other, beaming as though sharing a private joke. How such a quantity of food was consumed amidst so much chatter was a mystery; plates were passed, dishes handed out, tea and lemonade decanted and disposed of. At last came the time when words and laughter faltered, if only because everyone was too replete for further effort. Then Joe stood up and the champagne glasses were charged.

'Ladies and gentlemen of all ages . . . in senior position here today, I have the happy task of proposing this birthday toast to two of the loveliest ladies in the Principality.' Joe paused for murmurs of assent to settle.

'I have known both from babyhood, so no one can better extol their many virtues, while their weaknesses would not cover the statutory postage stamp. Many owe them much . . . I hope devoutly they are *not* a dying breed; but I've an idea, even so, that less folk today share their great strengths in such abundance.'

Joe paused again and his eyes became serious as he looked at his sister.

'It is my long-held belief that I owe my life to you, Han dear. We won't go into detail here, but you and I know how strong are the bonds between us, and today I salute you in all consciousness of them. And dear Flo, who supported my sister with such constancy over so many years, supported me, and also Tom through her. Others who have reason to love you both are here, and know their reasons well. They will join me I know in raising their glasses to you both, Hannah and Florence, lifelong friends, and in wishing you years of friendship yet. Hannah and Florence, with all our love.'

When everyone had cleared away and gone, and Jess was in bed, Carl and Hannah had a quiet drink together. Carl sat back against the cushions, looking more relaxed than she had seen him for some time. He smiled lazily at her, the diffused light of the June evening softening the thin, harsh lines of his features.

'It's been great today, Hannah. Thanks for letting me be here.'

'Thanks for coming.' She smiled back, more comfortable with this man now than she would have thought possible a decade ago. 'But you, Carl . . . I have a feeling of change in the air –?' Hannah paused, eyebrows raised. He nodded.

'However you know, you've hit it on the nail. Willow Hotels have turned the corner. The period of change is over and from here on it's routine. So.' He did not tell her of the money he had replaced in Jess's fund; the million dollars that before Liza's death he might well have considered fair game.

'So you're in search of new fields to conquer?'

He smiled again. 'You don't miss much, do you?'

Her turn to laugh. 'I try not to. So, any ideas?'

'Not yet. But I will consider looking back in the States as well as the UK. I'm open to all ideas. Just like a challenge I guess . . .'

'No harm in that. And Jess?' Hannah added quickly: 'About Jess, Carl . . . I want to say – well . . . you will need to be aware of her.'

'Her gift?' Carl prompted. 'It's OK, Hannah; I am aware. I'll handle that side of her very gently, you can be sure. Take every care. And of course we'll be in close touch with you, see you often. You'll be kept in the picture.'

'Thank you.' Hannah smiled, remembering. 'That's what my father did for me, you know. He was always aware; ready to understand. And it meant that I was never afraid.'

'I get that. All aspects of Jess will continue to be my first consideration,' he said firmly. 'Wherever we may go I'll see it's right for her. I owe Liza that.'

'And yourself, Carl.'

He took a drink and looked past her at the softness of evening dropping over the garden. She said softly:

'It won't be possible ever to forget her, Carl.'

'Who's asking to?' His voice was rough. Hannah nodded.

'No one, Carl. No one . . .'

Next morning Carl took flowers to Liza's and Matthew's graves, then drove the couple of miles further to Joe's house to take leave of his godfather. Hannah, at Jess's request, got out her car and drove them to the hill above Margam, where they could take in the panorama of Swansea Bay. Hannah used her stick to walk up a short way from the car; the climb seemed stiffer than it used to be. No . . . *she* was stiffer . . . she smiled wryly as Jess ran ahead.

'D'you seem to know some places *better* than others, Gran?' Jess had folded her legs round a tussock of heather and grass, and was observing the *morfa* below with unblinking concentration.

'I do indeed.' Hannah leaned on her stick to take in the vista.

'It's like that here. For me.'

'I thought it might be, sweetheart.'

A breeze off the sea lifted the heads of harebells, rustled grasses. A kestrel floated overhead on an air current before dropping soundlessly. Behind them the mountain ran in patched sun and shadow to a full fast sky. Hannah pointed with her stick, telling Jess what had changed in the landscape and what had not. She told of the beach picnic the first day of the Great War, when she was about the age of Jess, now. She told of the strikes in the 1920s, the lock-outs of the '30s.

Now, bad again; times Hannah had not thought to see back in her lifetime. Two and a half years ago, a steel strike over pay had lasted for ninety days. After it, workers had returned beaten and demoralised, with their unions accepting an offer that allowed no face-saving. Redundancies followed, though one in five jobs had already gone in the '70s. The new plan was called 'Slimline', and it was not negotiable.

Hannah felt a chill as the sun dipped into cloud. 'Slimline' had lost the town over 5,500 jobs in five months; Treasure Island had become Giro City. Losses followed thick and fast in every industry as recession deepened; large, medium, small businesses folded. Supermarkets, cinemas, medical centres, bank branches, all went to the wall. The last time Hannah had driven back over the Severn Bridge from London, it was scrawled with graffiti announcing defiantly WALES IS CLOSED.

But she had been here before, and she knew that Wales would never close. These people, her people, were the salt of the earth. Resilient to a degree, toughly humorous, supportive of one another and regarding none as their superior, as for certain no one was.

'We will wait, and work at what we may, and hope. We have each other, and our country.' She recalled these words from long ago, and now she spoke them softly, believing them as did so many, because she must.

Hannah watched Jess wander after a small blue butterfly. In her jacket pocket, her fingers found and curled about the pebble given her by Joe when he was five. Dear Joe. He had waited, and worked, and hoped. He had gone through fear, loneliness, doubt, and finally had come home. Joe, Tom; even Jonet, prickly, difficult Jonet, had found her way home. The family – her family – had moved out to the Americas, yet still was rooted here. How Dada would love to hear the story of Liza and Carl, and the making of a circle, the magic circle of a family.

Looking down the hill, Hannah knew that she was not, and never had been, isolated. She was an active participant in a continuous tapestry. She felt her father very close and now saw Dorothea a short way off in her old-fashioned dress, smiling at her. And there was Serena playing far down on the *morfa*, and Liza, who had never known her half-sister in life, was with her.

Jess, coming back stared at the *morfa* too, then at Hannah, with questions in her eyes. Hannah took her hand, washed over by a sudden, sublime release from doubt. No more of that. Yes, Jess inherited from both parents. Yes, those parents had in their various ways ill-used their own gift. But Hannah knew *now, here,* that regardless, their child had both a clean page before her, and the power in her to write upon it, a story of her own that would be full of grace and goodness. She nursed a great and growing hope that the Hywel gift, with which she had struggled all her life to come to terms, with which she believed Liza may only have played, and Carl used for personal gain, would in this lovely girl come to full and perfect flowering.

As they turned for the car, Hannah said: 'I have a book to show you when we get home. You may have it if you wish – it belonged to my great-grandmother.

She gave it to me when I was about your age.'

'*Nain* Hywel?'

'That's right. She wrote healing recipes down in it . . . they're rather interesting.' As they went down, Hannah spoke to Jess of *Nain*; of her lovely warmth, of her special skills. She knew that all those behind her stretched away in a shadowy but connected sequence of time, and that the sequence would run on through Jess, and far into the future.